THE PROMETHEUS OPTION

JEFF KIRK

THE PROMETHEUS OPTION

Maps created by the author.

Published by Jeff Kirk in the United States of America.

ISBN 978-0-692-68733-8

TABLE OF CONTENTS

BOOK ONE: THE BLACK BOX

BOOK TWO: THE BORROWED SWORD

ILLUSTRATIONS

BOOK ONE

THE BLACK BOX

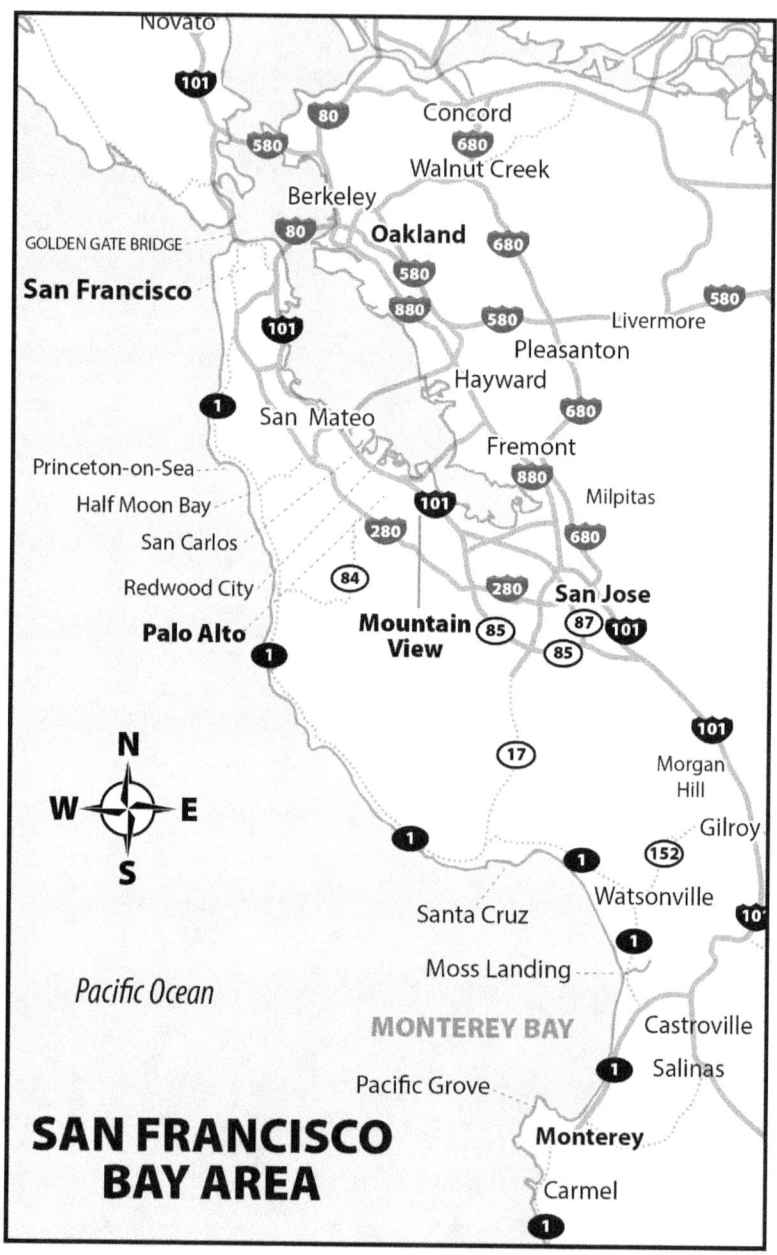

Figure 1: Map of San Francisco Bay Area

CHAPTER ONE

Princeton-on-Sea, California

June 23

The two men were of a kind.

They strode side by side across the deck of the deserted seaside restaurant. They were Silicon Valley royalty, and it showed.

They wore designer long-sleeved shirts, khaki slacks, Swiss watches, and Italian loafers. Their pockets jingled with the keys of cars worth as much as a house in some parts of the country. They clutched leather-bound laptop cases in pale, well-manicured hands.

There the resemblance ended.

One was tall, angular, weathered, and lean, with narrow cheekbones and a shoulder-length mane of dark brown hair. His thin lips bore a sardonic smile. Crow's feet stretched away from the corners of his pale gray eyes as he squinted into the mid-afternoon sun.

His companion was taller, older, heavier, and angrier. His face was smooth but spotted with age. His brown hair was well-groomed and oddly immobile in the hot summer breeze, his mouth bowed into a perpetual frown.

Men like them believed their destiny was to change the world—if not for the better, at least to leave their mark. Few would ever do so, unless one counted selling more ads among the great achievements of history.

These two would succeed, but not as they intended.

If they had known that their meeting would lead to war, they might have turned and fled before exchanging a single word.

Then again, they might not.

Even if they'd known that by taking this meeting, in a few months one of them would be dead, the other running for his life, and the very survival of humankind in doubt, they might have taken it anyway.

They were nothing if not arrogant. They'd have believed themselves more than capable of forestalling any unfortunate events.

The potential reward was just too great.

Alas, the restaurant was empty. No one was there to warn them off. And if there were any gods, they had given up teaching humanity of the perils of hubris long, long ago.

The restaurant sat atop a long, low hillside overlooking the placid surface of Pillar Point Harbor, separated from Half Moon Bay by a pair of curved, rocky breakwaters. Beyond was the Pacific Ocean, sweltering under a cloudless blue sky.

The waves were listless, hammered flat by a merciless sun. It was hard to believe that the Mavericks surfing competition was held here in what Northern Californians laughingly called "winter." Today the sea was as calm as a kiddie pool.

Peter Struve tried to ignore the hostile eyes of his companion as he crossed the restaurant's deck. The mid-afternoon sun glared at him as well. He shielded his face with his free hand.

A table and a trio of chairs awaited the two of them at the far corner of the deck.

Peter picked a chair and sat. He placed his laptop bag on the table, plucked a pair of aviator sunglasses from his dress shirt pocket, shook them open and put them on.

His sullen companion remained standing. He was a big man, powerfully built and imposing even after six decades spent mostly inside corporate board rooms. He swept a hand toward the expanse of empty tables. "You had to rent the whole place? We couldn't have just done this at my office? I thought those surfers waiting out front were going to lynch us."

Peter smiled up at him. "The sunlight will do you good. You look a little pasty." The low glass walls around the deck blocked the occasional hint of a breeze. He began to sweat.

The sullen man stared down at Peter for another few seconds and then lowered himself into a chair. He kept his own bag in his lap. "If we weren't in a public place I would punch you in the mouth."

Peter considered his response. His companion looked capable of making good on his half-serious threat. The hair beneath his expensive toupee was still brown. The long sleeves of his blinding white Stefano Ricci shirt didn't hide the muscles inside those age-thickened arms.

Without missing a beat, Peter shrugged. "Another good reason to meet here instead. Besides, I wanted to make an impression."

"You're into my fund for six hundred million dollars. You've already made a goddamned impression."

A waitress strode up to their table, her eyes on Peter's companion. "Mr. Struve? I'm Lacey. I'll be taking care of you today."

Peter cleared his throat. "He's Mr. Mayhew. Call me Peter."

"I'm sorry, Mister Str— I mean, Peter. Can I get you anything while you look at the menu?"

"Do you want some chowder, Phil? This place is famous for it."

"It's Philip," Mayhew snapped.

Peter said, "I don't think we'll be eating today, Lacey. Just bring us each an iced tea, and one empty glass."

"Yes, sir."

He winked an acknowledgement.

When she was gone, Mayhew leaned forward and growled, "Three years since we bought in and you still don't have anything to show me. Six hundred million, Peter. Alice Guest at Sequoia told me that you're into them for another four. Who else have you ripped off?"

"Sealock Capital, AMT and Gideon Hart, for starters. But *ripped off* is a pretty harsh term. They invested. So did you. Sometimes investments pay off. Sometimes they don't. You're not a child. You know the drill."

Mayhew sat back in his chair, gaping at him. After a long, silent moment, he said, "You are not going to sit there and tell me you pissed all my money down the fucking drain."

Peter *tsked*. "Language, Phil. You should relax. You don't want to have a heart attack. Sorry—*another* heart attack."

Mayhew's mouth tightened. "It's *Philip*. Don't crack wise with me, goddammit. I took a big chance on you. We all did. If you leave us hanging, you won't own StruvePharma anymore. We will. And we'll bury you so deep a geologist couldn't find you."

They both fell silent as the waitress returned with their glasses, two full and one empty. She placed them on the table. "Will there be anything else?"

"I'll wave when I want you to come back."

"Yes, sir."

Peter admired the sway of Lacey's hips as she walked away, but when she entered the building he forgot about her. He lifted his glass of tea to his lips. He surveyed the surroundings as he took a long swallow.

He'd visited the place yesterday to scout the sight lines. There was no clear view of their table from inside the building, nor from the paved walkway just below the edge of the deck. As directed, the restaurant staff had set up a tent-like pavilion along the side of the deck next to the parking lot, hiding their table from view. There was, however, ample sunlight and humid sea air—both necessary for the demo.

The afternoon heat had driven almost everyone indoors. The nearby waters of the lagoon were free of boats. There weren't even any fishing vessels out on Half Moon Bay proper. The only people in sight were hundreds of yards away: a gaggle of wet-suited idiots sitting on their boards in the lethargic surf, waiting vainly for a Mavericks-sized wave to roll in. Even the marine fog layer that usually hugged the coast in summertime had been driven away by the hot land breeze.

It was time.

Peter put the tea glass down, unzipped his laptop case and pulled out a small glassy slab the shape and size of a narrow paperback book. He placed it on the table between them.

"O ye of little faith," he said. A trickle of sweat rolled unpleasantly down his back. He shaped his mouth into what he hoped looked like a smile.

Mayhew mopped his forehead with a napkin. He leaned forward and peered at the slab, frowning. "A piece of glass?"

"A proof of concept." Peter pointed at the slab's face, which featured the white outline of a rounded square about an inch on a side. The letters "ON/OFF" were embossed in the center of the square. "Put this on top of the glass, face up, and turn it on."

Mayhew picked up the slab. "It's heavy," he grunted. His frown vanished and his brows furrowed. "What's this made of?"

Peter said nothing. An airplane on approach to the nearby Half Moon Bay Airport buzzed low overhead. He fought the urge to look up.

A ghost of Mayhew's familiar frown returned. He placed the slab across the top of the empty glass and tapped the square button.

The slab's face turned black—a black so perfect it might have been a window into empty space. The sides and bottom stayed transparent, as did as the area inside the button.

A pattern of fine golden lines appeared inside the slab. An elegant lacework of amber-hued whorls, loops, spirals and branches darkened slowly into visibility, filling the entire volume of the glass-like device. The lines converged to a spot on the bottom, centered beneath the transparent button.

Mayhew drew in a breath. He pushed his chair back from the table and lowered his head until his eyes were level with the slab.

Peter took another sip of his iced tea. He couldn't see it from this angle, but he knew what was happening: a bead of thick golden liquid was forming on the bottom surface of the device. He remained silent until he saw it fall into the glass. "It takes a minute to get going," he stalled. *Not as fast as I expected. I'll have a word with Emily about that.*

As if on cue, another droplet splashed down, followed by another and then another. Soon there was a steady patter of droplets splashing into a puddle of viscous amber fluid at the bottom of the glass. *There we go. Even better than in the lab.* Demoing it here had been the right choice.

"Jesus Christ," whispered Mayhew, staring at the device. "Is this for real? Is... is that what I think it is?"

Peter nodded, smiling. "It will work for forty-eight hours, starting from when you turned it on. If you want to see how much it can produce in that time, I suggest you get it to your lab."

"Two days? That's not long enough."

"Don't let your wizards try to take it apart. There are safeguards against tampering. We wouldn't want anyone to get hurt."

"Hurt?" Mayhew blurted, looking up at him.

"*Extremely* hurt." Peter drained his glass of iced tea, picked up his now-empty laptop bag and stood. "Speaking of which, turn it off before you pick it up. Don't touch the black surface unless you want to lose some skin. If it doesn't come back to us intact, my next call will be to your blabbermouth friend Alice at Sequoia. Maybe she'll be interested in footing the bill for Phase Two instead of you."

"Wait a minute. We need to talk!"

Peter felt his smile broaden. "Oh, we will. In forty-eight hours." As he passed the waitress on his way out of the restaurant, he pulled ten crisp hundred-dollar bills from his pocket and handed them to her. "Here's your tip. Don't let anyone else in until Mr. Mayhew leaves. And Lacey? I changed my mind. Get him some of that clam chowder."

He shrugged off her enthusiastic gratitude and threaded his way through the grumbling crowd outside the restaurant. He got into his white Tesla and sprayed gravel as he launched his car onto southbound Highway 1.

Astoundingly, the road in front of him was empty. For a blissful instant, there weren't even any surfers trying to walk across the road to get to the beach. He floored the accelerator. The car did its best to push him through the back of his seat.

His pasted-on smile vanished as the restaurant disappeared behind him. He gripped the steering wheel to keep his hands from shaking. He drew in a long, gulping, shuddering breath.

"Here we go," he whispered.

CHAPTER TWO

ZMPC Headquarters, Sunnyvale, California

June 23

Philip Mayhew stared at the glass as it slowly filled with thick golden fluid. Sweat dripped unnoticed from his forehead onto the table-cloth.

He leaned closer to look at the device, then drew his head back sharply. There was a small but perceptible draft coming from the side of the gadget.

He licked a finger and put it next to the device. Sure enough, he felt a constant, cooling breeze, yet the side of the glassy slab seemed just as solid as every other surface.

"Jesus Christ," he whispered.

He started violently when a steaming bowl of thick white soup slid onto the table in front of him.

"I'm sorry," the waitress said, giggling. "Mr. Struve asked me to bring it to you. Would you like some sourdough bread?"

He glanced up at her. "What?"

Her eyes were on the gadget, an uncertain smile on her lips. "What *is* that?"

Philip pressed the button on top of Struve's magic box. Its black top instantly became transparent. The golden lines inside the device faded away. The patter of drops slowed to a stop. "This? This is, ah, just a magic trick. Pretty cool, huh? Ha ha! How much for the glass?"

"Oh, Mr. Struve already paid for every—"

"Good." Philip unzipped his laptop case, jammed the heavy slab into it next to his tablet computer, grabbed the half-filled glass and fled.

He bulled through the crowd of hungry surfers outside the restaurant, ignoring their angry catcalls, hurdled into his Jaguar XK convertible—spilling some of the golden fluid on the passenger seat—and punched it.

As soon as he was on the highway, he inserted a noise-canceling Bluetooth earpiece and placed a call. "Rose? It's me. Call Ben Holcombe. Tell him it's about Project Eagle. Tell him to find a chemistry lab that will do a rush analysis for us." He paused, listening. "How the hell should I know? This is Silicon Valley, there has to be a goddamned chemistry lab somewhere!" He paused again. "Sorry, sorry. I'm just excited. Now stop talking with me and call Ben. Rose! Tell him he can't talk about this to *anyone*. Got that? Good. Have him meet me in Safe House in half an hour."

He roared into the parking lot of Zaggati Mayhew Pacer and Cho Venture Partners LLC in downtown Sunnyvale forty-five minutes later. He looked at the half-full glass of turgid liquid in the cup holder, and at the glistening trails left by the drops that he'd spilled on the leather of the passenger seat. He reached for the glass, but stopped before he closed his hand on it. *Don't want to steal my own thunder.* He raised the convertible's top, grabbed his bag, and locked the glass in the car.

He raced into the gleaming headquarters building, took the elevator to the fifth floor and raced down the hallway to his office. Executives and middle managers leaped out of his way.

He stopped in front of his office, next to Rose Maeda's desk. "Goddamned traffic," he panted.

"In the hallway?" she murmured, unflappable as always.

He ignored the gibe. "Is he here?"

"Waiting for you in Safe House. What's got you in such a lather?"

"I'll fill you in later, if this doesn't turn out to be a hoax. Speaking of which, call Andy Healy and tell him to get ready for the biggest lawsuit ever in case it does."

Rose smiled as she picked up the phone. "I'll do that."

Philip opened his laptop bag, removed his Surface tablet, left it on Rose's desk and strode down the hallway.

Like all the conference rooms at ZMPC, Safe House was named after a movie. Unlike the others, this one was true to its name. Its steel door and solid concrete walls were lined with a conductive wire mesh to prevent electromagnetic eavesdropping. Batteries supplied power for the lights and air conditioner. When the door was locked, the batteries were disconnected from external power. There were no Ethernet drops and no wifi. The only furnishings were a long oval conference table, sleek chairs, floor-to-ceiling whiteboards, and dozens of dry-erase markers.

The door was open. Ben Holcombe sat by himself at the long conference room table, reading a mathematics textbook. He was a fresh-faced thirty-year-old with a receding hairline and a perpetual expression of bemused wonderment. His knowledge spanned electronics, physics, chemistry, computers and biotechnology. What he didn't know about modern technology wasn't worth knowing. And unlike most of the many geniuses Philip knew in Silicon Valley, Ben wasn't an insufferable know-it-all.

Ben looked up from the book and smiled a greeting. "I found your chemistry lab, boss." He spoke with a relaxed Tennessee drawl that anyone who didn't know him might consider insolent.

Philip grunted, "Good." He wiped sweat from his forehead. He pointed at the framed poster on the wall at the far end of the room. "I want you to look at that."

The poster was a one-sheet for the *Safe House* movie, featuring a grim-looking Ryan Reynolds, a scowling Denzel Washington, and the words "NO ONE IS SAFE."

"That has never been more true in the history of this company." Philip turned back to make sure that Ben was looking. "Remember clause 5B of your contract. Not a word of this conversation leaves this room."

Ben sat upright at that. Clause 5B was the section that spelled out the savage penalties each of the senior staff members would pay if they breached their confidentiality agreements. The *Wunderkind's* smile faltered. "Criminy, boss. It must have been a hell of a meeting."

Philip nodded. He pulled the transparent slab of whatever-it-was from the bag and put it on the table. "This is from Struve."

"Holy shit," whispered Ben. "He actually had something to show you? After all this time? And it works?"

"It does something. Whether it does the right thing remains to be seen. As for *how* it works—well, your guess is better than mine. Don't touch the button until you get it to the lab or you'll make a mess. And keep your fingers clear of the top when it's running. It turns black. Struve didn't say what it would do to you, but it can't be good."

The young wizard picked the slab up and peered into it. "Wow. This thing is *heavy*. No batteries, that's for sure." He turned it around in his hands, carefully avoiding the white outline of the button. "It's not glass, or any plastic I know of. The index of refraction is too high. It's more like quartz, but there's no internal reflectivity at all."

Philip said, "It's solar-powered. It must pull the raw ingredients from the air. I don't know why else Struve would insist on doing the demo out in the sun next to the ocean, except that he's a chronic show-off. Steve Jobs Junior."

Ben was too captivated by the slab to notice the shop-worn slur. He rubbed its surface. "I can't tell if it's warm or cold. It's like it doesn't have a temperature at all." He let out an exasperated sigh. "You couldn't run a Fischer-Tropsch process in something this small. How in the world...?"

Philip glanced at his watch. "We have forty-seven hours to test it. Ben, do that voodoo that you do so well. You, Deepthi and Eric are the only people cleared for this. I'm not even going to tell the other partners until we know it's for real. No point getting their hopes up. And Ben? Don't try to crack it open. We have to give it back."

"What the hell, boss?"

"Struve said there were safeguards against tampering, and that it was dangerous. StruvePharma made drugs before they made *this*, remember? God knows what kind of horrible chemicals are inside that thing. You could blow up the building."

"But—"

"It doesn't matter if he was just blowing sunshine up my skirt. We can't afford to piss him off. We're not his only investor, just the biggest. If the gadget works as advertised, he won't have any problem raising the funds to bring it to market. So don't let Eric fuck around with it."

"Damn, I wish you'd given me a little notice, boss. The Cave doesn't have half the instruments I need to tell what's going on inside this little thing."

"You got as much notice as I did. I thought Struve was just going to string me along again. Don't sit! Go! I'm going to call Security and have a guard posted outside the lab." He tossed the laptop bag to Ben. "Here. Keep it out of sight until you get it to the lab. When you have something to tell me, find me here. I've got some planning to do."

Eleven hours later Philip had covered most of the whiteboards with half-legible calculations, to-do lists and business plans. There was a knock on the door. He opened it.

Ben Holcombe came in. He looked exhausted but happy. He carried a sheaf of papers in one hand. He closed the door before he spoke. "You were right, boss. It's solar-powered. It works best in strong white light, and it likes humid air. I put it in a plastic bag filled with CO_2 and the production rate went way up."

"Where did you get carbon dioxide?"

Ben smirked. "The soda machine in the cafeteria. The cooks were really pissed. I'm getting about three liters an hour from it now just on room air, by the way. The rate's as steady as a rock."

"What about the chemical analysis?"

Ben handed him the papers. "Here's the report. I practically had to fight my way out of that chemistry lab. They wanted to know how I got hold of it. It's a mixture of tri-1-hexene, tri-1-octene and tri-1-decene. Polyalphaolefins. A perfect one-third to one-third to one-third mix by *volume*, if you can believe that, and no impurities at all, and I mean *zero*. Do you know how impossible that is? Christ! It has to use a variant on the Ziegler process, but how could they get it into a package this small?"

"Ben," Philip said. "Do I look like a chemist? What the hell is it?"

"Synthetic oil." Ben said with an exaggerated Southern twang. "Black gold. Texas tea."

Philip's answering smile was so broad it actually hurt.

It didn't occur to him until hours later, as he crawled into bed next to his sleeping wife, to wonder how someone as young as Ben could quote the theme song of *The Beverly Hillbillies*.

Merlin's Cave smelled like old sweat socks, motor oil, and a delicate, floral perfume. The rank air was thick with humidity. It felt like Atlanta on a hot summer day. The only thing missing was sunlight.

The inventions they evaluated in Merlin's Cave were almost always anonymous-looking circuit boards, so the Venetian blinds were usually open. Today they were drawn. Even so, there was no shortage of light in the room. Every ceiling fixture was on, and the phalanx of six brilliant white LED spotlights aimed at the whatever-it-was created a fearsome glare.

The Gadget lay atop one of the workbenches. Reams of plastic-wrapped laser printer paper were stacked on either side to make a stable base for the binocular microscope propped over it.

Eric Dalton stared at the Gadget through the eyepieces, trying to understand what he was seeing. He was so tired he could barely stay on the lab stool. His attention wandered like a dog off the leash.

The microscope was wrapped in plastic, as were the two LCD monitors and the digital video recorder on the table nearby. Only the objective lens and the eyepieces were exposed to the open air. They had to keep wiping them with lint-free cloths to keep them free of condensation. Eric had replaced the standard HD cameras mounted near the eyepieces with ultra-high resolution RED cinema cameras. It was a pretty sweet rig.

They couldn't boost the Gadget's production with carbon dioxide in the open air of the lab without asphyxiating themselves. To compensate, they'd turned up the heat, flipped on every available light, and brought in six humidifiers. They'd removed most of the electronics as soon as they noticed the condensation.

Golden synthetic oil accumulated in the Pyrex beaker at a rock-steady rate. They'd been studying the internal structure of the Gadget through the transparent ON-OFF button in the center of its otherwise pitch-black top surface. After so many hours of intense but fruitless study in this stinking sweatbox, the magic was beginning to pall. All he could see through the scope was a bunch of looping hair-thin tubes filled with golden fluid, anyway.

"Get up from there, Eric. You aren't even looking at it anymore."

Eric started at the sound of Ben Holcombe's voice. He pulled back from the scope and rubbed his eyes. "It's only been a few minutes."

"Like hell. It's been half an hour."

Eric eased himself off the stool and tried to conceal his sigh of relief. He stood back from the long black lab bench and made way for his boss. His eyes burned. He rubbed them again and then wiped his sweating face with the gym towel he'd slung around his neck. "Ugh, it's so hot," he said as he pulled his sodden T-shirt away from his skin. At least his loose-fitting cargo pants were still comfortable.

Ben took Eric's seat at the microscope and mopped the eyepieces with an orange cloth. He peered into them, adjusted the focus knob and muttered a string of curses under his breath.

Eric exchanged a glance with Ben's other lab assistant, Deepthi Damodaran. "It's like a sauna in here. How can you stand it?"

Deepthi sat on a stool on the other side of the lab bench, resting her chin in her hands. She shrugged. "I grew up in Kolkata. This is like a nice spring day." Her eyes swiveled back to the Gadget. Her clothes were just as soaked as his, but she might have been sitting in the shade drinking iced water for all the effect the sopping air in the Cave seemed to have on her mood.

Eric's gaze lingered on her oval face, her gleaming brown eyes, her long, straight nose.

"What did you see this time, Eric?" Ben asked, not looking up from the microscope.

"Sorry, what?" Eric tore his eyes away from Deepthi. He glanced at the window in passing. The blinds were closed, but he could see thin blue slices of sky through the up-tilted slats. He looked at the wall clock. "Fucking hell, Ben. It's the middle of the afternoon. I've been up for, what, thirty-eight hours now! I need to go pee and take a shower. I smell like a draft horse."

Deepthi's nose wrinkled. "Yes, you do."

"You're no bed of flowers yourself, lady," Eric joked, but of course the jibe was untrue. Even his very real stench compounded by the reek of recently synthesized oil couldn't overpower her glorious scent.

He hadn't yet worked up the courage to ask her what perfume it was. He hoped he could do it before July. Her birthday was in July. He wanted to surprise her with a bottle of it. Maybe ask her out. He'd been told by some of the women he'd dated that he wasn't bad looking. Deepthi was way out of his class, but she might agree to go out with him. Stranger things had probably happened.

At least I could show her a good time. I've got the cash.

He could never tell Deepthi where the money came from, but if they wanted to fly to Paris or Tokyo on the spur of the moment, he could pay for it. Then again, if ZMPC paid her the same pittance they paid him, she'd wonder how he could afford it. Maybe he could tell her that he bought Apple stock before the iMac came out. But if he'd done that, why would he still be working at ZMPC? He'd have come up with a credible excuse.

"Earth to Eric. Come in, Eric," Ben said without looking up from the microscope. "Tell me what you saw. Again."

Ben growled, "This thing is supposed to stop working in a few minutes. I want your thoughts while they're fresh. Then you can go pee."

"A few minutes?" Deepthi said. "Good. We won't have to change the beaker again."

Ben snapped, "Come on, Eric! And press the RECORD button this time."

"Okay, okay." Eric pulled the slender Tascam audio recorder from his pocket, thumbed it on and held it in front of his mouth. Ben liked them to keep notes on everything, but Eric was a terrible two-finger typist, and the company forbade employees from using their smartphones to store confidential data.

"All right. The top's the absorption surface. Sucks water right out of your skin if you touch it when it's running." Which he had promptly done despite Ben's warning. He rubbed the Band-Aid on his right index finger with his thumb. "The Gadget won't absorb anything but CO_2 and water. Other liquids just bead on the surface and roll right off."

"Go on," urged Ben.

"The sides emit waste oxygen. You can really feel it coming out. Block the sides and it stops working." He glanced down the bench at the discarded pile of gray plastic brackets they'd made with the 3D printer to establish that fact. "No other waste products that we can detect with the gas chromatograph. It doesn't make any sounds. It doesn't emit RF. It's either perfectly shielded, or it doesn't use electricity."

"And? Use your words, Eric."

"And. Give me a sec." Eric's memory was clouded by fatigue. "When we hit it with ultraviolet light, it became reflective and turned off." For a terrible few seconds they thought they'd broken it. Fortunately, as soon as they turned off the black light, the Gadget's mirror sheen vanished. It continued making oil as if nothing had happened. Apparently, the UV in sunlight wasn't intense enough to trigger the mirror effect. They'd stuck to studies with white light from then on.

"What else?" asked Ben. "Come on, come on! This is for the record. What did you see?"

"Nothing but those tubes, or channels, or whatever you call them, that collect the oil and funnel it to the bottom of the Gadget." He faltered.

Deepthi came to his rescue. "But in polarized light you can see tiny spherical cells a few millimeters below the surface. They looked like alveoli in the lungs."

"Yeah!" said Eric. "Little cells full of colorless fluid, wrapped around channels that feed into bigger cells, and so on and so on. Channels get bigger, feeding into bigger cells. About three millimeters from the top, the liquid in the cells turns gold, and they empty into the tubes that converge at the bottom, where the oil comes out." And once again, he ran out of words.

Deepthi added, "It stays three point two degrees Celsius above ambient temperature when it's running."

"Right," he said, nodding to her. "And we had to use an IR thermometer to tell, because you can't feel how hot the damned thing is with your fingers." That was one of the weirdest properties of the device. Ben had speculated that its surface was so porous that your fingers never got a firm enough grip on it to be able to sense its temperature.

Ben said, "Did you see any moving parts? Pumps, wheels, cogs, anything?"

Eric and Deepthi spoke at the same time. "No."

Ben spoke as he continued to peer into the eyepieces. "Me neither. If only we had a lattice light-sheet microscope."

"What the hell is that?" Eric said. He looked at Deepthi, who shrugged.

Ben sighed. "I have no idea how this goddamned thing works."

Deepthi said, "It has to be nano—"

"Just slapping a label on it isn't good enough. We're paid to figure things like this out."

"We've never seen anything like it, Ben," Deepthi said, unperturbed.

Eric said, "No one has, until now. She's right. This is nanotechnology. All the good stuff is happening at molecular scale. We're never going to get anywhere with visible light observations. We have to crack it open."

Ben looked up from the scope and scowled. "That is not an option. I swear to God, Eric, if you had a pacemaker you'd cut it out of your own chest to see how it works." Then he slumped on the stool. "Besides, it's too late. Look."

Eric looked. The flow of oil from the Gadget had stopped. The glassy block was now a uniform, translucent milky white.

"Woah," Eric said. He stuffed the tiny audio recorder into a pocket, pulled the Gadget out from under the microscope and peered at it from all angles. The others gathered around to look as well.

"I'll be damned," Ben said. "The only detail left is the ON/OFF button. Goddammit!" He slapped an open hand down on the bench. In the quiet lab, the sound was like a gunshot.

Eric jumped and almost dropped the Gadget. "Jesus, Ben!"

"Calm down," Deepthi said. "You're just exhausted." She put a hand on Ben's shoulder.

Eric felt his face grow hot. He looked away. *She isn't seeing him,* he reminded himself for the hundredth time. The tenderness of her gesture was troubling, though. She'd been doing that more and more in recent days.

Eric grabbed the half-full beaker, stalked to the other side of the Cave, took an empty one-liter Nalgene bottle from the glassware cabinet and poured the oil in. He scrawled the date and time on the bottle's white plastic surface with a black Sharpie, screwed down the cap and put it on the counter next to the others.

He tried to regain his composure by counting the bottles. It took much longer than he expected. By the time he was done, he felt better. *She can't be seeing him. He's married. She's not that kind of girl.*

"That's it," he said. "A hundred and thirty-four liters, more or less." He turned back around in time to see Deepthi and Ben emerging from an embrace.

"Oh," he said.

They broke away from each other hurriedly and stared at him.

"Hey," he croaked. "Don't stop because of me."

"Eric," Deepthi said, stepping toward him.

He raised a hand and she stopped. "Doesn't matter. None of my business." He tried to smile and gestured at the counter. "A hundred and thirty-four liters. Not bad, eh? Not bad. Speaking of a hundred and thirty-four liters, I have to pee."

"Look, Eric," Ben began.

"Save it," Eric snapped.

He fled the lab.

They didn't try to stop him.

It was Sunday. With the building empty and the locks reset so that only Ben and his team could get in or out, even the security guy stationed outside the Cave had gone home.

Eric marched down the hall to the men's room.

When he finished, his bladder felt better, but the memory of Deepthi and Ben in each other's arms caused a crushing weight to descend on the back of his neck.

He imagined them going to her apartment. Laughing. Touching each other. Pulling each other's clothes off. Sliding under the sheets.

He shook his head to clear it of the images.

"That fucker," he whispered. "He's married. He's *married.*" Not that it seemed to matter to anyone around this place. If senior partners Elena Zaggati and Bruce Cho could have an affair and keep their goddamned jobs, the untouchable *Wunderkind* Ben Holcombe could get away with it.

"That's going to make this easier," he muttered.

He splashed some water on his burning face. He washed his hands and dried them under the Dyson Airblade tap without having to remove them from the sink.

He looked at the fancy faucet and gave a bitter laugh. ZMPC could afford the best of everything when it came to architecture and interior design, but they didn't pay their best technical people half of what they deserved.

It was a good thing he had another source of income.

When his hands were dry, he went to the door and locked it. He pulled his big phone from its designated pocket on his right thigh, started the web browser in "Incognito" mode, and typed in a long, obscure address character by laborious character. It took forever. The site's URL changed every week and it always began with a hard-to-remember TCP/IP address. He had to piece it together from clues in certain classified ads of the Sunday edition of the *San Jose Mercury News.*

"Goddammit," he growled, backspacing over his typos. "How could he do it? Why? He's *married*, for Christ's sakes!" He kept tapping on the phone's keyboard, deleting errors more and more often as he grew angrier. At long last the URL was correct. He tapped the "Enter" button.

The browser showed a bare-bones page consisting of two empty text boxes labeled USERNAME and PASSWORD and a button labeled LOGIN.

He keyed in his username, his forty-character password and tapped the button.

An even more spartan web page loaded. It held only an empty text box and a SEND button.

He typed:

IT WORKS.

He tapped the SEND button, quit the browser app, and jammed the phone back into its pocket.

"That'll show you, Dr. Benjamin Fucking Holcombe, Ph.D. Fuck *you*, fuck *her,* and fuck this *fucking* cheap-ass company." The weight on the back of his neck vanished. Betraying his betrayers felt *good.* He whispered, "This one will be worth a fucking fortune."

He walked into the corridor and stopped, considering his next move.

He couldn't go back the lab. He couldn't face them. Face *her.* It didn't matter. The Gadget had stopped working right on schedule. There was nothing left to do but send it back to Peter Struve and write up their report for Mayhew.

Let them do it, he thought. I need a shower and sleep.

He shuffled toward the exit, lost in thought.

They'd get a chance to learn more if—or more likely, when—ZMPC decided to fund Phase Two. They'd be crazy to pass up the chance to bring a real nanotech device to market, much less one that could make oil from thin air. It would change everything. *Everything.*

The sadness he felt at missing his chance with Deepthi faded as he considered the implications of this new technology. Besides, thanks to his nameless benefactor, he could afford to go out with anyone he liked, especially once the windfall from this latest betrayal was locked up in his safe deposit box. *To hell with Deepthi. Tomorrow I'll sign up for Match.com.* The Apple investment story might work on a girl who didn't work with him.

He got into his SmartCar, cranked the air conditioner up to its puny maximum, and drove to his one-bedroom apartment in nearby Santa Clara in a distracted haze. Once there, he stripped out of his reeking clothes in the living room, spent a luxurious half-hour in the shower, nuked and devoured a frozen chicken tikka masala meal, and then collapsed into his bed. He was asleep in moments.

He awoke seventeen hours later, when the policemen came.

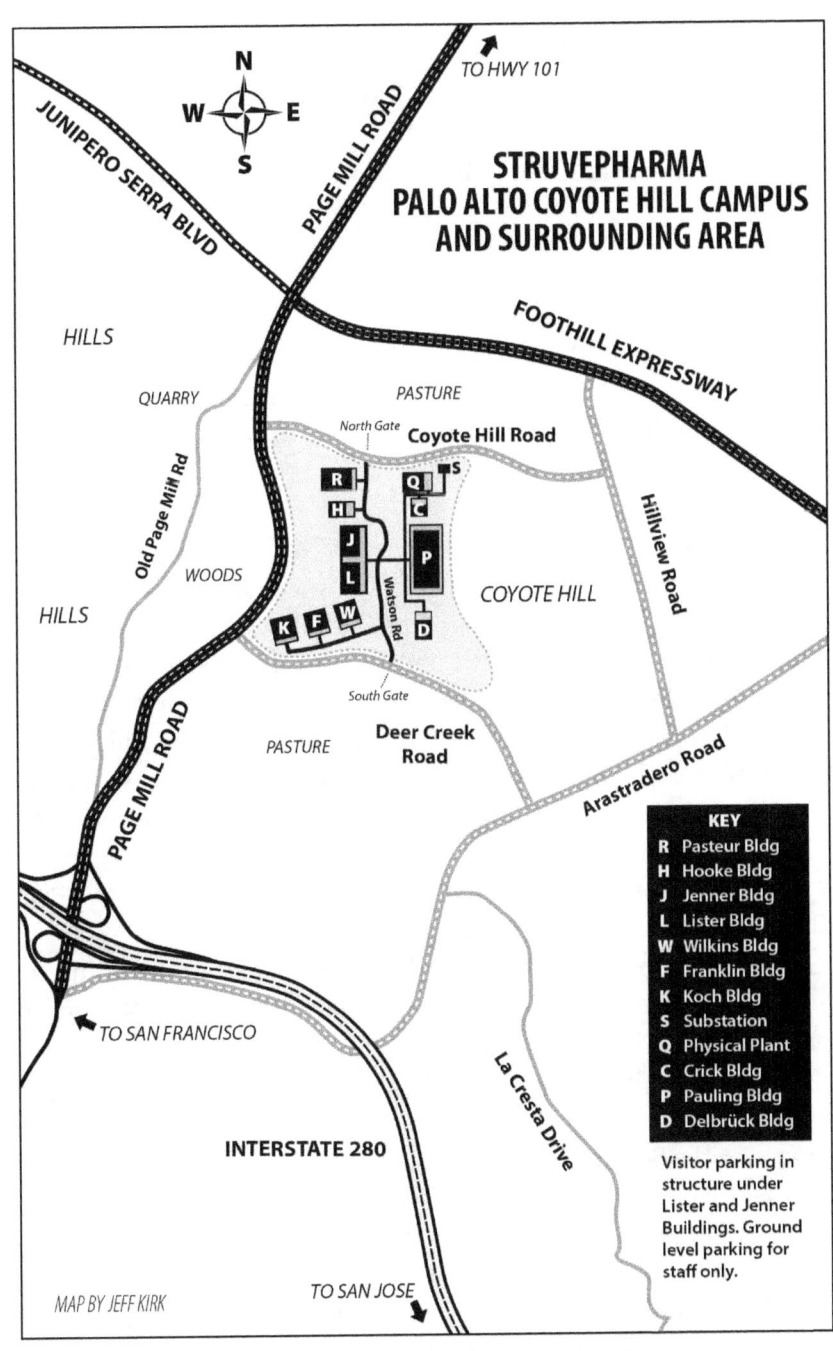

Figure 2: Map of StruvePharma Coyote Hill Campus

CHAPTER THREE

StruvePharma Coyote Hill Campus, Palo Alto, California

June 26

There was a knock at the door.

Emily Dura stopped typing. She peered over the top of the two huge widescreen monitors on her desk.

Peter Struve stood in the open doorway of her office.

"Well?" she prompted.

"They liked it." He smiled and waggled his eyebrows.

She laughed. "I thought they might." A wave of relief washed over her, nevertheless. Confidence was good. Certainty was better.

She glanced at the wall clock and then rubbed her eyes. After all these years of effort, she should feel something like triumph, but it was one thirty in the morning. All she felt was fatigue. Peter would want a better response. He might be twenty years her senior but in some ways he was like a little kid at Christmas. She forced a smile and said, "We did it. We really did it."

"*You* did it. You and the team. I was just the delivery boy." Peter walked in and held out the beta unit.

She took the heavy device from him and inspected it. Its interior volume was a creamy white, its glossy surface unmarred. "No obvious attempts to break in."

"They couldn't have cracked it without a diamond drill, but I'm glad they played by the rules. When can you have it ready for another run? I'm meeting the Sealock team tomorrow. I mean, *today*."

She tsked. "Better postpone it till Wednesday. It'll take at least thirty hours to recondition it. Maybe more if we run into problems."

"That's ten hours longer than last time."

She looked up from the device. "It gets less efficient every time you run it, just like I told you it would. It's a demo, not a production-ready oil refinery."

"At some point the investors are going to want to see something that just keeps working."

"This is the best we can do for now. You wanted something that would knock their socks off. Were they or weren't they?"

His grimace morphed into a smile. "Clear into Marin County. Mayhew was all over me to find out how we move to Phase Two."

She placed the beta unit on the desk. "Peter, how are we going to move to Phase Two without a functioning company?"

He sighed. "This, again."

"I'll stop asking when I get a good answer." She gestured toward the book-strewn couch.

He shoveled some journals aside and sat, his expression relaxing into his patented *I'm-listening-but-I-don't-really-want-to* neutrality.

She screwed up her courage. She'd needed to get this off her chest for months. "I know we're still making money on Amplacillin and Bortine and Allyvil, but you can't keep spending like this without any new drugs in the pipeline."

"We don't have the capital for a new study, even if we still had the people to do it."

"Exactly!" She held the spent beta unit aloft. "This is an amazing demo, but it cost a hundred and fifty million dollars to build it. A hundred and fifty million! You could buy a jet fighter for less. Everything you want us to build costs an insane amount of money. We've spent *billions*."

His expression didn't change. "Let me worry about the burn rate."

The ember of anger flared into a bonfire. She leaned forward and stabbed an accusing finger at him. "*Are* you worried about the burn rate? I sure am. How many people have you let go so we could make payroll? There aren't many cars in the parking lot anymore. We used to make drugs. This company's called StruvePharma. What's left of the *pharma*?" By the time she finished her last sentence she was almost shouting.

Peter stared at her, his face wooden. "Calm. Down."

She subsided into her chair, fuming. She crossed her arms under her breasts.

He looked down at his lap. When he spoke, his voice was hoarse with emotion. "I hated laying off all those people, Emily, but they got great severance packages. When we go public, their stock warrants will be worth a fortune."

Emily sighed.

He looked down at his clenched fists. "When Dad was dying, I promised him I'd be a good shepherd to his company. We're close to the goal line, Emily. When we go to Phase Two, we'll be rolling in money. I always planned to hire everyone back."

"How? Life goes on, Peter. They all work for Roche or Genentech or Gilead now. They had to make a living." She tried and failed to keep the sullen tone from her voice. *Dammit. I am no good at confrontation.*

"They'll come back. Emily, listen to me. Your discoveries made it possible for us to build *that.*" He pointed at the demo unit. "*That's* why Aidan brought you in. *That's* what the last seven years have all been about. So what if it costs a hundred and fifty million? It's the fix for our money problems, so we can solve the big questions once and for all!"

"Don't try to sell me, Peter. I'm not one of your venture capitalists."

"If I could've gotten us here without mortgaging the company up to my eyeballs, don't you think I would have? I believe in what we're doing. We might have a fifteen-year jump on the competition, thanks to you and Aidan."

"And to Jack," Emily said. Her former husband had played a huge role in inspiring her breakthrough. Without his insights, without the hundreds of discussions, arguments and even fights they'd had over the science, none of this would have been possible.

She swallowed the familiar lump of sadness and shame that rose in her throat whenever she thought about Jack. She'd never told him how much he'd meant to her work, but the circumstances of their divorce had been so awful she couldn't bring herself to face him. Even if she could, her non-disclosure agreement with SP would have kept her from discussing her breakthroughs with him. But she could remind others. Peter in particular never seemed to remember how important Jack had been to the work.

Peter shrugged. "And Jack. Fine. But think about it. We can make oil out of thin air! That by itself will change the world forever. No more dependence on Russia or the Middle East for energy. No need for fracking. No need for oil companies at all. It's even carbon-neutral! With all the other things we're working on, there's no limit to what we'll be able to do. We'll own the world."

"Peter. Everything is experimental. We can't even keep the demo unit running for more than forty-eight hours without having to take it apart to replace the reactants. It gets slower and less efficient every time we run it. Who knows how long it will take to work out the kinks? It could take years. There's still so much basic science to do!"

He stood. "I have faith in you. Just a few more dog and pony shows with investors and we'll have all the cash we'll ever need. Then we'll tell the pharmacy side about the Black Box. We can get the targeted MAB program back on its feet. Imagine what our drug designers will be able to do with this technology!" His face had taken on the sheen of true belief that Aidan O'Keefe called *The Messiah Look*. After the triumph with ZMPC, he probably wouldn't come down for days.

She kept her sigh to herself. There was no arguing with him when he was like this, but she had to try. "Okay, Peter. I'd better get back to it, then." She picked up the beta unit. "This thing won't clean itself."

He looked relieved. "Let's talk tomorrow. Come by around noon and we'll go downtown for lunch with Aidan and Sasha. How does Greek sound? I'm in the mood for some *moussaka*."

"Sounds good."

"I'll make reservations." He left, whistling a vaguely familiar tune.

Emily grabbed her white lab coat from its peg on the wall with her free hand. She followed him into the dimly lit hallway. The ceiling lights were low to save energy. "Peter? I want in on the business planning for Phase Two. I mean it."

"You got it," he said without turning around. He strode around the corner and disappeared from view.

Emily sighed. She'd heard it all before. No doubt, she'd hear it all again. She shrugged into her lab coat, turned in the opposite direction and walked to her lab.

The vast Pauling Building was as quiet as a mausoleum. Even the custodial staff had gone home. She ambled down the broad hallway known as Park Avenue.

The building was so large that its inhabitants had eventually named all of the corridors after streets. It was much easier to find the lab on the third floor at Cedar and 5th Street, for example, than to puzzle out the inconsistent room numbering scheme. The office manager had eventually installed signs on iron posts at the intersections, with swooping art-deco lettering inspired by the Metro station signs of Paris. The residents had even painted scenes on some of the walls.

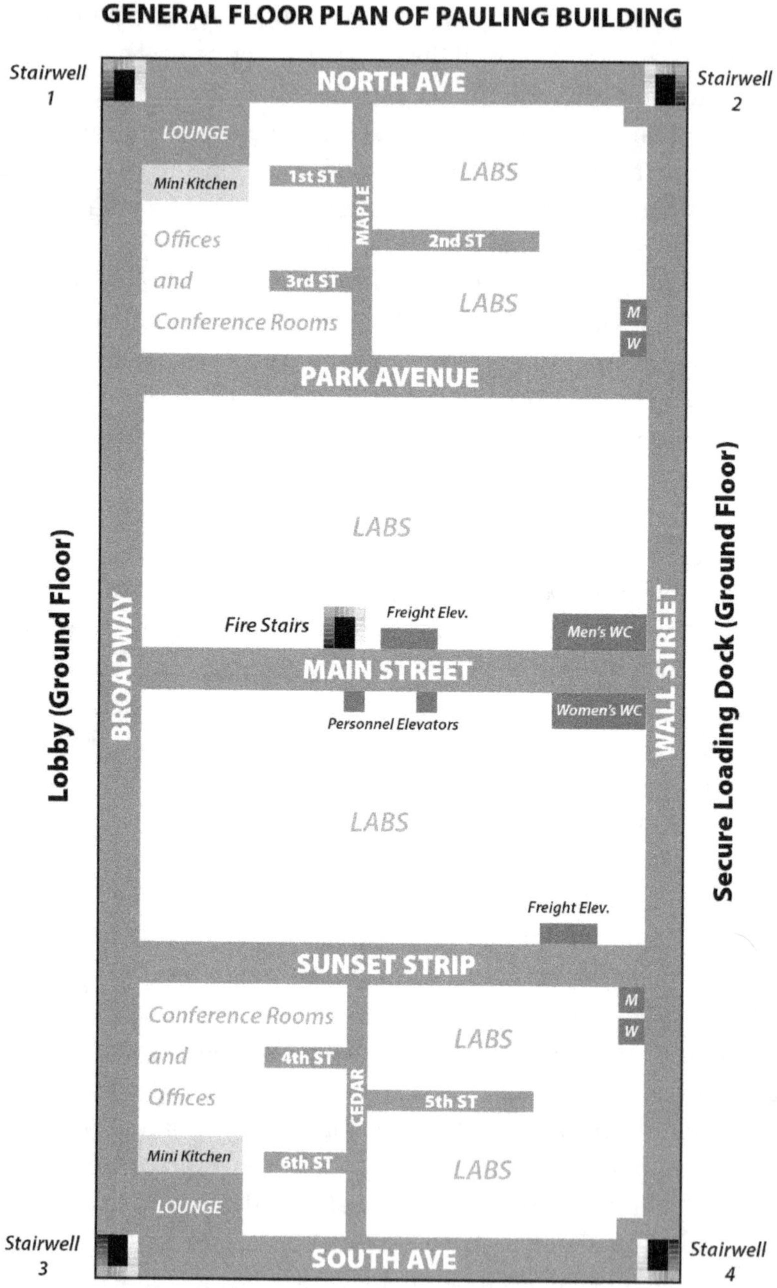

GENERAL FLOOR PLAN OF PAULING BUILDING

Figure 3: General Floor Plan of Pauling Building

Emily stopped in front of the heavy steel door just short of Wall Street, the corridor that ran the length of the east side of the building. "253" was stenciled on the door in flat black paint, but it was otherwise unadorned. It didn't even have a handle.

She pulled on the lanyard of her ID badge, clipped to a belt loop next to her right front pants pocket. She waved it in front of the magnetic card reader on the wall next to the door. It unlocked with a heavy *clang*. She let go of the badge. It zipped back to its spot on her belt. She shoved the door open and walked through.

There was a short hallway on the other side, lit by a pair of star-bright LED lights high above. The far end of the hallway ended in another metal door. Next to it was a wall-mounted biometric hand-scanner with a numeric keypad.

She walked to the far end of the mantrap and waited for the door to close behind her. When she heard its latch click, she placed her palm on the scanner and waited. There was a single beep. An air pump whirred. She yawned to ease the small drop of pressure on her ear-drums. Then she punched her security code into the keypad and waited again. Two beeps sounded a moment later. The motorized door swung open.

The lights went on as she stepped into her lab.

In contrast to the harsh blue-white brilliance of the mantrap, the Black Box was filled with gentle yellow light. It was kept at 77 degrees Fahrenheit, and just below one atmosphere of air pressure, like a biohazard lab. Any leaks in the containment would force air in, not out. The warmth was comforting.

Ten long rows of black benches filled the huge space—work areas for the chemists, biologists, engineers and technicians who reported to her. Above each station were shelves of bottles filled with chemicals, reagents, test tubes and beakers, computer monitors on adjustable swing arms, and a bewildering variety of electronic devices.

The walls were lined with cabinets full of dangerous chemicals, frag-ile glassware, and expensive instruments. The room hummed with the sound of ventilation pumps, refrigerators, heaters, and the low, smooth *basso* rumble of ultracentrifuges in the corner behind a wall of shrap-nel-proof Plexiglas.

Emily loved the lab. She even liked the odor of the mineral oil the techs used to polish the black epoxy lab benches. She closed her eyes, enjoying the warmth and the white noise of the machinery. She considered curling up in a corner to catch a quick nap. She had done it more than once when carrying out long experimental protocols. There was a cot, a pillow and a blanket in the closet. The notion was tempting, but after a moment's thought she shook her head. "You have work to do, girl," she said aloud. "There's a real bed waiting at home."

She crossed the full length of the lab, turned right and walked along the wall to the Revitalizer. The refrigerator-sized device stood in a space once occupied by a chemical fume hood. Its face was covered with flat-panel displays and controls arranged around a slot just the right size to accommodate the beta unit.

A tiny USB keyboard had been Velcroed to an empty spot on the Revitalizer's face. She smiled as she remembered the amused consternation on Aidan O'Keefe's face when she told him they'd forgotten to include a keyboard in the initial design. "Well, we won't be showing *this* to investors," the Chief Technical Officer had said. She and Aidan had split up years before, but she still appreciated his puckish sense of humor.

She stepped up to the Revitalizer and tapped a button labeled "INITIALIZE". The motorized door of the slot slid open. High-speed fans deep inside the device whined to life. She checked the orientation of the beta unit before feeding it into the slot. It disappeared, like a tape on her grandmother's old VCR. The slot slid closed.

A speaker emitted the first four notes of Beethoven's Fifth symphony: *dah dah dah DAH*.

She tapped the START button.

The Revitalizer beeped three times. The largest of the displays turned on.

```
OLEOSYNTH BETA UNIT REV 11.7 SER NO 001 CYCLE 7
ESTIMATED TIME TO COMPLETION: 31 H 17 M 11 S.
UNIT CANNOT BE REMOVED ONCE CLEANING CYCLE HAS BEGUN.
DO YOU WANT TO CONTINUE (Y/N)?
```

"Thirty-one hours," she sighed. It was worse than she thought. She tapped the "Y" button on the tiny keyboard.

The word "LOCKED" appeared beneath the countdown timer on the screen, and the "seconds" value began to decrease.

Two more displays lit up, showing camera views of the beta unit from different angles. It had already been lowered into a bath of dilute perchloric acid.

Emily watched as robotic manipulator arms descended into view and clamped the top edge of the beta unit in their grasp. All of the screens flashed as the device was bathed with a coded series of brilliant red laser pulses. The robotic arms carried the now-detached and dripping top plate of the beta unit up and out of view. The acid bath grew cloudy as the reactants from the unit began to flow out of its fluorinated nanotube capillary beds.

Emily murmured, "*Uh-buh-dee, uh-buh-dee, uh-buh-dee,* that's all, folks." Jack's Porky Pig imitation had been flawless. Hers was execrable, but it was improving. He'd had always made fun of her inability to imitate voices and accents. Even after all these years, though she hadn't spoken with him since the divorce, she still felt compelled to practice.

She turned away from the display. It would take hours for the spent reactants to be purged from the beta unit. It was interesting to watch—the first time, anyway. It wasn't as interesting as sleep. Nothing else would happen for another ten hours, and her bed was calling. She yawned as she made her way back to the door.

Just before she reached it, it beeped twice. Then it opened.

A man stumbled into the lab toward her.

Emily yelped and jumped back.

It was Jason Lackland, one of her technicians. He wore the same plain yellow T-shirt and denim jeans he'd been wearing when he left the lab at six o'clock that evening.

She reached out to steady him. "Jason? What are you doing here?"

He put his hand to his mouth, dropping his ID badge in the process. He didn't move to pick it up. He stared at her with wide, terrified eyes.

His mouth was bloody.

"What happened?" she blurted.

Then she saw the large man behind him.

A black balaclava obscured his face and hair, revealing only a pair of icy green eyes behind a pair of plastic goggles. Everything he wore was black: his jacket, his gloves, the bulging duffel bag slung across his back, and the giant silencer-equipped pistol he pointed at Jason's head.

"Don't shout," the man said. "It would be bad for both of you." His voice was deep, his accent northern European, possibly Scandinavian.

She stifled the scream before it could escape.

Calm down. Remember. Remember everything about him. The police will want to know. She'd been robbed and would have been raped when she was studying for her third Ph.D. at Cal Tech, but she'd pepper-sprayed her attacker and escaped. She had remembered enough about him to be able to identify him in a line-up and then in court. She could do it again.

"Who are you?" she whispered.

"Where is the unit?"

"What unit?" she said without thinking.

The stranger lunged forward and smashed the butt of his pistol across the back of Jason's head.

Jason cried out and went down in a heap. He clutched his head with both hands.

She reached forward to try to help him, but the man pointed his huge gun at her. She froze.

"No games, Dr. Dura. Where is the device?"

"I just put it into the Revitalizer."

"Remove it."

"I can't! It's being cleaned!"

The man stared at her for a long moment. Then he kicked Jason in the leg. "Stand up, or you will never stand up again."

Jason lurched to his feet. He held his head and groaned. Blood dripped from his blond hair onto his T-shirt.

"Show me," the man said to Emily. "Both of you. Walk ahead of me. Keep your hands where I can see them. I will not hesitate to shoot you." He spoke in a dull monotone. He might have been discussing the weather.

She didn't doubt his sincerity for an instant. She turned away from him and complied. Her heart felt like a hammer trying to beat its way out through her chest wall. "We'll do anything you want," she said.

Jason staggered as they walked back to the Revitalizer. She steadied him with her left hand. They halted when they reached the device.

The man said, "Turn around. Face me."

They obeyed.

He waved the pistol at the Revitalizer. "Explain it to me."

Emily said, "The cleaning cycle's engaged. It's removing the reactants. Look at the screen. It has more than thirty hours left."

"Stop the cleaning."

"I can't do that. It's locked. The beta unit's in an acid bath, in an argon atmosphere. If you take it out, the oxygen in the air will poison the unit. It will never work again."

"A broken device is of no use to me. You will give me the backup unit."

"There is no backup unit! This is the only one that works! We recycled the other prototypes to make this one!"

The man took two sidesteps to his right and pointed his gun at Jason's head. "The backup unit. Now."

Emily's voice rose to a near-shriek. "No! There *isn't* one! I swear to God, I'm telling the truth!"

"I told you!" Jason squeaked, still clutching his head. He looked at her, panic written on his face. "I told him, Emily!"

"You did," the man said. Then he pulled the trigger.

Emily screamed. The suppressed gunshot was loud enough to set her ears to ringing, but she still heard the thud as Jason's body dropped to the floor. She closed her eyes. "Oh, no, no," she moaned.

"Look," the man said.

She forced her eyes open.

She stared down the barrel of his gun.

He shouted, "Look at him!" His tone left no room for defiance.

She obeyed.

Jason sprawled next to the base of the Revitalizer, legs twitching. Blood fountained from his head onto the polished concrete floor, each pulse more sluggish than the last. His legs abruptly went still.

"Oh, my God," she said. *This can't be happening!* Then a different kind of panic seized her.

Jason had been standing in front of the Revitalizer.

She looked at the front panel of the refrigerator-sized device. It was intact. Then she saw the blood-spattered hole in the cabinet to the left of the Revitalizer. The gunman had shifted position to avoid hitting the machine.

A surge of guilty relief flooded her veins even as salt water filled her mouth. She fell to her knees and vomited her late-evening snack of strawberry yogurt onto the laboratory floor.

The murderer waited to speak until the final spasm passed. "One last time, Doctor Dura. Where is the backup unit?"

She wiped her chin with her right hand and snarled, "There. Isn't. One."

He lowered the gun. "Now I believe you. Come. There is another thing we must do before we go."

"I'm not going anywhere with you, you murderer!"

He blinked. "Go with me, or end up like him. I get paid more if I bring you in alive."

"You think I care how much you get paid?"

The killer sighed. "Shall we pay a visit to Mr. Struve? He has not yet left the campus. Do you care whether he lives out the night?"

That broke her fragile resolve. She wasn't going to get anyone else's blood on her hands. "All right," she said, tears filling her eyes. "All right."

He grabbed her arm, hauled her upright and dragged her into the mantrap. The door closed behind them. "Enter your code," he said. He forced her hand into the biometric scanner next to the door that opened on the hallway.

Her hands trembled so much she could barely enter her code. After her second failure, he pushed her away from the keypad, switched the gun to his left hand and slapped her across the face. "If you do that again it will set off the alarm. Do not make the mistake of thinking that I am stupid." He slapped her again, hard, before changing the gun back to his right hand.

"Okay!" she yelped. She rubbed tears from her eyes, focused all of her will, and entered her code. Her *second* code. Paradoxically, the gunman's slaps had cleared her mind. She'd finally remembered the emergency code. It opened the door, but it also triggered the silent alarm.

John Shea had trained her for this contingency. She'd never really believed that she'd have to use it.

She did now.

The killer pulled her back from the door as it opened. He leaned close and whispered, "If you try to run, if you make a sound, I will kill you. Do you understand? You will nod, or you will die."

She nodded, trembling.

Maintaining an iron grip on her right forearm, the killer pulled the door open a fraction, peered outside, and then put his head around the corner to look down the other end of Park Avenue. He pulled and she followed.

They made their way down the corridor. He stopped her in front of another heavy steel door. It bore the number "252."

Oh, no. He knows about the QUBE.

"Open it," the man whispered in her ear. His breath was hot and horrible.

She put her badge on the reader. The door unlocked. She pushed it open. The mantrap was identical to the one in her lab, but just a handful of people had access to this one. As SP's Chief Scientist, she was one of them.

The killer followed her into the mantrap.

She put her hand in the scanner. *They'll know I'm in here now, and under duress.* In the drills, John Shea's Rapid Response Team had arrived in three minutes, but it had been months since the last exercise. They'd all become lax about security as they neared the goal of delivering the demo. Emily wasn't sure the former SEALs were even on the payroll anymore. She couldn't remember the last time she'd seen any of the elite security squad on campus.

She prayed for the first time in her life. Please, God. Don't let Peter have downsized them.

She hit the ENTER button after she entered her code.

The door didn't open.

That was when she knew that someone, somewhere, was deciding whether to grant them access.

"What is wrong?" the killer demanded.

"Nothing. It... it just takes a second to process the request."

"It did not do so in the other lab."

"Well, this isn't the Black Box," she snapped. "This room has a different security clearance." She glanced up at the ceiling where she knew the tiny camera lens was hidden.

"This is taking too long," growled the killer. "Enter your code again."

"It doesn't work that way. Just give it a second." *Please open it,* she begged the person on the other end of the camera. *I want to live.*

At long last, the fans in the high ceiling began to whir. Dry, arctic air flooded into the mantrap. Emily's hair crackled.

Thank Christ, she said silently.

The door unlatched and ponderously swung open.

He shoved her inside.

The room was small and ice cold. The walls and floors were metal. Brilliant blue-white lights shone down from the fifteen-foot ceiling.

The only object in the room was a waist-high, stainless steel pillar with a featureless square top about a foot on each side. It looked like an oversized traffic bollard.

The man moved to the opposite side of the pillar, aimed the gun at her head, and watched her with unblinking green eyes.

The hole at the end of the silencer was *huge*.

"Shut it down and open it," he said. "Do not make a fatal mistake, Doctor Dura."

She didn't hesitate. She put her badge on top of the pillar. A musical triple chime echoed in the room.

"Command?" prompted a computerized female voice.

She cleared her throat and enunciated, "Rapid shutdown sequence." She began to shiver.

"Confirm rapid shutdown sequence authorization code."

"Authorization Emily Dura, Chief Scientist, StruvePharma, code one, one, alpha, two, bravo."

The computer voice said, "Rapid shutdown sequence confirmed. Three minutes to completion. Please stand by." The three chimes sounded again.

The killer lowered the gun. He pulled the strap of the duffel bag over his head and dropped it on the floor.

"Open it and remove the shells."

She knelt and did as she was told. Inside the bag was a pair of rectangular carbon-fiber shells about the size of two small shoeboxes side by side. In the center of each was a padded hemispherical cavity about four inches deep. Judging by their lightness, the shells were filled with some kind of insulating foam.

She looked up at him. "You won't be able to get it to work. The QUBE is only part of the system. Without the rest, it might as well be a paperweight." Her voice quavered as she began to shiver.

"Put them on the floor, with the cavities face up."

Either he doesn't know what the QUBE is, or he doesn't care. He's no scientist. "Why did you kill Jason?" she asked.

He surprised her by answering. "He was unnecessary."

"Am *I* necessary?"

"If you do not become a problem."

Emily couldn't bear to say anything else to him. She put the shells on the floor as he directed. She stared at them. The edges of their top surfaces were designed to interlock with each other. The rubberized cavities were shaped with extreme precision. They would fit the QUBE exactly. The craftsmanship was superb. Whoever put the killer up to stealing the QUBE and kidnapping her was clearly an insider. When she found out who it was—*if* she found out—she would make them pay.

She crossed her arms against her chest and tried to control her shivering.

They maintained a stony silence until the computer said, *"Rapid shutdown sequence complete."*

Motors below floor level whined. The pillar began to rise. The room became much colder as the square steel pillar grew taller. Her shivering grew almost convulsive.

The motors went silent. The pillar did not quite touch the wire mesh that hung below the ceiling lights.

There was a square opening in the pillar, about four feet above the floor. Inside was a silver sphere about eight inches in diameter, locked in place by four golden studs protruding from its base. A grid of tiny, glittering jewels covered the sphere's surface. It was otherwise mirror smooth except for four narrow thermal expansion slots that ran from pole to pole, dividing it into quadrants like the meridians of a globe.

The device looked fragile, but it was hardy enough to handle the transition from a fraction of a degree above absolute zero to its now merely Antarctic temperature in the space of three minutes.

"You have to be careful," she said, teeth chattering. "Until it reaches room temperature, it won't respond well to rough handling."

"I am well aware," the killer said. He pulled a pair of thin black gloves from his coat pocket and tossed them around the pillar to her. Long, thin wires ending with alligator clips were attached to the wristband of each glove. "Put these on, ground yourself, remove the device and put it into one of the shells."

As she pulled the gloves on, some still-rational part of her brain registered that they were made of Nomex. At least she shouldn't have to worry about frostbite.

She touched the pillar to discharge any remaining static electricity, then clipped the lead wires on the gloves to two of the four golden terminals protruding from the base of the QUBE. She pressed a button hidden inside the cavity. There was a click as the solenoids locking the terminals to the pillar were released.

With exquisite care, the slowly removed the QUBE from the pillar.

It was light as air and numbingly cold. She averted her face from it, but a few droplets from her breath condensed on its gleaming surface. They froze instantly, forming a constellation of tiny glittering beads.

She transferred the QUBE to the closest of the two shells. She forced her hands to remain steady in spite of her shivering. She didn't have to ask what would happen if she dropped it.

As soon as it rested in its form-fitting cavity, she unclipped the grounding wires and pulled off the gloves.

"Put the other case on top and press down around the edges, hard."

She did so. The carbon-fiber shells clicked together around the spherical device, making a box about ten inches on a side.

"Put it into the bag. Carefully."

Emily slid the encased QUBE into the duffel bag and zipped it closed. She rubbed her hands together and blew into them. The Nomex gloves had provided scant protection. The QUBE was *cold*.

"I am coming around. Move."

She backed away while he circled the pillar.

He slung the duffel bag across his back. "And now we go. Simple as that." He gestured with the gun. "Open the door."

Frigid air followed them into the mantrap, but when the door shut behind them it felt like a tropical paradise. She put her hand in the scanner and entered her second code again. The hallway door clicked open.

The killer moved behind her. "We take your car," he whispered in her ear. He pushed her into the corridor. "To the right."

She began to walk down Park Avenue.

He followed.

Her heart felt like it was about to burst. If the security squad was here, she should be seeing—

A small black puck-shaped object slid across the floor toward them.

There it is! She dropped to the ground, closed her eyes, opened her mouth and covered her ears.

The flash-bang grenade blast was so close it didn't matter. She felt like a boxer had slugged her in the face. Her sense of hearing just ceased to exist. Gasping, she tried to get her bearings. Closing her eyes had helped with the flash effect, but the hallway was too dark for her to see anything.

She felt something move very fast through the air near her head.

Gunfire!

She threw herself to the floor. She remembered her training. Lie flat and still and don't give them any reason to think you're one of the bad guys.

Then something lanced through her side.

She couldn't hear herself scream. The pain was colossal. Unbelievable. She contorted her body, clutching the right side of her chest. Blood gushed hot and sticky around her fingers. Cold terror flooded through her. *It's my liver.* "Don't shoot, don't shoot! It's me! It's me!" she screamed. She had no idea if anyone heard her. She couldn't hear herself.

Then she saw the black-clad killer. He lay on his back, clutching his gun and writhing in obvious pain. The duffel bag was on the floor beside him. He ripped off the balaclava and goggles, revealing a lean, handsome face contorted in agony. Blood streamed from a scalp wound somewhere in the thick of his short blond hair.

His merciless eyes locked onto hers. His bloody lips formed two words. She'd been deafened by the flash-bang, but his meaning was all too clear.

You bitch, he mouthed again and again.

Paralyzing agony spread like boiling oil through her veins, into her limbs.

The killer raised his gun. Smoke wafted from the silencer. Then she knew that it wasn't the SEALs who had shot her.

He pointed the gun at her.

She tried to get up, but the pain was too much. She collapsed. She heard rather than felt her head thump against the floor.

Black-garbed men with assault rifles ran toward the killer from the end of the hall, moving far, far too slowly.

The last thing she saw was the hole at the end of the silencer.

CHAPTER FOUR

StruvePharma Coyote Hill Campus, Palo Alto, California

June 26

Peter Struve paced back and forth across his huge corner office on the top floor of the Delbrück Building. He was too keyed up to sit down. Talking with Emily always did that to him. Hell, talking with *anyone* about his vision for the company did that to him. His detractors and even his friends sometimes talked about his "reality distortion field" when he went off on one of his rants about how he would change the world. Peter suffered the gibes without complaint. He knew better.

Thanks to geniuses like Emily Dura and Aidan O'Keefe, StruvePharma was a decade ahead of the competition. Maybe two. The giant gamble he'd made in liquidating most of his father's multi-billion-dollar pharmaceutical company was about to pay off—assuming his geniuses could solve the few remaining problems. He believed in them. They were geniuses, after all. That's why they were still on the diminishing SP payroll.

To be fair, he had harbored a few doubts. He'd slept only a few hours in the three days since the demo at Sam's Chowder House. Philip Mayhew hadn't called until long after the time limit of the beta unit's production run had elapsed—payback, no doubt, for the many months Peter had been forced to string him along. ZMPC had pledged half a billion more to fund Phase Two. Peter knew he should be ready to crash, but the adrenaline rush showed no sign of subsiding. *He'd done it!*

He wrenched his attention back to the present. Going home wasn't an option, not in his current mental state. He'd just toss and toss in bed. Yvonne would punch him in the kidneys if he kept her up all night again just because *he* couldn't sleep.

Then he remembered that Yvonne and the girls were in Italy. She'd made it clear that she might never come home again, unless Peter's giant bet paid off.

He sighed. He couldn't do anything about that tonight. He tried to put Yvonne from his mind. He had to write some emails. He had to get reservations at that Greek restaurant. He could do that online. The meeting with Sealock had to be rescheduled—and of course, so did the meeting with the Gideon Hart guy. He had to get back to Mayhew about Phase Two, and then he had to schedule demos with AMT and Red Rock and Sequoia.

He was deep in thought when his cell phone made a peculiar chirping sound. For a minute he didn't recognize it. It wasn't an incoming call. It wasn't an alarm sound.

"What the hell is that?" he murmured. He pulled his slender phone from his shirt pocket and glanced at its screen.

The whole face of the phone was red, except for the words "SILENT ALARM TRIGGERED" in bold white text.

"Holy shit," he whispered. He stood bolt upright. His chair crashed against the floor-to-ceiling window behind him.

Windows.

Why had he chosen an office with so many windows? He could be seen from outside from hundreds of feet away. He could be seen by *anybody*. And unlike the armored windows of the Pauling Building, these were just plate glass.

He bolted from his desk and wrenched open the door in the far corner of the office. Harsh white LED lights snapped on, revealing a concrete-walled room equipped with a desk, a chair, an iMac with a huge display, a phone and a toilet. A small USB fingerprint reader was next to the keyboard.

He pulled the massive door shut behind him and then slapped a switch on the wall. A thick metal shield slid across the doorframe, sealing him in. He didn't relax until he heard the heavy *chunk* of the locks. He'd thought the executive safe rooms an extravagance when Aidan O'Keefe proposed them, back when they were planning the Coyote Hill research campus six years ago. Not anymore.

"Oh, Jesus," he whispered. He sat at the table, pressed his thumb against the fingerprint ID reader, and stabbed the RETURN key on the computer's keyboard. The black screen came to life.

Argus, their custom surveillance app, was always running on this machine. It showed the views from four of the security cameras around the location where the alarm had been triggered. Each window showed a different angle of Emily Dura walking down a darkened hallway. A large man dressed in black walked behind her. He carried a huge pistol. It was pointed at her back.

"Oh, shit!" Peter yelped. He hit the speaker button on the desk phone. There was no dial tone. "God *damn* it!" The internal phone system was dead. He grabbed his cell phone. It still had a signal, thank God. His chief of security had insisted on installing battery-backed cell phone repeaters inside buildings all over the campus. Another expense Peter had grudgingly approved. "Bless you, John Shea," he whispered as he pressed the security chief's speed dial icon.

Shea answered on the first ring. "It woke me up too. What's going on?"

"There's a man with a gun. He's got Emily. Call the police! Then call Aidan!"

"They're already on the way. I have to login. I'll call you back."

"Wait wait wait! How do you know the police are coming?"

"If I got a call, they *got a call."* Shea's voice cut off with a click.

Peter lowered the phone and stared at the monitor. Emily and the gunman had stopped in front of a door. He couldn't tell which one. She waved her security badge in front of the reader and then pulled the door open. She vanished from view.

A few seconds later another window opened on the screen. It was labeled "PLNG 252B QUBE CRYO MANTRAP."

"Oh, no," Peter breathed. His blood ran cold.

The image in the window was the interior of a mantrap corridor as seen from a ceiling-mounted pinhole camera. Emily and the gunman were inside. Her hand was in the biometric scanner.

A dialog box popped up in the middle of the screen. "ALLOW ACCESS?" it prompted him. There were two buttons in the dialog: "YES" and "NO".

He put his hands over the touchpad and moved the pointer over "NO."

"What is wrong?" asked a harsh male voice.

Peter jumped in his chair. The voice had come from the computer. It was the audio feed from the mantrap.

"Nothing," replied Emily. Peter cringed to hear the quaver in her voice. *"It just takes a second to process the request."*

"It did not do so in the other lab."

"The other lab?" Peter whispered.

Emily said, "Well, this isn't the Black Box. This room has a different security clearance."

At John Shea's urging, Peter had practiced with the *Argus* security software for many hours. In an instant he had a new window open showing the interior of the Black Box lab. He jumped from camera to camera. Then he spotted Jason Lackland's motionless body, sprawled on the floor, surrounded by a vast pool of blood.

He was too shocked to curse. Bile rose in his throat. He felt faint.

"This is taking too long," the gunman said over the speaker. "Enter your code again."

Emily snapped, "It doesn't work that way. Just give it a second."

Peter tore his gaze away from the image of Jason's corpse. He could see Emily's eyes in the mantrap camera window, beseeching him. She knew someone was watching. Behind her, the black-clad killer raised the gun. He pointed it at her head.

"Fuck fuck *fuck*," Peter whispered, sweat rolling down his face. He moved the pointer over the "YES" button and pressed down on the trackpad.

On the screen, the door swung open. Emily and the gunman moved into the QUBE facility.

Peter's cell phone rang. He shouted in surprise, and then picked up. "Shea?"

"The building's in lockdown. The Rapid Response Team is on the way. ETA two minutes. Police are a few minutes out."

"Do you have the *Argus* feed? There's only one guy, as far as I can tell. He has Emily. He's after the QUBE." He swallowed, fighting nausea.

"I know. I'm watching it now."

"How the fuck did he get past security?"

"I'll find out. Why did you let them into the room?"

"Why?" Peter laughed, incredulous. "He already killed Jason Lackland. His body is in... in the Black Box. If he kills Emily...." He dropped the phone and bent over the toilet just in time. The wrenching spasms in his gut seemed to go on forever. When he was done, he sat back, grabbed a handful of toilet paper and wiped his mouth. Another handful of paper served to mop the cold sweat from his face. *Oh, Christ, this is not happening.*

He struggled to his feet, went back to the desk and collapsed into the chair. He stared at the screen. The gunman still aimed his pistol at

Emily. She had removed the QUBE from its connection pillar and was placing it into a hemispherical cavity in a black box on the floor.

He grabbed the cell phone and switched it to speaker mode. "Shea?"

"My men are in position."

"Did you call Aidan?"

"No. He can't do anything, and he'd just come down here and get in the way. We'll call him after that bastard's dead."

"No! Tell your men not to kill him," Peter shouted. "We have to know how he found out about the QUBE!"

Shea snarled, "If he hurts Emily, that fucker is dead meat, Peter."

On the screen, the gunman had backed Emily around the other side of the pillar and was shoving the box into a duffel bag.

Peter said, "We need to know who sent him. And for Christ's sakes, tell them not to hit Emily or the bag!"

There was a long pause before Shea replied. *"I'll tell them to try to take the tango alive, but shit happens, Peter. No guarantees."* Shea's Marine background was showing: *tango* was military shorthand for "terrorist."

Peter squinted at the computer screen as he listened to Shea relay his commands to the SEAL team, his heart beating like a kettledrum. The gunman had maneuvered Emily into the mantrap corridor ahead of him. "They're coming out."

"Shut up, Peter, I need to concentrate."

Peter bit his tongue. He might be John Shea's boss, but only an idiot would snark back to a veteran of Marine Force Recon.

Several of the *Argus* surveillance windows changed views. They now showed the dark corridor outside the QUBE facility. The images were grainy as the cameras struggled to make use of the dim green light coming from the EXIT signs. Peter saw Emily emerge from the lab, the gunman close behind her. He could also see Shea's black-clad former SEALs. There were two teams of four, crouching around the corners at either end of the corridor named Park Avenue, well out of sight.

"All right, Emily, remember your training," whispered Shea. Then, in a loud voice: "Team one, execute!"

Peter watched one of the SEALs crouch down and roll a flash-bang grenade down the hallway toward Emily.

There was a brilliant flash on the screen, accompanied by a crashing blast from the computer's speakers. He jumped in his seat and cringed away from the sound.

His recollection of the next events would always be incoherent, fragmented—somehow disconnected from reality, like half-remembered scenes from a fever dream.

He saw Emily's body, silhouetted against the bright white light of the flash-bang, captured in mid-fall as she dove to the floor. There was a fusillade of shots and a woman's agonized scream.

Peter jumped to his feet. "No!" he cried, holding his head with both hands.

"Don't shoot, don't shoot! It's me! It's me!" Emily shrieked.

There was shouting and confusion and another shot, then a rapid sequence of even louder shots. There was a brief silence, followed by more yelling.

"Shea!" Peter screamed. "*Shea!* What the fuck is going on!"

Endless seconds later, the lights brightened on Park Avenue.

The gunman was visible in one *Argus* window. The SEALs had removed the man's upper garments, revealing an expanse of pale white skin dotted with flecks of red. What looked like part of a bulletproof vest lay discarded on the floor nearby. One of the SEALs performed CPR on the intruder. Another pinched his nose shut and breathed into his mouth at intervals. A third pressed a thick gauze bandage against a bloody wound low in the gunman's abdomen. A fourth held his hand under the prone man's neck. Blood dripped through his fingers onto the concrete floor.

The duffel bag containing the QUBE was on the floor next to the wounded gunman. Struve couldn't tell if it was intact or not. He prayed that it was. Shame flooded through him. His first thought should have been for Emily. He scanned the other windows to find her.

In the center of another camera view, a group of four SEALs stared down at something on the floor. Their armored, motionless bodies blocked his view, but the spreading crimson pool near their feet told Peter everything he needed to know.

"Emily. Oh, my God," he croaked. He fell backwards against the safe room's rough cinder block wall, slumped to the floor and wept.

Sometime later—it could have been minutes or hours—he recovered enough to speak. "Will you call Aidan now, John?" His voice hitched with grief.

Shea's tone was gentle. "Come out of there, Peter. The police will be there soon, and they'll want to talk with you. I'm on my way."

CHAPTER FIVE

Millennium Tower, San Francisco, California

June 26

Aidan O'Keefe stared at the big iPhone vibrating on the glass surface of the living room table.

He put down the book he hadn't been reading and picked up the phone. On the screen was a picture of a smiling Peter Struve.

He glanced at the cheap plastic Korean-made phone resting on the table.

It was the "burner." It was the one that was supposed to have rung.

"Damn," Aidan whispered. He let his iPhone ring three more times before tapping the ANSWER button.

"Hello?" he said, slurring his words to make it sound as if he'd just woken up.

Struve was incoherent at first. Aidan spent the first five minutes of their conversation calming him down enough to understand what he was saying.

A strange numbness crept over him as he listened to Struve. He felt both hot and cold at the same time. Sweat broke out on his face. His stomach began to churn. *Is this fear?* he wondered. If so, he began to understand why Struve was gibbering. The sensation was deeply unsettling.

He talked Struve down, which took another five minutes, and told him he would be in as soon as he could.

Aidan lurched into the bathroom, dropped his bathrobe on the floor, turned the cold-water tap in the shower to full and stood in the frigid spray until his teeth began to chatter.

Emily was dead, as was Jason Lackland. The agent had been injured, perhaps killed. Worst of all, the status of QUBE Charlie was unknown. The carbon-fiber cases Aidan had designed would have shielded it from a fall, but bullets from semi-automatic rifles had flown in that corridor.

At some point the water did its work. The horrible amalgam of chills and heat faded away. Now he was just cold. He could think again.

He'd have to think fast.

It would take around thirty minutes for him to reach the StruvePharma campus down in Palo Alto. He'd have time to call Balestra, but he'd have to hurry. He couldn't delay his arrival at SP for long without attracting the wrong kind of attention from the wrong kind of people.

Aidan prided himself on his attachment to reality. He was under no illusions about the intelligence of the police. He assumed they would trace the whereabouts of everyone in SP's management chain, pull their phone records, maybe even put them under surveillance, once the true nature and scope of SP's research became clear. They would know when he spoke with Struve, and would notice any significant delay in his arrival on the scene.

Time was short. He wouldn't have another chance to talk to his Italian contact until he could be sure that the investigation had been completed. Even then, he would have to be very, very careful. The eyes of the police and who knows how many other government agencies would be on them all the time from now on. God and the NSA only knew how many security vulnerabilities there were in the cell phone network and the Internet. He'd have to resort to primitive but effective spy tradecraft to reach his co-conspirators now: dead drops and one-time pads to encrypt and decrypt printed messages. Fortunately, he'd already made all the arrangements.

In Aidan O'Keefe's world, there was no room for chance.

He turned off the tap and dried himself. He moved to the bedroom and pulled on the shirt and slacks he'd worn yesterday and thrown to the floor so they'd appear suitably rumpled today. He found his keys, wallet and both phones and stuffed them into his pockets. His gold Apple Watch still rested on its bedside charger. He decided to leave it, to enhance the appearance of a departure in haste. He took a deep breath, released it slowly, and then flung open the apartment door.

He ran down the hallway to the elevator, leaving the door ajar behind him. He stumbled once and caught himself before he could fall, wind-milling his arms to keep his balance. He pressed the elevator call button a dozen times. "Hurry, please, hurry!" he sobbed for the benefit of the surveillance camera in its domed enclosure in the ceiling behind him. There might not be a microphone in the hallway, but it was better to be sure. If the police had reason to suspect him, he didn't want to appear calm and collected on the building's surveillance tapes.

When the elevator arrived, he lurched inside and stabbed the button for the parking garage. The doors crept shut.

There was no camera in the elevator. He had to stop himself from smoothing down his tousled hair. *Look the part,* he reminded himself silently. As soon as the doors opened in the basement parking garage he barged through and ran flat out for his car.

He managed to escape the garage without hitting anything. He slalomed his Audi S8 through the downtown labyrinth of San Francisco high-rises, screeching around the few lethargic drivers out at this ridiculous hour.

He resisted the urge to floor it when he reached the southbound I-280 on-ramp. He had to leave convincing video evidence of his urgency to reach the campus, but he couldn't afford to be stopped and arrested for reckless driving before he made his call.

He set the cruise control at a high but still-rational velocity, turned the burner on, and tapped the icon for the encrypted voice-chat app that would connect him to Balestra.

It rang twice before the deep voice of the man who called himself Antonio Balestra resonated over the Audi's speakers. *"Yes?"*

"Your man tried to take Emily. She's dead, and so is one of her technicians. The QUBE might be damaged. Your man might be dead, too. The police have him."

The speaker sighed. *"That is most unfortunate."* His Italian accent was heavy but comprehensible.

"Unfortunate?" Aidan shouted. Unlike fear, he was well acquainted with fury. "The plan was to take the QUBE, not to murder the only person who knows how it works!"

"Be sensible. Who would have taken the device and not its designer? Who could make it work without her expertise? The police would have seen through your cover story in ten minutes. It had to be all or nothing."

Aidan's vision narrowed to a gray, red-tinged tunnel. He gripped the steering wheel with both hands. "He was supposed to use Jason Lackland to get in and take the QUBE. *Just* the QUBE! After we paid the ransom the Board would have taken the company away from Struve. They're almost ready to fire him right now! I'd be in charge.

Nobody else could run the place. Now you've fucked everything sideways. This was not the plan!"

"This was not your plan," Balestra said.

"Antonio. Listen to me. There's a reason I picked Jason. I hacked his security access so he could get into the QUBE facility. He didn't know the codes to call the Rapid Response Team. Only the executives even know the team exists! Your man didn't stand a chance against them. They're former Navy SEALs! If he'd followed my goddamned instructions, he would've gotten away scot-free. And he wouldn't have killed anyone!"

Balestra didn't respond for a long time. When he did, his voice was subdued. "And what if these boardroom—what is the word? Shenanigans? —did not go as you predicted?"

"I guess we'll never know now, will we, you damned half-wit!"

"My backers did not approve. Your plan was too subtle for them. You know they can be... a little rough. I am sorry, Aidan, I truly am, but this is immaterial. Surely you can depose Struve now. Dura's death alone should be enough evidence of his incompetence. My backers will provide the funds to build another QUBE if necessary."

Aidan spoke through gritted teeth. "QUBE Charlie is the only one that works every time. It's millions of times faster than the first two QUBEs even when they're running properly, and no one knows why. Do you have any idea what that means? Charlie has more processing power than every other computer in the world, put together, times a trillion. Emily was the only one who even had a chance of figuring out why it was so much better than the prototypes. Thanks to you her brains are all over the hallway. No amount of money is going to fix that!"

There was a long, silent moment. At last, Balestra sighed, *"Then it is over."*

Aidan took a deep breath. He let Balestra stew for a long moment before he said, "Struve has a contingency plan."

There was a snort of disbelieving laughter over the speakers. *"Struve is finished."*

"He'd better not be. He's the only one who can make it work. Thanks to you, we have to let it play out."

"Tell me his plan."

"No."

"Aidan—"

"No. This time I'm in the driver's seat. You'll find out where we're going when we get there."

"I swear to you; things will be different—"

It was Aidan's turn to scoff. "Listen to me very carefully. I have records. Audio recordings. Video surveillance. Bank transaction logs. I have employees of my own. They're watching you. If I disappear, or even if I don't check in with them regularly, every bit of that evidence goes to the FBI and Interpol. I can bring you down, and I will—unless you let me handle this myself."

"You do not know who you are dealing with, O'Keefe!"

"Oh, but I do," Aidan growled. "You'd be shocked by what I know about a sixty-one-year-old Milanese banker named Alberto Vincenzo di Mottura. And I assure you, if anything happens to me, you will not be pleased by what happens to your wife and children. Make sure they stick to their regular routines. If my people even suspect that you're trying to hide them, they're dead, and so are you. But not before they suffer. Especially Vanessa and Adriana." He crafted his voice to sound both lascivious and sad. "They're so lovely, Alberto. I might take a little trip to Italy myself to see them off. So to speak."

"You are bluffing."

"I. Don't. Bluff." After a long pause, he added, "Ever."

"I will kill you if you touch them," shouted di Mottura.

"Whether they live or die screaming is entirely up to you. Keep your distance and let me handle this, and we will both be unspeakably rich. And get rid of that gunman. If he talks, we're both sunk."

The answer was slow in coming. "He was hired through a cut-out. He knows nothing about us."

"He's a loose end."

"I do not have another operative in a position to do this."

Aidan sighed. "I'll have one of my men handle it."

"You've left a loose end yourself. What about Jason Lackland's security clearance? The change you made will be detected."

"Lackland never made it into the QUBE facility. No one will check his access. Why would they? In any case, I wrote most of our security software. All I have to do is revert the change." *And that is the sole bright spot in this whole fucked-up mess.* The bugs he'd introduced into the security software had contaminated the personnel database with inappropriate access privileges for more than a dozen employees, including Jason Lackland. Now Aidan could erase all evidence of those "bugs." Thank God he'd insisted on using an old source code control system that permitted such changes. It was tricky, but doable. If he'd bowed to the other engineers' demands to use *git,* he'd be sunk.

di Mottura snarled, "You have crossed a line today, O'Keefe. I will not forget it."

"That line has two sides, Alberto, and you crossed it first. Stay out of my way and I'll fix your mess. Interfere again, and I promise, you will be sorry, but not, alas, for very long. Meanwhile, no more calls. We're switching to the dead-drops. I'll be in touch."

Aidan held down the burner's OFF button. The old phone's display went dark.

He was still within the San Francisco city limits, but his Audi ate the miles like a lean black shark. In minutes the City was behind him, with nothing but tree-lined hills under starry skies on either side of the broad, curvy freeway. Come dawn the commuters driving south from San Francisco would choke the road, but at this hour it was almost empty.

Aidan pulled over to the shoulder and waited for the few cars in his rear-view mirror to pass. He got out and wedged the burner under the left rear tire. He leapt back into the sedan, used the dashboard controls to unlink the burner from the car's Bluetooth hands-free audio system, checked his mirrors, and then floored it.

The 520-horsepower engine roared. Black smoke from the tires, shredded plastic and bits of electronics spewed out behind the car as he thundered back onto the freeway.

He could afford to get a ticket now. It might even lend credibility to his cover story. He'd be expected to be frantic to get to the scene of the crime. He eased the car up to 120 miles an hour.

He felt immeasurably better after talking with di Mottura. He was back in control.

Struve's backup plan was a long shot, but it was the only option left. That meant suspending his relationship with the untrustworthy Italian and his backers, at least for now.

Aidan clucked his tongue. He hadn't wanted to get into bed with the Italians, but his takeover plan needed deep pockets unfettered by ethics or morality. Tom Reed had introduced him to "Antonio Balestra." Tom had done business with the Italian for years. Aidan had always known Balestra's name was fictitious. Tom had uncovered the banker's real identity and taken steps to ensure his cooperation if things went awry.

Aidan had appreciated his co-conspirator's foresight, but he'd never expected he'd have to use those safeguards. Until now, di Mottura had been the perfect silent partner. He'd earned Aidan's trust, and with one foolish move, he'd squandered it forever.

It didn't matter whether di Mottura or the vicious mobsters he called his "backers" were responsible for wrecking the plan. Aidan had to salvage the situation however he could. And if the banker chose to interfere again—well. Aidan had told him the truth. He did not bluff. Perhaps di Mottura would be more tractable if his eight-year-old son Agostino disappeared and was mailed back to him in a dozen little boxes. Aidan could always bring the Italian's wife and daughter to the States as his "guests" in case extra lessons were required. Tom's crew would certainly enjoy *that*.

He turned his mind to the future. It rankled him that Peter Struve would have to remain in charge of the company for the time being. Aidan couldn't possibly carry out the fallback plan by himself. He'd have to remain in the background, orchestrating events but not participating in them.

But he was nothing if not patient. He'd worked too long and too hard for this to let it all collapse now. He had to see it through. When the time was ripe, one way or another, Struve would be history.

Peter trumpeted the golden age the QUBE would usher in. He was entranced by the technology. He crowed over the ruinously expensive oil synthesizer demo, ignoring the dozens of more substantial inventions the engineers of Santa's Workshop had developed in the meantime. He had just enough imagination to appreciate Emily Dura's magnificent achievements, but he didn't have the stomach for the more immediate and profitable uses for limitless computing power.

Aidan had no such scruples.

He would not hesitate to do what was necessary—or to benefit from it in whatever way he could. He might become the most powerful man in history, and not just in business. He would have to be a very great fool to throw away that potential.

His heart resumed its usual slow cadence. He felt perfectly calm. This was a setback. Nothing more. He checked the clock on the dashboard. At this speed he'd be in Palo Alto in ten minutes.

He rubbed his eyes one at a time, hard, and began to practice his "anguished" expression. He and Emily had been together for three years, after all.

Everyone would expect him to look sad.

CHAPTER SIX

StruvePharma Coyote Hill Campus, Palo Alto, California

June 26

John Shea pushed his 1966 Shelby Fastback to its limit. The vintage car might need a paint job, but the upgraded V8 engine was good as new, and cranked out well over three hundred horses.

He took the long off-ramp from Interstate 280 onto Page Mill Road at a hundred and forty miles an hour. He took the corner expertly, braking and accelerating at just the right time to keep the speed as high as possible without breaking traction. The Mustang screamed up the steep hill that separated him from StruvePharma's sprawling Coyote Hill campus.

He took a deep breath. *Emily's dead. Killing yourself isn't going to help her.* At least he'd had the presence of mind to leave his .45 at home. He wasn't interested in a debate over his concealed-carry permit with keyed-up Palo Alto PD officers.

He let off the accelerator, letting gravity slow him until he reached the top of the hill. He swerved onto Deer Creek Road at a survivable speed. He screeched to a halt in front of a police roadblock at the south gate of the campus. In spite of his brake-scorching stop, the cops were calmer than he expected. He showed them his ID and was waved through.

He turned left onto Watson Road. He snaked the Mustang around the thick cordon of prowlers in front of the Pauling Building, found an unoccupied slot in the small executive parking lot, and shut the engine off. He got out, retrieved his gray sport jacket from the back seat and shrugged into it. The engine ticked and the acrid smell of hot brake linings filled the air. He slammed the door much too hard. The big car rocked on its springs.

Emily Dura's Prius was parked two slots over.

The little hybrid's clean silver paint glinted red and blue in the police car lights. Emily would never drive it home again.

"Oh, man," he whispered.

He took a deep breath and walked toward the Pauling Building.

Every light in the structure was on. Police officers were visible through the floor-to-ceiling windows on all four levels, shotguns shouldered and pistols holstered. John relaxed a bit. They must have cleared the building. There were five hundred eighty-four rooms in the giant laboratory, more than two hundred of those below ground level. He was surprised how quickly they'd gone through it, but there were a *lot* of cops. They must've called in reinforcements from nearby towns.

He tried to steel himself against what he was about to see. He'd been in too many situations like this one. He'd fought in Operation Desert Storm in Kuwait and Iraq. After he left the Marines, he'd become a consultant for Verity Services, a firm that provided private companies with security in dangerous foreign lands —which sometimes involved rescuing kidnapped executives, members of their families, or both. He'd been lucky: only one of his ops had gone bad, but it had gone bad in spectacular fashion. The Venezuelan gang had slaughtered the oil company executive, his wife, and his three daughters days before the rescue team found them. What they'd done to the women first—

John pushed the memory away. He didn't need that scene in his head again, especially not now. He couldn't help Emily Dura, but he could help find out who killed her, and with luck, take down whoever was behind tonight's awful events. Even if SP crashed and burned, he'd make it his business to find out who did this. He'd do it for free. Justice would be payment enough.

And if the court system didn't provide justice for Emily, he'd provide it himself. Just as he did when he tracked down the *jefe* of the kidnap gang. It had taken four months of personal leave, but John had found Juan Carlos Alvarez Bustamante y Garcia hiding in room over a liquor store in a slum in Caracas. Executive kidnappings suddenly became a lot less common in Venezuela once the news crews showed what was left of the *jefe* and his four bodyguards on TV.

John hadn't even known the executive or his family. He'd worked with Emily for years. She and Aidan had been to his house. Janine had cooked dinner for them. They'd played with his kids.

This was personal.

A squad of uniformed Palo Alto PD officers stood outside the entrance of the taped off Pauling Building, talking with each other. John walked up to them and held out his StruvePharma ID badge. "I'm John Shea, head of security."

A white-haired sergeant whose name tag read FERGUSON detached himself from the group. He scrutinized John's badge and nodded. "Detective Vieira told us you'd be coming. Follow me." He held up the yellow police tapeline so John could stoop under it. Ferguson then ducked under it himself and led John into the building and up the fire stairs next to the elevators. When they reached the second floor landing, the sergeant turned to him and held up a hand.

John stopped.

"Vieira said you were in the Army," Ferguson said.

"Marines."

"See any action?"

"Some." *More than my share.*

"Then you should know, it's a real mess in there. Fair warning."

"Thanks."

Ferguson opened the door onto the second level landing. He led John around the corner, down the glass-walled length of Broadway, and through the police officers milling around just beyond the corner of Park Avenue.

In spite of the sergeant's warning, John's stomach still did a slow, lurching roll.

The gunman's body was missing. Emily's was not.

She lay on her left side in a lake of congealing blood, her white blouse and blue jeans covered with gore. The left side of her head had been blown away. Fragments of skull, hair and brain matter had sprayed out behind her onto the concrete floor and the glossy white wall. Her sole remaining eye stared at nothing, dull and unblinking.

"Ah, no," John whispered, his heart sinking.

A strange, dispassionate part of his mind wondered at the sheer volume of blood contained in the human body. Murder scenes were never as antiseptic as they were depicted on film or on TV. In real life, there was always more blood, not just a dribble of red on the breast. TV couldn't convey the horrid, thick, hot-iron stench clogging your nostrils until you felt like you couldn't breathe at all.

John swallowed against the rising nausea. *Get control of it, man,* he told himself as he had so many times before. But this wasn't one of his soldiers on the floor, or a fallen enemy, or anyone who knew they might catch a bullet and signed on for action anyway.

This was his friend.

He turned back to the scene and stared at it, putting that alien, emotionless part of his brain to work on something other than dwelling on how horrible it was. He knew he'd have plenty of sleepless nights to do that later.

There was no trace of the man in black except bloody smears on the floor, a pile of discarded, red-stained gauze bandages, and a scattering of what looked like gold confetti.

Gold confetti.

John's stomach turned over again. Something about the glittering fragments on the floor disturbed him, but he couldn't think why. He swallowed hard, took a deep breath, and asked the room, "Where's the bad guy?"

A short, black-haired female plainclothes officer in her mid-forties walked up to him. She could be described as compact, or perhaps solid. A less charitable man might have called her a fire hydrant. Her lined face was as carefully composed as he knew his was.

She said, "John Shea? Detective Sergeant Allie Vieira." They shook hands. "He isn't dead, but he isn't breathing on his own. He's on the way to the Stanford ER."

"Any idea who the son of a bitch is?"

She shook her head. "No ID on him. We couldn't get a clear picture for the computer before they hauled him out to the ambulance. They had a tube down his throat and were bagging him. He's a real pro, though. He had Kevlar body armor—chest, arms, and even full leggings. Shot in the neck after he killed the female vic."

He couldn't intercept the scowl before it reached his face.

Vieira said quickly, "Sorry, I meant to say Dr. Dura. The perp probably won't walk again, if he lives."

"Too fucking bad for him."

She nodded. "A real shame."

"Speaking of my guys, can I talk to them?"

"After the interviews."

He nodded. It was standard police procedure to separate those involved in a crime and get their stories separately, to see if there were any inconsistencies. "I have to find Peter Struve. He's in the safe room in his office over in the Delbrück Building."

"He came down here a little while ago. My partner is interviewing him, just like I'm going to interview you."

"What about the black bag the perp had on his back?"

"Taken into evidence. Come on, let's find a quiet spot to talk."

John glanced at his watch. Dawn was still hours away. "The lounge. There's coffee. Your guys can help themselves," he added, loud enough for the other policemen to hear. He received some grateful nods.

He led Vieira down Broadway and to the spacious lounge next to the southwest corner stairwell, as far as possible from the carnage in Park Avenue. It looked a bit like a high-end Starbuck's. It was equipped with comfortable chairs, tables, sofas, and a full mini kitchen. There was a deli case full of cold beverages, shelves with wire baskets of chips and snacks, and a coffee bar. The lamp-lit grounds of the campus were visible through the thick armor glass windows. It was far enough from the crime scene that the stench of blood no longer clogged the air.

Vieira waited without visible signs of impatience while he pulled a cappuccino on the expensive espresso machine. He gave it to Vieira and grabbed a cup of black coffee for himself.

They sat at one of the tables and she debriefed him. She took notes on an old-fashioned Palm Pilot, scribbling rapidly on its grubby, scratched screen with a tiny plastic pen.

Officers wandered in and out at intervals, staring in puzzlement at the espresso machine for a moment before moving to the automated coffee maker for paper cups of industrial strength joe.

Eventually Vieira sat back, put her Pilot on the table, and took a sip of cappuccino. She made a face. "Yuck. Cold. How long have you worked here?"

"Five years? Maybe six. I'd have to check. Peter hired me after the Black Box Project was underway. I put together the security team."

"'Black Box?'"

"That's what we call it." He held out his hand. "Let me heat that up for you. Sugar, right?"

She handed him the cup, nodding.

He went to the sink, dumped the cup, and started to make her a fresh cappuccino.

"How did the perp get in?" she asked.

John's scowl came back. "He tail-gated Jason Lackland through an employee entrance in the back. The guys in the lobby were in the middle of a shift change."

"Pretty big coincidence."

"I don't believe in coincidence. When I find out who leaked the schedule, I'm going to collect a scalp." He returned to the table with her cappuccino.

She took a sip and nodded her thanks. "What about your surveillance operators?"

"They had their eyes on a fender bender right outside the south entrance. The two drivers looked like they were going to get into a fight. A couple of my men went over to check it out, but the drivers left before they got there."

"A diversion?"

"Maybe. Probably."

"Any way to ID the cars?"

Shea shook his head. "Generic beaters. No angle on the plates from any of our cameras, anyway."

Vieira looked over the rim of her cup as she took another sip. "Why do you have such a serious security force, Mr. Shea? Former SEALs? And you were a Ranger, right?"

He scoffed. "Marine Force Recon."

"Were you expecting an invasion?"

"What do you know about our research?"

"Not much."

"Let's just say it's worth protecting."

She squinted at him. "Can you be more specific?"

"Not without violating my confidentiality agreement."

"Okay, you're on record protesting my question, and I'm on record telling you that you could spend the rest of the night in the clink for obstruction of justice. Talk."

John thought about it. He could hold out, but Vieira didn't strike him as the kind of cop who made hollow threats. He shrugged. "Can you keep it on a need-to-know basis with the other detectives? If word of this gets out, we'll have to hire a *real* army to secure this place. I am not exaggerating. Do I have your word?"

"For what it's worth." She shrugged. "I can't vouch for what my Lieutenant does when he gets my report."

He sighed. "Well. It won't be confidential much longer no matter what I do."

She sipped her cappuccino. "It's hard to keep secrets in the age of Twitter. So quit stalling."

John leaned closer to her and murmured, "You ever hear of quantum computers?"

She shrugged.

"We built one. It solves certain kinds of equations millions of times faster than all of the rest of the world's computers put together."

Vieira's eyes narrowed. "Bullshit."

"It's true."

"Science fiction."

"Landing a man on the moon was science fiction before 1969. And then it wasn't." John took a long swallow of his tepid coffee. "That bastard who killed Emily was trying to steal it."

Vieira scribbled on her Palm Pilot again. "That thing in the bag he had on his back. That was this quantum computer?"

John's heart began to pound. "Did you say 'was'?"

"It caught a bullet. Looked like a broken Christmas tree ornament inside. Gold flakes came out. We sealed it back in the bag and turned it over to Forensics but some of the gold stuff got on the floor." Her eyes widened. "Is it dangerous?"

"I don't think so." *Gold confetti.* He'd known something was amiss when he saw it on the floor near Emily's body, but hadn't put two and two together. There was a lot of gold foil inside the QUBE. He closed his eyes and rubbed them with his fingertips. "God damn it to *hell*. That was QUBE Charlie."

"Cube? Looked round to me."

He opened his eyes. "Q-U-B-E. It's an acronym."

She took some more notes. "What does it stand for?"

"All I know is that we have—had—three of them," he hedged. "Alpha and Bravo weren't reliable. Charlie was. They cost about a billion dollars. Each."

Vieira's eyes widened.

"Jesus," he groaned. He slumped in his chair. "Emily was—" His voice cracked. He couldn't bring himself to finish the sentence. He looked down at his hands. They were clenched under the table, the knuckles white.

Vieira took another sip of her cappuccino and said nothing.

When John could speak again, it was in a whisper. He looked up at the detective. "Emily Dura was our chief scientist. Jason Lackland was one of her techs. It's my job to protect them." *Or it used to be, anyway. God knows how Peter's going to react to this cluster fuck.* "I'm damned if I'm not going to help find out who did this. Maybe thirty people inside the company know about the QUBE. I'll give you their names, but none of them would have spilled the beans."

Vieira snorted her disbelief.

John said, "You don't know these people. They've given everything to this project, and it stands—*stood*—to make them all billionaires." *Including me,* he reflected glumly. "It was probably someone at ZMPC. Big venture capital firm out of Sunnyvale. Peter did our first external demo for them three days ago."

Vieira's brow furrowed. "Venture capital? Why? SP isn't a startup. It isn't even publicly traded."

"You're pretty business-savvy for murder police."

"I do some investing. Have you seen how much houses cost in the Bay Area? I don't want to live in a cardboard box under an overpass when I retire."

John saluted her with his cup before he drained it. "You'll have to ask Peter Struve about the details. All I know is that he bought back all the stock and took the company private after he inherited control from his old man. We've been funding the Black Box Project on our own. It was expensive. Way too expensive. We've been selling bits of the company off to make ends meet. There isn't much left to cannibalize, to be honest. We need more money, and VCs have it. And with Emily dead and our one working QUBE destroyed, I guess we're pretty much fucked."

Vieira studied him for a long moment. "Okay, this is getting a little too deep for me. I'm going to have to call in some expert help." She produced an ancient flip-phone and stared at the screen in puzzlement. "Can't get a signal in here."

"This building's shielded."

"But we're right next to a window."

He shrugged. "If you need someone to call you, give them my number. Anyway, what happened to *need-to-know?*"

She put the phone away, frowning. "If what you're telling me isn't the plot of a Tom Clancy book, this isn't just an attempted kidnapping gone wrong. It's big time industrial espionage. A lot of people higher up the food chain need to know about it."

"Terrific," John said without heat. He'd told the executive staff a hundred times that keeping a lid on this kind of situation would be next to impossible, but it was disheartening to be proven right.

Vieira said, "I need to review your surveillance video."

"Let's go to my office."

"Can I use my phone there?"

"Yeah."

John led Vieira outside, away from the police cars and their flashing lights, and down the driveway that led to the executive office building.

Vieira dropped behind him to call someone on her cell phone as they walked. He couldn't make out her words, but her urgency was plain.

He moved ahead, both to give her privacy and to take some for himself. He unclenched his fists again and took a deep breath.

He looked up through the dense canopy of trees at the starry sky beyond them. There was no trace of the usual summertime marine cloud layer. It was cool and comfortable now, but another hot day was coming.

A motionless white spark hovered in the indigo sky, high above the predawn horizon. Venus, probably. The ancients had called it Lucifer. A solemn verse from Isaiah flitted through his mind: *How you are fallen from heaven, O Day Star, son of Dawn! How you are cut down to the ground, you who laid the nations low!* He glanced at his watch. The sun would be up in an hour, and Lucifer would be vanquished again.

He breathed deeply again, letting the air drain slowly from his lungs. Until today, this was a place of peace, quiet, and increasingly desperate productivity as Struve and his crew had sought to master the ultimate technology. A haven where John could put the violence of his early life behind him. A job that would guarantee his family's future. The spell was broken. Now it was just the place where Emily had been murdered.

He mounted the steps of the Delbrück Building. Vieira finished her phone call and caught up with him just as he opened the door.

Peter Struve was alone in John's third floor office. He sat in the visitor's chair, leaning forward, elbows on knees, staring at the carpet. He looked as if he lacked even the energy to vomit. He looked up slowly as John came in, eye sockets hollow with grief.

"Jesus, John," he whispered. "Jesus Christ."

John reached out a hand and pulled him upright.

Struve hugged him fiercely. "Poor Emily," he said into John's chest, his muffled voice shuddering. "Poor Jason. Dear God, what have I done?"

John let Struve clutch him for another few seconds before he gently disengaged. He grasped the shorter man by the shoulders and looked him straight in the eyes. "You didn't do anything. It wasn't your fault. But by God we will find out who did this, and we will make those fuckers pay. You have my word."

Struve sniffed, nodded, tried to smile, failed, and then seemed to notice Vieira for the first time. "You're the detective."

She shook his proffered hand. "Allie Vieira. Mr. Struve, I am sorry for your loss. Can you tell me where Detective Bosson went?"

Struve frowned. "Bathroom down the hall, I think."

A huge man dressed in an ill-fitting brown suit ducked into the office. "Did someone say my name?" he rumbled. He was florid, balding, muscular, and immense. The top of his head was at least four inches higher than Shea's six-foot-five. His hands were *huge*. He could have palmed a basketball with one of them.

John took an involuntary step backward.

"Oh, there you are, Bob." Vieira turned to John. "We'll be back in a minute." She led the giant back into the hallway.

John looked at Struve. "Sit down before you fall down. Do you want some coffee? Or something stronger?"

"No," Struve said. He lowered himself into the visitor's chair.

John rounded the desk and collapsed into his own chair. He could see Vieira and Bosson in the hallway outside the open door of the office. Vieira was already talking on her cell phone.

"What about operational security?" Struve murmured.

John shrugged. "There isn't any. The cops are everywhere."

"No way to stop them, I guess?"

"Not without getting locked up. This Detective Sergeant Vieira is pretty hard-core. I wouldn't test her. And they're calling in the Feds right now, if I'm not mistaken. Our best play is to cooperate, just like I've been telling you. Stonewall, and they might grab the whole project."

Struve scowled. "There's no legal basis."

"Did that ever keep a government from doing what it wants? When they find out what we've been working on, all bets are off. They could seize the company in the public interest. They could pass a law declaring it a strategic asset. The President could just issue an executive order. Face facts. The lid is off this thing. We need the government in our corner."

"Once they're in, we'll never get rid of them."

John hissed, "We need them to help figure out who killed Emily and Jason."

Struve raised his hands in surrender. He took a deep, hitching breath. "Did you call Aidan?"

"I did not, and I told you why."

"Well, I did. He's on his way."

"Goddammit, Peter. He wasn't here. He wasn't involved. He can't help."

"We need to figure out what to do next. We need him here."

John stared at Struve. "You've got to be kidding me. What's Aidan going to do but run around like a chicken with his head cut off for the next week? With good reason! Did the cops tell you that QUBE Charlie was destroyed?"

Struve winced and nodded.

"Then I'll tell you what we do next. Turn off the lights and go home!"

"No. There's a plan. We just have to make it work."

"You had a plan for *this?*" John asked, dumbfounded.

Struve looked at him, his face drawn and gray. "When you depend on a single person to make a key technology work, you take a risk. What if she choked on a sandwich? What if she got hit by bus?"

"Or shot by a kidnapper?" John added bitterly.

Struve ignored the interruption. "Emily knew she was the single point of failure. Her research is backed up ten different ways. Every thought she had went into a database. Every minute of every day she worked in the Black Box for the last five years is stored on video. Her name's on two-dozen papers and three hundred patent applications that are ready to go in the mail." A touch of pride crept into his voice. "There's never been a creative process so completely documented in the history of the world."

John sat back in his chair. He glanced at Vieira and Bosson in the hallway outside the door. She was still on her cell phone, gesturing furiously with her empty left hand. Her voice was too low to hear. Bosson watched her, grimacing.

John looked back at Struve, lowering his voice to a near whisper. "What about the QUBE?"

"We'll grow another one."

"Do you have a spare billion dollars that I don't know about?"

Struve frowned. "ZMPC is willing to put up another half-billion. All I have to do is demo the beta unit to a few more VCs with deep pockets. We'll be fine."

"How?" John barked.

Out in the hallway, Vieira glanced at him.

He lowered his voice. "Emily told me just the other day that building a working QUBE was like winning the lottery with the third ticket. Even she didn't know why the first two didn't work! What are we going to do, just build more and more of them and hope another one comes out just right? Is there that much money in the world?"

Struve's expression grew thoughtful. "We'll have to keep QUBE Bravo operational and Alpha on standby, but we can recycle Charlie for materials. Worst case scenario is we come clean to the government and they throw money at us to finish. They can *print* money, remember? And we might be able to get someone else to help—someone who already understands a lot of the science, who can pick up where Emily left off. It's a long shot, but maybe. Just maybe."

John gaped. "Look, I know I'm gonna get fired anyway, so I'm just going to say it. You are out of your goddamned mind. If you can keep SP from being nationalized, who would invest in us now? In case you missed it, two people were just murdered here. We're going to be national news by breakfast. We're radioactive!"

"No, we aren't," snapped Struve. He continued in a near whisper: "We have the most valuable technology in the world. It'll make computer chips look like *chocolate* chips by comparison. And I'm not firing you. You and your men did what you could, but we weren't thinking big enough. That's not your fault. It's mine. I'm going to need you to build up our security to handle any contingency. If a fucking *army* comes over the hill from 280, I want you to be able to hold it off. Unlimited budget."

"Unlimited?"

Struve nodded. "This is a bump in the road, but the road goes ever on and on. We're going all the way to the end."

John didn't know what to say to that. His head felt like it was wrapped in cotton. Nothing seemed real. He wanted to yell at Struve, to jar him out of that infamous "reality distortion field," maybe punch him in the nose and feel it break beneath his knuckles, but if he did that, it would be game over for sure. He'd never find an opportunity like this one again. He couldn't sacrifice his family's future to satisfy his urge to knock some sense into his boss.

If Struve was right, if they could somehow pull the company back from the edge of the abyss, if they could keep the government from seizing it—which seemed a pretty goddamned big *if*—the less he said now, the better. Shutting up had saved his career after a cluster-fucked rescue mission in Iraq. He could shut up again.

John put his hands in his lap, let them ball into fists, and kept his peace.

Vieira and Bosson chose that moment to come into his office. "We'll need a list of employees who know about this Black Box Project, and everyone who knows about it at that venture capital company, too. We've got a lot of interviews to do."

John glanced at his boss.

Struve returned his gaze. "How much did you tell them?"

"Everything I had to," John said flatly.

Struve sighed. "Give them the names." He turned toward the two detectives. "I hope you'll keep as much of this confidential as you can."

Vieira nodded. "We will, for what it's worth, but I just found out the case has gone Federal. Some investigators from the FBI and some Homeland Security department I never heard of will be here in a few hours. The Feds leak like a colander, so you can bet this whole story will be on CNN by lunchtime."

"Federal investigators? Why?" asked Struve.

Vieira said, "Kidnapping. Espionage. High-tech crimes. They'll throw everything at the wall to see what sticks."

"There might be an international angle, too," Bosson said. "Mr. Struve told me the perp had an accent. Maybe someone found out who he is."

Vieira threw her hands up in evident disgust. "Ours not to reason why, ours but to do whatever the hell our bosses tell us, so we don't get our asses fired."

"I heard *that,*" rumbled Bosson.

Vieira looked at Struve. "You're here until the Feds decide to let you leave, and you're not to talk to anyone who isn't on the premises at this very moment. Sorry. Don't use any computers for now, and I'll need your cell phones. We'll call your families and let them know where you are."

"This is illegal," Struve grumbled. "Prior restraint or something."

"Just do it, Peter," John said. He dug his phone out of his pocket and handed it to Vieira. She produced a plastic evidence bag from her scuffed leather purse and dropped it in.

Struve said, "Uh. About calling people. I already called Aidan O'Keefe. Our CTO. He's on his way."

Vieira said, "He arrived a while ago. He's being interviewed. Anyone *else* we should know about?"

"Someone should tell Jack," John said. At Vieira's blank look, he added, "Jack Dura. Emily's ex-husband. He shouldn't find out about this on the goddamned television. He teaches at Stanford."

"We'll send someone." She extended her open hand to Struve. "Your phone, please?"

Struve shook his head. "I need to call Sasha Khaimov, our HR director. We need her to tell the rest of the staff to stay home today."

Vieira frowned. "All right, but don't tell her why, and don't try to contact anyone else. I didn't fall off a truck yesterday."

Struve managed a weak smile. "I can see that."

Vieira said, "Make your call and then we'll take a look at that surveillance video. Might as well get some actual police work done before the Feds come in and fuck everything up."

CHAPTER SEVEN

Budget Inn, Inglewood, California

June 26

Laurel Wynn was sound asleep in spite of the boulder-sized lumps in the cheap mattress when her boss called.

"You have five minutes to shower and pack. There's a car waiting to take you to the airport. Get moving."

She'd hurled herself out of bed and toward the bathroom before she knew it on a conscious level. When you worked for Andrew Seigart, Director of Homeland Security's Joint Task Force on State-Sponsored Technological Espionage, when he said *jump* you didn't wait to ask "how high." You just jumped. After a while it was like a spinal reflex.

She emerged from the bathroom four minutes later, bleary-eyed and damp-haired. She had draped her clothes from the previous day across the back of a chair. She'd attended a low-impact social networking conference, so they were still presentable. She spent another thirty seconds putting them on.

She shot herself a glance in the room's dusty mirror as she bound her brown shoulder-length hair into a ponytail. Her blue eyes were tinged with red, and her face looked pallid instead of just pale. There wasn't enough time to put on makeup. It would have to do. Hopefully she'd get a chance to change on the plane.

She looked at her watch and cursed. She wouldn't even get a chance to brew a cup of Budget Inn's not-so-famous Budget Instant Coffee. Not for the first time, she wished her travel *per diem* was enough for her to stay someplace with decent coffee.

She piled her toiletries and her ancient plastic MacBook into her battered suitcase, slammed it shut, grabbed it and left the room without a backward glance.

She checked her watch again as she walked toward the motel office: 4:49 AM. This time the numbers actually registered. "Oh, Christ," she grunted. The low, orange-hued clouds hovering over Los Angeles showed no sign of the impending dawn. The night air was cold on her damp head.

A young man in a nondescript black suit, white shirt, black tie and a severe flattop haircut waited for her next to a big black limousine parked next to the office. "Good morning, Agent Wynn."

"Is it?" she snapped.

He hesitated before replying. "I'll return your rental car and check you out of the motel, ma'am. I'll take care of your suitcase, too."

She handed him the luggage and room keys.

He opened the rear door of the limo for her before putting her luggage in the trunk and walking briskly to the motel office.

She got in and pulled the door shut behind her.

The driver, sporting an identical haircut, said nothing as they surged out of the parking lot and raced through the almost empty streets. She was too caffeine-deprived to talk anyway. She stared out the darkened windows of the limousine and wondered what could be important enough for Andrew Seigart to roust her out of bed at the hellish hour of almost-five-AM. Whatever it was, it couldn't be good.

Minutes later the limo turned off at a private aviation terminal at LAX. They drove through the gates onto the tarmac and pulled to a halt next to a slate gray fighter jet.

She stared at it through the limo window. She recognized it instantly as a Navy FA-18F Super Hornet. Her father had been a career air traffic controller in the Air Force. He had dragged her to every airshow in a two-hour driving radius of wherever they were stationed until she was old enough to go to college. Willingly or not, she'd absorbed every factoid he emitted on every plane they ever saw together.

The jet was so sleek it looked like it could break the sound barrier just sitting there with its engines off. Its twin tails sported stylized logos of a black knight holding a kite shield and a sword. Its wings were heavy with long, teardrop-shaped canisters—presumably additional fuel tanks—but there were no missiles or bombs. The streamlined cylinder mounted on its belly had to be a cargo pod. Fuel tanks didn't come with hatches.

"What the *hell*," she whispered.

Another thinly disguised soldier in civilian clothes opened the door for her. "This way, ma'am," he said.

A pair of female aircrew members bundled her into an olive drab flight suit. They relieved her of her flats and replaced them with a pair of boots that were just a little too big. The ensemble was completed by a massive helmet with a dangling oxygen mask. She had to undo her ponytail to put on the helmet. She shivered as her cold, still-moist hair was pressed against her neck.

She soon found herself in the back seat of the fighter. An airman shouted instructions, mostly focused on what she should not touch—which was everything, except the air-sick bag, if necessary. *Just what in the hell am I in for?* she wondered dizzily.

The Navy pilot, one Lieutenant Commander Alan "Grease" McNally, spoke to her on the plane's intercom. *Aviator*, she reminded herself. *They like to be called aviators.* She heard his words but forgot them before they even started to taxi to the runway.

The roar of afterburners filled the cockpit. She was shoved deep into the heavily cushioned flight seat. The ground dropped away. They flew into the low orange clouds, emerging moments later into a flawless indigo sky. The marine cloud deck fell away. To her relief, Grease turned the afterburners off a few moments later.

Laurel wasn't prone to motion sickness, but she was grateful that the pilot didn't treat her to any aerobatics. She searched the enormous instrument panel in front of her for anything that looked familiar. A former boyfriend, Sam Something—or maybe it was George Something—had been a private pilot. She'd flown with him a few times in his little Cessna 152. She remembered the plane more clearly than the boyfriend, to her chagrin. It took her a minute to identify the altimeter, compass and airspeed indicators. They were already almost 10,000 feet up, doing 250 knots. Sam/George's plane couldn't manage that in a dive with the wings ripped off.

When they reached 12,500 feet, without warning, Grease kicked on the afterburners again.

Laurel was jammed back against her seat. It felt like a couple of grown men had landed on top of her. "Holy *crap*," she grunted.

Grease said over the intercom, "*Just breathe normally, ma'am.*"

"Easy for you to say," she growled.

They rocketed up to 50,000 feet in what seemed like seconds, then leveled off and turned north.

When the climb eased and she could turn her head without effort, she looked around and was shocked to see how far from land they were. The California coastline was just a line of black lumps silhouetted against a coppery band of light in the east. The ocean was too far below to make out any detail. They were suspended between two endless planes of blue-black. The few stars still visible were unwavering pinpricks of light.

The airspeed indicator now read an astonishing 1050 knots—well over the speed of sound. Almost ten times faster than Sam/George's Cessna. That explained why they were so far from the coast: to spare people on the ground the double sonic boom created by the jet's shockwave. *Fastest I've ever flown,* she marveled.

She'd read that you could still hear the engine noise from inside a supersonic jet. She was a little disappointed to find out that it was true. Of course, the sound was conducted to the cockpit through the airframe. The supersonic airflow around the jet was a low, continuous roar, brought to a manageable level by her helmet's noise-reducing headset. If only the sun were up! The view would have been stupendous.

It seemed like they'd been in the air for just a few minutes when they reduced speed and plummeted to a much lower altitude to rendezvous with an Air Force tanker. She craned her head to look around the back of the pilot's seat. She watched in fascination as an angular probe rose from the fighter's nose to mate with the fuel boom extended from the tail of the huge tanker. It only took moments for them to top off. Then they screamed back up to 50,000 feet.

Dawn broke over them. She lowered her helmet's dark visor. There wasn't much to see, this far from the coast. She kept herself busy trying to guess what the controls in front of her did, and worrying about this new mission. It must be pretty goddamned dire for Seigart to order her flown out on a military jet.

The only thing she learned from Grease was the origin of his call sign. One of his flight instructors had called him "Monkey" instead of McNally. Then someone put "grease" in front of "monkey." The second nickname was the one that stuck. Her other attempts to engage him in conversation didn't go anywhere. Eventually she stopped trying.

She didn't have much time to brood. Grease swung the jet toward land and reduced their speed. The sea and land far below were still shrouded in darkness, but she could make out the shape of the approaching coastline.

She smiled when she recognized the great elongated backward "C" of Monterey Bay. She knew the area well. To their right was the big town of Monterey, jutting out at the southernmost end of the Bay.

She'd attended the Defense Analysis program at the Naval Postgraduate School there. Further inland of Monterey were the sparkling lights of Salinas and the smaller towns sprinkled along Highway 101. It was still too dark to make out the fertile squares of farmland in the Salinas Valley. Just to the right, almost directly below, was a brilliant forest of orange lights beneath a giant pair of smokestacks at the Moss Landing power plant.

She craned her head to look over the left side of the fighter. In the middle distance was the resort town of Santa Cruz. She'd spent many hours on the Beach Boardwalk there, enjoying the sun, the sand, the rides, and the attention of three different would-be boyfriends, including Sam/George. Much further north was the San Francisco Peninsula. Haze concealed the beautiful city at its northern tip.

The jet plunged over the hills and down into Silicon Valley at a heart-stopping rate. The sun retreated below the hills to the east as they descended.

Laurel pushed her visor up to watch the landing. Ahead of them was Moffett Field, a former Naval Air Station and now a NASA base, located at the south end of San Francisco Bay. She spotted Hangar One, a huge lozenge-shaped dirigible hangar built in the early twentieth century. She'd heard that Google had leased the base and was planning to refurbish the hangar, but it looked like the work hadn't gotten underway yet. It was still just an immense skeleton of silvery girders to the left of the pair of parallel runways.

The landing was silky smooth. They taxied to a halt next to a pair of elderly white Gulfstream jets with NASA logos on their tails.

As the Hornet's engines wound down, the canopy rose out of the way and a new set of airmen rolled a ladder up to the side of the jet. They relieved her of her helmet and helped her clamber out. Her hair was dry but now it clung to her skull in unpleasant ropes, like the arms of a lazy octopus. Grease saluted her crisply and without apparent irony from his seat in the cockpit. She waved back at him before descending the ladder. She saw one of the airmen remove her bag from the cargo pod, and felt a moment of satisfaction at having identified it correctly. Her father would be proud.

An old Bell Jet Ranger helicopter was warming up a few hundred feet down the concrete ramp. A young man in a bland gray business suit ran toward her from the chopper. He had disheveled brown hair and a long, drooping nose that gave him a strangely woeful expression.

"Special Agent Robert Holmes, San Francisco Field Office. I'm your assistant while you're here, Senior Special Agent Wynn," he said, extending a hand.

She shook it. "Seriously? 'Holmes?'"

He grimaced. "I get that a lot."

"Hard name to live up to. What should I call you?"

"Bob, Rob, Robbie. Hey you. Dumb-ass. Anything but Sherlock. By the way, Bob Sheridan said to say *howdy*."

"Cowboy Bob is still in San Francisco? He was talking retirement when I left in 2004. And just call me Laurel, or you're liable to sprain your tongue."

The aircrew helped her doff the flight suit and boots. They returned her austere black patent leather flats along with her bag. She put them on, balancing fluidly on one foot at a time. She looked down at herself and sighed. The flight suit had really done a number on her blouse and slacks. She looked like she just crawled out of a ball pit at a kiddie restaurant. *Wrinkle-free, my ass.* She put her hair up in a messy bun with the ease of long practice.

Holmes said, "Shall we?" Without waiting for an answer, he picked up her bag and walked back to the helicopter at a brisk pace.

"What the hell am I doing here?" she shouted over the rising whine of the chopper's jet turbine.

"Coffee and information when we're on board," he shouted. He waited for her to climb in, pushed the suitcase into the compartment and closed the door after himself. The chopper's main rotor began to spin. When she was belted in, Holmes handed her a noise-canceling headset. Then he tapped the pilot on the shoulder and gave him a thumbs-up.

The chopper leaped into the air and tilted toward the North. The sun chose that moment to break over the hills, flooding the cockpit with reddish golden light. She squinted and turned her head away from the second sunrise of her morning.

They flew low over the already-crowded lanes of Highway 101. From the looks of it, traffic had gotten worse since she moved east. It was still better than the endless parking lot of the D.C. Beltway.

Holmes removed a large paper cup with a sippy lid on it from a plastic cooler next to his seat. He handed it to Laurel and then took another for himself.

"You are my hero," she said, positioning the helmet's microphone so she could drink. It was typical government-issue coffee: lukewarm, as tasty as crude oil and with a similar consistency, but it would be chock-full of caffeine, and that was all that mattered. "Okay, Mr. Holmes. Are these headsets on a private loop?"

"Pilot can't hear a thing over the engine."

"So what the hell is so urgent?"

"Some company named StruvePharma," he said. "One of their scientists and a technician were murdered last night. Not sure why that justifies sending you up here on a fighter jet."

Laurel's heart dropped into her stomach. "Oh, God. What happened?"

"Looks like attempted robbery and kidnapping gone wrong. The triggerman's at Stanford Hospital. The company had a bunch of former SEALs on their private security team. They shot the perp. A *lot*. A bullet clipped his spinal cord in his neck. They don't know if he's going to pull through. No ID on him yet."

"Holy shit. Who was the scientist?"

"Emily Something."

Laurel choked on her so-called coffee. "Not Emily Dura!"

"That's it."

"Oh, dear Christ. You're sure that was the name?"

Holmes nodded. "So you know her. I'm not up to speed on this company. Are they bad actors?"

Laurel stared out the window at the industrial parks passing below. *This can't be,* she thought. *This just can't be.* After a long moment of bleak contemplation, she said, "Do you have any briefing documents for me?"

"The Director said you knew all the players already. He wanted you to go in with an open mind and figure everything else out on your own."

She scowled at the floor of the helicopter. That's just like Andrew Seigart. Throw me in the deep end with an anchor around my neck.

It could have been worse. She had studied StruvePharma extensively. She had prepared several briefings on the company for Seigart over the last few years.

This semi-blank slate method had its advantages. She'd have to dig the facts out by herself, but if this investigation was like the last three she'd headed, she would have *carte blanche* to look into every nook and cranny with little or no interference from the head office. And she had solved all three of those cases. Every time she did, Seigart gave her more latitude and more responsibility. It was a huge advantage of being loaned out to Homeland Security, and having a boss who actually focused on results instead of office politics. Seigart was as high up on the ladder as he cared to be, and in spite of his near-incomprehensible job title, that was very high up, indeed.

"Agent Wynn?" Holmes prompted her.

She shook herself back to awareness. "Just Laurel is fine. Did you get a new code word clearance?"

"BLUE HORIZON."

She relaxed a bit. "Good, you're cleared for the whole picture. SP's been on the BAYLEAF watch list for a few years. It used to be a really big deal. Billions in revenue. You know that allergy drug, Allyvil? They invented it."

His eyes widened. "Seriously? That's some good shit, but their ads have the worst jingle ever. *Better take an Allyvil, if it can't help you, nothing will.* Goddamned earworm, is what it is. What's BAYLEAF?"

She took another sip of sludge before continuing. "It's a data mining project. It sifts public databases, press releases, news articles, even job sites like LinkedIn and Monster.com. It looks at employment trends to find potential targets for state-sponsored industrial espionage. SP's near the top of the list."

"Why?"

"Their president took the company private after his father died and left him the majority share. They've been spending a ton of cash on computers, weird hardware and hiring people who have no business working for a pharmaceutical company. Like Emily Dura." She sighed. "Jesus. I can't believe she's dead. It's like hearing Einstein just died."

"So who was she?"

"A genius. Scratch that. A *super* genius. Graduated from high school when she was eight. Had her first Ph.D. when she was twelve. She had a MacArthur Fellowship and a full professorship at Stanford by the time SP hired her away. She was only twenty-six at the time. By then she had four actual doctorates and a dozen honorary ones. Physics, chemistry, molecular biology and computer science."

"Holy crow. You know all about her, huh?"

Laurel nodded. "I wrote a bio on her for the task force a couple of years ago. Dura used to publish four or five papers a year, across all those fields, all of them important work. She's on the short list for the Nobel Prize. But she hasn't published anything since going to SP. No one there has published *anything* since she joined up. It's one of the reasons they came onto our radar. They stopped publishing. They stopped filing for new drug trials with the FDA. They stopped doing everything a pharmaceutical company does if it wants to stay in business, except cranking out their current products."

"Okay, that is weird," Holmes said.

"And Emily Dura wasn't the only genius they hired. Neurobiologists, materials science engineers, computer scientists—they hired the cream of the crop in a dozen different fields, none of which have much to do with drug research. Then they laid off most of the pharmacy types. They're spending a ridiculous amount of money on computers and network gear. They bought a big chunk of land close to Stanford and built a four-billion-dollar campus there, and it has crazy levels of security. Add it all up and they look like a prime target for espionage. They're doing something radical, and they're keeping a damned tight lid on it."

"Not tight enough," Holmes said. "The cops say the perp was trying to steal some super-expensive gizmo. Their chief of security just about had an embolism when he found out it was destroyed. The Palo Alto cops said he had some ideas about who might have tipped off the bad guys. We'll talk with them all when we get there." He looked out the window. "Which will be in about thirty seconds."

She followed his gaze. They were nearing the golden foothills that rose up from the flat, building-encrusted valley floor. Beyond them were the Santa Cruz Mountains, a densely forested, lumpy, low-slung series of what people from rockier parts of the country would call hills. The range ran the length of the San Francisco Peninsula, separating Silicon Valley from the cooling winds and foggy skies of the Pacific Ocean.

Just ahead of them was a lush green campus studded with angular, ultra-modern multistory buildings, nestled between a broad, snaky four-lane road and the slope of a knobby, oak tree festooned hill. A line of tall, narrow trees marched around the perimeter of the campus, which was thickly planted with other mature trees of all kinds. The campus hadn't been there long enough for any of them to grow that tall from saplings. Judging by the sparse, grassy fields on either side, Peter

Struve must have had them transplanted as adults, which was unusual and horrendously expensive.

She shook her head. He could've just installed blinds. She chalked it up to Struve's vanity. Like money, vanity was something of which billionaires never seemed to run short.

A single four-lane road ran the length of the campus, following the course of a narrow creek that divided it into two very unequal halves. The roofs of a number of smaller buildings protruded from the greenery on the larger side of the campus. The section next to the hill was dominated by a single long, glass-walled structure whose roof stood high above the surrounding trees.

Only a few small parking lots were visible, and those were full of police cars. Laurel knew that StruvePharma had once employed more than five thousand people at this location, though it had downsized radically in the last few years. The lots were adequate for only a couple of hundred vehicles. Most of the parking space must be underground.

She saw a huge white radio telescope antenna atop a neighboring hill to the north, on the far side of the busy four-lane boulevard. The giant dish pointed straight up. Half-remembered details from her stay in the Bay Area swam up to her conscious awareness. "That's the Stanford Dish," she said, pointing. "So that big street must be Page Mill Road."

"Yep," Holmes replied. He pointed at various buildings in the vicinity. "Xerox PARC. SAP. VMware. Tesla."

"You're a geek, too! Good deal," Laurel said, meaning it. She'd been using computers since she was old enough to smash her toddler's fists against a keyboard.

"Born and bred. That's probably why they assigned me to you," he said. He managed to look dour even while smiling. "I grew up here. Mom and Dad live just over the hill in Mountain View."

The police had blocked off an intersection for the helicopter. They touched down next to the west—*no, south,* she corrected herself, remembering that the San Francisco Peninsula was aligned at an angle—the south entrance of the campus.

As soon as they were solidly on the ground, Holmes unbuckled himself, opened the door and jumped out, hauling Laurel's suitcase in one hand and ducking to avoid the spinning rotor that was a good six feet over his head. Laurel followed on his heels, clutching her half-full cup of sludge. Holmes slammed the door shut and slapped it twice with his open hand before crouch-walking away from the chopper. It dusted off before they cleared the intersection.

They were met by a stumpy woman in her mid-forties wearing a gold badge on a lanyard around her neck. When the helicopter was far enough away for her to be heard, she introduced herself as Detective Sergeant Allie Vieira. She inspected their proffered FBI IDs, her mouth fixed in an uncompromising frown. "Welcome to Palo Alto," she said sourly. Her eyes scanned Laurel's wrinkled outfit. "Just get out of bed?"

"And flew here in a fighter jet. Didn't have time to change."

Vieira squinted at her. "Uh huh. Follow me." She briefed Laurel and Holmes on her preliminary findings as they walked.

They followed her down Watson Road, the main campus street, across a narrow, tree-lined creek and toward the hulking four-story building with silvered windows. A sign on the manicured lawn proclaimed it to be the Pauling Building.

As in Linus Pauling, Laurel presumed. She glanced around and saw names of other scientists, some familiar, others less so, on signs in front of the nearby buildings. She also noticed that the densest, tallest trees crowded close to the structures, obscuring them from view from nearby streets. Perhaps vanity hadn't played a factor in transplanting these full-grown trees. No one would be keen to work in windowless buildings, and the thick foliage provided good security from prying eyes.

Vieira impressed Laurel as competent and focused. Her briefing was as succinct as any she'd gotten from anyone outside the Bureau. As a bonus, she showed only a trace of the special resentment local cops usually reserved for Feds.

Laurel stopped when they reached the entrance of the Pauling Building. "Thank you, Detective, that's very helpful. We're not here to steal your case. We'll work together, but you're in charge of the local investigation. If there turn out to be serious Federal issues, I can't promise we won't take over, but that's not the plan."

Vieira's eyes narrowed. "That's... not what I expected. Why are you here then? I thought it was because of the attempted kidnapping."

"We work for a special group. We don't want any publicity. We don't want to tip the bad guys off that we're on the case. You and your department get to talk to the reporters. Just make sure you don't tell them about Robbie or me, or that the Feds have any interest in this case whatsoever." She offered her hand. "Deal?"

Vieira shook it. "Sounds good." Then she glanced up at the sky and frowned. "Well, shit."

Laurel followed her gaze. High above them hovered a helicopter, but not the one she'd flown in on. This one was bright red. Its nose was equipped with a shiny silver object that could only be a motion-stabilized camera pod.

Vieira said, "Looks like we'll be on the news sooner than I thought. They must have seen the squad cars." She gestured toward the door. "Shall we?"

Laurel tipped her cup of sludge into a trashcan and relieved Holmes of her suitcase before they went in.

She was glad she did. The crime scene on the second floor was a stomach-turning horror. Grim-faced photographers picked over the scene, taking close-ups with big digital cameras equipped with ring flashes. The bodies had been taken away, but the spacious hallway was still covered with gore.

Laurel had never enjoyed the sight of blood. Seeing so much of it, and knowing whose it was, was almost more than she could handle. Holmes' face grew even grimmer but he seemed otherwise unaffected. Vieira's expression was unreadable.

Laurel felt an all-too-familiar sense of being an imposter among professionals. She'd been recruited into the FBI right out of college. She'd gone through the standard rigorous training at Quantico, but she had spent her entire working career investigating fraud, cyber-crime and economic espionage. She had taken up martial arts and carried a gun, but she was happier with a computer keyboard. Murder scenes were not in her wheelhouse. She hoped she never saw so many that she grew used to them.

"Do you mind if I look around?" she asked Vieira. She hefted the suitcase. "I'd like to put this somewhere out of the way."

The detective shrugged. "You could put it in the lounge. Just around the corner and down the hall, near the stairway. The company's given us the run of the place. They disabled most of the door locks so we could clear the building. Struve promised total cooperation. Their head of security seems like a straight shooter. He asked us not to touch anything without clearing it with him first. They have a lot of expensive equipment. Also, you're being recorded. There are cameras *every-where*. They got the whole crime on video from a dozen different angles. I'll show you the footage later."

"Thanks," Laurel said, her stomach sinking. She didn't want to see the events that led to this mayhem from even one angle, but it was part of the job.

Holmes said, "Can I ask you some questions, Detective?" He produced a small notebook from a pocket with a stubby ballpoint pen riding in its spiral binder. He and Vieira moved toward a corner, murmuring quietly.

Laurel turned away from the bloody scene and walked down the hall, suitcase in hand. Robbie could learn the details of the murders from Vieira. Laurel was more interested in why they took place.

Given the secrecy the company had maintained for the last seven years, she found it surprising that there wasn't an army of lawyers and public relations specialists trying to run interference with the police. Vieira said the company was cooperating. Laurel wasn't going to waste time finding out why. She'd been dying to know what StruvePharma had been working on. Now was her chance to find out.

She got a sense of the giant building's layout as she searched for the lounge.

Three super-wide halls divided each floor into four more-or-less equal segments, arranged in a line. The innermost segments housed labs and larger workspaces. The end segments were divided into a multitude of offices, conference rooms, and utility closets.

Laurel found the lounge at one of the outer corners of the floor, next to a stairwell equipped with glass steps. The lounge was as big and well-furnished as an upscale coffee shop. She put her suitcase down in an out-of-the-way corner and resumed her prowling.

The corridors that ran around the perimeter of the floor were wide enough to fit a luxury sedan. Every intersection with another hall was marked with a street sign post. Laurel nodded appreciatively. The halls were nearly as wide as streets, so it made sense.

She walked up to one of the floor-to-ceiling windows that comprised the outer wall of the building. It was completely seamless, as if it had been poured into place. It was very thick, but had none of the dim murkiness or watery distortion she'd come to expect from ballistic armor glass. In fact, it was the clearest, cleanest transparent substance she had ever seen. She tapped it with a fingernail. It made a faint metallic ringing sound. She rubbed it. It was hard, cold, and slicker than oil. Her finger left no trace of moisture or prints.

Whatever it was, it wasn't any kind of glass she'd ever seen.

Laurel's appreciation of the building's security-conscious design grew by the second. The outer windows gave onto common areas such as atriums, break rooms and the glass-stepped stairwells located at each corner. The walls facing the windows were completely featureless.

Every door was deeply recessed in an alcove that opened only onto an interior hall. If an observer could somehow penetrate the thick veil of trees, he would never get line of sight into any room. Even the conference rooms and offices clustered at the far ends of the building were shielded from view.

Some doors featured narrow windows reinforced with wire mesh, like those of her high school classrooms. Most were windowless. All of them featured hand-stenciled numbers, a small white label with a terse description of the room's contents, and a fluorescent green sticker bearing the letters "PAPD." The police had evidently put them there as they cleared the building.

Her inspection led her back to Park Avenue, where the photographers were finishing their grisly work. She averted her eyes from the mess. It was then that she noticed that two of the doors in this corridor were made of metal. One was closed, but the other had been propped open.

She threaded between the photographers to get to the open door. Just as she reached it, a gurney bearing a black body bag was wheeled out.

She made way for the two men handling the gurney. They wore blue jackets labeled "Santa Clara County Medical Examiner." She watched them push the gurney down the hall until they rounded the corner.

Laurel sighed. Emily Dura wasn't the only person to die here. Her technician deserved justice, too.

She looked into the room. The door opened into a small entryway with a high ceiling. It ended with another metal door, also propped open. Beyond that was a yellow-lit laboratory filled with mysterious-looking equipment. The loud voices of many people echoed from inside.

She considered going in, but eventually decided to come back when it was empty. She didn't want to have to compete for access to anything interesting. The lab wasn't going anywhere.

She picked a room across the hall at random and read its label:

SURFACE PLASMONICS

"Huh," she said. She opened the windowless door and peeked in.

The room was big, about twenty feet by fifty. It was a mess, but the orderly kind of mess she associated with intense, driven minds. The walls were lined with open bins full of cables, electronic parts, and banks of tiny drawers like those of a hobbyist's toolkit. The broad black benches in the center of the open space were heaped with electronic gear. One table bore a collection of mirrors and prisms mounted on short metal stands.

She recognized some extremely old-fashioned oscilloscopes by their distinctive round displays. She wondered if the company was doing so badly they'd had to buy fifty-year old test equipment, but it was just as likely that the nerds who worked here were collectors of vintage electronics. One of her colleagues had a garage full of ancient computers and a hard drive the size of a washing machine, just because he liked them.

Nothing else in the lab was familiar. Few of the devices bore manufacturer's labels. In fact, much of the gear looked hand-made, stuffed into the kind of generic sheet metal enclosures you could buy at Fry's Electronics, a famous local nerd-supply chain.

Laurel withdrew from the room, intrigued but no better informed about surface plasmonics than she was before she went in. She wandered the hallways, reading each door's label in turn. Her mystification and excitement grew with every passing step.

She was an avid reader. She spent much of her little free time poring over high-tech journals, magazines and web sites. She prided herself on her familiarity with the techno-jargon of Silicon Valley, which fortunately evolved at a snail's pace compared to the nutty vernacular of pop culture. But the labels on these labs were like nothing she'd ever seen before.

She read the labels aloud as she passed them, struggling over the weirder terms. *"Syll Factory... Fluorotube Epitaxy... Symbrane Packing... Symport Stoichiometry."* She stumbled over the strange word. *"Q-Train Enigmatics.* That has to be a joke."

She peeked through the narrow window in the door, but was disappointed. The room was even more prosaic than the surface plasmonics lab. It was filled from floor to ceiling with racks of computer servers, all of them hand-built. She opened the door, and then closed it hastily as a wave of hot air and the low roar of hundreds of cooling fans filled the hallway.

"Well, crap," she breathed. *Q-train enigmatics* would remain a mystery for now, it seemed.

As Laurel scrutinized one mysterious lab after another, the novelty began to wear off, and she'd learned almost nothing. She was about to go looking for Vieira and Robbie Holmes when she spotted a narrow hallway near the elevators, next to the door to the fire stairs. The door at the end was windowless. She walked up to it. Its tiny label read "MISSION CONTROL."

"Now that's more like it," she said. She turned the knob and pushed. The door resisted, as if it were made of lead. She pushed harder. It opened ponderously.

Dim bluish lights snapped on as she walked in, illuminating a large room with a tiled floor and a high ceiling. The air was cool and smelled faintly of furniture polish.

It looked like a space mission control center, or at least a Hollywood set designer's idea of one. The wall to the left of the door was covered with huge flat panel displays, all of them switched off. The other walls were festooned with framed photographs, posters and logos, all related to spaceflight. There was even a huge blue NASA "meatball" insignia painted on the far wall.

She walked further in to get a better look. The door's latch clacked loudly as it closed behind her. The lights got brighter and whiter as they warmed up.

Four rows of six workstations faced the huge wall of displays, each row higher than the last, with a walkway up the middle. Each station was equipped with three flat panel monitors, set low so that anyone sitting behind them would still have a clear view of the big screens at the front of the room.

Just like a real NASA Mission Control room, each station bore a sign proclaiming its function.

POWER
NETOPS
CRYONICS
BUFFER SYSTEMS
CONVERGENCE
MONITORING
P-CONGRUENCE
MASS STORAGE

ENTANGLOTRONS
BEC PHASE CONTROL
Q-TRAIN METASTABILITY

And on and on, each label more obscure than the previous one. At last she spotted a sign that read FLIGHT DIRECTOR. It was affixed to the short wall in front of the workstation in the highest tier, at the very back of the room, just right of center.

"What the hell," she whispered, grinning.

"Not what you were expecting?"

She whirled.

Behind her was a very tall, muscular, unsmiling man in his late forties or early fifties. He held the heavy door open without apparent effort. He wore a dark gray sport coat, a wrinkled white shirt and gray slacks. He had short blond hair in a recently trimmed flattop that reminded her of her driver from the Budget Inn. His lean, tanned face was handsome but haggard, his lower jaw covered with blondish stubble.

He rubbed his chin. "Sorry. Looks like it's been a bad hair day all around."

She struggled not to glance down at her rumpled clothes. "And you are?" she said, too loudly. Her mortification deepened.

"John Shea, Head of Security. You must be Special Agent Wynn. Vieira said I might find you somewhere around here." He moved into the room, letting the door swing shut behind him, and extended his hand.

She said, "Senior Special Agent, actually. Sorry for barking at you. I didn't hear you open the door. It's been a stressful morning." *Christ, he doesn't need me to tell him that. I'm making a hash of this.* She realized then just how tall he was. She stood 5' 10" and didn't have to look very far up to most men. He topped her by seven or eight inches. She shook his hand, refusing to be intimidated. His grip was warm and predictably firm.

He released her hand. "What brings you to Mission Control, Senior Special Agent Wynn?" He scanned the big room in a kind of visual rhetoric. "Nothing happened in here."

"Maybe not, but something's happening at this company that's attracting the wrong kind of attention. Did Vieira tell you why I'm here?"

"I can guess."

"Don't. I'll need to work with you to try to keep a lid on things here, so I need you to be non-disclosed." Her eyes flicked to the closed door behind him, then to one of the ever-present camera domes in the high ceiling. "Who else has access to your video surveillance?"

"The senior staff. You'll meet them all later. I imagine you'll want to non-disclose them as well."

She nodded. "Okay, then. I work for a task force that looks for state sponsors of industrial espionage. SP's been on top of our watch list for a long time."

"Why?" he asked, his voice incurious.

"You hire a lot of people who don't usually work for pharmaceutical companies. You fired a lot of people who do. You spend *way* more than you earn. Rumor has it that you're working on something big." She swung her arm in a sweeping gesture. "You have a Mission Control center. And the smartest person who ever lived was just shot to death down the hall. Should I go on?"

He grimaced. "Can you?"

She nodded. "If we can find out this much about SP from public sources, you can bet that other governments can, too. Even if they didn't know about you before today, once news of Emily Dura's death hits the Internet, there are going to be a lot of curious eyes on this place. Some of them won't be friendly. We can protect you, but we can't do it well if we don't know what we're protecting."

His face became unreadable. "Do we need government protection?"

Laurel stared at him silently.

Shea looked away. After a moment, he gestured toward the rows of workstations. "They do computation runs on the cube from here. The decorations just started appearing one day. Peter Struve got into the swing of it and bought all those pictures and had the big logo painted on the wall. Lots of these nerds like space stuff. I do too."

"What's this 'cube'?'

"It's spelled Q-U-B-E. Another joke. They took it from that *Trans-formers* movie—the good one. It stands for *Quantum Unison Bioalgo-rithm Engine.* Don't ask me what it means. On a good day I can spell 'engine.'"

Laurel felt cold electricity run down her spine. "You are telling me that you have a working quantum computer? Not just experiments or a proof of concept, but a real, live, functional quantum computer that solves real world problems?"

"A quantum super-computer, and that's just the tippy-tip of the iceberg. At least, we did until last night." Shea's handsome face contorted into a scowl. "Now we've got two failed prototypes and a billion-dollar box of confetti."

Laurel's heart began to race. If it was true—if SP really had built the Holy Grail of computers—the implications were staggering. Quantum computers were the on the bloodiest part of the bleeding edge of technology. Theory said they could solve certain kinds of problems millions of times faster than traditional computers. *Like breaking codes.* Andrew Seigart must have known what SP was up to, or at least suspected.

Now she understood why he'd ordered her flown here on a military jet.

"And what is the rest of the iceberg?" she asked.

The tall man gave her a long, considering look. Eventually he nodded. "Let's go talk with Peter Struve."

CHAPTER EIGHT

San Carlos, California

June 26

The first few miles of Jack Dura's daily commute were the hardest.

His apartment was perched on a hill overlooking the mid-Peninsula community of San Carlos. The steep, twisty roads that led to Alameda de las Pulgas were great fun. The terrain between San Carlos and Stanford wasn't too challenging.

The drivers were another story.

In spite of his bright yellow jersey, the blazing orange pannier bag behind the seat of his fluorescent green recumbent bike, and a zillion flashing LEDs mounted all over its frame, San Carlos drivers never seemed to see him. He was forever being cut off or swerving to avoid the drivers who rode the right edge of their lanes too closely. They always had the same baffled expression when he shook his fist or yelled curses at them, their lips forming a silent "O" of surprise that a bicyclist would dare to use the clearly marked bike lane.

Weirdly, as soon as he passed Edgewood Road, where the bicycle lane disappeared, the drivers seemed to accept the presence of bicyclists on their precious street. In any case, they seemed less likely to try to run him down.

Today Jack counted himself lucky. Just three drivers tried to kill him before he reached the Edgewood Safety Zone, and only one of those came close to succeeding: a dirty white van that pulled into the bike lane in front of him and slammed on the brakes for no very obvious reason.

Jack swerved off the street, onto the shoulder and into a thick patch of Mexican feather grass, cracking his right knee against a wooden post hidden in the dry vegetation. The driver sped off before Jack could untangle himself from his bike. *Look on the bright side,* he told himself as he tried to walk off the pain. *At least there was a shoulder to roll into.*

Jack tried to ignore his throbbing knee and the itchy welts rising on the exposed skin of his calves as he finished the ride to Stanford. He speculated about the percentage of white van drivers who were serial killers, kidnappers, and/or drug dealers. By the time he rolled to a stop outside the Gilbert Building he concluded that the figure was at least seventy percent. He had the math to prove it.

He took his helmet off. He ran his fingers through his close-cropped, curly hair and shook off the worst of the sweat. Then he heard the sound of a helicopter somewhere to the south. It didn't sound like the Life Flight chopper that took off from and landed atop the Stanford Hospital a few times a week.

He peered into the sky. Sure enough, a bright red helicopter hovered over the hills to the southwest of the campus, a mile or two away. Then another chopper caught his eye. And another. "What the hell?" he said when he spotted the fourth and fifth helicopters.

A passing student said, "They've been there for a couple of hours now. Guess there was a big accident on 280 or something."

"Jesus, I guess so," Jack said, frowning. That was a lot of TV choppers for a car crash. *Must be a serious pile-up. Glad I ride a bike.* Being stuck on a highway during commute hours was pretty close to his idea of hell on earth. More white-panel-van-psychos at work, no doubt.

He locked up his bike, retrieved the bag from behind the seat, and limped inside. He scrubbed himself down in the faculty locker room's shower. The itching went away, but his right knee was beginning to swell. By the time he stepped out of the shower it had turned a delightful shade of purple. He changed into his everyday work uniform: ratty straight-cut jeans, a long-sleeved black T-shirt, tube socks and a very old but sturdy pair of Lowa hiking boots. He winced as his jeans constricted around his swollen knee when he bent over to tie his laces. He shoved his bag and his sweaty bike clothes into his locker.

On the way out of the bathroom, he scowled at his reflection in the mirror. He was still in good shape. He might drive a computer at work, but the terrifying bike commute kept an inner tube from forming around his waist. His long sleeves hid the shiny pink burn scars on his shoulders and arms.

He was still good looking enough to attract attention from women, which was a mixed blessing, considering his rudimentary relationship skills and the lurking danger of getting involved with a student. He'd made that mistake a couple of years ago. Even though she hadn't been *his* grad student, the affair had nearly cost him his job when she soured on him and lodged a complaint with the school. *Once bitten, twice shy.*

He'd dodged the male pattern baldness bullet: his black hair was as thick as ever. The skin he felt comfortable enough to expose was deeply tanned. On the other hand, the stubble on his jaw had more gray than he liked—more every day, it seemed. Too bad. He'd be damned if he'd bow to the urge to color it away. Without a girlfriend to insist, he was too lazy to shave more than twice a week.

"Fuck you," he growled at his beard's reflection. "Turn gray. See if I care."

He hobbled down the hall to his lab.

It wasn't really a lab, if he was honest with himself. It was more like an office crossed with a dorm room. It was small. There were no lab benches, chemicals, centrifuges, fume hoods or glassware. Jack's specialty was computational biophysics, which was a lot more about programming than experiments, but as a tenured full professor at one of the most prestigious universities in the world at the tender age of forty-one, he was determined to have a lab. Even if it was only a "laboratory of the mind," as Hank Drummond, his newest grad student, called it.

The "lab" had started life as a windowless seminar room. He had replaced the bookshelves, conference table and chairs with a low-walled, double-wide cubicle for Jack and four smaller ones for his students. There was a tiny area set aside for chats and the Friday beer bash, furnished with two dilapidated love seats, a glass-topped living room table, and a bookshelf stuffed with cheap booze and cheesy board games. The walls were covered with science fiction and fantasy movie posters, cartoons, and whiteboards filled with inscrutable formulas and computer code. An employee of any Silicon Valley startup would feel right at home.

The overhead fluorescent lights had been disconnected from the wall switches. LED strips lining the ceiling provided colorful mood lighting. Apparently today's mood was "green." But not just any green: a blood-curdling green, a green that spoke of cauldrons and eye-of-newt and goblets full of poison.

"Ugh," he said as he closed the door behind him.

"Don't blame me," said Terry Blau, whose cube was closest to the door. The hairy, pear-shaped postdoc didn't turn around from his huge flat panel display, which was filled with windows containing densely packed text. "It's Lizbeth's turn to pick."

"What's wrong with green?" Lizbeth Okome-Taylor protested. Her cube was opposite Terry's. She stood up, yawned, and stretched her arms high above her head.

Her ebony skin and dark clothing made her nearly invisible in the dim green light, which was probably a good thing. She was smart, sweet, single, spectacular, and as one of Jack's grad students, strictly off limits. Not being able to see her made it easier not to ogle her. "Seriously, Lizbeth?" he said, looking up at her shining eyes. "It's like the makeup of the Wicked Witch of the West. Did you know that actress died of skin cancer? Face rotted right off her skull. Right off her *skull*."

"True fact," Terry chimed in.

"You liars, she did not," Lizbeth grumbled. She sat back down, fiddled with her iPhone, and the lighting turned pink.

"No!" Jack and Terry said in unison.

"Okay!" she barked. The color changed to a warm sunset orange.

"Good enough," said Jack. Terry said nothing, which meant (a) he was okay with the color, and (b) he had dived back into his work and wouldn't be heard from unless the lights changed again. Terry was very focused.

Jack said to Lizbeth, "Have you been here all night?"

"Since about one AM." She tilted her head toward Terry. "*He* was already here, of course. We have to send the grant proposal to the NSF on Thursday, remember? It's easier to write when Terry's the only other one here."

"Hint taken," Jack said, laughing. Xu Chao-Xing and Hank Drummond wouldn't be in until noon at the earliest. They were working the late shift these days, trying to interpret the results from a simulation they'd run on the Sequoia supercomputer over at Lawrence Livermore. They'd probably be at it for months.

Jack sat down, pulled his ancient Steelcase chair closer to the desk, and logged into his computer. He banged his good knee against the corner of his desk and had to stifle a yelp. "Sonofabitch," he growled under his breath. "Now it's both of 'em."

He kept his desk clean, but his computer was a total mess. His three huge monitors were overflowing with windows containing half-read journal articles, half-written emails, and half-forgotten electronic sticky notes. He checked the clock in the corner of the menu bar. Just 10:00. He still had two hours to review Lizbeth and Terry's work on the proposal before he had to teach his graduate biomechanics seminar.

"Thank God for Google Docs," he whispered as he found the window containing their work-in-progress. He could follow along in real time as they collaborated on the proposal. He found an ancient, rewrapped, mummified Clif Bar in the top drawer, took a bite, and started reading. "Ugh. They made this one with real cliff." The taste didn't stop him from finishing it. He washed it down with lukewarm water from the stainless steel bottle on his desk.

He was deep into the document when a chat client window popped up on the screen. It was from Alastair Brodie, the head of the Biophysics department.

YOU THERE JACK

"Dammit," he grumbled as typed his reply.

Brother, have you heard the Good News about lowercase letters and punctuation? Hallelujah!

Brodie's answer was not long in coming.

NEED YOU TO COME TO MY OFFICE NOW PLEASE VERY URGENT POLICE MATTER

Police matter? Had he done anything illegal recently? Nothing sprang to mind, but he felt a premonitory chill nonetheless. He tapped CAPS LOCK and typed:

OKAY ALASTAIR KEEP YOUR UNDEROOS ON MAN

Then he smacked the RETURN key.

He struggled out of his chair in spite of the best efforts of his aching knees to keep him there. "Back in a few," he said over his shoulder to his oblivious students.

Five minutes later he learned why the helicopters had been hovering over the golden hills to the southwest.

CHAPTER NINE

StruvePharma Coyote Hill Campus, Palo Alto, California

June 26

Laurel Wynn exchanged mystified looks with Robbie Holmes and Detective Sergeant Vieira.

They followed a stone-faced Aidan O'Keefe down a brightly lit basement corridor of the Pauling Building. Peter Struve and John Shea trailed behind them.

This floor was like a set from a dystopian science fiction movie: vast, trackless and a little intimidating. It was at least twice the area of any of the above-ground floors, if Laurel was any judge of size at all. The walls were a featureless glossy white. The steel doors were unlabeled. There were no navigation aids of any kind. O'Keefe led them through the building using a moving map on his cell phone.

"Why aren't there any signs?" asked Robbie Holmes.

"Security through obscurity," said John Shea. "It's hard to find anything specific in the vaults unless you know exactly where it is."

O'Keefe stopped in front of an undistinguished door but made no move to open it. He clutched his big iPhone in his right hand and stared at it as if hypnotized.

Laurel looked sidelong at O'Keefe. Struve and Shea looked bad. StruvePharma's Chief Technology Officer looked worse. He'd known Emily Dura longer than anyone else at the company. He'd even been involved with her romantically. Her death had obviously hit him like a train. His eyes were red, his brown hair disheveled, his face sallow. His thick wire-rimmed glasses were slightly askew on his face. She felt an odd urge to straighten them.

"Are you sure you're up to this?" Laurel prompted him.

He did not respond.

Vieira cleared her throat. "The sooner we understand why you were attacked, the better."

"You're right," O'Keefe said abruptly. "You need to hunt down the bastards who did this." He pulled a photo badge from a pocket and waved it in front of a black square on the wall.

The door clicked open. Inside was a mantrap, sealed by a heavy door, secured by a hand scanner. The CTO led them into the tiny room. They had to squeeze in to fit.

Laurel was uncomfortably aware of the solid bulk of John Shea's chest against her back.

"Sorry," he whispered.

"Forget it," she whispered back.

O'Keefe did his thing with the hand scanner and the inner door of the vault clicked open. Fortunately, it was hinged so it swung open into the room beyond. The musty, cool air that swept over them carried a disagreeable odor of plastic.

The overhead lights snapped on as they walked in. The room was big, perhaps fifty by a hundred feet, punctuated with heavy diagonal girders and vertical support columns. It was filled with stainless steel racks of black plastic boxes. Every box was labeled with a long, cryptic number and a square, pixelated laser scanner code.

O'Keefe led them past three rows of shelves and down a long passageway, peering at his iPhone's screen the whole while. They were nearly at the end when he stopped, bent, slid a large box off a bottom shelf and lowered it gently to the floor.

Unlike most of the other boxes, this one was black-painted metal. Its lid featured nothing but a round, white button. O'Keefe put his thumb on it. After a few seconds there was a musical beep. The lid unlatched with an audible click. O'Keefe removed it and stood back.

Inside the box, nestled inside custom-cut foam padding inserts, were two spherical, metallic objects. Their surfaces glittered coldly in the storage room's blue-white light.

O'Keefe said, "QUBE Alpha and QUBE Bravo. Pound for pound the most expensive devices ever made. About ninety million dollars an ounce."

"Jesus," whispered Robbie Holmes. "What are they?"

"Quantum computers," O'Keefe said. "The most powerful computers in the world. Emily's design."

Laurel decided she didn't like StruvePharma's CTO very much. His voice was soft and gentle, but his diction was prissy and disdainful. His accent was Californian, but his word choices made him sound like he was trying to be an old Englishman. He had the overly precise pronunciation she'd come to associate with computer geeks, as if they'd learned English from reading instead of speaking.

She told herself to cut him some slack. O'Keefe had been through a lot in the last twelve hours.

"Don't sell yourself short, Aidan," said Peter Struve. "You had as much to do with their design as Emily did."

O'Keefe shook his head. "It was her breakthrough that led to it. Her genius. Hers and Jack's." He sighed. "I was just pinch-hitting for him. Maybe if he'd been involved from the beginning we'd have figured out how to make them work reliably by now."

"We tried," Struve said. "He wasn't having any."

"Back up a minute," Laurel said. "Can you explain exactly what these things do?"

O'Keefe knelt and picked one of the QUBEs up, holding it between the fingertips of both hands.

Laurel heard John Shea's intake of breath. She glanced at him. He was leaning forward, visibly tense. It occurred to her that she wouldn't want to make the big man angry.

"Please be careful with that, Aidan," Peter Struve whispered.

O'Keefe frowned at his employer. "I think I can manage to hold on to it." He shot a quelling glance at Shea. Then he shifted his gaze to Laurel. "This, Agent Wynn, is a Quantum Unison Bioalgorithm Engine. It's a quantum computer built to test large numbers of genetic algorithms simultaneously. We call them bioalgorithms because it fits the acronym better. Do you know what those are?"

Laurel nodded, her mind already spinning at the implications of O'Keefe's words.

"Well, I don't," said Robbie Holmes.

O'Keefe looked at the young FBI agent. "You've heard of evolution, I presume. It works at the level of genes. Parents pass on their genetic information to their offspring. Occasionally that information is altered, either by chemical mutagens or natural sources of radiation. But evolution is a very rough process.

"Most mutations are lethal, as you might expect. The machinery of life is very delicate. Some mutations have no obvious effect. An incredibly small number actually improve the organism in some way, usually small, sometimes large. Over the long run, the offspring with beneficial mutations tend to survive to breeding age more often than their less fortunate peers, and their offspring become more common. The species grows more fit for whatever ecological niche it occupies. Still with me?"

Robbie said, "It's been a while since biology class, but sure."

"Think of an organism as a kind of computer program. Its source code is its genetic code—the structured information in DNA that defines how to build and maintain an organism. The computer is the world itself, running all those genetic programs in parallel, so to speak. Organisms are born, live, and die. They interact with each other and with the world, just as do programs running on a network of computers. The program of life plays out over generations, over millennia, over eons. This is a gross oversimplification, and it doesn't take epigenetics into consideration at all, but you get the idea.

"Genes are problem-solving machines. They're always trying to improve the likelihood that their host will survive long enough to breed. That's all they do. Of course, this isn't purposeful. It's just a function of their construction. Genes are no more conscious than an architect's blueprint. Whether they become more common depends only on how they affect the organism's likelihood of reproducing. If the organism is successful, its genes are more likely to be perpetuated. Still with me?"

"Sure."

Laurel watched the CTO as he spoke. His grief seemed to fade as his enthusiasm for his lecture grew. She got the impression that he'd given the speech many times, probably to investors. He was very, very good.

It bothered her a little that he seemed able to set aside the horrible events of the last day so easily, but some men seemed able to compartmentalize their feelings without apparent effort. She couldn't do it herself, but she'd seen it often enough, particularly among geeks. She wondered if O'Keefe might be on the autism spectrum.

He continued, "Computer programmers have learned how to mimic evolution to solve certain kinds of very hard problems. *Optimization problems*, they're called. A famous example is the 'traveling salesman' problem: trying to create the shortest route between a number of cities. It's ridiculously time consuming to solve that problem with a linear computer program. Every city you add makes it exponentially worse. And there are any number of other problems that don't have *any* obvious solution.

"Take a two-dimensional maze. Each is unique. There's no obvious pattern you can exploit to solve it quickly. So how would you write a program to solve it? One way is to represent movement with four instructions: left, right, up or down. If you create a thousand random sets of movement instructions and test them against an actual maze, most of the time you get nowhere. But some of those instruction sets might make a bit of progress, purely by accident.

"So you take the solution that made the most progress in your first generation and 'breed' it. You use it as the basis for another set of a thousand programs, each of which is 'mutated' so it's different from the seed value. You test those 'offspring' programs against the maze. Some of them might be more effective at solving the maze than the parent. You keep the bits that succeed and throw away the bits that don't. Do this again and again and again, and eventually you will wind up with a program that runs the maze pretty quickly."

Detective Sergeant Vieira sighed audibly.

O'Keefe glanced at her but ignored the pointed hint. "It's a brute force technique. You don't wind up with a general-purpose maze solving program, but if you keep repeating the process, eventually you can solve that *particular* maze as quickly as theory allows. And along the way, you might learn something about the person who made the maze. Maybe he prefers left turns to right. You feed that information back into the model to generate variants with more left turns. You increase its efficiency even more."

The disheveled CTO was almost smiling now. "You see why they're called genetic algorithms now, don't you? The simple instructions—left, right, up, down—are like codons in genes. We mutate the algorithms and then test them to see whether they solve a 'black box' problem— one that doesn't yield to traditional mathematical analysis. We take the best solutions, mutate those, combine the parts that work best, and test them again and again against our fitness criteria, generation after generation, until we have an algorithm that solves the problem quickly."

"So Emily Dura discovered this genetic programming technique," said Vieira, impatience evident in her voice.

"Not at all. Genetic algorithms have been used in artificial intelligence research for years. Emily discovered how to build a compact quantum computer that could run them, in parallel, in massive numbers. She figured out a way to use quantum annealing to... Well, I guess the best way to put it is that the genetic algorithms help each other converge on the solution. I invented E++, the programming language we use to create them." He lifted the QUBE up so they could all see it.

"This is QUBE Alpha, the first one we made, four years ago. It's the baby. It only has 1024 qubits—quantum bits—but it was still by far the biggest quantum computer ever built at the time."

Laurel's mouth fell open.

"Is that a lot?" Robbie Holmes said.

O'Keefe answered before she could. "The biggest one outside of SP that we know of has five hundred and twelve qubits, and some people doubt that it really achieves quantum speed-up. QUBE Alpha *does*... about three percent of the time. But when it works, it *really* works."

Laurel gasped. A quantum computer of that size would be able to crack the most complex data encryption schemes faster than all of the rest of the world's computers put together. The NSA and CIA would go apeshit to get their hands on it, not to mention the Bureau's intel division. *"How?"* she squeaked.

Before O'Keefe could reply, John Shea snapped, "That's a secret."

"And one we don't have time for now," Allie Vieira growled.

Struve said, "Exactly. Agent Wynn, if you can give us a valid reason for us to show you the technical documentation, something that's pertinent to the investigation, we'll show you. But only after we talk with our lawyers. We're showing you this because you need to know why Emily and Jason were murdered. We're not offering to make you business partners."

Laurel said, "Fair enough." It was more than fair, if truth be told. She'd expected them to lawyer up as soon as she and Robbie appeared on the scene.

"Aidan, can you speed this up?" Struve said. "They're not investing. They just want the bottom line."

O'Keefe put the first QUBE back into its storage case and picked up the other one. "Alpha worked often enough for us to use it to design the next generation model. Bravo is a massively parallel upgrade of Alpha. And just like Alpha, it works about three percent of the time. Each entanglotron—each self-correcting quantum processor—has only 128 qubits, but there are over sixty-five thousand of them inside this unit. Charlie had four times as many."

"Holy crap," said Robbie. "How do they fit?"

O'Keefe shrugged. "They're small, and the QUBE is big. We used Bravo to design Charlie, which was far more powerful, but unlike the others, Charlie was completely reliable. There was something different about it. We still don't know what. Without Emily, I doubt we ever will."

If what O'Keefe was saying was true, the StruvePharma team was at least a decade, maybe two, ahead of everyone else in quantum computing. *Was Emily Dura really that much smarter than the best minds in computer science? She hadn't published a single paper in seven years.*

Laurel's astonishment shaded into outright disbelief.

Maybe this is a con game. Maybe her death had been staged to lend credibility to some kind of elaborate swindle.

She'd have to share that thought with Holmes and Vieira at the next opportunity. She'd seen nothing to prove that O'Keefe's claims were genuine. All she'd seen so far were some shiny, jewel-encrusted metal spheres.

"This is all very interesting," she said. "But this is a pharmaceutical company. Why spend so much time and money building this in-house? Why not get Intel or Samsung to build it for you?"

O'Keefe scoffed, "You can't just crank one out on a silicon wafer, though eventually that should be possible. We could barely do it ourselves, even with Emily and the best computer designers we could hire to work out the designs. In any case, the QUBE is largely optical, not electronic."

Laurel said, "Why did you build these things, anyway? What problem were you trying to solve?"

The CTO glanced at his boss.

Struve nodded.

O'Keefe said, "The protein-folding problem. One of the hardest problems in science."

Oh ho, thought Laurel. *It begins to make sense now*. A shiver of excitement ran through her in spite of her industrial-strength skepticism.

O'Keefe apparently noticed Robbie Holmes' blank expression. "Genes are sets of instructions for building structural proteins and enzymes—the basic functional units of living cells. If you understand proteins, you understand life itself. There is an equation to solve complex molecular structures. Schrödinger's equation. We might know the genetic sequence for a protein, but predicting the shape defined by that sequence is nearly impossible. The bigger the protein, the harder it gets. We've had some success with computer simulations, but—"

Laurel interjected, "It's one of those linear problems you told us about. Every new atom means the equation takes longer to solve."

O'Keefe looked at her shrewdly. "Exactly, Agent Wynn, and some proteins have hundreds of thousands of atoms. Shape determines function. Each amino acid added to the chain affects the structure of the whole molecule. Some amino acids are, ah, sticky, for lack of a better term. Some aren't. Imagine wrapping strips of double-sided sticky tape onto a string and tossing it into the clothes dryer until it wads itself into a ball. What would the final shape be? Protein folding is a bit like that, except in the real world, they always come out the same."

Struve said, "You can see why that would be important to a pharmaceutical company. I wanted a fast way to make monoclonal antibodies, tailored for individuals, to fight off infections directly and precisely. All the worries about antibiotic-resistant bacteria and viruses would go by the wayside. You'd even be able to target cancer cells with incredible precision."

"And SP would make a killing," said Robbie Holmes.

O'Keefe frowned. "Not the way I would put it, but yes. When Emily, her husband and I were at Stanford, we worked on the protein-folding problem. She came up with her new way to use genetic algorithms to model proteins, but it needed staggering amount of computing power. So she turned her mind to designing a new kind of computer, one built specifically for evolving quantum genetic algorithms at high speed." O'Keefe's voice fell to a whisper. "She was brilliant."

Struve cleared his throat meaningfully.

"Sorry," O'Keefe said. He wiped his brimming eyes with his sleeve. "Anyway. Emily and Jack had a stormy relationship. Their infant son was killed in a house fire. They blamed each other and got divorced. It looked like our team was finished. Emily's work was too important to waste, so I called Peter. He and I have known each other most of our lives. He'd just taken over SP after his father passed away. I talked him into offering her a job, and convinced her to work for him. He offered to fund our research if I joined her. We both left Stanford and came here."

O'Keefe placed the second QUBE back into its custom-fitted case and latched the lid.

Struve sighed as if he'd been holding his breath.

O'Keefe glanced at Struve. His face fell and shoulders slumped. "Would it really matter if I dropped it now, Peter? Emily's not here to bail us out anymore."

Struve's mouth tightened but he said nothing.

John Shea said, "Let's go."

They filed out of the storage room, cycled through the mantrap, and gathered in the hallway. The heavy door clicked shut behind O'Keefe.

"So now we know what the gunman was after," Laurel said. "How did he find out about it?"

O'Keefe said, "Someone inside the company must have leaked it. There's no other explanation."

Struve hissed, "I agree. God *damn* it."

Robbie Holmes said, "What about this venture capital company, ZMPC? Couldn't someone there have put the gunman up to it?"

"We're questioning them," Vieira said. "We'll know soon enough."

John Shea growled. "The perp knew exactly when the surveillance team changed shifts. He took Jason Lackland right to the Black Box, and he knew about the QUBE. The video proves it. Nobody at ZMPC could have known any of that. All they knew about was the demo unit." He shook his head. "Why would an insider be stupid enough to blab about the QUBE?"

They all stood there for a long, silent moment.

Laurel looked at the SP executives. They were asking the same questions she would ask in their place. If they were con men, they were among the best she'd ever seen. *Time to put this story to the test.* "What's this about a demo unit?"

O'Keefe said. "I'll show you." He led them back through the labyrinth of corridors to the elevator and pressed the call button. The door opened immediately, and they all filed in.

Laurel was at the back this time, next to Robbie Holmes. She exchanged a pensive glance with the young agent.

He raised his eyebrows as if to ask, *do you really believe this?*

She shrugged. At this point, she didn't really know what to believe. Or whom.

The elevator stopped. They exited into the central hallway of the second floor, also known as Main Street.

"The demo unit's being cleaned, Aidan," Struve said softly. "Let's show them Santa's Workshop."

"As you like." O'Keefe turned on his heel and marched down the corridor.

Laurel followed behind the rest.

Robbie Holmes caught her eye. "Santa's Workshop?" he mouthed.

She shrugged and whispered, "Geeks."

O'Keefe stopped in front of a metal door labeled "261." He waved his badge in front of the scanner to the left of the doorframe. The door clicked and opened onto another cramped mantrap. He cycled them through and led them into a huge workspace. Bright white LED lights flicked on as they entered the room.

"This is Santa's Workshop," O'Keefe said. "Where all our little toys are made."

The air in the vast workshop was cold and smelled of machine oil. The ceiling was at least as high as that of the Mission Control Room she'd visited earlier that morning. Long, waist-high workbenches divided the room into sections. The benches were covered with tubing, glassware, coils of cables, tools, electronic components, multi-testers, rolls of tape, Sharpie pens, and a hundred other things she could not identify. Between the workbenches were hulking, mysterious-looking machines of every shape and size. The only human touch was the collection of colorful, sequined Christmas stockings tacked to the walls.

Laurel had spent plenty of time in machine shops with her dad, who'd restored vintage cars. She'd even helped him secretly assemble a kit airplane at a rented hangar at the local airport. She'd been just as disappointed as he was when her mother found out about it and told him he could either divorce her or "sell that flying death trap." There was much in the room that was unfamiliar, but nothing inauthentic. It looked like a place where busy minds got things done.

O'Keefe said, "Peter, can you find an empty beaker?"

"Sure." The CEO walked to a nearby cabinet and rummaged around.

O'Keefe led them to a big black cabinet near the door. He opened one of the wide, shallow drawers. It was lined with black foam, like the QUBE storage unit in the basement. Five glassy rectangular prisms were nestled inside.

O'Keefe removed the one on the far left. The transparent block was about the size and shape of a large paperback book. He held it up for them to examine. Its only feature was a white square about an inch on a side in the center of its top surface. "This was one of the first things we made," he said. He took the heavy one-liter beaker from Struve, walked over to a nearby workbench, set it down and lay the block flat across its round top. He found a small work light on an adjacent bench, positioned it above the block and flipped its switch, bathing the device and the beaker with an almost painfully bright light.

"Watch carefully, now," he said, and tapped the square.

The top of the glass block turned black. Almost immediately, clear liquid began to drip into the beaker.

O'Keefe said, "This is a water condenser, powered by light. Pulls water straight out of the air. It took us nearly a year to figure out how to build this device, based on Emily's theories. It works by—"

"Aidan," said Struve sharply.

"Ah, yes," O'Keefe said. "Trade secrets. Well, you can see that it works. Imagine what this could do for the world. There's a surprising amount of water in the air, even in the desert. We tested this in Atacama, Chile. It's the driest place on Earth. Some weather stations there have never recorded any rainfall. Even there, this device can pull more than a liter of water out of the air every hour. All it needs is sunlight."

"Jesus," said Laurel. She stared at the beaker. It was almost a quarter full already, and the flow showed no signs of slowing. It couldn't be a fake. The volume of liquid was greater than the volume of the transparent block. The implications were staggering. "Why haven't you patented this and gotten it out into the market yet?"

Struve replied, "It still has certain... issues. We don't want to ship it until it's completely reliable."

O'Keefe said, "This is nothing, Agent Wynn. Emily's discovery was far more fundamental than we thought at first. Based on her work, we can now define a set of desirable properties, and the QUBE tells us how to make the molecule that has those properties. Say, the ability to split water into oxygen and hydrogen in the presence of sunlight." He pointed at another of the devices still in the drawer behind him. "That's what that one does."

Laurel felt the same electric chill she'd felt in the Mission Control room. If what O'Keefe claimed was true, the QUBE might be the greatest invention in all of human history.

O'Keefe folded his arms. "Satisfied, Agent Wynn? Or would you like to see something else? We have other demos that are much more advanced."

Detective Vieira said, "Including what you showed to ZMPC."

"Exactly. The water condenser is impressive, but not impressive enough." He pressed the button on top of the glass block. Its top surface became transparent again, and liquid stopped drizzling into the beaker. "All it does is concentrate a molecule that's already in the air. The hydrolysis unit is better. Free hydrogen fuel for your car or house. But it wasn't flashy enough for Peter. He wanted a demo that could *make* something, so that's what we showed to ZMPC. That's what the gunman was after. It's in the Black Box, being cleaned and refilled with reactants. We can show it to you tomorrow. It concentrates water and carbon dioxide from the atmosphere, and releases molecular oxygen... and synthetic oil."

A stunned silence filled the room.

Laurel was the first to speak. "Christ almighty. You're talking about nanotechnology."

"Much more than that—" O'Keefe began.

"—all of which is secret!" barked Struve.

O'Keefe frowned but he closed his mouth.

Robbie Holmes said, "No wonder the bad guys wanted the QUBE."

O'Keefe scoffed, "Magical thinking. If you stole Einstein's pencil, you wouldn't be able to think like Einstein. You'd need the cryo facility, the bioalgorithm library, the thousands of servers in the basement that process the data, and the scientists who interpret it. I think this was sabotage, pure and simple. Someone found out what we were doing and wanted to stop us."

Struve said, "Aidan, I don't think—"

John Shea's cell phone chirped. He pulled it from his sport coat's pocket and answered it. "It's for you," he said, handing the phone to Vieira.

She took it from him. "Vieira." She listened intently for a long moment. "Thanks, Angelo. I owe you a cold one." She handed the phone back to Shea. Then she smiled. The expression looked out of place on her gruff face. "Eric Dalton," she said with obvious relish.

"Who?" John Shea said sharply.

"One of the technicians at ZMPC. He was part of the team that did the technical evaluation of your demo unit. It looks like he's the one."

O'Keefe's face drained of color. "But how could *he* have known about the QUBE? Even Philip Mayhew didn't know!"

Vieira said, "Good question." She turned to Laurel. "Do you want to sit in on the interview?"

CHAPTER TEN

Palo Alto Police Department, Palo Alto, California

June 26

Laurel Wynn had attended the FBI Academy at Quantico. She graduated with high honors. She was an excellent marksman, especially for a member of what some of her colleagues called "the rubber gun squad," and she enjoyed martial arts training. She was a trained law enforcement agent who spent most of her working hours looking for criminal evidence in server logs, network packet dumps, bank records and spreadsheets.

She hadn't attended many interrogations, though. She seized every opportunity to do so. They were fascinating, though sometimes in much the same way that a train wreck is fascinating. They were real. They were human.

She sat to Allie Vieira's right. Eric Dalton tried unsuccessfully not to squirm in his chair on the other side.

His pudgy face was red. He rubbed his hands together compulsively. His black T-shirt was soaked with sweat, filling the room with an acrid, eye-watering reek. His eyes darted around the interview room, at the scarred wooden table in front of him, at the large one-way mirrors that occupied most of the walls—anywhere but into the eyes of his interrogators.

Detective Vieira studied the report of the officers who had invited Eric down to the station. Robbie Holmes and Detective Bosson watched from the other side of the interview room's one-way glass. Vieira had judged that Eric might be intimidated by the big men, but like many socially awkward geeks, he would tend to underestimate women—and be more likely to make a mistake.

The detective finally put the report down and looked up at Dalton, her lips pursed in the closest she could come to a smile. "I'm Allie Vieira, Mr. Dalton. Do you know why we asked you to come down here?"

"Uh, no. Not really," he said, staring at the tabletop.

"There was a bit of trouble at StruvePharma yesterday."

He frowned, looking up at Vieira for the first time. "What?"

"You didn't hear about it on the news? Or read about it on the web?"

"No. I went to bed early yesterday. Long day at the office."

"Working on a Sunday?"

"Yeah. We worked through the weekend. I was asleep when the cops—I mean, when your officers woke me up."

Vieira chuckled. "Most of us don't mind being called cops, Mr. Dalton, as long as it's said respectfully. Can I call you Eric?"

"Uh, sure." He looked down at the table.

Vieira said, "It was nice of you to let the officers search your apartment. You didn't have to do that. We truly appreciate it. That kind of cooperation goes a *long* way with us, Eric." She picked up the report and looked at it again. "The officers found something we'd like to ask you about. There was a digital voice recorder in your pants pocket. It had a property tag on it from your employer. ZMPC Venture Partners, isn't it?"

Dalton wiped sweat from his forehead. "Yes," he whispered.

"Ben Holcombe said you kept audio notes from your research work on it. He gave us permission to listen to them. Since he's your boss, and it's company property, we didn't need a warrant. We know about the demo unit from SP." She lowered her voice to a conspiratorial whisper. "Is it true that it really makes oil out of thin air?"

Dalton nodded dumbly, his eyes glued to the table.

Vieira shook her head. "Amazing. Anyway, the recording corroborates what your coworkers told us about the research."

"Well, good," mumbled Dalton. "Can I go now?"

"Did you know it was still recording after you left the lab?"

Dalton went utterly still.

Any paler and he'll go translucent, thought Laurel.

Vieira scrutinized him for a long, silent moment. "Guess you forgot to shut it off," she said at last.

Dalton shuddered but said nothing. Sweat poured from his forehead.

"Maybe you can explain what this means." Vieira removed a slender Tascam audio recorder from her pocket and placed it on the table. She pressed the PLAY button.

Dalton's voice emerged from the tiny speaker on the recorder. His voice had a hard, flat echo, and was occasionally muffled by a rustling sound, presumably from the fabric of his pants. *"That fucker. He's married. He's married! That's going to make this easier."* There was a sound of water splashing, followed by the whoosh of a hand dryer, then a metallic click. *"Goddammit,"* his recorded voice said a moment later. *"How could he do it? Why? He's married, for Christ's sakes!"* There was another short silence. Finally: *"That'll show you, Dr. Benjamin Fucking Holcombe, Ph.D., Fuck you, fuck her, and fuck this fucking cheap-ass company."* His voice descended to a barely audible whisper, obscured by the rustling sound. *"This... a fucking fortune."*

Vieira thumbed the recorder off. "It goes on for a while. Sounds like you drove home, dropped your clothes on the floor, showered, and microwaved something for dinner. Then you went to bed. The recorder was still on when the officers found it. Amazing device. I like the sound-activation feature. Saved us a lot of time when we were listening to your one-sided conversation, Eric. I'll have to get one when my Palm Pilot finally dies. These new lithium-air batteries last *forever*."

"Oh, my God," croaked Dalton.

"Do you know who this lady is, Eric?" Vieira said as she gestured to Laurel. "She's with the FBI. She investigates high tech espionage."

"Jesus."

"Eric." Vieira's voice grew low and serious. "The fact of the matter is that two people were killed at SP early this morning."

Dalton's eyes grew huge. He swallowed audibly. "Killed?"

"Well. That's kind of a gentle term for it. Slaughtered. By someone who was trying to steal something very valuable from them."

Dalton put his head against the tabletop. His back started shaking, but he made no sound.

Laurel felt a surge of sympathy for him. The interrogation had transitioned to "train wreck" stage some time ago. The poor man was utterly out of his depth. He was like a fawn staring into the headlights of an oncoming battle tank.

Vieira said, "Eric. We need you to explain what you meant on the recording. What was that about a 'fucking fortune?'"

Dalton looked up at her, eyes streaming. "I'm so sorry!" He put his head in his hands and sobbed.

* * *

"He's in custody now," Laurel finished.

She had taken refuge in an unoccupied interview room. She'd brought Andrew Seigart up to speed on the investigation so far. For a member of the "blinking 12:00 on the VCR" generation, he was pretty techno-savvy. He'd once been the head of a black technology group inside ATK—now Orbital ATK—a major defense contractor.

His stern face peered at her from the screen of her battered old MacBook. The Palo Alto Police Department had an excellent Wi-Fi network. The video was sharp and lifelike. The Stars and Stripes and the Homeland Security banner flanked Seigart's desk, their colors clear and crisp. The bright daylight beyond the window glinted off his expansive bald scalp. She could even see a bit of the Smithsonian Castle on the National Mall through the window behind him.

Seigart nodded. "That was good work."

"Vieira's, not mine. She's got real talent. And Dalton's not exactly a hardened criminal. When he found out about the murders he came unglued. Took us ten minutes to get another coherent word out of him. It was sad, really."

"So what's his story?"

"He's been in someone's pocket for a long time. He doesn't know whose. He was recruited over the Internet three years ago. He thought it was a joke until a big bundle of cash came by private courier. All of the contacts have been by email or through anonymous web sites. He gave us the passwords for his laptop. He says all the emails he's sent or received are on it, including the instructions on how to decode messages from his contact. He was supposed to delete them and securely erase the drive, but he never got around to it." She shrugged. "Typical amateur."

"Lucky for us even smart people are usually lazy about security."

"Yes. His handlers aren't lazy, though. They put twelve different personal ads in the *San Jose Mercury News* every Sunday. They mailed him a one-time pad with a different code for each week. The code phrases in the ads spell out an IP address for a web server. He logs in with a username and password decoded from a different set of ads, gets his instructions, passes on any new information, and then logs out. The server changes every Monday at 12:00 AM Pacific. Robbie Holmes is looking into the server Dalton connected to on Sunday, but I'd be surprised if it's still online. The IP address is registered to a porn website in Hungary."

"Of course it is." Seigart sighed and rubbed his eyes. *"What else?"*

"Dalton was paid about half a million dollars in cash for seven different tip-offs over the last three years. It's stored in three big safe deposit boxes in a Bank of America in San Mateo. We seized it. Maybe the bad guys left some forensic evidence on the money. We're trying to track down whoever bought the ads, but it's easy to fake out the online payment system, so it's probably a dead end. Dalton received all his money by courier. He says he's never had any personal contact with his handlers."

"Our opponents run a pretty tight ship."

"Yes, sir. The other thing is that Dalton says he didn't tell them about the QUBE. He didn't know about it. No one at ZMPC does, if you believe their statements. The only technology they've seen was this magical oil making machine. Struve and O'Keefe are the only SP executives who've been in contact with them, and they're both paranoid about keeping their trade secrets."

"Not paranoid enough."

"I think O'Keefe is right. An insider at SP tipped off the bad guys about the QUBE. I think they were waiting for independent confirmation of its effectiveness. Dalton was told that the oil synthesizer would be coming into the lab three days in advance, and that he should send a message right away to let them know if it worked."

Seigart's expression grew a bit less sour. "So the mole is someone who knew about the demo and the QUBE. That should narrow down the field a bit."

It was Laurel's turn to sigh. "Not as much as I hoped. There are twenty-four potential suspects, including the whole executive staff, minus Emily Dura and Jason Lackland."

Seigart said, "We'll get you some help doing the interviews. I want to nail these bastards, Agent Wynn. The task force is taking a beating in front of Congress. They're still up in arms about the cyber-attacks on Lockheed by that North Korean hacker group, and after the Office of Personnel Management hack, anyone involved with computer security has a big target on their back."

"That's hardly fair," exclaimed Laurel. "We weren't involved in the OPM investigation."

Seigart's eyes glinted. "Must be a problem with my Internet connection. I thought you used the word 'fair.'"

She could feel the flush suffusing her face.

Before she could formulate a reply, Seigart continued. "We're talking about politics, Agent Wynn. When Congress smells blood, everyone with a blood supply starts running. That includes us. The task force needs a win. See if you can get Dalton to help sucker his contacts into revealing themselves. They probably don't know about his arrest. Make sure it doesn't get into the public record."

"Yes sir. I thought you might have something like that in mind. I already floated the idea with the District Attorney. She seems agreeable."

"Good. Any ID on the SP gunman yet?"

"Last I heard he was still in surgery over at Stanford."

"You're in charge of this investigation until we have some concrete results. I don't care if it takes a year."

She wondered how dusty her apartment in Falls Church would be when she got back. *Good thing I don't have any pets.* "Yes, sir. What about SP? They've been cooperative up to now, but their CEO told me they're not interested in becoming, and I quote, 'indentured servants of the government.'"

Seigart sniffed. "Nice phrase. Tell him we'll beef up their physical security at no charge. We'll talk about partnerships later."

"No charge?" she echoed, eyebrows raised.

"Carrots before sticks, Agent Wynn. I'm pretty sure their technology is the real deal. Struve hasn't been as discreet as he thinks. Rumors have been flying about something big at SP for a long time. The President knows about it. We just met for two hours."

Laurel had to work to keep her jaw from dropping open.

Seigart didn't seem to notice. "We're under orders to be as helpful as humanly possible, but not to interfere with StruvePharma's work. We have every reason to want them happy and successful." He gave a single dry, scoffing chuckle. "The Joint Chiefs recommended that we should classify Struve's research and seize the company. The President tore a strip off the Chief of Staff an inch deep and a foot wide. There are a lot of campaign donors in Silicon Valley, for both parties. And nothing makes geeks run faster than the idea that the big bad government's coming to get them. Especially after that goddamned Edward Snowden," he added with a grimace.

She didn't have to ask his opinion of the notorious former NSA contractor who'd spilled so many secrets. She said, "That makes sense, sir."

"From what you've told me, Struve is on the edge of bankruptcy. If he can't get his funding, you're authorized to offer it. You're our liaison with them for now. The century's still young, Agent Wynn. There are a lot of people out there who want to knock the United States off her pedestal. SP's work could be just the thing to keep her there. Good work so far. Get back to it."

"Sir?"

He paused in the act of reaching for his laptop's keyboard. *"Yes?"*

"Do you think the Joint Chiefs were right? *Should* we seize the company?"

"Officially, that's above my pay grade. Off the record, I think SP might be a security risk, but they're cooperating with us and haven't done anything illegal, as far as we know. This is still the United States of America. The President made the right call."

She smiled, gratified. "Yes, sir." She felt the same way herself.

"Bring me some scalps, Agent Wynn. Good hunting." He disappeared from her screen.

She folded her laptop closed. Her stomach rumbled. She glanced at her watch. It was four PM. She was suddenly conscious of a powerful hunger and an impending headache. Her day had started more than eleven hours ago, and she'd had nothing but five cups of paint-thinner disguised as coffee.

She opened the door to the interview room, hoping to track down a vending machine. She heard several people shouting and instantly knew something was wrong.

"Don't just stand there!" she heard Vieira's voice over the sound of a small mob. "Get moving!"

She followed the shouts to the detective squad room. The door was flung open before she could reach for the knob. She leaped out of the way as the giant Bob Bosson and four uniformed officers pushed past her at a run.

Vieira was standing next to her desk, talking into a phone handset.

Robbie Holmes was watching her, his mouth agape.

"Yes..." said Vieira. "Yes... No, goddammit! There were two of them. Son of a *bitch*. What about the perp? God DAMN it!" she cried, slamming the phone down on its base.

Laurel's hunger turned to nausea. "What happened?"

Vieira snarled, "Two of my men were just killed, that's what!" She closed her eyes and took a deep breath. "Someone broke into the ICU at

Stanford. He killed the perp, the two officers who were guarding him, a doctor, and two nurses. Gunned them down and got away clean. Jesus H. Christ." She collapsed into her chair. "I've known Sam Martinez for fifteen years." Her voice was desolate.

Laurel felt like she'd been punched in the stomach. "Oh, my God," she whispered. "What the hell is going on?"

CHAPTER ELEVEN

El Carmelo Cemetery, Pacific Grove, California

July 7

When the service ended, the other mourners gave Jack their condolences and left him alone.

Emily's parents had died in a car crash a month after Emily filed for divorce. She had no brothers or sisters. Jack was the only family left to her, and they hadn't spoken since the break-up. He could say anything to her now, though. There was no one here to stop him. She'd have to listen, but she would never reply.

Emily had named Ramona Ochoa, SP's chief legal counsel, as the executor of her will. She and Jack had worked together on the phone to arrange her funeral in secret. Only a handful of Emily's closest friends had been invited. He didn't know any of them. They'd all looked shell-shocked, and had barely acknowledged him other than with perfunctory statements of sympathy.

Jack had flatly refused to allow Aidan O'Keefe to attend. "If he shows his face, I'll shove it up his ass," he'd told Ramona Ochoa, and that was the end of that.

Even now, almost two weeks after the event, the national media were still showing twenty-four-by-seven "up to the minute" coverage of the Struve-Pharma Massacre, as they called it. By some miracle the funeral had remained secret. Jack knew he would have lost it completely if it had wound up on CNN. There were no TV trucks, no satellite dishes, no helicopters hovering overhead. The only sounds were the quiet rustling of the leaves in the trees and the cries of seagulls from the nearby shore.

He stood in front of her grave marker, dry-eyed. Uncertain. Empty. He wished he could cry, but there didn't seem to be anything left in his tank.

"This is a beautiful place, Emily," he said at last. He looked around. The El Carmelo Cemetery was indeed beautiful. Low white clouds scraped the tops of the Monterey cypress trees that lined the emerald lawn. From time to time, beams of sunlight pierced the mist and stroked the mossy tombstones and monuments. A small herd of deer romped across the grass, bringing a short-lived smile to his face.

On the other side of Asilomar Road was the Point Pinos Lighthouse, just visible behind a row of carefully trimmed hedges. The elegant little lighthouse marked the northern tip of the Monterey Peninsula. It was the reason Emily had chosen El Carmelo as the final resting place of their son.

They'd brought him here once, when he was just a year old. Eddie had been oblivious to the charms of the rocky, wave-swept shoreline, and immune to the musical calls of seagulls. When they hiked past the lighthouse, Eddie's eyes had fastened on its slowly rotating beacon. He laughed like it was the funniest thing in the world. His tiny arms and legs beat against Jack's back as he cackled. When they left the lighthouse behind, Eddie started bawling. They had to go back. They waited forty-five minutes for Eddie to giggle himself to sleep in the baby carrier backpack, and then they moved on.

They had always wondered what their son had found so funny.

"You were right, Em," Jack said. He looked down at her grave marker, and then Eddie's, just to her left. "This is where he'd want to be. Take care of him." Jack had never been able to tell her that before. He hadn't attended the funeral. He'd been hospitalized, recovering from his first skin graft surgery.

He knelt, touched his fingers to his lips, and then pressed them against Eddie's marker. "I'll see you later, baby boy," he whispered. Then he did the same for Emily. "Goodbye, Em. I'll come back. I promise." He stood.

There was still space on Eddie's other side. He wondered vaguely how long it would be before he came here to keep them company forever.

He looked up at the clouds scudding overhead, and the dim white circle of the sun behind them. He whispered, "I can think of worse places to be."

He turned and trudged back across the lawn toward his car.

He stopped when he realized someone was standing on the grass in front of him. He focused on a pair of polished black shoes. His eyes moved up to take in the perfectly pressed pleats in the dress black pants, then the black suit coat, shirt and tie. His eyes finally came to rest on Peter Struve's narrow, weathered face.

"Jack, you have my deepest sympathy."

Jack should have been angry that Struve had the balls to show up uninvited, but he felt nothing but a great, gray weariness. "Get out of my way, Peter."

"I've been trying to reach you for two weeks."

"I didn't want to talk to you. Still don't." Jack tried to step around him.

Struve moved to block his path.

Jack sighed. "Did you know that I took up *kajukenbo* after my last skin graft? I've had a black belt for over a year."

"I have something for you. From Emily."

Jack noticed that Struve carried a manila string-tie envelope thick enough to hold the New York City phone book.

He shook his head. "I don't want it."

"Emily wanted you to have it."

"Emily wanted a lot of things. She wanted Eddie to grow up. She wanted to change the world. Did she ever get used to disappointment? You'd know better than I would." He stepped around Struve and walked toward his car.

"Jack," Struve called after him. "She wrote this for you. Her last wishes weren't in the will. She needed you to do something for her."

Jack stopped and slowly turned around. "I needed her to do something for me. I needed her to believe I didn't leave the burner on. I needed her to believe me, because it was true." Sudden fury blazed in his heart. He snarled, "And when I needed *her*, she left me."

Struve took a step back. "She was young."

"So was I!" Jack strode forward and grabbed Struve around the throat. The envelope tumbled out of his grasp. In an instant he'd pinioned the older man to the grass, his forearm across Struve's windpipe. "And you took advantage of her! She was naïve and vulnerable, but you weren't. You used her! You and that cocksucker Aidan O'Keefe! And then you got her killed!"

"Jack," Peter croaked. He made no move to escape.

"Hey, somebody call the cops," someone shouted.

Jack held his arm over Struve's throat for a long moment before releasing him. He stood up and looked down at Struve's supine figure.

"Leave me alone, you son of a bitch. There's nothing you have that I want."

Struve levered himself to his elbows. He gasped, "Emily's work!"

"What do I care about her *work?* I just put her in the ground!"

Struve struggled to his feet. "No, it's all right, Stu," he said to an onlooker who was punching a number into a cell phone. "Just a misunderstanding."

The man looked dubious but stopped dialing.

Jack was suddenly aware of a very tall man with close-cropped blond hair, dressed like Struve but built like a lumberjack. He had appeared behind Struve without making a sound. He looked to be in his early fifties but he moved with an easy, panther-like grace that Jack recognized from the sparring ring. The tall man brushed Struve's back free of grass and pinned Jack with a fearsome glare.

Struve said, "Thank you, John." He stooped and picked up the envelope. He stepped toward Jack but stopped well out of reach. "I'm sorry I had to come here. I really am. But I have to give this to you in person. It was her life's work. She wanted you to have it." He paused, holding the envelope in his outstretched hand.

Jack just stared at him.

"She did great things, Jack. Amazing things. She said you were the only one who could really appreciate them, or fully understand them. She included a letter for you. You owe it to yourself to read that, if nothing else. Please. Don't let her life have been for nothing."

"If I take it, will you leave me alone?"

"You have my promise. If you need to contact me, my card is inside."

"Don't hold your fucking breath," Jack snapped. He snatched the thick envelope from Struve's hand and stalked toward his car, acutely aware of the tall blond man's gaze on him.

"She *did* change the world, Jack," Peter Struve called. "When you read that, you'll know how."

A blue van with a folded microwave antenna mast on the roof screeched into the cemetery parking lot. A familiar-looking white-haired reporter jumped out and came toward Jack at a run, brandishing a hand-held microphone. "Wait! Dr. Dura!"

Jack flipped him the bird and shouted, "Too late, Cooper, you shithead."

He slammed the door of his rusty Geo Prizm. He cranked the feeble engine and lurched out the cemetery lot, trailing a cloud of smoke. He turned down several streets at random, leaving the TV van behind. He smirked at the impossibility of making a statement by peeling out of the cemetery parking lot in this ancient P.O.S. car.

It was then that the tears came, hot and heavy and irresistible.

He pulled over to the side of the road and wept.

When he had recovered enough to drive again, the low clouds had cleared. He glanced at the dashboard clock. It was just after noon. He was exhausted and unaccountably hungry. He'd skipped breakfast. Come to think of it, he didn't remember when he'd last eaten a meal. It was at least a two-hour trip back to San Carlos. If he tried to get home in his current state, he'd probably wind up in the ocean.

He wiped his face with the sleeve of his suit and drove deeper into the surrounding town of Pacific Grove. It took him a while to find a parking spot. He walked up and down the hilly retail district of the little town, peering at menus in restaurant windows, his stomach rumbling. Eventually he found himself in front of Peppers Mexicali Grill. He went inside and asked the waitress for *huevos rancheros* and a cold Negro Modelo.

When it arrived he ate with mechanical efficiency. He upended the beer bottle and drained it in one long, continuous swallow. He still felt like shit, and his taste buds appeared to be on strike, for all the flavor the food seemed to have, but at least his hunger was gone. He left three twenties for the pretty young waitress. She'd looked sad at his lack of enthusiasm.

He drove slowly around town, hoping against hope that his poor old Geo wouldn't die.

He visited Eddie's grave every year on the anniversary of his death, but he hadn't spent any time in Pacific Grove itself since that hike with Eddie on his back. He realized he'd missed it. He and Emily had visited the area frequently before and during their brief marriage. They'd even talked about buying a retirement home here someday, if they both made it big.

Jack was a confirmed desert rat. He'd grown up in Los Alamos, the son of physicists who worked at the National Lab. He didn't think he'd be able to handle the cold, foggy coastal summers, but he liked the charm of the little seaside town, the exotic look of the native Monterey cypress trees, and the sound of the waves on the rocky shore. Emily had loved it.

When Eddie died, all of those plans died with him.

He found himself on the Seventeen Mile Drive, a famous scenic coastal road that began near Pebble Beach Golf Course and ended in Carmel. He paid the auto toll with another twenty-dollar bill and told the attendant to keep the change. He drove slowly on purpose, drawing the ire of the tourists behind him. "No. Trust me. You do not want to hurry down this road," he said to his rear view mirror, and slowed even more.

He finally spotted his destination, a tiny parking lot next to a scenic overlook high above the blue-gray sea. He crept into one of the two available spots. A torrent of SUVs and sports cars rushed past him, horns honking, windows down, shaken fists and up-thrust middle fingers aimed in his general direction.

A newish but dirty black Camaro screeched into the other empty space, two cars down.

He waited for the backlog of cars to dissipate before he got out. He looked at the manila envelope on the seat next to him. He grabbed it and stepped out of the car.

"Hey asshole, the fuck you *doin'*, drivin' so slow?" said an angry teenaged voice.

Jack turned. The speaker was the muscle-bound, pimple-faced driver of the Camaro. He wore a grimy wife-beater T-shirt that had probably once been white, a flat-brimmed black hat featuring an orange San Francisco Giants logo and an "official merchandise" sticker, and a pair of baggy black jeans tied so low around his waist they were almost around his knees. The thug's skanky girlfriend observed from the safety of the Camaro's cabin.

"I buried my ex-wife today," Jack said mildly, meeting the thug's squinty gaze head-on. "Right next to our baby boy."

"Oh," mumbled the thug, clearly expecting a different response. His belligerence vanished, as if Jack had doused him with water. He wavered for an uncertain moment, and then said, "Well, uh, you oughta be more careful, like."

Jack nodded. "I'll do that."

The thug retreated to his car, holding his pants up with one hand. He struggled into the driver's seat, squealed back out of the parking space and rejoined the flow of traffic heading south into Carmel.

Jack turned away from the road, clutching Emily's envelope to his chest. He walked to the waist-high concrete fence that bordered the scenic overlook.

The sky was mostly clear now, aside from the perpetual wind-blown mist that hovered over the sea. Beyond the concrete rail, atop a rocky promontory silhouetted against the dark, deep waters of Carmel Bay, was the Lone Cypress.

The tall, elegant, ancient tree had been the emblem of Pebble Beach for so long they'd actually trademarked it. Cables wrapped around its forked, fire-scarred trunk kept it from splitting apart. Jack hadn't seen it since he and Emily had first discovered it on their way to their honeymoon in Carmel. It looked just the same. It was reassuring. *Some things should last.*

He moved along the overlook toward the tree. The concrete rail widened into a flat triangular space big enough to accommodate him. He clambered up and sat there, cross-legged, heedless of the damage he was doing to his only pair of black dress slacks. He put the envelope on his lap. He was half-tempted to hurl it into the ocean below, but he knew it would just wind up on the rocks. Some busybody would report him and he'd get a citation for littering. *It sucks to be a cynic.*

He debated with himself for five minutes before he finally untied the string that sealed the envelope.

Inside was a thick bundle of stapled documents. He opened the mouth of the envelope wider and saw a smaller white envelope inside. He fished it out. It was labeled "To Jack" in Emily's unmistakable, spiky handwriting. There was an old fashioned red wax seal on the flap, embossed with an ornate letter E.

He discovered that his hands were clammy. His heart was racing. He took a deep breath and let it out through his nose, repeating the action ten times, staring at the Lone Cypress without blinking. A measure of calm returned.

He slid a finger under the flap of the envelope, cracking the seal, and opened it.

The letter was on faded white stationery. He recognized it. It was from the La Fonda Hotel in Santa Fe. They'd stayed there on their last trip to visit Jack's dad, a year or two before the accident and their divorce.

It read:

Jack,

I know that you might not want to read this, but if you are, it's because I'm either brain-dead or dead-dead. I've written and rewritten this letter a dozen times already. I've decided the best way to tell you is just to tell you.

I don't blame you for Eddie. Not anymore. It had to have been an accident. We lost our son, and then we lost each other, and it's my fault for turning away. I'm sorry I couldn't be there for you during your recovery. I'm sorry for leaving. I'm sorry for being too ashamed to face you afterward. I never even thanked you for trying to save him. I can't say how sorry I am about that.

Those words seem pathetic, even to me, after all the pain I put you through. You know I was always better with numbers than words. I can't express my regret adequately, Jack, but I wanted you to know that I felt it every single day.

Tears blinded him. He looked away and let them stream down his face. The other sightseers standing near the rail went quiet.

He felt someone touch his shoulder. "Are you all right?" From the tone, it was an older woman.

He nodded, not looking at her. "It's been a really bad day," he said, his voice hitching. He nodded convulsively. "I'll be fine."

The woman murmured something and let him be.

When the surge of grief and pent-up rage subsided, he wiped his eyes and looked down at the letter again.

Peter insisted that I write this and keep it on hand in case I have an accident or die before our work is done. I hope he's just being paranoid. But in case he's not, I have something very important to ask you. I don't have any right to ask you anything, but I hope you'll keep reading anyway.

The work I've been doing at SP is important—more important than you can imagine. I discovered something new, Jack. Something I don't fully understand. Something so incredible you won't believe me unless I give you the evidence and let you draw your own conclusions. Now that I'm gone, you're the only one who can figure it out.

Inside this envelope are the key papers I wrote, up to the time of my death or incapacitation. As soon as Peter and Aidan decide it's the right time to send them out, the world will never be the same. Believe me when I tell you this.

I know you hate Aidan, and you're none too fond of Peter for hiring me away from Stanford. Please, for the love we once shared, listen to them. Read the papers. Come to your own conclusions. Help them, if you can. They may not deserve it, but they need it. The world needs it. You'll find out why.

Peter will ask you to join the team.

His hands clenched the letter. "God," he said through gritted teeth. It took him a full minute to decide what to do. He'd read this far. He'd finish it. He could always toss it into the ocean later. He'd gladly pay the fines.

He smoothed the letter flat, took a deep breath, and continued to read.

You're a hothead, Jack. Get mad now so you can think clearly later. Please don't reject Peter out of hand. Understand what you'd be passing up—and more importantly, what you would be denying the world. These papers will make everything clear.

There was another sheet stapled to the last page. It was on plain white printer paper. He folded it over and continued to read.

Jack,

There's one more thing.

My journal is in my personal document safe at SP. It's the capstone of my life's work. I update it every day. It ties everything else together. My theory raises more questions than it answers, and they're big questions. We've always said that's the best kind of theory, haven't we? It's what keeps us scientists employed.

You're the only one who can get into the safe. The code is a very long number—you know the one. Think "tequila." If the wrong combination is entered three times, the contents will be incinerated.

*Aidan and Peter know about the journal, but they don't
know what it's in it. I didn't put everything into the papers,
only the things we're sure about. Once you read it, once you
understand what we still don't know, what happens next will
be up to you.*

*You're a good man, Jack. Better than I deserved. All my
hopes and dreams now live and die with you. Make the right
choice. I believe in you. I'm sorry. Whatever you decide, I
wish you only happiness.*

Em

Jack stared at the letter for a long time. Finally, he refolded it and put it back in its small white envelope, which he put back into the large manila envelope, which he retied and placed gently on his lap.

"Jesus, Emily," he murmured. "You never did anything the easy way."

His rage slowly dissipated in the cool sea air.

The code is a very long number—you know the one. Think "tequila".

He didn't have to strain to remember it. He and Emily had had a tequila-fueled competition one night in Puerto Vallarta, before she got pregnant. They'd tested how impaired the other one was by memorizing the mathematical constant *pi* to as many digits as they could, and then repeating that number in reverse. Emily won handily, memorizing 140 digits without apparent effort. Jack could only remember thirty-five, but to this day, he could recite them all.

He stared at the Lone Cypress until the sun went down, whispering the numbers over and over.

Eventually he crept down from the concrete platform, brushed off his slacks, stretched to work out the kinks, got in his car, and drove down to Carmel. The right side of his face felt hot. It took him a while to work out that he'd sunburned himself. He pulled into the parking lot of the first hotel he could find. He flipped on the dome light and studied his reflection in the rear view mirror. Only the right side of his face was red.

"Nice," he said to his reflection. Then he went to the hotel's office. Luckily, they had a vacancy. At that price, he wasn't too surprised.

He went to his room, sat down at the desk, ordered a meal from a pizza delivery service, and removed the stack of papers from the manila envelope.

The topmost paper was a patent application. Its title would win no prizes for brevity, but its meaning almost made his heart stop.

A Method and Apparatus for Functional Modeling of Arbitrary Molecular Structures by Massively Parallel Quantum Annealing of Genetic Algorithms

Its principal authors were listed as Emily Dura, Ph.D., DSc., Aidan O'Keefe. Ph.D.—

—and Jack Dura, Ph.D.

"What the *hell...*?" he whispered, rubbing his burning, bestubbled cheek.

He picked up the paper and began to read.

CHAPTER TWELVE

StruvePharma Coyote Hill Campus, Palo Alto, California

July 13

Peter Struve sat behind his desk in his new office, a former conference room deep inside the fourth floor of the Pauling Building.

Laurel Wynn had urged him to move all of the employees at the Coyote Hill campus into the vast research facility. Guarding one building was infinitely easier than guarding twelve.

Struve had complied. It was a good idea, and the Pauling Building was by far the strongest structure on the campus. He'd been shocked at the number of offices and labs left empty after the move was completed. The building was designed to house sixteen hundred people. Fewer than three hundred remained.

Across from him sat Aidan O'Keefe, SP's Chief Counsel Ramona Ochoa, and Jay Kapoor, the beleaguered Chief Financial Officer.

Jay looked like he'd spent the night in a bar. His dark, thin face was unshaven. His deep-set brown eyes were rimmed with red. His gray suit coat hung from his bony frame as if from a wire hanger. He ran his hand through his sparse white hair and grimaced.

Ramona wouldn't be caught dead looking unkempt. Her business suit was immaculate. Her black hair was up in a bun. She smelled nice. Her makeup was close to perfect, but no amount of concealer could hide the bags under her eyes. She clasped her hands together so tightly her knuckles were white.

Peter's gaze shifted to Aidan O'Keefe. The CTO was the only one in the room who looked normal. Aidan wore a white long-sleeved shirt, a gray silk tie and matching slacks. His face was clean-shaven. He even looked as if he'd slept in the last week. The only hint of nervousness was the incessant drumming of his fingers on the arms of his chair. When he saw Peter looking at him, he cleared his throat and crossed his arms. "Sorry," he murmured.

Peter slouched in his chair and rubbed his chin. "So let me get this straight, Jay. We only have two months of operating capital left? *Two months?*"

Jay nodded slowly. "Philip Mayhew won't return my calls."

"Damn him," Ramona Ochoa whispered.

"They haven't formally canceled the letter of agreement," Jay said. "That's something. There's still a chance that they'll fund us."

Aidan said, "Fat lot of good that will do us if we keep losing researchers. I had to talk Dana Hughes down off a ledge this morning. No, not literally," he added, seeing Peter's eyes widen in horror. "She's gotten four offers since Emily died. I've lost eleven people since the attack, Peter. Most were poached. Some were scared. A few just gave up. Everyone's nervous. The word's out that we're hemorrhaging talent. The vultures are circling and we don't have a shotgun."

"Would more stock options help?" Peter asked, looking at Jay.

Jay shook his head. "They're all issued, except the reserve for this contingency plan of yours. You'd never get the Board to change the stock plan now. There's too much uncertainty about our future."

"What about another loan?"

Jay just looked at him.

Ramona said, "If we can't keep the doors open, what good are more stock options?"

Aidan snapped, "Why keep the doors open if we can't keep the scientists?"

"Enough." Peter stood, pushed his chair in, clasped his hands behind his back and began to pace back and forth in the inadequate space behind his desk. "When did he say he'd get here?"

"Two thirty," said Ramona.

He glanced at the wall clock. It was almost three. "Shit."

"How did he sound when you talked to him?" asked Aidan.

Peter sighed. "Hard to say. Not angry, at least. He didn't curse at me. That's a good sign."

Jay said, "Took him long enough to call."

"I'm surprised he called so quickly," said Aidan. "It would've taken me more than five days to read through those papers, and I helped Emily write them."

Ramona looked at Aidan. "From what Peter told me about the history between you two, I'm surprised he called us at all."

"Jack wouldn't miss this for the world." Aidan's tone was smug.

Peter said, "He and Emily worked on genetic algorithms and the theory that led to the QUBE. He got his own MacArthur Fellowship two years ago for the work he's done since their breakup. No one was as smart as Emily, but Jack's a genius in his own right. She reminded me often enough." He sighed again. "We've got to convince him to come on board."

"Then we'd better do it quickly," Jay said. "Peter, if we don't trim the staff or sell off more assets soon, we're dead. If ZMPC backs out, paying back the bridge loans will kill us. We'll be lucky to keep the production lines operating."

Peter stopped pacing and looked at his senior staff. "We do whatever it takes to get him. I don't care what he wants. We'll pitch in from our own shares if we have to. Jack's our moon shot. If we have to sell off the drug business, we'll do it. If he wants a hundred kilos of heroin and hot- and cold-running hookers, he gets them."

Jay and Aidan snorted.

Ramona flushed, clearly unamused by his hyperbole. She asked, "You can't just hire someone else who understands this stuff?" Her voice was plaintive.

Peter shook his head. "No one else can come up to speed in time. It's Jack or nobody."

The intercom on Peter' desk buzzed.

Peter punched the button. "He's here?"

"He's in the lobby," said the voice of his executive assistant.

"Thanks, Janice." Peter released the intercom button. "Okay, folks. It's show time."

He led the others to the elevator.

Jack waited for them in the atrium adjoining the spacious front lobby. Peter was astonished to see him in a sober but loose-fitting black suit and tie—the same suit he'd worn to Emily's funeral. Jack's face was gaunt but clean-shaven, a difficult feat for a man who could grow a visible beard in the space of an afternoon. The right side of his face was pink and peeling, as if he'd fallen asleep under a sunlamp. He looked like a marathon runner who'd gotten his second wind, beyond exhaustion and moving by will power alone.

"Thanks for coming, Jack." Peter stretched out a hand.

After a moment's hesitation, Jack shook it.

Peter introduced his staff.

Jack shook Ramona's hand gravely.

"It's nice to meet you in person," she said. "I'm sorry for your loss."

"Thanks for keeping Emily's funeral a secret." He shook hands with Jay, but merely glowered at Aidan, who lowered his hand without saying a word.

Jack looked at Peter. "You know why I'm here."

"Yes," Peter said. "Let's go." He led the group to the elevator for a short ride to the second floor.

Aidan stayed mum, as Peter had instructed. He was there in case Jack had technical questions, but Peter had made it clear that he was to speak only if spoken to. Peter was both gratified and surprised that Aidan agreed so meekly. The CTO could give mules lessons in stubbornness. Clearly the importance of mollifying Jack was not lost on him. Aidan's professional future was at stake too, and much more than that. Their discoveries would transform the world—but only if they could convince Jack to join them.

The elevator doors slid open. Peter led Jack to Emily's office, which had not been disturbed since the night of her death. He pushed the door open and held it for Jack. He waited for the others to file in as well.

"No," Jack said. "Just you."

"All right." Peter glanced at his colleagues. "Please wait here."

When the door clicked shut, Jack asked, "Where's her safe?"

Peter led Jack to the walk-in closet at the back of the disorderly office. It was filled with boxes, books and piles of paper. He pulled a box away to reveal a large floor-standing fire safe. It had a digital number pad and an LCD display to show the combination as it was entered.

He said, "Be careful. If you enter the wrong combination three times—"

"—the contents will be cremated." Jack finished. "I'm curious. Why did you ever agree to that?"

"I didn't. She had it installed and told us about it afterward."

Something like a smile ghosted across Jack's face. "That sounds like her." His lips turned downward. "Now leave me alone."

"She never let us read the journal, Jack. She said it was for your eyes alone."

"Get out, Peter."

Peter's heart began to race. "Will you tell us—" His voice caught in his throat. "Will you tell us what she wrote?"

Jack's face was unreadable. "Maybe."

Peter nodded. He moved to the door and grasped the knob. "I cared about her too," he said quietly. "I'm so sorry."

Jack did not reply.

He told Jack where he'd be waiting, went out into the corridor and closed the door gently. He looked at the others. "I'll text you when he comes out."

Ramona asked, "Do you want company?"

"No. Thank you."

They dispersed.

Peter ducked into the mini kitchen for a glass of sparkling water. He sat down heavily on a soft leather ottoman in the open lounge area and settled in to wait.

He tried not to dwell on the echoing emptiness of the building. In its heyday, this place had been a beehive. Now it was more like a tomb. He was vaguely aware of the sound of doors opening and closing, and of people occasionally walking through his peripheral vision.

After a time, he noticed that the glass of water had grown warm in his hands. He drained it in a few long swallows. He put the empty glass on the table next his chair.

He remembered.

When Aidan and Emily first approached him with the idea for the Black Box, he was skeptical, but after repeated attempts they finally convinced him. They seemed to know what they were doing. Their reputations were beyond question, and he liked them. He'd known Aidan's family for decades. He was willing to take a chance. If their theories turned out to be wrong, he might lose a few million dollars. He could pay for that out of his own pocket.

But they weren't wrong. Emily walked him through the experimental proof. The independent researchers he hired to double-check the results agreed. They really could build their quantum computer. All they needed was time, brilliant people to help them, and a ludicrous amount of money.

Peter was no fool. He was scientifically literate, for a layman. He read *Science News* and *New Scientist* regularly. He'd been reading science fiction since he was eight years old. The thought of being the man who brought Emily's and Aidan's discoveries to market was deeply thrilling. It would cost a fortune, but he had a fortune and a half. He knew a great opportunity when he saw it.

He hired the scientists and anchored their pledges of secrecy with piles of cash. He took StruvePharma private at enormous cost, spending much of his massive inheritance to do it. Being privately held, SP would no longer be subject to the regulatory scrutiny that would make it impossible to keep the research under wraps. Besides, sinking so much of the company's resources into a completely new field of science would never pass muster with the shareholders.

He was under no illusions that the secret would last forever, but he did everything in his power to keep it as long as he could.

He built the Coyote Hills campus to house the Black Box team, and hired John Shea to help him secure it. Few of the new employees knew anyone on the drug side of the business. Massive salaries, stock option grants, and Shea's draconian security measures helped keep their work away from prying eyes. Success followed success in the lab. The researchers were ecstatic.

Three years into the project came the first bump in the road. Neither Emily's nor Aidan's genius extended to relationships. Peter nursed them and the company through their tumultuous breakup. Their mutual resentment and anger occasionally flared into company-threatening bonfires.

After several desperate months, Peter got them back on track. In some ways, the new status quo was an improvement. They now felt free to criticize each other's ideas without having to dance around the other's feelings. They didn't hold back. Their arguments were frequent, loud, and sometimes alarming to the other members of the staff, but the results could not be denied. They made discoveries with almost magical speed.

Santa's Workshop became an engine of innovation that burned mountains of money. They built prototype after prototype of their quantum circuits. They needed exotic materials that were insanely expensive. Even worse, they needed a ridiculous number of traditional computers to interpret the results.

Security grew tighter as the world-shaking implications of their results became clear. They couldn't use cloud computers in Amazon or Rackspace. John Shea wouldn't hear of connecting the Black Box to the Internet. Their need for massive, low latency network bandwidth precluded an off-site install in any case.

A huge server farm took over two of the massive sub-basement levels of the Pauling Building. City power wasn't sufficient or "clean" enough. They hollowed out part of Coyote Hill to house on-site generators inside the electrically isolated footprint of the building. They bought miles of fiber optic cables and hired platoons of technicians to lay them. They bought ultra-fast routers and switches and a fabulously expensive cooling plant to keep the server rooms from melting. They needed this, that and the other thing, and everything cost money.

Then came more setbacks.

They spent over three billion dollars on the technology needed to build the first QUBE. It took four months to "grow" the device in the custom-designed assembler array—which itself cost nearly four hundred million. By then the technology had become so complex Peter could barely comprehend it, but he was all too aware that things did not turn out as planned.

QUBE Alpha was a huge disappointment. It worked only three percent of the time, and neither Emily nor Aidan could figure out why. QUBE Bravo was vastly more powerful—on paper—but it suffered from the same intermittent performance of its predecessor.

The revenue from their drug sales was not enough to fill the bottomless maw of the Black Box. They had to lay off employees in the pharmaceutical side of the business. Peter hated it. He hated seeing good people lose their jobs. He hated decimating his father's company, once the darling of high-tech drug manufacturers, now seen by the financial media as a privately-held, slow-motion train wreck.

More than anything, he hated being the cause of it.

It had been almost impossible to convince the rest of the Board to go along with his plan to privatize the company. He'd only succeeded because of Emily and Aidan's utterly convincing presentations, and because of the codicil he added into the company's bylaws: they could remove him as CEO if they believed he was leading them to ruin.

Keeping his job got harder and harder as costs mounted and results began to disappoint. It became clear that they would have to seek external funding to complete the work, which made no one happy, especially Peter Struve.

He consoled himself with the certain knowledge that the Black Box *would* succeed. It *would* justify the ruinous expense.

Long ago, the self-styled Elves of the Santa's Workshop lab had adopted Google's "twenty-percent" model. They spent a fifth of their paid hours working on blue sky projects of their own design.

Some of the things they created didn't even seem possible: a spray-on machine lubricant coating that was nearly frictionless, a kind of super-diamond fiber so thin it was invisible to the naked eye but strong enough to pull a truck up a hill, a nearly endless variety of new chemical compounds useful in industry, mining or medicine, and many other innovations that could revolutionize a dozen industries—provided they could figure out a way to produce them in quantity at a profit.

Reluctantly, and at dreadful cost to employee morale, he'd been forced to call a halt to the twenty-percent projects. They simply couldn't afford them. With the ever-shrinking work force to consider, they had to get all of their wood behind a single arrow. He told them to focus on the oil synthesizer. That was something he knew he could sell.

Any potential investor would understand the importance of oil. It wasn't used only for cars and trucks and planes. Oil was a feedstock for countless industrial chemical processes. It was used to make polymers and glue and aspirin and safety glass and a hundred other ingredients of everyday existence. Few people really understood how utterly dependent they were on oil, or that they would still need it, although in much smaller quantities, long after internal combustion engines were pushing up daisies.

Being able to make oil from thin air without drilling, without refining, without even having to transport it from the maker to the consumer, would change *everything*. Money would cease to be an issue. They would have the time and funding to perfect the dazzling "twenty-percent" demos now safely tucked away in the labyrinth of the vaults.

Emily and Aidan believed they'd solved the problems of QUBEs Alpha and Bravo. It took months of unpredictable compute runs, but they used Bravo to help design the circuits for the next generation quantum processor. Jay Kapoor sweated bullets to keep the money coming in.

This time the new QUBE worked perfectly. Better than either Emily or Aidan had expected, in truth. They spent a lot of time puzzling over that fact. It worried them, but Peter was not about to count the teeth of this particular gift horse.

They'd celebrated with a wild drunken party that had gotten them ejected from the Garden Court Hotel in Palo Alto. After her fourth glass of 1983 Henri Jayer Echezeaux Grand Cru, Peter's wife Yvonne took a swing at Aidan O'Keefe. Peter smiled at the memory. He didn't mind if she blamed Aidan for keeping her husband at the office until two in the morning every day for six long years. It was better than her blaming him.

His smile faded as he remembered how quickly the situation had grown desperate. QUBE Charlie might have been a glorious success, but the oil synthesizer was not. They built six prototypes, each more capable but more expensive than the last. They rebuilt the assembler tank, almost from scratch, at ruinous cost. They eventually solved the manufacturing glitches.

Even so, problems remained. The demo unit took longer to clean after each use, and worked for a shorter time before its output began to drop. They could only afford to build one more before they had to start soliciting funds from the VCs. Peter fumed at the setbacks.

Emily told him to be patient. "We're building an oil refinery the size of a book. Okay, a *Harry Potter* book. It's going to take some time to work out the kinks." In the meantime, the balance sheet dripped red.

They had always planned to spin the Black Box off as a pre-IPO company, with Struve and venture capitalists funding it as necessary. The timeline was moved up. The pharmaceuticals business was pared down to the minimum necessary to keep producing their drugs.

In spite of all their efforts, they were running out of runway.

They reduced the workforce even more. They sold off drug patents and physical assets. They took bridge loans at insane interest rates—anything necessary to keep the Black Box running.

People inside the project grew restless. They sensed impending disaster. Peter convinced them to stay, projecting a level of confidence that he did not feel. And at their monthly meetings, the other members of the Board stared at him with the red-rimmed glare of hungry vultures.

Never a big sleeper, his nights grew shorter still. Yvonne kicked him out of their bedroom. He tossed and turned in the guesthouse bed. He spent more and more time at the office. At one point, just before the seventh and final demo unit was finished, he slept on the couch in his office, using the men's locker room shower, sending his clothes out to the dry cleaner, working nineteen hours a day.

Six weeks ago, near the edge of total exhaustion, he picked up his phone to call a supplier and saw that Yvonne had left a voicemail for him. Aghast, he realized he hadn't even thought about her for an entire week. He couldn't remember when he'd last spoken with her. He listened to the message, his face burning with shame. She'd gone to

Italy on vacation with their two daughters, and didn't know when—or *if*—she'd be back.

Then he did the demo for Philip Mayhew. It was flawless. Better than he had dreamed.

He called Yvonne to tell her the news. Her response began with icy politeness, but she thawed a bit when she heard that the demo had gone well, and told him she might be home in a week or two.

Three nail-biting days later, that grim bastard Mayhew had smiled when he handed Peter the spent demo unit, shook his hand and pledged his funds for Phase Two. He'd actually *smiled*. Then Peter told Emily. His heart was light for the first time in months.

Less than an hour later she was dead, and QUBE Charlie had been shattered by a security guard's bullet.

Emily. Her name was an open wound in his soul.

She hadn't been perfect, by any means. She was far beyond brilliant, but she had a fiery temper. She had treated Jack cruelly, cutting off all contact with him after the death of their son. She had come to regret her intransigence, but apparently she had been too ashamed of her own behavior to admit it to her former husband.

From time to time, Peter broached the idea of her contacting Jack. He didn't know the man well, but he seemed a decent type, and he'd been horribly burned in his failed attempt to rescue their son. Emily always said that she wasn't ready to talk with him, and immediately changed the subject. Peter could see that she was consumed by guilt, and frankly he'd been afraid of pressing her. He was leery of breaking her laser-like focus on her work, and he had no desire whatever to be on the receiving end of one of her furious tirades.

Now, of course, it was too late.

The aftermath of the murders was unbearable. The news media had been languishing in a slow news cycle. Congress wasn't in session, the President was at Camp David, and people weren't slaughtering each other elsewhere in the world in numbers adequate to hold the attention of the American public. The full weight and power of CNN, Fox News, the BBC and a host of other networks descended on Palo Alto.

The police were mum about developments in the murder investigation, so the news channels focused on the rumors surrounding SP's secret research program. Soon the half-informed business pundits on CNBC and Bloomsberg and FNC were echoing the scuttlebutt across the globe, twenty-four-by-seven.

The blogosphere went into overdrive, trumpeting ill-informed speculation masquerading as well-known facts. The rumors were little more than vague hints about breakthrough technologies, insane expenses, and possible corporate malfeasance. Prospective investors suddenly became much harder to reach.

Peter refused all requests for interviews. He forbade anyone else from talking with the media, on pain of losing their jobs. Security held, but just barely. Shea hired a dozen more guards. They were ejecting reporters and other uninvited visitors from the grounds day and night. Peter had authorized the construction of a tall reinforced-concrete security fence just outside the line of Italian cypress trees that marched around the property, but the contractors hadn't even started yet. It would be weeks before they finished.

The incessant publicity was bad enough. The news from Mayhew was worse. ZMPC suspended the agreement until the police investigation was complete. They were already six hundred million dollars in the hole, but they wouldn't invest another dime until the source of the attack was identified. Peter pleaded with Mayhew, to no effect.

He couldn't blame the dour investor. Peter would be no less cautious if he were running ZMPC. He was less charitable toward his contacts at the other venture capital firms. They seldom returned his phone calls, replied to his emails, or responded to text messages. Even Yvonne abandoned him. She elected to ride out the bad publicity at their sprawling villa on Lake Como.

In his darkest moments, Peter wondered if she would ever come back.

Laurel Wynn was now a permanent fixture at the Coyote Hill campus, on the pretext of national security concerns. She had offered the full financial assistance of the Federal government.

Peter wouldn't go down that road unless he had no choice. His father had once cautioned him against working for the government. Grigoriy Sergeyevich Struve had grown up in Soviet Russia. He had seen at grisly firsthand what the government's "help" could turn into. The old man had once cautioned him, "Be careful, Pyotr Grigoriyevich. Even in the United States, they're like vampires. They can't come in unless you invite them, but once you do, they will never leave. One day you will wake up to find all of your blood missing."

Peter didn't think government was intrinsically bad, like so many of his friends on both sides of the political spectrum. He thought it was inept. He wasn't about to turn his company over to people who weren't qualified to run a beachside hot dog stand, much less vast Federal bureaucracies. He wouldn't watch his dream strangled in its crib by a serpent of red tape.

He and Aidan debated bringing the ZMPC techno-wizards in to see the rest of the toys in Santa's Workshop. Aidan was convinced Mayhew would hurl money at them regardless of the consequences once they saw the prototypes hidden away there. Peter decided to hold off. Even if ZMPC moved forward, their entire fund wouldn't be enough to pay for the construction of a new QUBE to replace the lost Charlie, even with the fragments of Charlie recycled for raw materials. They could build it if they sold off the drug business—but that would mean losing his father's company, and based on what Yvonne had told him when he broached the subject, very possibly his family as well.

Someone cleared his throat.

Startled, Peter looked up.

Jack Dura stood in front of him, clutching a thick three-ring binder in his left hand.

"Sorry," Peter said, lurching to his feet. "I was just thinking."

"I can see that," Jack said. His deep-set eyes glistened, and his voice was hoarse with emotion.

Peter instinctively reached out to steady the younger man, but stopped before he made contact. He lowered his hand, feeling awkward. "Can I get you something? A cup of coffee? Some water?"

"No."

Peter glanced at the binder.

Jack said, "It's going to take me a while to read it. I'm not ready to talk about it yet." He lowered himself into the chair across from Peter, leaning far forward. He kept the binder in his lap, gripping it with both hands.

Peter took his seat again. He waited for the younger man to speak.

"Why did she put my name on the papers, Peter?"

"She never told us. Not in so many words. But she told me once that she felt horrible about the way she treated you after... you know. After. I think this was her way of making it up to you. We'll honor her wishes. Your name will be on every patent application and every paper. You'll be rich, whether you join us or not."

Jack studied him for a long, silent moment. Finally, he said, "I have two conditions."

Peter's heart did a somersault. "Name them."

"My team from Stanford comes with me, as many as want to come. I need them. You figure out some way to convince the school to let us take an indefinite leave to work here. Endow a scholarship. Build a new wing for the hospital. I don't care what it takes. Do it."

Peter had deep family and personal connections with Stanford's current administration, and there was ample precedent of faculty members taking leaves to work at startups in the Valley. "Done," he said. "What else?"

"I want to punch Aidan O'Keefe in his fucking mouth."

Peter wasn't sure he'd heard Jack right. He blinked. "Uh, what?"

"You heard me."

"Are you serious?"

Jack stood and turned to go.

"Wait a minute," Peter blurted, leaping to his feet.

Jack stopped. "Do you want me to solve your little problems or don't you?"

"Can you?"

Jack nodded. "She missed something. I think I know what it is."

"What? What was it?"

Jack started for the nearby stairwell.

Peter shouted, "WAIT!"

The scientist stopped and looked back expectantly.

I can't believe I'm even thinking about this. "Didn't you say you have a black belt in some karate-mumbo-jumbo?"

"*Kajukenbo.* It's Hawaiian. A blend of *karate, judo* and *jiujitsu, kenpo* and boxing."

"Why don't you just... I don't know, challenge him to a fight?"

Jack stared at him, his face darkening. When he answered, his voice was so choked with emotion he was barely comprehensible. "If I fight him, I'll kill him. Did you know he was with Emily the day Eddie died? He'd already stolen my wife. She told me she was going out shopping, and had just put Eddie down for a nap. If she hadn't just left to be with him—" He stopped for a moment, his eyes closed. "Maybe Eddie still would've died. Maybe he wouldn't. I'll never know because *she... wasn't... there.* And it's Aidan's fault."

Peter covered his mouth with his hand. This was appalling. No wonder Emily couldn't face Jack after the divorce. "Jesus, Jack. I'm sorry. I didn't know."

"No one did, until now. It's the only reason I'm even considering working for you."

Peter thought about it for a long moment. "Just a single straight punch. All right?"

Jack nodded.

Peter pulled his phone from his pocket. "If he agrees."

"If he doesn't, I'm out of here. And I'm taking this with me." He brandished the binder like a weapon.

Fifteen minutes and one furious argument later, Peter, Aidan, John Shea, and Jack went outside onto the dry, scrubby slope of the hill behind the Pauling Building, beyond the line of cypress trees, out of sight of the omnipresent surveillance and the TV crews.

Aidan handed Peter his gray silk tie and his eyeglasses. "We can still afford dental coverage, right?" he asked sourly.

Peter nodded, dazed. He couldn't believe this was actually going to happen.

And then it did.

Aidan lay sprawled in the withered grass, blood dripping from his mouth. John Shea knelt by his side, checked his pulse, made sure he was breathing, and peeled up one of his eyelids. "Out cold." He looked up at Jack. "Hell of a punch for a biologist."

"Biophysicist," said Jack. "We're the supermen of science." He shook his right hand and then rubbed it with the other. Only a lunatic would have described his expression as a smile. "I've wanted to do that for seven years."

"Are you satisfied?" Peter asked coldly.

"No." Jack frowned at the unconscious computer scientist. "But I guess it will have to do."

Peter walked over to Jack and held out his hand. "Then you're with us? For the long haul?"

Jack hesitated. "If you come through on condition one. And a lot of money wouldn't hurt."

"Count on it."

Jack shook his hand.

Peter said, "Welcome aboard." No hint of a smile reached his lips, but relief gusted through him like a cooling wind. *Everything's going to be all right, after all.*

CHAPTER THIRTEEN

FBI Resident Agency, Palo Alto, California

July 14

Laurel Wynn said, "We have the name of the gunman."

Andrew Seigart leaned back in the visitor's chair on the other side of Laurel's borrowed desk. He squinted into the harsh light coming through the broad picture window behind her.

She quickly stood and lowered the blinds. The sky outside the Palo Alto resident agency was gray, but the sun was about to break through the low marine cloud layer. The glare was intense.

She knew that many in the Bureau and in Homeland Security considered her Seigart's protégée, but she still felt the same stomach-fluttering self-consciousness in his presence that she'd felt the first day she met him. He was a gruff, solid man with an air of deadly seriousness. It was easier to talk with him on the phone than to his face.

"Sorry," she murmured as she sat down.

He waved the apology away. "Which gunman are we talking about? StruvePharma or ICU?"

"SP. He was a Norwegian button man named Aage Folstad. Interpol had him down as a freelancer hooked up with the 'Ndrangheta Mafia." Her tongue stumbled on the strange word.

Seigart rubbed his bald head. "Hmm. Interesting."

Laurel nodded. The Calabrese clan with the odd name had supplanted the Sicilian Mafia as the most powerful crime syndicate in Italy in the late Nineties. "Folstad was implicated in the assassination of a Roman banker in 2007, but there wasn't enough evidence to convict him. Supposedly. There were rumors of judicial tampering and witness intimidation."

"A crooked trial in Italy? I'm shocked. Shocked."

Laurel snorted. "He was on the TSA watch list. We don't know how he got into the country. He sure didn't come through Customs."

"Why would the Mafia be interested in SP?"

"Well, they make drugs."

Seigart frowned. "Allergy drugs and antibiotics, not narcotics."

"True. Robbie Holmes is looking into it."

"How's he working out for you?"

Laurel smiled. "He's not as good as his namesake, but very good."

"I guess you can keep him, then. What about the hospital killer?"

Her moment of good humor evaporated. "Nothing yet. We're pretty sure he hid in a laundry closet around the corner from the ICU. We think he sneaked into the hospital, broke into the closet, and waited there for at least an hour before he hit Folstad. Most of the height and build matches we've found from the hospital's security recordings check out as solid citizens. The San Francisco office is still working the video. They're not hopeful."

"Forensics?"

"He was in a hospital laundry closet, sir. Fibers and hairs from every patient on the floor were in there. It'll take them a month just to sort them out."

"God damn it." Seigart's frown deepened. "What *do* we know about him?"

"He was a pro. Caucasian, medium height and build. He wore blue jeans, a black long-sleeve T-shirt, a flesh-colored ski mask, and surgical gloves. He had a suppressed nine-millimeter pistol. Bob Sheridan says it was a Glock 17C. He pushed right through the ICU doors and shot both of the PAPD officers before they could draw their guns. One shot each, right in the head. He took out the doctor and the two nurses before they could run, again, one round each. Then he put two into Folstad's temple. He was *fast*. He looked like a competition shooter. Total time in the room was seven point four seconds."

"Jesus. Maybe he *is* a competition shooter."

"We're looking into it."

"Ballistics? Anything interesting about the rounds?"

"No. He used 147-grain Federal American Eagle Parabellum ammo. This close to sea level they'd be subsonic loads. The suppressor was really good, and the civilians barely managed to shout before he killed them. No one outside the ICU even noticed anything was wrong until Folstad's EKG flat-lined. No DNA or fingerprints on the brass, either, just traces of latex and talcum powder. He was wearing powdered gloves when he loaded the gun."

Seigart sighed. "Where did he go?"

"He walked out a side door, still wearing the mask, hiding the gun under his shirt. Emphasis on *walked*. Could've been window shopping for all the hurry he showed. Someone in a stolen late-model Chevy Malibu picked him up. No pictures of the driver from the parking lot cameras. We found the car a few blocks away in a residential neighborhood. They must have transferred to another vehicle there."

"Let me guess. No witnesses, no dash cam videos, no home security system footage, nothing from the traffic light cameras, and nothing from forensics."

Laurel nodded.

Seigart thumped the arm of his chair. "We just can't catch a break on this one. Palo Alto PD is still on the case?"

"Yes sir. Detective Vieira's running their task force."

"Give her my compliments and extend the full courtesy of the department."

"Of course, sir."

Seigart stood and began to pace. He was a burly man with a rolling gait that testified to his long-ago years in the Navy. His perfectly tailored suit was at odds with his rough-hewn features.

Laurel shifted in her chair, uncomfortably aware of her off-the-rack business attire. "We do have some news on Eric Dalton, sir."

"Who?"

"The industrial spy at the venture capital firm, ZMPC."

"Right, right. What about him?"

She tried to tamp down her anxiety. "He's cooperating with our investigation. We haven't charged him yet, but we've examined all of his earnings. The money's as clean as a whistle, literally. No DNA evidence, no fibers, no latent fingerprints, and the serial numbers all check out. Whoever laundered it was an expert."

"Why am I not surprised," he grumbled.

"We convinced Philip Mayhew to let Dalton keep coming to work. He just sits in an office reading all day, but if he's under observation by his contacts, at least they'll think he's still employed."

"Any nibbles?"

"The bad guys are still placing their classified ads in the *Mercury News*. The *Merc's* web server logs track the transactions back to anonymized network addresses. They're paying with stolen credit card numbers. The web servers Dalton uses to send messages to them are in countries we don't have cyber-crime treaties with. This week's server is in Moscow."

"Shit. Is the Office of International Operations on this?"

"Yes sir, but they're not hopeful. For some reason the Russians don't want to lend a hand."

"Surprise, surprise." Seigart shook his head. "It seems like we just finished the first Cold War. I didn't think I'd live to see another one."

She couldn't think of a reply, so she just nodded.

His frown deepened. "What else?"

"Eileen Dupree at the Computer Forensic Laboratory did a linguistic analysis of the personal ads, Dalton's decryption key, and the emails the bad guys sent when they recruited him. Thank God Dalton never deleted them from his laptop. She found some similarities to a case we helped them with in 2012. Do you remember the Macao bank fraud?"

"The brain's old, but it still works," Seigart growled.

"Sorry. Eileen's pretty sure the same hacker group is responsible for Dalton's codes. *Dark Seoul.*"

"So the North Koreans are interested in SP. How sure is your friend?"

"Eighty-five percent."

"Not a smoking gun." Seigart's frown disappeared. "But close enough for government work. Good job."

Laurel's heart soared. Getting a compliment from Seigart was enough to justify the huge effort they'd put in to track down Dalton's contacts.

Seigart stopped pacing and went to the door. "Let's get some coffee and go for a walk."

They did so. The FBI office unrepentantly supplied Styrofoam cups, a serious no-no in eco-conscious Northern California. The office manager had confessed that their hoard of Styrofoam was dwindling, and they'd soon be switching to the same palm-searing paper cups everyone else used. Laurel and her boss affixed sippy lids onto their cups and walked outside.

The Palo Alto FBI resident agency was in an undistinguished, fortress-like two-story office complex close to Highway 101 and Embarcadero Road. The street was lined with similar bleakly functional office parks, partially hidden behind rows of broadleaf trees. The air was moist and cool. It smelled of diesel and car exhaust fumes from the freeway and the iodine odor of the nearby wetlands. The sun peeked through gaps in the low clouds, casting beams of sunlight through the misty air.

Seigart led Laurel out of the lobby, across the parking lot, over a short grassy berm and onto the sidewalk next to the frequently patched Bayshore Road. They began to walk to the south at an easy pace.

"This is not pretty," Seigart said, gesturing at the crumbling street and the obtrusive power lines high overhead. "I thought California was supposed to be pretty."

"A lot of it is," she replied. "Around here it looks like this. Welcome to Silicon Valley."

"Well, I hope you like it. You're going to be here for a while." Seigart sipped his coffee. "You're sure Struve and his crew are on the up-and-up? No funny business?"

Laurel nodded. "The Forensic Accounting team has been all over their books. They're so clean they squeak. They've spent eleven and a half billion dollars, but it was all theirs to spend."

"The President wants SP to succeed. From what you told me, it sounds like they're about to close the doors. Just two months of operating capital left?"

She nodded. "Struve won't take our money."

"I didn't expect him to." Seigart scowled. "We had to deal with a lot of these computer guys when I was at ATK. I wish Ayn Rand had never written *Atlas Shrugged*. I swear to God, every one of these geeks thinks he's the Second Coming of John Galt."

Laurel couldn't help but laugh. "Struve's not a computer guy."

"He's cut from the same cloth. He wants to rule the world."

"If their technology is viable, he just might."

Seigart scoffed, "All of these guys are megalomaniacs. Too Libertarian to take government assistance, too pig-headed to share the burden with other companies. They'd rather auger into the ground than let someone else call the shots. There are a dozen different ways Struve could pull out of this tailspin, but he won't, because he's too god-damned proud."

Laurel took a sip from her cup and grimaced. It was a far cry from the Blue Bottle blend they served at SP. She was getting spoiled.

Seigart said, "You said Jack Dura agreed to join the company. Tell me about him."

She took a deep breath. Luckily she'd written up her summary for her weekly report, so it was still fresh in her mind. "His full name is

Giacomo Taddeo Dura. Named after his paternal grandfather, an Italian immigrant. His parents were physicists at Los Alamos National Laboratory. His father worked on nuclear weapon initiators. His mother was involved in something I don't have the clearance for. Both are deceased. He had one sister, Elena, who died from something called Sanfilippo's syndrome when she was ten. Pretty horrible genetic disease, from what I've read."

"That's rough."

"Apparently her illness made Dura want to study biology. He won four science fairs, the first when he was twelve. He graduated from high school two years early and got his biophysics degree in three years at UCSD. He stayed there for his Ph.D. and then came up here to Stanford for his post-doc. They hired him as an assistant professor a year later. He was one of the youngest professors on staff until Emily Stollmeyer came along. She was only twenty, and she already had *three* doctorates. They met and got married a year later. They had one son. Edward. One day Emily left the house while Dura was mowing the lawn. The burner on the stove was on, and a dish towel caught fire. Kitchen went up in seconds. Dura didn't notice it until the house was fully involved. He took second- and third-degree burns on his arms trying to rescue the boy, but he had already died from smoke inhalation. He was only seventeen months old."

"Jesus," Seigart grunted.

Laurel nodded. After taking another sip of coffee, she continued. "Neither of them would admit to leaving the burner on. There wasn't any conclusive evidence, so it was ruled an accident. Emily wouldn't talk with Jack after the fire, and sued him for divorce. He recovered from the burns after eleven skin graft surgeries."

She paused as Seigart expelled a breath and shook his head. "Go on," he said.

"Emily went to SP. Jack eventually returned to Stanford, founded a world-class program in computational biophysics, won some big awards, and got his full professorship. He hasn't dated since the break-up, but there were some rumors of a fling with a grad student in another department. And now he and his whole team are going to work at SP." Laurel shook her head. "Peter Struve must be an incredible salesman. There's a lot of bad blood between Jack and Aidan O'Keefe, the CTO. O'Keefe was with Emily when the fire broke out. They'd been having an affair for two months."

Seigart's eyebrows went up. "She was screwing O'Keefe when her son died? No wonder she didn't want to face her husband. The guilt must have been killing her."

Laurel nodded.

"Did Dura know about the affair?"

"More than likely."

"And Struve thinks Dura can pick up where his ex left off?"

"He does, and so does Aidan O'Keefe. One of Jack's conditions for joining the company was that he could punch O'Keefe in the mouth, and everybody agreed to it. I couldn't believe it. I saw O'Keefe afterward. He had two broken teeth but he was smiling. It was pretty horrible."

Seigart gave an evil guffaw. "I'd like to have seen that."

"They did it away from the cameras."

"So, when does Dura join the team?"

"Next Monday."

They walked in a companionable silence for a few moments.

"What's the bottom line, Agent Wynn? Do you think SP's the real deal?"

Laurel considered her reply. "Yesterday Struve let me come with him on a demo for one of the other venture capital firms, Gideon Hart. They started returning his calls when he told them Jack Dura was joining the team. The oil synthesizer really works. Certainly the ZMPC people think it's real, but they still have cold feet because of the murder investigation."

"Okay," Seigart said. "I want you to meet with Peter Mayhew."

"It's Philip," she corrected without thinking. Irrelevantly, her mind dredged up the fact that an actor named Peter Mayhew had played the giant, shaggy Wookiee Chewbacca in *Star Wars*.

"Whatever. They need to get back in the ballgame. Tell Mayhew we'll make good on any funds he invests if SP crashes and burns. We'll even buy out his original stake, if it comes to that. Make the rounds of the other companies Struve was talking to and get them on board, too. Struve might not want us to invest in his company, but we can still back-stop the people who are."

"Yes sir."

"Then meet with Struve. If he won't go for the carrot, it's time to show him the stick. Tell him the Environmental Protection Agency is champing at the bit to find out what horrible chemicals they might have in their basement."

Laurel smiled. "The old *Ghostbusters* gambit, eh?"

"Oh, it's true enough. The only thing keeping them from getting search warrants is the President. God knows how long their investigation could take. Months. Years, maybe. Long enough for Struve's funding to dry up, in any case. If he wants to stay operational, he has to make you part of the core team. No more of this hiding behind trade secrets crap."

She stopped in her tracks. "But sir! I'm no scientist."

He halted as well. "You don't have to be. All you have to do is observe. Work with their security guy. Keep an eye on things from the inside. Look for moles. Find out if anything they're working on is actually dangerous."

"Sir, all that talk about nanotechnology turning the world into a pile of gray goo is just science fiction. What Struve's working on is more like miniaturized chemical factories."

He raised his eyebrows. "And chemical factories can't be dangerous? You're probably too young to remember the Union Carbide gas leak in India. It happened in 1984. You were what, six?"

"Five."

"Nearly four thousand people died, and thousands more were injured. Over half a million people were exposed to toxic fumes. The only reason we're not shutting Struve's campus down right now is that they're not doing anything at industrial scale. They've got the right permits for experimental research. Find out if Jack Dura feels the same way you do about how dangerous their work is. He's probably still pretty objective. If he has a problem with any of it, I want to know."

"Yes sir. I take your point."

"As you say, you're not a scientist. You need to be on the inside to look for more spies. If the Norks already have an eye on things, you can bet the Russians and the Chinese do, too—and maybe the Saudis, the Iranians, the Venezuelans, and every other oil producing country. Imagine what will happen to their economies when news gets out that oil might become cheaper than drinking water. The oil futures market is bad enough right now as it is."

For an instant, Laurel was dumbfounded. Then the implication hit her. "Holy crap."

He looked at her shrewdly. "If you own a gold mine, you're gonna want to knock off the guy who's breeding Golden Geese. You were hypnotized by the technology and you lost sight of the risks. Am I right?"

"Yes, sir."

"Well, I was too, for about ten minutes." He snorted. "When you get to my age, every Christmas present is just Pandora's box with pretty paper on it. You need a paranoia booster shot, Agent Wynn. This isn't just another microchip or software company. It's more like the Manhattan Project. Eight people have already died because of it. They might not be the last."

Her face grew hot with shame. "I'm sorry, sir."

"A lot of people higher in the food chain have lost a lot of sleep since you told me about the oil gizmo."

"I guess I will too, now."

"You're welcome." He paused, then peered at her closely. "I don't suppose Struve would be open to the idea of relocating them to someplace safer? Say, Lawrence Livermore?"

"No," Laurel said without hesitation. "I already floated that idea. We did some back of the envelope calculations, and even got their IT people in on it. It would take them a year just to disassemble their network. You should see it. You could tangle spiders with their network cabling. I don't know how it works right now. They built it fast and never planned to move it. The bottom two floors of that huge Pauling Building are jammed full of computers. The labs are full of fragile equipment that might not survive a big move, or so they say. And then there's the—"

"Okay, I get the picture. Moving them isn't an option."

"Not if they want to stay in business until they can solve the remaining technical problems."

"Shit." Seigart scratched his head with his free hand. "Well, it was just an idea. I'm glad you thought of it first. Maybe you don't need that booster shot after all. By the way, I've gotten word that some of the people who left the company recently have been Twittering and Facebooking."

Laurel fought to suppress a smile.

Seigart didn't notice. "They're hinting about the technology at SP but they're not saying anything specific. Still, interested parties might be able to piece it together. We've asked those people to shut the hell up, but a lot of them aren't big fans of the government. Big surprise. We're pretty sure someone inside the company is still leaking information. The rumors are getting close to the truth—too close for it to be an accident. Tell Struve he'd better file those research papers and patent applications he's been sitting on. This comes straight from the President."

Laurel swallowed against the lump that had formed in her throat. "That's going to make securing SP a lot harder. What's the rush?"

"Those asswipes at the *Guardian* are about to break the story. They're planning to submarine us, just like they did with Snowden."

"Oh, no," Laurel said. "How do we know?"

"We know," he said, glancing at her meaningfully. "They found someone who's willing to go on the record. Some disgruntled former employee, probably. Struve's cloak of secrecy is about to go bye-bye. He has about a week. He might want to hold a press conference and head the *Guardian* off at the pass. It would serve those pricks right. Pardon my French."

"Struve will shit a brick," Laurel said.

"I hope he does. The President can't *order* him to file. Silicon Valley bigwigs were really pissed off when Snowden's leaks about the NSA tapping their networks hit the airwaves. They can really hold a grudge. And what with the hacker attacks and this FBI thing with the cell phones, we're not winning any fans. Tell Struve he has the President's word that the Patent Office will fast-track those applications."

"Will do," Laurel said.

Seigart sighed. "Keep it strictly between you and him. Hopefully whoever's spying on SP doesn't have enough information to file first. When the world finds out what they're working on, it will set off a scientific arms race. It'll make the Space Race look like a soapbox derby. The President wants us to win it."

A soapbox derby? He really is old. "Can I get more security around the campus? They're having problems with crowd control."

"As much as you want. And see if Struve can convert one of the vacant buildings on the campus into temporary living space. Otherwise we'll rent a big house or a motel somewhere close by. Try to get Dura and his team to move in, and any other key researcher who'll do the same. Tell them we'll pay their mortgages for them, for as long as it takes. It'll be easier to guard the civilians if they're all in one spot. And you move in with them."

"Good idea." Blue Bottle coffee every morning, hooray.

Seigart checked his watch. He uncapped his cup and dumped the dregs into a nearby bush. "I have to catch a plane back to Washington. Keep me in the loop if anything develops with Dalton or his contacts. Get more security guys on board ASAP. You're going to need them. Once Struve files for those patents, Silicon Valley is going to be crawling with spies."

"Will do, sir."

She spent the rest of the day arranging meetings with the venture capitalists—no easy feat when their first instinct was to hang up as soon as she mentioned StruvePharma. The negotiations were draining but successful.

She went back to her hotel room, ordered dinner from room service—a foot-long hot dog, nachos loaded with jalapeños, and an ice-cold Electric Tower IPA—and watched the Giants game. They were playing the Nationals, her home team. Baseball just wasn't the same without a dog and a beer. The game was shaping up to be a real pitcher's duel, but her exhaustion got the better of her. She curled up on the motel room's stumpy couch and conked out sometime during the fifth inning.

She awoke to a late-night infomercial, jalapeño-induced heartburn and a dull thumper of a headache. She looked up the final score on her laptop, swore, switched the TV off and was about to undress and climb into bed when her phone rang.

"What!" she shouted into the microphone.

"Sorry for waking you up," said Robbie Holmes. His tone was grim.

Her stomach lurched. "What's wrong?"

"Eric Dalton is missing. The agents who were guarding him are dead."

CHAPTER FOURTEEN

Location Unknown

Date Unknown

Eric trembled in the dark.

He sat alone in a large, empty, echoing room. His hands and legs were zip-tied to his lightweight metal chair. He wore nothing but a T-shirt, boxer shorts, and a black cotton bag someone had put over his head. His mouth was stoppered by a huge silicone ball gag, secured around his head with a heavy elastic cord. The cold of a concrete floor leached through the thick plastic sheet beneath the bare soles of his feet. The air was chill and smelled of dust and motor oil.

The fabric of the bag was loosely woven, but there was little to see through the threads. The only light was the diffuse green glow of what had to be an EXIT sign over one of the doors. He guessed that he was in a warehouse or a machine shop, but there was no way to be sure.

Every now and then he heard a large truck drive by. He tried to shout, but no sound louder than a grunt made it past the ball gag. It was so big his jaw ached. Saliva dripped around the gag. He couldn't control it. He shivered as his shirt steadily grew moister.

He couldn't believe that he'd been kidnapped.

His heart had leaped when the Palo Alto Police transferred him to the custody of the beautiful FBI agent. His hope for leniency had crumbled when he discovered that Laurel Wynn was just as implacable as that bulldog Detective Vieira. The only chance he had of avoiding prison was pretending that everything was normal until the FBI could set up a sting to identify his confederates.

Everyone had assured him that he was perfectly safe. Two agents would be watching his every move. They'd have a car outside his apartment complex with their eyes on his doorway. There was no way anyone could get into the apartment without being seen—or so they'd said.

Apparently they'd been wrong.

It wasn't fair. He'd confessed. He'd played his part. He'd kept going to the office, enduring the stony silences and searing glares of his former coworkers. *People died because of you,* their expressions said when they looked at him, which wasn't often. It went without saying that he was no longer allowed to do any work. He itched to get his hands on the lab equipment again, to do something productive, to prove that he was still a good guy.

They wouldn't let him.

Ben Holcombe could barely tolerate his presence. Deepthi wouldn't even look at him. The first day he'd sequestered himself in a corner of Merlin's Cave and pretended to read while his former boss and lab partner tried to work. By lunch they'd had enough. Eric was banished to an unused office down the hallway. A rent-a-cop had been stationed outside Merlin's Cave to make sure he didn't come back. He started taking lunch to the office so he wouldn't have to go to the cafeteria. He usually tossed it in the trash, uneaten, at the end of every endless day.

A pair of nameless FBI agents tailed him to and from work. They never spoke with him on the phone. They didn't email him. They worked on the assumption that the bad guys could intercept any electronic communications. Eric was entirely alone. The sense of isolation was suffocating.

On weekends he maintained his usual pre-nightmare behavior pattern. He drove north to Millbrae, boarded a BART train to San Francisco, and got off at the Civic Center station. He threaded his way through the streets to Isotope Comics, where he pretended to browse through the latest graphic novels. Laurel Wynn or her sour-faced partner, Agent Holmes—whichever one had drawn the short straw, he supposed—would be there, perusing the shelves as well.

Eric would pass the agent his hand-written notes from the last week, and in exchange would receive his orders for the next. They were always the same: to keep doing what he was doing—that is to say, nothing. He would stuff the orders into his pocket, choose some comics at random and buy them. When he got home, he would drop his purchases on the living room floor, undress, lie down on top of his unkempt bed, and stare at the ceiling.

People died because of me.

The last time they'd met, Agent Wynn had actually spoken. She'd told him to wash his clothes and to eat. She'd also given him a bottle of little blue pills that guaranteed at least eight hours of sleep. When he got home he'd studied himself in the mirror for the first time since the murders. He looked like he'd lost ten pounds. Then he got on the scale and discovered it was closer to twenty. His skin had turned a waxy yellow. It seemed to droop from his face. He looked like he'd contracted malaria.

The rank odor in his apartment convinced him to follow her advice about washing his clothes.

He put the sleeping pills in the medicine cabinet and forgot about them.

He kept telling himself that he wasn't a bad guy, but there were seven innocent people dead because of his greed. He wanted to prove himself. He wanted to help the FBI find the real bad guys. Most of all, he didn't want to spend the next twenty years taking it up the ass in a maximum-security Federal pen.

He remembered eating a microwaved meal, sitting in front of the TV until exhaustion got the better of him, and going to bed. He woke up here, alone, tied to a chair, with a brutal headache and without a clue as to how he got there.

All he knew is that he had trusted the FBI to protect him, and they'd failed.

He sat in the dark, terrified, cold, and alone.

As the terrible hours ticked away and his bladder grew painfully full, the idea of prison became positively alluring.

Eventually he heard the door open. Gray morning light filtered through the weave of the bag.

Eric shrieked as loud as he could, but the only sound that got past the giant ball gag was a mewling whimper. He wrenched his hands and legs against the zip-ties, rocking back and forth in the chair until it tipped over backward. The back of his head struck the unyielding concrete floor.

The sharp smell of ammonia brought him around. He jerked his head away from the odor, and wished he hadn't. Stars cascaded through his vision. Spider webs of agony radiated from the back of his skull.

"There, there. You don't want to tip over again."

The speaker's voice was soft, male, tenor, and oddly muffled.

It finally dawned on Eric that the bag was no longer on his head, and that someone had levered his chair upright.

The blur in front of him gradually resolved into the face of a white man, clean-shaven, with medium-length brown hair and thick wire-rimmed glasses that weren't quite level. His lower lip was split and puffy. A yellow-green bruise the size of a shot glass discolored the left side of his jaw.

The man sat in a folding chair a couple of feet away, peering intently at Eric's face. He dropped a used smelling salts capsule on the plastic sheet under Eric's chair. "Are you all right? That was quite a fall."

Eric nodded, wincing as bolts of pain shot through his head.

"I want you to look to your right," the man said. His voice was soft and gentle, though his injured mouth made him mumble.

Eric looked around groggily. His guess had been right. He was in some kind of warehouse. The wall behind the gentle-voiced man was a huge, heavy-looking roll-down garage door wide enough to accommodate four cars side by side. Bare fluorescent tubes flooded the room with sickly bluish light. The vast space was empty aside from a dusty black late-model Honda pickup truck.

"Look to your right, Eric," the man repeated calmly.

He obeyed.

A hard-looking blond man of average size stood about ten feet away, between Eric and the truck. He was screwing a heavy black silencer onto the barrel of a heavy black pistol.

Eric tried to say, "Oh, Jesus Christ." What came out was "*Hmm, Hmm-mm Hmmm.*"

His eyes snapped back to the man in the chair. It was then that he noticed the plastic apron over the man's blue chambray work shirt and denim jeans. He held a pair of elbow-length rubber gloves in one hand.

A wheeled metal tool cart with an open drawer stood nearby.

The man rose and pulled the cart close. "Want to see?"

Eric looked.

The drawer was full of surgical instruments.

Oh, Jesus Christ almighty, no! The agony in Eric's head spiked as panic filled him. Piss ran down his legs.

The gentle-voiced man sat down again. He looked at the man with the gun. "Aren't you glad we put the plastic down *before* we got started?" He chuckled.

Eric began to sob. Snot accumulated in his nasal passages, making it harder and harder to breathe. He couldn't inhale around the ball gag.

He turned his head away from his interrogator and blasted his sinuses clear. Then he wept again.

"Now, Eric," the man said after Eric had spent himself. "It's Saturday morning. You can scream your head off, but no one's going to hear you. We checked. So I'm going to take out this gag and we're going to have a conversation. If you tell me everything—and I do mean *everything*—we'll let you go. If you don't tell me the truth... well, things are going to get a little messy in here. Messier, I mean," he said, glancing down at Eric's soiled crotch.

In spite of his terror, Eric felt a hot wave of shame.

"Believe me when I say that I'll know if you're lying," the man said.

Eric nodded convulsively.

"Will you keep your voice down and talk to me like a man?"

Eric nodded again.

The man removed the gag.

Eric talked and talked, responding to the soft-spoken man's occasional probing questions, holding nothing back. He even revealed the one thing he'd kept from the FBI: the email code for the emergency signal that would request an in-person meeting with his contacts. He'd hoped to shake his shepherds and make use of it himself, to get help escaping from the country, but the opportunity had never arisen.

His interrogator looked happy when Eric swore that he'd told no one that little detail.

That made Eric happy, too. For a while.

The man did not stop asking questions, however. Eric's voice grew hoarse from repeating the same details again and again in a different order. The man gave him a drink from a bottle of mineral water the gunman brought in. The windowless room grew warmer, then stuffy, then oppressive as the hours crawled by. The urine on his legs dried up, but some had collected in a chill, acidic pool beneath his buttocks. He squirmed as it began to burn his skin. The stench was unbearable.

At last the man seemed satisfied. "Thank you, Eric," he said, smiling warmly.

"You're... you're welcome," said Eric, venturing a hesitant smile of his own.

The man stood up. In a single lightning motion, he shoved the ball gag back in Eric's mouth and cinched the strap tight.

He tried to scream. *You promised!* But some part of him had never really believed it.

"Stop fussing, Eric," said the man as he resumed his seat. "I want to believe you. I really do. But I need to be sure. I need to find out who put you up to spying on SP. You haven't even mentioned the mole inside the company. You've been most unhelpful in that regard." He pulled on his heavy rubber gloves.

Eric's eyes felt like they were going to bulge out of their sockets. He didn't know anyone inside StruvePharma. He shrieked against the gag.

The man looked at him quizzically, then laughed. "Oh, that's right. You probably thought your contacts sent *me*. No, no. I need to find out who *they* are. But most importantly, I want to know the name of the mole. And we are not leaving here until you tell me." The man stared at the drawer of tools for a long minute, then removed a pair of heavy shears that looked like a giant pair of wire cutters.

Eric fought against the restraints, bucking and kicking. The gunman seized him by the neck and shoved him down with iron-hard fingers.

The gentle-voiced man frowned at him. "Be good, Eric, or I might get angry. Emily Dura was a very dear friend of mine."

Eric slumped in the chair, whimpering against the gag.

The man hitched his chair closer. "I recently had some dental work," he said, rubbing his discolored jaw with the tip of a gloved finger. "It was quite painful. It reminded me of *Marathon Man*. Did you ever see that movie? Dustin Hoffman? Laurence Olivier as the Nazi dentist? Great movie. Inspirational, you might say. But unlike Dr. Szell, I don't know anything about dentistry, and I don't need you biting my fingers off while I ask you questions."

Eric's tears obscured the man from view, but he could still hear him.

"So let's start with these. What are they called?" He held the shears close to his eyes. "*Bone cutting forceps*. Just the thing. Made in Solingen, Germany. Very nice! Thank you, Tom. This equipment really is top-notch. Now Eric, I've only done this once before, and it wasn't on a human, but I suspect there's nothing like snipping a few fingers off to loosen the tongue. Tom, keep that butane torch handy, will you? We don't want him to bleed out."

Eric's bladder let go again, and this time, so did his bowels. He closed his eyes and wept.

The man's whisper was hot in Eric's ear. "We'll keep the gag in for now, until I'm sure you're ready to tell me what you've held back. Oh, and I'm sorry, but I told you a bit of a fib, earlier. We're not letting you go. If you convince me you've told me everything, I'll let Tom put a bullet through your head, just like all those people at the hospital and your two friends from the FBI."

Eric screamed against the gag. *NO NO NO NO NO!*

The man waited him out. "You really want to convince me, Eric. If you don't—well, I might be rusty at this, but I'm a quick study, and I've got all weekend. I'm pretty sure I can make you last at least twenty-four hours."

CHAPTER FIFTEEN

Mayang-Do Island, North Korea

July 16

The landing was going to be rough.

The Mi-24 juddered in the wind as it descended toward the hilltop helipad. General Guo Qiang could see little from his seat in the troop compartment of the Soviet-era helicopter. Perhaps it was a blessing that the only thing visible through the small windows was the dark gray sky.

There wasn't much to see in any case. He had been here twice before. He knew that the submarine base at Mayang-Do Island was even uglier than the mainland of North Korea—if such a thing were possible.

Guo clutched the shoulder straps and offered a silent, half-jesting prayer to Fei Lian to deliver him from this rusting deathtrap in one piece. Of course, as a loyal member of the Party, he professed to be an atheist, but in this instance he felt an exception could be made.

The North Korean Admiral seated to his right appeared to be mumbling a prayer of his own. The sound was lost in the whining roar of the jet turbine engines.

To Guo's left, the Colonel seemed to be taking the rough flight in his stride. When he saw Guo looking at him, he smiled, nodded and averted his eyes. Unlike most of these Korean dogs, Ryu Sang-Chul was smart, skillful, and obedient without being a footstool. His Chinese was excellent, as was his English, as required by his work. He was the diametric opposite of the obsequious Admiral Ahn Kyung-Tae, whose only redeeming virtues were the ease with which he'd been recruited and the tiny bribes required to secure his shaky loyalty.

"Helicopters do not bother you?" Guo shouted to Colonel Ryu.

"No, sir. With respect, I have flown in them many times."

"I myself have not," Guo conceded. "But it is better than the boat." The strait between the mainland and the island was usually placid, but the storm had whipped the seas into a heaving mass of foam. The air was just as turbulent, but the flight would at least be brief.

"Yes, sir!" said Colonel Ryu. He translated the General's words for the Admiral, who nodded agreement. Predictably.

In spite of Guo's fears, the landing was surprisingly smooth. A single hard bump and they were on the ground. The engines spun down immediately. The door slid open and a single uniformed Korean People's Army soldier helped them climb out.

General Guo removed his earplugs and put them in a pocket. Perhaps Fei Lian had granted his prayer, half-serious though it was. The monsoon rain had stopped. The heavy gray overcast remained. Clouds scudded low over the churning waves in the harbor. It was warm but not oppressively so.

They clambered into a Chinese-made armored car that had been old when Guo had graduated from the National Defense University. The soldier who'd escorted them from the helicopter took the driver's seat. Ryu sat next to him after helping Guo and the Korean Admiral belt themselves into the back.

Guo shifted painfully. The padding beneath his buttocks had been flattened by decades of constant use.

The car's engine sputtered to life. They followed an open truck with a heavy machine gun mounted on its roof down the hill to the submarine base. The road was so pocked with holes they might have been better off driving straight down the unpaved slope.

Guo stared at Ahn, who turned a gratifying shade of umber.

I should be more forgiving, Guo told himself. They spend all of their money on arms and missiles. They can barely afford food, much less decent roads. "It is of no consequence," he said. "All that matters today is learning the result of the sea-trials."

Colonel Ryu repeated Guo's words in the barking Korean tongue.

The hapless Admiral's face lit up. He would have bowed if the shoulder restraint had permitted it.

The road grew smoother as they approached the base. There was little worth seeing along the way. Short, ugly trees. Ramshackle peasant shelters next to terraced fields of stunted crops. Rusting corrugated metal warehouses. Missile bunkers placed well away from the buildings along the perimeter of the base. Waterlogged troopers of the Korean People's Army, who saluted the car as it rolled past.

General Guo returned the salutes absently. His mental eye was turned inward.

The weather was perfect for today's operation. The American satellites might be miracles of optical technology—miracles Guo had been trying to steal for more than two decades—but even they could not penetrate such a powerful storm.

The car stopped next to the dock. Guo climbed out, followed by the Admiral and finally Colonel Ryu.

The test engineer and his team of a dozen juniors awaited them, their backs to the harbor, trying to stand still in the buffeting wind. Two squads of NKA troopers flanked them on either side, their rifles held at port arms.

The engineer's name was Kim Hae-Jin. He was undistinguished by Chinese standards, but he fit the part assigned to him. He was competent, if not innovative. He was enthusiastic, which counted for much. He'd seized on the opportunity to work on technology the North Koreans would not be capable of for decades. He'd proven a careful steward of *Zhāngyú*. The reports he'd sent to her builders had been detailed and comprehensive.

Kim held the nominal rank of Captain, but in spite of the insignia on his loose-fitting drab green uniform, he was a civilian through and through. His posture was terrible. His salute was sloppy. The engineers standing behind him raised their hands to their foreheads belatedly, and with equal lack of precision.

General Guo might be seventy-one years old, but he could still salute as smartly as a new recruit. He lowered his arm, stepped forward and took Kim by the hand. "It is a pleasure to see you on this beautiful day," he said in his tobacco-roughened growl.

Colonel Ryu translated.

The engineer beamed and bowed. After an instant of hesitation, his team copied him.

Behind him, Admiral Ahn chuckled.

Guo released the engineer's pathetically thin hand. Kim looked a decade older than his forty-eight years. His smiling face was wan and pale, and his crooked, yellowing teeth were in a deplorable state. Guo forced himself not to look away in disgust. "Tell me, Kim. How fared *Agwi?*" He used the Korean code name. The Chinese name of the project was unknown to everyone here but Colonel Ryu.

Kim's reply took a long time. Ryu translated.

Guo paid scant attention to the details. He had difficulty keeping himself from fidgeting. He looked over the Engineer's shoulder at the strait between Mayang-Do Island and the dreary city of Sinp'o. *City* was a generous name for the slovenly village, Guo reflected. In China it wouldn't even qualify as a hamlet.

The undistinguished freighter carrying *Zhāngyú* was at anchor perhaps three kilometers from the shore, nose to the wind, rocking in the choppy waters. *Zhāngyú* itself was not visible, of course, but it was comforting to know it was there. The project had taken years, and its success or failure would depend on Kim's report. Guo mastered his impatience and watched flecks of sea foam blow from the wave tops in the harbor until the Engineer wound to a close.

Colonel Ryu's broad smile was all the summary Guo needed. "Kim says that the sea trials were a complete success, General! *Agwi* performed flawlessly."

"Wonderful!" said Guo, his enthusiasm unfeigned. "Tell Kim and his team that I could not be more pleased with them. Their reward will be great. Ask him if he has the final technical report ready for me."

Ryu translated. Kim's hideous smile grew broader. The members of his team exchanged happy glances with each other. Kim's reply this time was succinct.

The Colonel said, "There is a single hard copy under guard in the harbormaster's office, as you directed. All others have been destroyed."

"Well done, Colonel." Guo turned to the Admiral. "Conduct the team to debriefing. We've set up a room for you in building C-1. You will personally take their reports." He pointed to an undistinguished looking warehouse on the waterfront, perhaps two hundred meters to the east.

After Ryu finished translating, Admiral Ahn bowed, looking slightly puzzled. "Sir? I thought I was to return to Sinp'o with you."

Guo understood enough Korean to take Ahn's meaning, and he was prepared for the question in any case. "I trust you, and only you, to take their final reports," he growled. "There are refreshments inside. Take your time. Captain Kim is a thorough man, but there may be details he did not include in his report. Your reward will be as great as theirs, Admiral Ahn. You have done my nation good service. Now, see to it. Take the driver with you. He could probably use some hot food as well."

Ahn bowed more deeply once Ryu finished speaking Guo's words. His salute, at least, was worthy of a military man.

Guo returned it.

Ahn barked orders at the engineer and his team. They and their armed escort followed the Admiral down the waterfront, trailed by the soldier who'd driven the armored car from the helipad.

Guo watched them go. He looked around. He spotted the soldiers guarding the fence perhaps three hundred meters up the crater-pocked road to the helipad. There was no one else in sight. He nodded to the Colonel. They inserted their earplugs and waited in silence.

The Admiral, the engineers and the soldiers disappeared into the building. The outer door closed behind them.

General Guo removed the remote control from the pocket of his greatcoat, extended its antenna, and pressed the button.

The building exploded.

A vast plume of searing orange flame billowed into the air. Guo turned his face away from the heat. The sound reached them an instant later: a flat, heavy blast of astonishing volume in spite of the earplugs. Its force pummeled his body. Had there been any unshuttered windows nearby, they surely would have exploded as well.

The Colonel leapt into motion. He ran to a nearby building. Soldiers were spilling out of the door before he got there, looking around in confusion. He shouted instructions to them—or so Guo assumed. He removed his earplugs and put them back into his pocket for the return trip to the mainland.

Troopers converged on the burning building from all directions. Wind-swept clouds of black, ember-filled smoke engulfed the adjacent buildings to the east.

Well upwind of the conflagration, Guo wandered closer to the dock to watch the spectacle. A trio of decrepit fire trucks eventually arrived and trained their hoses on the wreck, but the building and its far-too-knowledgeable inhabitants were a complete loss. The rain-drenched roofs of two neighboring warehouses began to smolder but were doused before they burst into flame.

Perhaps an hour later, an unsmiling Colonel Ryu returned. He carried a plastic document binder in his left hand. He saluted with his right. "It is done, sir. There could be no survivors. Here is the hard copy of Kim's report."

Guo returned the salute and took the proffered binder. "Well done, Ryu. Now it is time to depart. Do we have a new driver?"

"I will drive you myself, sir."

"Very well." *There is no point in sacrificing another soldier*, Guo reflected. The helicopter crew was under strict orders not to interact with the passengers. Guo had considered having them liquidated anyway, but eventually decided against it. An accidental explosion on a military base was not unheard of. The loss of Admiral Ahn would raise eyebrows but not suspicions. He had not been well-loved. The disappearance of two highly qualified pilots in an Air Force that could not spare them would be harder to explain away.

Guo smiled. It was well done. The American satellites could not have observed the procession of engineers marching to their doom. All the National Reconnaissance Office would see when the skies finally cleared would be a pile of charred timbers where a warehouse had once stood.

Lukewarm rain began to sluice down on them before they reached the helipad. Ryu helped Guo into the helicopter and closed the hatch behind them. Guo shed his rain-soaked greatcoat before sitting in the uncomfortable jump seat. The Mi-24's hull pinged under the barrage of fat drops of monsoon rain.

Ryu helped Guo fasten his harness and then sat next to him. His face was flat and unreadable as he cinched his seat belt tight.

"You disapprove, Colonel?"

Ryu shook his head. "No, sir. It was unfortunate, but necessary. No one who cannot be trusted can know of *Zhāngyú*."

"Of *Agwi*," Guo corrected sharply. "You must never use that other name again. If it is ever revealed, the world must know that is a Korean project."

Ryu's face paled. "Yes, sir. I am sorry."

"It is a small lapse, Colonel. One I trust you will not repeat." He had to raise his voice as the helicopter's huge engines whined to life. He stuffed his earplugs back in. He peered at the young man and spoke loudly. "You should not be concerned that you will meet a similar fate. You are far too valuable, Ryu, both to me and your Korean masters. Why else would you have been entrusted with running their computer intelligence program? You are a unique asset. I do not question your loyalty to me. You will go far."

Ryu looked relieved, but he frowned nonetheless.

The helicopter shook itself into the air.

Guo shouted, "Speak your mind, Colonel! You need not wait until our scheduled briefing."

"Last night we received an email from Eric Dalton." At Guo's quizzical look, he added, "Our contact in the venture capital company in California."

"The one who is being shadowed by the FBI."

"Yes, sir. At least, we *think* the message was from him. Our experts tell me that the wording was unusual. More formal. He says he wants a meeting."

"Out of the question," Guo snapped. "We cannot show our hand so openly. It would be better to eliminate him."

"That's just it, sir. We may not be able to. Adam says Dalton has fled. We do not know where he is. The car with the FBI agents was not outside the apartment this morning, either. Dalton's message says he has gotten access to the schematics of the advanced computer developed by SP."

"Is this possible?"

"I do not know, but he claims to have proof."

Guy considered Ryu's words. SP's security had proven too strict for their mole to smuggle out any schematics, though he had been directed to do so if humanly possible. *Could he have gotten Dalton the plans somehow? Supposedly they were completely ignorant of each other.* Guo gave an exasperated sigh. If Dalton's message somehow proved to be authentic, the opportunity could not be allowed to slip away.

At last he said, "Tell Adam to send someone expendable, with no traceable connection back to us. If Dalton has the schematics, we will make some effort to accommodate him. He has been reliable, after all. If it is a subterfuge... well, we did not build *Agwi* for nothing."

Ryu's face turned ashen. "Surely it will not come to that."

Guo turned a hard eye on his spy. "Our enemy cannot be allowed to own this new technology, Ryu. If he does, we will never surpass him. The Marathon will fail, and we will live under the American thumb forever. We will use every tool we know to prevent that from happening, but we cannot attack him openly. This is not our way. You were not trained in our *Thirty-Six Stratagems*, but you know of them now. Do you know the one most appropriate to this situation?"

Ryu thought for a moment. "Make a sound in the east, then strike in the west?"

Guo smiled. "A good guess, but no." He let his smile fade. "*Kill with a borrowed sword.*"

CHAPTER SIXTEEN

San Carlos, California

July 17

Jack's phone bleeped him awake at 6:00 on the dot. He tapped the ten-minute snooze button twice before he remembered that he had to be ready at 6:30.

He sprang out of bed, jumped in and out of the shower, and was half-dressed when he heard a loud honk through the open bathroom window.

"Just a minute!" he shouted through the sweatshirt he was pulling over his head. He found a threadbare pair of hiking shorts wadded up next to the nightstand. He looked around for his boots but couldn't find them in the chaos of his bedroom. He swore and stuck his bare feet into a pair of battered brown deck shoes. The horn sounded twice more before he found his keys and wallet.

A long black van waited for him on the street. A muscle-bound man in his early thirties wearing a plain gray sweatshirt and black jeans opened the rear compartment door for him. He frowned. "You're wearing *that?*"

"What's it to you?" Jack said as he scrambled inside.

The man said, "Ohhhh-kay." He slammed the sliding door closed and jumped into the passenger seat.

The rear of the van was empty except for a pair of padded benches along the windowless outer walls. Jack chose a spot in the middle of the bench opposite the door and buckled himself in.

The driver, a tiny Asian man probably in his mid-sixties, peered at Jack via the rear-view mirror. His expression was half-smile, half-grimace.

"Good morning?" Jack ventured.

"We're late," the driver barked. He checked the side-mirror and stomped on the gas.

The van careened around the corner and down the hill. By the time they reached Terry Blau's apartment building in downtown Redwood City, a thoroughly rattled Jack had sworn a silent and solemn oath never to be late again. He thought about asking the driver if he drove a white van in his off-hours, but after a long internal debate, he finally decided he'd rather not know. He didn't want to wind up at the bottom of a well in the driver's basement, a la *Silence of the Lambs*. He muttered, "*It puts the lotion on its skin, or else it gets the hose again.*"

"What's that?" asked the beefy young man.

"Nothing," Jack said, shivering.

Terry trotted down the front steps of his building as soon as the van pulled up. The driver greeted him warmly as he clambered into the back and took a seat opposite Jack.

"First day of school, eh boss?" Terry said cheerily. He was barely recognizable. His usual oversized tie-dyed shirt, plaid shorts and Birkenstock sandals were nowhere to be seen. He wore a clean white button-down shirt, khaki slacks, brown leather shoes, and an ostentatious silver belt buckle that would have made a rodeo champion proud.

Jack goggled at Terry. "I know someone who sounds exactly like you! His name is Terry Blau! Do you know him? Are you *Darth Blau*, his evil corporate-suck-up twin brother?"

"Why yes! Nice to meet you, sir," Terry said breezily. "I've never held an actual job before. I thought I'd dress nicely at least *once*." He peered at Jack's faded AC/DC sweatshirt. "I'm pretty sure the teacher is going to want you to stay after school, young man."

For a wonder, Highway 101 wasn't too crowded. They made good time down to Palo Alto.

Hank Drummond shared an old house with six other students in a neighborhood not far from Stanford. He was waiting on the street. The lanky blond Georgia Tech grad was dressed like a normal person, in Jack's estimation. He wore a Homer Simpson T-shirt, faded blue jeans and weathered Converse sneakers. He jumped in the back. The driver floored it as soon as he was buckled in.

"Tell me why I couldn't ride my bike, again?" Hank drawled. "It's just up the road from here."

Jack grumbled, "I had the same question."

"You'll see," said the beefy man in the passenger seat.

A few minutes later they were on Page Mill Road. It was jammed. It took them ten minutes to creep from El Camino to the top of the hill overlooking Foothill Expressway, the last major north-south cross street before Interstate 280. The whole way Jack and Hank pointed out how much faster they'd have gotten there on their bikes. They exchanged evil grins as they watched their driver squirm angrily in his seat after every gibe.

When they topped the rise, they saw why they were making such slow progress.

TV vans lined both sides of Page Mill Road. Reporters and photographers darted around the cars, aiming their cameras into every passing vehicle.

Jack, Hank and Terry looked at each other, then simultaneously unbuckled their seat belts and crowded forward to see.

The beefy man turned to look at them. "Get back!" he barked. When they hastily complied, he reached over, grabbed one edge of a thick black curtain Jack hadn't noticed before, and drew it closed across the width of the cabin.

"They're looking for you," the beefy man said. "And we don't want them to see you. Please be quiet." Technically it was a request, but his tone made it an order.

"Fine," Jack snapped. "At least turn the light on."

"No."

They sat in near darkness, fuming silently. Jack dug out his iPhone and checked the local traffic on Google Maps. Every street for blocks in all directions was drawn as a solid red line. The backup was even slowing traffic on the nearby Interstate 280.

The van crept forward and stopped, crept forward and stopped, again and again and again. To Jack's amazement, the driver didn't use the horn once. At long last the van surged forward and made a sharp left turn.

A few seconds later they turned right and stopped. They heard the driver roll down the window.

"Hey, Sam," said a male voice from outside the van. "How's the cargo?"

"Pissed off, like me," the driver snarled. "On Page Mill for thirty minutes! What the crap!"

"Can't say as I blame 'em. Okay, go ahead."

Sam punched it. The van turned right and pitched down sharply. Then it turned right again, and kept on turning.

The brawny passenger pulled the curtain open. "Sorry about that," he said. "I'm Alex Southall, by the way."

Jack said, "What the hell is going on?" He saw through the front window that they were spiraling down a parking garage ramp.

Southall frowned. "Didn't read your email yesterday?"

"I don't read email on weekends."

"You might want to start."

Terry mumbled, "Jeeze, I don't feel so good. Getting car sick."

"Whee," said Hank Drummond. "C'mon, Terry. This is fun. Whee."

The van had gone down at least three levels so far and showed no signs of stopping.

"Hang on, Terry," Jack said. "So, what's the story?"

Southall grimaced. "The bigwigs found out that some limey newspaper is going to publish a story about us. About the research program, and Emily, and everything else. Sorry. I know she was your wife."

Jack took a deep breath and let it out slowly. "Yes. She was. What about the story?"

"They're holding a press conference to head the newspaper off at the pass. Seems like every reporter in the country is going to be there. You're the guest of honor." He glanced as his wrist. "And it starts in six minutes."

The van finally straightened out and headed into a well-lit but mostly empty parking level. Terry heaved a sigh of relief, but now it was Jack's turn to feel sick. He looked down at his AC/DC sweatshirt and ratty shorts.

"Oh, shit," he whispered.

The vast parking level could have held hundreds of cars. A scant dozen were parked there now. The nearest wall featured a glassed-in security booth. Next to it was an access way blocked by a heavy-duty roto-gate turnstile. A uniformed security guard stood next to it. He rested his right hand on the butt of his holstered pistol.

The van screeched to a halt near the guard. Southall leaped out and opened the passenger compartment door. Hank piled out, followed closely by Jack and Terry.

Southall led them to the gate. "I vouch for 'em, Doug. Let 'em through."

The uniformed guard waved something in front of a black box on the turnstile. There was a heavy, metallic *clack*. "Okay, it's open," the guard said. "Have a good one."

"You too. After you, gents," Southall said, gesturing to the turnstile.

Jack pushed on the bars of the rotary gate experimentally. It moved without resistance. He went through.

The broad hallway beyond the turnstile was at least a hundred yards long. He wondered why there wasn't an airport-style conveyer belt walkway.

A beautiful, tall, slender, angry-looking brunette in a light blue blouse, black skirt and matching blazer waited for them at the end of the long corridor. Behind her was a closed elevator door.

Next to her was Peter Struve, also dressed to the nines. "Jesus, Jack!" he said. "What the hell are you wearing? Didn't you get the email?"

"I don't check email on weekends," Jack retorted. "Why didn't you just call me?"

"I did! Do you ever listen to your voicemail?"

"Not on weekends!"

Struve threw his hands in the air. "Goddammit. Well, come on, we've got to find you something to wear." He turned around and punched the call button. The doors slid open and they all filed in. Southall followed them and hit the door close button repeatedly.

Jack eyed the brunette. "I'm Jack Dura," he said, offering his hand.

She shook it without enthusiasm. "Laurel Wynn."

What a knockout, he thought, gazing up at her face. She was several inches taller, which he found extremely sexy. She was a bit willowy, but her figure was a perfect blend of graceful curves. Her features were finely chiseled, delicate but strong. Her long brown hair was bound into a ponytail, and her disdainful eyes were the color of the sky. *Holy cow, I'm in love.* "Do you work here too? Things are looking up."

Struve growled, "You can flirt later, Jack. We're having a press conference in five minutes. I'll do all the talking. You're just there to... oh, brother. To look pretty. God *dammit.*" He sighed meaningfully.

"I'm sorry, already," Jack said, tearing his eyes away from Laurel Wynn. "I promise to read my email every day from now on, okay, Dad? By the way, what's the big idea of hiding us in the back of a van if we're starring in a press conference?"

Wynn answered. "They're not going. Just you. We want to keep your team out of the limelight as much as possible. It's for their own safety."

Terry Blau said, "Um, what do you mean, exactly?"

She shook her head. "We'll talk about it later at the security orientation. At length."

"Great," Terry said. His earlier ebullience had vanished.

"Don't sweat it, Terry," said Jack. "At least you don't have to go out in front of an audience wearing grubby old hiking clothes."

They exited the elevator on the fourth floor. Southall remained in the elevator. He said, "Good luck," and punched another button. The doors slid shut.

Struve led the rest of them down the ridiculously wide hall to an office. The label on the door read AIDAN O'KEEFE. Struve went in without knocking.

Everyone but Jack followed him inside.

"Fuck this," he said, folding his arms across his chest.

"Don't be a baby," Struve snapped. "Aidan keeps a spare change of clothes in here. I'd ask him first but I couldn't get hold of him this weekend, either. What the hell is wrong with everybody? You're about the same size in the chest. He's taller but we can deal with that. Come on, Jack!"

Reluctantly, Jack entered. The windowless room apparently had been converted from a conference room in the very recent past. A big, off-center whiteboard dominated the wall behind the desk. Its surface was covered with inscrutable equations.

In spite of Jack's hatred of Aidan, the unfamiliar symbols on the wall piqued his interest. He moved toward the board to get a closer look.

"Nope, nope, nope," said Struve. "No time for that now. Try this on." He had taken a sober gray suit from a wardrobe that stood in the corner.

Jack peeled off his AC/DC sweatshirt and put on the proffered white dress shirt. The material was cool and smooth against his skin. He caught Laurel Wynn looking at him. He waggled his eyebrows at her with what he hoped was a devilish smile.

She turned away, blushing ever so slightly.

"That bastard does have good taste in clothes," he said. "It even kind of fits."

Struve handed him the pants. "Ms. Wynn, would you mind waiting in the hall?"

She vacated O'Keefe's office hastily.

"You're no fun," Jack said, mock-peevishly.

"Three minutes. Come on!"

The pants were too long, but Jack solved that problem by rolling the hems up. Struve *tsked* loudly and knelt, unrolling the hems and tucking them under to make the adjustment less obvious. "That'll have to do. Can you tie your tie?"

"Uh."

"Well, of course not. What am I thinking." Struve did the honors, shaking his head and frowning. He cinched the tie much too tight.

Laurel Wynn's voice drifted in from the hallway. "*One minute.*"

Jack loosened the tie a notch and shouldered into the sport coat. It fit surprisingly well, considering Jack's muscular build. "Belt? Socks? Shoes?"

Struve shook his head. "Just try to keep your feet out of sight, okay?"

Jack slipped his bare feet back into the deck shoes. "Not sure how to do that, exactly, but I'll try." He retrieved the battered-looking black belt from his pants and put it on. The pants were much too loose, but it was too late to do anything about it. He tightened the belt to compensate.

Hank said, "Gray suit? Check. Black belt? Check. Brown shoes? Check. Stylish, boss."

"You're fired," said Jack without heat.

"Already? You usually wait 'til Wednesday to fire me."

Terry Blau said, "And it's a *neeeeeew* state record."

Struve led them back to the elevator at a trot. Wynn had anticipated him and was holding the doors open.

When they closed, Struve said, "Just remember, Jack. They're going to have a lot of questions. Don't talk. Leave it all to me."

"Fine. What about the boys? And where are Lizbeth and Chao-Xing?"

Hank scoffed, "*Boys,* he calls us."

"First floor lounge. There's a TV. They can all watch from there."

They descended quickly to the ground floor. Laurel Wynn beckoned to Terry and Hank. They turned to the left and walked away.

"Well?" Jack prompted Struve. "Let's go."

Struve watched the trio disappear around a corner. He turned to Jack and spoke in a low voice. "Listen. I'm really glad you're here, but for God's sake, will you tone it down? Please? This is probably the biggest news conference of our lives. I have to go public. I don't know how much detail they have, so I have to tell it all. If I don't, and the *Guardian* breaks the story before I can spin it, I don't know what will happen. If the investors get spooked, we could lose everything, and we'll do it on live TV. That would be the end of this company, the end of my career, and the end of any chance we have of finishing Emily's work. Got it?"

Jack backed up a step. "Sure, Peter. Got it. I'll keep my lips zipped."

Struve rubbed his eyes. "Sorry. I haven't slept much for the last seven years." He glanced at his watch. "Okay, let's do it." He turned and walked away.

Jack followed at a discreet distance.

The low roar of voices echoed down the hallway, peaking in volume as he reached the atrium leading to the lobby. To his left was a double door opening onto a large lecture hall. A sign above the door read *Pauling Auditorium.* A pair of sturdy looking men in discreet black suits guarded the entrance. Jack noticed their wireless ear-buds. They looked like Secret Service agents.

A middle-aged African-American woman clad in chic business wear waited there, impatience graven into her handsome face.

Struve stopped near the guards and conferred with the woman. Jack was too far away to overhear their whispered conversation. The woman looked Jack up and down and frowned. He shrugged and smiled apologetically. She rolled her eyes and turned back to Struve.

Jack sighed. *Way to make a first impression, you doofus,* he scolded himself. He'd been even worse with the lovely Laurel Wynn. He knew he tended to come on too strong when he was nervous, and he'd seldom been as nervous as he felt right now. He promised himself to apologize to her later.

He peered around the guards into the lecture hall.

The stage was on the left, facing seven tiers of comfortable-looking seats arranged in a long, shallow arc. In every chair sat a reporter. A gaggle of—*no, not a gaggle; what do you call a group of tame paparazzi? A clutch? A murder?* He finally settled on *grovel*—a grovel of photographers sat or crouched on the floor in the carpeted space between the stage and the first row of seats

On the stage was a microphone-festooned podium facing the audience. Beyond it was a low table draped with a dark blue cloth. Five chairs, five empty glasses, five microphones, and a crystal carafe of iced water completed the set.

Suddenly Jack began to sweat. He had spent a good fraction of his life teaching students in rooms like this one. Crowds didn't faze him, but he was used to being in charge. Now his fate was entirely in Peter Struve's hands, and he'd been told to keep his mouth shut. Even worse, he'd agreed. There were few things Jack hated more than being told to shut up. He thought about fielding a few questions from the reporters, just to make a point.

Then he remembered Emily's final letter.

The allure of pissing Struve off in front of the cameras dimmed and vanished. He had to remember Emily. She'd given her life for this research. The questions in her journal still needed answers, and Jack was the only one who could find them.

A psychologist friend of his once told him that he used humor as a weapon to mask his own insecurity. Jack had just laughed, but the comment had carried a painful sting of truth. He often said things he found himself wincing about later. Emily's death had stirred feelings he hadn't entertained consciously for years. Ever since reading her final letter, he'd felt a little unhinged. He'd been acting out even more than usual. Demanding to be allowed to punch Aidan O'Keefe in the mouth, however justified that might have been. Leering at Laurel Wynn. And now, actually thinking about sabotaging a press conference just to score points in a game only he was playing.

He felt himself flush with shame. *Grow up, Jack,* he told himself, just like Emily had told him so many times during their short, tumultuous marriage.

Grow the fuck up.

He rubbed his face as if to erase the evidence of his embarrassment, then shoved his hands into the pockets of Aidan O'Keefe's sport coat.

Two people walked past him. One of them was a petite, curvy Hispanic woman wearing a suit very much like Laurel Wynn's. He struggled to remember her name. She was Struve's chief legal counsel, and had helped arrange Emily's secret funeral. Her companion was an older man with suspiciously thick brown hair. He tapped Struve's shoulder.

Struve turned. "Philip. Glad you're here." He shook the older man's hand—a bit reluctantly, it seemed to Jack. Struve turned to the Hispanic woman. "Ramona. Thanks for coming."

Her name finally popped into Jack's head. *Ramona Ochoa. That's it.*

Struve searched the hallway. "I guess Aidan's going to miss it. Where the hell could he be?"

"Traffic is really bad out there," the older man growled. "You might want to think about putting in a helipad."

Struve looked at his watch. "Well, we can't wait any longer. I'll go out first and introduce you. Come in when I say your name, take your seat and don't answer any questions unless I give the sign. The presentation will take about an hour, and we'll hand out a press kit afterward. Ready?"

Everyone nodded. Jack joined in belatedly.

Struve cleared his throat, shot his cuffs, adjusted his tie, and said, "It's show time." He stepped out into the lecture hall.

After the scattered applause died down, Struve made the introductions. The African-American woman was Barb Johnson, the VP of Public Relations. Next came Ramona Ochoa. The hairpiece was Philip Mayhew, the head of a venture capital firm with a dauntingly long name. They all walked out and took the seats closest to Struve's podium.

Jack lurched into motion when Struve called his name. He squinted as he walked into the bright lights. Struve held out his hand before Jack could walk past him. He paused belatedly and shook it. Struve's hand was like a cold steel claw, freezing him into immobility.

There was a low murmur from the crowd. A barrage of strobes from the cameras all but blinded him. Blinking away the hot blue afterimages, he tried to smile and waited for Struve to release him. He stumbled slightly on his way to his chair.

He was grateful for the floor-length blue drape around the table. *At least they can't see my shoes.*

Jack's memory of the press conference would always be hazy. Struve spoke for a long time. He talked about the founding of StruvePharma, and what his father had wanted: a company that would do good works for everyone on the planet. At length he began to tell the story of the last few months, and why this press conference had been called in the first place.

Struve's voice was calm, his cadence unhurried, his wording precise and assured. Jack couldn't keep his mind on any of it.

The lights were hot. The atmosphere in the overcrowded room grew stale in spite of the best efforts of the overburdened air conditioning. He tried to count the people in the audience and lost track somewhere in the mid-five-hundreds. Someone nearby—either Philip Mayhew or the pudgy photographer sitting cross-legged on the floor in front of his table—had eaten a lot of garlic recently. The body odor made Jack's eyes water.

As Struve's hypnotic voice droned on and on, Jack began to suspect that his chair had been made by Torquemada and Sons, and had played a prominent role in securing confessions during the Spanish Inquisition. He squirmed, rolling his weight from one aching butt-cheek to the other, and tried to look calm.

Then Aidan O'Keefe arrived.

The CTO walked onto the stage as if they'd all been waiting just for him. He paused next to the podium while Struve introduced him, then mumbled a half-hearted apology into the microphone. The bruises around his mouth had been concealed with makeup, but his lip was still swollen, which pleased Jack to no end. He left the podium and took the last seat at the table—right next to Jack.

"Nice suit," O'Keefe whispered as Struve resumed his presentation.

"Really baggy in the ass, though," Jack stage-whispered. "How's the teeth?" He subsided when Mayhew favored him with a poisonous smile.

Jack's concentration, always in short supply when it came to anything he didn't want to do, was now shot. He could barely sit still. Struve went on and on and on. Jack heard none of it. The spotlights at the back of the room blazed down at him like miniature suns. He loosened his tie and his collar, praying that he wouldn't sweat through the sport coat—then remembering whose it was, and hoping he would. *Stop being an asshole,* Jack told himself for the millionth time, and for the millionth time, he knew it would be close to impossible. He'd spent his whole life perfecting his evil brand of humor.

When Struve said his name, Jack's attention snapped back into place.

"—on loan from Stanford University, has agreed to head our research division. We want to welcome Jack to the company, and wish him every success."

Struve and the others sharing the table beamed at him and began to applaud. A few people in the audience clapped as well.

Jack stood belatedly, almost overturning his chair. He smiled, took a shallow bow, and quickly sat down again.

Struve stopped clapping. "And now I'll take a few questions."

The room erupted.

To Jack, who had never attended a press conference before, it seemed like every reporter in the room was screaming at the top of his or her lungs. Certainly, every photographer was focused on him, flash units blasting away at full speed. The afterimages smeared into a giant, pulsing, star-hot blob. He held his hand in front of his eyes to avoid permanent blindness.

Before Struve could restore order, Jack somehow saw the very tall, muscular man who'd accompanied Struve to Emily's funeral walk onto the stage. He stopped short of Struve's podium, looked in Jack's direction, and made a beckoning motion. No one else seemed to notice him.

Jack pointed at himself and mouthed, *Me?*

The man nodded emphatically and pointed at Aidan O'Keefe as well.

Jack stood, tapping on O'Keefe's shoulder and tilting his head toward the beckoning man. He'd much rather have hit Aidan again, but the dozens of cameras still snapping away were an effective deterrent.

Jack preceded O'Keefe offstage. He blinked in the sudden darkness. "Something wrong, Mister...?"

"Shea. John Shea. We've met, Dr. Dura."

"John! Right. Sorry. I'll remember your name after we're introduced to each other ten or fifteen more times."

The tall man waved the apology off. "Sometimes I have to check my driver's license to remember my own name. And nothing's wrong. Peter arranged for me to rescue you from the conference."

O'Keefe snorted. "He didn't want us answering any questions, you mean."

Shea shrugged, but a smile tugged at the corner of his mouth. He gestured toward the stage. "You want to go back?"

"No!" Jack and O'Keefe said in unison. The tumult in the room had not lessened. If anything, the departure of the two scientists had caused the uproar to grow.

"Sorry, folks," Struve was shouting. "They need to see to some experiments. Please, everyone, calm down. Please. I'll be happy to answer any questions—"

Jack turned his attention back to John Shea. "What now?"

"Now you change out of those nasty work clothes and go to new employee orientation."

"Yay," Jack said. "Paperwork. My favorite."

O'Keefe mumbled, "You can keep the suit, Jack. It looks good on you. Maybe take the pants in a little bit. I *do* need to hit the gym." He walked over to the elevator. The door opened as soon as he pressed the call button. He walked in, favored them with a tight-lipped smile, and gave a little wave as the doors hid him from view.

Shea said, "Well, he's in a good mood."

"Probably ran over a bicyclist on the way to work," Jack growled. "Does he drive a white van, by any chance?"

Shea stifled a laugh. "Okay, Dr. Dura, let's get you a badge."

"Call me Jack."

* * *

As it turned out, there was no paperwork. StruvePharma was very modern. The forms were on gigantic iPads. All Jack had to do was read, tap checkboxes, and sign his name with his glossy new Apple Pencil. There were a lot of forms, though. It took a good half hour for everyone in the crowded conference room to fill them out.

Jack finished early. He took the opportunity to duck into the bathroom and change back into his old clothes, which Alex Southall had brought down for him. He stuffed Aidan's clothes into the trash bin.

Back in the conference room, he fetched a cup of black coffee from the sideboard, ignoring the bagels, muffins, and plastic-wrapped fruit plates. He returned to his seat, took a sip and cast an eye at the others sitting at the table.

Lizbeth, Terry, Hank and Chao-Xing huddled together to his left, looking ill at ease in these corporate surroundings. A fit-looking man with receding brown hair in his late twenties or early thirties sat across from them, next to a drop-dead-gorgeous Indian woman of about the same age.

The spectacular Laurel Wynn sat at the end of the table, immediately to Jack's right. She was reading something on her iPad, not filling out forms. She glanced up and returned his gaze impassively.

He was the first to look away. He shivered and said "Brrr." Out of the corner of his eye, he saw her frown. He suppressed a satisfied smile. He scribbled aimlessly in a notepad app on his iPad until the others finished their "paperwork."

The woman from HR said, "You get to keep the iPads. Each of you will find a MacBook waiting for you at your desks. And now shall we go around the table and have everyone introduce themselves?" She looked at Jack.

He said his name, folded his arms, and nodded to Lizbeth. His former students introduced themselves. The unfamiliar man and woman turned out to be Ben Holcombe and Deepthi Damodaran, technologists at Philip Mayhew's venture capital firm. They'd been appointed to join the team as a condition of ZMPC's funding. Jack hoped they wouldn't be a burden on his whiz kids, but they seemed sharp enough at first glance.

Laurel Wynn went last.

When she said she was with the FBI, Jack's eyebrows nearly climbed off the top of his skull. He enunciated, "What. The. Hell."

"She's here as an observer," John Shea said as he closed the conference room door behind him. The big man was stealthy. Jack hadn't heard the door open. "She's with a counter-espionage group that's investigating... well, we all know what they're investigating. She's here to help us keep it from happening again, and we're glad to have her."

Laurel smiled a little at that. "Thanks, John. I won't get in your way, Dr. Dura."

"I hope not," Jack said frostily. He looked at Shea. "Jesus, joining the private sector and getting a big ol' heaping dose of Big Gubmint in the same day isn't my idea of a great start. When can we get to work?"

"Tomorrow. We have a full slate of events scheduled for you today. Next up is the security briefing. Settle in, folks. This is going to take a while."

Shea wasn't kidding. The security measures at SP went well beyond "paranoid."

They would do all of their work in this giant building, which was quite literally a fortress. It was made out of a special ceramic and carbon fiber reinforced concrete that the government was starting to use in foreign embassies. The windows were five-inch-thick ballistic glass made from a fused alumina compound, interleaved with layers of gel-like polymer and a secret material designed by SP's engineers. Shea claimed it would stop .50 caliber rounds all day long. Jack shook his head, wondering how much that must have cost.

Once the press conference ended, the lobby doors and the employee entrances at the corner stairwells would be permanently sealed. The only access to the building would be through a secure delivery area at the rear and through the freight elevator to the underground parking garage, which had not one but three separate vehicle traps that could be engaged to stop unauthorized access.

The security guards were former Navy SEALS. They were being joined by a plainclothes group of FBI and other government agents as well as civilian contractors. They were going to build a fifteen-foot high steel-reinforced concrete fence around the entire campus just outside the tree line. They planned to install gatehouses with active vehicle barriers that could be raised in less than a second. They should be able to stop a tank.

Jack's blood pressure rose steadily throughout Shea's presentation, but he kept his peace. By the time Shea finished describing the mandatory security procedures, he was pretty sure his head would explode.

"Let me get this straight," he said, quivering with rage. "No cell phones. No personal computers. We can't take our machines home at night. We can't dial in and use the fucking company's computers. There's no Internet access in this building at all! We have to change clothes and go through fucking security scanners any time we come in or leave. Why don't you just install cameras in our foreheads so you can make sure we're not fucking around in the fucking break room all fucking day?"

Shea returned Jack's furious stare with steely resolve. "Do I really have to remind you what happened here a few weeks ago? You, of all people?"

Jack's retort jammed in his throat. He realized then that he'd been shouting, and that he'd stood up and raised his fist. He looked around. His former students were staring at him in shock, as were the two newcomers from ZMPC. Laurel Wynn's face was composed, but her eyes seemed filled with pity.

Jack unclenched his fist and lowered himself into his chair, face burning. He'd done it again. *What the hell is wrong with me?* Maybe he really was coming unhinged.

Shea said, "I understand, Jack. I really do. I was here that night. I saw what that bastard did to Emily and Jason. They were my friends. I'm not about to let anything happen to you. You have my promise on that. But I'm going to need your cooperation to make it work."

Remember Emily, Jack told himself. Remember her journal. You're the only one who knows. The only one. You can't fuck this up. For once in your lifetime, stop being an asshole. "Forget it," he grated. "I apologize. Let's get on with it."

John Shea took them to the security office to "get their badges," a lengthy process which involved giving a blood sample, fingerprint, iris, and retina scans, getting photographed by a weird camera with three lenses, and endlessly repeating code phrases into a microphone in a phone-booth-sized anechoic chamber until their voiceprints could be recognized.

While he waited his turn for the voiceprint booth, he saw that everyone seemed to be walking on eggshells. It was his fault, he realized. He'd nearly lost it during Shea's briefing. He trotted out a few of his better curmudgeonly jokes to try to lighten the mood.

His students responded as usual, and were soon chatting with each other amiably. They laughed when he told them his pass phrase would be "My voice is my passport. Verify me." It was a line from a pretty good old hacker movie with Robert Redford and Sidney Poitier. They'd watched it together on Friday Movie Night in his "lab" at Stanford a couple of months ago.

The two ZMPC techs stood together to one side of the office, regarding him with no small amount of suspicion. He couldn't blame them. His students knew he could be an asshole, but his assholery didn't usually last very long. It would take the new kids a while to get used to him.

Laurel Wynn, on the other hand, clearly disliked him, and he clearly hadn't helped himself with his earlier flirtation. Well, she was just a tool of Big Gubmint, though a gorgeous one. He didn't have to be her friend.

The female security guard on duty handed each of them a lanyard attached to a bright orange temporary badge with a large white letter "T" emblazoned on it. She said, "Wear these until we get you your permanent badges. They should be ready after lunch."

Next, Shea took them to the loading dock and showed them how to enter and leave the building. There they found more armed guards, more body scanners, and another floor-to-ceiling turnstile gate, all of which looked recently installed.

When his crew had completed a full security sweep to make sure no stragglers from the press conference remained, the personnel elevator to the parking level would be shut down and permanently disabled at the top floor. They were installing barriers in the shaft to prevent its being used to gain access to the rest of the building. The only way to or from the garage would be via the spiraling fire stairs or the freight elevator.

Shea gave them a tour of the huge, well-equipped exercise gym, the basketball court, workout and weight rooms. He then showed them the locker rooms, where they traded their personal clothes for impersonal gray underwear, socks, jumpsuits and comfortable loafers provided in their sizes. This would be their standard issue uniform while they were in the building.

Shea changed from civvies right along with Jack and the other men, and showed them how to secure their belongings in fingerprint-keyed lockers. Jack presumed Laurel Wynn was doing the same for the women.

Jack noted that a small LCD panel on each locker lit up with the name of its user. At least he wouldn't have to remember which was his. He had to admit that SP did a hell of job with their security—so good, it was a little daunting. If only they'd shown a similar level of commitment before Emily was killed.

He tried to put that thought aside. From everything he'd learned about the attack, the bad guy had help from inside. They still hadn't found the suspected mole, but the security measures had been ramped up so much it seemed impossible that a similar event could occur now.

If what they'd built here was worth so much time, effort and money to defend, it must be beyond spectacular.

Jack was itching to get into the lab.

But first, it was time for lunch.

They regrouped in the hallway on the other side of the locker room. Shea took them to the cafeteria on the second floor. The big room could easily have accommodated five hundred people. Perhaps a quarter of the tables were occupied. They stood in line for food. Cooked and fresh vegetables were abundant, but starches and sweets were in short supply. Off to the side was some vegetarian *ersatz* meat dish that looked about as appetizing as cat food, to Jack's jaundiced eye. The broiled cod and rare roast beef looked and smelled amazing. His stomach growled loudly enough for everyone nearby to hear.

They all laughed.

Jack plucked at his gray jumpsuit and growled, "Well, I had to pick out my clothes, you know. I didn't have time for breakfast."

Even Laurel Wynn cracked a wintry smile.

He glowered comically before chuckling a bit himself. The residual tension from his outburst in the conference room was finally broken.

Shea led them to a long table bearing a folded cardboard placard that read RESERVED FOR NEW EMPLOYEES. They sat down and dug in.

John Shea took the seat opposite Jack's and attacked his food with as much enthusiasm as anyone else.

Lizbeth said, "Hank, you should try some vegetables. You know, those *green* things."

"You know what I always say: vegetables aren't food. Vegetables—"

"—are what food *eats*," the rest of Jack's students finished for him.

A few minutes later, stomach suitably appeased, Jack waved a forkful of cod at John Shea. "Look, I'm not trying to be an asshole—*don't say it*, Hank—but why did we just give blood?"

"Good question," Shea said. He'd already hoovered his plate clean. "They started doing that a couple of years ago. Some of the chemicals in the labs can cause severe allergic reactions. They check your blood to see if you're susceptible before letting you in. The results should come back at the same time we get the badges."

"Allergic reactions?" prompted Xu Chao-Xing. The diminutive Taiwanese woman looked alarmed.

"Yeah. About one in every ten thousand people can't handle it, or so the eggheads tell me. We've only had the one incident. Poor guy's face looked like a whole hive of bees had stung him. It wasn't life threatening, but it was pretty scary."

"Glad I asked," Jack mumbled around a mouthful of fish.

Laurel Wynn said, "While you're all in such a good mood, I want to make a proposal."

"The answer is *yes*," Jack said instantly. "We'll honeymoon in Tahiti. I know this really great bar—"

The FBI agent stared at him, her mouth compressing into a flat, lipless line.

Jack kicked himself mentally. "Sorry," he muttered. "I'm an asshole. Everyone knows that. Go on."

Her eyes flicked away from him dismissively. "You all saw how hard it was to get to the office today. It's probably going to be like that for the foreseeable future. Mr. Struve is converting some rooms in one of the nearby buildings into temporary housing. We wanted to find out how many of you would like to relocate."

Jack managed to keep his voice calm. "You mean *move* here? Permanently?"

"Until things settle down, at least. It would make it a lot easier on the security teams. We're renting a bunch of RVs for you until the housing conversions are finished."

Jack said nothing. *Just count. One-one-thousand. Two-one-thousand.* He raised another forkful of fish to his mouth and chewed it with great deliberation. He'd reached fourteen by the time anyone else at the table spoke.

"Rent-free?" asked Hank Drummond.

"Of course," said Laurel Wynn. "Mr. Struve tells me the conversions will be luxurious. The only downside is that the bathrooms will be communal. They can't install plumbing everywhere."

Terry Blau said, "I just signed a one-year lease."

Shea said, "SP will pay it off, and pay for your move. You won't even have to pack."

"Would we have Internet access? Cable?" asked Lizbeth.

Shea said, "I don't see why not. We'll pay for that too. Room and board, cable TV. Pet sitters. Pizza delivery. Laundry service. If you own a house, we'll make your mortgage payments. Whatever you like. Once you get going in the labs, you probably won't be doing much but sleeping there, to be honest. No commute means more productive hours in a day, and it would save us a lot of trouble in the long run, not having to shuttle you back and forth."

Try as he might, Jack couldn't find anything wrong with the idea. His own apartment was nothing special, aside from its location. San Carlos was a great place to live. He growled, "Are the RVs nice, at least? Not like the one Walt and Jesse drove around in the desert in *Breaking Bad?*"

Shea actually laughed. "We spared no expense, but absolutely no meth cooking, okay?"

"Dammit," said Jack, thumping the table in mock disappointment.

After that it was just a matter of details. All of them agreed to move in. None of them had families, though most had boy- or girlfriends. Jack didn't, nor any pets. Maybe the mold growing on the takeout leftovers in the fridge would miss him. The idea of avoiding the Commute of the Daily Near-Death-Experience was appealing. He was surprised to hear Laurel Wynn say that she would be moving to campus as well. He wasn't too keen on having the FBI agent as a neighbor, but she would certainly improve the scenery.

The mood was considerably lighter when they left the table.

John Shea took them around the building, starting at the bottom-most level and working their way up. The parking garage turned out to be under the buildings across the street. The six basement levels of the Pauling Building were even larger than the stupendous four-story structure above ground.

They donned noise-canceling headsets with tiny microphones and walked through a huge room in the lowest level of the basement. It contained six giant Diesel-powered generators. They were connected to massive cylindrical flywheels energized by the municipal electrical grid. If the city power dropped out, the flywheels would keep the generators spinning until the engines could kick on.

Shea claimed that they could run the whole campus at full capacity for more than a week without refilling the huge fuel tanks dug into base of Coyote Hill. The generators weren't just for backup. They supplied smoother power than the municipal grid. They were turned on whenever they used the QUBE.

Next, they toured the water treatment and air conditioning plants, which Jack was not prepared to be interested in. The amount of cooling required by the lab was prodigious. The brightly colored pipes in the huge room were a nice change from the bland white glossiness of the rest of the building.

Above the HVAC plant were two levels of servers. The tall racks of computers seemed to stretch to infinity in all directions. Arm-thick bundles of zip-tied optical fibers ran from the servers to a single, two-story-tall central chamber and into banks of handmade-looking network switches. The blazing light from a galaxy of blinking red, green and blue LEDs made Jack's head hurt. He tried to imagine what it would be like to track down a single broken cable among these tens of thousands. The techs probably didn't even bother. They'd just add another fiber.

They skipped what Shea described as a purely mechanical and support level. After a quick, mystifying peek into one of the two labyrinthine levels of what Shea called "the vaults," he took them upstairs, back to the security office.

The guard handed the badges out and assured everyone that they'd passed the allergy tests with flying colors.

Each badge featured a holographic photo of its owner on the front, and a tiny fingerprint sensor on the back. Shea demonstrated their use. "We just installed this system last week. We're still breaking it in, but it works pretty well so far. Once you're inside, activate the badge by holding your index finger down on the sensor for about five seconds. It detects your fingerprint, your body temperature and your pulse. It's called a *proof-of-life* badge. No one will be able to cut off a finger and get in by pretending to be you."

"Cheery," muttered Hank Drummond.

Shea smirked. "It'll stay active as long as it's within a foot of your body. Wave it in front of any badge reader. If you have access privileges, it will unlock. Take it off for more than ten seconds and you'll have to reactivate it. Leave it off and you'll trigger an alarm. You can wear it on a lanyard or clip it to your belt. I recommend the belt. You'll have fewer false deactivations. The battery should be good for a year, but if it stops working just bring it back here and we'll replace it. The outer doors are guarded twenty-four-by-seven, and you won't get in without an iris scan and a voiceprint."

The group followed Shea to the elevator. They went up several floors. He led them down a broad, brightly lit hallway and stopped in front of a blank metal door labeled with the number 261.

Laurel Wynn was still with them. Jack wondered vaguely if she was worried that one of *them* was a spy.

Shea intoned, "And now for the moment you've all been waiting for."

He waved his badge in front of the reader. The door clanged open.

A handsome older woman with strong Mediterranean features and dark, shoulder-length hair emerged. She wore a white lab coat and carried an iPad.

She said, "I'm Amber D'Agostino, the Chief Elf. Welcome to Santa's Workshop."

She held the door open.

They all walked in.

CHAPTER SEVENTEEN

StruvePharma Coyote Hill Campus, Palo Alto, California

July 17

When Laurel last visited Santa's Workshop, it had been cold and vacant. Not so today. The vast space was warm, brightly lit, and full of gray-clad geeks.

"Let me introduce you to the Elves," said Amber D'Agostino.

The Elves were a group of around fifty scientists and engineers, most of whom she'd never met before. She'd probably recognize their names from the reams of background reports she'd been reading for the last few days. They stood in a rough semicircle behind the long black lab bench closest to the door. A dozen more engineers sat on tall chairs at their workstations, still focused on their tasks.

More than half of the Elves were women, Laurel noticed—unusual for tech jobs in the male-dominated Valley, but women were better represented in life science careers. Fewer than half were Asian or Indian, which was also a little unusual. Six black faces were visible, aside from Lizbeth Okome-Taylor's.

The expressions of the assembled Elves ranged from eager to disdainful. Most seemed distantly curious about their visitors. They applauded semi-politely after D'Agostino finished introducing the newcomers.

It was hardly the enthusiastic greeting Laurel had been expecting Jack Dura, at least, to receive. Maybe they'd seen him squirming in his chair like an antsy four-year-old at the press conference.

On second thought, it was probably just that the trauma of losing two coworkers and the ensuing media circus had turned everyone's personal and professional lives upside down. They probably resented the attention focused on the newcomers, who had done precisely nothing but were being paraded around by Struve and the other executives like war heroes returning from the front.

She flashed on her dad's favorite movie, *The Right Stuff*, where the tried-and-true test pilots at Edwards Air Force Base sneered at the introduction of the Mercury astronauts as demigods long before any of them had ever boarded a spacecraft.

The bench between the newcomers and the Elves was covered with paperback-sized glass blocks and a variety of other objects. A bright white lamp on a flexible stalk shone down at the tabletop.

"Now it's time for a little show-and-tell," D'Agostino said with obvious relish.

SP's newest employees moved closer to the bench. Laurel was about to join them when she felt a tap on her shoulder

It was John Shea. He beckoned her aside.

Laurel didn't want to come with him. She'd seen a handful of the demos, and they were always fascinating. She'd wanted to watch Jack Dura's smug expression give way to blank amazement when D'Agostino turned on the oil synthesizer, which had been freshly revitalized especially for this occasion. With a sigh, she followed Shea to a nearby, unoccupied corner.

Shea murmured, "So what do you think?"

"I think he's a *prima donna*," Laurel said. "And he swears like Jeff Lebowski."

Shea grinned, clearly recognizing the movie reference. "The Dude got under your skin a little bit, eh?" He did a passable imitation of Sam Elliot's laconic cowboy accent.

"He doesn't get under yours?"

He shrugged. "Monster egos in the Valley are a dime a dozen, and my drill instructor helped me get over the cussing thing my first day at Parris Island. Peter tells me Jack's almost as smart as Emily, so his ego's probably about the right size."

Laurel gave a snort of laughter. "Maybe." Her tone said, *Yeah, right.*

"What about the rest of them? Did Sherlock finish the background checks?"

She winced. "Don't say that where Robbie can hear. The students are clean. Hank Drummond just broke up with his long-time girlfriend, a geneticist at a startup in Santa Clara. Xu Chao-Xing's boyfriend is a mechanical engineering grad student. They're both Taiwanese. Her grandparents escaped from the mainland right after Mao took power, and her father is a major player in one of the anti-Chinese parties. Quite wealthy, too, so she wouldn't have any financial motives to spy for anyone. Terry Blau's boyfriend is a commercial horticulturist, so no worries there. Lizbeth Okome-Taylor isn't seeing anyone, believe it or not. She's a serious workaholic."

"What about our new friends from ZMPC?"

It was Laurel's turn to shrug. "I was with Allie Vieira when she told them about Eric Dalton. They were shocked. They didn't want anything to do with him when he came back. They both have good reputations with their coworkers, and ZMPC takes security pretty seriously."

Shea muttered, "Not quite seriously enough."

"Well, no," Laurel admitted. "Why are they here, anyway?"

"Philip Mayhew really bent Struve over a barrel for Phase Two. He insisted that his people get places on the core research team. ZMPC is liquidating most of their assets to fund us. I heard they boosted the commitment to over a billion dollars. They signed the most vicious non-disclosure agreement Andy Healy could come up with. I was there." He smirked. "If they violate it, they'll have to hand over their first-born children."

Laurel made a show of widening her eyes in amazement. As Andrew Seigart's representative to ZMPC, she'd bent Mayhew and his partners over that very same barrel just two days ago. They hadn't wanted government money any more than Struve did, but they couldn't refuse a no-strings-attached bailout if SP went down the tubes. She hoped Mayhew was circumspect enough to keep that news from the Fed-o-phobic Peter Struve.

She said, "Holcombe and... Damo... Sorry, I can't pronounce her last name. Deepthi. They both passed their background checks. The only thing we learned that they didn't tell us is that they're shacking up. Holcombe and his wife are separated. Her idea. She moved back to Chicago four months ago. He and Deepthi started seeing each other a few weeks later." She shook her head. "Eric Dalton was pretty crushed when he found out about it. He had a thing for Deepthi."

"Too fucking bad," Shea snapped. "Speaking of which, any leads on him?'

Laurel sighed. "No. All we know is that the bastard who killed Dalton's guards was the same guy who killed the people at the hospital. Ballistics matched the bullets, and there were traces of talcum powder on the brass. Otherwise, nothing. At least we've been able to keep it out of the news."

When the agents failed to check in on time, a heavily armed team responded. They were dead in their car, with one bullet hole each, centered in the forehead. To kill two agents with two bullets at such close range was almost unheard of. If the killer didn't turn out to be a competition shooter, Laurel would eat her badge. Bob Sheridan, the grizzled chief of the San Francisco office, agreed with her. His agents were scouring the databases for possible matches, but the population of semi-pro shooters was surprisingly large, even in California.

Shea's face grew tight with anger. "So they have Dalton. They're rolling up their network. Not much chance of seeing him again."

"No. Not much."

"Jesus," Shea said. He rubbed his chin. "The body count just keeps going up."

Laurel sighed. "I'm glad you could talk everyone into moving to the campus. It'll be a lot easier to guard them."

Shea's handsome features twisted into a frown. "That leaves two hundred and sixty-two people who have to get here by car or bus every day. Including me. After today's press conference, those reporters might camp out here forever."

"I'll talk to Allie Vieira and see if PAPD can shoo them off. Did we get the temporary RVs yet?"

"They're on the way. We'll park 'em next to Delbrück. There aren't any water hookups, but we can run electricity and network cables from the building. Give 'em public internet access, anyway. Everyone can use the showers in the locker room in the meantime. The room conversions in Crick won't be ready for two or three weeks."

"Good," Laurel said. No matter how nice the RVs were, she couldn't imagine living in one indefinitely. "I'll be glad when the remodeling is done. We can use the service tunnel to go back and forth. If our mystery shooter is as good with a rifle as a pistol, he could take someone out from the hills on the other side of Page Mill."

Shea frowned. "We planted full grown trees to prevent surveillance, but it will do a pretty good job of foiling a sniper, unless he's shooting at someone on a roof top. Even then he'd have to be on top of a hill to get a decent angle. When that fence is up, there won't be a clear shot from ground level. Believe me. I used to do that kind of thing for a living. I'd have installed ground sensors, too, but we don't own the land outside the tree line. The neighbors take a dim view of shady characters like me digging trenches in their hillsides." He checked his watch.

"Crap. I have a meeting with the contractors to talk about that very fence. Can I leave the kiddies with you?"

"Sure," she said. "I'll sync up with you later."

"Tell them there's a beer bash downstairs in the cafeteria at five o'clock. Pizza from Blue Line."

Laurel had been there once. "Make mine sausage and pepperoni."

Shea gave her a thumbs-up and made his way to the door.

Laurel returned to the newcomers. Amber D'Agostino was wrapping up her introductory talk. The Stanford Five were staring at her with open mouths—even, Laurel was gratified to see, the ill-tempered Giacomo Taddeo Dura. The Elves had abandoned their sour expressions. Most of them were now smiling proudly. Ben Holcombe and Deepthi Damodaran shared a knowing look.

D'Agostino picked up a transparent block from the table. "So much for 'tell.' Now it's time for 'show.' I guarantee this will blow your mind." She turned to one of her colleagues. "Blaise, hand me an empty beaker, would you?"

Laurel couldn't keep the smile off her own face as she watched oil begin to drip slowly into the beaker.

"All right," said Ben Holcombe. "I've been dying to ask this question for weeks. How in the *hell* does it work?"

"Oh, it's very simple," said D'Agostino, and all of the Elves laughed. "All we did was reinvent biology from scratch." Then she began to talk very quickly indeed.

Laurel tried to filter the key points from the torrent of technobabble.

Five years ago, Emily Dura and Aidan O'Keefe invented a way to model the behavior of almost any conceivable molecule using their quantum processors and genetic algorithms. The engineers, biochemists, and materials scientists whose job it was to turn those models into reality decided to adopt a proven but radical technique: mimicking the way proteins and enzymes were built inside living cells.

The first two generations of their synthetic enzymes were in fact made from the same ingredients as proteins: chains of amino acids. They performed the same function as natural enzymes, namely, to act as catalysts, making inefficient chemical reactions possible using a fraction of the energy required by the crude bulk processes of modern industry.

The first generation of synthetic enzymes could produce only tiny quantities of output. The Elves designed protein-based enzyme "toolkits" to build tougher and more efficient successors. They boot-strapped their way through six generations of "synzyme" technology, each one faster, hardier, and more efficient than the last. The lessons they learned about the real-world behavior of their custom-made molecules were used to improve the computer model.

SP's synzymes could function across a much wider range of temperatures and chemical conditions than their naturally evolved counterparts. The Elves were laying the groundwork for the seventh generation when Emily and Jason were killed.

D'Agostino described how the loss of QUBE Charlie had paralyzed SP's development work. She carefully avoided mentioning Emily's murder in her description of their current woes. It was a wise move, in Laurel's opinion. Reminding Jack might send him into another furious tirade. Based on his reaction in the security briefing, his hair trigger had a hair trigger.

They were trying to make progress with QUBE Bravo, but the old prototype wasn't powerful enough to run the current generation of quantum genetic algorithm code—what the Elves called *E-ware*, as in "e" for "evolution." Until they had a replacement for Charlie, they had to make do with an earlier, less efficient version.

As she reached the end of the story, D'Agostino made the mistake of pausing for breath. The newcomers showered her with technical questions, all talking at once. The Chief Elf looked stricken.

Jack bellowed, "Hey, hey, hey! One at a time."

Lizbeth seized the momentary silence. "About the oil synthesizer. Ben said there were only three chemicals in the output. How can you get such purity?"

"It's all about compartmentalization," D'Agostino said. "We isolate the products from each other as we funnel them from one stage in the synthesis pipeline to the next. It's like a molecule-scale assembly line. Cells do the same thing, only they use membrane-bound chambers. The endoplasmic reticulum and the Golgi apparatus. We do it with seals."

"Seals?" said Jack Dura, looking baffled.

"S-Y-L-L-S," spelled out D'Agostino. "Synthetic cells. *Sylls*. Get it? Little hexagonal chambers filled with synzymes for a specific reaction, say, carboxylation, or hydrogenation. Each one is packed with one or two synzymes, either in liquid solution, or embedded in a silicone-polymer membrane—"

"Let me guess: a *symbrane*," said Terry Blau.

"Exactly—a symbrane, highly folded to increase its surface area, and three layers thick, unlike cell membranes. Then we pack the sylls together in sheets. All of the sylls in the same layer make one and only one modification of the productant." At their blank looks, she added. "The target molecule under assembly at each stage of the pipeline. Sorry. It's shorter than saying *intermediate product*. I haven't had to explain this to newbies for a long time." She frowned. "We haven't had any new hires for years."

Terry waved her apology off. "Please, go on."

"All right. So. Every syll in each layer makes one modification to the productant, which is moved to the next layer by symporters—one-way gates, essentially, that move a specific molecule from one syll to the next. The next layer performs a different operation, and so on and so on. We just stack them together in the order we need. The final layer exports the finished product, be it hydrogen, water, oil, or what have you."

"Wow," said Hank Drummond.

D'Agostino said, "Of course in reality it's a lot more complicated. There are strips of sylls that carry reactant molecules to the sylls, and others that take waste products away for storage or reprocessing. We had to figure out how to efficiently collect gases from the air. That was *really* hard. Waste heat's a problem, but we have ways around that." D'Agostino smiled. "We developed a thermal superconductor."

"What?" gasped Lizbeth Okome-Taylor. *"How?"*

The room erupted. Everyone shouted questions at everyone else.

Laurel looked around helplessly. Her eyes met Jack Dura's.

He had a silly grin on his unshaven face that made him look ten years younger. He mouthed the phrase "HOLY SHIT" at her and shook his head in obvious amazement.

She knew a smile was plastered on her face as well. It was all so strange, like her life had taken a left turn into a science fiction movie. Another thing occurred to her then: when he wasn't being a self-absorbed asshole, Jack was very good looking. She buried that thought as soon as it popped into her head. *You're an observer,* she reminded herself silently. *Observe.*

Eventually calm was restored.

"Holy Christ," said Ben Holcombe into the sudden silence.

Jack Dura nodded. "You said it, brother. This is amazing. So how do you power it all? Enzymes and these symporters might not use much energy, but they use *some*."

"Photovoltaics and *proticity*," said one of the Elves standing nearby.

D'Agostino said, "This is Blaise Thierry. He's our lead molecular designer."

Jack nodded across the bench at the Elf, who was in fact rather elf-in: slim, blond, medium-height, beardless, and blue-eyed, with sharp features and a somewhat otherworldly appearance. He reminded Laurel of someone. She struggled to place his face.

Thierry nodded back to Jack. "The key components are powered by a proton current. Proticity. Or a strong acid gradient, if you prefer. It's the same mechanism that powers the molecular motors in bacterial flagella or the tails of sperm cells. A single such motor can operate at up to 17,000 revolutions per minute, and it can drive a bacterium through water up to sixty cell lengths per second." His accent was French, or perhaps French-Canadian. Laurel found it a little hard to follow him.

"Sixty per second. Is that a lot?" she ventured.

Thierry smiled, a bit condescendingly. "A cheetah can manage about twenty-five body lengths per second. If our bacterium were the size of a cheetah, it would travel at about a hundred fifty miles an hour."

"That's a lot," chortled Jack Dura.

"Jesus," said Hank Drummond, the lanky Southern student. "If I saw a bacterium the size of a cheetah, I'd be the one doing a hundred and fifty."

Thierry pursed his lips and waited for the laughter to die down. "Proticity is much more efficient than electricity. The work function of the proton is—"

Suddenly Laurel had it. Thierry looked a little like Herbie, the elf who wanted to be a dentist in *Rudolph the Red-Nosed Reindeer*. She had to cough to cover a snort of laughter.

Jack looked at her curiously before returning his gaze to the engineer.

Thierry's words washed over her in an accented wave. Jack's face betrayed his consternation as he struggled to follow Thierry's explanation. It was sprinkled with terms like "photo pumps" and "reverse osmosis" and "plasmonic induction." He rattled something off about converting light into electricity into proticity, and the acid ions being collected in the outermost symbrane compartment. The rest of the explanation might as well have been in Turkish.

Eventually the Elf's lecture wound to a close.

Jack said, "I see." He was clearly struggling to keep his face straight.

"That explains why you didn't want us opening the demo unit," said the Indian woman, Deepthi of the unpronounceable last name. "The acid would have been very dangerous."

Thierry folded his arms across his chest and smiled smugly. "You would have found it difficult to get through the case. The demo unit is made from bonded layers of a special kind of graphane. That's like a sheet of diamond, Agent Wynn. We can make sheets of any size."

Another uproar greeted this pronouncement.

Laurel considered telling the snooty Dentist-Elf that she knew about graphene and its cousin graphane—she'd read about them in *Scientific American*—but by the time the hubbub died down the moment had passed.

"Let me show you. We developed this for John Shea," Thierry said. He picked up a thin sheet of glass about a foot square. Two other Elves put on plastic gloves and held the glass vertically above the bench. Thierry uncapped what looked like a tube of toothpaste. Another Elf placed a thick wad of paper towels on the bench beneath the glass.

Thierry ran the end of the "toothpaste" tube across the top edge of the glass, leaving a thick bead of yellow gel behind. The gel clung like glue. Thierry put the squeeze tube down and picked up a spray bottle. He squirted the gel with the liquid in the bottle at close range.

The gel turned bright red and liquefied. Crimson fluid ran down both sides of the glass, but not in blobs or drops. The leading edge of the liquid was ruler-straight. The red color spread to the edges of the glass. The assisting Elves shifted their gloved fingers to let it coat the spots where they'd been holding it.

A few seconds later, as suddenly as if a switch had been thrown, the red color faded. Tiny droplets of colorless liquid drizzled from the glass onto the paper towels. The sheet was no longer glossy, but otherwise it looked unchanged.

Thierry said, "This glass is now coated with multiple layers of FQG. Fluorinated Q3-graphane, that is, under high tension."

"Q3?" said Jack, clearly mystified.

"A new conformation of carbon we discovered, considerably stronger than diamond. We can make fibers as well as sheets." Thierry ignored the astonished murmurs and nodded to his assistants. One of them removed the paper towels. The others dropped the glass sheet. It bounced on the bench with a hollow metallic sound. When it stopped bouncing, it slid across the tabletop as if it were coated with oil. Thierry's helpers laughed as they struggled to catch it before it fell to the floor. They had to corral it by pinching the corners with their fingertips. One edge was starred with cracks, but the sheet held its shape.

Thierry said, "This used to be ordinary window glass. Now it can resist a shot from a small handgun. The material is much tougher than we expected. We used a similar process on the Class 10 bulletproof windows of this building, putting down layer after layer, with shock-absorbing elastomer gel in between. Mr. Shea shot a test article with an armor-piercing round from a .50 caliber Barrett sniper rifle. It didn't even leave a mark." Thierry's eyes glowed with pride. "The surface is almost frictionless. It would take an artillery shell or a shaped-charge explosive to get through the windows of this building. They are in fact tougher than the walls—or were, until we reinforced them, too."

The excited babble started again, at twice the previous volume.

Laurel watched in bemusement. She knew more about graphene than Blaise Thierry would have believed. It was a simple but incredibly tough molecule: pure carbon, a single atom thick. Companies across the world had struggled to produce it in commercial quantities since it was first synthesized in the lab in the early 2000's. It was a hundred times stronger than steel, a superb electrical conductor, and a promising candidate to replace silicon and other semiconductors for ultra-fast computer processors. This Q3 variant sounded even more astonishing.

The last vestiges of her Seigart-fueled skepticism faded away. If what Thierry was saying was true, SP was going to be the wealthiest and most powerful corporation on Earth.

Don't be a fan-girl, she told herself. An instant later something that had been troubling her for days finally swam up to her conscious awareness. She put up her hand. "I have a question," she announced. She had to repeat herself twice before the chaos settled to a low roar.

"Yes, Ms. Wynn?" prompted Amber D'Agostino.

"If you can make this Q3 stuff so easily, why don't you just commercialize it? You could make billions on that alone. What are you waiting for?" She felt Jack Dura's hawkish brown eyes on her as she spoke.

The buzz in the room died away. Most of the SP veterans looked uncomfortable. Some looked angry.

Ben Holcombe came to her rescue. "I was wondering the same thing."

Jack Dura nodded. He looked askance at D'Agostino.

The Chief Elf's face was carefully composed. "It boils down to a business decision. We're focused on the oil synthesizer because we need a sustainable source of income, and it's probably the most commercially viable technology we have. We can make all of these things in the laboratory. We can even make some of them to scale. But everything is monstrously expensive."

She picked up Thierry's half-empty squeeze tube. "Take the FQG poly-gel. As a technology demo, it's hard to beat, even by the oil synthesizer. But it can't be commercialized in its current form. It took eleven months and forty million dollars for Blaise to produce enough for John Shea to armor this building. This tube of gel costs about three thousand dollars."

Hank whistled. "You won't be running down to Home Depot to buy *that* anytime soon."

D'Agostino smiled wryly. "No. The list of problems is endless. Symbrane polymer is cheap. The equipment to pack it into sylls is horrendously expensive. Symbranes just don't want to fold up into tiny hexagonal compartments. It took us six months to solve that little problem. The thermoconductor is even more expensive. We can only make it in tiny quantities, and almost all of it is in the QUBEs and the oil synthesizer. There just isn't much dysprosium-156 on Planet Earth."

"Wait a minute," interjected Lizbeth Okome-Taylor. "You need a *radioactive isotope* to make it?"

D'Agostino shook her head. "No. It's stable. Half-life on the order of ten to the eighteenth years. It's just incredibly rare. The more abundant isotopes of dysprosium don't work at all. The mass of the nucleus makes all the difference. No one would *ever* have guessed that. It flies in the face of everything we thought we knew about chemistry. We discovered it by accident. The E-ware wasn't programmed to ignore nuclear mass. Thank God. The bioalgorithms sometimes pick the weirdest and most expensive ingredients around, and we have no idea why. The only thing we really know is that they work."

Jack gave a single, barking laugh. "So this is all a big cheat. The QUBE gives you the recipes but you don't really understand the physics behind half of it."

D'Agostino nodded. "A lot more than half." She paused to rub her eyes. "Once upon a time we had more money than we knew how to spend. Ha. That's no longer an option. Even if it were, just throwing money around won't solve our problems, at least not directly. There is so much basic science left to do."

Blaise Thierry picked up the thread when D'Agostino fell silent. "We can't fabricate sylls fast enough. They must be absolutely uniform at the atomic level to pack correctly into layers. About eight percent of our production meets that requirement. If there are gaps, there will be leaks. Leaks mean inefficiencies that quickly grow out of control. Leaks mean reactants mixing with the wrong stage of the productant, which can ruin the yield or wreck the syll chain. I could name a dozen other problems we have no idea how to solve. Without a fully functional QUBE, we may never solve them."

Ben Holcombe held up a hand. "Dr. Thierry, with all due respect, this is the wrong approach. Every new technology takes years to perfect. You can't wall yourselves away from the world and expect to solve it all yourselves. You don't even have Internet access here. You can't do this kind of work in a vacuum. You need to open-source it. Get everyone on the planet involved."

The Stanford crew began to nod as Holcombe spoke.

"This is a company, not a college," snapped Blaise Thierry. "There are trade secrets involved!"

The debate grew hot. Laurel watched the faces around the work-bench carefully. The newcomers enthusiastically supported Holcombe. The SP engineers were divided. Some, like Thierry, adamantly opposed the idea of sharing the technology with the world. A few, including D'Agostino herself, defended Struve's cautious approach of releasing just enough detail to secure the commercial rights to the technology, while protecting the key technologies as trade secrets.

To Laurel's surprise, Jack Dura said nothing. He watched the others with interest, but he never expressed an opinion, never smiled, never nodded or shook his head. His eyes met hers for an instant, but his expression didn't change.

What does he know? Laurel wondered. What isn't he saying?

"Enough!" shouted Blaise Thierry. "It does not matter what we may think as individuals. We work for StruvePharma. We do what Mr. Struve says. The patent applications have been filed. The papers are out for review. The world will know what we are doing soon enough. In the meantime, we have problems to solve."

Jack spoke into the sudden silence. "He's right."

His students stared at him.

Jack returned their looks calmly. "Like Dylan says, 'you're gonna have to serve somebody.' Struve pays the D.J., so we dance to his tune. And I have some ideas."

Every eye in the room was focused on Jack now, Laurel saw. His students looked like he'd hit them with bricks. Evidently, agreeing with the management wasn't something he did often—or perhaps *ever*. Even the engineers who had ignored them when they entered Santa's Workshop were watching him.

"You all know that once upon a time, Emily was my wife," Jack said in quiet, measured voice. "She and I worked on the protein-folding problem together. We came up with the ideas that eventually led her to build the QUBE." He looked down at the bench. "I read her papers. All of them. I think I found her mistake. If I can fix it—and with your help, I think I can—then we can solve all of these problems. We can make these inventions viable. And maybe a whole lot more. A *lot* more." He gestured at the demos on the bench top. "These are miraculous. You should all be very proud. But if I'm right, you ain't seen nothin' yet. If I'm right, the work we're doing here will change everything. And I do mean *everything*."

Everyone in the room was smiling now. Including Laurel.

Jack looked up. His eyes scanned the room, locking on hers. "Let's not waste time debating. We're here. We're all we've got. And we've got a lot of work to do. So let's fucking *do* it."

CHAPTER EIGHTEEN

Westfield Centre, San Francisco, California

July 23

San Francisco was one of the few US cities with an extensive underground public transit system. It was not much to speak of, compared to that of a European city, but the standards were different in car-crazy America. Aidan didn't use it often, but it was handy when he needed it.

He used limo services like Uber or Lyft when it wasn't practical to take his big Audi, or when he wanted an independent record of his journey in case he needed an alibi. He'd walk three miles up and down San Francisco's steep hills rather than get on a cramped, odious Muni bus or train. Just thinking about the bus made him want to take a shower.

The Bay Area Rapid Transit system, on the other hand, was just tolerable.

The system started operations in 1972. The trains were spacious and, considering the age of the cars, in a reasonable state of repair. The seats were comfortable, if occasionally decorated with gum, crumbs or dried spots of mystery fluids. Some stretches of rail screeched like tortured witches when the cars rolled over them, but the tunnels beneath San Francisco's Market district weren't too noisy. Aidan had found that he could endure short rides on BART, as long as he avoided commute hours.

Fortunately, today was a Sunday. The seats were full of slack-bellied, selfie-stick wielding tourists, resplendent in their logo-bedizened T-shirts and fingerprint-smudged ball caps. Aidan stood next to one of the car's two doors to avoid soiling his tailored sport coat and slacks.

He tried not to probe the temporary bridgework in his mouth with his tongue. The dentist wouldn't have the replacement tooth ready to implant until next week, and it still hurt in spite of the Vicodin. At least the bruise on his cheek had faded.

The car braked hard as it pulled into Powell Street Station. Aidan braced himself, gripping the vertical hand rail next to the door. He sauntered out when the doors slid open.

He walked slowly to the escalator, as befitted a well-dressed man on a leisurely weekend shopping run. He suffered the long slow ride up to the mezzanine level of the station. He waited behind the confused mass of tourists at the exit gates as they struggled to figure out which end of their prominently labeled magnetic tickets to insert into the reader.

He mastered his urge to stride ahead of the phalanx of giggling teenaged girls sauntering eight abreast through the underground entrance of the Westfield Centre. The shrieking mass of girl-flesh veered onto the escalator ahead of him instead of going into the crowded food court. He followed them at a comfortable distance.

Patience, he counseled himself.

He didn't think he was being tailed. Laurel Wynn had given no sign that she suspected him or any of the other SP executives of malfeasance. A week had passed since Jack Dura and his team had joined the company. Wynn spent much of her time observing the newcomers and looking for moles in the ranks of the scientists and engineers already on staff. She consulted with Aidan on every employee. He knew whom she suspected and whom she thought above reproach. To all appearances, Aidan was in the latter group.

A less cautious man would think himself home free. He was not that kind of man.

He checked his gold Apple Watch. He was half an hour early. He stepped off the escalator and went shopping.

Clutching the handle of a Nordstrom bag, he arrived at the café one minute before the scheduled rendezvous.

The upscale coffee shop was directly beneath the glass-paned dome atop the high-end indoor shopping center. Trendy restaurants full of well-dressed diners surrounded the uncrowded café. It was quieter here than the basement level food court, and a more credible destination for a crowd-averse gentleman to avoid the *hoi polloi.*

About half of the tables were in use. Most of their occupants were busy with phones, tablets or laptops.

Tom Reed sat alone at a small round table. The slender, blond gunman wore a casual short-sleeved cotton shirt and black slacks. He sipped something from a paper cup and studied the screen of his old-fashioned Blackberry. A Bluetooth earpiece protruded from his right ear.

Al Sanderson sat on the other side of the coffee bar. Reed's muscular lieutenant wore a gray shirt and blue jeans, and was likewise playing with a cell phone.

Aidan spotted three more employees of Ableman Security, Reed's more-or-less legitimate business. There was little chance of their target doing anything stupid in such a public place, but there was no reason to be overconfident.

Aidan got in line behind a young couple pushing a stroller and pretended to examine the pastries. He felt a buzzing in his jacket pocket just before he got to the register. He pulled out a large gold iPhone and studied it casually. It looked just like his personal phone, but this one was registered under a fictitious name. The risk of being caught with it was low compared to leaving an electronic audit trail of his communications on his personal cellular account.

The message was from Tom's number. It read:

> HES @ UR 9:00, @ END OF BAR, FACING ME. WHT,
> BRN HR, BLU SHRT, BLU JNS, LAPTOP. NOONE
> FOLLOWD U.

Aidan put the phone away. If *Tom* hadn't seen anyone trailing him, he knew he was safe. He ordered and received a paper cup of black coffee to go. As the barista rang him up, he inspected the café's patrons with a casual eye.

He spotted their target quickly. He was an inconspicuous-looking man, much like Tom, in a way: slender, average in height and build, thoroughly unremarkable—a perfect conduit for Dalton's anonymous masters. The man sat between two empty tables with his back to the coffee bar. He looked nervous. His hands rubbed the surface of the closed PC laptop on the small round table in front of him.

Aidan paid for the coffee with cash. He strolled over to the man's table, looked down, smiled, and said, "Hello."

The man's eyes flicked up to Aidan's face. "Hey," he grunted, and looked away.

Aidan asked, "Do you mind if I join you?" He sat down without waiting for an answer. He placed his Nordstrom bag on the empty chair to his left.

The man stared at him. "Yeah, I do mind. I'm waiting for someone."

"Oh, I know," said Aidan, still smiling. From the corner of his eye, he saw Alan Sanderson slide behind the empty table to the target's left. An instant later, Tom Reed took the chair to his right.

The man's eyes widened.

Aidan glanced at his colleagues. "Don't worry. We're not with the police. Ah yes. I'm supposed to say *situation bright orange.*" He took a sip from his paper cup and made a face. "Dear me. I'll have to have a word with the proprietors about this coffee."

The man sat back and eyed Aidan's companions warily. "What do you want?"

"I have some bad news for you. Eric Dalton is no longer..." He made a show of groping for the right word. "*Available.* Yes, that's a good way to put it. He told me all about his arrangement with your employers before he suddenly became... unavailable. I trust I don't need to elaborate?"

The man's face grew stony.

Aidan rolled his eyes. "Oh, please," he scoffed. "I just want you to take them a message. Describe me to them. They'll know who I am. Tell them if they're still interested in what I have to offer, they can reach me here." He pulled a card from the inside breast pocket of his sport coat. On its surface was a long, cryptic, laser-printed email address. He held it out.

The man took it.

Aidan's smile broadened. "You see? That wasn't so hard. And tell them not to shed any tears over poor Mr. Dalton. They are trading up."

"Who are you?" the man said.

"I'm their knight in shining armor. Have a nice day." Aidan stood, collected his coffee cup and his shopping bag, and walked away.

Tom Reed joined him on the escalator. They descended to the mall's BART station entrance in silence. Aidan dropped the coffee into a recycling bin, handed his bag to Reed and availed himself of a public hand sanitizer.

Reed murmured, "Do you think they'll bite?"

Aidan rubbed the cold gel over his hands briskly. "Have you been watching the news?"

Reed shook his head.

"Peter's press conference on Monday was long on claims and short on substance. The press raked him over the coals all week. Apparently they couldn't make heads or tails of the technical papers he gave them. *There's* a shock. The state of the press these days... So Peter tried to help them understand. He went on CNBC Friday afternoon and demoed the oil synthesizer."

"Holy Christ."

"I tried to talk him out of it, but once he's made up his mind, you can't reason with him. He's worse than Emily was. Looking back, though, I think it helped us. *Us.* Not SP." He held out his hand expectantly.

Reed gave him the shopping bag. "So? What happened?"

"The TV people were amazed. Then they started talking about what would happen to the oil industry. After that it was pandemonium." He laughed. "Turn on any TV, go to any web site, and you'll see the demo. The pundits think the bottom is going to fall out of the energy futures market. The stock market might follow. The government is petrified. The President called Peter and asked him not to do any more demos. Industrial spies will be on SP like a plague of locusts. So, do I think Eric Dalton's paymasters will bite?" Aidan smiled wolfishly. "Yes, I believe they will. I'll be in touch when they do."

Reed nodded and walked away.

Aidan pulled his BART ticket from his pocket and girded himself for another trip on the bacteria-riddled train.

CHAPTER NINETEEN

StruvePharma Coyote Hill Campus, Palo Alto, California

August 7

It was time for rounds.

John Shea shouldered into the heavy gray armored jacket. It had been designed to his specifications, but he'd put on a couple of pounds since he'd been measured for it. He pinched the fabric around his midriff so he could pull the underarm zipper all the way up. Letting the jacket out wasn't an option. It was made in Santa's Workshop, and it was made to last. You couldn't exactly order a bigger size from Amazon.

"Getting a little slack around the middle, eh, Gunny?" quipped Alex Southall as he closed his locker. The smirking punk was already dressed. Wearing mottled gray from rolled-up-balaclava-covered head to combat-booted toe, he looked like the SEAL he once was: chiseled, muscular, and disgustingly good-looking.

John growled, "You want to go a few rounds in the ring tomorrow, squid?" He jokingly used the Marine's not-so-nice nickname for sailors.

"Not me, boss. I like my chin right where it is."

"All right then." John zipped the tight jacket closed. He might be a bit thicker around the middle, but his fists and his reflexes were just fine. His biggest problem was finding sparring partners who would get into the ring with him more than once.

"Don't forget your badge," said Alex.

John replied, "Way ahead of you, sonny boy." His San Mateo County Deputy Sheriff's badge was already pinned to his jacket.

Laurel Wynn had talked to her boss, who'd leaned on every law enforcement agency in California to get John's security force official recognition. Eight days ago the members of John's original core team of former special forces operatives had been sworn in. Laurel's contractors were still restricted to traditional security guard duties.

Emergency deputation was almost unheard of in this day and age. Given the number of deaths in the wake of Emily and Jason's murders, no one could argue that the security situation at StruvePharma was anything less than an emergency. Homeland Security had agreed to take the PR heat if there were any mishaps, so the sheriff's department reluctantly agreed, with one hard and fast requirement: John's crew had to pass an accelerated Police Academy course.

The core team was exhausted from pulling double shifts to complete the course. Every person on John's staff could have taught the sheriffs a thing or two about tactics and firearms, but using them in a civilian context meant a lot of relearning. Memorizing all the statutes and codes was a serious bitch, and there was no end in sight. Everyone had developed a healthy new respect for the amount of classroom work required to become a police officer. In the meantime, they still performed their usual bimonthly rotations through day, swing, and graveyard shifts. It was wearing on them all.

Still, he preferred the way things were now to the relaxed way he'd run things before the attack. There had been far fewer people on staff then, distributed across eleven buildings. They hadn't run any of the executive code level response drills for months before that fateful night. Even so, his Rapid Response Team had formed up at the Pauling Building quickly enough, and they'd done their best to save Emily.

Sometimes the dice just come up snake-eyes. He told the men that and hoped they believed him. He told himself the same thing every night before collapsing into bed next to his already-sleeping wife. He repeated it every minute of every hour he lay there until he finally passed out. Maybe, someday, he'd actually believe it himself.

In the meantime, he and his team reviewed every element of their response plan. They'd fixed every flaw they could find. Shift changes were faster and better. They'd instituted the proof-of-life badge system, and they tested it every shift. They'd installed even more cameras and sensors, and added contractors from Verity Services to fill in the gaps.

To test the new measures, every one of the former spec-ops guys had tried to break in. Every time, they'd been caught. And they'd worked themselves to exhaustion to complete the police training. They'd have to ease off soon. Tired people made dumb mistakes. But for now, it was balls to the wall, all ahead full.

Alex failed to stifle a yawn.

"Stop that," John said, and then yawned himself.

They left the locker room and went to the armory, where they put on their heavy duty belts and selected their weapons.

"Loaded for bear," said Alex as he holstered his 9mm SIG MK25.

John sniffed. "With that pea-shooter, you'd better take Boo-Boo. I'll get Yogi."

Alex rolled his eyes. "Whatever you say, boss."

John's weapon of choice was his prized Kimber 1911 .45, a Custom TLE/RL II. He'd won more than a few of the friendly matches they held every month down at Reed's Indoor Range in Santa Clara. Most of his crew favored the pistols they'd used in the service. John wanted to be sure that if he had to take a shot, the guy on the receiving end wouldn't get up again. Besides, the 1911 model .45 was a classic design. It was hard to improve on Browning perfection. He racked a round into the chamber, set the thumb safety, and holstered it.

He checked his belt. It had a ridiculous number of ballistic nylon pouches containing every conceivable thing he might need while on duty: his holster, a pouch for his radio, handcuffs, pepper spray, a Taser, flashlights and weapon lights, spare magazines, a collapsible rod called an Asp, a folding knife, and even a first aid kit.

He clipped his radio's speaker-microphone to his shoulder loop, gave Alex a cursory eye to see if he was done—he'd finished first, as usual, the punk—and nodded. "*Now* we're ready for bear. And hey, hey, hey! Let's be careful out there." He smiled at Alex's baffled look. He was way too young to remember Sergeant Esterhaus' daily post-briefing instruction on *Hill Street Blues*.

They stepped out into the security office. Even at 11:45 PM, the big conference room was like a beehive. Cord Walker, a fellow former Marine sergeant, was delivering the graveyard shift briefing to a crew heavy on newbies.

Cord stood a shade over six feet tall. He was as dark-skinned as John was pale and was built like a battle tank. His gentle, cultured baritone voice was accompanied by a laser-like drill instructor stare he'd used to great effect on dozens of classes of terrified Marine recruits. He tossed John an up-and-down alpha-male nod without breaking cadence.

John nodded back. He preceded Alex to the surveillance room. It was a mess. They'd knocked down a wall to expand it, and construction wasn't finished. Two sharp-eyed staffers sat in the original half of the room, in front of a wall of professionally mounted flat panel displays. They could watch the entire perimeter of the campus from here.

His eyes strayed to the unfinished half of the room, which would house the next-generation surveillance technology from Laurel Wynn's government buddies. The new wall unit wasn't close to being finished. Bundles of zip-tied cables poked out from the wide rectangular holes where the screens would go. Soda cans and empty bags of chips had been left on the console by the installers, who worked banker's hours, judging from the glacial progress of their work. The whole assembly was offensively junky. He grabbed the refuse and tossed it in a trash can.

John had spent enough time in the private sector that anything with "Government Issue" stamped on it made him wince, but Laurel had assured him that the technology was anything but cheap. The NSA had its own version of Santa's Workshop, which was probably more like Vulcan's forge. He was eager to find out what the new gear could do.

He turned to Ana Katsumata, the lead surveillance operator. In a former life she'd been an Air Force battlefield intelligence operator, flying in MC-12 Liberty surveillance aircraft. She'd even gotten the Bronze Star for something in Afghanistan that she didn't talk about.

"Evening, Ana. Sitrep."

She brought up the activity log on the widescreen display directly in front of her keyboard. "At 22:45 we caught a local reporter and a photographer trying to sneak down from the top of Coyote Hill," she said. "Perimeter patrol intercepted them and escorted them back to their vehicle. And we zapped a quad copter that overflew us about half an hour ago. It crashed in the trees by the Wilkins Building."

"Ha," said Alex. "Told you so, boss."

John sighed dramatically. "I'll pin a gold star on you later." The prototype high-power microwave unit on the roof had been Alex's idea. He had a buddy who worked for a British defense company that preferred to go nameless, and had talked John into agreeing to beta test their product on the sly. Alex called it the Zap Gun. It wasn't powerful enough to hurt anyone on the ground, but it would be hell on airborne electronics inside a three-mile radius. The targeting controls were complicated, but Ana had gotten the hang of them after a few hours of practice. It probably wouldn't be the last drone they'd fry with it.

Ana said, "The Greek checked it out. Looks like a civilian model, a DJI Phantom 3, 4K camera, no special modifications. Kinda dumb to be flying it around at night without an IR sensor."

"Wow," said Alex. "Nice rig. Somebody's gonna be pissed. Hope they don't call the FAA on us."

"Fuck the FAA," replied John. "Laurel Wynn can handle them."

Everyone in the room nodded. The willowy FBI agent had impressed them all, especially once they saw her practicing Krav Maga routines in the Pauling Building gym. She sparred with members of the security team regularly now, and gave as good as she got.

John said, "What else, Ana?"

"Nada. Zip. Zero."

"Seriously?"

"So far," Ana said. "I think the TV twits are starting to get the picture."

"Jeeze, I hope so," muttered Alex. "It's been two weeks since our coming-out party. It's gotta be pretty damned boring standing out on the street watching lookie-loos drive by."

"Some people do not learn very fast," said John. He checked the views from the perimeter surveillance cameras.

The Palo Alto Police had finally responded to Struve's constant complaints about employees not being able to get to and from work. They'd reclassified the entire length of Coyote Hill Road as a tow-away zone. The reporters tried to stand their ground, but as soon as a few of them forked out the specially jacked-up fees to recover their vans from the impound lot, they caved. The road bordering the north side of the campus remained blissfully empty.

The reporters seemed to be getting tired of staking them out in any case. There were gaps in the row of vans parked in the designated part of Deer Creek Road, on the south side of the campus. A scruffy-looking man and a nattily-dressed woman stood in one of them, smoking cigarettes.

John said, "I guess CNN can only show so many hours a day of armed guards on patrol."

Ana said, "One more week on the new fence and they won't even see that. I'm looking forward to racking out through my shift again."

John laughed. "I'll pretend I didn't hear that." He started for the doorway, Alex on his heels.

"Hey, what's that?" said the junior surveillance operator, a newbie whose name escaped John at the moment.

"Wait a sec, boss," Ana said sharply.

John turned on his heel and strode back to the console. "Show me."

Ana pointed at a screen located about halfway up the wall. It showed a sparkling green night-vision image of a grove of trees.

"Bring it up on the tactical display," said John.

An adjacent screen lit up. It showed a 3D computer map of the terrain around the campus. A bright red arrow indicated the camera. It was mounted on a pole in the middle of the cypress trees that bordered the SP campus along Page Mill Road. A pair of dotted green lines started at the red arrow and slanted across the screen to the left, forming a wedge to show the direction of the camera and its field of view. The wedge ended in a lumpy blob of trees on the far side of Page Mill Road.

The grove was in an elongated, tree-filled plot of land between the expressway and a short, one-way lane named Old Page Mill Road—a segment of the original street that still persisted after the modern version was laid down on a different path. On the near side of the grove were a few small buildings at odd angles to each other: stalls for the horses that roamed the fenced-in paddock next to the busy street.

They all watched the screens. Nothing moved in the grove.

"So?" said Alex.

Ana said, "Keep watching the trees."

A moment later, John saw it: a human figure carrying something long and narrow in both hands. The figure crouch-walked slowly through the thick brush.

"Bingo," said Alex.

"That's no reporter," said John. "Ana, can you get a better picture?"

"No sir. This is the only camera with this angle."

"Get Mikey in the air."

"Sir," said Ana. She flipped a few buttons on her console. A joystick popped up from its hidden enclosure to the right of her keyboard. Another controller rose slowly from a panel to her left: an odd hybrid of a throttle lever and a thumb-operated controller pad.

The display in front of Ana changed. The top two-thirds of the screen went blank. A smaller pane took up the rest. It featured digital instruments John remembered from his sole frustrating attempt to play Microsoft Flight Simulator back in the Nineties.

Ana pressed some keys in quick succession. The top part of the window lit up with a false-color image from Mikey's infrared camera: a rainbow-tinted view of distant hilltops, cut off at the bottom by the lip of the drone's rooftop enclosure. She did something with the joystick and the throttle controller. The enclosure slid down, passing out of view. Dark blue ground and light blue trees fell away as the stealthy electric hexacopter gained altitude.

"We're airborne," said Ana unnecessarily. She twisted the joystick and pushed forward. The bluish hills slowly grew bigger.

John followed Mikey's progress on the tactical map display, which was closer to his eye level. It showed the angles and targets of all of their surveillance cameras in a single view, superimposed on a 3D map of the terrain surrounding the campus.

"God bless the Greek," John whispered, not for the first time.

Stathis Sotiropoulos was one of Santa's Elves: a rock-star computer whiz and materials scientist who'd invented the magical window armor, among many other things. The Greek was also a passionate drone builder, military historian and war gamer. He loved to hear stories from the combat veterans on staff. He spent a lot of his spare time with John's crew, trying to figure out ways to make their lives easier. One trip to Reed's Indoor Range had been enough to convince everyone to keep him far away from anything resembling a gun. The Greek more than made up for his shortcomings as a marksman by building incredible tools, like the tactical display John was watching.

Mikey's bright yellow icon slid across the tactical display. It flew west from the roof of the Pauling Building, crossed above the trees and over Page Mill Road.

"Keep Mikey high, Ana," John said. "We don't want him hearing it." The likelihood of that happening was small, considering the noise cancellation system the Greek had built into the drone, but there was no point in taking chances.

Ana said nothing, but the tops of the bluish trees below the drone began to shrink. Then a yellow speck appeared in their midst.

John barked, "Stop! Zoom in."

A fuzzy yellow blob suddenly filled the screen. The thermal imager auto-focused. The blob became the outline of a man walking slowly through the trees, as seen from almost directly overhead. He wore a cap with a long brim that hid his face. The glowing object in his hands was unambiguously a rifle. It had an oddly shaped grip and stock as well as a monstrous telescopic sight.

"Fuckin' A," said Alex. "That's a Savage 110BA, sure as shit. Guy Harris has one. Shoots .300 Winchester or .338 Lapua. Bolt action, very accurate."

John's felt a familiar tightness in his chest and balls. "Ana. Silent lockdown, right now."

Ana lifted the yellow-and-black striped cover on a button on the console above her keyboard. She pressed it. The room lights turned red. John's smart watch tapped a drumbeat on his wrist. Everyone else on duty would be receiving the same silent alert. On the screens above, the patrol officers moved to cover without appearing to hurry.

"That's a big goddamn gun to hump through the woods at night, boss," said Alex. "A pro would keep it in a case until he found his shooting position. It's got a bipod mount, and it needs it. And what the hell is he doing down in those trees? He'd have to be on the hilltop to hit anyone but a reporter or a guard on the perimeter. The fence is mostly finished along Page Mill. This guy's an amateur."

John turned to his partner. "I think you're right. That makes him even more dangerous." A pro would know when to give up. An amateur might not. "Get Cord, and tell him to bring one more guy. Then call Diego. We're gonna need four e-bikes out back, ASAP."

"Roger that, Gunny," said Alex, and disappeared.

Ana said, "All posts report lockdown secure."

"Anyone out in the RVs?"

"No sir. The scientists are still in the lab."

"Good."

"The campers aren't visible from those trees, sir," said the junior operator, whose name chose that instant to pop into John's head. *Leo Patrusky*.

"That's true, Patrusky, but I'm still glad they're inside the building."

Ana said, "Laurel Wynn's coming down here."

John glanced at a display that showed the lab's floor plan. Glowing dots with tiny labels showed the active proof-of-life badges. Most of them were in the Black Box or Santa's Workshop. One of them was on the move.

"We don't have time to wait. She can watch from here."

"Should I call the police?"

"We *are* the police, remember?" John touched his badge. "I don't want PAPD coming in here running sirens and lights, scaring this guy off. We'll try to take him in and find out who sent him. Then we'll call the city cops." If the same bastards who killed Emily and Jason were behind this new threat, he was damned if he was going to pass up the opportunity to find out.

He left the office on the run.

He met Alex and Armando Diego by the secure loading dock at the rear of the building. Diego was on sentry duty at the turnstile gate and wasn't dressed for a night op. He had already rolled two of the big Lightning LS218 electric motorcycles out of their shed next to the trees. He and Alex hustled back to get the other two.

Their sleek frames and aerodynamic fairings were coated with charcoal-colored paint, courtesy of the Greek. They called it infra-gray in honor of its heat-absorbing properties. Even the chrome had somehow been tinted infra-gray. The Greek tried infra-black first, but it turned out to be easier to see in night-vision goggles. It absorbed too much heat, leaving a silhouette. Black stood out against nighttime backgrounds to the naked eye, too. Everyone had been disappointed. Black was a lot sexier.

John looked up at the sky. "Perfect," he whispered. It was a warm night, clear, breezy, and moonless. There was no marine cloud layer to provide the bad guy with reflected orange city light.

He removed a balaclava from a pocket in his too-tight jacket and pulled it down over his face. Then he put on a pair of gray Nomex gloves with leather padding on the palms.

Cord Walker and Alex's buddy Sy Hamilton emerged from the building on the run, fastening their body armor as they went. Cord's ebony skin made him nearly invisible inside his dark gray armor. Diego and Alex wheeled the last two e-bikes up. Diego ran back to the building. Alex moved to John's side.

"What's the plan, Gunny?" said Cord. "Alex filled us in."

"We'll leave by the north gate. You and Sy loop around on Arastradero and come up Page Mill from the south. Turn off at Old Page Mill Road and dismount before you get to the trees. Alex and I will come in on Old Page Mill from the north. We'll surround him in the trees and arrest him there. Hopefully."

Cord said, "We're gonna roll up on him just with hand guns?"

John considered it for an instant. "Four-to-one odds, Superman vision and the best body armor in the world? I think we can handle it."

Diego returned with four heavily padded gray tactical helmets with curved face visors. They provided no protection against neck trauma, but no bullet short of a .50 cal would do much against the FQG material of the helmet or the visor. It would still feel like getting hit in the head with a baseball bat. You might wind up with a concussion, but at least your head wouldn't pop like a water balloon if you did catch a round. And they'd all taken live shots against their Elf-made body armor during practice. It was like getting thumped by the end of a two-by-four, but the force was so well distributed by the exotic materials it didn't even leave a bruise.

John said, "I'll do the talking. Keep an eye on your tac map and keep good crossfire discipline. Mount up."

They switched on the electronics in their helmets, strapped them on and mounted their bikes. They powered them up and made sure all lights were off. Then they all flipped the switches that disabled the high-pitched pedestrian alert sound circuits.

A section of the inside of John's visor lit up. The tac display showed the locations of the other members of his team on a schematic map of the area. It also showed the roads and an elevation map of the terrain. It would zoom in and out as distance between the team members changed. The dim red color wouldn't wreck their night vision, and some of Santa's magic made the tac display invisible from the other side of the visor.

"God bless the Greek," John heard Alex murmur over the intercom.

"Roger that," John said. Then: "Ana, comm check."

"Loud and clear, boss. How do you read?"

"Five by five. Give us the target's location." A pulsing red dot appeared in the visor's tac map. The intruder hadn't moved. "Perfect. Let's roll." He leaned forward to grab the handlebars and grimaced. *Twice a day in the gym till this fucking jacket fits right,* he told himself.

The men at the north gate lowered the newly installed vehicle barrier to let John and his team roll through. The only sounds the bikes made were nearly inaudible electric whines. The supple rubber tires were effectively silent.

John led them in a right turn onto Coyote Hill Road, away from Page Mill and the grove that concealed their quarry. The street was still empty. When they reached Hillview Avenue, John and Alex turned left. Cord and Sy turned right and vanished into the night.

With a hill between them and the grove where the tango lurked with his rifle, John switched on his headlights. Alex did the same an instant later. They swooped down the hill to Foothill Expressway. Seeing no one, they turned left and powered through the red signal light without slowing down. They did the same thing at the intersection with Page

Mill, but had to swerve to avoid a truck. They switched off their lights as they approached their turnoff.

John angled his bike through the tiny entrance to the narrow lane of Old Page Mill Road, ignoring the "WRONG WAY" sign. Alex was close behind him. There were no streetlights to guide them.

John tapped a button on the left side of his helmet. His visor's heads-up display switched to an "augmented reality" 3D view of the landscape created by the thermal/night-vision cameras on either side of his helmet. The dim red image was infinitely better than the bulky infrared goggles he'd used in combat, and preserved his night vision, to boot. The original tactical overhead view shrank to a small square in the right corner of the visor.

John steered the e-bike down the dark, narrow lane, keeping an eye on the tac display. When they were about fifty meters from the tango's position, he said in a low voice, "Pull off here, Alex." He rolled onto the narrow grassy shoulder and dismounted. The ground was firm and dry. He eased the bike onto the heavy-duty kickstand. Alex followed suit.

The grove concealing their target was just ahead.

John watched the tac display. He waited until the square icons that marked Cord Walker and Sy Hamilton stopped moving on the far side of the grove. The icons changed to arrowheads, indicating that the men had switched their visors to night-vision mode.

"We're ready, John," came Cord's murmur in John's ear.

Alex added, "Loaded for Boo-Boo, Gunny."

John growled, "Secure that shit, Alex. Not the time for jokes. Okay. Move in."

They moved.

John followed the road toward the grove, Alex at his heels. A steady breeze riffled the leaves in the trees overhead. He smiled grimly. The tango would be unlikely to hear them approach over that sound. Even with the sensitive stereo microphones in his helmet, John couldn't hear his own footfalls, much less Alex's. His team could talk in low voices over the intercom, which was easier and faster than using hand signals. He reminded himself for the thousandth time not to whisper. The sibilant hiss of a whisper carried further than low-volume speech. Resisting the urge was still difficult even after more night ops than he cared to remember.

They picked their way through the gravel scattered across the left edge of the road. They stopped short of the next obstacle: a wire fence that came up to the middle of John's chest. A single strand of barbed wire ran across the top of the loose wire grid. It was bound to the metal fence posts with rusty clips, so electrification wouldn't be an issue. It would be impossible to cut or climb it without making noise, but they were still more than thirty meters from the target.

John examined the wire. It was old but still looked strong enough to bear his weight. He said softly, "Ana, be ready to drop a flash-bang on the tango if he runs."

"Roger that, sir."

He looked for a clearing on the far side of the fence. Spotting a grassy area that was relatively free of twigs and other debris, he moved toward it, took a knee and gestured for Alex to climb over.

Alex didn't hesitate. He put a heavy, booted foot on John's armored thigh and pushed himself over the fence in a forward somersault that ended with him landing in a crouch. Leaves crunched but there was no other sound. John studied the tac display. Their target had not moved.

John muttered, "Good job, Alex." *Goddamn show off.* "I'm going to have to climb over. I think we should only risk this once. Cord, you and Sy take backup positions on the road. Ana, time for the crickets."

A pair of quiet *"Yes, sirs"* sounded in his earphones.

John waited for Ana to move Mikey upwind to deploy the "crickets." Another gift from the Greek, they were tiny noisemakers with remote control circuits. The Greek had crafted them into tiny winged plastic darts that could be dropped from a drone onto an unsuspecting target. The curved wings stabilized the darts as they spun down, and kept their airspeed to a gentle five miles per hour. Mikey would be shining an infrared designator on the target. The crickets were smart enough to veer away from it so they didn't drop onto the enemy's head. In the dark, with this breeze, the tango would never sense them until they went off.

"They're on the ground, sir," Ana said a minute later. "The tango still hasn't moved. FYI, Mikey has about ten minutes left in the air. I'll launch Norbert in five."

John put his right boot into a gap in the wire fence. He tested it with his weight. It held, but it began to creak when he put more weight on it. He eased off. "Give me a countdown and let her rip in five seconds."

"Roger. Five..."

Alex moved closer to lend a hand.

"...four..."

John grabbed the wire atop the fence, positioned his hands between the closely spaced barbs, and waited.

"...three...two...one...mark!"

They could hear the fusillade of cricket sounds even from this distance. A youthful male voice yelped, "What the fuck!"

John scaled the fence as quickly and quietly as he could. It squealed in protest when it took his considerable weight, but it held. Alex grabbed the fence and steadied it while John lowered himself to the ground. He pulled his boot from the wire mesh just as the crickets began to slow down, their chirps becoming softer and more regular, in imitation of real insects.

John squeezed Alex's shoulder and gave him a thumbs-up. He stared at the tac display in his visor. The tango jittered but hadn't moved far from his original spot.

"He moved about five feet," Ana said in John's earphones. "But he's still in the grove. He's looking around for the crickets. Uh oh. He has night-vision goggles, sir. I couldn't see them before because of his hat."

Dammit. "Okay, Ana," he murmured. "We need to get a little closer. See if you can draw his attention away from us. We're going silent. Alex. Pistol." He sure as hell wasn't going up against someone carrying a big game rifle with a Taser. If the tango was wearing body armor and the tips didn't penetrate it, they'd be sitting ducks.

He and Alex drew their weapons and moved quickly but quietly toward the grove. The trees thickened up ahead. The sound of crickets surged again and grew louder as they approached the target's location. Alex moved away to the left.

Finally, John could see their target in his augmented-reality visor: a man with a medium build, wearing a dark jacket, a baseball cap, and cradling a rifle in his arms. He was about thirty feet away, facing the other direction, evidently straining to find the source of the noise.

John checked the tac display. Alex was about twenty feet from the tango on the left. Cord and Sy were still on the road, covering their quarry's escape route in that direction. They were arranged in a ragged line. No one was in anyone else's field of fire, just as he'd directed.

He considered the tactical situation. The ground cover here was thick with branches. It was a miracle they'd gotten so close without the tango hearing them, but getting any closer without alerting him would be impossible. Not even the crickets turned up to eleven would be enough.

If the shooter was a pro, he'd probably give up immediately. If he was an amateur, God only knew what his reaction would be. He might turn and shoot. He'd have enough time to do it, if he didn't take too much time to aim. Taking a .338 Lapua round, even with their exotic body armor, would be like getting kicked by a mule. Getting nailed in the helmet could cause permanent damage, or even death.

Damn it all, thought John. He couldn't afford to take a chance, no matter how much he wanted to interrogate this guy.

He raised his pistol, thumbed the safety off, and pointed it at the tango, who still hadn't turned.

He roared, "Sheriff's Department! Freeze!"

The tango's head snapped around. His body swiveled, and he began to raise the rifle.

"Drop it!" shouted Alex. "You're surrounded!"

The man quickly swung the rifle toward Alex.

John screamed, "Drop it or we will shoot you!"

The rifle came up to the man's shoulder.

John and Alex fired simultaneously.

The tango jerked as the bullets struck him. He reeled backward. He fired the rifle. The sound was like a thunderclap compared to their pistols. The shot went high. He dropped his gun, teetered, and fell onto his back.

John and Alex converged on the gasping man. His hat and night vision goggles had fallen off. He'd have been handsome if his face weren't twisted in agony. He couldn't have been more than twenty-five years old.

Alex kicked the rifle away from the fallen man's outstretched hand. He said, "tango is down, repeat, tango is down!"

Cord Walker and Sy Hamilton came crashing through the trees, guns drawn.

John safetied and holstered his .45. He knelt next to the man and unzipped the heavy leather jacket. Underneath it, the man wore a light-colored shirt and nothing else. A dark stain centered on the man's breastbone spread rapidly across the expanse of pale fabric.

John snarled, "Son of a bitch. No vest. Ana! Call PAPD and an ambulance! Now!"

"Yes, sir!"

He pressed hard on the man's chest to try to staunch the flow of blood. "Who sent you, you stupid bastard?" he said. "Who are you?"

The man smiled, grunted, then coughed. He tried to breathe. His eyes widened with panic. His chest heaved once, twice. Blood gushed from his mouth. Then he went very still.

John tore off his blood-soaked gloves and checked for a pulse. There wasn't one. "God *damn* you!" he screamed into the tango's face. "What is this, some kind of sick fucking *joke*?"

He sat down heavily a few feet away from the dead man and heaved a sigh.

Sirens began to wail in the distance. There were shouts from the direction of the TV vans parked across the road from the campus.

Alex edged close to him. "Gunny? Are you okay?"

"No, I am *not* okay! I want people to stop dying around here! For Christ's sakes, look at him. He's just a kid." His voice cracked on the last word.

The four ex-soldiers waited in silence until the cops arrived.

CHAPTER TWENTY

StruvePharma Coyote Hill Campus, Palo Alto, California

August 8

Peter Struve said, "Christ, I need a vacation."

Laurel looked at the CEO closely. The LED lighting in Struve's large, windowless office wasn't flattering to begin with, but he looked like he'd aged five years in the last week. He wore his customary black suit, white shirt and tie, but his suit coat was creased, his shirt was rumpled, and his tie was decorated with a tiny blob of dried ketchup. She wondered when he'd last had it cleaned. Lunchtime was still two hours away.

The other SP executives sitting around the conference table looked as exhausted as Struve. Jay Kapoor, the CFO, slouched in his chair, staring at the tabletop. The chief counsel, Ramona Ochoa, leaned forward with her elbows on the table, her hands propping up her head. She'd figured out how to conceal the bags under her eyes, but they were still red-rimmed with fatigue. Barb Johnson, the VP of PR, looked calm enough, but one of her cheeks had developed a nervous twitch. She squinted in a vain effort to control it.

Even Jack Dura looked worn out. Like Laurel, he wore a gray worker-bee jumpsuit. He sat with one leg draped over the arm of his chair, but his heart didn't seem to be in his studied insolence today. His arms were crossed over his chest, and his lips were drawn downward. The perpetual stubble of his beard seemed a bit grayer.

John Shea was conspicuous by his absence.

Laurel had watched the events from the surveillance office. John had taken the shooting hard. Alex Southall had seemed as calm as a cup of water, but it might have been macho SEAL bravado. She didn't know him well enough to be able to tell the difference. Struve had ordered them to go home after the police interviews were finished. He'd sent veterans from the security team to keep them company.

The only person in the room who didn't look defeated was Aidan O'Keefe. The sandy-haired CTO was as dapper and imperturbable as always. Laurel's eyes fixed on his uneven glasses. *He's wearing a $10,000 gold smart watch. Why can't he afford glasses that fit right?* Then she finally realized why they looked off-center: one of his eyes was higher than the other.

O'Keefe said, "You *should* take a few days off, Peter. Spend some time at the beach house. We'll keep an eye on things for you."

Struve shook his head. "No. I'll take a nap later." He gestured at Laurel. "Go ahead, Agent Wynn."

She cleared her throat and looked at her spiral-bound notepad. "His name was Ivo Maskowicz," she said, struggling with the unfamiliar pronunciation. "Born in Pittsburgh. Moved to New York City when he was three years old, lived there ever since. Father was a surgeon; mother was a socialite. He got involved in the Green movement when he was in junior high. He joined Greenpeace and worked for PETA when he was in college. He was kicked out of both groups because he was too radical."

O'Keefe snorted, "Too radical for PETA? Is that even possible?"

"Apparently. He was arrested when he was twenty-three for breaking into a cancer research lab at Columbia University. He let a bunch of rats loose and ruined a major study. His parents got him released, but he did the same thing at SUNY Stonybrook a month later. This time he spent a year in jail. When he got out, he broke parole and disappeared. There were some rumors that he was involved with an ultra-radical eco-terrorist group in Oregon, but he managed to avoid capture. Until last night."

"Capture?" Jack said. "Is that what you call it?"

"You saw the video," she said coldly. "They gave him every chance to give up."

Struve snapped, "Do we really need to argue about this? What's done is done. What do the police say, Agent Wynn?"

"Allie Vieira says we don't have anything to worry about. It was a righteous shoot. We had it on two helmet cams and the thermal imaging feed from the drone, complete with audio."

"Thank God for Stathis Sotiropoulos," said Ramona Ochoa. "Peter, we should give him a raise."

"I agree," said Barb Johnson. "Who knows what would have happened if we didn't have that footage to show the police—or the press, for that matter." She sighed. "We're back to square one with the networks. They're still trying to decide whether to make us out to be heroes or villains. And there are more vans out there than ever. We've got to hold a press conference, Peter. We've got to take control of the narrative before it blows up in our faces."

Struve nodded distractedly. "What the hell was this kid planning? Was he going to shoot one of the scientists? Was he the one who shot those people at the hospital?"

Laurel shook her head. "No. He doesn't match the video images we have of the hospital killer. He was way too tall. Allie Vieira called me a little while ago. Maskowicz had the key to a room at a fleabag in Redwood City. He checked in five days ago. He didn't leave a note, but there weren't any other guns on him or in his room. He couldn't even have seen the Pauling Building from those trees, but the south entrance to the campus was right across the road. If we hadn't spotted him, he could've found a good shooting position and waited there all night. He might have decided to take someone out as they drove into the office. He might have been targeting an executive, Peter. Maybe even you."

Struve's face turned white. "Why in God's name would he want to kill me?"

O'Keefe leaned forward. "Haven't you been watching the news? Every Green from San Francisco to Seattle wants your head on a spike. Peter. You demonstrated an oil synthesizer on TV. An *oil synthesizer*."

"Why? It's carbon-neutral!" Struve roared. "It takes carbon dioxide *out* of the atmosphere! And it was just a demo! We could make hydrogen fuel just as easily! Why me, anyway? I didn't invent the damned thing, you and Emily did!"

Laurel interjected, "Maskowicz was unbalanced. You shouldn't assume that every environmentalist is out to get you."

O'Keefe turned his lopsided gaze on her. "Don't be too sure of that. The surest way to make a Green go up in smoke is to use the word 'chemical.' And your demo on CNBC was all about chemistry, Peter. I wish to God you had let me go with you. I know how to talk to these cretins. They don't even know that they're made out of chemicals *themselves*. You have to speak in soothing tones and use a lot of little words or they bring out the torches and pitchforks."

Barb Johnson said, "That's enough, Aidan!"

O'Keefe glared at Johnson for a moment, then settled back into his chair. "As you like. It doesn't change reality. If you haven't been following the media on this, you're in for a shock. The eco-freaks want Peter's head. That is a fact. It might be a *stupid* fact, but it's still a fact. And so do the presidents of every petroleum company in the world. Brent crude oil futures are down $25 a barrel since the demo. The Dow is down nearly five thousand points."

"What the hell is wrong with everybody?" snarled Struve. "Nothing is in production. It'll be years before we can commercialize any of these inventions."

O'Keefe said, "You publicly cut the legs out from under a dozen industries on cable TV last week, Peter. It doesn't matter that it will take years. Everyone knows that it's *going* to happen. No one wants to be the last one holding the bag. And every country that depends on oil as its primary source of income is buying guns. Who's going to buy it from them when you can make it in the comfort of your own home?"

Struve made a disgusted sound. "Christ. Does anyone still think I spent too much on security?"

Jack Dura stood abruptly and went to the door. "I don't have time for this navel-gazing bullshit. I've got work to do."

"Jack!" called Struve, but it was too late. The door swung shut behind him.

Struve sighed and looked at Laurel. "Anything else?"

She shook her head. "I'd recommend switching to buses to get people in and out of the campus. All of the tech companies around here use them, so they'll blend in on the roads. We can use some of your magic window spray on them to make them safer."

"Fine. And?"

"The fence and the vehicle barrier at the south gate should be finished at the end of the week. We'll be able to bring most of the security team inside the walls. The TV crews won't be able to see anything anymore."

"Good." Struve scribbled notes on a small spiral-bound notebook. "Are you finished?"

"Yes."

Struve looked at Aidan O'Keefe. "I was going to ask Jack how things were going in the lab. Do you know? I hardly ever see you down there."

O'Keefe frowned. "You might have noticed that Jack and I aren't exactly close."

Struve's face turned red. "Do you have a report, or don't you?" he grated.

O'Keefe's eyebrows rose. "The newbies are still learning the ropes. They haven't made any breakthrough discoveries yet. Every time I ask Jack if he's figured out Emily's mistake, he says, 'When I know, I'll tell you.' I think he's brushing me off. I'm not sure he really knows where we went wrong with the QUBE design. It might take him a year to figure it out."

Jay Kapoor cleared his throat. "We don't have a year. Even with ZMPC's funding, we're spending at an alarming rate, and now that Ramona's little army of intellectual property lawyers are negotiating with the Patent Office, it's getting worse. Let me show you these figures—"

Laurel pushed her chair back. "If you don't mind, I have some other things I need to do, too."

"Fine," Struve said in a flat voice. "Go on, Jay. Your turn to fuck my day up beyond all recognition."

She left, closing the door softly behind her. She turned to go to the elevator.

Jack Dura said, "I was hoping you'd come out soon."

She jumped.

He was slouched against the wall behind her, his arms and legs crossed.

"You don't want to startle me," she snapped. "You might not like what happens."

"You have better control than that. I've seen you in the gym. You're pretty good at that Crab McCoy stuff."

"Krav Maga," she corrected him, nettled. "Did you have something to say, or did you just want to piss me off?"

"You look like you could use some coffee."

She rubbed her eyes. She'd gotten a grand total of three hours of sleep, and was in no mood for Jack Dura today. "Can't this wait?"

"No. Sorry."

She sighed. "Fine."

He led the way to the closest mini kitchen. Unsurprisingly, they were the only ones there. Only a few of the offices and labs on the fourth floor were occupied.

Jack grabbed a Coke from the deli case while she waited for the pre-fab coffee maker. He took one of two swiveling chairs in the far corner of the sunny lounge.

The coffee machine beeped. She grabbed the brimming paper cup, carefully snapped a lid onto it, and joined him.

"The kids are scared," he said without preamble. "Frankly, I am too."

She studied his stubbly face. None of his usual arrogance was in evidence. She said, "It's a scary situation."

"Are there other nut jobs with guns after us?"

She considered how to answer him.

Jack sat back in his chair and popped the top of his Coke can. "That bad, huh?" He took a noisy sip.

"It's not good," she hedged. It was a lot worse than *not good.* Robbie Holmes had complained to her yesterday about the volume of death threats the local field offices were investigating, and that was before Ivo Maskowicz embarked on his ill-fated nighttime hike.

"Let me guess," he said, smiling wryly. "You're trying to figure out how much you can tell me without scaring me and my students off for good, am I right?"

She took a sip of her coffee.

Jack sighed. "Maybe Peter doesn't watch TV, but I do. Internet access in the RVs, remember?"

"I didn't think you went there to do anything but sleep for a couple of hours a night."

"Ha. I wish. Sometimes I can't sleep at all. When I can't, I fire up the iPad and check the news. I guess I've become a kind of celebrity. I'm learning all kinds of things I didn't know about myself." He smirked. "Apparently I had an affair with some trashy singer I've never even heard of. I wish I could remember that. She's built like a brick laboratory."

She smiled briefly.

His grin faded. He leaned forward again. "Look, Agent Wynn—"

"You can call me Laurel."

"All right. Laurel. None of us are planning to leave. We're on the verge of something so big I can't even describe it to you."

"You've been saying that for a while."

"It's the truth."

"Aidan thinks you're blowing smoke because you don't know how to fix Emily's mistake, whatever that was."

"Fuck Aidan. I solved *that* problem before I first put on this lovely jumpsuit. I haven't told him because he's an evil schmuck. Trust me.

I'm way beyond that now. *Way* beyond. You couldn't pry me loose with a crowbar. That goes for my team, too. Level with me. What's going on out there? What do you know about who killed Emily and all those people at the hospital? Who's out to get us?"

She shifted uncomfortably in her chair. "Why don't you ask John Shea?"

"He's not here. You are. And he's a company man. I like him, but he'll tell me whatever Struve tells him to say."

"If you can say that with a straight face, you don't know him at all."

"Maybe so, but he's still not here."

"So why trust me? I work for *Big Gubmint*, as you put it so kindly on my first day here." *And you really don't know* me, *either.*

He had the grace to look ashamed. "Yeah, well. Sorry about that. Being an asshole is a hard habit to break." He took another sip of his Coke. "I guess it boils down to this: You seem like you're on the level. John and his team think the world of you, and those guys are salt-of-the-earth types. And... I like you."

Laurel considered her response. She didn't like him. He seemed like a typical entitled techno-geek, with a silver spoon thrust into his mouth by virtue of his special knowledge. She knew better than to fall for his flattery, but Andrew Seigart had told her to try to get his confidence, and he'd just served up the opportunity on a golden platter.

He sighed. "Look, Laurel. I'm sorry I was a gaping sphincter the first day I met you. I was really nervous. I know I can come on pretty strong. Can we let that go for now? This is important."

"I'm listening." He even seemed earnest, for a change.

His voice dropped to a murmur. "If this discovery turns out to be what I think it is, it's way more than SP can handle by itself. Struve's going to want to own it, but he can barely control things around here as it is. Did you see them in there? They look like they're on the verge of a nervous breakdown. Except Aidan O'Keefe, of course."

"Why 'of course'?" she said.

He stared at her. "Because he's a grade-A psychopath. Am I the only one who notices this? Nothing *ever* gets to him. He's a robot."

"Ah."

"I'm serious. He's bad news. He was smiling after I popped him in the mouth, for Christ's sakes."

"Okay."

He frowned. "I know you think I hate him because he took Emily away from me. He gave me the heebie-jeebies from the day I met him. She hadn't even joined the faculty yet. Do me a favor? Humor me. Keep an eye on him."

"All right, Jack. I will. I promise. So, you trust me. Thanks. Why should I trust you? How do I know you aren't blowing smoke?"

His smile returned. "I wondered when you'd ask that. I show you mine, and you show me yours. Agreed?" He held out his hand.

She shook it. "If I'm convinced."

"You will be. Come on. Let's go talk with the kiddies. No drinks allowed in the lab." He drained his Coke and tossed it in the recycling bin.

She took a long sip of her coffee before chucking it in the trash. She followed him to the elevator, walking past Struve's office. She could hear shouting through the door. Jack pointed at it in passing and raised his hands with open palms as if to say, *see what I mean?*

Laurel glanced sidelong into Janice Feldman's office as she walked by. Struve's executive assistant was on the phone, but her eyes followed Laurel as she passed.

They waited in silence for the elevator to arrive. When the doors closed behind them, she said, "You know I'm going to have to brief my boss on all of this."

"I know," he said. He punched the button for the second floor.

"So why are you telling me?"

He looked at her. "I'm no fan of Big Gubmint, but I don't see any alternative. Believe me, I've been trying to think of one for weeks. This discovery is too big to leave in the hands of a single company. It will change everything. And it's not like we can just take over the building and stage a sit-in. This isn't Stanford. John Shea would just pepper-spray us and haul our asses off to jail. We need to be here to make sure the right things are done with this technology. Telling you is the least-worst alternative, Laurel. And frankly, if I don't tell someone, my brain is going to pop."

"Your team doesn't know yet?"

"They're about to. And so are you. Welcome to the soon-to-be inner circle."

In spite of her mixed feelings about Jack, goose flesh rose on her arms. She rubbed the evidence of her excitement away.

The elevator door opened and they walked into the hallway.

He moved close to her. "I need you to do something."

She resisted the urge to back away. "What?"

He leaned close to her ear and whispered, "I need you to shut off the surveillance in the Black Box."

Now she did back away. "Why?"

"I know that Struve captures everything in there on video and audio," he said, still whispering. "I need this conversation to be off the record. I need to be able to talk openly with my people and with you. And I need to make sure that fucker Aidan O'Keefe doesn't learn about it. I don't trust him as far as I could throw a hippo. I don't want him seeing the math. You can judge whether you need to tell Struve about it afterward, but I ask you not to unless there's a really good reason. Believe me, this is some serious shit."

She stared at him. "This verges on paranoid, Jack."

He shrugged. "This place inspires paranoia. Are you in? If you say no, I'll just work around you. I don't want to do that."

She thought about it. She had super-user privileges on *Argus*, SP's in-house security system. She'd needed them to carry out the audit she and Eileen Dupree of the Computer Forensic Laboratory had done after the break in and murders. Andrew Seigart had seen to it that she kept those privileges.

Argus was remarkably well-designed. Coverage of the Black Box in particular had been extraordinary. There were forty cameras and as many audio pickups distributed throughout the lab. Virtually every square inch of it could be seen. It would be impossible to have a truly private conversation there as long as *Argus* was watching.

She looked at Jack. She was surprised to notice that he was several inches shorter than she was, and she was wearing company-issue flats today. He seemed taller from a distance. She said, "Aidan will find out about it. He wrote a lot of that software."

"I don't care if he knows we talked. I don't want him knowing what we talked about."

She threw her hands up in the air. "Can't you just take everyone outside?"

"Getting them all outside might be a little tricky, with eco-snipers in the trees. Anyway, there's something I can't take from the lab that I have to show everyone, and I need a whiteboard. Don't worry. It's not like Peter can fire us. You don't even work for him."

She sighed heavily.

"Laurel. Please. Trust has to start somewhere."

She thought about it. If Struve had a fit over the missing surveillance video, she would just wheel in the artillery piece labeled *Andrew Seigart*. "Okay. Let's go."

His eyes widened in surprise. "Don't you have to sneak in to the security office or something?"

She couldn't suppress a snort of laughter. "No. All I need is a terminal. You watch too many movies, Jack."

"I guess."

She followed him to the Black Box. He and his team had appropriated Emily's former laboratory. Jack wouldn't allow anyone but his students in until they learned everything they could about SP's technology by themselves. He said he didn't want them to take on the same preconceived notions about the limits and capabilities of Emily's work that the existing employees shared.

Laurel was surprised to see Ben Holcombe and Deepthi Damodaran huddled together at one of the lab benches, staring down at a circuit board in evident puzzlement. She looked askance at Jack.

"They're good," he said. "They ask the right kinds of questions. They might work for ZMPC, but their hearts are in the right places, and they've got top-rate minds." He lowered his voice to a whisper. "Do you know something about them that I don't?"

"No," Laurel said quickly. "As far as we can tell, they're just who they seem to be."

"Good," Jack said, looking relieved. "Okay, please turn off the cameras now."

Laurel found a free Linux workstation at a lab bench near the door. She took a seat and logged in. She brought up a web browser and a terminal window.

The many days she'd spent with SP's Network and Computing Services group paid off. She used a web browser to login to the NCS monitoring server. It ran an off-the-shelf alerting system called Nagios. Laurel had used it before, and had even set it up once on an FBI web server at her own office in Alexandria, Virginia.

She used her super-user privileges to put the alerts for the *Argus* security servers into maintenance mode. As soon as she disabled the cameras in the Black Box, *Argus* would start throwing errors like mad, but the Nagios software would ignore them until she returned the servers to "production" mode. Then she fired up the *Argus* command line tool, typed in her sixteen-character password, and typed a few commands.

She looked up at the mirrored camera domes on the high ceiling, and tapped the RETURN key. The tiny red LEDs mounted at the bases of the domes winked off. She typed a few more commands that told *Argus* to send her a direct notification if anyone turned the cameras back on.

"That's it," she said to Jack.

"Good work. How will we know if they switch the cameras back on?"

She brandished her iPhone. "I'll know."

Jack smiled. "Perfect. Hey, how come you get to keep your cell phone and I have to lock mine up every morning? And how do you get calls in here, anyway? I thought this building was one big Faraday cage."

"Privileges of being on the security team," she said. She breathed on her fingernails and polished them on her sleeve. "There's a private cell phone repeater system in the building. You have to know the right people to get an account. Which I do."

"Nice. Hey, everyone! Gather round."

Jack's students and the two ZMPC engineers drifted together to form a semi-circle around Jack and Laurel. She studied their faces. All of them seemed fresh and alert in spite of the crazy hours they'd been putting in—a stark contrast to the obvious bone-weariness of the veteran SP employees. Then again, the newcomers had only been here for a few weeks. The old-timers had been grinding away at it for years.

She smiled a bit when she saw Terry Blau's outfit. The rotund, bearded scientist was wearing suspenders over his gray jumpsuit and a Greek fisherman's hat on his head. She wondered how he'd talked those past security.

"I want to welcome George R. R. Martin to our gathering today," intoned Jack, to gales of laughter from everyone but Laurel, who missed the reference.

Terry bowed from the waist.

"And I want to welcome Laurel Wynn here as well. You might be wondering why I've asked her to be here. Well, it's pretty simple. We needed her to disable the surveillance system."

Their cheeriness faded. They all looked up at the cameras.

"What's going on, Jack?" said Ben Holcombe.

"We might not have a lot of time, so I'll make this quick. Roll that whiteboard over here, would you, Hank?"

The gangly Southerner obliged.

Jack grabbed the eraser.

"Wait, wait!" yelped Xu Chao-Xing. "I need to write that down!"

Jack glanced at the board's contents. "Uh, no, you don't. Believe me." He erased it.

Chao-Xing said, "Hey! I was working on that for six hours!"

"Sorry. It's not going to matter in a few minutes anyway. Okay, everyone. You've read Emily's papers. You've been boning up on quantum theory and genetic algorithms and E++ programming for weeks now. You're starting to beat your heads against the wall because you're just as stymied as the Elves as to why QUBE Charlie worked so well. Right?"

There were nods and grunts of assent.

"Then watch this." He turned and began to scribble equations on the whiteboard as fast as he could.

Even if Jack's handwriting had been legible, the terms and symbols he used were wholly unfamiliar to Laurel. Her last math class had been second-semester calculus at the University of Florida. Her instructor was a graduate student who didn't much like teaching undergrads. Especially female undergrads. She'd scraped through with a C-. That horrid class had caused her to switch majors from computer science to criminology, and it had nearly cost her the *summa cum laude*.

The equations clearly meant something to the others in the room. Terry Blau said, "Yes, yes," at intervals. Ben Holcombe interrupted with questions about the symbols from time to time, and Jack redrew them so they were clearer.

The only one who looked as puzzled as Laurel was Deepthi Damodaran. She stared at the board with furrowed eyebrows.

Laurel made her way over to stand next to the beautiful Indian woman. "What is all this?" she whispered.

"I've no idea," Deepthi whispered back. "I studied mechanical engineering. This is way beyond me."

Laurel sighed. She found a stool and sat down, checking the surveillance cameras from time to time. The RECORDING lights stayed off, and her cell phone remained silent.

About ten minutes after Jack started, Ben said, "Wait. That's not right."

"Yeah it is," said Jack without slowing down.

"No, it isn't. You transposed the terms."

Jack turned around and stared at Ben. "Just wait. You'll see."

Ben looked like he wanted to argue, but he subsided.

Jack turned back to the nearly full whiteboard and kept writing. He proceeded to fill it from edge to edge. The notation he used was completely alien to Laurel: a lot of vertical lines and "greater than" symbols with groups of up and down arrows between them. His letters grew smaller and fainter as they neared the corner of the board. He threw his fading dry erase marker to the floor and uncapped another one. He said, "I need another board."

Hank Drummond fetched another rolling whiteboard from the far corner of the lab and positioned it to the right of Jack's.

Jack drew a long arrow connecting the bottom right to the old board to the top left of the new one, then kept on scribbling equations. He added something that looked like an electrical circuit diagram.

Laurel looked up at the ceiling cameras. They were still off. She checked her watch. Jack had been writing steadily for twenty minutes now.

Terry Blau had been standing near the board the whole time. Now he edged even closer and peeked around Jack to see what he was writing. Suddenly he grabbed his hat and threw it to the floor. "No. Fucking. Way."

Jack turned around, a brilliant smile on his face. "Yes. Fucking. Way." He turned back to the board and kept writing.

Everyone crowded closer.

Lizbeth Okome-Taylor drew in a sudden, sharp breath. She put both hands to her mouth. She said, "I don't believe it!" Her eyes shone.

"I do," said Ben Holcombe. "Holy Mary, Mother of God. I do. Jack. Do you have the original schematics?"

"I thought you'd never ask." Jack charged over to his workstation and pulled a large rolled-up sheet of paper from a drawer. He unrolled it on the surface of the nearest workbench. His students held down the corners. He and Ben bent over the sheet, which was covered from edge to edge with circuit diagrams.

This was what he couldn't remove from the lab, Laurel realized. The QUBE schematics were the most closely guarded intellectual property SP had. They were also printed on a sheet of an incredibly tough substance that looked like paper but wasn't, and which had a tiny RFID tag embedded in it. Removing any documents printed on that "paper" would set off an alarm as soon as they came within range of the hallway sensor network.

"You see?" said Jack, pointing at something with the dry erase marker. "Here. And here. It's the same in every diagram."

"My God," Ben said. He stared at the schematics. "But how do the phase probes propagate across world lines? How the hell is this possible?"

"I don't know," said Jack. "I just don't know. It's a mystery. But everything works out in the end."

Ben's face broke out in an incredulous smile. "Aren't you supposed to say 'eureka' or something?"

"Eureka or something," said Jack.

Ben stretched his hand out across the schematics.

Jack shook it.

Then everyone was talking at once. Laughing. Cheering.

Laurel and Deepthi exchanged a bemused look.

"Hey!" Laurel said. "What the hell is this?"

"The answer," Jack said. His face bore a beatific smile. "But first I have to tell you about the question." He replaced the cap on the dry erase marker and placed it back in its tray. "A long time ago, a physicist named Hugh Everett had a brilliant idea. A brilliant, untestable idea—at least, untestable at the time."

Deepthi gasped, and her eyes grew large. "You mean—?"

Ben held a finger up to his lips. Deepthi closed her mouth, but now she was smiling too.

Laurel shouted, *"What?"*

Jack said, "Quantum physics is based on the notion that at the most fundamental level, everything is probabilistic. You might have heard of the Heisenberg uncertainty principle? You can't measure both the position and the velocity of a fundamental particle of matter like a photon or an electron to 100% precision. The act of observing it requires you to interfere with one or the other, because you can't observe it without bouncing a particle off it. And that changes the result."

"Hence the uncertainty," piped Hank Drummond.

Jack nodded. "The world of the very small is the world of the very strange. Matter is probability. Things are only where we think they are and doing what we think they're doing when we actually observe them.

Even then we can't be certain. Why does a particle choose to be in one place at one velocity and not another? Wheeler proposed that it doesn't. He said that every particle makes *every* possible choice."

Laurel felt the same defensive anger that she felt in her long-ago calculus class. She crossed her arms. "What the hell does that mean?"

"It's like Yogi Berra once said: *When you come to a fork in the road, take it.* Everett's idea was that every choice, every *possible* option at the quantum level is in fact taken. Our universe is just a particular cross-section of those alternatives. Everett's theory came to be called the Many-Worlds Interpretation. John Wheeler and Richard Feynman popularized it, and a lot of people have forgotten Everett even existed.

"It's been revised many times but it boils down to this: every quantum event represents an infinite number of universes in which every possible choice is realized. Microscopic events can have macroscopic consequences. There's a universe where I didn't cap that dry erase marker. There's a universe where I didn't get up in time to have breakfast. There's a universe where Emily didn't—" His voice cracked. He took a deep breath. "Where Emily didn't die. And there are infinitely more universes where the fundamental laws of physics are completely different.

"Our world, our history, is a line traced back through infinite possible variations, all the way back to the beginning of time itself. Think of that, Laurel. Infinity on infinity, forever and ever. Only we can't directly prove the existence of these parallel world lines." He paused. His smile returned. "Or at least, we *couldn't.*"

The hair on Laurel's neck began to rise. "You mean...?"

"Exactly. Now we can. Listen. Emily left me something: her private journal. I'm the only one who's read it. That's where I found the first hint of the solution."

"Holy cow," said Terry Blau. "Let *us* read it!"

Jack shook his head. "It's in my safe deposit box, and besides, it only hints at the answer. Emily knew something was different about QUBE Charlie, but she didn't know what. I looked at her math. I looked at the schematics. I looked at the server logs. I looked at everything. And I read her journal, again and again. Some of her equations were very subtly wrong. A couple of weeks ago, I figured out why. I'd been thinking on similar lines for a long time, but from a different perspective. That's what led me to her mistake.

"It was a fluke. There was an error in the system they used to manufacture the entanglotrons—the self-correcting interferometers that contain the quantum processors. She missed it. Everybody missed it. They didn't know that the entanglotrons weren't interferometers. They weren't built right. They were quantum rectifiers, for lack of a better word." He gestured at the whiteboard. "The math proves it."

"Rectifiers?" Laurel said blankly.

"Antennas. Trans-world-line antennas. Sort of." Jack threw his hands up in a gesture of disgust. "I don't have a good word for it yet." He turned to the whiteboard and began to erase it.

"Wait!" cried everyone but Laurel.

Jack kept erasing. "Who knows when they'll turn the cameras back on? This is our secret for now. We'll decide when and how much to tell Struve once we've gotten a chance to talk it out. But not here. Keep this under wraps. Don't write it down. Don't make notes about it on your computers. Anyone could log into them and then we'd be sunk. The implications are too big. We need to decide what to do."

"Antennas," repeated Laurel. "Antennas for what? Jack. What does it mean?"

The whiteboards were bare again. Jack put down the eraser. "Emily was a Copenhagenist. She didn't believe in the Many Worlds Interpretation." He shook his head and laughed. "We got into a few fights over it. She wasn't looking for it, so she didn't see it. Charlie behaved like a *classical* computer, but the entanglement wasn't between qubits inside the processor. It was happening between universes—across an *infinity* of parallel universes on an infinite number of parallel QUBEs."

"An infinity of parallel universes," she said numbly. "You're not talking about some abstract theory, are you? It's real. It's really *real*."

Jack nodded. "Up to now the only force that theorists believed might be able to cross world lines was gravity. Clearly that's not the case. I don't know how this parallel-universe entanglement works yet, but the math proves that it's real. The QUBEs just didn't have enough processing power to do what they were doing entirely in our local continuum."

"Holy Christ," said Terry. "You might have detected a new fundamental force of nature."

"Maybe. But it also means that we *can* build QUBE Delta. It will be better than Charlie. We should be able to extend it to perform classical computational operations. The giant server farm in the basement might be completely unnecessary. We might be able to make a portable QUBE. This will open up whole new areas of science that haven't even been conceived of yet."

The others, including Deepthi, looked like they'd been struck with hammers.

Laurel said, "This is a joke, right? Big joke on the only scientific illiterate in the room? Ha ha, very funny?"

"No," said Lizbeth. "If anything he's understating it. This might be the biggest thing since the theory of relativity."

The only sound was the low hum of machinery and ventilation fans.

"How did you do this, Jack?" asked Deepthi. "I thought you were a biophysicist."

"A little light on the *bio*, but very heavy on the *physicist*. Emily taught me what I didn't learn on my own. We worked out the theory that led to the QUBE together. I've been thinking about it ever since. That's why I noticed the problem. She must've kept up with my work. That's why she wanted me to come here, if anything happened to her."

"Jack," Laurel said, feeling very small. "Why did you ask *me* to see this? I'm not a scientist."

"Because I trust you. You don't have a dog in this hunt. You seem like you're on the level. And I'm going to need people I trust to help me decide what to do. Everyone I know I can trust is inside this room. Peter's an all-right guy, but he's never going to think of anything but the bottom line. Aidan O'Keefe is Satan incarnate. Laurel, if my math is right, if we can build this device, it could solve almost any conceivable problem in no time at all. It would be an infinite computer. We've got to make sure it doesn't wind up in the wrong hands. And I can't think of any hands wronger than Aidan's."

CHAPTER TWENTY-ONE

StruvePharma Coyote Hill Campus, Palo Alto, California

August 8

Aidan would've liked to have followed Laurel and Jack away from the endless executive meeting, but it wouldn't have been seemly. He was the CTO and Vice President of Operations, after all. He tried to focus on what was probably the thousandth wrangling argument over money. He knew every line of every participant by heart, though his heart wasn't in it, much less his head.

He played scenarios through his mind and let the increasingly angry argument drift away from his conscious awareness.

Tonight he would talk with one of Dalton's masters. It had all been arranged.

The go-between he'd met at Westfield Centre would have described Aidan to his superiors. They would certainly have identified him by now. They would believe that they had the advantage.

They would be right.

He would have to play his hand very carefully. Eric Dalton's masters had known about the oil synthesizer unit before it left the SP campus. They had told him when to expect it, and to let them know if it worked as advertised. Now, thanks to Peter Struve and his reckless TV appearance, the whole world knew about it. There was no question about its authenticity. That would strengthen Aidan's hand, but only a little.

The biggest problem was the elusive mole inside StruvePharma's walls. Eric Dalton hadn't known who it was. He would've confessed to killing Julius Caesar by the end. He'd been told when to expect the demo unit to arrive. The information had been correct almost to the hour. There *was* a mole. He or she would probably still be active—and telling Dalton's mysterious superiors things Aidan would not want them to know.

He would have to tread very lightly indeed.

Then he felt a subtle tap on his left wrist.

He glanced at his golden Apple Watch. It showed a notification from *dathan*—a monitoring system that kept tabs on every other monitoring system in the Coyote Hills research complex. He'd named it after the traitorous Hebrew overseer who'd betrayed Moses to Rameses in *The Ten Commandments.*

Aidan took a breath. It was the first time *dathan* had tried to get his attention for anything other than a test.

He'd designed the program to hide itself from all other security systems. Its network traffic was not logged by the routers. The custom kernels on all of the Linux servers would not show processes belonging to *dathan,* and would send an untraceable alert to him if anyone looked for them.

No one but Aidan, Peter, and Luke Tso, the head of Network and Computing Services, knew anything about *dathan*—and only Aidan would receive *this* kind of notification.

Someone had tried to disable the AV feeds in one of the labs.

Could it be the mole?

He stifled an urge to leap from his chair and run down the hall to his office. Instead, he cleared his throat.

Peter and Jay broke off their argument to look at him.

He tried to look embarrassed. "I'm sorry. I have to visit the... uh... I'll be back in a few minutes."

"Don't bother. We're done here," Peter snapped. He turned a gimlet eye on Jay. "No more arguments. Make it happen."

The aged CFO's face was ashen. He stood unsteadily. He looked like he was about to collapse. "This is a mistake."

"Noted." Peter frowned at everyone still seated at the table. "Get out. I have calls to make."

Aidan walked to the door and held it open for the others. They shuffled out. He cast a puzzled glance back at Peter.

The CEO had not moved from the conference table. "I'm done talking about it, Aidan," he said, his voice hoarse with emotion. "This is the only option left."

Mystified, Aidan nodded as if he understood. He followed the others into the hallway.

They were waiting for him.

As soon as the door closed, Jay said, "Do you agree with this?"

"I have to think about it," said Aidan, truthfully. *When I find out what it is.*

Jay's face fell. "I don't know what to say." He turned, opened the door to his office, and shuffled inside.

Before Barb Johnson and Ramona Ochoa could rope him into a discussion, Aidan said, "Excuse me, ladies. I really have to go." He quickly walked down the hall to the bathroom.

Fortunately, it was vacant. The fourth floor was mostly unoccupied. All of the action was in the second and third floor labs and workshops.

He retreated into the big stall reserved for disabled employees, closed the door behind him and took his iPhone from his sport coat's inner pocket. "Damn it," he whispered when he turned it on and saw the wallpaper pattern of his burner iPhone. He put it back and hunted for the real one, with the authorized copies of his office apps. He found it in the right outer pocket.

He turned it on, entered his password, opened a secure terminal app and logged into the *dathan* server. He thumbed commands into the tiny text window. In moments he was reading the logs.

It wasn't the mole. It was better. Laurel Wynn had tried to shut down the cameras and microphones in the Black Box.

He smiled. He'd been waiting for something like this.

He logged out, put the phone back in his pocket, washed his hands and left the bathroom. Barb and Ramona hadn't waited. The hallways were empty. He quickly went to his office and locked the door behind him. He plugged a pair of earbuds into his tiny gold MacBook and logged into *dathan*'s secret web server.

All Laurel Wynn had achieved with her ham-handed hacking was to turn off the red "recording" LED lights on the cameras. *Argus* would tell the FBI agent that the cameras were off, but their streaming video files were still being written into the giant Hadoop cluster in the basement, and were available only to Aidan.

He picked a camera at random and watched.

The angle wasn't good. Jack Dura and the rest of his clique were clustered around a whiteboard. Dura was drawing equations on the board with a green marker. The camera didn't pick up enough detail for them to be legible. They might as well be in Sanskrit.

Aidan cursed and hunted for a better angle. Cameras were everywhere in the room, but the detail of the video wasn't high. It couldn't be, considering how much data was being stored, and how tightly it was being compressed to conserve disk space. It was good enough to tell whether someone was trying to steal something. It had been clear enough for Emily's clean block lettering, but she'd been striving for legibility.

It wasn't good enough for Dura's minuscule chicken scratches.

Aidan got up and found the large widescreen monitor that had been moved from his old office but never plugged in. He placed it in the center of his desk and hooked his MacBook up to it, and then reinserted his earbuds.

He hunted through the video feeds for a clear view of the whiteboards, to no avail. If the text was legible, someone (usually the fat man with the beard) was blocking the rest of the board. If the board was fully visible from another angle, the camera was too far away, or the writing was a blur of fuzzy green pixels.

He watched the video with mounting frustration. Dura's marker eventually ran out of ink. He tossed it, and asked one of his students to bring over another whiteboard. The writing in the lower right corner of the first board was too faint for any of the cameras to make it out.

"*Damn* it," Aidan breathed.

When at last Dura stopped writing and began talking, Aidan forgot about the board.

What Dura told Laurel Wynn was impossible. Flatly impossible. Absolutely, without question, *impossible!*

His tie suddenly felt like a noose around his neck. He took it off.

"It's not that simple," he whispered to the people capering on the screen. "It can't be that simple. Emily would've seen that. She would've *seen* it!"

Then Jack Dura picked up an eraser.

"*No!*" Aidan shrieked. He stood up from his desk. The earbuds tore at his ears. He nearly pulled the tiny laptop off the desk. He grabbed it before it fell. He yanked the earbuds out, heedless of the pain. He shoved the laptop back on the desk. His heart hammered in his chest.

He waited, staring at his door. No one came. No one had noticed. Peter had his own issues. Based on Jay Kapoor's defeated expression, the other executives might also be screaming in the privacy of their offices.

He forced himself to sit down. He reinserted the earbuds and watched the rest of the video.

When Jack Dura said that they could now build an even better QUBE, Aidan felt faint. When Dura said that it might not even need the server farm, Aidan thought his heart might stop.

If it was true—if a truly portable QUBE could be developed—the plan would have to change.

A new universe of possibilities opened up in his mind.

He forced his attention back to the screen.

Dura told his cronies to get back to what they were doing before the talk, though not without an acid reference to Aidan as "Satan incarnate." They dispersed throughout the lab with evident reluctance. Dura asked Laurel Wynn to enable the cameras and asked her if she could further disguise any evidence that they'd been turned off in the first place. She typed for a long time.

When she was done, Aidan reviewed her work. She was good. She'd covered her tracks very neatly. If it hadn't been for *dathan* and Aidan's secret archive of video clips, she would have gotten away with it.

Aidan decided to give her a hand. He didn't want Luke Tso stumbling across any gaps in video coverage. His secret video archival job would clean everything up for him, but it wasn't scheduled to run until midnight.

He paused for a moment to consider the risks, then launched a program he'd used several times before to eliminate footage of events he didn't want anyone else to see. It replaced the missing video files with fakes filled with garbage data that would look like errors caused by a buggy video compressor.

There was in fact a bug in the video compression codec Aidan had written for the security system—one he'd introduced deliberately. Occasionally it would "act up," producing glitched video that affected all the feeds for a particular room for a certain amount of time.

There were many files with similar "errors" sprinkled around the video archive randomly to create the impression that there was a bug. They'd never been discovered for the simple reason that very few of the millions of video files had ever been reviewed by a human being. Up to now, there hadn't been any reason to do so.

Aidan's fakes had valid timestamps and checksum values. If by chance someone were to run across a glitched file and raise the alarm, Aidan would "discover" some of the other damaged files, pretend to track down his bug, and "fix" it. No one would ever be the wiser.

"It's not a bug," he said aloud. "It's a feature." It might be tricky to explain just how so many glitched files from the Black Box happened to show up at the same time, but if anyone ever noticed, he could always blame it on Laurel Wynn's buffoonish hackery. He'd think about a way to pin it on her later.

Aidan started the video sequence again, this time watching from a single camera. He made note of the precise instants when Jack began and ended his secret meeting.

He started a text editor and began to code.

Aidan was a ferocious programmer. He could type over a hundred words a minute when writing prose. He was scarcely slower when coding. He knew a great deal about image processing. He'd been an intern at NASA's Ames Research Center during his second summer in college. He'd written image analysis programs to enhance photos from orbiting telescopes. He'd been able to apply some of that knowledge to the development of the QUBE, and of course, to *dathan*. Stathis Sotiropoulos had even asked him to help with the imaging software they'd written for the security drones.

In a little over three hours, his four-thousand-line program was debugged and complete. He ran it.

He went down the hall to the mini-kitchen.

The job would run in parallel on the 23,300 machines in the two stupendous server farm levels in the sub-basement. Each computer in the Hadoop cluster would digest chunks of each video file to reduce the processing time needed to extract the data Aidan sought. The machines were mostly idle these days, since QUBE Bravo could only feed them with useful data three runs out of every hundred. The *dathan* program would conceal the system activity and redact all of the log files to prevent anyone from detecting Aidan's job.

The new program would analyze every frame in every fragment of every video clip, finding the edges of the whiteboard and extracting the contents. It would mathematically "flatten" the images to remove geometrical distortions caused by the camera angle. The frames would then be "stacked" on top of each other to produce a composite image. Sensor noise and blurs would be removed and details enhanced. Then the program would stitch the cleaned-up fragments of the whiteboard together. With luck, he would then have a legible image of Dura's formulas. Amateur astronomers with modest telescopes used a similar technique to create images of deep space objects. The best of them rivaled the work of professional observatories.

Aidan returned from the mini-kitchen with a glass of sparkling water.

The result of his work was already on the screen.

He took a long swig from the glass, sat down, and scrutinized the image.

Most of the left-hand whiteboard was clear, except the section in the lower right where Dura's dry erase pen had run low on ink. It was still a murky mystery.

He looked at the image of the right-hand whiteboard. At least a third of it was obscured by a dark, blurry form that could only have been the fat, bearded geek wearing the Greek fisherman's hat. Dura had sketched something resembling a circuit board, but only its left edge was visible.

Frantic, Aidan scanned his code for errors. It didn't take him long to conclude that there weren't any. This was the best image the program could generate.

"Well," said Aidan. He took a deep breath and exhaled it slowly. "That is very DISAPPOINTING!" He stood, unplugged the earbuds and monitor cable, and with great deliberation hurled the laptop across the room. It smashed into the wall next to the door. He threw the half-full glass of water after it. It shattered as it struck the door. Water went everywhere.

He waited.

No one came.

He sat, closed his eyes, and breathed in and out, deeply, slowly, fifty times in a row. His heartbeat slowly returned to normal.

He couldn't afford to get emotional. He had to think.

Aidan had planned the theft of the QUBE solely to depose Peter Struve. It was to have been a flamboyant example of Peter's inability to protect the company's secrets. Alberto di Mottura had supplied Aage Folstad to carry out the robbery. Instead, Folstad had taken Emily captive as well as the QUBE, at di Mottura's behest.

Aidan had expected more from John Shea's celebrated Rapid Response Team. They should have reacted faster. He didn't expect them to intercept Folstad as he entered the building, but he certainly thought they would kill him before he could escape. He hadn't shared that little detail with Alberto di Mottura.

Perhaps if he had, he would have detected the Italian's intent to kidnap Emily, and arranged for her to be out of the building. Whether Jason Lackland lived or died was immaterial. He was a nonentity. Emily was indispensable. The SEALs had been hampered by their need to keep her from being injured, but they had fumbled that job as well. Folstad managed to shoot her twice before John Shea's team could disable him permanently.

In spite of what he had told di Mottura, Aidan never intended for Emily to die or for the QUBE to be stolen, much less destroyed, but he'd adapted. He'd encouraged Peter to pursue Jack Dura, who was the only person who might be able to complete Emily's research. He had consented to Dura's brutal punch in the face, and was still painfully aware of the dental consequences. Against all odds, Dura had signed on. Now he claimed to have achieved something far beyond what Aidan had wanted, but his solution remained a mystery.

It was infuriating.

Aidan had never pretended to be a physicist. His expertise was in computer programming. Even if the formulas had been clear as day, he would need a physicist's help to make sense of them. He needed Emily, but she, like Eric Dalton, was "no longer available." He'd have to maneuver Dura into explaining it.

Aidan began to relax. Dura would *have* to come clean eventually. The exotic materials required to grow a new QUBE would devour much of the funding Peter had secured from ZMPC. Recycling the dysprosium-156 from QUBE Charlie wouldn't be enough. There were dozens of other crazily expensive materials to purchase. Peter wouldn't authorize building another one without a very good reason.

Jack Dura might think of Aidan as Satan incarnate, but he would still need Aidan's approval for a new design—and that wouldn't happen unless Dura disclosed his theory. Aidan would make certain of that. Being forced to divulge the details would drive Dura up the wall. Aidan would enjoy that very much.

"Satan, am I? Better to rule in Hell than serve in Heaven," he whispered.

There was a knock.

Aidan went to the door and opened it.

It was Peter. He clutched a sheet of paper in his right hand. The exhausted CEO's eyes widened when he saw the splinters of glass and the wreckage of the laptop.

"Sorry," Aidan said, trying to sound embarrassed. "I had a bit of a tantrum."

Peter pushed his way into the office. He handed Aidan a sheet of paper. "Read it."

Aidan obeyed.

FOR IMMEDIATE RELEASE

STRUVEPHARMA TO BECOME STRUVE TECHNOLOGIES
Pharmaceutical Business to be Sold

Much of the press release was breathless PR boilerplate. Aidan scanned through it. No buyer was mentioned.

Compared to Jack Dura's discovery, this was small potatoes, but Aidan tried to look suitably impressed.

"Jay doesn't see it," Peter said. "He did everything he could, but even with all the VCs along for the ride, we just can't pay for it all. We don't know how long we'll have to wait before Jack solves the QUBE problem. Our burn rate is calamitous. We have to pay off the bridge loans *now*. The interest alone is bleeding us dry. If we reduce the staff to the bare minimum, we might have a chance."

"We're already at rock bottom in the technical staff, Peter."

"Then we'll trim somewhere else. We need every penny. Selling the drug line will net us two or three billion in cash."

"And cut off us off from our only source of revenue."

Peter's mouth tightened. "Do you believe in what we're doing, Aidan? Do you think Jack can figure it out? If not, just tell me now and I will pull the goddamned plug. I swear to Christ I will."

Aidan made a show of considering Peter's words. He didn't believe them for a second, after all these years, but it would be politic to pretend that he did. "What will the Board say?"

Peter stared at him like he'd sprouted horns. "Weren't you listening in the meeting? Who do you think suggested this? They won't let me bring any more investors in. They won't accept further dilution of their shares. It was hard enough to get Philip Mayhew a seat at the table. And none of them wants the government to become our partner. It was either this or give up the Black Box forever."

"Ah. Well, then. I guess we don't have much choice."

Peter looked pointedly at the smashed laptop.

Aidan shrugged. "I was in a snit. I'll get over it. As long as Jack rides to the rescue."

"If he doesn't, this was a lost cause anyway." Peter went to the door.

"Do you have a buyer yet?" Aidan asked.

Peter turned the knob. "I'll let you know." He pulled the door closed.

Aidan picked up his phone and punched in a number. "Luke? Aidan. I need a replacement laptop. Sorry about that. I, ah, dropped it."

The rest of the day passed quickly. He took the remains of his old laptop down to the e-waste room in sub-basement three. He fed it into the ravenous maw of the hydraulic shear shredder they normally used to dispose of dead hard drives. It gobbled the aluminum laptop like a dog wolfing its dinner. Then he collected his new machine from IT and spent what was left of the afternoon configuring it for his use.

When he was done, he checked his watch. There was plenty of time until the call with Eric Dalton's masters. He picked a destination at random and decided to take the scenic route.

It wasn't even a challenge to elude the TV vans that peeled out after him when he rocketed away from the SP campus. He barreled off Interstate 280 at the Woodside Road exit and wended his way up Highway 84 into the verdant coastal hills. He found a bit of peace in the seclusion and grandeur of the ancient redwood forest. On impulse, he stopped at a grocery store in the tiny village of La Honda and got a cup of surprisingly good coffee.

When he returned to his car, he turned off his personal iPhone, dropped it into an aluminized Mylar bag, and put it in the glove compartment.

He drove on.

Highway 84 ended at the Pacific Coast Highway. He turned south, then took an immediate right into the half-full parking lot at San Gregorio State Beach. He paid the attendant and parked in an empty slot well away from the array of dinged-up beachcomber SUVs.

He checked his watch. It was almost time.

He locked his car and wandered down the path toward the beach. The marine cloud layer was dark and low today, and the wind was brisk. He walked along the short bluff that overlooked the beach and found a spot well away from the few desperate morons trying to frolic in the chilly sea air.

The burner vibrated in his coat pocket.

He pulled it out and answered it.

"Hello," he said cheerfully. "Do you know who I am?"

The reply was several seconds in coming. *"Yes."* The voice was flat and inflectionless.

"Are you disguising your voice?"

Another long pause. *"Yes."*

"I was told by a mutual friend that I should say this: 'All the birds have flown up and gone.' You're supposed to say something back. Let's hope your computer pronounces it properly, or this conversation will end."

There was noise on the line, then a human male voice spoke. *"A lonely cloud floats leisurely by."* The voice carried a distinct Asian accent—Chinese, probably—with a hint of British inflection.

Aidan smiled. *As I suspected. Hong Kong, without a doubt.* "You were our mutual friend's superior?"

"His... supervisor. What has happened to him?"

"Do you have a name?"

"You may call me Adam."

Aidan's lips twitched. "An interesting choice."

"The name was picked at random."

"A good omen, nevertheless. Adam, I happen to know the location of the Tree of Knowledge. I am waiting for it to bear fruit. I can offer you that fruit if you can supply me with support."

"What happened to our mutual friend?"

"Alas, he has shuffled off this mortal coil, as they say, but your chances of getting what you want have just improved dramatically."

"What do you want?"

"I have a team that needs to be paid. My original sponsors wrecked my attempt to take control of the company. I'll need you to deal with them as well. But most of all, I need your word that if I can deliver the technology to you, that I will remain in charge of it."

"It is a possibility."

"It's a condition. If you can't meet it, I'll look elsewhere. I can make sure that you never acquire the technology. I can also guarantee that your secrets will get out if my condition isn't met."

"That would not be wise."

"It won't be necessary if we can come to an accommodation. The public demo of the oil synthesizer has ensured that there will be no shortage of potential buyers."

"Do not be hasty. A deal is possible, but it will have to be approved by my superiors. I will inquire. I believe they will agree. It will take several days."

"Very good. There is one more thing. I know you have a mole inside the company. I want to know who it is, and now. A show of good faith on your part."

There was another pause. *"Please wait."* The line went quiet.

Aidan checked the phone's display to make sure the connection was still live. It was. He waited for several minutes, pacing back and forth along the bluff, scuffing his shoes in the wind-blown sand.

The phone came back to life. "What do you plan to do with this information?"

"That is my business."

"Our contact is highly placed and very useful. We do not want to lose him like we did our former mutual friend."

"If your mole is that useful, then I'll make use of him as well. It'll be good to have an ally on the inside. As a show of good faith on *my* part, I promise I will not hurt him."

"Very well. You may speak with him. He is with me now."

A moment later, a familiar Belgian-accented tenor voice said, *"Bonjour, Aidan."*

Aidan couldn't help but laugh. "Blaise Thierry! As I live and breathe. How *very* nice to speak with you. We must have dinner tomorrow. I'll make the arrangements. Would you kindly put Adam back on the line?"

"Certainly."

There was a pause. Then Adam's voice said, *"Are you satisfied?"*

"Absolutely. Blaise will be an exceptionally useful partner. Please contact your superiors and see if they will agree to my condition. I'll wait for your call."

"I shall be in touch."

The line went dead.

Aidan pocketed the burner. He looked at the wine-dark sea and smiled.

Blaise Thierry. That little weasel. I never suspected him. Thierry was smart. Smart enough to hide his espionage from Aidan. And his talents as StruvePharma's lead molecular designer would be extremely useful, in the short term as well as the long. He'd worked closely with Emily as she developed and refined the molecular modeling code in the QUBE's E-ware. Blaise could verify whether Jack Dura's breakthrough was real or just wishful thinking. He would understand the quantum mechanics. Perhaps he could even help decode the missing elements of Dura's circuit diagrams.

He wondered at Blaise's motivations. The Belgian was exceptionally well paid, and had a mountain of stock options. Surely it could not be ideological. Blaise had never shown the slightest interest in politics in Aidan's presence. He made a mental note to find out. The reason could become a useful lever on the scientist, should Aidan ever need one.

Mind racing, he returned to his car, singing softly to himself. "Gray skies are gonna clear up, put on a happy face. Brush off the clouds and cheer up, put on a happy face!"

The long drive home was very pleasant.

CHAPTER TWENTY-TWO

Struve Technologies Coyote Hill Campus, Palo Alto, California

September 22

Peter followed an unusually well-dressed Jack Dura into Mission Control.

It had been a long time since Peter had been here. Since just before Emily was killed, in fact. Three months.

It felt like a lifetime.

The rest of the Board of Directors followed him.

At 68, Sanjiv Krishnamurthi was the oldest and most senior member, second only to Peter. He was the CEO of a genetics startup in nearby Santa Clara. His face was lit by a dazzling white-toothed smile.

The elegant Darlene Smith's day job was running a high-profile charitable fund for science and engineering education for women and inner-city minorities. She had also been the Chief Operating Officer of a large aircraft and defense company in her native England.

Sam Bollard was the second-most junior member of the Board, having joined six years ago. He had owned a Texas-based semiconductor company that had been bought by Intel back in the 1990s. Now he ran a variety of software businesses and a startup incubator in the trendy South of Market area of San Francisco. He was tight-fisted, domineering, abrasive, and hugely successful.

Bringing up the rear was Philip Mayhew of ZMPC, the newest member of the Board. His frown was thoughtful rather than dour today. As well it might be. Today his massive investment in Struve Technologies would bear fruit—or end in abject failure.

Today they would test QUBE Delta.

Peter stopped in front of the bank of giant flat panel screens that dominated the front wall of the massive space. Jack moved off to join the small crowd of his former students, the two ZMPC engineers, and the ever-present Laurel Wynn. Aidan had taken to calling them the "Dura Party." Everyone wore business attire instead of the usual bland jumpsuits. The HR director, Sasha Khaimov, had arranged a party in the cafeteria. There would be a lot of booze. If the test went well, Peter would invite everyone to celebrate.

And if it doesn't, they can toast me at my wake.

Peter surveyed the room while his companions stared in fascination at the colorful graphs, inscrutable log messages scrolling by, and the blinking status indicators that had been deliberately designed to look like the annunciators in a nuclear power plant.

The faces of all twenty-four operators were visible from here. Their workstations were arranged in four tiers, their monitors positioned low to give them unobstructed views of the front wall. The operators wore headsets with tiny microphones in front of their mouths. All of them looked happy, excited, and busy. Few seemed to notice the bigwigs enter the room.

"Very fancy," said Sam Bollard. He pointed at the huge red NASA logo on the far wall. "What's with all the spaceship stuff?"

Peter said, "We let the employees decorate their spaces any way they like."

Bollard frowned. "You should put a big ST logo up there."

"Visitors aren't allowed in here. No one but us will ever see it."

Darlene Smith said, "Sam, be a dear and stop growling at people. It's too early in the day."

Bollard checked his watch. "It's ten to five PM!"

Smith smiled. "Exactly."

"Is all of this crap really necessary?" said Philip Mayhew.

Peter said, "Don't be a spoilsport, Philip. In the early days everything was prone to failure. It was great to have all of the team leads in one place to troubleshoot problems. Everybody likes being here, especially when we roll out a new QUBE. Most of the time it's empty. The operators are staff engineers and scientists."

"You could automate it. Use the room for something else."

"Did you count the cars in the parking garage? We're not exactly short on space."

Mayhew frowned but went silent.

Emily had once asked him the question he'd just asked Mayhew, the same night she was killed. He pushed the surge of anger and sadness back into its hole. He knew it would come out to play again as soon as he touched his head to his pillow.

He spotted Aidan O'Keefe. The CTO was talking with the heavyset, balding, bearded "Flight Director" Ed Black, whose console was at the very back of the room. Black was the biggest space nut in the whole company. He loved running the tests with an audience. He'd even donned an expansive off-white vest with a NASA mission patch on the left breast, *a la* Ed Harris playing Gene Kranz in *Apollo 13*.

Peter said, "Aidan! Please come down. Jack, could you join us, please?"

Aidan ambled down the steps.

Jack detached himself from the Dura Party and came over with evident reluctance. He stood next to Aidan and crossed his arms, frowning.

Peter turned to the Board. "You all know Aidan. I want to introduce you to Jack Dura."

Predictably, the ebullient Sanjiv rushed forward. "Our savior!" He grabbed Jack's hand and pumped it vigorously.

Jack's frown turned to a small, embarrassed smile. "Hopefully."

Sanjiv released Jack's hand. The others shook hands with him as well, except Philip Mayhew, who exchanged nods with him. Peter remembered vaguely that the two had met at the press conference.

Darlene Smith said, "I can't believe you were able to solve the technical issues so quickly, Dr. Dura. You've only been with us for two months!"

Jack shrugged. "I had a lot of help. And the problems weren't that difficult to solve, as it turns out. You just had to look at them from a different perspective."

Sam Bollard snorted. "That's not what Aidan tells us."

Jack's smile froze on his lips. "Oh?"

"He says you're some kind of super-genius, just like your ex-wife. That you created a whole new kind of quantum theory. I'd like to hear more about that."

"Ah," said Jack, glaring sidelong at the CTO. "He might be exaggerating a bit."

Aidan smiled. "Oh, not at all. Jack is too modest. His theory will open up whole new areas of science that haven't even been conceived of yet." He put a hand on Jack's shoulder.

Jack gaped at Aidan. Inexplicably, his eyes grew stormy.

Peter felt a sinking sensation in the pit of his stomach. *Christ, what fresh hell is this?* "Aidan, why don't you fill the others in? Jack, I've been meaning to ask you something." He grabbed Jack by the forearm and led him to an unoccupied corner.

Jack was staring back at Aidan, his face turning red.

"Jack. Look at me."

The scientist slowly turned his gaze toward him.

Peter hissed, "What the *hell* is wrong with you? And before you answer, remember that the goddamned Board of Directors is standing ten feet away."

Jack took a deep breath. He released it slowly, but said nothing.

Peter rolled his eyes. "Is this another one of your *Aidan O'Keefe is the devil* complaints? This is getting old. Tell me how Aidan paying you a compliment makes him a bad guy."

"I heard him say—" Jack threw his hands in the air helplessly. "Nothing. Never mind. It doesn't matter." His voice was repentant but his face was still taut with anger.

Lord above, please give me patience. "I get it, Jack. I do. He ran off with your wife, but that was as much her fault as his." Peter thought for a moment before he tried a different tack. He sighed. "Maybe I didn't tell you. Yvonne filed for divorce."

"Who?"

"My soon-to-be-former wife."

Jack's eyes widened. "What? Why?"

"Why?" Peter barked. Heads turned in his direction. He lowered his voice to a whisper. "Why shouldn't she? She told me that if I sold off the pharmaceuticals business that she'd leave me. She's as good as her word. She thinks I just gave away our children's legacy. She doesn't believe in what we're doing. I do. I'm in it too deep to give up on it now. Thanks to you, and yes, thanks to Aidan, we have a shot at changing the world, but don't you *dare* think for a single goddamned second that you're the only one who's suffered for this."

"Jesus, Peter. I'm sorry."

"Don't be sorry. Just be polite, for Christ's sake."

Jack nodded, looking thoroughly ashamed. "Okay."

It worked! He'd neatly sidetracked Jack's inexplicable fury. Peter kept the exultant smile from reaching his face. He decided to relent. "Look. This is supposed to be fun, right? Just enjoy yourself. If this thing works, it really will be a new age. Forget about Aidan for a while."

"I'll try."

"Good. Now I have to get back to the Board."

"Just a sec. If it does work, the team needs a break. I was thinking of an offsite, a long way from here, for a few days. They need to blow off some steam. Maybe a trip to Vegas."

I should have thought of that. Gets him away from Aidan, if nothing else. "If John and Laurel sign off on the security arrangements, fine, but Vegas is out. You guys are too much in the public eye. If the paparazzi see you in a casino, they'll be all over you. I saw that article about you and that singer. How did you find the time?"

Jack snorted laughter. "Okay. I'll find something with a low profile."

"Find something *without* a profile."

Jack wandered back to his students, evidently mollified. For now.

Peter allowed himself a sigh of relief and rejoined the Board. They were gathered in a semicircle around Aidan.

Darlene Smith said, "I don't understand, Dr. O'Keefe. How could you possibly build such a complex device in only six weeks?"

"We didn't start from scratch," Aidan said, smiling indulgently. "We had already built three QUBEs and expect to build more. The fab—the fabrication engine—was ready to go when Jack unveiled the fix for the entanglotrons. We spent quite a while testing prototype circuits. Jack's new design is far more efficient than the ones Emily and I came up with."

Peter was surprised at Aidan's evident delight at that revelation. He wished Jack had seen it. It might have put some of his paranoia to rest.

Aidan continued, "We use the same fab to grow our demo units and experimental prototypes. It's not like making computer chips or other electronic devices. The fab uses a combination of 3D printing and self-assembly of molecular components. It takes about a week to grow a QUBE from scratch, and another week for it to cure in a low-temperature annealing oven to drive off the volatiles and relieve stress in the materials. The QUBE has the equivalent of forty quadrillion transistors. There's no way to manufacture something like that perfectly. We spend a day or two just mapping the defects so we can program around them."

Sam Bollard said, "If all of this equipment was just sitting here, why in God's name does it cost half a billion dollars to make a new QUBE?"

Aidan's smile broadened. "The raw materials are very expensive. This time we reused the remnants of QUBE Charlie. We had to buy about half of the world's annual production of dysprosium to extract enough of the isotope we need to create the first three QUBEs. We started reclaiming Charlie's raw materials as soon as the police released it to our custody. Otherwise Delta would have cost about twice as much."

Mayhew frowned. "I begin to see where all my money is going."

Aidan nodded. "We are also testing brand new technology that might make the next generation QUBE independent of the server farm. If it works, we'll recycle the first two prototypes to build what Dr. Dura calls the HyperQUBE. It will be identical to the one we're testing tonight, except for a few key components."

"And what will this HyperQUBE do?" Darlene Smith asked, eyes glittering with anticipation.

Aidan's eyes took on a faraway look. "Anything," he breathed.

Before he could elaborate, Ed Black's amplified voice came over the room's public address speaker. *"We're about to get started, everyone. Please take your places."*

Peter ushered the Board members to the row of conference chairs lined up in front of the first tier of operator consoles, facing the wall of screens.

Aidan went back up the stairs to take his place in front of his control console.

Jack and his Party took the chairs on the other side of the center aisle, to Peter's right. Their earnest conversation dropped to a whisper but didn't stop.

Jack's continuing problems with Aidan bothered Peter more than he let on. He'd had his own fair share of issues with Aidan O'Keefe. He remembered how uncomfortable he'd been after Aidan revealed to him that he'd been having an affair with Emily. The future CTO had been trying to recruit her for an independent venture for months before the accident that cost her son's life and sent Jack to the hospital.

Emily had been vivacious, brilliant, and attractive. Peter knew that she and Jack had a stormy relationship—hardly a surprise, given how strong-willed they both were—but her abandonment of her husband had shocked him. As far as he knew, she'd never even tried to contact Jack in the hospital as he recovered from the burns he'd suffered in trying to rescue their son. He'd always suspected that Aidan had a hand in keeping the two of them apart. As the primary beneficiary of Emily's departure from Stanford, guilt nagged at Peter for months after she joined the team.

Peter wasn't blind to Aidan's shortcomings. Aidan was a wizardly programmer whose productivity left the staff computer scientists slack-jawed with awe. He was also fussy, patronizing, demanding, inflexible, arrogant, and utterly indifferent—or perhaps simply ignorant—of the feelings of anyone who got in his way.

The Valley was brimming over with self-involved geek *prima donnas*, but Aidan took it to the next level, and beyond. He'd always been polite and obedient to Peter, and somehow he'd been able to woo Emily Dura, which was nothing short of astonishing, but handling the complaints of his subordinates kept the HR department very busy.

Half of the programmers nearly walked out when Aidan insisted on using an antique source code control system. Only an agreement to use *git* for the QUBE-specific software, accompanied by substantial spot bonuses, had soothed those ruffled feathers. To this day Peter occasionally heard programmers grousing about it, and he'd never managed to get Aidan to explain his intransigence.

Trying as he was, Aidan got results. Peter appreciated that. He'd been able to placate Aidan's direct reports with bonuses. He'd managed to keep both Emily and Aidan productive during the rocky dissolution of their improbable relationship. The struggle to build the QUBEs had consumed them all. The difficulties of the past had faded away as they celebrated triumph after technological triumph.

Peter's days and nights were filled with the constant struggle to pay for it all, but as the months became years, Sasha Khaimov came to him less and less frequently with Aidan-related personnel issues. He'd hoped that Aidan had finally figured out how to work with others peacefully. Even after Emily and Jason died, Aidan remained on his best behavior.

Then Jack arrived.

Peter had taken a secret, guilty pleasure in watching Jack deck Aidan. Jack's revelation that Aidan had been with Emily when their son was killed explained his bone-deep hatred for the CTO. Peter had hoped that the act would be cathartic, and they would be able to figure out a way to work together. No such luck. If anything, repeated exposure to Aidan made Jack even more surly. His distrust of Aidan now bordered on full-blown paranoia. Aidan, in the meantime, was as agreeable and easy-going as Peter had ever seen him. As far as Peter could tell, the problem was now entirely one-sided.

Six weeks ago, Jack came to Peter and told him that he and his team had solved the mystery of the QUBE. He tried to talk Peter out of telling Aidan the details. Peter had blown his top. His memory of the next half hour was nothing but a red-tinged blur. He vaguely recalled describing Jack's own personality defects to him in excruciating detail. "Keeping the Chief Technology Officer of the company from knowing how our technology works *is not a fucking option!*" he roared.

He'd expected the volatile scientist to go up like the *Hindenburg*.

Instead, to Peter's utter astonishment, Jack wilted.

He'd borne the brunt of Peter's fury with a resigned frown, sinking deeper and deeper into the chair on the other side of Peter's desk. When Peter finished his diatribe, Jack was silent for a long minute. Then, in a quiet voice, he said, "I had to try." He slouched out of the office, returning a few minutes later carrying a thick, handwritten report on college-ruled notebook paper, fastened with a huge paper clip. "It's all there." Then he left again.

Since then Jack had been compliant. Unhappy, but compliant. Two days after Peter's rant, at Peter's specific direction, Jack briefed the engineering staff in the Pauling Auditorium. Peter attended to make sure Jack behaved. Aidan was there as well, sitting far in the back, smiling benignly. The math went so far over Peter's head it might as well have been in orbit, but the mounting excitement of the audience was obvious.

The Q&A session was four times longer than the talk itself. To Peter's surprise, the normally reticent Blaise Thierry asked most of the questions, firing them at Jack in rapid succession like a prosecutor grilling a hostile witness. Jack's answers were slow in coming and short on detail. Thierry kept at it, though, and eventually broke the logjam. The audience gasped at some detail that Peter missed completely. After that it was bedlam. Everyone shouted questions at Jack at once. He sighed and began to speak more freely. He even seemed to warm to the subject.

When his voice began to give out, he called an end to the session.

The whole audience arose as one and applauded, shouting, hooting and whistling. Jack should have been triumphant. Instead, he looked utterly defeated. He put down his dry erase marker and trudged out of the auditorium, his former students crowding close like a nerdy version of the Praetorian Guard.

The grim mood of the veteran staff engineers had finally lifted. Jack had given them something concrete to do, a new and exciting goal to aim for.

Jack himself fell into a funk that had taken him weeks to recover from. Aidan sneeringly referred to it as "*post-partum* depression."

Peter thought there might be a grain of truth to that notion. It worried him. Jack's moods ran the gamut from obnoxious to paranoid. He might be brilliant, but his erratic behavior was another reason for Peter to lose sleep, and he could scarcely afford to lose any more.

Peter glanced at the cranky scientist. He and his cadre were still deep in conversation. They were almost always together. They worked from dawn to well past midnight, every day, retreating to the luxurious bedrooms in the renovated Crick Building only when completely exhausted.

Irrationally, Peter chafed at that. He'd gone to a lot of trouble and expense to refit an office building to house them in ridiculous comfort. They'd probably have been content if he'd given them sleeping bags, a quiet corner to sack out in, and fed them take-out sandwiches from Togo's. However, since he was the primary beneficiary of their overwork, he let it slide without comment.

Laurel Wynn was with Dura and his clique as often as not. Peter glanced at her. She was with them now, and was as deeply involved in their whispered conversation as any of them.

Peter's frown deepened. He'd have told her to leave long ago if not for the relentless pressure from Andrew Seigart at Homeland Security to keep her here. She didn't contribute to the work. Her recommendations for enhancing security had been acted on. Ostensibly, she was still researching the staff, conducting interviews to find this hypothetical mole, and coordinating security arrangements with John Shea, but Peter was damned if he knew why she couldn't do that from the Palo Alto FBI office.

He was well aware that Andrew Seigart's stated reason for keeping Agent Wynn on site was just a pretext. She was the government's eyes and ears inside SP. *No, not SP, now it's ST, dammit.* Name change notwithstanding, Peter's business was completely above board. Laurel Wynn was agreeable to work with, but it irked him to have a state-sanctioned spy inside the campus walls. It didn't make him feel any better that she'd suggested that he build them. Walls could keep people in as easily as out.

Ed Black's amplified voice brought him back to the present.

"All right, we are proceeding to final systems check. Power?"

"Off grid and on generators, smooth and stable," replied one of the infrastructure leads from her console.

"Network ops?" said Black.

"Green board, Flight Director."

"Cryonics?"

"Laminar superfluid flow. Laser cooling at one hundred percent. Entanglotron mean temp is 0.035 K. We are go."

"Mass storage?"

"Twenty-three thousand, two hundred and nine servers are green, ninety-one red. Three point three four exabytes of disk, nineteen petabytes of RAM. We're good to go."

"Buffers?"

"Go at full capacity."

"KV store?"

"Go, Flight."

"E-ware?"

"Test suite loaded, ready to execute."

The roll call lasted a long time. Even after all these years, most of the "preflight" tasks were a complete mystery to Peter. He wished he had time to bone up on the science. He knew who to hire to make all of this possible, but he was still an outsider. Management. The Pointy-Haired Boss.

At last, Ed Black announced, "This is the Flight Director. All systems are go. We are proceeding to the systems test. T-minus ten seconds."

Peter smiled. The first time they did this, Ed had insisted on going through a full sixty-second countdown because it was more dramatic. Ten seconds was enough. In fact, zero seconds was enough. All they had to do was press a button. But it was tradition, and he had to admit that it was fun. There'd been too little of that around here lately.

"Nine."

He glanced at the members of the Board. They looked thoroughly bemused.

"Eight."

He looked at the Dura Party. Jack flashed him a confident smile. The others were spellbound, staring at the huge countdown clock on a display at the front of the room.

"Seven. Six."

Peter's heart began to pound.

"Five. Four. Three. Two. One. Zero."

The wall of displays in front of him went wild. Lights flashed. Graphs showed massive spikes in activity. Log messages scrolled down windows faster than he could read them.

A second later, it all stopped.

Peter leapt to his feet, his heart lodged in his throat. *That's not long enough. Not* nearly *long enough!* He squeaked, "What the hell?"

"Stand by one," said Ed Black. "Everyone, I need your system status, by the numbers, on the private loop." He cut off the PA microphone with an audible click.

Jack joined Peter. He said, "What's the problem?" His voice was normal enough.

Peter looked at the log window. It had stopped accumulating messages. The last line was:

PROGRAM EXITED WITH CODE 0 AT 1.827763 SEC

He walked up to the wall and pointed at the message. "What does this mean?" he asked Jack.

Before Jack could reply, Ed Black's amplified voice rang out, "I can't believe it. It finished. Peter! It didn't abort. It worked! It's done!"

"That's impossible," Peter said. "Charlie took five or six minutes to run the same test!"

Aidan came down the stairs wearing an incredulous smile. He walked up to Jack. "The tests passed. All of them. In *six* iterations. If I hadn't seen it, I'd never have believed it. Delta is nearly two hundred times faster than Charlie. Your new design worked." He extended a hand. "Congratulations."

Under Peter's withering eye, Jack shook it.

CHAPTER TWENTY-THREE

Lake San Antonio, California

September 26

"We're here," Jack said as Sy Hamilton shut down the engine.

Everyone got out and stretched.

The other three big RVs pulled in next to theirs. The four vans containing their camping supplies and the rest of the security team were close behind.

Jack took a deep breath. The late afternoon air was breezeless, bone dry, desert-hot, and dusty from the arrival of the vehicles. It was also filled with the strange, pungent scent of the tall, moss-festooned trees that studded the campground. There was little other vegetation except for tufts of dried brown grass.

Sweat popped out on Jack's brow. He went back into the RV and got his wide-brimmed Tilley hat and sunglasses.

There were plenty of empty parking spaces in the Redondo Vista campground. Best of all, there was no competition for the water, electrical and sewer hookups for the RVs. It was just as he'd hoped. School was back in session. The late September heat wave was proving a deterrent for all but the hardiest—or craziest—weekday vacationers. Lake San Antonio met Peter's requirement of a place well off the beaten path, and that was all that mattered. That, and the fact that the vacation coincided with the annual end-of-the-season star party Jack always attended.

"Gotta hand it to you, boss," said Hank Drummond, blinking in the harsh sunlight. "This is pretty much the shittiest campground in California."

Lizbeth said, "Shut up, Hank. You want to wind up in Death Valley?"

The rest of the vacationing scientists and engineers emerged from their RVs and walked over to join them. Everyone from his team had come along, though Ben and Deepthi had required some extra encouragement. They'd wanted to stick close to the lab during the week-long vacation Peter had declared after the successful test of QUBE Delta. Jack suspected they just wanted time alone. He'd convinced them to come anyway. They needed to talk, well away from the perpetual surveillance on campus.

Laurel Wynn looked particularly fetching in her form-fitting Defense Language Institute T-shirt, shorts and hiking boots, but her expression was just as grim as everyone else's. "Wow, Jack. This place is totally awesome. Much better than, oh, I don't know, Big Sur or Yosemite."

"Okay, okay," Jack said, raising his hands in a placating gesture. "I know it doesn't look like much, but the lake is just over the hill. We can go running or swimming or rent row boats. Stathis brought some drones to fly. There's a day trip over to Hearst Castle the day after tomorrow. That's pretty cool. You'll be sleeping most of the day, anyway. The real action will be at night."

"Uh-huh," Hank said in a weird, low, chortling voice. "Uh-huh. You said *action*."

Jack frowned. "Are you making fun of my star party, Beavis? You're fired."

"You fired me before we got on the RV. And that was Butthead, not Beavis."

"Okay, you're hired, and now you're fired again."

Hank shrugged. "Fair enough."

"Jesus. That was on TV when *I* was a kid. When did you ever see *Beavis and Butthead*?"

"They have this thing called the Internet, Gramps. Mike Judge is God."

"Can't argue with that. Okay, you're rehired."

Laurel looked around. "I don't see any telescopes."

Jack said, "The astronomers set up in the overflow parking area, just down the road a ways. They're pretty strict about keeping the lights off at night. I imagine some of you would rather get drunk and sing songs instead of looking through telescopes, like real scientists."

Hank quipped, "Well, get drunk, anyway."

Jack gave him a mock-fierce scowl. "Don't overdo it with the booze. It screws up your night vision. Anyway, when you see the skies tonight, you'll change your tune."

"Uh-huh," said Hank, using his "Butthead" voice. "Uh-huh. You said *tune*."

Terry asked, "Could you please fire Hank again, Jack?"

They spent the better part of three hours getting the camp set up. The security guys pitched their tents around the RVs in a loose circle. They erected portable screen houses around the picnic tables to keep out the bugs. They set up gas-powered barbecues and suffered the park ranger's inspection with good grace.

She told them not to make any open camp fires. "After the rainfall we had last winter, there's a ton of dried vegetation out there. This whole place will go up like an atom bomb if a fire gets out of control."

The scientists booed and hissed, but the ranger stood firm. Jack was relieved when she finally moved on. If she'd known how many guns the security guys had brought into the camp, they'd have been kicked out, if not arrested on the spot. Shea and his men might be deputy sheriffs now, but they were way out of their jurisdiction.

Jack pitched his tent beneath one of the mossy trees, and was pleased to see Laurel set up her newly purchased REI dome tent nearby. Most of the others elected to sleep in the RVs. The accommodations were luxurious enough. The big vehicles had slide-out compartments, comfortable sleeping areas, satellite TV and Internet access. The private bathrooms and showers would take a lot of the sting out of "roughing it" for those who weren't keen on camping to begin with.

Dinner was simple but tasty. They made bison burgers and grilled vegetables on the designated vegan barbecue for those who didn't eat meat. Chips and salad and beer were plentiful. Once people had a chance to sit, eat, drink, and relax a bit, their mood began to improve, as Jack had predicted. At length the food disappeared, as did the sun. As the sky turned purple and stars began to emerge, they sat around their Coleman lanterns, drank, and shot the breeze.

"Okay Jack," said John Shea at one point. "Why the hell did you drag us out here, of all places?"

"Hey, *you* asked *me* if you could come."

"My wife took the kids to visit her parents in Montana. I didn't have anything better to do."

Jack made a noncommittal grunt. *Sure. You just wanted to keep an eye on the problem children.* He took a swig of beer. "You really want to know or are you just trying to score points, like that joker?" He pointed at Hank Drummond.

"Scoring points is a perfectly sound motive," Hank drawled.

Shea shrugged. "There's got to be some good reason."

"Well, it's dark." When the pity-chuckles died down, Jack continued, "No, seriously. This is one of the darkest spots in California. It's easy to get to. It's comfortable at night. The new moon is tomorrow. We're only a few miles from the coast, believe it or not, so the 'seeing' here is good. The air traveled all the way across the ocean without going over land masses. Land makes thermals, and thermals make turbulence. The more turbulence, the twinklier the stars, which is pretty, but not so great for imaging. This time of year the air is as smooth as glass. Once the temperature near the ground drops, you can shoot amazing pictures of deep-sky objects. Astronomers love it. You'll see."

"You didn't bring a telescope," Laurel pointed out.

"No shortage of them here already. These folks are *serious*. I can't compete with my crappy old Celestron. You should see some amazing stuff tonight. I checked the Heavens Above site before we left. Both Jupiter and Saturn are up. And if Ray Batista is here you might even get a close-up look at the International Space Station. It's making a pass just after full dark."

Well before the last hints of blue faded from the sky, Jack decided it was time to pay the astronomers a visit. Of the small group who chose to go with him, Stathis Sotiropoulos was the only one who looked genuinely excited. Jack sighed. He handed out small red LED flashlights to everyone. "Don't shine them in anyone's face, just use them to find your way around. Red light won't ruin your night vision. There's a 'no light allowed' area further to the south. We'll just stick to the main camp site tonight. Just ask before looking through anyone's scope. They'll probably want to tell you all about their gear. Let 'em. It's a small price to pay for some amazing sights. And try not to kick up too much dust."

John Shea and a handful of his men joined the group as they made their way to the access road. Jack knew they were armed. The bulkiness of their light jackets made him think they were armored as well. "Are the gorillas really necessary?" he murmured to Laurel Wynn, who walked next to him.

"Only way Peter would agree to let us out in public," she whispered. "That would-be sniper really rattled him, Jack. This might be the last chance we get to spend time off-campus for a long time."

"Huh? Why?"

"Have you been keeping up with the news?"

"I've been too busy revolutionizing science. Why?"

"Let's just say that things are getting a little crazy out here in the real world."

He glanced at her sidelong. He could barely see her silhouette against the indigo sky. "What do you mean?"

She hesitated. "I'd rather not repeat myself, and everyone needs to hear it."

"Fine. We need to have a group chat tomorrow anyway. We need to decide what to do next."

"Okay, what do *you* mean?"

He mimicked her in a high, girlish voice: "I'd rather not repeat myself, and everyone needs to hear it."

She punched him lightly on the arm. "What are you, five years old?"

He chuckled. "Four."

The sounds of excited astro-geeks grew louder as they approached the overflow parking area.

He said, "You ever been to a star party before?"

"No."

"They can get pretty rough. Stick close to me, kid, and I'll show you a good time."

Laurel laughed and punched him again.

Jack grinned. She'd definitely warmed up to him since the revelations in the Black Box. She had a great laugh. Genuine. Musical. Sexy as hell. He could stand to hear it more often, even if it cost him a punch in the arm now and then.

The overflow parking area was a big clearing next to the dirt road from the main campground. There was just enough light to see the thirty or forty cars, trucks and campers parked in no particular order, surrounded by tents, pavilions, and elaborate telescopes of every description. Everyone had red flashlights. Some people had set up dim red lights on their tripods to keep people from stumbling over them in the dark.

The astro-nuts were as friendly as Jack had predicted. He saw a few old friends, who were eager to hear all about his work at ST. He deflected their questions as gently as he could, citing his nondisclosure agreement. He introduced Laurel as his bodyguard and said she'd beat the hell out of him if he spilled any secrets. "She already hit me twice tonight, so I gotta be on my toes," he said, rubbing his biceps. Laurel told him to shut up the fourth time he used that joke.

Also as predicted, the astronomers were eager to talk about their gear. It ran the gamut from little hobbyist scopes, usually operated by earnest youngsters "making their bones," as one of Jack's friends put it—prompting peals of laughter from Laurel—all the way to huge motor-driven refractors on massive, pillar-legged equatorial mounts. Inexpensive, hand-steered, mortar-like Dobsonian reflectors were everywhere. Their huge mirrors were installed in big black boxes mounted close to the ground on cheap-looking swivels. Many of them had tubes so long their eyepieces could be reached only by ladder.

It didn't take Jack long to find Ray Batista. His booming laugh could be heard from a hundred yards away.

They navigated through the obstacle course of campers and tele-scopes, trailed at a discreet distance by the ever-vigilant John Shea, and in moments they'd found his barrel-chested friend.

"Hey Jack!" said Ray, pumping his hand with a vise-like grip. "Good to see you! And you have a girlfriend! Jesus, took you long enough. Nice to meet you, miss...?"

"Laurel. She's not my girlfriend," Jack said.

"I'm not his girlfriend," Laurel said at the same instant.

Ray laughed. "You keep telling yourselves that. So. What do you think of the new rig?" He shined his own red flashlight on his gear. His scope was in fact two scopes: a pair of long white five-inch refractors mounted side-by-side on a hulking motor-driven tripod. The optical tubes terminated in bulky black boxes instead of eyepieces. Cables snaked from the boxes to a big laptop resting atop a flimsy-looking folding table surrounded by a group of kids.

Laurel said, "Very nice."

"Fancy!" said Jack enthusiastically. "How's the binocular setup working?"

"See for yourself. You're just in time for the ISS pass. It's gonna be a good one." Ray's voice became declamatory. "Look to the skies!" He added in a softer tone, "To the west. Near the horizon."

Jack followed Ray's instructions. He relaxed his focus, letting his peripheral vision do its thing. Seconds later he saw a tiny, brilliant white spark scaling the band of dark blue near the horizon. He leaned close to Laurel and pointed. "There it is!"

She laughed. "I saw it before you did. That's the space station?"

"Yep," said Ray. He leaned over his laptop and tapped a button. The motors on his scope whined to life. The heavy binocular telescope slewed and tilted skyward.

Jack peered at the swiftly rising dot. "Wow. It's so bright. It's hard to believe it's more than two hundred miles up."

The motors on Ray's scope grew quieter, but not entirely silent.

Ray laughed maniacally. "Ha! Nailed it! Take a look. This is gonna wreck your night vision, but it's totally worth it."

They looked. The image on the laptop rippled and wavered, but it was clearly identifiable as the International Space Station. It was shaped roughly like the letter "H", except for a narrow silvery tube protruding from the cross-bar. The vertical bars—enormous solar panels, Jack knew—were tinted a reddish gold. Reflected sunlight flowed across one of the panels as the Station tilted slowly on the screen.

Laurel pointed at a small, brilliant white object not far from the Station. "What is *that*?"

"A Dragon capsule," said Ray. "Full of trash and getting ready for its deorbit burn. Great timing! Wow, this picture is even better than I'd hoped it would be. Wait 'til you see what it looks like after I process it. I'll post the link on the CalStar web site."

Laurel said, "How did you *do* this, Ray?"

"Adaptive optics, custom CMOS cameras, ceramic-bearing motors with active vibration cancellation, real-time image analysis, and custom-designed software."

Jack said, "Ray owns a couple of companies, but he spends all his time building telescopes."

"Man, it *has* been a while since I've seen you. I own four companies now. Speaking of which, are you guys taking any new investors? I've been reading about you online."

Some of the kids clustered around the laptop turned to look at them.

"Shh," Jack said. "We're on vacation. We're supposed to be on the down-low."

"Aw, come on, man. Hook me up. I'll give you this scope!"

"Ha. I'll see what I can do."

"My man," Ray said. They bumped fists.

The binocular scopes were pointed high in the Western sky now. The image of the station grew dim and red as it entered the Earth's shadow. In seconds, it faded into darkness.

They thanked Ray, promised to visit him tomorrow night, and made the rounds. It took a while to regain their night vision. Jack told her about the San Jose Astronomical Association and some of the star parties he'd attended, as close to home as Monte Bello Open Space Preserve atop the hills near Palo Alto, and as far away as Mount Shasta. Laurel told him about getting a tiny refractor for Christmas when she was a kid, and promptly dropping it on the icy steps in front of her Minneapolis house in her eagerness to show it off to her next-door neighbors.

They spent the rest of the evening moving from scope to scope, greeting passionate hobbyists, hearing their stories, and peering at planets, star clusters, nebulae and the faint wisps of distant galaxies.

Laurel's ambivalence slowly turned to enthusiasm. They both began yawning much sooner than they expected, though. The day had started before dawn so they could escape from the ST campus in their fleet of blacked out vans, elude the reporters, and converge on the RV rental company in south San Jose to start their journey to the lake. Then they'd spent two motionless hours on southbound 101 near Gilroy, waiting for an overturned big rig to be cleared from the road. Everyone had ribbed Jack mercilessly as the scenery became increasingly sere and desolate. They were all a little testy at the end of their journey, and Jack knew better than anyone how much energy it took to stay cranky for any length of time.

He was about to suggest they head back to the camp when the elderly owner of one of the huge Dobsonian scopes crowed, "Take a look at Saturn! I just got a new Tele Vue eyepiece, and *man* is it sharp. Just take a look! Quick, it's about to set. It's a little wobbly but it still looks great! I've got this baby hooked up with an auto-guider. No need to keep re-pointing it."

The six-foot-plus tube of the massive scope was pointed just above the trees. Laurel stooped to look through the eyepiece.

Jack asked the owner, "How big is the mirror in this bad boy?"

"Twenty-five inches," said the man proudly.

"Oh, my God," said Laurel. "I've never seen anything like it. It could be right next door! Jack! Take a look!"

She relinquished the eyepiece. He took her place.

The pale yellow planet was huge and brilliant. Its rings were spectacular. It was so close to the horizon that it shimmered like it was immersed in a shallow dish of water. In spite of that, the sense of the majestic planet's immensity was palpable. You could look at pictures of Saturn taken by the Cassini space probe all day long, but there was nothing, *nothing* like seeing it live. "Damn," he breathed. "That is amazing." They took turns watching the giant planet until it disappeared into the trees.

On the walk back to the camp, he said, "We'll have to check that out tomorrow night, earlier, when it's higher in the sky. Then you'll really see something."

"It's a date."

Jack chuckled. "So, what do you think of my choice of vacation spots *now*?"

Laurel said, "It's growing on me." He could hear the smile in her voice.

"It sucks," said John Shea.

Jack jumped. He'd forgotten Shea was still trailing them. The big man was as silent as a ghost. He said, "Jesus Christ! Is there a defibrillator in the RV?"

Laurel laughed and said, "Try looking through the telescopes tomorrow, John."

"I'm too busy keeping an eye on you two love-birds."

Jack snickered, but his chuckle became a yelp when Laurel landed a solid punch on his biceps. "Yow! Save that for the sparring ring, lady."

"What an excellent idea. Know any Krav Maga?"

"Nope. Kajukenbo, Emperado method. Second degree black belt."

"Huh. Okay, it's a date. When we get back."

John Shea made a comical tweeting sound. "Two little lovebirds, sittin' in a tree—"

"Shut up," they both said to him.

They were all yawning uncontrollably by the time they returned to camp. Jack bade the others farewell, found his roomy tent, pulled off his dusty boots, crawled into his sleeping bag, briefly wondered what it would be like to share the bag with Laurel, and sank into an exhausted slumber.

It was close to noon by the time everyone had awakened and taken their turn in the cramped RV showers. The security team nixed the idea of using the campground's restrooms. They could control access to the RVs. Jack chafed a little at that, but his objection was *pro forma*. He'd bathed in icy mountain creeks when the only other option was to use a public campground bathroom. No matter how clean they were, they always had that *smell*.

He chatted amiably with the others until lunch was served.

Jack asked the members of his inner circle to gather beneath a big shady tree about a hundred yards from the RVs, well away from the other campers. They grumbled good-naturedly but followed, carrying their food and folding camp chairs. They gathered in a loose circle around a big red beer cooler. A trio of security men followed as well, but kept watch just out of easy earshot.

Laurel brought John Shea with her. Jack nodded to the tall security chief. Unlike everyone else, Shea looked no less alert than he'd looked last night. Before the trip, Jack and Laurel had argued for several hours about the wisdom of letting him into the inner circle. She'd reminded Jack that Shea had even less scientific training than she did. He couldn't blab secrets he didn't understand.

If what Jack suspected about the ST surveillance system was true, they'd need John Shea's help. Laurel maintained that they'd get it only if they could convince him that their motives were pure. Jack eventually relented. His relationship with Shea was cordial but distant. That would have to change. He'd have to be diplomatic, which was as natural to him as riding a bicycle was to a barracuda.

The food was a repeat of the previous day's menu, but no one seemed to mind. Jack wolfed his bison burger and Doritos. He looked at the others in the circle as he ate. Deepthi and Ben sat together, as always, looking insufferably happy with each other. Terry Blau wore a blinding Hawaiian shirt, plaid shorts, flip-flops, and dark bags under his eyes. He hadn't slept much in the last few weeks. Chao-Xing, Lizbeth and Hank Drummond sat together, giggling about something. Lizbeth wore a brilliant white tennis outfit that hugged her athletic body almost lasciviously. She caught him looking and smiled. He smiled back, took a big bite of his burger to cover his embarrassment, and quickly looked away.

The compact, dark-haired Stathis Sotiropoulos, better known around campus as the Greek, perched on the front edge of his chair, talking earnestly with John Shea. Jack had learned of the Greek's role in designing custom technology for the security team. His help would be invaluable—and inevitable, if Jack could convince Shea of his case. The Greek plainly worshipped Shea, and would do anything he asked.

Laurel sat between Shea and Jack, wearing a loose fitting T-shirt and baggy cargo shorts, much to his disappointment. She caught his eye, glanced at her watch, and arched her eyebrows meaningfully.

He nodded to her, took a deep swig of Firestone ale, smacked his lips contentedly, cleared his throat, and said, "You're probably wondering why I gathered you here today."

Terry Blau said, "To amuse us with mystery movie clichés?"

"Not exactly." Jack lowered his voice. "We need to talk."

"You guys don't do anything *but* talk," groused John Shea.

Jack ignored the gibe. "First, I want to congratulate you. What you've done in the last three months is—well, I wouldn't have believed it if I hadn't lived through it. You made history. They'll write books about you. You're all going to be filthy, stinking rich. Cheers." He raised his beer.

The others did as well, smiling and laughing. "Cheers!" they echoed in a ragged chorus. Terry Blau shouted, "FILTHY, STINKING RICH!" and they toasted that as well. Even John Shea cracked a smile.

Jack clinked his bottle against Laurel's and drained it, putting it on the ground next to his chair. "I don't want to ruin your vacation. God knows you've earned it. I didn't drag you out here just to look through telescopes, though. I need to tell you some things." He looked at John Shea and the Greek. "You two weren't there for it, but about a month and a half ago, the rest of us had a secret meeting in the Black Box. I asked Laurel to disable the *Argus* system's video and audio feeds. Which she did."

John Shea's eyebrows rose. He looked at Laurel.

She nodded, blushing.

Jack said quickly, "It was my idea. I needed to make sure my team had a chance to learn what I'd discovered, off the record. I read Emily's journal. I'd figured out the math behind the error in the entanglotron design a week before. I put it all up on a whiteboard for everyone to see. I showed them the schematics of the old QUBE design to prove it. We danced and hugged and held hands. And then I erased the board and Laurel turned the surveillance system back on."

Shea's eyes were cold. "Why did that have to be off the record? Didn't you give a five-hour talk about it in the auditorium to the whole staff?"

"I'll get to that." He looked around the circle. "Do you remember what I said about this new theory during our secret talk? About what it would lead to?"

Ben said, "That it could be the biggest thing since the theory of relativity?"

"Nope, something else. And Lizbeth said that."

Chao-Xing said, "This will open up whole new areas of science that haven't even been conceived of yet."

"Exactly! What a memory. Did I talk to you or coach you to say that? I'm asking for John's benefit."

Chao-Xing frowned. "No."

"Do the rest of you remember me saying that in the Black Box?"

Most of the people nodded, including Laurel.

"Did I say anything like that in the lecture to the staff?"

They looked at each other in confusion.

"I don't think so," said Lizbeth.

Jack said, "I didn't. I watched the recording twice to make sure. But what do you think Aidan O'Keefe said to me just before we did the first test run on QUBE Delta? Almost exactly what I said to you in the Black Box. Word for word. I don't know if he was trying to let me know that he had seen something that shouldn't even have been recorded, or if it was just a slip, but he said it."

John Shea sighed, sat back in his chair and crossed his arms. "And that couldn't *possibly* be a coincidence."

Laurel looked down at her lap.

"I know," Jack said, looking steadily at Shea. "I'm a broken record. I'm the boy who cried 'Aidan O'Keefe.' He stole my wife. I'm not objective. I'm paranoid, *et cetera, et cetera*. I get it. I'm not asking you to *trust*, John. I'm asking you to *verify*. Laurel told me you have access to the surveillance archive. Stathis, you know your way around the company's computer system as well as anyone, right? You can check out the footage from the Black Box. When Laurel hacked the system, the lights on every camera in the room went off. They shouldn't have been recording at all. Right?"

The Greek nodded.

"So there should be a half-hour gap in coverage on that date from every camera and microphone in the room. If there isn't, it means those cameras stayed on, and Aidan watched the whole conversation."

"So what if he did?" barked Shea. "You weren't supposed to be fucking around with *Argus* in the first place. It's there for a reason. Everything in that room has to be recorded!"

Jack took a deep breath. "If you can't trust that you've turned off the cameras when *Argus* says you did, you can't trust anything. God knows what else that system is recording. Did you guys put cameras and mics into our bedrooms in the Crick Building?"

"No!" snapped Shea, eyes flashing.

Stathis said, "Wait. Turning the cameras off should've fired a Nagios alert."

Laurel shook her head. "I disabled the alerts and then went back and edited the log files after I turned them back on."

Stathis smirked. "Very clever."

"Very goddamned irresponsible," growled Shea, glaring at Laurel.

Jack said, "John. It's my fault. Don't blame her. I convinced her to do it. I told her I wanted her on the inside, but that we'd work around her if we had to."

"You trusted *her*? An FBI agent?"

"Yes."

"I thought you academic types were all about how evil the government is!"

"I don't trust the FBI. I trust *Laurel*."

"Because you're hot for her."

Jack fought his rising temper. "Because she's smart and capable and objective. Because she's not bought and paid for by the same company that hired Aidan O'Keefe." He didn't add, *And* also *because I'm hot for her.*

Shea scowled. "Peter Struve has never asked me to do anything I'd be ashamed of."

"Jesus, John, why do you think I invited you here? Don't you get it? I know what you did to protect us from that sniper. I know you would've given your life to save Emily and Jason. I trust you, too! Would you cool down? If Aidan's a bad guy, he's a danger to Peter and you, too, you know. Not to mention everyone else who works at ST. Anyway, that was only one of the two things that didn't seem quite right."

Shea stood up, but it was only to get another bottle of beer from the cooler. He popped the cap with a church key and took a swig before sitting back down. "Okay. Lay it on me." His voice was calm, but his eyes were flinty.

"Laurel noticed something in the last executive staff meeting. You ever notice that Aidan wears one of those crazy-expensive gold Apple Watches? He's always looking down and fiddling with it. It dings when he gets a message or a meeting notification. I even saw him answer a phone call on it once."

Shea said, "A lot of people have those *Dick Tracy* watches." He brandished his left wrist. "I have one, myself. What's your point?"

"He almost never looks at his phone. He keeps it in his coat or in a pocket. Can't blame him. The thing's the size of a waffle. But he is *always* looking at his watch. Except in the last executive staff meeting. Laurel. Tell him."

She said, "I heard his phone buzz in his pocket. He took it out and answered a call, saying that he was busy and he'd call whoever it was back. His watch didn't make a peep."

"Big deal. It could've been in silent mode."

She shrugged. "Maybe. I've heard it ding a dozen times a day, every day, but let's say he put it into silent mode, just this once. It bothered me. I didn't know why until I had a chance to think about it later. I had a smart watch for a few months just after they came out. I took it off at the gym and someone stole it. You get used to wearing it. You get dependent on it for notifications, emails, and messages. When you wear a ten-thousand-dollar watch, you are going to look for a reason to use it."

Jack added, "Which he always does. He loves flashing that thing around. But this time, he didn't. Why?"

Shea's frown became speculative. "He has a second phone?"

Jack nodded. "That's what we're thinking. One that's not linked to his watch. But that raises another point. Those armor glass windows make the Pauling Building into a Faraday cage. There isn't even Internet access. I have to get my phone out of my locker and go outside just to check my personal email. But I've seen Aidan, Peter and Laurel use theirs. I know how it works, but maybe you can tell the others how some people can use cell phones inside the building, John."

"There's a repeater connected to an antenna on the roof. It feeds a microcell network inside the building. Only VP-level execs and members of the on-duty security team have phones that can use it. And Laurel." He looked at her reproachfully.

"And *Argus*," said Laurel. "You used it to get access to the video feeds *that night*." She didn't have to say which night.

John shook his head. "Not anymore. We unhooked *Argus*' cell connection when we moved everyone into Pauling, since we have more staff on site now."

Laurel leaned forward. "Who has access to the repeater?"

"Luke Tso and me. It's on an isolated network. You can't login to it remotely. It's in a restricted wiring closet on the fourth floor."

"Does it log every call?"

"Yes," he said slowly.

Jack said, "John, when we get back, I'd like to ask you to check two things. Look for the video from the Black Box cameras. Laurel can give you the precise times the video should be missing. Stathis can help you with the computer work. If the footage is in the archive, it means someone compromised the *Argus* system's command line tool. And who wrote *Argus*, John?"

Shea's frown returned. "Aidan O'Keefe."

"You should also take a close look at that cell phone repeater. When's the last time you checked it out physically, in person?"

"Shit, I don't know. Sometime last year. Luke Tso was the last person to touch it, to add Laurel's phone."

"I think it's time, don't you?"

"It couldn't hurt."

The relief flowed over Jack like a physical wave. John wasn't enthusiastic, but he was coming around. "Good. I'll track down the exact time of the executive staff meeting. Laurel and I both saw Aidan take that phone call. There should be a log of it on the repeater. If there isn't, you have a problem. And if you do see it, you should see one more phone registered in the system than there should be."

"And if it shows his regular phone got the call?"

"Then I'll drop it. We'll just build the HyperQUBE and write a new chapter in the history of science. But I think you'll find something."

Laurel said, "And remember this, John. Someone inside the company told Aage Folstad about the oil synthesizer and the QUBE. Until now, we haven't even had a good suspect."

"So you buy this crazy story, then? Aidan's the goddamned CTO!"

Laurel glanced at Jack. "Let's just say I think it's worth checking out."

Jack suppressed a smile. "That's all I'm asking for."

Shea took a swig from his beer bottle. "All right. I'll play detective, if only to shut you the fuck up about Aidan O'Keefe. Stathis, can you lend a hand?"

"Absolutely!"

Shea turned his steely gaze back on Jack. "You never did say why you wanted to keep your big nerd talk in the Black Box off the record."

It was Jack's turn to fetch a new bottle. "Because I don't trust Aidan O'Keefe. Obviously. I tried to talk Peter out of letting Aidan in on the science. He blew his stack and made me give the talk to the whole staff."

Laurel said, "Listen, everyone. This might be the last time we get away from the campus for a long, long time. If Aidan's the mole, he's connected to people who won't hesitate to kill to get this technology. The world is getting scary. Everyone's acting like the oil synthesizer is production-ready. The stock market goes up and down a thousand points a day, entirely on rumors. OPEC is breaking up. Russia's economy is crashing. There's a counter-revolution in Venezuela. Radical Greens are ready to storm the campus. God knows how many more nuts like Ivo Maskowicz are out there. Half of the countries in the Middle East are preparing for war. Hell, the North Koreans are threatening to nuke the entire West Coast."

"So why not quit?" blurted Deepthi Damodaran. "If we're looking down the barrel of a gun, maybe we should get out of the way of the bullet."

Jack said, "That's just not an option, Deepthi. Not for me." He took a long drink from his bottle. "Look. We built the most advanced computer in human history, using scientific principles we barely understand. By all rights this thing shouldn't work at all. It seems to violate the second law of thermodynamics. We're running computer programs across parallel universes." He paused, shaking his head. "That news will turn the scientific world on its head. If the HyperQUBE works, God knows what we'll be able to do with what amounts to infinite computing power.

"The thing is, it might just turn out to be the tip of the iceberg." He lowered his voice. "I'm working on something. I call it N-dimensional quantum continuum manifold theory—or *quantinuum theory*, if you like. If it turns out to be true, we'll be rewriting a good chunk of modern physics. The quantinuum is... well, it's weird. Counter-intuitive. *Anti-*

intuitive. If the math works out, we'll be able to do things you can't imagine."

He paused as the possibilities flickered through the back of his mind. No. I can't share this with them yet. If I'm wrong, I'm going to sound like the world's biggest crackpot. But if I'm right...

He shook himself back to the present, picking his words like a soldier crossing a minefield. "I'm working on some programs to run on the QUBE that will help me test the equations. I'm going to need all your help to figure it out."

They goggled at him silently.

His throat was dry. He took another swallow of beer. "The world knows that this kind of technology is possible, even if they don't know the theory behind it. Someone else will figure it out eventually. There are a lot of smart people out there. You can't keep reality secret. If bad guys get there first, the consequences could be... unimaginable."

He swept his gaze around the circle. "Look. I'm not going to lie to you. Things could get bad. They already have. People we care about have died. If I'm right, we're on the edge of a scientific revolution like nothing we've ever seen before. It will reshape the world and everyone in it. We might pay a terrible price for that knowledge, but somebody has to pay it. Zeus took fire away from humanity, then chained Prometheus to a rock with a vulture tearing out his liver for giving it back. But fire made our world possible. Would you want to live in a world without warmth and light?"

They stared at him, the import of what he was saying plain on their shocked, wan faces.

"Look. I'm not angling for martyrdom, here. Quantinuum theory is my baby. I want to bring it into the world. For me, quitting isn't even a possibility. I'm committed. You aren't. That's why I'm talking with you today. You don't have to choose the Prometheus option, but I'm asking you to do it anyway. I can't work this theory out on my own. I need your help." He around the circle. "And I need all of you to help me keep this knowledge from falling into the wrong hands. We're not ready to unveil this to the world yet. We barely understand it ourselves."

He took a deep breath. "Okay. I've told you everything I know. Make your own decisions. But please, keep what I've told you today to yourselves," he said. He looked at John. "Even paranoids can have enemies."

Shea nodded, but he was obviously far from convinced.

Jack stood and drained his bottle. "I'm going for a swim. Think about it. Debate and discuss it. We're here for two more nights. Don't stay in the RVs watching TV. Come outside. Look at the stars. There are worlds out there, just waiting to be discovered." He hesitated, then decided to share just one hint of what might be possible. "If we can work out the kinks in the math, we might even be able to go there."

He met each pair of eyes and saw the dawning recognition in them that he was absolutely serious. Then he folded his lawn chair, carried it by one leg, and walked back toward the camp to get his towel.

Laurel caught up with him. "I'm with you."

"Good. The water should be nice and cool."

"No, Jack. I'm *with* you."

He looked into her shining blue eyes and smiled. "Well, that's even better."

CHAPTER TWENTY-FOUR

Struve Technologies Coyote Hill Campus, Palo Alto, California

September 27

Aidan knocked quietly on the office door.

"*Entrez*," replied a male voice from within.

Aidan eased the door open and slipped inside. "Burning the midday oil, I see."

Blaise Thierry sat at his desk, behind three huge flat panel displays arranged like segments of a castle wall. "I have been working on our project."

"I have news. My Italian friend is no longer a concern."

Blaise nodded. "I read about it on the web this morning. Your 'friend' was one of the so-called innocent bystanders killed at the attack on the cafe?"

"He was. Adam says most of the 'Ndrangheta leadership was wiped out as well. Everyone who knew about my arrangement with di Mottura, in any case."

"Did so many true innocents have to die as well?"

Aidan shrugged. "It had to look like something a rival gang would do. They aren't known for subtlety."

"I suppose not." The Belgian scientist's face was glum.

"Don't let it get to you, Blaise. Restaurant bombings in Europe are a dime a dozen these days. *Arrividerci*, Signor di Mottura. Our new allies have come through for us. Now it's time for us to deliver."

"I think I have it."

"Already?"

Blaise gestured an invitation for Aidan to come around and look at his screens. Amid the dozens of terminal windows and editors filled with E++ program code was a complicated, colorful "ball-and-stick" model of a massive spherical molecule.

"Very pretty," said Aidan.

Blaise sat back in his chair and crossed his arms. "I worked with the immunology group when we were still a pharmaceutical company. I have copies of their research. We worked on host-specific synthetic viruses for use in gene therapy for years, with limited success. But now that QUBE Delta is fully operational, I've made rapid progress. Modeling the capsid proteins is child's play now."

Aidan smiled. "Excellent. How is it triggered?"

"It's keyed to the target's major histocompatibility complex antigens, the ones that are used for tissue typing for transplant patients. The virus will bind to the MHC-I molecule. If the match is perfect, the virus will inject its RNA into the cell. The trigger will be pulled, so to speak. Death is inevitable."

"What is the chance of a false match?"

"Effectively zero. The receptors on the virus coat are designed for the target's tissue type. These genes are highly polymorphic—extremely variable, in other words, across members of our species. For our purposes, they're unique enough to guarantee a match. We will need to sequence the target individual's genome, of course. A single hair or a cheek swab would be enough for the polymerase chain reaction. A quantity of blood or a tissue sample would make things easier. In either case the match will be precise."

Aidan peered at his co-conspirator. "Complicated. Maybe too complicated."

"Not at all. The immunology group already had a working protocol for synthesizing the virus. That's why I chose it. They already proved much of this in the lab. It will work."

"How long will it take?"

Blaise waggled a hand in an *I'm not sure* gesture. "It will take two days to perform the sequencing. The most difficult part is isolating the MHC-I genes, but this is simple enough with the proper restriction enzymes."

"If you say so. Can you do all of this work by yourself?"

"It's mostly automated. Will the lab be free? I do not want to be observed."

"All research projects were frozen when Peter announced the sale of the pharmaceuticals division. Most of the scientists over there have already found new jobs. The rest should be on vacation this week, just like we're supposed to be." He chuckled. "They're not strongly motivated to work overtime. How soon can you start?"

"As soon as I get a sample of the target's DNA."

"Excellent. So, you've developed the trigger. What about the payload?"

Blaise looked at his computer. "The virion is airborne. Once inhaled it will infect the pulmonary cells of the lungs, but only if it matches the target's MHC-I genotype. Then it reproduces and spreads into the blood stream. After ten generations the cells infected by the virus will start to produce a toxic polypeptide. It's based on *kappa*-conotoxin PVIIA—one of the cone shell snail poisons. My version should be about five hundred times more effective. It blocks the potassium channels in cardiac muscle fibers. Death should be swift if not painless, several hours after the initial exposure."

Aidan frowned. "An airborne, heart-stopping virus? How safe is this, Blaise? We don't want to be killed by our own creation."

Blaise frowned, "Perfectly safe. Why else would I choose an immune molecule as the trigger? You could not hope for greater selectivity."

"The toxin can't be detectable in an autopsy."

"When the target dies, the acidity of the blood increases. The toxin changes to an autolytic conformation. It self-disassembles. The digestion products won't be detectable on any toxicology screen. The amount of toxin required is incredibly minute in any case. On the order of micrograms."

"How long will it take you to synthesize the virus?"

Blaise rubbed his chin. "Once the design is complete, a week, perhaps two. The difficulty is in the scheduling. Once Mr. Struve's holiday is over I will have to work late at night, when everyone has gone home. I don't want to arouse suspicions. If anyone asks what I am doing, I will say it is a research project. Which it is. Of a sort."

Aidan considered. "Two weeks is fine for a proof-of-concept, but our new allies will want to be able to deploy this weapon at short notice."

Blaise sniffed. "The capsid proteins are a commodity part. We could synthesize them in bulk quantities. All that would be needed at that point is to add the target-specific receptors. We might be able to get the whole process down to three days. Perhaps two. But this will never be a battlefield weapon, Aidan. The primary design goal was stealth."

Aidan studied Blaise. The molecular designer seemed to have accepted Aidan's taking control over their conspiracy. Adam had not shared the reason for Blaise's betrayal, and the Belgian was singularly unwilling to discuss it, but his obedience to Adam and his Chinese masters was beyond question. The assassination virus had been his idea, though he'd shared the notion with obvious reluctance. Aidan had seized on it with unconcealed glee. Nothing would prove the capabilities of the QUBE more effectively than demonstrating an untraceable, target-specific biological weapon.

Aidan said, "I must admit, Blaise, I am impressed. You seem to have thought of everything."

Blaise shrugged with unusual modesty. "Without QUBE Delta this would have been impossible. I've tried optimizing as many as five properties at once, and the compute runs don't take much longer than if I were only optimizing against one. Charlie would have bogged down at two. The potential for this device is unlimited."

"If Jack can build his HyperQUBE, that will be true, quite literally. Very well, then. I approve. I'll send an update to Adam. Are you ready to begin?"

Blaise hesitated for a long moment before nodding once.

"Shall we get some lunch before you go to the lab?"

The Belgian's eyes widened. "You already have a target in mind?"

Aidan smiled. "We need to stop by cold storage to pick up the blood sample."

CHAPTER TWENTY-FIVE

Struve Technologies Coyote Hill Campus, Palo Alto, California

October 1

John Shea asked Laurel to drive back to the ST campus with him in one of the vans, before the others, and alone. He didn't waste any time with chit-chat. They started to argue about Jack's paranoid theory before they even left the campground, and they didn't stop until they pulled into the underground parking structure.

He turned the key and the van went quiet. He studied her. "You don't *look* like a crazy person."

"I'm not sure Jack's right. But you can't deny that he makes sense."

"The craziest people are the ones who seem to make sense. Then they go and annex the *Sudetenland*."

She snorted. "Look, I'm about a week ahead of you on the 'believing Jack's not a paranoid' curve. He might be wrong about what Aidan said to him, I'll give you that, and Aidan could just brush it off as a coincidence, but this thing with the phone and the watch pushed me over the top. I was there. I *saw* it. Jack's interpretation fits the facts. All we want you to do is check the logs on the microcell concentrator. It should only take a few minutes."

"Okay. Let's do it now."

She looked surprised. "Seriously? It's almost ten o'clock."

"It's either that or I don't sleep a wink tonight, not knowing."

"So you do believe him."

"I'm on the fence, and it's pointy and uncomfortable." He opened the door and got out.

She followed him. "John, let's not talk about this near any microphones."

"I was just about to suggest that very thing. You'll need your laptop."

In short order they found themselves outside the IDF closet on the Pauling Building's fourth floor. John waved his badge in front of the scanner and the door clicked open. He flipped the light on and led Laurel inside. She closed the door after herself.

The closet was small, noisy, and stuffy. It was just big enough for a pair of two-post Chatsworth racks filled with network switches, a few small servers, and a gigantic high-performance router mounted close to the floor. Bundles of multicolored cables descended from huge conduits in the ceiling, down the sides of the racks, and fanned out to connect to the ports on the fronts of the switches. Eye-searing blue LEDs blazed on every device. Tiny green lights blinked above every connected port, showing network activity.

"We can talk in here. No mic and a lot of insulation in the walls," John said loudly, to be heard over the router's fans. He pointed at one of the devices mounted high in the rack. "That's it."

It was a small, handmade-looking metal box outclassed in looks by the gaudy commercial devices surrounding it. The only feature on its front panel was a small, oblong port.

"How do I connect?" asked Laurel.

John pointed to a gray cable hanging from a hook on the wall.

She grabbed the cable. "This should do. DB-9 on one end, USB on the other." She plugged it into the server, then looked around the room. "Uh. No place to put this while I type."

John found a folding chair behind one of the racks. "Have a seat."

He went to one knee beside her chair and watched as she opened her old MacBook, plugged the USB cable in, and started a terminal program. "Is this a null modem cable? And what settings do I use?"

"Hell if I know, and beats me."

"I'll try 9600, eight, one and none."

"Whatever that means."

"9600 baud, eight data bits, one stop bit and no parity."

"Thank you, that's very helpful," he said dryly.

She typed *minicom −s* and tapped the arrow keys to select *Serial port setup* from the primitive-looking text menu that appeared. She entered the settings. Garbage characters appeared. "Crap," she muttered. "Maybe fifty-seven six? Ha. That's it."

The screen now showed this:

```
* * * * * * * * * * * * * * * * * * * * * * * * * *
*          STRUVEPHARMA MICROCELL AUTH & RELAY HOST         *
* COPYRIGHT © 2013 STRUVEPHARMA NETWORK & COMPUTER SVCS *
*                                                          *
* AUTHORIZED USE ONLY --- CONTACT LUKE@STRUVEPHARMA.COM *
*                                                          *
* Login: _                                                 *
*                                                          *
* * * * * * * * * * * * * * * * * * * * * * * * * *
```

"*This* I can help with," he said.

She angled the laptop so he could type.

He keyed in his username and the long password that had taken him weeks to memorize, and silently thanked God that they were still months away from the annual password reset.

He coached her on how to navigate the device, but she didn't need much help. The repeater ran BSD, a variant of UNIX popular for network devices, both commercial and home-grown. It was clear that she'd used it before. In moments they were looking through the call logs.

She said, "Okay, I've found the time of the meeting. Oh, wait, these are UTC time stamps. Thank God they're not in seconds from the epoch."

"Yeah, thank God for that."

She didn't respond to his sarcasm. "Let me see... okay, *now* I found them. Let me copy this to a file." She selected the contents of the screen, tapped some keys, opened an editor and pasted the text into a new document. "Now I just need to know where the config files are. Hopefully the usernames are listed next to the IMSI numbers. Any ideas?"

"No. Sorry. Luke usually drives. One of his guys wrote the software."

She frowned and started typing commands. "Hmm. Nothing in the usual places. Let me see... Oh, good. Someone installed ellsoff. Now we're getting somewhere."

"What the hell is ellsoff?"

She spelled it out. "*L-S-O-F*. A command that lets me see what programs opened what files. Hang on a minute, John, please." She tapped rapidly.

John stood up and stretched. He decided to inspect the equipment. He went behind the rack to inspect the microcell repeater's connections. It took him a few minutes to ensure all of the wires were still independent of the corporate network. All of them were coated with a layer of fine dust.

"No signs of tampering," he said at last.

"Okay, I found the config file," Laurel announced. "Let me see..." She trailed off. "Son of a bitch."

"What?"

She typed more commands into the laptop and did something with the trackpad. Then she reversed the laptop. "Take a look."

He took a knee and looked. The small screen contained two windows, aligned side by side. The one on the left showed a configuration file, formatted for use by a computer, but human-readable. He saw the names of the eleven authorized users, including himself. Each line also included a pair of very long strings of letters mixed with numbers.

Laurel said, "That long number is the cell phone's IMSI—its international mobile subscriber identity. The code next to it must be the phone's hardware ID. I forget what they call it. No user has more than one cell phone on the list."

John nodded. "That's the policy. If your phone's not on the list, you can't get on the cell network. So they tell me."

"Exactly. Now check out the log file on the right. I grepped out every call that matched Aidan's phone."

He followed her instructions. The window on the right showed the time and duration of a call, the phone's ID numbers, whether the call was incoming or outgoing, and a string of geeky abbreviations. He looked up at her. "So?"

Laurel said, "I double-checked it. He didn't send or receive any calls on his one authorized phone until 3:32 PM—more than five hours after the executive staff meeting."

John stood and brushed off his pants. He took a deep breath, trying to remain calm. "You're sure you're looking at the right time and date?"

She pulled her iPhone from her pocket, tapped on it for a few seconds, and showed it to him. It was her Calendar app, showing her schedule from the day in question. The slot between 10 and 11 AM was labeled EXEC STAFF.

"Were there any calls made during the meeting?"

"If there were, they aren't in this log file."

He scratched his head. "Shit. I don't remember this meeting at all."

"I think you were doing the final check of the new vehicle barriers."

"Oh. Yeah." He peered at her, considering. "So either he somehow hid the call, or both you and Jack are lying, crazy or mistaken. Jack's clearly crazy, but you aren't, and I don't think either of you are liars."

"Maybe I didn't tell you earlier. *I* was the first to notice Aidan's watch not beeping. Not Jack. I asked *him* if he noticed anything weird about that meeting, and that's how I phrased it. He remembered the phone call, and he mentioned Aidan's watch. Without my prompting him."

He sighed. "So, not mistaken, then."

She was tactful enough not to smile, but her eyes glowed triumphantly.

"Sheeeeiiiiiiiiit," he growled. "Okay. I believe you."

She turned the laptop back around, typed a few commands, closed it and detached the USB cable, handing it to him.

He unhooked the other end from the server and put the cable back on its hook on the wall. "We're going to have to find out how Aidan got around the phone security."

She stood up. "He probably hacked the software on this box to conceal his second phone. Everyone says he's a wizard programmer. Does he have physical access to this room?"

John rubbed his hands through his short hair. "He has access to everything. Jesus Christ, Laurel. If Aidan O'Keefe is the bad guy, who knows who else he might've recruited." He paused for an instant, thinking furiously. "I don't want anyone in Luke's group to know we're looking. We've got to keep this quiet."

"I'll bring in Eileen Dupree. My friend from the Computer Forensic Laboratory. If she can't figure it out, no one can. But I have to tell my boss. He'll get the whole FBI behind this."

"God almighty. Why would Aidan do it? He's the insider's insider. He knows *everything* about what we're doing here. Why would he set Emily up to be kidnapped or killed? They were together for three years! And everything was going so well!"

"I don't know," Laurel said. "But I want to find out, and fast. If he is the Big Bad, he belongs behind bars."

"Or in a fucking hole in the ground."

"Steady, now," she said, looking alarmed.

He couldn't claim he'd been kidding. She'd been honest with *him*, after all. "If he *is* the mole, we can't trust anything he ever touched, and he touched everything. He wrote our surveillance software. The whole security system here would be compromised. Let's figure out how to nail the bastard, and fast."

"Could you sweep the dorms for bugs? It might be a little suspicious if we're always going into a network closet to talk."

"First thing tomorrow." He sighed. "Dammit. I was hoping we'd be able to eliminate Aidan as a suspect. Now I won't sleep for a week."

"My prescription is beer. Lots and lots of beer."

"We're going to have to be careful. If Aidan thinks we're on to him, he could erase every bit of evidence in the computer system."

"Don't worry. *This ain't my first rodeo*, as Cowboy Bob would say. Can you and Stathis look for the video from the Black Box talk tomorrow?"

He nodded. "We will, but I'm not too hopeful. My guess is that Aidan covered his tracks somehow. He's scary-smart."

She smiled smugly. "Not as smart as Jack. He was way ahead of us on this."

John snorted. "Lord, don't tell *him* that. He already has trouble getting his head through the door." He looked at her speculatively. "You know, I was just kidding about you two being lovebirds, back at the lake. But *are* you getting serious about Captain Cussword?"

She laughed and looked at the floor.

He sighed. "Be careful. He might not be a paranoid, he's still a hothead. Keep this phone thing between us until we get some admissible evidence, okay? I saw him doing *kajukenbo* forms in the gym a couple of weeks ago. It's weird but it's no joke. He'd probably march right up to Aidan and break his neck for him." *If I don't beat him to it.*

CHAPTER TWENTY-SIX

Struve Technologies Coyote Hill Campus, Palo Alto, California

October 2

"Here we are," said Laurel. She fished a key from her pocket, slid it into the lock and opened the door.

The storage room lacked a badge sensor, which meant that people going in and out wouldn't attract any unwanted attention from anyone with access to *Argus*. She and John Shea had swept it for bugs earlier that morning. The shelves of janitorial supplies had been shoved together into one corner of the room. Someone had brought in a stubby folding table. It took up most of the scant floor space.

Stathis Sotiropoulos was there, sitting at the table, facing the door. He looked up from his giant Alienware laptop and smiled. "Hey, Laurel."

Behind him, a pair of long gray cables ran from the table, up one wall, and into the space above the drop ceiling. A tile had been pushed aside to make room for them. One of the long cables connected to the tiny network switch on the table. The other led to the back of the Greek's laptop.

"Hey, Stathis." Laurel led Dupree into the room and made the introductions. "Eileen's helped me with a few other investigations over the last five years. She's as sharp as they come."

"Pleased to meet you, Stathis," Eileen said. She didn't have any trouble with his name. "Laurel's told me a lot about you. I'm sure we'll get on like a house on fire."

He blushed furiously and stammered an incoherent reply.

Laurel suppressed a smile. Eileen had that effect on a lot of guys. She had a pleasant, freckled face, a great figure and a spectacular head of curly auburn hair. She had charisma to spare, a lively intelligence, and an operatic contralto voice that melted straight male geeks like butter under a blowtorch.

They got right to work. They set up their laptops on either side of his. There was a power strip and an eight-port network switch.

"Don't use the Wifi, and don't connect to the switch yet," said Stathis, finally recovered from his initial encounter with Eileen. "It's hooked up to the sniffer port on the core router down the hall. I started looking at the network traffic about an hour ago."

"Find anything?" said Eileen.

"Yep." The Greek's awkwardness had vanished now that they were talking shop. "The router is lying."

He showed them the Wireshark scans he'd collected. "I was going to look for the video files you wanted, but I got sidetracked by this. See? These packets have non-standard type IDs. And there are a lot of them. That's not the weird part. We move a lot of data using private protocols and strong encryption. It's part of the security design. Even if a hacker were to break into the network somehow, they'd just see a lot of gibberish hauling ass on the net. Sorry," he said, blushing again and looking quickly at Eileen.

She dimpled and said, "I've heard worse."

He returned her smile shyly. "The weird thing is, the router doesn't seem to keep track of this packet type at all. It's not showing up on the stats table. It doesn't matter how much of this traffic there is. It isn't counted. If I weren't hooked up to the router's sniffer port directly, I'd never know it was there."

"Show me," Eileen said. All traces of humor were gone from her face.

Laurel watched as Eileen and the Greek puzzled it out. She followed their logic easily enough, but the speed with which they characterized the problem was nothing short of astonishing. It took them only minutes to prove that the router was doing everything it could to hide the existence of these packets to a casual observer. The suspicious packets originated only from Linux servers, not from laptops or portable internet devices.

Eileen said, "Someone went to a lot of trouble to hide his tracks. Really nice work tracking this rogue traffic down." She beamed at Stathis.

He blushed. "If John Shea hadn't unlocked the wiring closet for me so I could cable it up, I'd never have seen it. I'm guessing the bad guys were counting on no one getting the authorization to plug straight into the sniffer port."

Eileen laughed bitterly. "My job was so much easier when everyone used hubs."

"*Hubs*," scoffed the Greek.

They all chuckled. By today's standards, hubs were as antique as buggy whips and bed warmers. Any device connected to one would be able to "see" all of the network traffic from all the other connected devices, but they were incredibly slow.

Eileen said, "Who made your routers?"

"They're custom-built," replied Stathis. "Aidan's idea. Saved us a ton of money, or so he said."

Eileen nodded. "Uh huh. Sounds like BS to me. Does he have any experience with embedded systems programming?"

"Writing router firmware is kind of a black art. He probably con-tracted it out."

Laurel said, "If he did, there'll be a record of it. Great work, Stathis. Eileen, what do you think?"

"I think we need to log into these Linux boxes and see what's what."

Laurel considered it. "Risky. If Aidan's this careful, he probably set up tripwires."

"We'll never know unless we try."

Stathis shook his head. "It doesn't matter. None of us have direct root access. Or do we?" He peered at Laurel.

She shook her head. "Just *sudo* privileges."

"How secure is the authentication?" asked Eileen.

The Greek scowled. "There's no way to get in without being detect-ed. You need a hardware key and a one-time password to get root access, unless you're a member of Network and Computing Systems. All access is logged in the ELK stack, anyway. Come to think of it, so is the command-line interface on the router. Crap. He might know we logged in already."

"Spilt milk," Eileen said, patting his hand and provoking another feverish blush.

They sat back, defeated. They looked at each other. After a time, it became clear that no one had any ideas.

"Well, shit," said Laurel at last. "Let's go talk to John Shea."

Laurel led them to the security office on the first floor. John Shea was watching the installers put the finishing touches on the expanded outdoor surveillance system. When he saw Laurel's companions, he jerked his head toward the open door of his office. He closed it after them. There were only two chairs in the office, so they all stood in a loose circle near the door.

Laurel looked up at the ceiling meaningfully.

"It's clean. We can talk in here," he said.

His expression became grim as they explained their findings.

Laurel said, "We need to take a look at one of these servers. Can we sweet-talk Luke Tso into giving us access?"

"He's the Chief Information Officer. I can't make him or anyone in NCS do anything they don't want to do. And they won't want to work around the security rules we put in place five years ago. I was the one who insisted on them. Luke's a nice guy but he'll just laugh at me and call Peter."

"Then let's talk to Peter first."

John folded his arms and frowned. "Is your evidence solid enough to make a case against the CTO? Because if it isn't, we could find our asses out on the street."

Laurel said, "He can't fire Eileen or me. If I have to, I can call in my boss. I briefed him on our theories about Aidan last night." She held up her thumb and forefinger, a hair's breadth apart. "He's *this close* to sending in the troops. If he finds out that Peter's blocking the investigation, he'll declare a national security emergency and take control of the facility. The whole place will be shut down while every Federal law enforcement agency goes through it with a fine-toothed comb. If Peter doesn't cooperate, that could drag on for months. Or years."

She didn't think John's expression could get any bleaker. She was wrong. "Jesus, Laurel," he whispered. His shoulders slumped.

"I'm sorry, John. Seigart's been on a war footing ever since the Chinese hacked the Office of Personnel Management. That was a huge black eye for the department, and God help you if you ever mention it in his presence. He's my boss, and his boss' boss is the President of the United States. If they find out what we discovered today, they'll peel this company like an apple to find out who's responsible. We don't have a choice."

"I guess we don't." John heaved a sigh, straightened up, and looked at the Greek. "You up for this?"

Stathis glanced at Laurel and Eileen uneasily. "Yeah, I guess so. No offense, Laurel, but we can't let the Feds come in. You heard Jack at the lake. The team needs more time to work out the theory. We've got to give it to them."

Laurel said, "No offense taken. I agree."

John slapped Stathis on the back. "You are a steely-eyed missile man."

He beamed in response. "Whatever it takes. If that means I lose my job, well, I guess I'll brush up my LinkedIn profile. DuPont's always trying to recruit me, anyway."

"What theory?" asked Eileen, looking at Stathis.

John glanced at her and quickly said, "Might as well get this Charlie Foxtrot over with. Let's go talk to Peter." He opened the door and strode out. They followed him.

"What theory?" Eileen asked Laurel.

"Uh, I'll tell you later." Laurel hurried to catch up with John. "Are you sure you want to do this?"

They stopped in front of the freight elevator.

John punched the call button. "They'll be lining up to hire Stathis, but who's going to want to rent an old jarhead like me?"

"I'll fix you up. *Semper fi*, Devil Dog."

"Oorah." His sardonic smile faded all too quickly.

Peter Struve was in his office. He'd returned from a quick trip to Italy to visit his wife and daughters the previous night. As usual, he looked exhausted, but the worried frown he'd worn constantly before the successful test of QUBE Delta was absent.

He welcomed Laurel and John readily enough, but his expression grew quizzical when the Greek and Eileen Dupree followed them in. They sat at the round conference table in futuristic but uncomfortable rolling chairs.

John started talking before Laurel could utter a word. He didn't stop until the whole story was laid out. He spoke without emotion or inflection, as if he were briefing a superior officer on a battle action gone wrong. Laurel reflected that he'd probably done that very thing at least a few times during his career. She let him talk without interruption, and glanced meaningfully at Stathis and Eileen to make sure they did the same.

Peter's face hardened when John mentioned Jack's suspicions about Aidan. He turned bright red when John described the secret meeting in the Black Box, and Laurel's role in hiding it from the cameras. He avoided looking at her until John told him of the suspicious call Aidan had taken during the staff meeting, and how she and Jack had convinced John to look at the cell phone repeater logs. Then the CEO glared at her fiercely. He tried to speak, but John asked him to wait. Peter folded his arms and nodded, his lips turning white with the effort needed to bite back the words.

John told Peter how they'd failed to turn up evidence in the logs of Aidan's cell phone call. "I know, absence of proof isn't proof of anything, but it made us think. That's why we brought Eileen in to look at the network. She and Stathis turned up something today that scares the crap out of us. Laurel?"

Laurel cleared her throat and described their findings: the mysterious encrypted packets, the routers failing to count them, and the destination addresses that went to nowhere. Winding to a close, she said, "Something really weird is going on, Peter, and it looks like Aidan's at the center of it."

"He is."

Laurel, John and the others exchanged shocked looks.

"What?" said John.

Peter frowned at him. "He and Luke set up a backup surveillance system called *dathan*. You ever hear the expression, 'who will watch the watchmen?' For us, it's *dathan*. It's wired into everything. It tracks everything. Or so they tell me."

"How long has this been running?" asked John.

"Since we built this campus."

"Jesus. And you never told me anything about it."

"It was strictly on a need-to-know basis," Peter said coldly. "And you didn't need to know. You still don't, as far as I'm concerned. And if you breathe a word of this to anyone outside this room, you are history." His eyes shifted to Stathis. "Both of you."

The Greek nodded miserably and sank deeper into his chair.

"What about Aidan's call?" Laurel blurted. "If he used his real phone, there should be a record of it. If not, he shouldn't have been able to take the call at all, not in this building."

Peter looked at her as if she had just passed wind. "That is the *only* reason I haven't thrown you out on your ass, Agent Wynn. I want the answer to that question, too. Wait here." He stood up, stalked to the door, and slammed it shut behind him.

They looked at each other for a long time in utter silence.

"Jesus Christ," breathed Stathis.

Eileen reached over and squeezed his wrist. "Steady."

Laurel looked at John. "Are you all right?"

His face was blank. "I'm fine. That went better than I thought it would."

"It did?" whispered Stathis.

"We didn't get fired, did we?"

The door opened. Luke Tso walked in, followed by Peter. Luke wore a light blue short-sleeved shirt and khaki Dockers. Laurel had met the CIO only once. He was of Taiwanese extraction, of medium height and slight build, and in his mid- to late-forties. As usual, he wore a sunny smile.

Peter closed the door after him. He turned the lock and returned to his seat. "Aidan's not in his office. I asked Janice to find him."

Luke took the sole remaining rolling chair, between John and Peter.

"What's going on?" said Luke.

Peter said, "They discovered *dathan*."

Luke's smile vanished. He looked around at the others. "Hmm. Had to be Stathis, right? How?"

John said, "I let them hook up to one of the core routers." He gestured at Stathis and Eileen. "They saw the traffic."

"That's a serious breach of security protocols," said the CIO, frowning.

Peter said, "He's already been spanked, Luke. All right, Agent Wynn. Fill him in. Don't leave anything out."

Luke's face darkened as she recapped the story of their investigation, but went blank when the subject of Aidan's suspected duplicate cell phone came up. "I was in that meeting," he said when Laurel finished. "I remember that, too."

Peter's frown deepened. "Aidan's watch didn't ring when he took the call?"

"That's right," Luke said. His face was growing worried now. "He's always bragging about his watch because he can answer the phone on it. And that time, he didn't."

Peter's desk phone bleated. He picked up the receiver and listened.

Laurel shot John a triumphant look. He noticed, but gave a tiny shake of his head. She mastered her reaction with difficulty. *Right. Not time to celebrate yet.*

Peter's frown became a scowl. "Okay, thanks." He hung up the phone. "John, would you see if you can track Aidan down? Janice can't find him anywhere."

"Sure." He left the room.

Laurel's satisfaction at being corroborated by Luke withered and died. *Uh oh. Maybe Aidan found out we were on to him.*

Stathis said, "What about the video footage from the Black Box lab? Luke's here. He should be able to find the files, if there are any."

Peter nodded to the CIO. "Do it."

They gathered behind Luke's chair and watched him work. It didn't take him long to find the files from the date of Jack's secret talk. His web browser showed a list of files with long, cryptic names. He said, "There's one compressed file generated per camera per hour, stored in triplicate in the Hadoop cluster. The room, camera number and timestamp are part of the file name."

Laurel said, "If I switched off the cameras in *Argus*, should there even *be* any files?"

"No. They should end at the time the camera was turned off, and start up again when the camera's turned on."

She leaned close and looked at the listing on the screen. "They all start at the beginning of the hour."

He scanned the list as well. "They do. And they're all about the same length. They shouldn't be, if you turned the cameras off. How long was Jack's talk?"

"The cameras were offline from 12:23 to 12:57."

Luke shook his head. "The files starting at noon should be smaller. But they're not."

"Can you bring one up on the screen?"

"Give me a minute." He typed out commands with the staccato speed of a well-seasoned geek.

Laurel looked at Peter. "There were eight people in the Black Box who'll swear to the time and date of Jack's meeting."

He returned her gaze with stony silence.

"Here it is," said Luke. He tapped the RETURN key.

A window popped up in the middle of Luke's screen. It was filled with random blocks of color that shifted and moved across the screen in waves.

"What the hell," Luke whispered. "Let me try another one." He typed again. Another window popped up. It too was filled with tiny colored squares.

"Macro blocking," Eileen said. "Looks like a bug in the video compression. Are you using H.265?"

Stathis said, "No, we wrote a really lossy codec to get better compression. A lot of unsharp masking to bring out edge detail. Try one of the files from earlier in the day."

Luke did so. A view from one of the ceiling cameras appeared. It showed Ben and Deepthi sitting side by side at one of the lab bench workstations, peering at a laptop screen. The image was a little grainy but clear enough. Deepthi kissed Ben's cheek at one point.

"Fast forward it?" suggested Laurel.

Luke complied. The video was clear all the way to the end of the file. They spent another minute verifying that there were hour-long files from every camera in the Black Box. Every one they checked was filled with random blocks of color.

Peter said, "I don't understand. What the hell does this mean?"

Eileen replied, "Either there's a bug in your video compression software that just *happened* to affect every single camera in the Black Box at the exact time Jack gave his talk, or someone screwed up and replaced the original files with fakes that are too long."

"There isn't any bug!" The Greek's voice was outraged. "I helped write that codec! We tested the shit out of it."

Eileen asked, "Who did you help, Stathis?"

His eyes narrowed. "Aidan O'Keefe."

Peter looked at Luke.

The CIO shook his head. "No way is this accidental. If Laurel turned off the cameras, there should be a gap in the coverage, and there isn't one. Those files are fakes." He looked down at his laptop screen. "Oh, shit."

"What is it?" said Eileen.

"They're gone." He clicked the Refresh button in his web browser and looked at the results again. "All of those video files. The ones with the glitches. They've just been deleted."

"God damn it," grated Peter. He looked at Laurel. "Okay. I believe you. Find that son of a bitch *now*."

Laurel grabbed her cell phone and tapped in a number. She turned on the speaker. "John? Any luck?"

"Not yet. He's not in any of his usual hangouts. I just got to the security office," he said. His voice grew quieter as he said to someone, "Find Aidan O'Keefe on the badge tracker." There was a pause. "Okay, then check the gate logs." Another pause, longer this time. "Fuck! Laurel, he's gone. He left campus almost an hour ago."

"Goddammit!" snarled the Greek. "That's my fault."

"It's no one's fault," said Laurel. "He must have been monitoring the routers. He did have a tripwire. You couldn't have known, Stathis."

"John," said Peter loudly. "Lock him out until we get to the bottom of this."

"Will do."

"I've got to call the San Francisco office," Laurel said. "He might have gone home. John, I'm hanging up."

She found Robbie Holmes in her phone's "favorites" list and dialed him. She could arrest O'Keefe on suspicion of conspiracy now. There was enough evidence for that, even if it might not hold up in court. She just prayed they were in time.

CHAPTER TWENTY-SEVEN

San Francisco, California

October 2

Aidan walked calmly from the elevator to his apartment and opened the door with casual deliberation.

Once inside, he went into overdrive.

He tore off his work clothes and put on a black San Francisco Giants T-shirt, blue jeans and battered-looking cross-trainers. He removed his glasses and inserted a pair of contact lenses with brown false-color irises. A gray hoodie sweatshirt went on last.

He grabbed his "go" bag from the top of the closet. It was a big green gym bag with a white Nike swoosh down the side, complete with grooming kit, change of clothes, fake IDs and an envelope stuffed with cash.

He retrieved his MacBook from the desk in his study, powered it down and put it in the bag, along with the hardback he'd used to hide the one-time pads he'd once used to communicate with Alberto di Mottura. The encryption pads themselves were long gone, but he didn't want to have to explain a book with hollows cut into the pages.

Before he left the ST parking garage, he'd shut off his phones to keep anyone from tracking him via cell towers. He'd gambled that no one had installed a GPS tracker on his car in the short time since Laurel Wynn and John Shea had been back from their vacation. He'd have to abandon the car anyway. His exit plan called for him to travel light.

He ejected the SIM cards from his phones with a small, bent paper clip. He unrolled six feet of toilet tissue, wadded it up, and ran cold water over it from the faucet. He thrust the tiny chips into the damp wad and flushed it, then flushed again for good measure. He put the phones into the bag along with his gold watch and eyeglasses. He disguised the white band of skin on his wrist with a cheap Timex he'd bought at Walgreens a few weeks earlier. He completed his new ensemble with a black Giants baseball cap.

He took the freight elevator to the parking garage and left the building via a stairway. The door opened onto the driveway behind the building. A high wooden fence separated the driveway from the massive construction project next door, where the new Transbay Terminal was being built.

The marine cloud layer was close to the ground today, accompanied by a chill breeze. He put the hood up over his hat and crossed the busy street. *I'm just another work-a-day schlub with too much time on his hands.* He forced himself not to look around for anyone who might be watching him. *Blend in. You are a schlub. Think schlub thoughts. Be the schlub. Go, Giants.* He sauntered to the temporary bus terminal a block away, smiling vacantly.

His apartment building was a block and a half from the terminal. As he waited there, he saw a pair of black SUVs screech around the corner from Market Street and park slantwise in front of the parking garage exit. A pack of men and a few women in off-the-rack suits raced into his apartment building.

He was both elated at the ease of his escape and infuriated by the need for it. That bitch Laurel Wynn had found him out, all right.

The *dathan* agent on the microcell repeater had told him about her snooping as it happened the previous night, sending an encrypted text message to him over the cellular network. Worrisome, but not of itself enough to trigger his escape plan.

As soon as he arrived on campus at ten o'clock this morning, he watched the *Argus* videos of Wynn and John Shea emerging from the IDF closet on the fourth floor the previous night. While he did that, another alert came in. Stathis Sotiropoulos had logged into the second-floor core router. That had been truly alarming. Aidan searched through the surveillance logs. Seconds later, he watched footage of Laurel Wynn and the investigator from the Computer Forensic Lab walk into a janitorial closet on the second floor.

He was never one for second thoughts. Even before Stathis had a chance to log out of the router, Aidan launched his fail-safe programs and headed for his car. The programs ran on a dead-man switch. If he failed to stop them within an hour, they would begin to erase all evidence in the server farm that could possibly incriminate him.

He could explain a sudden departure in the middle of the workday. He might be able to explain the glitched video files. Explaining how and why thousands of files had suddenly vanished from the Hadoop cluster would be impossible.

He checked his Timex. The fail-safes would have begun deleting files a few minutes ago.

It didn't matter. The agents pouring into his apartment building were enough evidence of that. His days at ST were over.

If Aidan had been in any way religious, he would have thanked God that the commute traffic had ended before he'd been forced to flee the campus.

A bus pulled into the terminal. He mastered his disgust and got on without checking its destination.

It took him to the west side of the city—the Sunset District. He got off near the northern entrance of Golden Gate Park. He walked across the lush green meadows. At length he found himself in front of the California Academy of Sciences.

He paid cash for a ticket, went inside, found a disabled-only bathroom, and locked himself in. The room was spotless, to his immense relief. The odor of bleach was still thick in the air.

He pulled a plastic garbage bag and a battery-operated hair trimmer from his go-bag. He spread the bag out on the floor, set the guard on the trimmer to a quarter of an inch, and quickly shaved his head, catching the hair with the bag. When he was done he examined himself in the mirror, touching up the areas he'd missed. He *tsked* with disappointment. He hadn't worn a buzz cut since he was in elementary school. It was not a flattering look. He looked like he'd just been released from prison. *Better than just checking into one,* he mused.

He pulled a blue windbreaker, a flat woolen cap, and a white button-down shirt still in its wrapper from the go-bag and changed into them. He removed the contact lenses and put in another pair, this one with false green irises. He put the phones, his eyeglasses, his watch, and the envelope of money into his jacket pockets. The hair trimmings bag went into the trash, along with the wadded-up schlub disguise and the "go" bag. He left the building carrying nothing but his laptop and the book formerly containing his one-time pads.

He found a cab outside the museum. It took him to the nearest BART station. He dropped the hardback into a trash can before buying a ticket.

The southbound train was lightly traveled, but he stood near a door anyway, ready to bolt if it opened and there was any sign of pursuit—and to keep from soiling his clothes, humble as they were.

He was in plain view of the cameras spaced at intervals along the ceiling of the car, but there was no way to avoid them. He presumed they were connected to video recorders, not sending their signals straight to the home office. At least he hoped that was the case. It would be hard to send that much data reliably with the trains constantly going in and out of tunnels, and very expensive, to boot. The more he thought about it, the more relaxed he became. Even if the FBI thought to examine the tapes, he would be well away by the time they collected them, much less recognized him.

Aidan took the time to unlink his Apple Watch from his phone and reset all the devices to factory defaults before turning them off. He suspected that a forensics expert could recover the phone's memory, but if he was caught before he reached his destination, he didn't want to make it easier for them.

When he reached the end of the line in Millbrae, he transferred onto Caltrain. He mounted the steps into the car and gasped when he smelled the air inside. It stank of urine. It was all he could do to keep from vomiting. He went forward two cars to get away from the rancid stench, but he couldn't escape the chemical reek of vinyl seat cushions. The ride down the peninsula took an eternity.

He called Tom Reed from a payphone at the San Jose Diridon station. Then he took a taxi to the nearby Valley Fair Mall.

He bought fresh clothing at Nordstrom, paying with cash. He breathed a huge sigh of relief as he changed into his clean, comfortable new purchases in the public restroom. He flipped the contact lenses into the trash and put his glasses back on. His gold Apple Watch and the cheap Timex went into the trash as well.

He sighed as he strapped on his new Citizen chronograph. It looked like gold, if you squinted, but it just wasn't the same.

Tom, sporting his ever-present Bluetooth earpiece, met him in the hallway near the parking structure entrance. He led Aidan to his dark green Hummer H2 SUV. Aidan got into the back. The heavily tinted rear windows would conceal him, but he folded himself into the space behind the passenger seat and covered himself with a black blanket just in case.

Tom drove for about half an hour, choosing streets at random. At last he said, "My guys say we're clear. If you had a tail, you lost him. What the hell happened?"

Aidan pushed the blanket off and buckled himself into the rear seat. "I'm burned. Laurel Wynn started digging. No idea what got her attention, but she was clearly on to something. I got away from the apartment a couple of minutes ahead of the FBI."

"Son of a bitch," Tom breathed. "What do we do now?"

Aidan thought about it. "Blaise is still inside. They can't know anything about him. I made sure there's no evidence of our collaboration. He's safe. We need to get rid of these phones and then visit a few safe deposit boxes. In the meantime, call Adam. We need to meet."

Their Chinese contact had rented a suite for their meeting at the Fairmont in downtown San Jose. Tom ferried Aidan to the hotel and went in with him while four of his most trusted men kept watch in the lobby and outside on the street.

"Adam" opened the door for them. He ushered them in. He exchanged an impassive nod with Tom, who took up a position next to the door.

Adam's real name remained a mystery, but Aidan could guess at his background. He was taller than average, and in his mid-thirties. He was fit, trim, and moved with the same casual fearlessness as Tom and his highly-trained men. If he carried a weapon, it was well-concealed. Based on his accent and elocution, he was either from Hong Kong or had learned English in the UK, and was well educated. With luck, that would work in Aidan's favor.

Blaise was already in the hotel room, panic inscribed on his face. He rose from his chair in the suite's sitting area and blurted, "What the devil is happening, Aidan? There was a company meeting this afternoon. They announced that you were fired! And what happened to your hair?"

Aidan sat and poured himself a glass of water from the carafe on the low table. "Sit down, and I'll tell you."

Adam took the remaining chair. His face was wooden throughout Aidan's terse summary of the day's events.

By contrast, when Aidan finished his tale, Blaise's expression bordered on hysteria. "Aidan!" he shouted, red-faced. "What am I to do now? I am alone inside that company!"

"Be calm," snapped Adam. "You heard him. They do not suspect you." He turned his gaze on Aidan. "The real question is, what are *you* to do now? Your value to us has dropped considerably."

"On the contrary," said Aidan. He sat back in his chair and folded his hands in his lap. "I'm more valuable to you than ever. I know more about the software architecture of the QUBE and its support systems than anyone in the company."

"And how will we make use of that knowledge?" said Adam. "Have you forgotten the reason for our trial run? You were to prove that you could use the QUBE for our purposes without anyone inside the company learning of it."

Aidan glanced at Blaise. "When will the product be ready?"

Blaise gaped at him for a moment before responding. "Another week. Perhaps two, if security grows more intrusive."

"You *will* be able to smuggle it out?"

"Yes. They are only looking for electronics and RFID-tagged documents."

Aidan returned his gaze to Adam. "When it's ready, we'll complete the demonstration. You and your masters will have proof that we can do what we claim."

"Even if it works, it is irrelevant now. You cannot get within a thousand meters of the QUBE."

"Then we'll have to go in and get it."

The Chinese agent gave a single, scornful laugh. "Do you propose that we steal the entire Pauling Building? How would we get it through Customs?"

Aidan looked at his fingernails. "Sometimes I wonder if you actually listen when I talk, Adam. Jack Dura's team is designing the HyperQUBE. His theory was proven by QUBE Delta. The HyperQUBE will contain a new type of entanglotron. If Jack's theory works, it won't need the network, the buffer systems or the server farm, just a few dozen commodity machines to collect and correlate the results. All you need is the processor, the schematics, the software, and someone who knows how to use them. Someone like me. You can be up and running in a matter of months."

"You are a fool," Adam said. "How would we get in? You yourself have told me that the building is virtually impregnable by anything short of an army."

Aidan looked at Blaise. "We still have a man inside."

Blaise paled.

Adam scoffed, "Of what value is that against their security team? Do you think Blaise can smuggle the HyperQUBE out in his jumpsuit pocket? Can he defeat John Shea's SEALs? Can he open the gates to us when there are fifty armed guards on patrol at all times? And what new security measures will they enact now that they *know* they have been penetrated by a spy?"

Aidan sat back in his chair and folded his arms. "Tell me, Adam: what was your plan when Blaise Thierry was your only asset inside the company? Were you just going to sit on your hands and watch as SP created the most valuable technology in the history of mankind?"

"The situation was entirely different then!" Adam snarled. "Emily Dura was still alive! The QUBE was still unproven, but their guard was down! A small strike force could have seized her and her research. Now, thanks to your foolishness, they are ready for anything."

"No," Aidan said. "They are most certainly not ready for *anything*." He stood and went to the window. The orange-pink sodium vapor lights and stunted skyscrapers of downtown San Jose stretched out below. A Southwest Airlines plane swooped overhead on its way to a landing at the nearby airport.

He turned and locked eyes with the Chinese spy. "You need to think of the future, Adam. The not-very-distant future. What happens when the U.S. government gets its hands on the QUBE? If you believe this technology will remain in private hands, then you're the fool, not I."

Adam scowled but said nothing.

Aidan slowly walked closer to the Chinese agent. "Can you imagine what will happen when the black magicians at Langley and Los Alamos and Lockheed get their own QUBEs? They will unlock every secret of the natural world. No technology will be outside their reach. They could build spy robots the size of gnats that could penetrate every secret facility in China, or make hypersonic stealth missiles that could rain down on you without any notice at all. Every tank, airplane, ship and missile base in your country could vanish in a moment.

"And they don't need anything that exotic. Do you think Blaise is the only person who could design a targeted virus? It took him a week, working by himself. Imagine the chaos if the whole Standing Committee dropped dead at the same time. Or every soldier in the People's Liberation Army."

"They wouldn't dare." Adam's voice was shaky.

"Why wouldn't they, if they thought they could get away with it?" Aidan stopped next to Adam's chair. "Even if they don't build a single weapon—*that's* a laugh—they'll still be able to torpedo your economy. Who would buy anything from China when the U.S. could make everything better, faster, and infinitely cheaper? That's the real danger, Adam. Your superiors know it, even if you don't. You'll be reduced to a nation of beggars."

Adam stared up at Aidan, but he said nothing. Perspiration glistened on his forehead.

Aidan's voice dropped to a murmur. "The world knows that the QUBE can be built. It's only a matter of time before someone else builds one—years, perhaps decades, but it *will* happen. The U.S. could use that time to dominate the world in every area that matters. But remember this: as soon as they test the HyperQUBE, if it works, our window slams shut. The government will move the device and the researchers to a secure location. In a few years they'll have dozens of QUBEs. The U.S. could destroy the economies of every other nation and laugh while doing it. The rest of the world will be third-class citizens for the rest of history."

The room was silent for a long time.

"What would you have me do?" said Adam at last.

Aidan kept the triumphant smile from reaching his lips. "Contact your masters. We will need every assistance they can give. It's just a matter of weeks before Jack grows the HyperQUBE. Blaise will be able to tell us if it works, and keep us up to date on their new security measures. You must be ready to strike, and to strike hard. You have to take it, while there's still only one, before they can move it offsite, and make sure they can't build another one for as long as possible." He glanced at Tom, who had a tiny smile on his lips. He looked back down at Adam. "You said we'd need an army to breach ST security."

"Yes."

"Then get us one."

BOOK TWO

THE BORROWED SWORD

CHAPTER TWENTY-EIGHT

Pacific Ocean

October 22

The BCL *Barinthus* was named after an obscure Celtic god of the sea. She was Baskin Container Line's newest vessel, if not its biggest. She floated out of Samsung Heavy Industry's Geoje dock in 2014. Her decks were piled high with stacks of colorfully painted intermodal shipping containers.

The narrow twenty- and forty-foot steel boxes could be unloaded by crane and placed onto trains and trucks for shipment overland to their final destinations. Most were filled with Japanese cargo bound for the United States: electronics, books, packaged foods, furniture, toys. *Barinthus* could carry a staggering 8,500 twenty-foot containers, making her mid-sized by today's standards. She was too wide to fit through the Panama Canal, but could be accommodated at most deep-water ports around the rim of the Pacific.

Like all of Baskin's ships, the *Barinthus* was registered out of Monrovia, though Baskin's headquarters were in the City of London. The Liberian "flag of convenience" allowed Baskin to run the ship at a much lower cost, since she was not bound by the labor laws and tax regulations of the United Kingdom.

Much of the savings came from reduced payroll. Ships registered out of Liberia could hire crews from anywhere. By contrast, ships on a national registry were required to hire the majority of their crews from that nation. Ships on open registries were free to set their wages at whatever price the market would bear. The practice was not popular with labor unions, but it was common nonetheless.

Baskin was a young and relatively small company, but it was growing fast. It paid its employees more than most open-registry shippers, having realized early that a well-compensated crew kept their expensive ships delivering on time. Baskin lived in the gap between the underpaid and the (by their standards) grossly overpaid. The strategy worked. The Baskin work force was affordable and yet competent. It recognized an annual savings of over three million dollars on the *Barinthus* payroll alone.

The company's reputation for on-time delivery was peerless, and that reputation was largely responsible for its meteoric growth in an industry fallen on hard times in recent years. Baskin traded on it by charging a small premium for faster delivery. Baskin paid every crewman time-and-a-half for every full day the cargo could be brought into port early. The bonus for the skipper was a five-percent per trip bump on his or her annual salary. The surcharge per container was small, but it more than made up for the bonuses.

It was therefore a matter of considerable annoyance to Captain Anneke van den Broeke that her ship had a problem. They were a week out of Singapore and had been just over one knot slow the whole way.

They had offloaded a considerable weight of dense dry-bulk containers in Yokohama in favor of relatively lighter cargo bound for America. The lesser load meant the ship would ride higher in the water. The smaller surface area of the hull below the waterline meant reduced drag. The result was a higher top speed, but she was still making one knot below her rated maximum of twenty-three with this load.

Anneke had commanded *Barinthus* since she was still under construction. This was the first time her vessel had ever given her cause for concern. Something was very wrong.

Chief Engineer Pat Stearns and his mates had found no problems with the two monstrous diesel engines. Everything was running normally. The drive shaft was making 147 RPM at full power. They'd double-checked the rotations using a timing light, similar to the type used for car engine tune-ups. The gigantic six-bladed screw should be pushing *Barinthus* through the waves at the same speed she always did with this load, yet the ship's instruments and handheld GPS receivers all agreed: she was about one knot too slow.

At breakfast this morning, Stearns jokingly suggested that *Barinthus* had contracted a bad case of barnacles while they were tied up in Singapore. Anneke hadn't had her morning coffee yet, and a decaffeinated Captain was a dangerous Captain. She'd pinned his ears back with a verbal barrage that would've left a more junior officer shaking in his boots. Stearns had sailed with her for many years, though. All he did was raise his eyebrows. The unflappable American gathered his crew and headed back to the engine room for another day of searching for the cause. The rest of the small crew was still walking on eggshells, which suited Anneke just fine.

The new Third Officer, Liu Wenlan, was responsible for the stowage of the cargo. Anneke ordered him to take charge of a small detail of seamen to verify the positions and manifests of every container on the ship. An improperly stowed load could cause the ship to ride lower by the bow or stern, impairing her ability to cut through the waves. The vessel's level sensors didn't indicate an imbalance, but no one could imagine what else it could be. Maybe the sensors weren't sensitive enough to pick it up.

Anneke was grimly determined to know the cause of the slowdown, even if she couldn't do anything about it underway. If there *was* a fractionally unbalanced load, she planned to decorate her cabin wall with the scalp of the person responsible.

At this point the job was far from complete. Checking thousands of containers on a ship the size of a small aircraft carrier took a long time. No significant discrepancies had been found yet.

If nothing else, it gave Anneke a chance to see how Liu handled the stress. He'd replaced their former Third Officer, Ole Alfredsson, who had been arrested and jailed for public drunkenness and fighting in Singapore. Liu carried out his duties quickly and efficiently. He was a bit cold to the junior officers and crew, but Anneke put that down to his unfamiliarity with them. She was sure the ice would break after a few weeks at sea. In the meantime, the quest for the cause of the slowdown went on, without results.

Anneke's confusion mounted by the hour. The unbalanced cargo scenario seemed less likely every time she thought about it. She'd checked the specs of the level sensors, re-read the instruction manuals, and even placed a satellite call to the manufacturer. If *Barinthus* were that far off-balance, the tilt of the deck should be detectable. It wasn't.

The only explanation left was increased drag on the hull. Some of the facts argued against it. The ship had no tendency to drift to one side or the other when the rudder was feathered. If there was something stuck to the hull, it was well below the waterline. The very notion was ridiculous, though. If there were a large object stuck to the ship, it would have to have been welded there, or else the tremendous force of the water running under the keel would have stripped it away.

Stearns' barnacle theory was equally ludicrous, but Anneke found herself mulling it over during the few quiet moments in her frenetic daily schedule. The ship's hull was built for speed, albeit by the ponderous standards of container vessels. It was far too soon since her last scraping and repainting for barnacles to have grown back, and the new paint contained tiny amounts of a potent toxin called ivermectin. The bottom-fouling marine animals couldn't tolerate it.

In any case, barnacles wouldn't just sprout full-grown everywhere on the hull during a single port call. Anneke wished that she'd had time to send down divers to inspect the bottom, but the slowdown had almost made them miss their appointment for the slip in Yokohama Harbor. She'd been pressed with making up the lost time, and none of her people could be spared from their usual in-port duties. Naturally they could not perform such an inspection in the open ocean, even if they had scuba gear onboard. Time was too precious a commodity, and they had less of it by the hour.

She wouldn't have any choice when they arrived in the States. She had to know why her ship was running slow. A stem-to-stern hull inspection would be mandatory. She'd already radioed in to make the arrangements. It all meant delays, missed bonus objectives, and an unhappy crew.

By late afternoon, *Barinthus* was about seventeen hundred nautical miles from Japan, three days out of Yokohama and a little more than a third of the way to America, in cold and unusually calm seas south of the Aleutians. Anneke was on the bridge at the end of the twelve-to-four watch, grumpily reviewing their course with the navigator, when the First Officer cursed aloud.

"*Godverdomme,*" said Wim Achterop, a fellow Netherlander.

Anneke's head whipped around. She was no prude, but she had never heard Wim swear in private, much less in public and on duty. "*Wat zei je?*" she demanded.

He was staring out the window. "Captain. Look! Three points off the starboard bow."

She followed his gaze. On the horizon was a small black cloud, rising from the waves on a dark stalk of smoke.

She grabbed a pair of image-stabilized binoculars from the bookshelf at the chart station, moved closer to the window, and peered at the expanding cloud.

Something was on fire, undoubtedly a ship, but it was still hull-down due to the curvature of the Earth. All she could see was orange flame under billowing clouds of black smoke. Then white light stabbed into her eyes. She jerked the binoculars down. Even to the naked eye, the titanic explosion was bright against the horizon.

"Sound the alarm," she rasped, blinking the afterimage away. "All hands to fire control stations. Mr. Hironaka, steer for that ship, all ahead full. Wim, try to raise them on the radio. Mr. Liu, call it in." The crewmen leaped to obey.

Anneke prayed that the crew had been able to escape in their life boats. In these icy waters, an unprotected crewman could die of hypothermia in minutes.

The burning ship did not broadcast a Mayday or an SOS, which Anneke took as a very bad sign. The *SPAR*, a U.S. Coast Guard buoy-tending cutter, was about ten hours away from the accident site at top speed. The only other ships in the area were also cargo vessels, none of them well suited to getting men out of the water, much less providing them with the kind of medical help they would need.

The Coast Guard had to rely on *Barinthus* to get a fix on their location, since the burning tanker's emergency position-indicating radio beacon was also apparently out of order—another very bad sign. If the EPIRB was damaged or destroyed, the mishap could be nothing short of calamitous.

By the time they arrived on scene, a little over half an hour after the explosion, it was clear that they had arrived too late. The tanker was fully engulfed. The burning oil slick surrounding it had expanded to a circle a quarter-mile in diameter. The wreck's hull was punctured in a dozen places, disgorging countless thousands of gallons of crude into the fire.

Anneke brought her vessel no closer than half a mile from the wreck. Even from that distance, the radiant heat was incredibly intense. The smoke billowing up from the burning oil was so thick that they couldn't even see the ship's name on her stern. There was no hope of putting this conflagration out, but Anneke kept the crews at the hoses in case they encountered any survivors menaced by the flames.

They strained for a glimpse of an orange-hulled life boat. They saw none. They circled the infernal mass to find crewmen in the water. There were none. They blasted the giant ship's horn again and again. There were no answering cries over the bubbling roar of the fire as it changed sea water to steam. The only sound on the VHF emergency frequency was static.

After three hours of fruitless effort, Anneke called a halt to the search. She ordered *Barinthus* moved two miles away from the wreck, positioned well upwind. They would remain until the Coast Guard arrived to take over the rescue effort in five hours.

Anneke shook her head ruefully. They had probably been too late even when they first arrived. Anyone who could have made it out of the fire surely would have perished from hypothermia by now.

In the meantime, she and the bridge officers watched the fiery wreckage of the tanker as it slowly disintegrated.

At length the ship's back broke. The bow shook loose and plunged below the waves in less than a minute. The stern section floated for a while, perhaps half an hour, before a bulkhead gave way inside its blazing interior. A massive gout of flaming oil surged out of the truncated hindquarters of the ship, which settled lethargically in the water until it sank. The oil remaining on the surface would burn for hours—perhaps days.

Anneke and the rest of her officers stared in horrified fascination at the floating inferno until well after sunset.

They did not see their newest crew mate, Third Officer Liu Wenlan, surreptitiously press the button on a small transceiver in his right front pocket.

They could not see the twenty-four curved, ridged, magnetically anchored baffle plates drop away from the flat bottom of *Barinthus'* hull, eventually to smash into the ocean floor miles below.

They were not watching as three huge, dark, rounded triangular objects glided slowly up from the depths to attach themselves to the spots vacated by the baffle plates. Pairs of scuba divers clad in insulating dry-suits held on to the ends of each thirteen-meter "wing," letting go as they drew close to the bottom of the ship.

The streamlined objects nestled against the steel hull like a row of remoras on the belly of a shark. Their long, curved wings folded upward to lie flat against the gently curving hull. Their bulb-nosed, twenty-meter-long cylindrical cargo pods were aligned precisely along the ship's keel. The wings deployed powerful rare-earth permanent magnets, locking them to the steel hull with implacable force. Nothing short of a tsunami would dislodge them now.

The six divers checked that everything was secure and aligned. Two of them found the dangling ends of the two antenna cables that had been connected to the baffle plates, still magnetically attached to the side of the giant ship's hull. The thin cables were positioned precisely along a weld to make them harder to spot. They ran to points three meters above the waterline on either side of the ship, ending in flat GPS array antennas painted to match the vessel's red hull. One of these very divers had placed the antennas the first night *Barinthus* was docked in Singapore, even as Ole Alfredsson was being arrested for drunken fighting—the fight having been provoked by another Chinese agent.

The divers attached the free ends of the antenna lines to the submersible mounted closest to the bow. Just as he had triggered the baffle plates to detach, Third Officer Liu would now be able to signal the drone subs by radio to drop away if they were in danger of discovery.

The other four divers linked the other two subs to the first one via similar magnetic cables. Their work was completed in less than five minutes. They swam back into the depths to board the stealthy diesel-electric attack submarines that had ferried them here.

From a distance, had they been visible at all, the objects attached to the bottom of the container ship would have looked like manta rays. The resemblance was not coincidental. In Chinese, their code name was *Zhāngyú*. In Korean, the code name was *Agwi*. The meaning was the same: *devilfish*.

Their skeletons were made of non-ferrous metals, carbon fiber and ceramics coated with sonar-absorbing polymers. In the unlikely event that a Devilfish was captured by the enemy, every marking on every wire, circuit, component and weapons system was in Korean, save for generic parts available on the open market.

The Devilfish were nearly invisible to sonar. Their manta-like shapes were highly streamlined, allowing them to cut through the water with minimal resistance. Their articulated, folding wings were filled with argon-pressurized polymer foam calculated to offset the weight of their cylindrical payload sections.

The Devilfish would not weigh *Barinthus* down, but there was no way to conceal the drag they would create as the ship plowed through the sea. Hence the baffle plates. They had been designed to produce the same amount of drag as three Devilfish.

The one-knot reduction in speed had plagued *Barinthus* all the way from Singapore. Assuming they even thought to check their massive data warehouses, intelligence operatives in the United States would be unable to deduce where or when the Devilfish had been attached to the hull of the ship.

Neither Singapore nor Yokohama's harbors were deep enough for the Devilfish to have been mounted while in port. Positioning the heavy but relatively thin steel baffle plates at night had been hard enough. It had been easier to arrange for the *Barinthus* to halt in mid-ocean long enough to attach the Devilfish. Captain van den Broeke was a scrupulous sailor. She would never have ignored a ship in distress, much less a ship on fire.

The unfortunate crew of the crude oil tanker *Mariposa* had perished at the hands of an agent who had joined the crew as a replacement cook in Dubai. The poison he added to the morning meal had made quick work of most of the crewmen. His skills with a blade had done for the rest. He had brought the ship to a halt in the sea lanes ahead of *Barinthus* to await the container ship's arrival.

The divers had completed the task. The old double-bottom tanker had been built to sustain a moderate speed collision. Her designers could never have protected her from limpet mines or incendiary charges. The evidence of sabotage—along with the charred body of the expendable agent—was now cooling in the infinite night at the bottom of the Pacific Ocean.

Six hours from now, scuttling charges aboard the three PLA Navy submarines would send them and their hapless crews to the crushing depths as well. General Guo Qiang would be the only human left alive who knew anything about their mission.

Barinthus resumed her westward course, her three new and unwelcome stowaways safely hidden beneath the waves.

CHAPTER TWENTY-NINE

Struve Technologies Coyote Hill Campus, Palo Alto, California

October 23

Laurel's final day at ST dawned clear, bright, and hot.

She showered, dressed, and emerged from the Crick Building trailing her suitcases at precisely 8:00 AM. She winced as she walked out of the office-building-turned-dormitory. The underground walkway to the Pauling Building was closed until the rainy season, so she was forced to schlep her luggage through the miserable heat. It was nothing compared to the sweltering hell of the summertime East Coast, but she'd been in California long enough to have "gone native," as far as the weather was concerned.

The heat wave was in its third day and showed no signs of abating. October was often hot in the Bay Area, she knew. In other parts of the country, autumn was in full swing, and leafy trees were turning red or gold. Here, the trees were green, the hills were yellow, and the heat was stifling. In a month or two the rains would come, if Californians were lucky, or would divert north to fall on Oregon and Washington if they weren't. She would probably be back in D.C. starting her next assignment long before the hills turned green.

She walked around the back of the Pauling Building, exchanged pleasantries with the security guards, badged and voice-printed and iris-scanned in, and took the elevator down to the parking garage to put her suitcases in the trunk of her rental car. Then she went back up to the first floor locker room to change into her "worker bee" gray jumpsuit for the last time. After Aidan O'Keefe's dismissal, not even top executives were allowed to wear civvies or bring personal items, including cell phones, into the lab.

John Shea, similarly dressed, sat by himself at one of the tables in the sparsely populated cafeteria, wolfing down his breakfast much as he must have done in boot camp. She brought her raspberry yogurt, English muffin and coffee and sat across from him.

He looked up at her. She made a *go-on* gesture, so he continued scarfing his eggs and bacon. She took a few desultory bites of her muffin, sighed, put the uneaten portion down and said, "Aidan didn't leave any clues behind. Nothing we can arrest him for, even assuming we found him."

John put the final forkful of eggs into his mouth, chewed twice, and swallowed. He finally raised his eyes.

She continued, "Eileen's been over every system with a fine-toothed comb. He cleaned up after himself, but good. He left back doors in a dozen systems. He clearly eavesdropped on Jack's talk in the Black Box, and he probably bypassed the security system for his burner phone. Firing offenses. Grounds for a civil suit, sure, but not for arrest."

He stared at her. "You don't believe for one second that Aidan O'Keefe is innocent."

"No, but I don't have any direct evidence that he was behind the attack. Even the program that deleted all those files is gone, and there's nothing in any log file to show it even existed."

"But—"

"John. Here's the problem. If this building had an Internet connection, with all the security back doors Aidan installed, we'd be able to nail him. But this building is a Faraday cage. I haven't seen a better job of air-gapping outside of a military installation. The only system that sent any data outside the building is *Argus*."

"He helped write the thing!"

"He did, but he didn't compromise it. Eileen spent two days checking it. All it does is send the most active video feeds to servers in Amazon's cloud and respond to camera and door lock commands. The code on the cloud server is pristine. The logs don't show any sign of use except for the monthly tests and during the night of the break-in, and *you* were the only person using it. There's no sign of tampering, and no evidence of anyone logging in since you disabled *Argus'* cell connection after the break-in. We physically traced all the fiber optics carrying *Argus* feeds from the rest of campus to the security office. They're separate from the rest of the network, and they're still secure."

He dropped his fork onto his plate. "Well, fuck."

"He probably thought sneaking data out on the repeater network was either too risky or too slow. It would've been easier for him to copy privileged data to his cell phone. Or phones. I'd be amazed if his phones even exist anymore. We even thought about him using a laser to transmit the data out through a window, but the armor glass won't let concentrated laser light go through. It just turns reflective and sounds an alarm."

"Yeah. Another of the Greek's little tricks."

She said, "None of Aidan's back doors were accessible from outside. That's the point. He wrote a lot of the security software. Installing back doors might be a bad practice, but it isn't illegal unless you're doing it on a government system."

John expelled a disgusted sigh. "Goddamned legal system. It was easier on the battlefield. You see the enemy, you shoot him. Next case."

Laurel hastened to add, "We have a warrant out. Fleeing from the investigators is enough for us to detain him for questioning. If we can tie him to Folstad or the break-in beyond a reasonable doubt, we'll make him pay. He can't stay underground forever."

"You hope."

She looked down at her coffee cup, raised it to her lips and sipped.

John sighed. "Nothing turned up in his apartment, I suppose."

"Not yet. Robbie Holmes is on it. Unfortunately, it looks like Aidan took his laptop with him, and he didn't have any other computer gear. He didn't even use a cloud based backup service. We checked."

"You can't tell me you didn't have a tap on his internet connection."

"You're right. I can't tell you."

"Of course not." John picked up his last piece of bacon and made it disappear.

"Sorry." Laurel was barred from discussing domestic Internet surveillance in any capacity, privately or publicly, but in fact there had been no tap on Aidan's home network link. She'd requested one after Jack convinced her that Aidan was acting suspiciously, but the approvals hadn't come through in time. Events outpaced the sluggish legal process, as they so often did. She expected to receive the now-pointless approval sometime next week.

It probably wouldn't have made a difference in any case. Aidan was too smart to have used his home network for anything that might incriminate him. And there were twenty cafés with free wifi within a three-block radius of his apartment building.

John cleared his throat. "So. You're out of here, huh?"

"Not much reason for me to hang around now. Aidan's our only suspect, and he's in the wind. I'll be coordinating the effort to find him. Eileen will keep working with Stathis and Luke to see if we can turn up any solid evidence. That could take weeks or months. I might drop by from time to time."

"Well. We'll miss you."

She smiled wryly. "Peter won't."

"Don't take it personally. He's just bitter about Aidan. He blames himself for not seeing it sooner."

"Nobody did but Jack, and none of us believed him until it was too late."

"Yeah, well. Jack wasn't exactly objective, was he?" He looked at her shrewdly. "He'll miss you most of all, you know."

She felt a blush creep slowly up her face. "I know." She sipped her coffee to camouflage her embarrassment.

John stood and picked up his tray. "Drop in to say goodbye to the crew before you leave, would you? You made a lot of friends here. Give Sherlock my best. See you later, crocodile."

She smiled up at him. "In a while, alligator."

She looked out the cafeteria window at the bright blue sky instead of watching him leave. At length she ate her muffin and yogurt, regretfully polished off the excellent coffee, put her tray in the dirty dishes cart and went looking for Jack.

He was in the Black Box lab, as usual. He was alone, sitting at a workstation under the warm yellow lights, staring at his laptop's screen. It was filled with mysterious looking mathematical formulas. He didn't turn around when she came in.

She walked up and touched him on the shoulder.

He gave a violent start and jumped out of his chair. "Jesus, Laurel!"

She couldn't help laughing at his terrified expression. "Remember when you surprised me outside Peter's office? Just returning the favor."

His look of outrage turned into a rueful grin. "Help me find my heart, would you? I think it landed in that sink over there." His eyes were red, his unshaven chin almost bristly enough for a trimming.

She clucked with disapproval. "You look like crap. When's the last time you had a good night's sleep?"

"What is this word, *sleep?*"

"Be serious for once."

"Okay. You want serious." He squinted at the wall clock. "Is that PM?"

"AM."

He sighed wearily. "Then I was up all night again."

"Again! How many nights in a row?"

"Um. I don't remember. Two? I hope it was just two."

"You're going to have a psychotic break if you don't get some shut-eye."

"I took a nap on Sunday. I think."

"Jesus, Jack. Even God took a break after six days."

"All He did was create the universe. *I'm* trying to figure out how to use the latest version of *Mathematica*." He pointed at the equations on his laptop screen. "I almost have it, Laurel. Almost."

"What?"

A smile spread slowly across his face. "Something wonderful."

"Last time I heard that phrase, some aliens turned Jupiter into a second sun."

"Wow, you saw *2010*, too?" His smile became impish. He chanted, "With fingernails that shine like justice, and a voice that is dark like tinted glass."

"Uh, what?"

"Old song. *Short Skirt/Long Jacket*. It's sort of about the perfect woman."

She laughed, but felt a flush rise to her cheeks. "I came to say good-bye, at least for now. I'm moving out today. I'll be working out of the Palo Alto resident agency."

His face fell. "Oh. Hell. I've been so busy here, I completely forgot. I'm sorry. We didn't have a goodbye party or anything."

"I'll drop by when I can. If I can."

"Still looking for Aidan O'Keefe?"

"Yes."

"Break his neck for me when you see him, okay?"

She smiled. "I would if I could."

"We never did find time for that sparring match," he said.

A silence stretched awkwardly between them.

He rubbed his eyes. "Laurel, I—I've got too many things to say, and I'm too tired to figure out what to say first."

She smiled wanly. "You don't have to say anything." She leaned forward to kiss him on his scratchy cheek.

He moved his head, and she found her lips meeting his. He pulled her into a fierce embrace. The kiss was deep, blissful, and all too brief.

She pulled away gently.

He released her with evident reluctance.

She murmured, "I can't get involved with someone who's part of the investigation. You know that."

"Well, I do now." His smile was tinged with bitterness.

"I have to go, Jack. When this is all over—" She couldn't finish.

He nodded. "When this is all over."

She left then, before the tears came. She wiped them away almost angrily as she strode down the corridor to the elevator. *Damn him for kissing me,* she thought. She had to fight the urge to go back and kiss him again, and never stop. He was a cranky, paranoid, difficult, arrogant, brilliant, infuriating, insanely attractive man.

She veered into the bathroom before she reached the elevator. She rinsed her face three times with hot water, bringing it from the faucet to her face with cupped hands. Fortunately, she wasn't wearing any makeup. *Why can't I fall for a simple, sane guy, just once?*

She dried her face with a handful of paper towels, took three deep breaths, and went to Peter Struve's office.

He opened the door at her knock and gestured to a chair in front of his desk. He sat down, folded his hands across his narrow jump-suited chest and returned her gaze without speaking. He no longer had the hollowed-eyed look he'd had before the confrontation with Aidan.

She said, "You must have finally gotten some sleep."

"Xanax helps."

She brought him up to speed on the O'Keefe investigation. He nodded several times but didn't interrupt her. When she wrapped up and asked him if he had any questions, he merely shook his head.

"There is one more thing," she said. "Andrew Seigart is offering you the use of a refurbished lab complex over at Lawrence Livermore—"

"No," he said curtly.

"Peter, if the HyperQUBE works, there won't be any need to move the whole facility. It's much more secure than this campus, even with the new fence. And it's ready to be used, right now."

"No, thank you, Agent Wynn. Tell your boss I appreciate the offer, but under no circumstances will I relocate these people to a government laboratory. This is *our* work, and if the Feds want to use it they will by Christ license it the same way everyone else will."

"That's pretty much what I expected. I'll let him know."

"Now if there isn't anything else?" He went to the door and opened it.

She rose. "Two more things."

He frowned. "Please make it quick. I have a meeting."

"One: make sure Jack gets some rest. He looks terrible. Maybe give *him* a Xanax. Have John conk him on the head if you have to."

"Fine. And?"

"I have a message for you from the President. Your patents will be issued tomorrow morning at 9:00 Eastern. Forty-three of them, anyway. The major ones. The rest should be granted within six months. There's no prior art to research when you've invented the whole category. Still, I don't think you know how many strings had to be pulled to make that happen."

Peter's mouth fell open.

She controlled the urge to laugh. "The President's coming to tour the lab on Friday. There will be a black tie dinner party at the Four Seasons in Palo Alto that evening. I'll email you the details and the list of invitees." She looked around at his Spartan office with its IKEA furniture and total absence of wall hangings. "You might want to get somebody in here to spruce the place up. And would you please get Jack a tux that fits? That old AC/DC sweatshirt isn't going to fly."

Peter continued to gape at her as she walked out.

CHAPTER THIRTY

Pacific Ocean, South of the Farallon Islands, California

October 27

The BCL *Barinthus* emerged from the coast-hugging fog bank just before sunset.

From the bridge, the duty officers could see the spiky tops of the Farallon Islands to the north and the rocky headlands of California to the east. With binoculars they could even make out the tops of the towers of the Golden Gate Bridge, silhouetted against the red sky near the horizon.

They chattered to each other excitedly. They were scheduled for a week-long stay while Baskin's hired divers inspected the hull to find the cause of the mysterious slowdown. San Francisco was a favorite shore leave destination. They'd missed their bonus on this leg, but the extra time in port should make up for it.

Far below the waterline, the hindmost of the three Devilfish prepared to drop away. The signals relayed from the concealed GPS antennas told the robot sub that the time for departure was nigh. It warmed up its fuel cells, powered by liquid oxygen and hydrogen extracted from diesel oil.

Some of the argon gas in the rubberized foam ballast chambers of the wings had been allowed to bleed away during the journey, to be replaced by heavy seawater. The hindmost Devilfish was now ballasted for neutral buoyancy at a depth of one hundred meters—just below the oceanic thermocline. The cold water upwelling from the depths would impede sonar from surface vessels and sonobuoys that might be dropped from anti-submarine aircraft. The tactic had been used by ballistic submarine skippers for decades.

It signaled that it was ready to depart.

The second Devilfish detached its end of the data cable, which dangled free in the powerful current beneath the ship. The tiny electronic brains of both drone subs began a one-minute countdown.

The third Devilfish began to retract the powerful rare-earth magnets in the tips of its wings, currently folded against the shallow curve of the bottom of the ship's steel hull. The articulated wings came free, starting from the tip and working inward, section by section. As they did so, the Devilfish angled each section to slice into the current with minimum possible resistance. Soon the only magnets holding it to the hull were the ones along the top of its tube-shaped cargo pod. They were barely adequate to the task.

The one-minute countdown ran out.

The third Devilfish retracted the payload-section magnets. It was free.

The wings angled down. Propelled by its inertia, the Devilfish arrowed into the murky depths below *Barinthus*, clearing the ship's churning six-bladed screw easily. It ripped the dangling magnetic data cable free of the ship as well, only to jettison it an instant later. The cable coiled up on itself and dropped away into perpetual darkness, followed by dozens of the small, powerful magnets the Devilfish had used to secure itself to the ship.

The two Devilfish still locked onto the *Barinthus* deployed flaps on the trailing edges of their wings, compensating for the drag that was lost when the third Devilfish detached. The top speed of *Barinthus* would continue to be about a knot below its normal maximum. There would be no telltale change in speed to indicate where the drone sub detached from its unwitting carrier.

Devilfish Three reached its resting depth and waited for five minutes, carried south by the California current, checking its passive sonar systems for evidence of any other shipping traffic in the area. Satisfied that there was none, it deployed a tiny, transparent, globe-shaped device on a long, lightweight, carbon-fiber reinforced cable. The sensor buoy bobbed to the surface. It contained a 360-degree panoramic camera, a satellite radio antenna, and a GPS receiver.

Devilfish Three analyzed the images fed to it by the tiny camera. It pieced together a panoramic image of the nearby sea. Its sensitive phased-array antenna picked up no signals from any ship-borne navigation radar transmitters. It received Automatic Information Service data on a satellite channel, giving it the positions, courses and speeds of every known oceangoing vessel in the area. All of the data agreed: with the exception of the *Barinthus*, now several miles to the east, Devilfish Three was alone.

It started to move, propelled by a trio of electrically powered thrusters placed deep inside the drone sub's body. Their ceramic turbine blades had been designed to move water gently enough not to produce noise. Their intakes and outlets were carefully sculpted to prevent detection by the U.S. Navy's Integrated Undersea Surveillance System. The IUSS was sensitive enough to hear aircraft traveling high above the ocean's surface many miles away. The top speed of the Devilfish was only two knots, but then again, speed was not its purpose. It was designed for endurance. It was built for stealth.

The Devilfish towed the sensor buoy on the surface, getting its bearings from the GPS receiver. It angled its wings to correct its course.

The swift current carried it south.

CHAPTER THIRTY-ONE

Four Seasons Hotel, Palo Alto, California

October 27

Blaise Thierry submitted to the Secret Service agent's pat-down with studied indifference.

The carefully folded silk handkerchief in his tuxedo's breast pocket would not merit a glance from a security agent, and of course it was immune to the hastily-installed metal detector in the lobby entrance. Nevertheless, there was a chance that the handkerchief's contents might be detected by an airborne particulate scanner. Blaise hadn't seen such a device, but that didn't mean there wasn't one nearby. The weave of the silk was so fine that the chance of a leak was small, but not zero.

He screwed an ironic smile onto his face. "You would think the metal detector would suffice," he said over his shoulder.

Behind him in the line was his boss, Amber D'Agostino, wearing a lovely black Italian dress. She arched an eyebrow. "I would, but apparently *they* don't."

"Sorry about this," said the agent, a handsome young man with chiseled features and the dead-eyed expression of someone who issued perfunctory apologies too many times a day. He finished patting down Blaise's legs and stood up. "Thank you, sir."

"Think nothing of it," Blaise said. He cocked an eyebrow at Amber and said, "Do enjoy yourself." He moved forward into the corridor outside the closed doors of the dining room to join the others waiting to go in.

Behind him, he heard the agent say to Amber, "Ma'am, there's a female officer who will take care of you. If you'll just walk this way?"

No alarms sounded. No agents rushed up to tackle him. He'd gotten through the security cordon. He took a deep breath and mastered his fears.

The corridor outside the dining room was filled with well-dressed people. He recognized a few of them: luminary businessmen and women representing the whole spectrum of Silicon Valley companies. The Struve Technologies Board of Directors was here, of course. Most of the others were unfamiliar older people, though all of them reeked of money and influence. *Magnates of the military industrial complex, no doubt.* A few sported charismatic young companions on their arms—borrowed or rented for the occasion.

He walked up to the Dura Party. They were "dressed to the nines," as they said in America. Except for the stunning African-American girl, they also looked tired, isolated, and acutely uncomfortable in their non-shabby clothes. They had preceded him and the other ST veterans in the security line.

Blaise supposed he should resent their taking the center stage away from people who had been laboring to bring Emily Dura's work to life for years. Many of his colleagues felt that way. Instead, he pitied them. If Aidan's plan worked—and Blaise had no doubt that it would—Jack and his team would soon find themselves in much less comfortable surroundings.

He sidled up to Jack and said, "Can I speak to you privately for a moment?"

"Sure," said the exhausted but nattily attired scientist. He followed Blaise to a spot about ten feet from his clique.

"My compliments on the tuxedo," Blaise said. "Much better than Aidan's last minute hand-me-downs."

"Gee, thanks." Jack pulled at the bow tie. "I'm glad it *looks* good. I think this thing is trying to strangle me."

"Are you sure you are up to this?" Blaise whispered. "You look like you haven't slept in a month."

Jack sighed. "*Et tu*, Frenchie?"

"'I'm not a Frenchie. I am a Belgie.'"

Jack stared at him blankly for a moment, then gave a startled laugh. "*Touché.* You just jumped a notch in my book, Blaise. Not many people I know can quote *Murder by Death*."

Blaise faked an indulgent smile. "I'm glad to hear it. The question remains. You look half-dead. The rest of your crew doesn't look much better, except of course for Lizbeth. Enjoy tonight, but do take the weekend off."

"Yeah, we've been burning the candle at both ends, and the middle, too. Don't worry, Mom. I'll go right to bed after dinner and a few dozen drinks."

"Very good. Be sure to taste the Bâtard-Montrachet chardonnay before you start swilling down the Pabst Blue Ribbon. Peter ordered it especially for this occasion. He has an announcement to make that concerns you."

"Oh?"

Blaise smiled enigmatically and rejoined Amber and the handful of others who had been invited from Santa's Workshop. They availed themselves of appetizers and cocktails and talked shop until the guest of honor arrived, preceded by a phalanx of Secret Service agents, who regarded the guests with bone-deep suspicion. One never knew when the President might be attacked by someone wielding a canapé toothpick.

Blaise drifted away from the crowd nucleating around the President. He saw Peter Struve in the center of the crush, to the President's right, shaking hands alongside the Commander in Chief as if he were a high ranking dignitary in his own right. *In fact, that is what he is, as the CEO of what stands to become the most revolutionary company in human history.*

A man dressed as a butler appeared, tapping the side of a glass to get their attention. He intoned, "Ladies and gentlemen, dinner is served."

The doors to the dining room opened. The party moved inside.

The dimly lit chamber beyond was a large, windowless conference room, selected for security, not for its décor. Every table sported name tags, white cloths, precisely arranged silverware, cannily folded napkins, and a single burning taper. The chairs were surprisingly well-padded, especially for a hotel meeting room. The floor-to-ceiling flat panel displays on every wall were lit with panoramic scenes of the nighttime Bay Area skyline, creating the impression that they were in a high-rise far above the streets of San Francisco. The effect was both silly and oddly powerful.

Blaise and his colleagues were seated well away from the long, raised table at which the President, Struve, Dura and a number of unfamiliar older men and women presided. The President sat next to Struve. They spent much of the dinner in conversation. Dura was at Struve's left, and was clearly having trouble staying awake. His lady friend, the far-too-perceptive FBI agent, was not there, though John Shea was seated close by with some of the members of ST's Board. Blaise had always felt like a rodent crossing an open field when Laurel Wynn's falcon-like gaze fastened on him. Her absence should make his task easier.

When he met with his co-conspirators two nights ago, Aidan had insisted that Blaise deploy the virus at the dinner party. If they could demonstrate the use of their weapon in spite of the elaborate security measures attending the presence of the President of the United States of America, the impact would be infinitely more powerful on their new benefactors. Adam had agreed.

Blaise could not refute Aidan's logic, but it was *his* neck on the line. An ember of resentment had smoldered in the pit of his stomach ever since that discussion. He wished for the hundredth time that he knew precisely how Aidan and Adam were going to extricate the QUBE and the researchers from the country. They had excluded him from the planning, claiming that the less he knew, the less he could reveal if he were compromised.

That, too, was logical. That, too, rankled him, but it was much too late for second thoughts at this point. He'd entered into his original arrangement with "Adam" of his own accord, years ago, when Emily and Aidan's break-up was threatening to bring down the company.

Adam had recruited him out of the blue. Blaise had shared a few harmless secrets and made good money. Why not, when the Black Box Project could collapse at any moment? Then Peter healed the breach between the two top scientists. The research got back on track. Blaise began to realize how revolutionary their work would become. The lure of Adam's money palled. He tried to withdraw from the arrangement.

Even now, four years later, the memory of how naïve he'd been brought heat to his face. He was still well paid, but Adam had made it clear to him that his participation was no longer voluntary.

Then, to his utter astonishment, Aidan O'Keefe became a member of their conspiracy. The Chinese agent told Blaise to do everything Aidan asked of him, with a reminder that he was truly answerable only to Adam. Blaise dutifully obeyed them both.

In spite of his wish to end his career as a spy, his *de facto* demotion to henchman grated on him.

Aidan had invited Blaise to his apartment for dinner the night after he learned that Blaise was the mole. The food was delicious and the wine plentiful. They brainstormed on ways to impress their Chinese benefactors. After hours of fruitless rumination, Blaise tossed out the idea of a lethal, genetically targeted virus. He never thought Aidan would insist that they actually make it.

He'd balked at moving forward, but he'd buckled under Adam's unsubtle threats. As before, when he'd tried to sever ties with the Chinese, the agent hinted that any hint of disobedience on Blaise's part would be met with the unfortunate release of a large number of highly incriminating documents.

Blaise was left with no alternatives. He had no interest whatsoever in spending the rest of his life in solitary confinement, or worse, to be found floating face down in San Francisco Bay.

The road ahead was rocky, but he had to ride it out.

He tried to put it out of his mind. He had a mission to accomplish. He had to focus. It would all be over soon, in any event. The Elves had started growing the HyperQUBE prototype only days after the successful debut of QUBE Delta. It would soon be ready for testing.

The dinner was long, the food superb, the wine exquisite, the speechifying tiresome. Blaise sat back and nursed a glass of exquisite Montrachet while the President spoke for nearly an hour, extolling the virtues of Struve and his company, the near-magical technology they were pioneering, and how it was the key to a brighter future.

The President seemed to understand the practical effects of ST's technology, sounding a cautionary note about how it might disrupt the existing economy. A few glares greeted the President's warning that the advances would have to be brought to market gradually, so that existing industries could adapt to them. Ruffled feathers were quickly smoothed by cheerful predictions of clean power, clean air, and the environmentally friendly factories of future America, all made possible by Struve Technologies.

It was all very inspirational—or would have been, had Blaise not known that it would never come to pass.

At one point the President mentioned Jack Dura by name, praising him as the kind of innovator America needed now more than ever. Jack's head was propped up on one hand, his eyes firmly shut.

Peter Struve tapped him on the shoulder.

Jack jerked awake and looked around wildly. Apparently realizing where he was, he yawned and rubbed his eyes.

Peter whispered something in his ear.

Jack smiled, leaned forward and nodded to the President, who smiled back and joked that Jack might want to cut back to an eighty-hour work week.

Some of the other veterans at the table rolled their eyes, but Blaise stared at them, unblinking. Eventually they had the good grace to look ashamed. Blaise understood the ramifications of Jack's discoveries, perhaps more fully than anyone else in the room. They owed a great deal to Jack Dura. He was killing himself to work out the math of his so-called quantinuum theory. It was a pity that the fate in store for him and his students was not a kinder one. They deserved better.

Guilt gnawed at him. He brooded, unhearing, through the rest of the speech.

The President finally sat down, to thunderous applause.

Peter Struve took his place at the podium. His speech was short and to the point. He thanked the President for visiting, for hosting the dinner, for ramrodding the patent applications, and for the kind words. He then told the weary crowd that he would only have one more thing to say: he announced his offer of the currently vacant role of Chief Technology Officer and Senior Vice President of Operations to Jack Dura, who would be second only to himself in the ST org chart.

Dazedly, Jack stood up and came to the podium. Struve shook his hand before he could say anything. The members of the Dura Party stood and whooped their approval of the move, applauding and whistling. After an instant, the rest of the audience joined in.

When the applause finally began to wane, Jack cupped his hands around the microphone and said, "Well, I can't say no after all of that fuss, can I?"

"NO!" chorused the audience, and began whistling and cheering all over again.

Blaise stood and smiled and applauded along with them, his heart growing heavier by the instant. He *liked* these people. Even the cantankerous Jack Dura.

It took another hour for things to quiet down a little. Blaise continued to sip his wine, pretended to listen to his table-mates as they grew drunker and less coherent, and watched Peter Struve. He, Jack and the President huddled together for another thirty minutes.

At last, the President stood, shook their hands, and turned to the door. A ring of agents condensed around the Commander-in-Chief and moved into the corridor.

Blaise watched Peter as he leaned toward Jack and said something. Even from halfway across the room, Blaise could read Jack's lips as he replied, *Me too*. Jack patted his belly. They both laughed and set out for the hallway.

Blaise stood and followed them, moving quickly but trying not to look rushed.

As he entered the main corridor, he glanced to the left. The President's entourage was moving into the hotel's main lobby. He looked to the right, and saw Peter preceding Jack into the men's room at the other end of the corridor.

He followed them.

Peter stood at one of the urinals. Jack had evidently gone into one of the stalls. Baroque music blared from ceiling mounted loudspeakers, mercifully camouflaging the sounds from within.

Blaise glanced around the room. If there had been a particulate sensor in here, the Secret Service had taken it with them.

He availed himself of the urinal next to Peter. By the unspoken etiquette of the American male bathroom, no words were spoken until he stood next to Peter at the sink. The CEO was washing his hands.

"A marvelous dinner, Peter," he said. "I enjoyed your speech most of all."

Peter looked up at him in the mirror. His smile looked like an actual smile and not a death's head rictus. He looked infinitely better than he had a mere week ago, just after he dismissed Aidan. He said, "Brevity is the soul of wit, as they say."

"Indeed." Blaise wrinkled up his nose, then covered his lower face with his hands and pretended to sneeze. "Excuse me," he said. He turned away and snatched the carefully folded handkerchief from the inside pocket of his tuxedo's jacket. He blew his nose noisily.

Even from his closest of vantages, the tiny white puff produced when he blew into the handkerchief was almost unnoticeable. Propelled by the force of his breath, in seconds tens of thousands of the powdered virus particles would diffuse through the air in the bathroom. He would inhale many of them himself, but that was no cause for concern. In all the world, there was only one person whose body would prove fertile soil for the virus' lethal fruit.

Blaise stuffed the handkerchief back into his pocket and washed his hands.

Peter dried his on a paper towel. "Allergies, or a cold?"

"Allergies, I think," Blaise replied.

"Better take an Allyvil," said Peter in a sing-song tone. "If it can't help you—"

"*Nothing will,*" Blaise finished, forcing himself to echo Peter's chuckle.

Peter tossed the used paper towels into the trash bin. "I always hated that jingle, but it does stick with you. See you later?"

"Indeed you will," said Blaise, smiling tightly.

Peter pushed the bathroom door open and disappeared.

Blaise stared at himself in the mirror, fighting the wave of nausea that threatened to spill all of that precious Chardonnay into the sink. *I'm so sorry, Peter,* he said silently. *At least it will be quick. May God forgive me.* Then he dried his hands, wiped the tears from his eyes, crossed himself, and followed Peter back to the party.

CHAPTER THIRTY-TWO

San Francisco Bay, California

October 27

Eleven miles from the Golden Gate, *Barinthus* rendezvoused with an orange-and-white San Francisco Bar Pilots launch.

Captain Anneke van den Broeke was gratified to recognize the pilot. Lori Bell was a longtime friend and former colleague from her years at Carnival Lines. Lori was a topnotch sailor and one of the few women employed as a bar pilot on the West Coast.

They spent a happy few hours maneuvering the big ship across the treacherous bar and into San Francisco Bay, chit-chatting about old friends and acquaintances in the few spare minutes afforded by that complex task.

As *Barinthus* slid beneath the Golden Gate Bridge under one-quarter power, the hindmost Devilfish detached from her hull. It dropped to the bottom of the deep shipping channel.

Fifteen seconds later, the sole remaining Devilfish pulled free as well, pulling the magnetic GPS antenna lines off the hull along with it. The scraping sound was inaudible over the rush of water along the ship's sides. The divers who would soon be inspecting the hull would find no evidence to explain the one-knot reduction in *Barinthus'* top speed.

The small but sophisticated computer brains of each Devilfish went to work. Their passive sonar arrays detected many targets in the area, in spite of the late hour. Soon both Devilfish had a complete inventory of the locations, courses and speeds of every nearby surface vessel. They settled in to wait for the flood tide, and for the activity on the water to lessen.

They were programmed with detailed models of the currents in the San Francisco Bay, as well as databases that would tell them when the tides were favorable. They would move only when tide water was surging into the Bay, so as to conserve power, and then only at night, if at all possible.

The makers of the drone subs had judged the risk too high to ride the bottom of the carrier vessel any further into the Bay. If the ship happened to stray too close to the shallows, one or both of the Devilfish could be disabled. There was ample time for both subs to reach their destinations.

Devilfish Two would get there in a matter of hours: a spot to the southeast of the infamous former prison island of Alcatraz, just offshore of the city of San Francisco. The waters here were deep enough that there was little danger that it would fail to reach its destination.

Devilfish One had a more difficult task. Its destination was in the much shallower waters at the southern end of the Bay. It would take several days to reach its station, traveling only at night, using the twin RACON navigation transmitters on the Bay Bridge as guideposts, steering well clear of ships whose drafts were deep enough to pose a risk of running into the Devilfish's two-and-a-half-meter diameter cargo pod.

It would have to navigate down a deep but progressively narrower channel to its final resting place beneath a disused, permanently open swing bridge, once part of a Union Pacific railway that had connected the towns of Newark and East Palo Alto.

Worse, the drone sub would have to move in and out of the shallows to avoid any ships or pleasure craft that might venture nearby. The chances of it running aground or striking some hidden, submerged object were not small. Agents with boats and divers were on standby to pull it free if possible, though such an operation would be incredibly risky.

The designers of the Devilfish had relished the challenge of placing a robot submarine so close to an enemy city without being detected. Their solutions were many and ingenious.

The surface of the Devilfish was covered with a layer of transparent, sonar-absorbing polymer on top of sheets of tiny interferometric modulator display cells. The designers christened it *chameleon skin*. The technology had been stolen from a Californian company that was offering it for use in ultra-low power electronic book readers.

Each cell of the chameleon skin contained a pair of tiny squares of transparent semiconductor material, one fixed, one moveable. The distance between the sheets could be tuned very precisely by the application of a minuscule electric charge. The color of light reflected by the cell depended on the width of the gap between the sheets. It was the same principle by which butterfly wings produced brilliant, iridescent color without the use of pigments.

The first version of chameleon skin used tiny LEDs to produce camouflaging color, but the power consumption was unacceptably high. IMOD technology solved that problem. Once set to a particular color, an IMOD cell held it, using power only when a new color was selected.

During the day, the top surface of the Devilfish would take on the color of whatever was below, providing a poor man's version of invisibility. At night, it was set to an inky black. The illusion was not perfect, but in the murky green water of San Francisco Bay, it didn't have to be.

The sea trials performed by the Korean engineering team had proven that the Devilfish was invisible to boats and aircraft in turbid waters as shallow as four meters. It would be less likely to fool the eye in transparent tropical seas, but a third generation of chameleon skin was under development. The designers were hopeful that they could conquer that problem as well.

The magnetic signature of the payload section was the real problem. Anti-submarine aircraft and ships were equipped with sensors called magnetic anomaly detectors. MADs could detect the ferrous metals used in submarine hulls even through significant depths of water.

The wings of the Devilfish were built from non-magnetic metals and synthetics. However, the robot sub's power plant, motors, cargo pod, liquid oxygen and diesel fuel tanks contained significant quantities of steel and copper—not to mention the payload. Disguising them from airborne MADs had taken the best weapons engineers in China nearly a decade.

The solution was a sheath of exotic and ruinously expensive anti-magnetic metamaterial. Its composition and even its existence were closely guarded secrets. It required a continuous supply of electricity, but when it was active, it could conceal even extremely intense magnetic fields from snooping ships or aircraft.

The massive steel hull of the *Barinthus* had provided cover for the Devilfish as they crossed the open ocean. As soon as they detached from the ship, they turned on their magnetic cloaks. The amount of time they could conceal themselves was limited by the capacities of their liquid oxygen and diesel oil fuel cells.

The designers estimated that Devilfish One could reach its station and remain shielded for at least ten days. Even if its magnetic cloak failed, the heavy steel swing bridge under which it would come to rest should conceal its unusual magnetic signature. Devilfish Two, with a much shorter distance to travel, could maintain its cloak for three weeks.

At local midnight each day, both Devilfish would deploy their floating sensor buoys and transmit status messages using a commercial satellite phone network. To foil eavesdroppers, their encrypted messages were encoded into innocuous, pre-recorded digital voice conversations using a technique called steganography. Their programs for the next twenty-four hours would be transmitted back during the same automated "conversation."

If the operation were called off, the Devilfish would move back out to sea as stealthily as they arrived, to find themselves watery graves off the continental shelf. If possible, they would be retrieved by deep-sea robots at some future date.

Devilfish One could act on an abort order only if it was received by the seventh day. After that, it would not have enough power left to escape, even by taking advantage of the Bay's powerful ebb tides.

If they did not receive abort orders by midnight on the tenth day, their fail-safes would engage.

Twelve hours later, precisely at noon, the Devilfish would complete their missions.

CHAPTER THIRTY-THREE

Struve Technologies, Palo Alto, California

October 28

Jack sat bolt upright in his bed, covered with sweat and salt-water flooding into his mouth.

He scrambled down the hall to the bathroom, banged open the door of an unoccupied stall, knelt in front of the toilet and lifted the lid before nature could no longer be denied. He would not have been surprised to see a week's worth of meals in the bowl by the time his heaving stomach finally relented.

"You okay, boss? I heard some noise," he heard Hank Drummond say. The words were whispered but they thundered in his ears as if Hank had used a loudspeaker.

Jack spat into the bowl. "Do I look like I'm okay?" he growled.

"Wow. Very barf. So hangover."

Jack grabbed the handle and flushed the incriminating evidence. "Oh, Christ," he gasped as he sat heavily, panting. It was then that he realized he was completely naked. He silently thanked God that it was Hank who'd come to investigate, not Lizbeth, Deepthi, or Chao-Xing. He leaned against the stall's cold metal wall, eyes closed against the harsh LED lights. "I will never ever drink anything but water ever again, so help me."

"And coffee."

"Well, yes."

"And probably Coke."

"Shut up or die now."

"Shutting up. Need a hand?"

"Yeah."

He held out his hands, letting Hank pull him upright and brace him by the shoulders as he wobbled unsteadily on his feet.

He cracked an eyelid. When he saw Hank's unfeigned expression of disgust, he groped his way to the sink.

Hank scrubbed his own hands in the adjacent sink. "Eww, naked-boss cooties."

Jack rinsed his mouth and face with cold water several times before he spoke. "Thanks. If you can make the bathroom stop spinning, I won't make fun of your horsie pajamas."

"Hey, these are made from 100% genuine synthetic fibers. At least I didn't get the ones with footies."

Hank guided him back to his bedroom. He closed the door and tottered around in the dark, trying to find something to wear. Eventually it dawned on him to try the dresser. He dug out some jeans, a pair of boxer shorts, and a long-sleeved Black Sabbath sweatshirt. He dressed, put on a pair of flip-flops and meandered with half-closed eyes down the hall to the mercifully unoccupied kitchen.

The Crick Building had once been full of mid-level management and professional offices. After the attack on the campus, it was converted into a luxury dorm for what the execs called "mission-critical personnel." The third floor was reserved for Jack and his team. The break room had been expanded to a kitchen worthy of an Iron Chef. It was kept stocked with fresh food. For the lazier scientists, the cooks in the company cafeteria prepped ready-to-reheat meals for weekends. Most importantly, from Jack's perspective, the kitchen had the same life-giving Nespresso coffee maker as the break rooms in the Pauling Building.

He fed the machine a disc of coffee sealed in an aluminum envelope, punched a button and waited for his oversized mug to fill with coffee. He topped it off with organic, artisanal, free-range, fair-trade, shade-grown Half and Half and sat down at the nearest table, staring at the mug, shielding his eyes from the overhead lights with one hand, waiting for the whirlies to go away.

Some indeterminate time later, he looked down and realized that his cup was empty. He shuffled into the kitchen. He raided the first aid cabinet for a packet of migraine-strength aspirin. He grabbed a big bottle of water from the deli-style chiller, popped the aspirin in his mouth and drained the bottle in one, long, continuous swallow. His head was starting to clear, but his stomach still quailed at the idea of eating. He was confident that he'd be okay in a little while. He'd always recovered from hangovers quickly, if he hydrated himself properly. He refilled his coffee cup and sat down again.

At length Hank and Lizbeth came into the kitchen, dressed in shorts, T-shirts, sandals, and holding hands.

Holding hands?

Lizbeth was laughing, but she stopped abruptly when she saw Jack staring at her. She released Hank's hand and put hers behind her back, like a kid who'd been caught raiding the cookie jar.

Jack managed a weak chuckle. "Oh, Lizbeth. You went and fell for Hank. What charmed you the most, the goofy accent or the comic book collection?"

"The comic books. He made me read *Y: The Last Man*, and I knew it was love."

She said it jokingly, but there was a glint in her eyes when she looked at Hank. The same glint was reflected in his.

Jack sighed and made the sign of the cross. "Blessings on you, children. Now. Please make your old professor and CTO some breakfast, and he won't rat you out to HR for having an undeclared personal relationship. Maybe some oatmeal?"

They obliged him.

He watched as they busied themselves in the kitchen. He didn't ask why they'd kept their relationship secret, or how long it had been going on. He was glad for them. Lizbeth was a relentless workaholic, even by the elevated standards of his team. The fact that she'd found time to have *any* kind of personal relationship was astonishing. And Hank was a great guy, even with the endless supply of sardonic jokes and one-liners. He was lucky to have her.

Jack even felt a twinge of jealousy until Laurel's face popped into his mind.

They'd been right on the verge of starting something. He'd hoped it might happen during the trip to Lake San Antonio. Her support after the Big Talk had been invaluable. His idiocy on the day he'd met her seemed to have been forgotten, or at least forgiven. They'd spent a lot of time together for the next two days, swimming in the lake, revisiting the star party, and even going for a run around the campground on the morning of their departure, trailed by a pair of John Shea's athletic security guys. The opportunity for concentrated alone-time had never come up.

And when they returned to the ST campus, the shit really hit the fan. Aidan O'Keefe's treachery was discovered. He vanished and was promptly fired. Jack knew Laurel had to focus on tracking Aidan down and finding out who he was working for. When she came to say good-bye, Jack had done the responsible thing. He'd let her go with a smile and a promise. *When this is all over*, he'd said, and watched her go. But the memory of their kiss burned in him. He'd felt her body soften against his, and would never forget the look in her eyes as he released her. She'd wanted him, too. But it wasn't the right time.

Christ, when will *it be?* he thought, polishing off his second cup of coffee.

It had been too long since he'd been in a real relationship. The end of his marriage to Emily literally could not have been uglier. He'd lost his son, his wife and very nearly his life that dreadful summer afternoon. It had taken years and many surgeries to restore him to a semblance of normalcy. He still wore long-sleeved T-shirts to cover the shiny pink scar tissue.

The wounds to his heart might not have been physical, but they were even more severe than the ones to his body. A year after his final surgery, he'd recovered enough to have a brief, ill-advised romance with a post-doctoral student in another department. Things started going south as soon as she discovered the scars beneath his sweatshirt. She accused him of lying to her by concealing the extent of his injuries. Then she stormed out. The next day she lodged a complaint with the school that had almost gotten him fired. If she'd been his student, he certainly would have been. He'd never felt so humiliated or alone. Since then he'd avoided situations where he would be likely even to meet women, plunging entirely into his work.

His closest friends, few though they were, knew better than to badger him about dating. He tried to convince himself that he didn't need anyone in his life, but he'd known it was a lie from the start. The side-effects of his isolation were visible even through his self-generated veil of denial. His patience grew shorter and his temper fiercer with every passing year.

He was a life scientist, so he tried to think scientifically about everything, even his own relationships. Primates needed to satisfy their basic drives. He was a primate, therefore he had the same needs. But he also had responsibilities, duties to his students, and problems to solve. He told himself he'd get back to that part of his life when he had time, when the needs of work weren't so pressing, when he'd learned the answer to that last nagging question.

For a long time, the delay tactics had worked. But when he saw people in love, like Hank and Lizbeth, the reality he'd been denying slammed home. He didn't just need companionship or sex. Satisfying the basic drives just wasn't enough. He needed love.

Letting Laurel go had been incredibly hard. *When this is all over,* they'd said. But when would that be? He was forty-one years old now. He was in great shape, scar tissue notwithstanding, but he was all too aware that there were probably fewer years ahead than behind. He'd never been sharper mentally. The work here had challenged him like nothing else in his life. He'd already made discoveries that anyone in their right mind could look back on with pride. But there were so many new questions, so many unexplored implications of his quantinuum theory—would one lifetime even be enough? Would he die with the most important questions unasked, much less unanswered?

Would he die alone?

His thoughts left him in a black and all-too-familiar mood. He consumed the oatmeal he'd extorted from his former students without enthusiasm.

They joined him at the table after they'd prepped a more traditional breakfast of eggs, bacon and pancakes. The aroma of the bacon brought him back to himself. His stomach had settled enough for the smell to be enjoyable. "What is that?"

Hank handed him a strip. "Thick cut, black pepper bacon. From Prather Ranch."

Jack took a bite. "Ooh. Oh, my God. You get a raise."

"I cooked it," Lizbeth said.

"You get one too," Jack said around a mouthful of bacon. He looked at Hank's plate and donned a comically mournful expression.

Hank sighed, stood, and returned to the kitchen. "Told you," he said to Lizbeth.

"Believed you," she said, mimicking his tone.

Hank brought an untouched plate of bacon, eggs and pancakes and set it down in front of Jack.

Inexplicably, Jack found his eyes swimming with tears. He smiled and blinked them away. "Thank you," he whispered hoarsely.

"You had a rough night, what with dining with the President and all," Hank said, but there was a touch of emotion in his voice as well. "You're welcome, boss."

They ate in companionable silence. The aspirin started to take the edge off his hangover. After a while Jack felt his mood lighten.

No one else came out to join them, as they usually did on weekends. Laurel, of course, was gone and wouldn't be back. He shunted that painful thought aside. He wondered briefly where Terry and Chao-Xing were, until he remembered that Terry and his boyfriend were touring Napa Valley wineries (along with a pair of ST security guards). Chao-Xing and her fiancé were on a plane to Taiwan to visit her family, also in the company of a pair of brawny escorts.

Peter had told everyone to take some time off while the HyperQUBE prototype baked in the annealing oven. He wanted them fresh and ready to put in some long hours testing it when it emerged. As usual, Jack had no intention of complying. He was headed back to the lab to work on his theory as soon as his brain felt up to it.

When their plates were empty, Hank gathered them up, scraped them into the sink DisposAll and loaded them into the dishwasher. He brought orange juice for Lizbeth and a fresh cup of coffee for Jack.

Jack said, "Keep this up and I'll write you into my will."

Hank chuckled.

They spent another half-hour chatting as Jack's brain warmed up. They quizzed him about his conversation with the President. He couldn't tell them much. Peter had made him promise not to talk about it. The President had offered all kinds of government help, and Peter had politely but firmly refused. He was willing to accept help securing the Coyote Hills campus, but that was all. The idea of relocating the lab to Lawrence Livermore came up, and Peter spent a good fifteen minutes explaining why it was logistically impossible.

At one point, Jack had started to reply to the President's question of what new innovations they had in the pipeline. Before he could utter more than a handful of words, Peter shot him a warning look and smoothly injected himself into the conversation, speaking in generalities about everything except the HyperQUBE. It was clear that he had no intention of telling anyone outside the company about that technology.

Jack could understand his reasons: it was still far too early to know if it would work, though all of the experimental evidence indicated that it would. And if it did, would it really be a good idea to let the government know about it?

A grim thought trudged into Jack's slowly awakening mind. *What if Laurel already told them?*

She was no scientist, but she was extremely sharp. He'd made a point of explaining his theory to her during their conversations at the lake. The math might have been beyond her, but she'd had no trouble understanding the broader implications. What if she'd told her superiors? What happened if the HyperQUBE test was successful? Would CIA goons flood into the building and take over? Would they spirit him and his former students away to some ultra-classified laboratory at Area 51, never to be seen in public again? Or would they just put everything into a big wooden crate and shove it into a stadium-sized warehouse, next to the Ark of the Covenant?

No, he decided. Laurel wouldn't do that. She's one of the good guys.

"I gotta get some work done," he said at last. He changed to his grumpy-old-man voice. "Thanks for indulging your poor old teacher. You kids have a good day. And stay offa my lawn."

They laughed.

"Anytime, boss," said Hank, then made a show of reconsidering. "Well, not *anytime*. That was pretty gross. Maybe once or twice a year."

Jack rinsed out his cup and put it into the dishwasher. He shaved, showered, and added a pair of dirty old sneakers to his ensemble. He took a walk around the campus on the sidewalk next to the high concrete fence that now surrounded the property. Normally he'd run the circuit, but his brain was still just a little tender.

The sky was clear and the scent of dried grasses was thick in his nostrils. There was still a hint of coolness in the morning air, but they were headed into Indian summer—the home stretch of the California fire season.

It had been bad this year. The Bay Area had been spared, but smoke from forest fires in the Northern California redwoods had blanketed the region for weeks on end. He remembered watching TV coverage of the Oakland firestorm of 1991. It had happened during a hot dry spell like this one. Fierce winds had fanned the flames, causing it to spread faster than firefighters could contain it. Thousands of homes in the Berkeley and Oakland hills had been destroyed. He looked at the nearby peak of Coyote Hill, and the parched golden grasses beneath the motionless branches of the oak trees. If that were to happen here—

"Morbid much?" he asked himself. "Get your ass inside and do something productive."

He turned and walked through the trees toward the Pauling Building, thinking about his theory. The team had been burning the midnight oil to help him work out the math. He was so close to buttoning it up, he could taste it.

A few more days of concentrated effort and he might be there. The allure of discovery, of the indescribable, incomparable feeling of knowing something absolutely new to science—something no one in the entire history of the world had ever known before—was so strong that every other concern paled into insignificance. His worries about the fire season and Laurel's trustworthiness faded as his mind slotted into the familiar paths of his work.

As he crossed a small foot bridge over Deer Creek, he saw John Shea's red Mustang pull into the empty executive parking lot.

Shea slammed the car door and started toward the building, but evidently saw him. He stopped to wait as Jack turned toward him.

Jack sped up to a trot. He stopped a few yards away from the big man.

Shea looked terrible. He'd been at the party, but he'd been on duty, so whatever was bothering him, it wasn't a hangover. He wore a rumpled T-shirt and jeans. His arms hung listlessly at his sides. His unshaven face was bleak and somehow feral. His sunken, bloodshot eyes swiveled toward Jack.

Oh, Jesus. What happened? Jack's blood began to pound in his ears. "Is it Terry or Chao-Xing? Are they okay?" *Please God, don't let it be Laurel.*

"They're fine," Shea croaked. "It's not them. It's Peter."

CHAPTER THIRTY-FOUR

FBI Resident Agency, Palo Alto, California

October 28

Laurel was combing through the reports from the agents searching for Aidan O'Keefe when her desk phone rang.

She glared at the obnoxious device and said, "Goddammit." She'd been in the zone, taking full advantage of the uninterrupted time at her desk today. *So much for that idea.* She grabbed the receiver and snarled, "Wynn here."

"Sorry to bother you, boss. Something came up."

"Robbie, my stomach flips over every time you call me. What is it?"

"Peter Struve died last night."

She sat bolt upright. "What? How?"

"He was driving home after that big shindig at the Four Seasons. The President was there, you know? Anyway, he was up in the hills on Woodside Road, probably driving home, and he just went off the street into some trees. Some neighbors heard the crash and called the sheriffs. They found him slumped against the air bag. The front bumper was caved in but the crash wasn't bad enough to hurt him. Those Teslas are built like tanks. There weren't any skids or brake tracks, and he didn't have one of the new models that have autopilot. The police are thinking heart attack. The autopsy is scheduled for this afternoon."

She sighed deeply. "Could you call me with some good news, just for a change of pace?"

"Hey, at least it wasn't a mass-murder this time."

She closed her eyes. It was hard to believe Peter Struve was dead. He looked damned healthy for a guy nearing his sixties. He was fit, trim, and spent an hour in the gym on the elliptical trainer and the Stairmaster every day. Then again, he'd been under an impossible level of stress trying to keep his company afloat. He'd been near the edge of total exhaustion for the whole time she'd known him.

"You still there, boss?"

Holmes' voice in her ear startled her out of her reverie. "Sorry. I was just thinking. Make sure I get a copy of the autopsy report, would you? I should go over to the campus later and see how everyone's dealing with this."

"Will do. There's something else. We've been digging into O'Keefe's known associates. He doesn't have any friends outside of work. No social media accounts that we know of, and no indication of a love interest since he broke up with Emily Dura."

"With his warm and fuzzy personality? No way."

Holmes snorted. "Yeah. Well, we had to go a long way back in his history, but we ran across someone you might want to interview. One of his childhood buddies, name of Thomas Albert Reed. They lived next door to each other in Los Altos Hills. They were always hanging out with each other. Inseparable, apparently, but they parted ways when O'Keefe went to college and Reed joined the Army."

"What's so special about this guy?"

"Three things. His father was abusive. Mom always had a lot of bruises. The boy suffered a broken collarbone when he was twelve. Cops investigated but no one would press charges. The dad fell down a stairway and broke his neck when Reed was thirteen."

"Any chance Reed was involved with that?"

"No. He and his mom were visiting relatives in Florida, but when he was fourteen, he was accused of torturing a dog to death in the hills near their house. The witness was a neighbor girl about twelve years old, name withheld. She eventually recanted, so the charges were dropped. The police suspected that Reed bullied her into changing her story, but once she did, they couldn't get a peep out of her, so Reed skated."

"Huh." Violent criminals frequently started as childhood animal abusers, visiting their pain on something too weak to fight back. "Was Aidan O'Keefe involved?"

"He wasn't mentioned, but there's a sealed report in the file. I'm trying to get a court order to open it."

"Okay. Let me know if you run into any red tape. I'll ask Seigart to call in an airstrike. What's the second thing?"

"Reed did eight years in the Army. Qualified as an expert sharp-shooter in Basic. Not well liked, but very competent. Went to Sniper School. Did one tour in the Middle East, logged a bunch of kills, then joined something called the Army Marksmanship Unit, based in Fort Benning, Georgia. He had a solid reputation as a firearms instructor. He won the Interservice Rifle Championships twice. Apparently it's a big deal."

"Wow," blurted Laurel. "I've heard of it. It is a big deal."

Holmes continued, "When he mustered out—"

"Wait. Did you actually say 'mustered out?' What side did he fight for, the Blue or the Gray?"

"That's still what they call it," said Holmes in an injured tone.

She rubbed her eyes with her free hand. "Sorry, Robbie. I've spent too much time around Jack Dura. Go on."

"Anyway, he joined Ableman Security in San Jose. They provide protection to Silicon Valley bigwigs. He took over the business when the owner retired six years ago. And get this: he's a semi-pro competition pistol shooter."

"Ho-lee shit."

"That's what I said. He won a ton of awards. He was even on a TV show called Last Gun Standing. Kind of like Survivor, except for marksmen. Came in second, but only because he pulled a muscle when he ran down a hillside in the finals. And his physical description is consistent with the gunman who hit the Stanford ICU."

Her heart was rapping a tattoo against the inside of her breastbone. "Is Ableman Security open today?"

"It is."

"Are you in the City?"

"Yep."

"Get down here. I want you with me on this. We're gonna pay him a visit. Arrange for backup, full tactical gear."

"Roger that. See you soon."

Laurel fired up a web browser on her MacBook and Googled *Last Gun Standing*. It was on one of those channels that used to broadcast cultural and educational programming, but now did nothing but "reality" TV and sleazy infomercials. Their web site contained a backlog of full-length episodes, including the one from two seasons back in which Tom Reed lost the competition.

She flipped through the show while she ate some Fritos from the vending machine down the hall. Surprisingly, the program was pretty well made. Unsurprisingly, most of the competitors were men, either current or former law enforcement or military, greying around the temples, and developing a bit of a paunch.

Reed was an exception. He looked younger than his then forty-two years. There wasn't an ounce of fat on his wiry body. He reminded her of the craggy actor who'd played Mercury astronaut Alan Shepard in *The Right Stuff*, her dad's favorite movie. The only difference was that his hair was a dusty blond instead of brown.

Reed smiled a lot. He was popular with the other competitors. They clapped him on the back and said, "Too bad," and "Damned shame, brother," when he hobbled across the finish line. He lost by eleven seconds. The winner was a recently discharged Army Ranger ten years his junior.

She scrubbed through the video to find clips of Reed in action. It might have been her imagination, but it seemed that his ready smile never quite reached his blue eyes. He was demonically fast in the pistol competitions, and just a fraction slower with long guns. The only weapon that gave him any trouble was the javelin, and only on his first throwing attempt. By the end of that event, he was as good as any of the others. He was clearly a natural-born warrior.

Laurel stopped watching the show and brought up the video of the attack in the Stanford ICU. She'd lost track of how many times she'd seen the clip, and it never failed to make her queasy. She watched the gunman take out the two policemen, the doctor and the nurse with a single sweeping motion of his pistol, pausing only long enough to point at a new target between pulls on the trigger. Then he moved to Aage Folstad's side and pumped two shots into his temple.

Reed moved with a similar machine-like precision in the *Last Gun Standing* episode, but then again, so did all of his competitors.

"Dammit, I don't know," she whispered. She might not *know*, but deep in her gut, she was beginning to believe.

She wrote an email to Harry Chisolm, an Academy classmate who now worked at the FBI Laboratory in Quantico, Virginia. One of his pet projects was computer analysis of human kinematics—the study of the motion of human bodies. He was trying to create "fingerprints" of the way people moved from surveillance videos. She'd kept up with his work, and it was starting to show real progress.

She asked him to analyze the hospital video of the gunman and compare it to the footage of Reed from *Last Gun Standing*, to see if his program concluded that they were the same man. The technology was still under development, but she wasn't looking for evidence that would stand up in court. Her gut might be saying that Reed was their man, but she wanted someone else's brain to confirm it.

She sent the email, and then looked up Ableman Security on Yelp. It had only a handful of reviews, but they were very positive. She checked the business hours. Their Santa Clara office was open today from 9 to 5. She closed her laptop and went to the armory to find a vest.

Robbie arrived by 1:05. A bevy of backup agents in FBI-standard tactical gear showed up a few minutes later. She drove the big, black, up-armored Chevy Suburban. Robbie rode shotgun and four more agents sat in the back. Another SUV followed, likewise filled with agents.

Ableman Security was located near San Jose Airport. It was the anchor tenant of an unglamorous industrial park just off the busy Highway 101. It had a large four-bay garage with sturdy-looking roll-down doors, currently closed. The only vehicles in the spacious, recently-paved lot were three late-model Mercedes limousines, a red Tesla Roadster, a blue Mini Cooper, and a dusty, dark green Hummer H2 SUV. A neon OPEN sign blazed in the single, narrow window of the small office next to the garage.

Robbie preceded Laurel into the office, followed closely by a pair of unsmiling agents. Several more waited outside the door, while the others fanned out to surround the building.

An attractive, well-dressed Hispanic woman in her mid-twenties sat behind the desk in the reception area. "Can I help you?" she said. Her eyes widened as she saw the agents outside.

Laurel quickly scanned the office. It was much classier than the industrial setting promised. The waiting area was well-appointed with modern furniture, plants and a big salt-water aquarium. The walls were covered with framed photos of celebrities and business types posing with a slender blond man wearing a coldly precise smile. One closed door presumably led to an inner office. A heavier metal door was on the wall shared with the garage.

Laurel looked at the receptionist. "I'm Senior Special Agent Wynn. This is Special Agent Holmes. We'd like to talk with Mr. Reed."

"Mr. Sanderson?" the receptionist called.

The door to the interior office opened. A muscular white man in his mid-thirties wearing a well-tailored business suit walked out. "What is it, Daniela?"

"These people are here to see Mr. Reed," the receptionist said. "They're from—"

"The FBI, yes, I can see that," he said, eyeing the agents behind Laurel in their tactical gear. He walked forward and offered his hand to Robbie Holmes. "I'm Al Sanderson, vice-president of Ableman."

Robbie didn't take it. Instead, he looked at Laurel.

She extended her hand. "Senior Special Agent Laurel Wynn."

Sanderson pivoted smoothly toward her and grasped her hand in a gentle but firm grip. "Sorry about that," he said with a smile. "I guess sexism isn't as dead as we'd like it to be."

Laurel released his hand and said, "We'd like to talk with Mr. Reed. Is he coming in today?"

The receptionist laughed. "It's the first weekend of duck season."

"Can he be reached by phone? It's urgent."

"I'm sorry," Sanderson said, smiling. "Every year he takes three weeks off and goes into the boonies to hunt. The best performing employees for the last year go with him. It's a big deal for them. They like to camp out. They don't tell us where they're going. They don't even take their cell phones. They just pile into his RV and hit the road. Last year they went to Montana."

"I heard him say something about Idaho," added the receptionist.

Laurel frowned. Given Reed's background, a hunting trip was at least plausible. "When will he be back?"

"Two weeks from Monday. Is there something I can help you with?" offered Sanderson.

"No," said Laurel. She pulled a card from a vest pocket and handed it to him. "Please have him call me as soon as he gets in touch."

He took the card. "Will do. You all have a nice day, now."

Back in the parking lot, she assembled her team. She peered at Robbie. "What do you think?"

"Seemed on the level," he grumbled. "Maybe a little too smooth. Most people are rattled when the FBI walks into their office."

"Mm-hmm. Pretty convenient timing, too."

"They didn't know we were coming," he said. "That didn't seem like an act to me."

"Yeah," she muttered. "Run the plates on these cars. Get a BOLO out on Reed's RV, and anything else he drives."

"Will do."

She got back in the Suburban and slammed the door angrily. She was tired of being two steps behind. "I have a bad feeling about this guy," she said when Robbie got in next to her. "We need to track him down."

She went to bed that night exhausted and irritated from hours of fruitless searching. The teams she'd sent to Reed's apartment had found no sign that he'd been there recently. The "be on the lookout" advisory on the RV had turned up nothing. The green Hummer in front of Ableman was Reed's. Judging by the accumulated dust on the windows, it looked as if it hadn't moved in a while. Many of the Ableman employees were missing. They *could* be out hunting, she admitted to herself, but she didn't really believe it. Her gut instinct was that something was very wrong.

She dug a Unisom tablet out of her overnight bag, dry-swallowed it, and flopped down on the Budget Motel's lumpy mattress to wait for it to take effect. She missed her Sleep Number mattress back at the ST campus. It was only then that she remembered that she hadn't even called Jack to see how he was doing, much less stopped by. Nor had she checked her email for the autopsy report on Peter Struve.

She checked the clock. "Damn," she whispered. No one would be grateful for a sympathy phone call at midnight, and she knew she'd be up for another hour or two if she cracked open her MacBook to read the report. She sighed and tried to compose her mind, but it was hard. She felt bad about Peter. She missed the Greek and John Shea.

She *really* missed Jack.

It took her a long time to fall asleep, and when she did, she dreamed of Tom Reed's mechanical smile, and the icy glint in his bright blue eyes.

CHAPTER THIRTY-FIVE

Moss Landing, California

October 28

"Thanks, Al. I'll keep my eyes open."

Tom Reed closed the ancient burner flip-phone and dropped it into his shirt pocket. He put one booted foot up against the grimy dashboard and stared out the window of the old Ford pickup at the hills next to Highway 101.

They were stuck in the usual slowdown between Gilroy and the California Road 156 exit toward Castroville, well south of San Jose. Once they turned west they'd be able to travel at the speed limit. He frowned. *Goddamned traffic.* It got worse every year.

"Problem?" asked Gonzo Rodriguez.

Tom looked at his driver. "Did Coop put the Winnebago in the garage before we left Morgan Hill?"

"'Course."

"Then there's no problem. Keep your mind on the road."

Gonzo shrugged. "*Listo, patrón.*"

"Jesus. Knock that shit off. Ever since you watched *Narcos* you think you're some kind of fucking drug lord. You've never even been to Mexico."

"Okay, boss," Gonzo said in his normal third-generation California-native accent. His great-grandparents had crossed the Mexican border around 1900.

Tom's thoughts turned inward. Al had said it was the same FBI bitch who'd fingered Aidan. She'd come to the office heavy, with one plain-clothes guy and at least eight agents in full tactical gear. He scowled. He'd been made, or as close as made no difference.

It didn't really matter. The compound in the foothills west of Morgan Hill was their new base of operations. It couldn't be traced to him, to Aidan, or anyone else in their crew. They'd picked it because of the huge metal tractor sheds where they could hide their work on the trucks from prying eyes. The owner had run a farm equipment business. He, his wife, and his four employees were buried in a deep grave under the barn. Tom's crew was careful to avoid running too many vehicles to and from the ranch at any one time. So far, none of the neighbors had paid them the slightest attention.

Tom took a deep breath and let it out slowly. Events were in motion. The timetable didn't have much flex in it. He and his crew just had to keep their heads down until that Belgian faggot at ST gave the signal. After that, the FBI would have a lot more to worry about than finding Thomas Albert Reed—or so Aidan said, but he didn't say why. Tom understood operational security. The fewer people who knew the whole plan, the better. If Aidan said the diversion would be one hundred percent effective, Tom believed it, especially after he saw what Aidan had ordered done to the trucks.

Nor did he have any doubts about his own men. They were reliable. Even Gonzo, with his stupid fake Colombian accent, was as solid as a rock. The only problem was, this job demanded a much bigger force. *Much* bigger. Luckily, Adam's mercenary "contractors" were shaping up well, especially considering how fast the Chinese agent had gotten them to Northern California.

Then again, Adam had mentioned that his original plan was to send a strike force into SP to secure Emily Dura and the QUBE—a plan had been derailed by the late Alberto di Mottura and his Norwegian henchman. Tom supposed Adam had just reconvened the same people he'd assembled for that strike force, with a few dozen additional members.

Tom didn't know any of the mercs. That was surprising, given how deep his contacts went into the underground world of military contractors and wet-work specialists. Most of them were South African, judging from their accents. Older guys, for the most part, but still in great shape. They all spoke English and they were all ex-military. They knew how to take orders. They knew their guns. He'd watched them field-strip, clean and reassemble them enough times to know.

Tom had taken them in batches on field trips to an outdoor range in the Central Valley to assess their marksmanship with long guns. None of them were up to his standards, of course. Only his own man, Bobby Boykin, could give him a run for his money. The contractors were good enough. They were seasoned pros. Even considering the competition, he believed they'd do.

The cars ahead of them finally started to creep forward. Eventually Gonzo turned off the freeway toward Castroville. After that they made good time. The rest of the detail would arrive later in the afternoon, assembling at the Motel 6 on the northwest corner of the little farming town. Bobby had already called to assure him that everything was in place. They were all set.

Tom and Gonzo reached the motel at 2:30 PM. They checked in with fake IDs but genuine cash, got their keys and went to their rooms, overnight bags in hand. Tom wasted no time. He stripped, showered, and got into bed. He fell asleep instantly.

He awoke when his watch alarm went off at 11:00. He showered again, dressed in street clothes, ate the sandwich and chips he'd packed in his bag, and washed them down with a bottle of spring water. He wiped down every surface he'd touched with disinfectant towlettes before he closed the door. At midnight he went downstairs to the truck.

The rest of the men were waiting. There were nine of them: five of his, including Gonzo, and four of the newbies. He'd picked them from the sixty-odd increasingly impatient men waiting for action. It was time to see how they worked under pressure.

Tom and Gonzo departed first. The others would leave a few minutes later in a pair of big black GMC Yukon SUVs. They staggered their departures and arrivals to keep from attracting attention from the motel's other guests.

Their destination was the tiny fishing port of Moss Landing, just three miles north on Highway 1. Tom had looked the place up on Wikipedia. It was what they called a *census-designated place*—not even big enough to be a village. It was located on the mouth of the Old Salinas River, a big name for a narrow ditch that paralleled the beach for a mile or so before joining Elkhorn Slough and hooking left to empty into Monterey Bay. A small harbor had been built on the west bank of the river, in the shadow of the Dynergy natural gas power plant. Its two huge smoke stacks could be seen for many miles in every direction.

Highway 1 was almost deserted at this hour. Tom spotted the smoke stacks long before he and Gonzo reached the tiny town. Plumes of steam drifted up from them to merge with the low marine cloud deck that blanketed the shoreline. Blazing orange lights from the power plant lit the clouds like a bonfire. Tom winced. The light was a problem, but if they did their job right, they'd be in and out before it mattered.

They turned off the highway and threaded their way through narrow streets to the northern end of the harbor. Gonzo pulled into the parking area behind a marine repair shop. The blue Mazda minivan Bobby Boykin had stolen earlier that day was there, parked to the left of a big truck with a gray tarp tied down over the cargo box.

Bobby and Nick Satriale leaned against the truck, smoking and trying to look casual. The two men could've been twins: tall, black-haired, stubble-chinned and olive-skinned. They even dressed alike, in dark jeans and sweat shirts. The only features they didn't share were Nick's widow's peak and Bobby's once-broken Roman nose.

Gonzo parked the truck to the left of the minivan.

Tom got out. "Any problems?" he asked Bobby in a low voice.

"Nah," Bobby said. "Had to take out the owner of the shop and his old lady. Bodies are inside." He shrugged. "Didn't expect anyone to be here so late."

"Where's the boat?"

"Right there," said Bobby, pointing.

The big fishing boat was just south of the shop, tied up alongside a pier that ran parallel the harbor's main waterway. Bobby and Nick had paid the mystified owner to get it scheduled for a motor overhaul. He had moved it next to the shop earlier that afternoon.

To the left of the boat was the reason they'd chosen this location: a parallel set of piers that extended into the channel, creating an elevated runway for a marine travel lift: a big, box-shaped crane sitting on motorized truck wheels. The shop's now-deceased owner had used it to pick boats up out of the water for repair. The lift had been rolled out as far as it could go. It straddled the narrow stretch of water between the piers.

"Good," Tom said. "How about the boat's captain?"

Nick gave a feral smile. "At room temperature. Even got the payoff money back." He patted his back pocket.

"And the extra thing I asked you to pack?"

"In the galley."

One of the black Yukon SUVs pulled into the parking lot and parked on the other side of the minivan. The other one arrived thirty seconds later.

"Okay, Nick, you and Bobby keep an eye on the place. Call me if anything goes sideways. I'll let you know when to bring up the truck. Come down and give us a hand with the lines."

"Will do." Nick dropped his cigarette on the pavement and stubbed it out with a toe. Bobby did as well.

Tom joined the others. They opened the backs of the SUVs and took out the bags containing their jackets and guns.

Tom led the group down the pier to the boat.

He couldn't tell what color it was in the weird orange glow from the power plant. It was dark, and that's all the mattered. *Sea Conqueror* was painted in white block letters on the side. *Sea Pig* might have been more appropriate. It was what they called a purse seine trawler, built for scooping up fish in nets that trailed behind the boat. Supposedly it was on the small side for its purpose, but it was still a lot bigger than he'd expected. It sat high in the water, probably because its refrigerated hold was empty. The boat was butt-ugly and streaked with rust, but it would serve.

A heavy-duty crane loomed over the rear half of the boat. A huge pulley dangled from the end. The pulley was secured by a line so it wouldn't swing free. If it got loose and hit you, it was game over. It made Tom nervous.

He'd picked the four contractors because they said they had experience on commercial fishing boats. Two of them were divers. Tom frowned. They'd prove it tonight, or they'd wind up at room temperature, too.

He climbed up the short ladder at the back end of the boat. The rest followed him, except for Nick and Bobby, who stood by on the pier. Gonzo climbed up to the wheelhouse while the others pulled on olive drab Air Force-surplus flight suits over their street clothes. Warm fleece jackets went on over those. It would be cold out in the Bay, and just in case some busybody with a long lens and night vision cameras took pictures of them, Tom didn't want any personally identifiable clothing visible. "Leave your guns in your bags and take 'em into the cabin," he told them.

Two of the contractors stripped and started putting on wet suits while the rest of them obeyed Tom's orders. As a confirmed landlubber, Tom didn't envy the divers their task, but they'd volunteered for it readily enough.

The boat's engine roared to life. From somewhere close by, sea lions barked in protest.

Gonzo emerged from the wheelhouse and gave a thumbs-up.

Tom called, "Cast off."

Bobby and Nick unhooked the lines from the cleats. The contractors reeled them in and coiled them up on the deck. The boat drifted slowly away from the pier.

Gonzo gassed it.

The *Sea Conqueror* accelerated like the pig she was. They passed a half-sunken pier with a dozen fat sea lions crouched atop it, all of them barking like mad. Tom chewed his lip. As far as he knew there was nothing illegal about taking a boat out this late, but it might attract unwanted attention from the harbormaster. Well, Nick and Bobby would take care of him, if it came to that.

They turned west and exited the harbor. Gonzo kept the boat well clear of the two long jetties on either side of the channel. Darkness closed in as the cloud-reflected light of the power plant fell behind. The boat's running lights were off, too, which didn't help. The deck started to pitch up and down as the ship entered the open water of Monterey Bay.

Tom grabbed a rail to steady himself. As he waited for his night vision to adapt, he thought about the mission. So far everything had gone by the numbers, but he didn't like snuffing so many civilians.

Taking out the cops at Stanford and the FBI agents guarding Eric Dalton's house was different. They were in the game. They knew the risks. Waxing Aage Folstad had been a real pleasure, considering how badly he'd fucked everything up by wasting Emily Dura. But crossing off the doctor and nurses in the ICU weighed on him.

He wasn't naïve enough to think of himself as a good guy. He knew who and what he was. He was a killer, but he took pride in doing it right. He'd never capped a civilian during his tour in Iraq, as far as he knew. Shit-tons of *hajjis*, but not one sheep. Since Aidan O'Keefe had tracked him down and enlisted him in this adventure, he'd killed four.

Okay, technically Aidan had done Eric Dalton, but Tom had been the one to administer the mercy shot. And then there was that first one, years ago, just after Aidan got back in touch with him, just after he'd taken over Ableman Security from his retiring former boss. That one had *really* been bad. He'd almost managed to purge that one from his memory. Now it came roaring back into his brain like a migraine headache.

So, five, then. Five innocents dead at his hands. Five too many. He didn't count the owner of their new compound in Morgan Hill, or the people who'd died here in the last twenty-four hours. He hadn't been involved, not directly. He put those on Aidan's growing tally.

Killing Dalton hadn't troubled him. The kid probably would've thanked him, if he'd still been able to speak. But the look on that last nurse's face as he turned the gun on her—she'd known what he was going to do, because she'd just seen him kill four people in two seconds. Her eyes pleaded with him not to do it, but he'd just gone and done it anyway. He didn't hesitate. He didn't even slow down to watch her fall before moving to Folstad's side and double-tapping him. And that, more than anything, was what woke him up at night, lying in a pool of sweat, heart pounding like he'd just run a marathon. That look in her eyes, and his robot-like indifference to it. He didn't want to experience that, ever again. But he was afraid he might have to.

It didn't comfort him to think that this was just the tip of the iceberg. Aidan was determined to get hold of this crazy computer they were building at ST. Their new Chinese allies certainly seemed to want it badly enough. Adam's backers were pouring a metric shitload of money into the effort.

It didn't make Tom happy to be working against his own country— the country he'd served in battle. But if Aidan was right, they'd all be richer than Bill Gates if they could get this magic whatsit out of the country intact. It was hard to argue with that.

Aidan had always been able to talk him into anything, even when they were kids. But his planned diversion was over the edge. Just thinking about it made even Tom's admittedly cold blood run a little bit colder. There was no walking back from *that*. *That* was every chip in the pot. *That* was all-fucking-*in*.

He fought to regain his concentration. He didn't have time for self-pity now. He had a goddamned job to do. And he owed Aidan his life.

When Tom was twelve, his father Hal had been laid off from Intel. He hadn't been able to find a job that paid nearly as well. He'd always been a mean drunk, but now when he was home, he was drunk more often than he was sober. He took out his frustration on his wife, and when that wasn't enough, he took it out on his son. He'd broken Tom's collarbone in a drunken rage one night. His mother had begged Tom not to tell the police. He couldn't understand why, but when he read about something called "battered wife syndrome" decades later, it made more sense to him.

He hadn't told the cops, but he had told his friend Aidan.

Aidan was a weird kid. Tom knew that well enough. Aidan was bookish, withdrawn and strangely unemotional about most things. When he spoke, he sounded like an old British guy instead of a kid who grew up in California.

Tom didn't mind. He didn't have many friends of his own, and Aidan was interesting. He knew a lot, and he liked to talk about science. Other kids thought he was a braggart, but Tom knew that he just enjoyed talking about that kind of thing.

He stood up for Aidan against bullies at school. He beat the living crap out of a shit-bag named Kyle Stern after he'd pushed Aidan down during P.E. class. Aidan never said anything, but Tom knew he was grateful.

So he told Aidan about his drunken father. What he did to his mother. What he'd done to Tom.

His dad's drinking had gotten so bad he'd nearly fallen down the stairs. Tom had saved him, pushing him back to the second floor landing. For that, he'd gotten the beating that ended with a broken collarbone.

Tom told Aidan that he was worried. If his dad kept doing this, he didn't know if he or his mom would survive it.

It wasn't right.

Aidan didn't respond. He just seemed to file it away in his memory. Tom was disappointed, but not surprised. It felt good to get it off his chest.

Just after Tom turned thirteen, he and his mom flew out to visit her sister in Miami Beach. They had to come back the day after they arrived. The police had called. Hal Reed had been found at the foot of the stairway by a neighbor. His neck had been snapped. Alcohol had certainly been a factor.

When he saw Tom after the funeral, Aidan said, "Now you don't have to worry about anything anymore. You watch out for me. I'll watch out for you."

Tom had been a little scared, but exhilarated, too. He kept Aidan's words to himself. His collarbone healed. His mother's bruises faded. Life was better.

There was a bad patch a year later when he came across Aidan in the woods near their neighborhood. He'd been doing things to a dog. Terrible things. Theresa Walker, a neighbor girl, saw him but didn't see Aidan, who managed to sneak away.

Tom took the fall. He didn't blame Aidan, though he'd been creeped out by what his friend had been doing. He'd managed to get away. Good for Aidan. No reason for them both to get into trouble. Just bad luck. Aidan had dealt with his father, hadn't he? Tom would return the favor. It wouldn't be so bad. He was a kid. They didn't punish kids as severely as adults. His mother's appalled reaction to his arrest was harder to handle than the prospect of juvenile hall.

But then Theresa changed her testimony. The charges were dropped. The report was even sealed. Aidan had to have had a hand in that, too, but Tom never asked him, and Aidan never volunteered how he'd done it. Aidan's father was a high-powered attorney, but he'd always been kind of snooty. Tom couldn't imagine Roger O'Keefe lifting a finger to help him. He always suspected Aidan had threatened Theresa somehow, but whenever he saw her from that time forward, she made herself scarce.

The fact remained that they'd stood up for each other in the only way that really counted. They had each other's backs. Aidan had gotten in touch after Tom left the service. He'd explained the science of what he'd been working on. Then he'd explained his plan.

"Some eggs will undoubtedly need to be broken," he'd said in his soft, clipped, mechanical voice. "I need a man who won't hesitate to break them. I need a man who can find other men like him. I know what you did in the Army. A hard duty, but you did it very well. You watch out for me. I'll watch out for you. If we succeed, we'll be richer than kings." He'd offered his hand.

They'd shaken on it.

Tom didn't regret signing on, even now. He just hadn't realized how many eggs there'd be.

He took a deep breath and shook his head to clear it of this shitty woolgathering. *Fuck it. It's Aidan's show. All I have to do is make sure we win.*

Tom hauled his heavy bag up the ladder to the wheelhouse to get out of the cold wind. Gonzo stood at the controls, his upper body lit by the GPS display on his smart phone. He'd used a giant black document clip to clamp it to the—*what do you call it when it's in a boat? —*the dashboard.

"Did you shut off the radar transponder?" he asked Gonzo.

"Natch."

Tom looked out the windows. There were some bright lights from boats in the distance, probably fishermen attracting anchovies or squid to the surface, but nothing nearby.

"How long?" he asked.

"Ten minutes, maybe. Depends on the currents and the wind."

"Gotta hand it to you, Gonz. You sure know how to steer."

"*Gracias, patrón.*" Gonzo's teeth shone in the orange glow from the instruments.

Tom knelt next to his bag, unzipped it, removed a Swamp Fox magazine harness and shrugged into it. He inserted four of the long, curved magazines into the sling's pouches. Then he pulled out his weapon and began to check it as best he could in the semi-darkness.

"That is one weird-ass gun, boss," said Gonzo.

"The Belgians do two things right: they make good beer, and they make good guns." The FN F2000 *was* weird-looking: a short, bulbous thing made of black polymer, with a bullpup design that put the action and the thirty-round magazine well behind the trigger, nestled into the gun's heavy stock. The stumpy rifle was great at close quarters and good at a distance. The top rail held a large laser rangefinder. A single-shot, pump-action 40mm grenade launcher projected forward and below the rifle's muzzle like a blunt-ended bayonet.

Tom opened a black plastic ammo case and considered his choices. "If things go tits-up, I think this one will do." He held the stubby, red-painted grenade up to show Gonzo.

The wanna-be Colombian laughed. "*Caramba.*"

Tom pushed the grenade into the launcher's breech and shot it home. He slung the rifle across his chest and watched through the wheelhouse window for unwelcome guests.

Eventually Gonzo reduced their speed and turned to the left. A minute later he set the engine to idle.

"We're here," he announced.

Tom went out on deck. They were well away from shore, though he couldn't say exactly how far. The power plant at Moss Landing was an orange glow in the distance, but it provided just enough light to see by. The few boats nearby kept their distance.

Chucky Van Camp stood near the rail, looking around with a pair of night-vision goggles clamped to his broad, ugly face. His real name was Roland, but with his sparse tufts of red hair, sunken eyes, melon-shaped head and half a trillion freckles, his resemblance to the homicidal doll in the *Child's Play* horror movies was too strong for anyone to call him anything else. "There," he said, pointing. "About a hundred feet out."

"Good driving," said one of the wet-suited contractors. He and his partner waddled to the back end of the boat—*the stern*, Tom reminded himself—in their ungainly diving fins, fastened masks over their faces, sat on the side and dropped backward into the water.

Chucky guided the divers to their destination as quietly as he could. Sound carried a long way over the water. Then he relayed directions to Gonzo via walkie-talkie.

Gonzo backed the boat up slowly until they were almost on top of whatever-it-was. Then Chucky signaled to shut the engine down.

In the sudden silence, Tom heard waves slapping against *something* in the water next to the boat. He went to the stern and looked over the rail.

"I'll be damned," he muttered.

In the dim orange light from shore, he could just make out the divers sitting astride a long, featureless black cylinder with rounded ends. It projected directly away from the end of the boat. The top of its curved surface was perhaps three feet above the waterline. The waves on either side of it were oddly listless, as if there were large, flat objects just beneath the surface robbing them of strength.

Tom reached into his pocket and removed the transmitter Adam had given him. He pressed its single large button.

A pair of doors opened down the length of the black cylinder, like the doors on the Space Shuttle's cargo bay. Greasy black fluid flooded out of the chamber and into the sea. A weird metallic odor drifted across the water.

One of the divers slipped off the end of the sub as the liquid gushed over him. He couldn't climb back on top. It was too slippery. The two South Africans operating the crane pulled the diver out of the water and lowered him into the chamber. One of the operators tossed the diver a heavy coiled line and tied his end loosely to one of the stern cleats.

Aidan had explained why this was the best spot for the rendezvous. Below them was the end of a huge marine canyon. It had been carved out of the sea floor by the cold water of the Old Salinas River. The robot sub had hidden there, waiting for the appointed time to come to the surface and offload its burden.

Tom felt a chill that had nothing to do with the cold, wet breeze. If Aidan's Chinese friends were ballsy enough to pull this off, there wasn't much they couldn't do.

They lifted twenty-three long, heavy black boxes from the sub's cargo chamber, hosed them down to remove as much of the oily black shit as possible, and lashed them together on deck.

Then Gonzo spotted the incoming boat. He shouted a warning.

Tom pulled himself up the ladder and into the wheelhouse. He didn't have to ask where the boat was. It was perhaps three miles out and coming fast, lights blazing.

"Fuck," he growled. "Coast Guard or Navy. Get ready to move."

Gonzo fired up the engine.

Tom leaned out of the wheelhouse. He shouted, "Abort! Prepare to repel!"

His men didn't hesitate. One of the contractors shouted at the divers to unhook the line and get aboard. The others ducked into the galley to get their guns from their bags.

Tom ducked back into the wheelhouse. "Where'd they put it?" he snapped.

"What?" said Gonzo, eyes wide.

"What do you fucking *think?*"

"Oh. Sorry. Nick said it was in the galley."

Tom jumped down the ladder and opened the door to the lower deck. The dirty vinyl flooring was spattered with spots of blood. He found what he was looking for on the floor of the galley, along with the boat's owner. His body had been shoved into the space under the small dining table.

Tom grabbed the handle and hauled the heavy box out to the deck. He set it down, flipped its latches and opened it up.

He heard Chucky gasp, "Jesus."

Tom wrestled the blocky, bazooka-like MBT-LAW out of its case. He grabbed the three-foot-long Swedish anti-tank weapon by its handle and moved to the side of the boat closest to the incoming vessel.

"Get everyone clear from behind me," he told Chucky as he levered the weapon onto his shoulder.

Chucky looked around, panicked. "Where?"

"Just go *inside*, for Christ's sakes! Move!"

He counted down silently from ten to zero. The incoming boat's engine grew louder with every passing second. Men scrambled behind him and he heard the cabin door close.

A spotlight atop the oncoming ship turned on, scouring the *Sea Conqueror's* rust-streaked wheelhouse with glaring white light. An amplified male voice boomed, *"This is the US Coast Guard! Shut down your engines and prepare to be boarded!"*

Tom took a deep breath and rose up. The ship was no more than a hundred yards away now. He'd practiced with the weapon's controls, but it was the only one they had, and he hadn't had the luxury of test-firing it. And it was meant for a tank, although the dealer who'd sold it to him had sworn it would work just as well on a ship. He propped the end of the tube on top of the rail, sighted directly into the spotlight, whispered "This better fucking work," and fired.

The missile burst out of the launch tube, propelled by a charge of compressed air. Its motor ignited and it blasted away from him, covering the distance to the oncoming Coast Guard boat in less than a second. It arced over the top of the boat and exploded.

The spotlight winked out. The sound of the blast followed an instant later. The concussion was astonishing.

Tom dropped the spent weapon over the rail, unslung his rifle and trained it at the still-oncoming boat.

Its massive engine still howled, but now it was punctuated by a guttural cough. The boat veered slightly away from the *Sea Conqueror*. Perhaps the pilot had seen the missile coming at the last moment.

Tom stared at it as it raced by.

The wheelhouse of the patrol boat was a splintered ruin. Flames erupted from the boat's stern section, trailing behind the boat like bright orange pennants. No one moved on deck. The boat flashed by and kept going, heading toward shore. Somehow it missed the drone sub.

"God *damn*," Tom snarled, as much in jubilation at hitting the boat as anger at having been interrupted. He smashed his fist against the closed door of the galley. "Get the divers on board, right now! Get rid of the sub!"

His men leaped to obey.

The two divers climbed up the ladder at the rear of the boat, apparently having ditched their swim fins. One of them must have pushed the emergency abort switch inside the sub's cargo compartment. Adam had told them about it in case they needed to get away in a hurry.

Tom leaned over the rail and caught a glimpse of the sub's long cylinder vanishing into the water, the cargo doors still open. The long black boxes they'd been offloading were far too dense to float, he knew, but they'd left at least a dozen still on board. Some of those unlabeled crates were way more important than others.

He hoped they'd gotten the right ones.

They turned back to shore, engine on full. They passed the Coast Guard boat on the way in. It was adrift and ablaze. Liquid fire poured onto the water from the fully-engulfed vessel.

Even at full speed, it seemed to take forever to reach Moss Landing.

Gonzo backed the boat into the narrow slip under the travel lift. Bobby and Nick helped tie the boat down and then ran back to the street to keep watch.

Gonzo jumped down to the slip, raced to the travel lift's controls and lowered the pair of cradle lines. They were meant to go beneath the hull of a boat. Instead, the contractors hooked the mesh of nylon webbing they'd lashed around the crates onto the cradle lines with huge steel carabiners.

Gonzo waited for everyone to get out of the boat before he started the crane's noisy engine and began to lift the crates. The webbing held fast. The travel lift took the load easily. The assembled mass of crates lifted free of the fishing boat's deck. Gonzo backed the lift slowly off the piers. He stopped it next to the cargo truck, lowered the crates to the ground, and shut off the engine. The sudden silence was broken by the barking of sea lions and angry yells from the nearby RV park, complaining about the racket.

"Move fast," Tom said. Someone probably already called the cops. He thought about sending somebody out to reinforce Bobby and Nick, but they'd need every man to move these heavy crates.

They cut the webbing around the crates and manhandled them onto the heavy-duty tailgate lift and then into the big truck. They worked as fast as they could, all ten of them straining under the monstrous weight of the icy metal boxes. Tom told them not to put more than one crate onto the lift gate at a time, fearing that it might buckle under the load.

Adam had assured him that the truck could take the weight of the entire shipment, but the back of the truck sagged visibly with every new crate.

They were almost done when Tom heard the wail of approaching police cars. The sirens stopped short of the shop. Then they heard automatic weapons fire punctuated by pistol shots.

"Put the crate down!" Tom grunted. They quickly obeyed. He jerked his chin at the two men on the end closest to the truck. "You two, go help them!" He took cover behind the crate, raising his rifle. The others followed his lead.

The two men ran toward the battle, machine guns at the ready. A minute later there was a huge burst of gunfire. The sudden silence that followed was punctuated only by shouts and screams from the RV park.

One of the men he'd sent came trotting back, smirking. "No problem, boss. Our guys are healthy, but we gotta blow."

"No shit," Tom growled.

They heaved the last box into the truck, tied it to the others, slammed the doors, and got on the road. They passed two stationary police cruisers on the way out of Moss Landing, the officers' bullet-riddled bodies sprawled beside their open doors.

Tom and Gonzo went south in their pickup. The two Yukons went north, to guard the truck and make sure it got back to Morgan Hill via back roads.

They reached Castroville safely, found their change car and left town at a safe-and-sane speed. Tom knew the others were doing the same, cutting the tarp free from the truck to reveal a meticulously hand-painted Bimbo Bread company logo—a common sight in this Mexican-dominated agricultural region—and swapping the SUVs for old Chevrolet sedans. Tom just hoped the obvious overloading of the truck escaped notice. No baked goods ever weighed a truck down like that.

As they left town, a pair of CHP black-and-whites screamed past them from the south, obviously heading toward Moss Landing Harbor. Tom kept in touch with the other vehicles by SMS messages using burner cell phones. No one mentioned any encounters with police.

Only when they reached the Morgan Hill compound did Tom allow himself a smile of satisfaction. The "Bimbo Bread" truck was there, safely hidden in the huge machine shed, as were the two Chevys.

They hauled one of the long boxes out of the truck and opened it.

The crate was filled to the brim with a familiar packing grease. Tom exchanged a knowing look with the others who'd been in the military. He knelt next to the box. The smell of Cosmoline filled his nostrils. He reached in, fished around for a moment, and then pulled out a stubby, hideous rifle with a short stock and a massive barrel.

Tom cleared some of the grease away. He took a deep breath when he read the markings on the side of the heavy gun. "Holy shit," he breathed. "Merry fucking Christmas."

He placed the weapon back in the open box, stood up, and smiled at his men. "Good job, everyone. Get that truck unloaded. I want everything cleaned and inventoried by twelve hundred hours. Asses and elbows, ladies! Move it!"

His men leaped to obey.

CHAPTER THIRTY-SIX

Woodside, California

October 29

Buck's Restaurant was a Silicon Valley legend. It was a few miles north of the venture capital mecca of Sand Hill Road, just off I-280 in the deceptively folksy town of Woodside, where you couldn't throw a cell phone without hitting a millionaire. Nobody knew how many famous companies had gotten their start as business plans sketched out on napkins at the eclectic roadside restaurant. The number was not small.

Philip Mayhew arrived in time to get the big oblong table in the conveniently empty back room. It was Sunday morning, and still a bit early for the crush of customers he knew would be here later. He asked to talk with the manager. With a judicious application of cash, he arranged to reserve the entire back room for his party.

The bittersweet memory of Peter's having rented the whole outside deck of Sam's Chowder House for the two of them came unbidden into his mind. It had taken Philip some time to forgive Peter for that showboating demo, but he had to admit it had worked beautifully. He wished he could tell Peter that now. It would have made him smile.

He took a chair at the table facing the entrance and peered at the inexplicable décor as he waited for the others to arrive.

The walls were festooned with photographs, posters, cavalry sabers, a giant harmonica, a hippopotamus head, and myriad glass cases containing any number of bizarre knickknacks. Crystal chandeliers and fairings from high-speed bicycles hung above the tables. Atop the short wall between the front and back rooms was a diorama containing meticulous models of various species of redwood trees. Mounted above it was a narwhal tusk. The toothy nose of a sawfish occupied pride of place on the wall to his right. Behind him was a large glass class case containing a pair of accordions, labeled with the words "IN CASE OF

EMERGENCY, BREAK GLASS, SAVE ACCORDIONS." Philip thought the public use of those instruments should be a hanging offense, but even he had to admit they were beautifully made.

The rest of the Board of Directors arrived together. Philip rose to greet them.

Darlene Smith looked tired and wan. Sam Bollard looked tired and angry. Sanjiv Krishnamurthi seemed alert enough, but his eyes were rimmed with red. They sat and ordered cups of coffee.

"Who else is coming?" Sam Bollard said, gesturing at the remaining empty chairs.

"John, Jay, Ramona and Jack." Philip took a sip of the scalding hot coffee. "They deserve a voice in this."

"Why here?" said Darlene Smith, looking around dubiously. "It is... charming, I suppose, but we could have met at the ST campus."

Philip frowned. "Frankly, I'm not sure how private our conversations there are. The whole place is wired for video and sound, and I don't know who gets to watch it. I wanted this off the record. And I've sealed more than a few deals here. It's got good karma."

The waiter delivered more cups of coffee. He vanished after Philip told him to come back when the rest of the party arrived.

Philip felt a growing sense of discomfort as the minutes ticked by. The other members of the Board seemed content to sip coffee in brooding silence.

The team from ST eventually came to his rescue. Everyone but Jack Dura wore business-casual for the occasion. Jack wore gray sweat pants, running shoes, and a black, long-sleeved sweatshirt featuring a faded Talking Heads logo. Philip sighed. He wished Jack had taken his appearance seriously for a change.

They crowded around the table. The waiter materialized, took orders, and departed.

John Shea spoke first. "The autopsy report on Peter came in last night. Heart attack."

Darlene Smith made a *tsking* sound. "Such a shame. He looked perfectly healthy to me."

"He was under terrible stress," said Jay Kapoor. The diminutive Indian man looked like he had one foot in the grave himself. His skin was waxy and his eyes so sunken that they had nearly disappeared beneath the overhang of his brow. His hands trembled as they cradled his coffee cup.

"When is the funeral?" asked Sanjiv.

Shea said, "His wife and daughters are flying back from Italy. They haven't announced a date yet. Probably by the end of the week."

The moment of uncomfortable silence that followed was eventually broken by Jack Dura. "Not that I mind getting away from campus, but why did you call us here, Mr. Mayhew?"

"It's Philip," he said automatically. "We need to make plans. Peter's gone. I'm sorry to say it, with him not even in his grave yet, but we have to appoint a new CEO. We have to figure out our next steps."

Darlene Smith said, "I'd have thought that was obvious. Sam's the only possible choice."

Sam Bollard looked at her with wide eyes. "Hell, no. I have enough on my plate with my own companies. All I know about ST's technology is that it cost a fucking fortune. Philip should do it."

Sanjiv said, "Philip's a venture capitalist, and he has a full time job, as well. We need someone who understands what ST is trying to do, who already knows the technology and the people. We can't take time for an executive search."

Philip nodded. "Science class was a hell of a long time ago, and I got a C, anyway."

"What about Darlene?" said Sam, stabbing a finger at the elegant British financier. "She was the COO of a defense company, for Christ's sakes! Or you, Sanjiv! ST used to be a pharmaceuticals company, and you've been working in genetics for decades."

Darlene smiled sweetly. "But I don't *want* to do it, Sam."

Sanjiv shook his head. "I'm about to retire. I'm moving back to Bangalore next year."

Sam growled, "Well, I'm not gonna let you railroad me into this job." The Texan sat back and crossed his arms, looking for all the world like a pouting four-year-old.

Philip watched the ST people as the others wrangled with Sam. John Shea looked thoroughly bemused—no doubt wondering why he'd been invited to this goat rodeo. Ramona Ochoa's face was a study in careful neutrality. Her dark, lovely eyes glittered as she watched the argument rage back and forth across the table. Jay Kapoor sat back with no appearance of interest.

Jack Dura, by contrast, looked bored and impatient. He looked around at the restaurant, his eyes lighting on every weird decoration.

He checked his wrist-watch several times. Eventually he pulled an oversized iPhone out of a pocket and began to play with it.

It was the moment Philip been waiting for. "How about Jack?" he blurted, as if he'd just thought of it.

The conversation came to an abrupt halt.

"Uh, what?" said Jack, looking up from his phone.

John Shea's mouth twitched. "You want *Jack Dura* to run ST?"

The rest of them just gaped at him.

The food arrived at that moment. Philip tucked into his breakfast with gusto. He showered his eggs Benedict with Tabasco sauce and shoveled them into his mouth, ignoring the baffled stares directed at him from every seat at the table. He waved his fork encouragingly. The others began to eat as well.

When he'd finished the delicious food, he took a long sip from his coffee cup and finally began to speak. "Who knows more about the technology than Jack Dura? Nobody." He paused and glanced around. Only his guests were in earshot, and the noise from the front room had increased as more customers arrived. He continued in a low voice. "Who turned the team around and solved the problems with the *you-know-what*? Jack. Who invented the *new* you-know-what? Jack. Who exposed Aidan O'Keefe? Jack. No one else has his credibility with the public. He's being compared to Albert Einstein in the press. Albert goddamned *Einstein*. It's Jack or nobody." He didn't add that as the primary funder of the company, he could insist. Judging from the icy expressions of his fellow Board members, he didn't have to.

Darlene Smith said, "Philip. ST isn't a startup. Don't you think the day of the *enfant terrible* Silicon Valley CEO is over and done? No offense," she added, glancing at Jack.

He shrugged it off. "None taken. I'm a scientist, dammit, not a businessman."

Philip said, "And you'll continue to be one, just with a few more responsibilities. CEO's just one rung up the ladder from CTO."

Jack snorted derisively. "A *few* more responsibilities! Jesus Christ! Peter just made me CTO the day before yesterday! What I don't know about running a company would fill the Grand Canyon."

"We'll help. All of us," he said, glaring at the other members of the Board. "We'll advise you on strategy. Jay, Ramona and Barb Johnson can help with the day-to-day stuff. Barb's going to pitch a fit when she finds out she's got to do PR for *you*, Jack. And once you test the..." He stopped himself before he said *HyperQUBE*. "When you test the new *you-know-what,* we can move the research group over to Lawrence Livermore."

"Huh?" blurted Jack.

John Shea's eyes narrowed. "You don't think I can maintain security at the campus?" he hissed.

Philip threw his hands into the air. "I don't want us to find out the hard way. I'm getting a lot of pressure from the government. I got a wake-up call at five AM from Andrew Seigart. Laurel Wynn's boss. This thing that happened out on Monterey Bay last night really has them spooked."

The others exchanged baffled glances with each other.

Philip sighed. "Don't any of you read the news? The attack on the Coast Guard boat? Seven sailors dead? One of them jumped overboard and got picked up by a fisherman, half-dead from hypothermia. She said the bad guys were on a fishing boat. They took the Coast Guard ship out with a rocket. A fucking rocket! There was a shoot-out in Moss Landing a half-hour later. Four cops and three civilians murdered. The attackers loaded a big truck with *something* and got away clean."

John Shea blanched. "And Seigart thinks it's connected to us?"

"What do you think?" Philip said acidly. "Hasn't every mass murder in the last few months been connected to this company in some way? I'd prefer the Feds to be too paranoid than not paranoid enough."

"Why did this Seigart guy call you?" said Jack. "You're the newest member of the board. Why not Sanjiv?"

Philip felt blood rise to his face. "Because... ah, because he and I had some dealings before we agreed to invest in ST."

"What kind of dealings?"

There wasn't any way to soft-pedal it, so Philip just said it. "The government underwrote ZMPC's investment. If ST went under, the Feds promised to reimburse us. Laurel Wynn practically shoved the deal down my throat."

Now it was Jack's face that turned red. "Holy Christ," he grated.

"Before you blow a gasket, hear me out," said Philip, raising a hand. "They didn't contribute. Every penny we put into the company was ours. They don't have a say in what we do with it."

"Like hell," Jack snapped. "They're telling you to move us to a god-damned government lab!"

"They're encouraging it. I think they're right. I'll tell you something Seigart told me, but you have to keep it at this table." He leaned forward and gestured for the others to do the same. He whispered, "The Navy does passive sonar research in Monterey Bay. They have some of the most sensitive detectors in the world there. They picked up something like hull-popping sounds, but a hundred times quieter than usual. That's why they sent the Coast Guard boat out to investigate."

John Shea leaned back from the table. "Holy shit," he breathed.

"What? What does it mean?" asked Ramona.

"A submarine," John whispered. "When they come up to the surface, the drop in pressure makes their hulls pop."

Even Philip felt a chill run through him when John said the words.

Jack turned pale. "Christ on a crutch. If they have *submarines*, God knows what else they have."

"Exactly. I know the Pauling Building is like a fortress, but it doesn't compare to the security around a nuclear weapons lab. That's why the Feds aren't really giving us a choice," Philip said in a more normal tone. "They're going to reinforce your squad, John. And they're telling us to leave ST voluntarily."

Jack growled, "I guess they don't know what *voluntarily* means."

"In this case, it means we get to choose when we go, as long as we do it within a week. Is the new *you-know-what* going to be ready?"

Jack shrugged. "We're testing it on Wednesday."

"Can you do it sooner?"

"No." Jack's face twisted into a sudden, wry smile. "'I cannae change the laws of physics, Captain,'" he said in a terrible Scottish accent.

Philip snorted. He'd watched repeats of *Star Trek* after school every day when he was a kid. "If it works, can we relocate to Livermore?"

Jack sat back and looked thoughtful. "*If* it works. If it doesn't, we're stuck in Palo Alto until we make one that does. It's completely experimental. This is the first design based on my new theory. The old, ah, the old *you-know-what* won't work without the server farm. There's no way they're relocating *that*. It would take a year."

"How confident are you that the new gadget will work?"

Jack pursed his lips. "About ninety percent."

"Can you get your people ready to go as soon as the test is over? If it's successful, that is?"

"Probably. We'll have to scramble to copy all the data onto hard drives. There's a shitload of modeling and research data we'll need to keep handy. I think we *could* do it."

Philip grunted, "Good. We'll need backup copies of everything at a secure location, anyway. I've always been nervous about Peter's idea of keeping all of the research in one goddamned building, no matter how bulletproof it is. He wasn't expecting John to fight off an actual army. Nut-ball protestors and whack-job criminals, maybe, but not a full-scale armed assault."

Jack nodded. "Makes sense. I'll have to talk to Amber and Blaise. They know the systems better than I do. But I want an ironclad fucking guarantee from the Feds that they won't try to take this project away from us. It's ours, by God."

"You'll get it." Philip looked at the others around the table, who were gaping at them in evident amazement. "So. Does anyone think Jack *isn't* the right person to run ST?"

They shook their heads slowly. After a long, considering stare at Jack, even John Shea shook his. "Talk about your meteoric rises," he muttered. "From new employee to CEO in four months. That's gotta be some kind of record."

Philip looked at the ashen-faced scientist. "Jack, I might not like your sloppy clothes or your snotty attitude, but your heart is in this. No one else will protect my investment the way you will. You're a natural leader. You *are* the right man."

Jack stared at him. "If I do this... *if* I do this... I won't be a figure-head."

"No," said Philip, unleashing a rare smile. "That just wouldn't be *you*."

CHAPTER THIRTY-SEVEN

The Refuge, San Carlos, California

October 29

Laurel Wynn sat at the booth at the rear of the gastro pub, looking for Jack. He'd asked her to meet him here, which was odd enough, considering how seldom he left the safety of the Struve Technologies campus these days. The tone of his voice on the phone had been different, too. Terse. Tense. Almost unfriendly.

It worried her.

She glanced around. She faced the front of the restaurant so she could see Jack come in. Lambent October sunset light slanted in through the windows, casting a ruddy glow on the cheerful crowd. The bar to her left was packed with people watching the San Francisco 49ers game on big flat TVs. Up-tempo hipster music blared from the overhead speakers. It was noisy but not uncomfortably so. The scent of pastrami drifted past. Her stomach rumbled. She hadn't eaten since getting back from Moss Landing. She sipped her iced water and tried to push the memories of the awful scene out of her mind.

Jack arrived a few minutes later, preceded by a trio of John Shea's men, including Alex Southall. The waitress pointed at her. She beckoned to Jack, smiling and standing up to greet him. His guards stayed outside, waiting for an empty table near them, she guessed.

Jack's unshaven face was grim.

When he came close, she pulled him into a hug. His arms went around her, but there was no urgency in them. She pulled back and looked at him. "What's wrong?"

"Let's talk," he said, gesturing to the booth.

She sat opposite him, uncertainty gnawing at her. "What is it, Jack?"

"Why didn't you tell me you and Andrew Seigart strong-armed Philip Mayhew into investing in StruvePharma?"

Uh oh. She took a second to compose herself. "I had orders not to."

"And you just obey orders like a good little soldier."

"Every legal one," she snapped. She tried to remain calm. "And it wasn't exactly strong-arming. If we hadn't offered to reimburse ZMPC if Struve went down in flames, they'd never have invested, and you'd be back at Stanford, Jack. Is that what you want? What's wrong with you?"

He sighed. The anger seemed to bleed out of him. "I wish I hadn't found out from Mayhew."

"I didn't have any choice, Jack."

"Yeah, I know. There's a lot of that going around these days."

The smiling waitress arrived and asked for their orders. "Try the Reuben," Jack suggested.

She shrugged and said, "Fine."

"I'll have one, too, with garlic fries. And a North Coast Pranqster." He glanced at Laurel. "Make that two. And bread pudding for dessert."

When the waitress departed, Jack leaned back against the booth's backrest and rubbed his eyes with both hands. "I'm sorry, Laurel. This day's been FUBAR'ed from the time I woke up. They made me CEO."

That doused the anger simmering in the pit of her belly. "Uh. What?"

He described the breakfast meeting at Buck's. When he finished, she became aware that she'd been gaping at him. She shook her head and closed her mouth. "Holy shit," she breathed.

A table opened up near their booth. Alex Southall and the other guards took it. Laurel exchanged a nod with Alex. He grinned at her, looked at Jack meaningfully, and waggled his eyebrows.

She hid the smile behind her hand.

Jack growled, "Yeah, I'd be laughing too if I wasn't stuck with this job."

She didn't care to explain Alex's recognition of her interest in Jack, not when he was still being a jerk. "Look. I'm sorry I didn't tell you about the deal with ZMPC. Seigart offered to backstop him if the investment went bad. Okay, he offered really hard," she amended when she saw the skeptical look creep back into his eyes. "My boss and his both know what a gold mine ST will be for the economy. They wouldn't do anything to jeopardize that. They just didn't want you to run out of money."

The beers showed up then, served in little bulbous glasses that looked a bit like brandy snifters. Jack took a long swallow from his.

She brought her glass to her nose and sniffed. Cloves. She'd never cared for Belgian beers, but she took a cautious taste. It was delicious.

Jack noted her reaction and tried a smile. "I wouldn't steer you wrong."

She nodded, put the glass down, and stared into his eyes. "I wouldn't steer you wrong either, Jack. I promise."

He put his glass next to hers and reached across the table. Their fingers entwined. "I'm really sorry, Laurel. This really has been a hellish day."

"I can guess," she said as softly as she could and still be heard over the din of the crowd. She squeezed his hand. "I'm sorry about Peter. I meant to call yesterday, but things just got away from me."

"I know what you mean. I can't believe this is all happening." He looked at her sharply. "I know you heard about the mayhem in Moss Landing."

She shivered. "Seigart sent me down to take a look. It was... horrible." It was a lot worse than that. The four deputy sheriffs had been chewed to bloody ribbons by machine gun fire. They'd found the body of the captain of the fishing boat stuffed under the table in the galley, his brains strewn across the floorboards. The owner of the marine repair shop was sprawled face down in the locked garage, his hand clutching his wife's. They'd been dead at least twenty-four hours. Then she'd seen the smoldering hull of the Coast Guard boat. It had been towed into the harbor, what was left of it.

Jack winced at her expression. "Was there really a submarine out in the Bay?"

She shrugged. "Some witnesses from a KOA campground nearby said they saw men unloading huge crates from the fishing boat and putting them on a truck. We've got video from a restaurant next to Highway 1. It showed a truck with a gray tarp on the back driving into the harbor late Saturday evening. When it drove out again, just after the attack, it was riding on its axles."

"Could they be drug smugglers?" he asked, almost hopefully.

"Jack... I don't think so. There's never been a drug sub this far north, and with the sonar the Navy has in Monterey Bay they'd have picked it up before it got anywhere close to shore. Drug subs aren't high-tech. They're more like submersible barrels. We have to assume the worst case scenario. It was probably a shipment of weapons, and from someone with a very advanced submarine. That means a nation-state's involved, not just criminals."

"Well, shit."

"Yeah. The Navy's flying in some planes to see if they can find the sub. They're pretty sure it hasn't left Monterey Bay. The surviving Coast Guard said the bad guys were lifting a crate from it when they were interrupted. Maybe some of the cargo went overboard. The Monterey Bay Aquarium volunteered their ROV, so they're going to search the undersea canyon. They're even bringing a big NOAA ship down from Newport to look for it with high-res sonar. There's no shortage of small arms for sale in America, Jack. Whatever was in those crates is probably heavy-duty stuff. Rocket-propelled grenades, maybe, or worse. We need to relocate you all to Lawrence Livermore, ASAP."

He nodded sourly. "Philip Mayhew already told us. We can't move until Wednesday. The new *you-know-what* is coming out of the annealing oven tomorrow. We've got to cool it down, get it into the deep freeze, and test it before we can be sure we're portable."

"You can't test it at Livermore?"

"Not a chance."

"Shit."

"I need three days. I've already got the Elves copying data and schematics onto hard drives. I'm almost certain the Hyper—sorry, the new gizmo—I'm ninety percent sure it will work first-time. If it does, we can relocate."

"And if it doesn't?"

His mouth twisted into a frown. "Santa's Workshop is the only place I can fix it, Laurel. If we have to spin up another one... there really is no other place to do it."

She sighed. "We're working under the assumption that this attack was related to your work. I tried to get regular soldiers from outside the Bay Area, but there's a lot of push-back. There's a big legal fight on Capitol Hill over the Posse Comitatus Act. The governor's sending in some National Guard troops to reinforce John's men until it's settled. Don't argue, it's already in work. They're going to shut down traffic everywhere in the mid-Peninsula area until they can get you out of there."

"That'll make the commuters happy."

"*Fuck* the commuters," she snapped. "We're talking about *you*, Jack."

"Woah, there," Jack said into the sudden silence.

She looked around. She must have spoken a lot more loudly than she'd thought. Half of the people in the restaurant were looking at them, some of them with expressions of dawning recognition. A few raised cell phones. LED flashes went off.

"We're getting out of here," she said. "Alex."

"Right," the guard said, standing up. He looked at his companions. "Guys, get them to the truck. I'll pay the bill and bring the food."

They threaded between the tables and emerged from the restaurant into golden sunset light. Shortly they found themselves sitting together in the back row of one of ST's up-armored Suburbans. Alex was only moments behind them, toting a big paper bag.

They drove back to the campus with the mouth-watering odor of pastrami and garlic fries filling the cabin. There was little conversation. Jack's face was pensive. His usual insolent grin was missing altogether. She grabbed his hand and held on tight.

Soon she found herself sitting at the dining table in the third floor kitchen of the Crick Building. It had only been a few days since she left, but she'd missed it terribly—or rather, the people who lived there.

Jack reheated the sandwiches in the microwave. He brought them out on paper plates. He went back for a couple of glasses of chilled sparkling water. "Not exactly North Coast Pranqster, but they'll do in a pinch," he said with a ghost of a smile.

The pastrami was the best she'd had since she'd last visited New York. The mood lightened as they ate. She stole some of his garlic fries, and he guarded the rest with mock ferocity. Then he made her try the spicy sauce on the fries. Her taste buds did handstands and somersaults. They shared the bread pudding. It was the best she'd ever tasted.

They moved to the lounge afterward, closing the door when they heard Ben and Deepthi talking in the nearby kitchen. As they talked, the twilit sky outside the thick bulletproof windows gave way to inky blackness. She told him everything she knew about the bad guys, about Aidan's secret history, her suspicions about Tom Reed—everything she thought he might need to know.

In turn, he told her about the dinner party at the Four Seasons, the last time he'd seen Peter, being appointed CTO, and finding out about Peter's death the following morning. She tried to draw him away from the topic, but the conversation kept looping back to it.

He said at one point, "You know something? I was sitting up there next to Peter and the President of the United States, way up at the high table, under the spotlights, everybody applauding me, and the only thing I really wanted was to see you walk into the room." He smiled. "Maybe wearing some slinky dress that showed off your legs."

She felt the faint beginning of a blush creep into her face. "I wanted to be there, but... you know. Work."

"Yeah. Work."

"I think... I think we might work a little too much, Jack."

"I was just thinking the same thing." His smile faded. He paused for a long moment. "I never really apologized for how I acted the first time we met."

"Yeah, you did. You said something like 'it's hard to get out of the habit of being an asshole,' or words to that effect."

He laughed. "That sounds like me. I really do apologize. That was a rough week."

"I remember."

"I must have seemed like a total creep for asking to pop Aidan in the chops."

She didn't say anything.

He lowered his eyes. "Yeah, pretty much what I figured. Not my finest hour, for sure. Even though he turned out to be just as bad as I was telling everyone, I still feel a little guilty about that."

"Don't." She smiled at him. "I wish you'd knocked his head off."

He returned the smile, then grew serious. "And I owe you another apology. I'm really sorry for not knowing if I could trust you. That's why I had to see you tonight. I had to be certain. I couldn't stand it if... if I didn't know."

"And do you?" she whispered.

He nodded. "I do."

A silence yawned between them. Her heart began to race. His pupils were huge, and his face was flushed.

Don't do it, girl. You're not supposed to get involved. Look away. Look away. LOOK AWAY. She looked away. Then she happened to see the wall clock. She blurted, "Holy shit!" and leaped to her feet.

"What?" he said, startled.

"It's ten PM! I have to get one of your guys to drive me back to my car. Seigart's flying into Moffett tonight. I have to be there to pick him up."

"When's he due?"

"Twelve thirty, I think."

"Two and a half hours. Plenty of time."

Her face grew warm. "Plenty of time for... what, exactly?"

He stood and moved close to her, smiling. "For some very serious *not-work*," he said. He offered his hands.

She took them and let him pull her close. Then she leaned in and kissed him hungrily, wrapping her arms around him, ignoring the furious catcalls from her conscience. His body was as solid as an oak. His strong hands on her back felt like they were on fire.

"You're right," she said, panting, when the kiss finally ended. "That *is* plenty of time."

She let him lead her to his bedroom.

CHAPTER THIRTY-EIGHT

San Francisco Bay, California

October 30

The millions of people who lived around San Francisco Bay were largely ignorant of the staggering volume of water that surged in and out of the shallow Bay under the influence of the sun and moon. Ship's captains and pleasure boaters knew about it, of course. Even they wouldn't have spared a thought to the problems a drone submarine would have in fighting those currents. They would have scoffed at the very idea of a sub remaining concealed in the single infrequently dredged channel that gave access to the South Bay's marinas and ports.

Devilfish One's propulsion system was too weak to resist those tides. Each time the ebb tide began or a big ship got too close, the Devilfish was forced to settle to one side of the channel, its cylindrical cargo pod positioned well away from the center to keep it from being struck by the keel of a ship. Its wings were draped across the bottom so that the friction of the mud kept it from being dragged back toward the Golden Gate, where the Bay waters emptied into the ocean.

The unfortunate combination of tides and traffic had stranded the Devilfish at the bottom of the channel just south of Oyster Point, near San Francisco's big, busy airport. Its program allowed it to move only at night, and only then if the tides were high enough to give it a comfortable margin for navigating these shallow waters.

At midnight, Devilfish One deployed its sensor buoy to pick up the nightly message from the heavens.

The Devilfish decrypted and authenticated it. If the onboard computer had been capable of emotion, it might have panicked. The deadline had been moved up. It had to be in place no later than Tuesday night—just forty-eight hours to reach the abandoned rail bridge in the shallows of the South Bay.

The Devilfish ran a series of calculations to determine whether it could meet the new schedule. It had to be several miles further south before it settled in for the next low tide. It was two days before the new moon. The tide was nearing its lowest point right now. If it hadn't been for the early departure of a tanker that had been moored almost directly above it, the Devilfish wouldn't even have been able to raise the sensor buoy safely, much less get under way.

Its computations ended. Meeting the schedule was just possible, if it ran the propulsion system at 100 percent, and if absolutely nothing went wrong. There was no margin for error.

Devilfish One transmitted its acknowledgment of its orders, including its new ETA to its destination, and then pulled in the sensor buoy. It waited another hour for the outbound tide to slacken. When its sensors began to register the beginning of the flood tide, it pumped argon gas into the foam-filled chambers of its articulated, manta-like wings. They pulled free of the bottom muck lethargically, lifting the long cylindrical cargo pod free as well.

An hour and a half after receiving its new orders, Devilfish One was on its way. It made good progress. It deployed its sensor buoy to calibrate its inertial guidance system against its GPS coordinates. It computed that it would be able to shelter in the waters just to the east of Palo Alto for the day, and embark on the final leg of its journey at the next flood tide after sunset.

At 3:38:07 AM, Pacific Daylight Time, north-northeast of Redwood City, its propulsion system at maximum and making excellent time as the flood tide continued to swell, the Devilfish was impaled by the tip of a submerged metal pole.

It was the mast of a decrepit wooden clinker-built sailboat that had sunk at night in the channel several months earlier. Its young cheapskate of an owner had gotten it for a steal, but it turned out that the real thief was the seller.

The first owner had neglected crucial repairs in the hull. The new owner hadn't noticed the water streaming in between the rotten planks until it was almost too late. He'd escaped in an inflatable rubber raft. The sailboat had never been located. It was far enough to one side of the channel that it hadn't been encountered by the vessels that kept to the center. It now lay on its side, its mast angled slightly up, directly in front of the Devilfish.

The unyielding steel pole rammed through the front edge of the thin, rubberized fiberglass shell of the port wing like a needle pinning an insect to a cork board.

The propulsion system reversed as the shudder of the collision ran through the sub's frame, but the inertia of the Devilfish carried it forward, pushing the port wingtip down into the mud at the edge of the channel with slow, inexorable force.

The Devilfish began to pivot around the point of impact. The slow-motion collision punched the base of the mast out through the bottom of the sailboat's hull. The long pole speared deep into the bottom mud and stopped, fetching up under a submerged boulder. Frozen in place, the mast sheared through the fragile armature of the wing like a knife. Control lines were severed. Circuits were broken. All readings from the sections of the wing past the point of impact went dead.

Emergency programs kicked in. The sensor buoy was reeled in fast, so that it would not become entangled in the obstruction. The drive went to maximum, but the cylindrical cargo pod was as long as a freight train car and just as massive. Its momentum carried it forward with slow inevitability.

With its wingtip wedged in the mud and the cargo pod still moving, the wing sheared apart along the tear created by the mast. Once freed, the wing floated away, rising to the surface to be carried away by the currents.

The Devilfish was now badly unbalanced. It heeled over, the buoyancy of the foam-filled starboard wing forcing the cylinder onto its side. Without the lift provided by the left wing, it couldn't hold its former depth.

The nose of the cargo pod plowed more than fifteen feet into the muddy bottom of the channel. The passive sonar pod at the bulbous tip of the cylinder was smashed. Water flooded the nose section, destroying the primary computer and guidance system. Mud rammed into the nose-mounted intake vents, driving sea water at high pressure before it. The mud fouled the propulsion system's delicate ceramic turbines, clogging them hopelessly.

When it finally came to rest, the Devilfish lay on its side, the stump of its port wing crumpled uselessly beneath it. The twenty-meter long cylinder was jammed into the bottom of the channel at a forty-degree angle. It had rotated two-thirds of the way around. Its tail now pointed in the general direction of Redwood City. The rear end of the cylinder was a scant meter below the surface.

The drone sub's backup computer analyzed the damage. The cargo cylinder had been built tough. The payload was not compromised, but the crucial navigation instruments in the nose were a total loss. Mud clogged the outlets of the forward ballast tanks. Worse, the primary sensor buoy had been housed in a compartment in the nose. It was no longer operable. The chameleon skin system was likewise disabled. It could no longer match the color of the water surrounding it. After daybreak, anyone in a boat or a plane would spot the dark bulk of the submarine immediately.

The backup computer's options were limited. Its programmers had anticipated a large number of disaster scenarios. The turbidity of the water might be enough to conceal the Devilfish if it could come to rest at the bottom of the channel. The payload bay doors still tested as operational. The mission could still be completed.

The computer's remorseless little brain calculated the best chance of getting the vessel to a horizontal position was to eject the starboard wing. It didn't hesitate. It opened each section in the remaining wing to let the argon gas bubble out to fill the voids in the plastic foam with heavy sea water. Then it jettisoned the wing. It slowly drifted to the bottom of the channel a few meters away.

The cylinder's angle dropped slightly, but it had been driven too deeply into the mud to shift much further. The computer flooded the rear ballast tanks, which helped, but not enough. The stub of the left wing jammed into the bottom. After every option had been exercised, the vessel remained tilted up at an angle of thirty-four degrees.

It had been decided at the top level not to equip the Devilfish with an automatic self-destruct. Its mission was too delicate. An untimely detonation would be more ruinous than allowing the sub to be discovered. The Devilfish had no remaining options. It deployed the backup antenna float from the rear section of the cargo pod. It connected to the satellite phone network and sent its distress message to its makers.

The engineers pored over the Devilfish plans, sweat dripping from their faces, trying to find a way to coax the sub into dropping to the bottom of the channel. They tried repeatedly emptying and flooding the rear ballast tanks. The sub's angle declined half a degree, but it would go no further.

When they finally gave up, three increasingly desperate hours had passed. The lead designer was just about to call General Guo's office to inform him of the disaster when the satellite telemetry from the Devilfish abruptly ended.

The engineers scrambled to reestablish the connection, to no avail.

They did not know that a few seconds before, the captain of the Indonesian heavy bulk carrier *Pride of Balikpapan* had left dock in the South Bay port of Redwood City. The ship's hold was full of shredded scrap metal. High tide had just passed, but there was still ample water under the keel in mid-channel for the fully-loaded vessel to depart—or would have been, had the Devilfish not been in the way.

The bulbous bow of the ship struck the Devilfish squarely on the end of its up-tilted cargo pod.

The low speed of the collision was irrelevant. The force of thousands of tons of ship and scrap metal moving at six knots was more than sufficient to tear the drone sub apart.

Caught between the unyielding floor of the Bay and the unstoppable mass of the cargo ship, the cylindrical cargo pod burst open along the long seam of its doors. The formidable but delicate contents of the payload bay were crumpled, smashed and strewn across the bottom of the channel.

The helmsman tried to turn the ship away from the collision, but only succeeded in running her aground in the shallows to the east of the channel. When the crew spotted strange looking debris floating next to the ship, they called the harbormaster, who spent the rest of the morning on the phone.

A team of divers from the National Transportation Safety Board arrived in Redwood City by mid-afternoon. What they found beneath the now-anchored *Pride of Balikpapan* sent them scurrying back to the surface, their eyes bulging with panic.

The NTSB supervisor, Callie Howard, was waiting for the divers on the harbormaster's launch. When they told her what they'd found, her face drained of color. At first she didn't even know who to call. She had to look the department up on Wikipedia. She gripped the boat's rail tightly and closed her eyes as she waited for the call to be answered.

"DOE NNSA, how may I direct your call," said the bored operator.

"Get me the NEST hotline," she said without preamble. "This is not a drill! This is Callie Howard of the NTSB!" She recited her government ID number.

"H-hold please," the voice said. The line clicked. Muzak that had been old when she'd been a kid began to play.

Holy Mary, mother of God, she thought, fighting the urge to throw up. She'd worked for the NTSB for twenty-three years. In all that time, she'd never imagined she'd be the first person in the history of the agency to call in the Nuclear Emergency Support Team.

CHAPTER THIRTY-NINE

Struve Technologies Coyote Hill Campus, Palo Alto, California

October 30

Blaise Thierry and the other Elves watched Amber D'Agostino and one of her technicians pull the ceramic tray containing the HyperQUBE out of the annealing oven. Even from ten feet away, he could feel the gentle heat radiating from the open chamber like sunlight on his face.

They transferred the tray with exquisite care to the top of the closest workbench. Blaise knew the HyperQUBE was clamped to the tray by the four golden thermoconductor studs that emerged from its base. Even so, it looked like it might roll off at any second. He didn't breathe easily until the tray lay flat on the bench. There was a scattering of applause, which Amber acknowledged with a dark chuckle.

The gleaming eight-inch silver sphere looked identical to its predecessors. Its closely spaced grid of optical data interconnects glittered like bands of tiny sapphires in the bright light of Santa's Workshop.

"Did anyone call Jack?" Blaise asked the room.

No one replied.

"Oh, crap," Amber said. She looked at her technician, who nodded, went to a nearby lab bench and picked up an interoffice phone.

Jack appeared twenty seconds later. He must have been next door in the Black Box. The Dura Party trailed him like a pack of eager puppy dogs. Blaise made room for Jack next to the workbench. The others crowded in wherever there was space.

"Welcome," said Amber, looking at Jack. "Now we get to see if your baby is healthy and happy, or if we get to grind him up and try again."

Jack winced and said, "Ouch."

Silence filled the room as Amber placed the diagnostic "hat" onto the north pole of the spherical QUBE: a small, concave metal disc connected to a bundle of hair-thin optical fibers wrapped with bands of black electrical tape. The hat was magnetic, so it stayed in place when she released it.

The bundle of fibers ran to a small black device that looked like an electronics hobbyist's digital multi-tester. Amber pressed a button on its face. Its small LCD display came to life. Lines of text too small for Blaise to read scrolled quickly up the screen as it began to exercise the HyperQUBE's optical data pathways. Amber stared at it intently.

Jack growled, "Well?"

Amber looked up. "So far, so good. Give me a minute, Jack." She turned her attention back to the display.

There was a rustling in the crowd as they watched with growing impatience. Blaise had never been to the debut performance of a new QUBE before. It was surprisingly anticlimactic. The full-scale tests in Mission Control were far more intense. But if the device was a failure, if for whatever reason the auto-assembly process had gone wrong or some flaw had developed in it while it baked in the annealing oven, Aidan's schedule would be wrecked.

A trickle of sweat rolled down his back.

At last the text stopped scrolling on the diagnostic machine's screen.

Amber looked up at Jack again, smiling broadly. "Congratulations. It's a boy."

The room erupted in cheers, laughter and shouts of glee.

"Awesome!" said Jack, beaming. "Start defect mapping right away. We don't have a minute to lose."

"Filthy, stinking rich!" bellowed Terry Blau, raising a fist in the air triumphantly.

The rest of the Dura Party echoed him.

The bemused Elves eventually joined in. Soon the laboratory was ringing with the words. "Filthy, stinking rich! *Filthy, stinking rich! FILTHY, STINKING RICH!*"

Blaise remained at the celebration in the cafeteria until a few others called it a night. He excused himself, walked to the nearby locker room, changed out of his dull gray jumpsuit, and went to his car.

Blaise chose the most direct route to Morgan Hill, straight down Oregon Expressway to Highway 101. Traffic moved freely until he approached Moffett Field.

There was a lot of activity at the former air base. Floodlights illumi-nated the tarmac. Every other time he'd driven past at night, the abandoned flight line was dark. The Naval air station had been shut down years ago. Only NASA and Google used it now, or so he thought. The viewing angle was not good from the southbound side of 101, but he could tell that there were many aircraft parked along the runway. Usually there were none.

He jumped in his seat as a thunderous roar filled the world. The car in front of him braked to a sudden halt. He slammed on his brakes as well, cursing.

A squadron of six big aircraft passed low over the freeway, one after the other, silhouetted against the low, orange cloud deck. The noise they produced was incredible. They looked like some kind of weird blend of airplane and helicopter, with giant propellers attached to up-tilted engines at the ends of their stumpy wings. They passed over the end of the runway at a ridiculously slow rate. He watched, mouth agape, until the driver behind him leaned on his horn.

"Merde," he whispered as he put his foot on the gas pedal.

He drove the rest of the way to Aidan's new compound in a cold sweat.

The guards at the gate looked nervous. They let him through after shining a flashlight in his face, wrecking his night vision. He parked next to one of the huge metal sheds, blinking the afterimages into submission. He heard men talking inside, and the clatter of tools on metal.

One of Tom Reed's men let him into the former owner's office. Aidan had appropriated it as his headquarters. He and Adam were inside, leaning over a table, staring down at a large paper map.

The guard cleared his throat.

Aidan looked up and smiled thinly. "Blaise. Glad you could join us."

The Chinese agent folded the map before Blaise could see what was on it.

Blaise walked slowly into the room. The guard closed the door after him.

"The HyperQUBE came out of the oven this afternoon," he told them. "It passed the initial diagnostic tests. They're putting it into the cryo facility to take it down to operating temperature. The first full test run will be Wednesday at ten AM."

"Perfect," said Aidan.

Adam scowled. "Why not tomorrow?"

"The QUBE is only functional at temperatures close to absolute zero," said Aidan. "They lower the temperature very slowly the first time they test a new unit. They have to be sure there aren't any structural flaws that will cause it to crack. The processor armature is instrumented with strain gauges. If it contracts uniformly while it's being cooled, we'll know it's safe to bring it back to room temperature quickly."

"Which means...?"

"That we'll be able to steal it," Aidan said, as if speaking to a child.

Blaise nodded. "They plan to move the HyperQUBE and the researchers to Lawrence Livermore as soon as it passes the functional benchmarks. We've been copying data onto hard drives for the last two days."

Aidan shrugged. "Don't worry, Blaise. We anticipated this."

"I drove past Moffett Field on the way down here, Aidan. There is a great deal of activity there." He described the squadron of bizarre aircraft touching down.

Adam's frown deepened. "Those would be MV-22 Ospreys," he said, copying Aidan's mocking enunciation. "Tilt-rotor troop transports. Usually operated by the Marine Corps."

Aidan's smile faltered. "Unfortunate, but unsurprising."

Blaise cleared his throat. "What is going on?"

Aidan waved at him dismissively. "Believe me, Blaise, it's better that you don't know. We've taken care of all contingencies." He gestured to a chair. "Let's discuss the new timeline. Would you like something to drink?"

Blaise left the compound well after midnight. He knew he would have to take a sleeping pill if he were to get any rest at all. His mind roiled with uncertainty as he drove north.

He knew his role, and he knew he could carry it out, but the crucial moment was approaching like an oncoming freight train now, and he felt like he was standing on the tracks.

No one had acknowledged it, but he knew that the events in Moss Landing were connected to Aidan's crew. Aidan had as much as admitted that the activity at Moffett Field was also involved, but he didn't say why. That worried Blaise more than anything. If the military was stirred into watchfulness two full days before they made their move, what chance did they have of escaping with the HyperQUBE, much less all the critical personnel Aidan planned to take as well?

A giant transport plane crossed low over 101 as Blaise approached Moffett Field, this time from the south. Even at this hour, traffic was slow. He spared a quick glance at the tarmac as he topped the low rise of the Ellis Street overpass. The field was crowded with military aircraft, wheeled vehicles, and soldiers. Hundreds and hundreds of soldiers.

"Mon dieu," he said. Sweat began to bead on his forehead. He wiped it away with his free hand.

As he approached the Woodside Road exit in Redwood City, he saw the ripple of brake lights, then the red sparkle of safety flares on the side of the freeway, and the unmistakable strobe of emergency vehicle lights. Cars were backed up for a mile before the Seaport Boulevard off-ramp.

Blaise kept his car in the center lane and kept pace with traffic to ensure that he attracted no attention from the police. He rolled down the passenger side window to see if he could hear anything.

As he crept past, he saw that the exit was closed, but he didn't see an accident. Two CHP cars were parked across the exit, forming a road-block. At least another half-dozen police cars were parked nearby, their flashing blue and red lights painfully bright at this short distance. Officers stood on the roadside. One of them carried a shotgun.

Far beyond them, four helicopters hovered above the small seaport, their searchlights sweeping back and forth. Even from half a mile or more away, their engine noise was stupendous. They were much too large to be police or television helicopters.

When he reached his apartment in downtown Burlingame, he switched on the TV. Channel 2 had live coverage of the events. Apparently a ship leaving Redwood City had struck something just outside the channel early in the morning. Now the area was swarming with police, NTSB investigators, and an unnamed team of uniformed people who'd arrived at the port by helicopter, landing on the disused salt flats across from the seaport. There were unconfirmed rumors that they were from the Nuclear Emergency Support Team.

Nuclear, Blaise thought. His blood congealed in his veins. *No. It cannot be.*

The young Asian anchorman stopped in mid-sentence, looking down at the monitor recessed into the desk in front of him. *"I'm sorry, I'm just getting word that—"* He looked at someone off-camera. *"Are you sure about this?"*

Blaise heard a faint voice reply, *"Yes!"*

The anchorman looked at the camera with a stricken expression. "I've... We've just received word that the United States military forces have been put on full alert. There are unconfirmed reports that the Pentagon has declared DEFCON 2." He looked back down at his screen. "Defense Condition Two is the second highest level of military alert. It has only been declared twice before, once at the beginning of the 1991 Gulf War..." The anchorman swallowed visibly. "... and during the Cuban Missile Crisis of 1962. We don't know the reason for the alert yet, but we are making every effort—"

It was then that Blaise abandoned all hope of sleeping. He collapsed against the cushion and stared in horror at the screen for the rest of the night.

CHAPTER FORTY

Morgan Hill, California

October 31

Aidan stood outside the office. The dawn was gray and cold. He shivered under his windbreaker and made a mental note to have someone go to the Wilson's outlet down in Gilroy to buy him a new leather jacket. At least his close-cropped head was warm under the nice woolen cap he'd bought at Nordstrom.

He watched the last of the trucks leave the huge tractor shed. The rest of them were either already in place or on their way via back roads. The man at the gate closed and latched it, then trudged back up the short hill to the shed.

Adam came out to join him. The Chinese agent wore blue jeans and a black turtleneck sweater. The cold, damp air didn't seem to bother him. He handed Aidan a freshly brewed cup of coffee.

Aidan nodded his thanks. He took a sip. "Happy Halloween."

Adam said nothing.

"The forecast calls for rain tomorrow night. Good timing."

"If so, it's the only good timing we've enjoyed so far."

"Don't be churlish, Adam. It's unfortunate that we lost some of the crates from the sub, but we have enough to do the job. More than we need, really." Aidan checked his plebeian Citizen chronograph. "Thirty-four hours to go, assuming the HyperQUBE test is successful."

"It does not matter whether the test is successful," Adam said curtly. "This is the only opportunity we will have. We are committed. The only thing left to do is wait for our final orders. They will come at midnight."

"But if the HyperQUBE isn't portable—"

"It does not matter, Aidan! The military is on the ground now, and they have teams diving on the Devilfish. They've closed the waterways but I have observers watching from the East Bay hills with telescopes. The divers removed the warhead from the wreck."

"Hmmm. That *is* unfortunate."

Adam shook his head. "You have a gift for understatement."

"Lots of practice." Aidan took a long swallow of coffee. "We're lucky it didn't go off in the collision."

Adam scoffed, "You clearly know nothing about nuclear weapons. They don't just *go off*. And it would have been foolish to set this one up with a booby-trapped detonator. It is much too close to Palo Alto."

Aidan's heart skipped a beat. "Just how powerful is it?"

"Powerful enough."

That gave Aidan pause. Redwood City was miles from the Coyote Hill campus. He hungered to know more, but Adam clearly was in no mood to be drawn out on the subject. Aidan sighed. "At least they won't blame your homeland, once they examine the wreckage. And it's unlikely that they'll discover the other one before H-hour."

"They are sending a sea-floor mapping vessel down from a port in Oregon. It was going to Monterey Bay. They will certainly divert it to San Francisco in light of this development."

"With the new timetable, it will probably arrive too late."

"We'd better hope so. I don't like our chances of getting the HyperQUBE and the data drives out of the building, much less to the cargo sub, if we have to resort to the fallback plan."

The so-called "Devilfish" that had brought Tom and his men their wonderful gifts had reported its healthy status to Adam's masters the previous night. Tom had worried that the sub's cargo bay had not been properly sealed when they were interrupted by the Coast Guard. Those worries were unfounded. As programmed, it had dumped the rest of its cargo into the submarine canyon before departing Monterey Bay.

Aidan said, "Don't worry. The Navy will be looking for it near Moss Landing. It should be nearing the extraction point now." He sipped his coffee. "That just leaves the prisoners. It shouldn't be too hard to get them out overland. Relax, Adam. Even if the Army closes down the highways, they won't be able to keep them closed."

"Assuming they don't find the remaining Devilfish."

"This negativity is beginning to wear thin, Adam. Perhaps you need some breakfast. Cheer up! Tomorrow is the dawn of a bright new age for your nation. The Hundred Year Marathon will end a few decades early."

Adam's eyes widened. "You know about...?"

"It's not a secret. I've done my homework. There was even a book published on the subject not too long ago."

Adam's mouth turned downward.

Aidan laughed. "You shouldn't worry. People in this country don't read, and if they do, they're more interested in stories about which half-wit celebrity is screwing whom than in anything of real substance. I don't think Chairman Mao could've conceived of a technology like the HyperQUBE. Not only will it enable China to supplant America as the world's greatest power, but it will bring prosperity even emperors could never have dreamed of."

"*If* it works."

"Even if it doesn't, we will need only a few years to recreate the support infrastructure at ST. We'll take QUBE Delta too, just to be safe. But more importantly, we need the scientists—and most especially, we need Jack Dura." He rubbed his chin. "Peter forced him to disclose the theory behind the HyperQUBE, but there's something he's not telling us—something much bigger that he didn't want me to know. I must find out what it is."

"The way you found out about us from Eric Dalton?"

"There are other levers to pull on Jack. I know just how to motivate him. Every care must be taken to ensure he and his former students are not harmed."

"Do not tell me my business."

Aidan clapped the younger man on the shoulder. "Come on, my grumpy friend. I'll make some French toast."

CHAPTER FORTY-ONE

Moffett Federal Field, Sunnyvale, California

October 31

Laurel felt a nudge on her shoulder. She blinked awake.

She lay on a cot next to the curving interior wall of Hangar Two, well away from the huge, partially open door.

Robbie Holmes stood over her, holding something in his right hand.

She removed the pair of orange foam earplugs she'd been given by a passing soldier last night. The noise of activity in the vast, echoing space became painfully loud. She clutched the rough woolen Army blanket to her chest and tried to focus.

"Robert Stephen Holmes," she rasped. "You woke me up. Again. You live to wake me up."

"Happy Halloween," said Holmes, handing her a paper cup of the steaming brown fluid the Army optimistically called "coffee."

"Ugh," she responded, grasping the cup.

"You're welcome. Bigwig briefing in ten minutes. Seigart wants us to attend. I'll come find you." He left her alone.

She sat up on the cot, trying not to spill the "coffee" before she could drink it. She took a sip as she checked her watch. It was just after eight o'clock. She'd managed to sleep almost six hours in the echoing din of the ancient wooden dirigible hangar.

She threw the blanket off and stood up. Her business-casual blouse and slacks had picked up a static charge from the woolen blanket. They clung to her body unpleasantly. She found her blue FBI jacket folded up under the small pillow on the cot. She shrugged into it, took a sip of magma, and looked around.

The Army had borrowed the hangar from Google, the current operator of the former Naval Air Station. Hangar One was still skinless, just a giant framework of shiny steel girders, and therefore of no use to the military. Hangar Two was the emptier of the two old but intact structures the Navy had built on the field back in the 1930s to house what they mistakenly believed would be the first in a long line of dirigibles. Google's big jet had been moved out to the tarmac.

Before Andrew Seigart had directed her to get some rest the previous night, she'd seen men on the curved roof tying down a giant white flag with a huge red cross that could be seen from the air—perhaps even from orbit. When she entered the hangar, searching for the promised cot and blanket, she saw that the front half of the vast hangar's floor was being converted into a combat support hospital.

The rear half of the floor had been kept open, but the hundreds of black plastic crates aligned along the edge labeled "BODY BAGS, FIELD USE, HEAVY-DUTY, QTY 50 EA" left little doubt of its intended purpose.

The implications had kept her awake and shivering for hours.

All of the tents had been erected now, their guy ropes attached to eye bolts that had been drilled or driven into the concrete floor. *How the hell did I sleep through that?* The answer was obvious enough: before she found her way to the cot, she hadn't slept since meeting Seigart at the airport the previous night, just after she left Jack.

Heat and a slow smile crept into her face as she remembered.

The pleasure drained away as she regarded the scene in front of her. She prayed this was all for nothing, and that the hospital and the field morgue behind it would never see use.

She watched the soldiers moving purposefully around the space as she drank her coffee, trying to wake up and trying hard not to brood, until Robbie Holmes returned for her. He led her out of the hangar and into the chilly gray morning air.

The concrete apron was filled with aircraft on both sides of the two parallel runways. The aircraft models and types popped into her mind unbidden, the information drummed into her brain by her airshow-fanatical father.

She recognized two huge C-17 cargo planes, offloading pallets of plastic-wrapped supplies; a squadron of gray National Guard F-16s; a big, sinister-looking C-130 turboprop cargo plane, painted all in black, with a huge bulbous device mounted on its stubby nose; a number of Marine MV-22 tilt-rotor planes; and dozens of helicopters of every description. There were even a few Navy FA-18 Hornets, like the one she'd taken to this very airport four months ago. It seemed like a lifetime had passed since then.

Robbie led her across the apron to a dusty, scrubby field that had until recently been used as a parking lot, based on the tire tracks leading into and out of it. The field was now covered with closely spaced, frame-supported tents.

The biggest was long, tall, and dark green. Its top and sloping sides were covered by a huge rip-stop nylon rainfly. It was surrounded by soldiers, mostly older men, wearing tan combat boots and blue-gray fatigues with an odd, pixelated camouflage pattern, their officers' insignia on a patch on the breastbone. They stood in loose groups with deadly expressions on their stern faces. The whine of a nearby generator drowned out their low voices.

Robbie excused himself as he led Laurel through the mass of officers into the tent. The interior was surprisingly bright. Fluorescent light fixtures hung from cords at intervals along the length of the tent. Long, narrow tables had been set up along both sides. Young soldiers of both sexes sat in front of them, working on laptops.

The back half of the giant tent had been set up as a briefing area, with perhaps two hundred folding chairs arranged in a neat array facing three huge reflective screens, currently dark. Projectors were suspended at the ends of long booms that jutted from the tops of the screens toward the audience. A lectern was positioned well to the right, so as to leave a clear view of the screens.

Andrew Seigart was there as well, wearing a dark suit, crossed arms and a forbidding expression. He and a quartet of male senior officers stood in a tight group between the chairs and the projection screens. Seigart saw them and beckoned them over with a curt gesture. When they arrived, he made the introductions.

Three of the four officers wore two stars on their insignia badges. Two were Major Generals from the Marines and Air Force: the short but powerfully-built Everett "Dutch" Holland, distinctive in the darker camouflage uniform favored by the Marine Corps, and the lean, angular Kenneth Cook. Another was a Navy Admiral, a thin, sour-faced man named Patrick Miller.

Their commander's badge had three stars. Lieutenant General Brad Dorsey of the US Army was the deputy commander of USNORTHCOM, the unified combat command responsible for defense of the United States. He had short-cropped brown hair, still thick in spite of his age, and a nose like a hatchet in the center of a weather-beaten, kindly-looking face.

The officers nodded soberly to Laurel and Robbie. Dorsey glanced at his watch and looked at Seigart. "Five minutes until the briefing. Make this quick."

Seigart nodded. He glanced at her. "Agent Wynn, fill them in on Ableman Security."

Laurel coughed nervously. "Excuse me," she said, taking a quick sip of coffee to clear her throat. "All of the Ableman crew have disappeared, except for the secretary. She's being questioned, but we think she's innocent. She was at home with her kids and didn't even try to get away. Seemed more annoyed at having to get a babysitter than anything else."

General Dorsey looked at her. "Mr. Seigart told me your theory about Tom Reed. I looked him up. I know who he is. I saw him win the Interservice Rifle Championship. He was a hell of a shot, and his service record was outstanding."

Laurel swallowed. "It was just a hunch at first, after seeing the footage of him from *Last Gun Standing*. A colleague of mine at the FBI Laboratory ran a comparison of video of Reed on the show and the clips of the gunman who took out the people at the Stanford ICU. The result was a ninety-six percent probability of a match."

"Not one hundred percent," said the Marine general.

"The protocol is still experimental, but we've been testing it internally for a couple of years. Ninety-six is as high as it ever gets."

Dorsey frowned. "Still sounds thin to me."

"Sir, with the exception of Daniela Esperanza, every employee of Ableman Security is off the grid. Almost all of them are single men. The families of the ones who were married have disappeared as well. We have BOLOs out on them but it looks like they fled the area well before the news about the sub got out. We're canvassing their neighbors. Their cars and trucks were packed like they were going on a trip. That *can't* be a coincidence."

The Air Force general said, "You don't have any other suspects?"

Laurel said, "No, sir."

"Hang on a minute," said the Marine general. "If they're going after ST, why the fuck would they put a nuke in a sub inside the Bay so close to their objective?" A distinct Oklahoma twang colored his pronunciation.

Laurel said, "I don't know, sir. It could be to cover their tracks once they steal the QUBE, or maybe to destroy the facility if their attack fails. Or it could be just to deal the tech economy a knockout blow."

"Hmm." Dorsey glanced at Seigart. "You vouch for Agent Wynn, here?"

Seigart nodded. "I do. She's the best field investigator I know. That's why she works for me."

If Laurel had been less exhausted, the rare praise from Seigart would have made her blush. As it was, she had just enough energy to nod to him.

Dorsey's mouth twisted with doubt. "Hmm. Okay, Mr. Director, I'll think about it."

"General," she said before he could turn away. "If ST *is* the reason for these attacks, we need to reinforce their defenses." She quickly outlined the numerous reasons they could not move the scientists to their new home at Lawrence Livermore.

"My hands are tied on that at the moment, but I'll keep it in mind, Agent Wynn." Dorsey squinted at the officers beginning to fill the seats in the briefing area. "You'd better grab chairs unless you want to stand." He looked at the other senior officers, jerked his chin, and led them off for a private conversation.

Seigart led Laurel and Robbie to chairs in the middle of the otherwise empty first row. The backrests were labeled with strips of masking tape and their names scrawled in black.

Seigart's chair was on the right. Laurel sat next to him. "Thank you, sir," she breathed.

He looked at her sidelong. "You have the best theory, Agent Wynn. Right now it's the *only* theory. I just hope to Christ we can find these bastards quickly. Excuse me," he said. He pulled an ancient government-issue Blackberry from his inside coat pocket and scanned its screen.

Laurel and Robbie took the opportunity to check their messages while the briefing area filled with officers. Laurel had a dozen messages from other agents, none of them encouraging. Sarah Hardy at the Palo Alto resident agency had sent her a summary of Daniela Esperanza's interrogation. Esperanza had finally run out of patience with the questioning and asked for a lawyer, but she'd said nothing to implicate herself in any wrongdoing. She'd also failed to disclose anything that might clue the investigators into where Tom Reed and his crew might be.

Laurel scanned through the other messages. No sightings of the suspects had come in from the CHP or local police forces. Agents from the San Francisco and Watsonville FBI offices had been poring over the crime scenes in Moss Landing, collecting forensic evidence, fingerprints, and brass from the hundreds of rounds exchanged between the criminals and the slaughtered policemen. So far, no results, but she hadn't expected any. TV shows like *CSI* to the contrary, forensic investigations were not measured in minutes or hours. Everyone was working as fast as they could, given the circumstances, but forensic laboratory work was by nature slow, requiring careful, painstaking analysis. It usually took weeks to months to yield useful results.

She was about to put her phone away when she saw a notification of a new email. It was from Jack. She glanced quickly at Seigart and Holmes to make sure their eyes were on their own business, then brought her phone close to her face and clicked on the message.

Laurel,

Just wanted to wish you a good morning, hope you're OK. Didn't hear from you yesterday. I know you're busy. So am I! We're going to test the you-know-what tomorrow morning at 10. Come by if you can. I'm the CEO now, I can let you in. There will be a party before we pack everything in the trucks and head over to goddamned Livermore. We can sneak over to my room, ha ha. Seriously, let's sneak over to my room. You are amazing. Can't wait to not-work with you again.

Jack

She smiled, unable to suppress the blush, and quickly put the phone down.

A loud male voice bellowed, *"Ten-HUT!"*

The soldiers in the room leaped to their feet. Laurel, Robbie and Seigart belatedly copied them.

General Dorsey and his colleagues came into view next to the lectern. He said, "As you were. Captain Morton, let's get started." He and his officers sat next to Seigart as a female Navy officer in her mid-forties walked forward. There was a rustling sound as everyone else resumed their seats.

"Thank you, sir," she said. She took the portable microphone and introduced herself as Deborah Morton, Naval Intelligence. She said, "This briefing is classified Top Secret under keyword HAILSTORM BRAVO. Anyone without that clearance is directed to leave the briefing immediately." No one did. Laurel and Robbie had just gotten their clearances yesterday afternoon.

Captain Morton asked someone in the back to turn on the projectors.

The three screens lit up. The two on the left showed maps of the San Francisco Bay Area. The middle one was a satellite view of the area around the port of Redwood City. A red dot had been placed just offshore of a swampy-looking oblong of land labeled "Bair Island".

"The dot shows where the *Pride of Balikpapan* hit the drone sub. Most of the wreckage has been recovered. The warhead was disarmed and removed by the NEST divers last night around 1:30 AM."

A restless sigh escaped from many members of the audience.

"The wreckage was moved to an empty warehouse in the port of Redwood City. The NTSB team has been reconstructing it nonstop. It's a sophisticated design, very stealthy, equipped with a diesel oil and liquid oxygen fuel cell. Electric propulsion, which explains why it wasn't detected. The water intakes and exhausts were baffled to reduce noise. The warhead was shielded to reduce neutron and gamma emissions. There was a tungsten tamper and about a metric ton of lithium hydride around the missile. The most important thing we've found is that most of the markings on the components are in Korean."

"Son of a *bitch*," Laurel heard someone growl.

"The missile was cracked and flooded in the collision. The warhead was mounted on a very short-range booster rocket, solid-fueled. It was clearly meant for a local target. It's been taken over to Lawrence Livermore for analysis. Every breeder reactor generates a unique combination of radiogenic and non-radiogenic isotopes. It's called an isotopic fingerprint, and we can use it to try to identify whoever made the warhead's plutonium. We have samples from North Korea and Iran, and no end of samples from Russian reactors. We should get the results back in a few hours."

"What if it's Chinese?" said the Marine Lieutenant General, Dutch Holland.

Captain Morton shook her head. "They have way more reactors than we have samples, sir, and more every year."

General Dorsey said, "Is there an estimate of the weapon's yield, Captain?"

"I think so, sir," she said. She went to the podium and picked up a ruggedized tablet computer. She swiped at the screen for a few seconds. "The scientists at Livermore say it's a two-stage thermonuclear weapon, and a big one. It's an old-fashioned design, but functional. They think its nominal yield is between two and five megatons."

The audience grew very still. The only sound was the whine of the generator outside the tent.

Mother of God, thought Laurel. She crossed herself. She hadn't done that since she was in elementary school.

"The Norks can barely explode an A-bomb," snapped the Admiral Laurel had met a few minutes ago. "The last test was just a few *kilotons*, if I remember right. How the hell could they field an H-bomb, much less sneak it right up to our goddamned coastline?"

"We don't know, Admiral Miller," replied Morton. She looked down at her tablet. "There have been a lot of rumors flying that they're getting ready to test a hydrogen weapon. A real one, not that firecracker they claimed was an H-bomb. There's a contingent of high-level Iranian nuclear scientists visiting Pyongyang right now."

The Admiral made a growling sound. "Iranians. Even those camel-fuckers couldn't build an H-bomb without a hell of a lot of help from somebody, and my bet is his address is in the fucking Kremlin."

There was a moment of embarrassed silence.

"Go on, Captain," said General Dorsey, aiming a glare at the bellicose Admiral.

Morton said, "That's all the information we have about the sub at this time, sir. We have boats looking for any other subs, but we don't have any assets with side scanning sonar in the area, so we can't map the bottom in any detail. All normal shipping traffic on the Bay has been suspended. Inbound vessels have been redirected to other ports on the West Coast. A NOAA survey ship should arrive in San Francisco this afternoon, and we can start searching for any other subs that might still be here." She went on to describe the plethora of destroyers, cruisers, amphibious assault ships and even submarines converging on San Francisco Bay.

Morton added, "Sir, we are also getting reports of cyber attacks on infrastructure targets everywhere in the country. They're trying to hack programmable logic controllers in power plants, dams, and even hospitals."

"Any damage?" asked someone in the row behind Dorsey.

"No sir, not yet. Most of the vulnerabilities were patched as part of the HERMES BROADHEAD program we started a year and a half ago."

"Point of origin?" snapped Dorsey.

"We're not sure, sir. Attacks are coming in from Eastern Europe, South America, and even Africa. The one place they're *not* coming from is North Korea, at least not directly."

Laurel cleared her throat. "That's consistent with some of the more successful North Korean hacker attacks I've investigated."

"And you are, ma'am?" said Captain Morton, peering at her quizzically.

"Oh. Sorry. I'm Senior Special Agent Laurel Wynn. I work for Director Seigart, Joint Task Force on State-Sponsored Technological Espionage." She tilted her head toward her boss.

Morton nodded. "Thank you. As you say, it's consistent with Nork activities, but it's not definitive."

General Dorsey leaned forward and looked down the row at Laurel. "How much experience do you have with these bastards?"

"Quite a bit, sir. I was lead investigator on the *Dark Seoul* attack on the bank in Macao back in 2012."

"Good. I'd appreciate it if you could pitch in. We need to track down whoever's doing this to us, ASAP. See Captain Morton after the briefing."

She glanced at Seigart, who nodded. She said, "Absolutely, sir."

General Dorsey stood up and turned to the audience. "Director Seigart and Agent Wynn think the reason the nuke was here has something to do with this super quantum computer thing they're building at ST. They also think the attack on the Coast Guard boat in Monterey Bay is related. This new computer is a major strategic asset for the United States. We don't have a better theory as to why this shit is happening, so we're going to assume they're right. You're to give them every assistance." He glanced at Seigart. "Good enough?"

"Outstanding," Seigart said with a wolfish grin.

Dorsey nodded and returned to his seat. "Let's move on, Captain."

Laurel sat back and took a shuddering breath. The briefing continued. She was vaguely aware of Morton's rundown of National Guard deployments, the President's planned declaration of martial law, highway closures, the shutdown of the local airports, and interactions with local media.

Laurel belatedly realized why General Dorsey was reluctant to commit ground troops to defend ST. The Constitution stood in the way. Without a declaration of martial law, regular military troops could not be deployed to enforce civil law. It was one thing to marshal them at the site of a former military base. It was quite another to deploy armed soldiers in contact with civilians.

Captain Morton said that the governor had insisted that the National Guards would be enough. Laurel prayed that he was right. Seven million people lived in the San Francisco Bay Area. The demands of enforcing the curfew and highway closures around the Bay would stretch the Guard thin. She hoped that the President would issue that declaration as soon as humanly possible. God knew how many lawyers were wrangling over the precise wording right now.

Her mind churned with anxiety. There wasn't much more she could do to locate Tom Reed and his colleagues. Dozens of agents were on it already. Some of them, like Cowboy Bob, had far more field experience. The stakes were now infinitely higher than a simple bank fraud case. She couldn't screw this up. If she made a mistake, if she implicated the wrong enemy, it could lead to war.

She looked at the people around her. Their faces were drawn but determined. Someone had parked a hydrogen bomb in San Francisco Bay. It was only through blind luck or the grace of God that it had been found in time. If it hadn't been, if the bomb had gone off, the scope of the disaster would have been incomprehensible. It would have made 9/11 pale into insignificance.

Laurel had been stationed in San Francisco when the Twin Towers came down on 9/11. She'd watched the events unfold on television with the brutal inevitability of a waking nightmare. She'd wept hot tears, and she'd sworn to help track down the psychopaths who thought killing thousands of innocent civilians was a legitimate act of resistance.

She'd done her part, but she never felt that it had been enough. She was too new, too raw, too inexperienced then, and her assignments had been minor and unfulfilling.

Everything was different now. She'd been given the lead by the deputy commander of USNORTHCOM himself.

A furious, steely resolve formed like armor around her heart.

She would find whoever did this.

They would pay.

CHAPTER FORTY-TWO

Struve Technologies Coyote Hill Campus, Palo Alto, California

October 31

Halloween morning was turning out to be a bitch.

Jack spent most of it with John Shea, going over the security for the move. If the HyperQUBE test tomorrow was successful, they were going to warm the device up and transport it to Livermore in a brawny-looking truck called an MRAP. There would be four such vehicles: one for the HyperQUBE, one for QUBE Delta, and two carrying decoy payloads. Each would have a separate convoy of heavily armed escort vehicles, and would take different routes to the national lab.

Jack suggested using a helicopter, but Shea and the National Guard liaison vetoed that notion before he'd finished speaking the sentence. The bad guys had already used anti-tank missiles. If they had anti-aircraft missiles too, a helicopter was the last thing you wanted to transport a mission-critical cargo.

He shook his head. Holy shit. Mission-critical cargo. Emily's life work. My friends. Me.

The conversation dragged on and on. The details were many and mind-numbing. Every action he took as CEO reminded him of whose shoes he was trying to fill.

He and Peter Struve hadn't been close, but Jack had come to respect him. His sudden death had been shocking. He felt a surprising lump of grief form in his throat when he thought about Peter, which was all too often. It compounded with the constant sadness over Emily's death and the way they had parted. He'd missed his chance to say goodbye to her in person by years.

By lunchtime Jack had a headache the likes of which he'd seldom experienced.

He had to excuse himself before the meeting with the National Guard officer ended. Shea had everything under control, as always.

He went back to the Crick Building, popped two tablets of migraine-strength Excedrin, downed them with a bottle of Mexican Coke (made with cane sugar, not that vile high-fructose corn syrup crap), and lay down on one of the recliners in the third-floor lounge.

The rest of his team was in Mission Control, learning from the veterans of Santa's Workshop how to operate the consoles for tomorrow's big test, including a near-comatose Xu Chao-Xing, who had gotten on a return flight from Taipei an hour after she'd landed. The only sound was the quiet whoosh of the air conditioner. He drifted to sleep as heavily filtered sunlight crept across the room and bathed him in amber warmth.

He slept hard.

When he awoke, the headache was gone. In its place was a shining realization: he had made a mistake. A huge mistake. A magnificent, glorious, *brilliant* mistake.

He leaped up from his recliner and bolted for the door.

Minutes later he was in the Black Box, alone and cackling like a mad man. He grabbed a portable whiteboard, smeared it clean with his bare hands in spite of the big red magnetic "DO NOT ERASE" sign someone had stuck to it, and began to scribble equations as fast as he could.

When he filled the third board two hours later, he stood back, eyes wide, heart beating like a jackhammer, and laughed like a hyena. The equations were right. The mistake had not only been eliminated, but had led him to a whole new way of conceiving of the quantum universe. It linked special relativity, m-brane theory, dark matter and energy, and even the theory of gravitation into a single, cohesive, astonishing whole. Everything was there, boiled down to a handful of admittedly non-trivial equations.

He'd never known such a moment of clarity. His theory was right. He paced back and forth in front of the whiteboards, trying to find a flaw. *It can't be this simple. It can't be.*

He sat down in front of his laptop and began to enter the equations into *archimedes*. It was something they'd been working on since returning from Lake San Antonio: an E-ware package that would run his formulae on the QUBE using a near-infinity of alternate inputs, checking each run to make sure the results agreed with theory. Every member of the team had contributed to it. He was proud to be a part of this group of incredible people.

He looked over the code one last time and then checked it in. He opened a web browser and kept tabs on the progress of the unit and integration tests. A few minutes later the server gave the green light. His equations weren't buggy, at least.

He clicked the button that would cause the server to build an *archimedes* executable to run on QUBE Delta. It was still in the deep freeze, running jobs for Santa's Elves until the HyperQUBE defect mapping was complete. Amber D'Agostino had told him it still had about ten hours to go.

More minutes ground slowly by. When he received the email message that the job was done, he logged into the QUBE control software, halted the program already in progress, and substituted the new package. He ran it.

The results came back after three endless minutes.

Harnessing the staggering power of QUBE Delta, *archimedes* had run one septillion—one followed by twenty-four zeros—iterations of his test program varying the inputs, exploring the multidimensional phase spaces of the permitted solution sets, checking the results for inconsistencies.

Even one would have been enough to invalidate his theory.

There were none.

"Holy *fuck*," he said. He thought his cheeks might crack from the force of his smile.

From this day forward, everything would be different. Today was an inflection point in human history. He'd just changed the course of science. And for this one perfect moment, Jack Dura was the only person on Planet Earth who knew it.

He crowed, "Yes, *yes*, *YES!*" He danced in a little circle. He slapped himself on the butt and said, "Hot stuff!" He chanted in a low, dopey sing-song: *"I am so smart! I am so smart! S-M-R-T! I mean, S-M-A-R-T!"* He wanted to get the recordings from the *Argus* surveillance cameras later. He laughed when he imagined some poor graduate student fifty years from now, watching that footage for his thesis and trying to figure out the origin of the song. Then again, at this rate *The Simpsons* might still be on the air.

"Thank you, Emily," he whispered. "And thank you, Peter."

Then he ran down the hall to Mission Control to get his former students.

He chivvied them into the lab in spite of their grumbling and complaining. "I'm the CEO, so what I say goes! Get in there! Grab chairs, sit down! No, in front of the whiteboards! Hank, don't make me fire you!"

Jack turned around and saw that behind the row of stools occupied by his students, almost the entire complement of Santa's Elves had followed them in. Even Blaise Thierry was there. He looked like he hadn't slept for a week. Everyone else looked spooked. Jack had caught the news before breakfast, and couldn't blame them.

Xu Chao-Xing stared at him. She pointed at the whiteboard. "You did it again, Jack! You erased all my work!"

"I'm really sorry," he said, meaning it. "In a little while you'll know why. Okay, folks. Crazy things are happening out in the world and everybody's scared to death. I am, too. But tomorrow we test the HyperQUBE. It will work. I know it. I know it because of what I just drew on these boards, and because I just ran a simulation that tells me I'm right. But I'm a scientist, and I need to ask you a favor. This might be the most important thing you ever do. Prove me wrong." He pointed at the whiteboards. "I will give one hundred thousand dollars to the first person who can find a flaw in these equations. I'm the CEO now. I can sign the check. I am *dead fucking serious*. Go."

Four hours of argument and counter-argument ensued. Chao-Xing and Terry found a way to simplify some terms, and he promised them a thousand bucks each, but no one could refute his logic.

Eventually the room fell silent.

"Give up?" he asked.

Everyone stared at him with undiluted awe.

"How?" asked Lizbeth. "How did you come up with this?"

"It came to me in a dream..." he began in a spooky, mystical tone, waving his hands dramatically. Then he laughed. "How the hell should I know? I had a headache, I took some aspirin and drank a Coke, and when I woke up, I had the answer. Don't tell me caffeine isn't a miracle drug."

"What does it mean?" asked Deepthi Damodaran. "I still don't understand half of this gibberish after studying it every day for months."

"It's the formal proof of Jack's quantinuum theory," said Lizbeth.

"It's a lot more than that," said Ben. He stood, walked over to Jack and extended his hand. "Congratulations. This is the Grand Unified Theory. You've unlocked the Universe." He tilted his head expectantly. "You know what to say."

Jack shook his hand and deadpanned, "Eureka or something."

From the corner of his eye, through the bedlam of scientists and engineers cheering and jumping up and down, Jack saw Blaise Thierry smile wearily at him, then burst into tears and flee the room.

He's just tired, thought Jack. The craziness outside ST's walls was getting to everyone. *He'll feel better tomorrow, after the test.*

He put Blaise out of his mind. It wasn't every day he changed the course of human history. He intended to enjoy it, for a little while, at least. He already had some ideas on how to improve the E-ware for the test tomorrow.

He gave himself ten minutes to rejoice in the biggest breakthrough in science since... *Since ever, really.* Then he'd get back to work.

CHAPTER FORTY-THREE

General Staff Headquarters, People's Liberation Army, Beijing, China

November 1

General Guo Qiang looked out the window of his modest fourth-story office at the busy street below.

It was mid-afternoon. Crisp autumn winds had temporarily cleared the city of its permanent pall of smog. Pedestrians hunched under coats, scarves and hats, walking briskly along the crowded sidewalks, not pausing to enjoy the clarity of the air. *Pity,* thought Guo. There had been a time when the air above the great metropolis was clean and healthful. He was old enough to remember it. That day would come again.

He returned to his desk and sat down carefully. The arthritis in his right hip was flaring up. He took a pain pill from a small plastic box in his coat pocket, lifted the cup of green tea to his lips and took a cautious sip. It was cool enough to drink. He popped the pill and took a longer sip of tea to wash it down.

The clock on his desk read 2:51. He would have to transmit the order to his subordinates no later than 2:55 to ensure that the sole surviving Devilfish would receive it at local midnight.

He ordered his thoughts and reviewed the situation.

The Devilfish had still not been detected, in spite of the arrival of the sea floor mapping vessel in San Francisco Bay. Its hiding spot in the depths next to Alcatraz Island had been chosen carefully. It was concealed from sonar except from a narrow cone directly above its location. His experts told him that the probability of detection was low, as the ship was focusing its search on the shipping channel. Still, the possibility remained. His agent in America, Charles Wu, known to his American collaborators as Adam, had promised it would be dealt with.

The loss of the other Devilfish had been distressing, but it was not a fatal blow to his plan. He grimaced. It would not have been used until the QUBE and the scientists were in hand and well away from Palo Alto. The primary blast radius was to have encompassed both the ST campus and the row of venture capital companies on Sand Hill Road, but of course the damage would have been far more widespread. At the optimal height for the airburst, buildings throughout the lower Peninsula would have been flattened, and the thermal effects would have been far more extensive.

He was not foolish enough to believe that incinerating the heart of Silicon Valley would have destroyed the American technological economy, but the loss of so many venture capitalists, engineers and computer professionals would have set them far back. More importantly, the arrogant nation's morale and economy would have been severely damaged. The American belief in their own invincibility would have been undermined, perhaps permanently.

General Guo shrugged unconsciously. It did not matter. The Americans would be scarcely less furious to receive only one blow instead of two, and the North Koreans would receive all the blame.

By all reports, Colonel Ryu had done his work well. Guo had expected no less. Ryu's dissident parents had died in North Korean concentration camps. They had bought time for him to get away at the cost of their own lives. He had been found as an orphan by Korean operatives working covertly for Guo. He'd been taken in, gifted with a false history to disguise his rebel ancestry, and raised by those operatives. Every day they indoctrinated him with what was, after all, the truth: that the Kims were insane, leading North Korea toward inevitable destruction, and deserved to be put down like the mad dogs they were.

Ryu had risen high in the North Korean military, with help from his sponsors in Guo's cabal. He might well have done so without assistance. He was smart, ruthless, and focused entirely on vengeance for his lost parents. He had distinguished himself in his role in the electronic espionage wing of the Korean People's Army. For more than a year he had been planting evidence that the Americans would eventually uncover, implicating the young Dear Leader and his clique in the coming attack. As Guo had told Ryu, they had not built *Zhāngyú* for nothing. The QUBE had merely accelerated Guo's schedule.

In the last week, Colonel Ryu had released computer viruses targeting American infrastructure targets—viruses that were almost certainly doomed to fail, but which would be traced back to the hacker group in which Ryu was embedded. He had been extremely careful not to overdo it. An excess of evidence would be more suspicious than its absence. The CIA and the NSA must be made to work for it. Having expended significant effort to have traced down the culprit, they would be all the more convinced that they had the right one.

Once Guo gave the word, Ryu would begin the final phase of his disinformation campaign. In American eyes, the evidence of Korean guilt would be damning. Their President would have no choice but to retaliate, and massively. At long last, China would be rid of the worse than useless parasites of the Kim dynasty.

In its death throes, North Korea might even take a substantial portion of South Korea with it. Guo's underlings had assured him that the effects on China would be modest at best. The cloud of fallout would drift westward, falling mainly on Japan—an unexpected bonus—and largely would have dissipated by the time the global circulation of wind in the Northern Hemisphere returned it to China.

If the Chinese President had known of Guo's plans, he might have approved. But he did not know, and never would.

The President was a princeling: a descendant of a glorious figure of the Revolution. His power derived largely from his ancestry, like the decadent emperors of old. His military background was insubstantial. As China mantled itself in the trappings of a modern economy, the power, wealth and influence of the princelings grew and grew.

Guo was no ideologue. He knew that the Communist government was rife with corruption from top to bottom. But the corruption introduced by the princelings was of another kind. It was corrosive to their national identity. In Guo's view, China must be foremost in the leader's minds.

After his accession to the head of the government, the President's commitment to the nation had been displaced by a devotion to himself. He had forced many of the generals of the PLA to swear personal allegiance to him. He cultivated his supporters and waged what amounted to open war on his political enemies.

It had been the doctrine since the time of Mao Zedong that members of the Politburo Standing Committee were not subject to prosecution for misdoings while in office. No longer. The President had arrested and jailed several of his rivals. The charges might have been trumped up, or might not. The effect was the same. His rivals receded and he continued to prosper. More and more he conducted himself like an emperor.

Guo was not among the top rank of Generals in the PLA, but he was highly placed. Many of his friends shared his disdain for the princelings. They believed, as he did, that China's dominance in the world was assured by Mao's Hundred Year Marathon, but only if the runners stayed on the track. The corruption of the princelings had grown so gross that they seemed to have forgotten Mao's goal of pulling the United States off its pedestal.

The military, on the other hand, had forgotten nothing. They were dedicated to the goal of avenging China's many humiliations at the hands of the foreign devils and establishing their nation as the world's sole great power by 2049—one hundred years after Mao first took power.

The Marathon had been a guiding principle of Chinese strategy for more than half a century. Some few foreigners knew of it, but their warnings had fallen on deaf ears. The leadership of the West continued to believe that China's leaders were just like them, and that the Middle Kingdom would eventually fall prey to the same blind consumerism that had robbed their nations of their own vitality. They balked at putting limits on China's expanding dominance over its rightful domain.

China's leaders had encouraged this perception with every means at their disposal, including the careful planting of propaganda in the Western press, and the suborning of political movements favorable to them.

The Russians had done much the same during the long years of the Cold War, but their efforts had lacked sophistication. The Chinese were subtler, and their agents were everywhere. The people of the West had grown so cynical that they would never believe that their opinions were susceptible to manipulation on so grand a scale. They could only believe the worst of their own governments. Time and again, their bone-deep cynicism was turned against them. All it took to diffuse suspicion of an aggressive action was a press release and a propaganda campaign on the Internet. A few dismissive comments planted in the public forums—the surlier the better—and curious eyes looked elsewhere.

And now the excesses of the princelings threatened to overturn all of this progress. The people could not be trusted to govern themselves:

this much was obvious. Strong hands were needed at the tiller. Yet the back-stabbing and corruption at the top levels of the Chinese government threatened to bring down the carefully crafted order. It threatened the Marathon.

The Princeling-President seemed to believe he could govern like an autocrat of the twentieth century. Even if this were true, it brought too many suspicious eyes to bear on Chinese affairs at a time when their export-based command economy was beginning to falter.

It had to be stopped.

Guo's friends looked to him for guidance.

In his capacity as one of the heads of foreign industrial espionage, he had come across evidence of the technology under development at StruvePharma. His network of agents in America had corrupted one of the top scientists in the company, who had reluctantly revealed to them the true scope of the work underway there.

Guo was no scientist. He belonged to a generation which had difficulty operating modern computers, much less understanding the technology that went into them. But one did not need to be a gunsmith to be able to shoot a gun.

Guo was quick to understand the implications of the quantum computer being developed in America. His advisors impressed upon him its ability to crack codes, and of potentially developing completely secure means of communication using something called "quantum entanglement." Moreover, if this QUBE could be used to design devices like the oil synthesizer so recently demonstrated by Peter Struve, it could guarantee China's energy independence forever.

He kept the knowledge of the QUBE to himself, and began to develop a plan. It was four years in the making.

First, he suborned the top-secret *Zhāngyú* program. It had been developed as a secret first-strike weapon, to be used only under the direst of circumstances, to be sure. According to their spies, the Russians were building something very similar. The Americans were toying with the idea as well. China wasn't about to be left behind.

Since Guo headed the *Zhāngyú* program, it was only natural for him to adapt it to his purposes. It had been kept secret even from the Politburo, its funding siphoned from hundreds of weapons systems budgets. Corruption was rife within the ranks of the bureaucracy, so he made use of it. He bribed the functionaries to silence. When bribes failed, men with knives succeeded.

His agents had eliminated everyone who knew the true nature of his program, including a couple of Guo's own friends on the General Staff. It was regrettable, but necessary. If even a whisper of his plan were to reach the ears of the CIA, his country might one day be bathed in nuclear fire.

The few remaining scientists and engineers were sequestered in a bunker in the arid hills near Jinchang. Once the Devilfish had performed their tasks, they, like the Korean engineers who had tested the Devilfish, would perish in a ball of fire.

Guo arranged for North Korea to receive the stolen plans of an old Chinese thermonuclear weapon. They had built such a bomb using the plutonium created in the breeder reactor at Yongbyon, which had been produced in quantities far in excess of Western estimates. Enough plutonium had been stolen from the North Korean's hidden cache to build two more weapons of the same design. These had been loaded into two of the three Devilfish bound for America.

The underground test firing of the sole remaining North Korean H-bomb had been scheduled for next week. Guo had managed to get it moved up to earlier this morning. *That* had been very difficult, involving blackmail and threats, but the officials in charge eventually caved in. The weapon had performed as expected. Seismographs all over the world had registered its might. The North Koreans had made risible claims about having fusion weapons in the past, but now there could be no doubt of it.

The Americans would now be in a panic. The discovery of the wrecked Devilfish and its deadly payload would deepen that anxiety. Colonel Ryu's disinformation campaign was working perfectly. Already Guo had word of submarines in the seas off North Korea's coast. The joint American and South Korean forces were ready to mobilize. The aircraft carrier USS *Ronald Reagan* had set sail from its Japanese home port, along with its battle group. Dear Leader was screaming bellicosity from the hidden TV studio beneath his palace, unaware that this time the Americans were coming for true.

And in the Bay Area, "Adam" reported that Aidan O'Keefe's team and their crew of expert former military contractors were in place and ready to go.

Guo looked again at the clock on his desk. It read 2:54, nearly midnight in California. He picked up the phone, dialed the number slowly, and spoke a code-phrase.

The final chain of events was now in motion.

As he put the phone down, he allowed himself to smile. After all this work, there had never really been any question of the operation proceeding. Evidence of the "theft" of the Chinese thermonuclear bomb plans had been planted long ago. The United States would be incandescent with fury, but even they would think twice about going to war with China. They would settle for disposing of North Korea, once and for all.

If the operation to secure the QUBE failed, America would still have been dealt a savage blow, and North Korea would be no more. Mao's Hundred Year Marathon would still proceed.

And if O'Keefe and his men could bring the QUBE and its builders secretly to China, they would sprint to the finish line.

Assuming he lived long enough for his plan to bear fruit, he, General Guo Qiang, would use the power and wealth conferred by ownership of the QUBE to lever himself into the Presidency. If not him, then one of his like-minded confederates.

China would again have a leader it truly deserved.

CHAPTER FORTY-FOUR

San Francisco Bay Area

November 1

Blaise woke to someone pounding on his apartment door.

His eyes were crusted shut. He rubbed them open. His head felt as if someone were hammering on it instead of the door.

He levered himself slowly to a sitting position in his disheveled bed. He was naked. The blanket and sheets were mostly on the floor. An empty bottle of red wine stood upright in the middle of the spotless white carpet.

A male voice shouted, "Doctor Terry! Are you there? Blaze Terry!"

He was halfway to the closet to get his robe when it finally dawned on him what day it was. *Could it be the police? How would they know?* He hadn't done anything to attract attention. His heart began to smash against his breast bone. He staggered into the hall as he tied his robe shut and stopped next to the door, listening.

"Doctor Terry!" shouted the man again. In a quieter voice, he said, *"What if this asshole ain't home?"*

Another, rougher male voice said, *"Then we track him down."*

"Like we don't got better shit to do."

Blaise peered through the peephole. Two helmeted soldiers stood in the hallway, one black, one Hispanic, both in camouflage gear with rifles slung over their shoulders.

Soldiers! What are they doing here?

The black soldier banged on the door again. *"DOCTOR TERRY!"*

Blaise jerked his throbbing head back from the sound. "I'm Doctor Thierry," he said, emphasizing the proper pronunciation.

"Thank You, Jesus," the soldier said in an undertone. Then he shouted, "WE'RE HERE TO TAKE YOU TO THE LAB!"

"Oh, my god," Blaise whispered, dizzy with relief. Now he remembered. Jack Dura had sent email to everyone on the staff. The roads were closed. Only official traffic was being allowed to use the freeways. He'd arranged for National Guard escorts for the few who would be attending the test who didn't live on campus.

Blaise opened the door and ushered the soldiers in, ignoring their undisguised horror at his appearance. He glimpsed the irritated face of his next-door neighbor glaring at him from her half-open door. "I'm sorry, Sarah," he said. Her mouth tightened and she vanished, slamming the door behind her.

It doesn't matter, thought Blaise. I'm never coming back here.

He turned to the soldiers. "I'm sorry, I was asleep. Let me put on some clothes. I need a few minutes." He gestured to the couch. "Please, have a seat."

He rushed back to the bedroom, closed the door, and frantically pulled on a clean change of clothes. He didn't bother with a tie. He went to the bathroom, scrubbed his face in the sink with hot water, quickly brushed his teeth and rinsed with mouthwash. The clock on the bathroom counter read 7:25. The HyperQUBE test was in two and a half hours.

He looked at his bleary reflection in the mirror. His face was unshaven, though its blond color disguised the worst of the stubble. The bags under his eyes were dark and puffy. And his eyes—even he had difficulty looking at them. They were so red he wouldn't have been surprised if he'd been weeping blood. He looked *terrible*.

He opened a bottle of aspirin, shook some into his hand and swallowed them, gulping water from the faucet. A terrible thirst consumed him. He noisily slurped water until he thought he would explode, but his thirst did not abate. Then he turned the faucet on hot and scrubbed his face until it felt as though it would slide off into the sink.

He wiped his red, streaming face with a hand towel and looked at his reflection again.

"You just have to get through this day," he whispered. "Just one day, and the nightmare will be over."

Even as he said it, he knew it was a lie.

The nightmare had not yet begun.

He left the apartment in the company of the soldiers. They explained that they were National Guardsmen. They had a huge, hideous truck, the original military version of the boxy Hummer SUV. He climbed into the back seat. The Hispanic soldier closed the heavy door after him.

For such a big vehicle, there wasn't much room inside. The transmission was mounted high in the cabin, presumably to protect it from mines, explosives or obstacles. Behind him was an unmanned but intimidating turret where a soldier could operate the big roof-mounted machine gun. The small square window in the door was thick and so scratched up he had difficulty seeing through it. He could tell that the skies were clear and the sun was shining brightly, and that was all. The cabin smelled of dust, sunbaked rubber and machine oil.

They rumbled out of his apartment complex onto the street. The air quickly grew hot. The driver flicked on the loud air conditioner. The temperature plummeted until it reached a comfortable level, and kept dropping. He decided not to ask the soldiers to raise it.

He ignored their desultory attempts to talk to him. They gave up with obvious relief and turned on a local news radio station. Blaise strained to hear it over the roar of the engine.

As they drove through largely deserted streets, periodically passing checkpoints manned by armed soldiers, he learned what had happened since he fled the laboratory yesterday afternoon, drove home and opened the first of three bottles of wine.

The reports of the military being put on full alert had been confirmed by the Secretary of Defense: the nation was at DEFCON 2. At four AM, Pacific time, the President had finally declared martial law in Northern California. The nation's airports were closed. All domestic and international flights had been canceled until further notice, the first time that had happened since September 11, 2001.

The President had enlisted the aid of the regular military to enforce the daytime curfew. This had outraged civil libertarians across the nation, and particularly in the ultra-liberal Bay Area, the only metropolitan area where the military had actively deployed. The Attorney General claimed that she had made that request as required by law, but this did not satisfy those already incensed.

In defiance of the curfew, and because of the government's few, uninformative news releases—deliberately kept vague so as not to cause a deadly panic, Blaise presumed—a number of protestors had begun to congregate in the streets in Oakland, Berkeley and San Francisco.

There was talk of a march being organized to occupy the Golden Gate and San Francisco-Oakland Bay bridges. So far it was just talk. Almost everyone was obeying the orders of the government and staying off the roads, but the burst of military activity in the area, coupled with the declaration of martial law, had the population on the edge of hysteria.

The reporters discussed the armada of aircraft that had appeared at Moffett Field, many of which were now constantly in the air. FA-18 aircraft orbited the Bay Area at high altitude in what the Air Force called a "combat air patrol." Countless black helicopters patrolled along the shores.

Several distinctive-looking turboprop aircraft with long booms projecting behind their tail fins had been flying low over the surface of the Bay. The KCBS aviation expert described them as P3C "Orion" anti-submarine warfare planes, and noted that they were very old. Evidently all of the newer P8 "Poseidon" aircraft were deployed overseas, involved in a spat with the Chinese over a speck of dirt named Scarborough Shoal.

There was also something new, something none of them recognized: a modified C-130 Hercules cargo plane, painted black, wings loaded with lozenge-shaped fuel tanks. Its nose sported an alarming spherical bump. The aviation expert speculated that it was a surveillance plane, but that there was an outside chance it was actually an experimental laser weapon platform. The plane circled endlessly above San Francisco at low altitude.

A National Oceanic and Atmospheric Administration ship named the *Fairweather* had been patrolling the waterways of the Bay as well. The task was made easier by the suspension of all boating traffic. Police and Coast Guard boats were stationed off all of the ports and marinas ringing the Bay.

There was a report that a commercial fishing boat had tried to escape from the marina in San Leandro. The police had given chase and fired on it, critically wounding the pilot. A flotilla of destroyers and cruisers was headed to the Golden Gate, between the mainland and the Farallon Islands, and were believed to be conducting anti-submarine warfare drills.

The reports of the collision between a ship in the South Bay port of Redwood City and some unknown object, combined with rumors of the arrival of the Nuclear Emergency Support Team and the undeniable presence of anti-submarine aircraft, had led the panel of reporters and experts to draw some alarming conclusions about what was happening.

Sweat ran freely down Blaise's face. It had drenched the collar of his shirt by the time they arrived at the ST campus.

They passed through three checkpoints on the roads immediately around the Coyote Hill campus. The guards at the gate had to lower the huge wedge-shaped vehicle barrier to let their Hummer enter the grounds.

The vehicle came to a stop in the middle of Watson Road, directly in front of the Pauling Building. It was too wide to enter the underground parking garage.

The Hispanic Guardsman opened the door for Blaise. His eyes grew very round. "Are you okay? Do you need a doctor?"

Blaise tried to smile.

The effect must have been appalling. The soldier actually backed up a step.

"I'll be fine," Blaise gasped as he lowered his feet to the ground. "I, ah, drank a little bit too much last night. Halloween party, you know."

The soldier exchanged a dubious glance with his partner. "I don't know what you got to celebrate with all this shit going on, but I hope you had a good time. Man, your skin is *gray*. You sure you don't need some help?"

I don't deserve your help. "Thank you, no. I will be fine. Have a nice day." He walked with painstaking deliberation to the rear entrance of the Pauling Building.

I should go, he thought. They'll know something is wrong. I'm jeopardizing the mission. I should just go. Turn around and walk away and never come back.

But his shaky legs carried him to the entrance anyway.

The ST guards were just as shocked at his appearance as the soldiers had been.

Alex Southall walked him to the lounge on the first floor and instructed him to sit down at a table. Instead of the mandatory gray jumpsuit, Southall wore the same kind of blue-gray camouflage uniform the soldiers had been wearing, but with patches bearing the seven-pointed star of the San Mateo County Sheriff's Department instead of rank insignia.

Blaise looked up at the tall young security guard. "Could you get me an espresso, please? A strong one?" he asked, his voice cracking.

Alex obliged him. As he placed the tiny ceramic cup in front of Blaise, John Shea walked in, wearing a similar camouflage uniform. A radio microphone was clipped to the epaulette on his left shoulder. The coiled black cord connecting it to the radio at his belt drooped across the front of his chest like the tail of a sleeping serpent.

The big man sat down opposite Blaise and frowned.

Blaise tried to focus on the espresso. He brought it to his lips with shaking hands. There was a growing pressure in his bladder, but he ignored it.

"What's going on, Blaise?" Shea asked in a calm, level voice.

He knew he couldn't lie to John Shea, with his merciless blue eyes eating away at him like lasers. He put the cup down, keeping his eyes on it. He tried to laugh. Another mistake. It came out like a strangled cough. He said, "I drank too much last night. Way too much. This situation, you know? All of these Army people, and the planes, and martial law. I watched too much of the news on television. I have never seen anything like it." His voice dropped to a whisper. "I am afraid." *Truth, if not the whole truth.*

Shea took a deep breath and released it slowly. "You look like hell. You should have stayed home."

"Oh, yes, perhaps you are right. But I had to be here for the test. I had to see if it works. It will be a momentous day."

John Shea's hand snaked into view. He pinched Blaise's minuscule cup between two oversized fingers and moved it away. "Tell you what. I'm going to ask Alex to walk you over to Crick. You should take a nap. Maybe take a shower. There are two empty bedrooms there. Never been used. Clean sheets. There's still two hours till the test. I'll send someone over to get you. We'll send over a fresh jumpsuit, too. What do you say?"

It sounded like an excellent notion, and the big man's tone brooked no argument. Blaise nodded.

He let Alex lead him to the dorm building, with a brief but welcome detour to the restroom.

When the door was closed, he lay down on the bed without removing his clothes. The unpleasant dampness of his sweat-soaked collar pressed against his neck.

"Oh, Blaise," he murmured. "What have you done."

He was asleep before he spoke the last syllable.

CHAPTER FORTY-FIVE

Struve Technologies Coyote Hill Campus, Palo Alto, California

John Shea closed his office door.

His nerves were jangling. He didn't much care for the stuffy Belgian scientist, but he respected him. He'd been a key player in the success of the QUBE technology. Blaise had never come to the office with a hair out of place or any indication of an emotion stronger than long-suffering disdain.

And neither had Aidan O'Keefe.

John had learned to trust his instincts. Right now they were smacking him in the back of the head. Something was very wrong.

He picked up his cell phone and dialed Laurel Wynn's number.

She picked up on the fifth ring. "John? How are things over there? Did you get those Guard reinforcements yet?"

"Hi Laurel. Yep, they're here. Got about a hundred and fifty men around the perimeter now, roadblocks on every street."

"General Dorsey's ordered Marines in from Pendleton but they won't get here until early afternoon. The President's order wasn't finalized until about four AM."

"I think we're good to go. Thanks. But that's not why I'm calling. Blaise Thierry came in today, half drunk, sweating. He hadn't shaved. Have you ever seen *him* with a stubbly face? He looks like something the cat barfed up. He's been acting jumpy the last few days. He said he was scared about all the shit that's going down around the Bay, but I don't buy it."

"He'd have to be crazy not to be scared."

"He's not just scared. He's close to a breakdown. He wouldn't look me in the eyes. I've known him for six years, Laurel. I've never seen anything faze him. I've got a bad feeling about this. I think you should talk to him, pronto."

"Jesus," said Laurel. The implications obviously weren't lost on her. "I'm really busy, John. I've got a briefing at 10:30. I could probably get over there by one o'clock."

"Can you skip it? We've gotta find out what's up with him, sooner rather than later. If he's working with O'Keefe... Well, my interrogation style might be a little on the aggressive side for this. You're a real cop. I just play one on TV."

She snorted. "Let me check." He heard muffled sounds as she spoke to someone. "Okay, I'll get someone to drive me over. I'll be there in half an hour. I'll see if I can get Allie Vieira to come, too. She's scary as hell in an interview, and I promised her that we'd let PAPD work the case."

"Sounds good. I'll let the crew know you're coming." He hung up the phone. He touched the SEND button on the mic clipped to his shoulder loop. "Attention, everyone. This is John Shea. I want two armed guards on Blaise Thierry, right now. He's in room 112 in the Crick Building." He released the button and paused for a moment, considering. He clicked the mic button again. "I'm declaring a red alert. Everyone get to your action stations. Spread the word. This is not a drill."

CHAPTER FORTY-SIX

Palo Alto, California

Tom Reed waited in the kitchen of the rental house, watching CNN. Gonzo was outside in the truck. It was painted with Allied Van Lines logos. They'd parked it next to their house, at the end of a tree-lined *cul-de-sac* in an upscale neighborhood a few blocks from Page Mill Road. They were less than a quarter of a mile from the Struve Technologies campus.

Halloween night had been strangely devoid of trick-or-treaters, which was fortunate, since none of them had thought to buy candy.

A pencil-neck neighbor had come over to complain that their truck was blocking the parking spots in front of his house. Tom reminded him about the driving curfew, but the geek hadn't had the sense to let it go. So they'd had to deal with him.

The geek had been hosting a party, apparently, because they'd had to deal with his guests, too. They walked up to the geek's house from around the neighborhood, all of them unattractive thirty-something males of the nerd variety. Unfortunately for them, they arrived one at a time. Nick Satriale and Chucky van Camp had been waiting inside. A quick blow to the back of the head, a little of the old garrote action, and that's all she wrote.

Eight bodies had accumulated in the back room before the guests stopped arriving. Nick had checked their IDs and done a little web research. None of them had families, to no one's surprise.

Stupid, thought Tom. If the first guy hadn't bitched about parking spots that were going to go unused anyway, he and his idiot friends would still be alive. Well, considering what was about to happen, maybe they were better off. At least they'd had good taste in beer. After the geeks had stopped ringing the doorbell, Tom and the men grilled their Johnsonville brats. It was a hell of a lot better than the TV dinners they'd brought from Safeway. Good German potato salad, too, nice and vinegary. *Waste not, want not.*

His teams were in place, their trucks parked in neighborhoods all around the ST campus. Most of them were next to the houses the team members had rented through an Internet home-sharing service. The biggest trucks, extra-wide flatbeds carrying the two bulldozers, were parked in a leaf-strewn lot behind a defunct high tech business a couple of blocks away. The tanker was parked there as well.

Gonzo had risen early and gone out to wait in the truck. Something about how the house gave him the willies.

Tom shook his head. Shooting people was fun and games to Gonzo, but an empty rental place creeped him out. Tom had been tempted to say something like "You could've stayed with Nick and Chucky over in Dead Geek Manor," but he'd let it slide. Gonzo was a freak, but he was a hell of a driver.

Tom made two cups of instant coffee and carried them outside. Gonzo sat at the wheel of the truck, one arm resting on the open windowsill, looking downcast. He took the offered cup and nodded gratefully. "I hate this," he groused. "The waiting is always the worst part."

Tom said nothing. He'd seen serious action in the Middle East. He wasn't anxious to be in the shit again, and with every passing hour the shit ahead got deeper.

The reports from the guys watching the campus weren't encouraging. Reinforcements had been arriving throughout the night. There were three rings of roadblocks now, and machine gun nests behind stacks of sandbags at the street corners. Tom was pretty sure they still had enough firepower to handle them, but considering how much of their arms shipment had wound up in the drink, it was no longer a sure thing. He hoped the diversion would siphon off enough of the defenders that they'd be less of a factor.

Tom checked his watch. Three hours until *H-hour*, as Aidan insisted on calling it. Assuming, of course, that Aidan didn't call him to get things started earlier, or that events on the ground didn't force Tom to do likewise.

He sighed, said *"Hasta la vista"* to Gonzo, and went back inside to watch TV. CNN was great for keeping tabs on military deployments. He didn't want to miss anything important.

CHAPTER FORTY-SEVEN

Struve Technologies Coyote Hill Campus, Palo Alto, California

Laurel Wynn finally managed to get away from Moffett Field an hour later than she'd planned. She sat in the passenger seat of an Army Humvee driven by a taciturn, red-faced MP corporal named Berry. He'd made no secret of his displeasure at being forced to drive a civilian woman around. *Screw him*, she thought. Life was full of little disappointments.

For the sake of convenience, she'd traded her civvies for an Army Combat Uniform, though hers lacked rank insignia. She wore her hair up in a tightly coiled bun beneath a camouflage fatigue cap. She'd more or less moved into Hangar Two at Moffett Field now. The ACUs helped her blend in with the ever-growing military presence there. They also seemed to increase her credibility in the eyes of the officers she worked with—that and the increasingly damning evidence that she'd collected, confirming North Korea's role in the current crisis.

General Dorsey had accepted her latest report with a white-lipped nod, and had immediately gone off to an unoccupied corner to phone his superiors. His intensity made her nervous. Friendly-grandpa-face notwithstanding, his gaze could strip you to the skin and expose your deepest secrets. She was glad she worked for the comparatively mild-mannered ogre named Andrew Seigart.

In spite of her sullen driver, she was glad of the opportunity to get away from the Field, even if only for a little while. The prevailing mood at the base was blackly grim. They'd had no luck finding any other drone submarines in the Bay, which would have been encouraging if you were an optimist, but there were no optimists on Captain Morton's intelligence staff. In the absence of contrary evidence, they just assumed they'd missed it.

The P3-C Orion anti-sub planes had been flying low over the Bay for hours. They'd found nothing with their magnetic anomaly detectors aside from already-charted underwater obstacles, pipelines and unrecovered wreckage from old ships.

The search might be in vain in any case. The analysts at Lawrence Livermore reported that the cylinder of the wrecked sub had been coated with a new material that might have blocked its magnetic field from airborne sensors. That news made all of the naval officers extremely nervous.

A pair of RQ-4 Global Hawk reconnaissance drones had been flown all the way from Grand Forks Air Force Base in North Dakota. They were orbiting the Bay Area at high altitude. So far they had not uncovered visual evidence of anything unusual beneath the Bay's calm waters. The morning skies were clear, but the forecasts called for overcast starting around noon, followed by an unseasonably early rain storm. The window of Global Hawk effectiveness was going to close all too soon.

The sea floor mapping ship *Fairweather* hadn't completed its survey of the shipping channel yet. There were some technical problems with their towed side-scanning sonar array. If there was another sub, it had so far eluded their best efforts to find it. A stealthy drone sub could have taken refuge in the shallows where no ship the size of the *Fairweather* could find it. If its missile had a fuel load comparable to the one found in the wrecked sub, it wouldn't spend more than a few seconds in the air before its warhead exploded.

Worst of all, though few had voiced the thought aloud, it was always possible that there was more than one sub. The Generals were drawing up some contingency plans, but they hadn't shared them yet. Laurel had no illusions about her rank in the sprawling, makeshift organization that had formed to deal with this event. She didn't have enough "juice" even to ask.

They all hoped that the XC-130J prototype aircraft orbiting San Francisco would be able to bring down a missile if, God forbid, one were to be launched. Laurel had learned about it at the midnight briefing. She'd seen the plane taxiing for a takeoff yesterday after the big briefing, and had mistaken it for an AC-130 Spectre gunship. Its experimental solid-state fiber laser was powered by a dedicated jet turbine generator mounted inside the fuselage. Though its official designation was "Medusa," everyone called it "Gort" after the death-ray-eyed robot from the classic sci-fi movie *The Day the Earth Stood*

Still. Some wag had painted the words KLAATU BARADA NIKTO in dark gray block letters beneath the faceted cockpit windows.

Whimsical name aside, Gort was a very serious weapon. It packed a punch of over two hundred kilowatts, combining the output of many smaller lasers into a single powerful beam. Two hundred kilowatts was at the top end of the power range for a street car engine. It didn't sound like much, but focused onto a point a few millimeters in diameter, it was devastating.

Gort could shoot down drones, aircraft, and even artillery shells in mid-flight, though its area of coverage wasn't wide enough to act as a point defense for the plane itself. They'd supplied its targeting computer with data about the missile's conformation, pinpointing the best spot on its casing to strike the warhead, which they presumed was identical to the one recovered from the wrecked missile. Then all they could do was hope. The aircraft had performed flawlessly in tests, but its very existence had been a closely held secret until circumstances had forced the Air Force to bring it to the Bay Area. It had never fired a shot in battle.

Gort's laser was powerful enough to burn through any missile casing in a fraction of a second. There was only one problem: the laser might touch off the chemical explosives packed around the plutonium sphere at the core of the warhead.

The result would be an asymmetrical explosion. Implosion weapons required a perfectly symmetrical blast wave to compress the plutonium so it would reach critical mass—the point at which the neutrons emitted by the radioactive isotope would begin an unstoppable chain-reaction.

An asymmetrical explosion would produce what atomic weapons specialists called a *fizzle*: a radical reduction in the output of the weapon. The experts at Lawrence Livermore described the North Korean bomb as a two-stage weapon. The first-stage fission warhead must explode perfectly to ignite the far more powerful second stage deuterium fusion reaction with concentrated X-rays.

A fizzle could range from a complete failure to achieve fission to a mere reduction in the efficiency of the fusion reaction. Even cleaning up the debris from a best-case result would be a deadly task, but the laser weapon was their only real option. Anything was better than the bomb exploding at full yield.

If Gort was in the right spot, if it was traveling in the right direction, if the weather conditions remained favorable, if the missile was detected the instant it broke the surface and was close enough that the beam didn't spread too much, and if there was only one target in the air at a time, they had a fighting chance of burning through its warhead fast enough to disable it.

There were far too many *ifs* in that equation. There was only one Gort, and it had to rendezvous with a tanker every few hours to refuel. If someone on the ground managed to shoot it down, or if a missile were launched while it was out of range—

Laurel tried to put the endless chain of *ifs* out of her mind. The Army was placing Patriot anti-missile batteries along the shores of the Bay. Hopefully they would be operational in time, and would be fast enough to make a difference if Gort failed.

She was startled out of her reverie when the driver took the ramp from the eerily empty Highway 101 too fast. He scraped the left front fender against the guard rail of the Oregon Expressway overpass before slowing to a rational speed. She shot him a resentful look, but he ignored it.

The expressway was a tree-lined, four-lane boulevard that led to Page Mill Road. It was vacant except for a number of police cruisers patrolling slowly in either direction. Long concrete barriers called K-rails blocked every intersection to provide a clear path from ST to the freeway. The heavy, thigh-high rails were normally used along roadside construction projects to protect workers from traffic. They could stop any vehicle short of a tank.

When they crossed El Camino Real, the long, usually busy street that ran the entire length of the San Francisco Peninsula, they saw an angry confrontation between local police and a handful of drivers. Corporal Berry slowed the Humvee to a crawl to watch.

A small convoy of three compact cars apparently had been trying to drive across the sidewalk at the corner to bypass the K-rails and get onto the expressway. Their roofs were piled high with luggage tied down with bungee cords or ropes strung through the open windows. The lead vehicle was a tiny Mitsubishi sports car with very small, sporty wheels. It had high-centered on the curb. As they watched, the drivers of the two cars that were still mobile got back into their vehicles and drove away, ignoring shouted orders to stop. The first driver tried to flee on foot. He was quickly caught by the two policemen, who wrestled him roughly to the ground.

Berry said, "Hmm," and picked up the pace.

Laurel was gratified by the number of National Guardsmen and Guardswomen they drove past as they neared the Coyote Hill campus. They were highly visible, heavily armed, and in their greenish-gray ACUs, body armor and Kevlar helmets, they were intimidating to say the least. They had a battle-hardened look that spoke of real-world deployments. There weren't many in the Guard who hadn't seen action, after so many years of war in the Middle East. That, too, was gratifying. These were no "weekend warriors." These were the real deal.

The Humvee finally reached the campus. It was ringed by National Guard troopers, some crouching behind ramparts of damp-looking sandbags, some walking with their M4 carbines at the ready. Humvees with roof-mounted machine guns were parked at each corner of the campus, probably more for show than for effect.

They stopped in front of the north gate. The huge, heavy wedge-shaped vehicle barrier slowly dropped until it was flush with the street. They drove in.

The first thirty feet of Watson Road was lined with HESCO bastions: nine-foot tall wire-mesh containers holding heavy, tight-woven fabric bags filled with water-soaked dirt. They were proof against small arms and explosive devices, and had been used to protect fixed bases of operation throughout the Middle East for years.

The soldiers, contractors and permanent Struve security staff beyond the line of HESCOs gazed at her impassively as she drove through. She saw Sy Hamilton and waved, but he did not respond. Everyone looked tense, and they held their weapons at the ready. Laurel felt a surge of adrenaline just watching them. *What's happened now?*

She glanced at her watch as they pulled to a stop in front of the Pauling Building. It was already 9:35. *Dammit,* she thought. "Wait here," she told Berry, ignoring his wordless grunt of acknowledgement. She jumped out and walked quickly to the building's rear entrance.

Cord Walker was supervising the guards manning the gate. He smiled slightly at the sight of her ACU battle dress and asked her to wait. He called John Shea on his radio.

Shea came at a trot. Allie Vieira followed, struggling to keep pace with him. Vieira's partner, the massive Bob Bosson, brought up the rear.

"He's in Crick 112, asleep and under guard," Shea said without preamble. He led them across the grass at a fast walk. Vieira and Bosson brought up the rear.

Shea asked, "What kept you?"

"Sorry. I can't talk about it. Classified."

"Jesus," he grunted. In a low voice, he added, "This is turning into a real shit-show, you know that?"

"You have no idea," she said under her breath. "Let's just pray it doesn't get any worse."

He badged the door open and let them all in. He led the way to Blaise's room on the first floor. The two bored-looking security contractors guarding the door looked up with relief plain on their faces.

"Anything?" Shea prompted them.

They shook their heads. One of them, a short, muscular man with close-cropped, curly black hair and a serious widow's peak, said, "Not a peep. We checked him a few times. Sound asleep. Or just passed out."

"Okay, you guys get some coffee or something, but stay close."

They nodded and went down the hall to the kitchen.

Shea eased the door open. They followed him in.

Blaise Thierry lay on his stomach, his face to the wall. Shea went to one knee next to the bed while everyone else looked on. He shook Blaise's shoulder.

The Belgian stirred and groaned, but that was all.

"Blaise, wake up," Shea barked. "Right now."

Blaise rolled over and looked up. His red eyes widened and his already pale face turned white. He closed his mouth and wiped a string of drool from his lips with the back of his hand.

"You know why we're here, Blaise," said Laurel in a gentle voice.

The Belgian scientist levered himself into a seated position with his back against the wall. He said nothing, but two fat tears rolled down his cheeks.

Son of a bitch, Laurel thought. John was right. He's not just afraid. He's terrified.

She looked at Allie Vieira.

The PAPD detective sat at the end of the bed. She crossed her arms. "Time's running out," she said, her voice gruff. "I can tell you don't want to be involved with this. You know what's going on. Tell me."

Shea stood up slowly, standing very close to the bed, looking down from his full height.

The giant detective Bosson moved to stand behind Shea. He clenched his huge fists. The cracking of his knuckles sounded like gunshots in the stillness of the room.

Blaise closed his eyes as tears began to stream from them. "Oh, God," he whispered. "Forgive me."

Fighting back sobs, he began to talk.

CHAPTER FORTY-EIGHT

Near the Rimjin River, North Korea

Colonel Ryu Sang-Chul drove past the checkpoint after flashing his credentials. The nervous-looking guards knew him well. As a senior official in charge of electronic intelligence, his duties included inspecting the listening posts stationed along the demilitarized zone. The band of no-man's land between North and South Korea was less than a kilometer south of the checkpoint, hidden behind a thickly forested ridge.

Beyond the DMZ were the combined troops of the Republic of Korea and the United States. On this side, the vastly larger Army of the Democratic People's Republic of Korea waited for relatives and former countrymen, sworn enemies of more than sixty years, to break across the border.

Ryu stifled a yawn as he drove away from the checkpoint. He'd spent the long, cold day preparing his vehicle and supplies, and he was very tired. He checked his wrist watch. He had less than thirty minutes to carry out Guo's orders.

He eyed the dented metal bottle in the passenger's seat. It was filled with Kona coffee, smuggled at great expense into the country. It was the reason the guards at the listening posts looked forward to his infrequent, unannounced visits. He couldn't keep himself from salivating at the prospect of a cup of the delicious brew, but this particular batch was not for him.

Ryu could have delegated the onerous task of checking the gear to a subordinate, but he had good reason to do it himself. He had established his behavior pattern more than two years ago. No one questioned his reason to be there, even in the middle of the night during a time of high alert. The listening posts would bring the first word of any movement by the ROK armies. They must be kept operational, day and night, especially now. Dear Leader had been warning of impending invasion for days. For the first time, his televised speeches conveyed not bravado, but fear.

He drove another ten kilometers into the hilly countryside. He pulled the old *Kozlik* over to the side of the winding dirt road that led to the listening post and switched it off. The poorly-tuned engine of the Jeep-like transport eventually dieseled to a coughing stop. Cold wind blew into the gaps under the canvas flaps that covered the rear half of the vehicle. Without the heater, it would have been intolerable.

The country near the Rimjin River was steep and hilly, a hard place to make a living by farming, but extensively cultivated nonetheless. The listening post was located on a hilltop with a clear view to the south, high above the wide, treeless swath of the DMZ.

Beyond the fortifications, fences, land mines, and vigilant troops was the prosperous South Korean farming county of Yeoncheon. The countryside was dark all the way to the horizon. Evidently the South Koreans were nervous, too. Normally he would see the twinkle of distant farm villages and houses, spraying light into the night sky with reckless disregard of the cost, while north of the border, his country languished in darkness until the power was restored the next day.

My country.

The very phrase was like a cut to the heart.

His parents had given their lives that he might survive. He'd sworn to avenge them against the tyrants who'd so callously destroyed his family. General Guo had put that power into his hands.

Ryu had no illusions about Guo's motives. He knew the contempt that the General held for his poor nation. Ryu's own contempt was mixed with pity. The Kims were demons in fleshy human form. They and their cronies had brought nothing but ruin and despair to the people who'd been unlucky enough to be born in this land.

The time of their reckoning was at hand.

Ryu got out of the truck, buttoning his coat's fur collar against the cold. He took a scuffed leather attaché case and the coffee bottle with him and walked up the deeply rutted road to the listening post.

Two guards stood next to the antenna-festooned metal shack. They wore heavy winter clothes and warmed their hands over a smoky oil fire inside an old steel barrel. Ryu knew them: young, foolish conscripts, too stupid to understand that by standing so close to the ruddy light of the fire, they had ruined their night vision and exposed themselves to potential enemy sharpshooters. They might as well fire signal flares into the starlit night.

It didn't really matter. The position of this highly visible listening post had undoubtedly been pre-sighted by enemy artillery.

The guards saluted smartly when they saw Ryu trudging up the road. They smiled when they recognized him, their eyes on the coffee bottle.

He exchanged pleasantries with them, raising his voice to be heard over the drone of the gas-powered generator.

The guards watched as he poured the coffee into their tin cups. They guzzled the coffee gratefully, waving off his apology for its being only lukewarm.

Less than a minute later, in mid-laugh, one of the guards slumped to the ground. The other one had time only for an accusing look and a choking gasp before he joined his fallen comrade. The cyanide had done its work.

Ryu sighed. He could not afford to leave them alive to report on his arrival at the listening post. His refuge was too close by. It was bad enough that the guards at the checkpoint had seen him, but they were very close indeed to the DMZ. They would soon have other things to worry about.

"I am sorry, comrades," he said to the two motionless bodies. He bowed to them, his heart leaden. "Yours will not be the only sacrifices this night."

For a moment, Ryu thought about saving the rest of the coffee for later. *No,* he decided. *I will live with the consequences, whatever they may be.* He tossed the half full coffee bottle into a clump of scrubby bushes. It clanged as it rolled down the rocky slope beyond.

He produced his heavy steel key ring and quickly found the one he needed. He opened the door, pulling hard to overcome stiff resistance from its rusty hinges. The guards were not allowed into the shack under any circumstances, and it had been some weeks since his last visit.

The shack contained a rack of old but serviceable console radios, most of which dated back to the 1980s. A more recent addition occupied the top shelf of the rack: a digital audio recorder. It collected the recorded voices of ROK and US military forces on the other side of the border, compressed the files, encrypted them, and transmitted them on the packet radio network so they could be analyzed by the DPRK intelligence agency. It was primitive compared to the fiber optic systems used in the West, but it served. Ryu himself had designed it.

Ryu opened his attaché case and pulled out a tiny portable laptop of the type called a "netbook" in America. He plugged an Ethernet cable from the rack's network switch into the netbook. He ran a script which linked him into the packet radio network. That done, he ran another script that connected to the secret daemon program he had installed on the master server in Pyongyang, where the audio files were collected for processing and analysis.

He paused. Millions would die, both here and in America, if he completed his task.

He was indifferent to the plight of so-called innocents abroad. The world had known about the Kim regime and its infinite evils for decades and had turned a blind eye to them. In any event, he could not stop Guo's plan. At best he could merely delay it. But if he entered the final command, the West would surely annihilate his homeland.

Better a quick death than a lifetime in chains.

His decision had been made years ago. He felt no further compulsion to review it now.

"For you," he whispered to the spirits of his parents. "And for the millions who went before you."

He typed the command and hit the ENTER key.

The secret daemon on the master server would now begin its fateful work.

Ryu had provided it with a secure path to the Internet via the same egress servers he used in his everyday work as a spy. It bypassed the ironclad safeguards the repressive government held in place to keep its slave labor force from learning how badly off it was.

The program would copy hundreds of files to a server in Japan. The files held genuine evidence of the North Korean hydrogen bomb program, along with the Dear Leader's detailed plans to strike against his enemies both near and far. Mixed in with that evidence were a few subtle falsehoods.

Ryu smiled with grim satisfaction. He had included up-to-date forged emails from Kim to his obsequious general staff, ranting about the discovery of the Devilfish in the waters of the South San Francisco Bay, and promising to execute the responsible party by his favorite, grisly method: 20mm anti-aircraft fire. In reality, of course, Kim was unaware of the existence of the ultra-secret drone submarine program.

A trove of supporting data would be provided as well—details of every element of the North Korean electronic surveillance program; source code for the viruses they occasionally unleashed on Western societies in hopes of bringing down infrastructure targets like hospitals or power plants; deployments and disposition of troops and weapons along the DMZ—all of it quite real. With so much actionable intelligence surrounding it, the false data would not be questioned until it was far too late.

The Japanese server would then copy the data to other machines throughout the world. Those machines would in turn email those files to every news bureau and foreign intelligence agency for which Ryu could find addresses. Much of it would be intercepted and discarded as spam. Enough of it would get through to its intended recipients.

The daemon's final task would be to send a message to the sole remaining Devilfish via its satellite phone link.

Ryu had signed the letters with his own name, and explained why he was betraying his homeland. The evidence of the conspiracy was fake, but if he were somehow to survive the events of the next few hours, he would swear to anyone who cared to listen that it was all true. With luck, there would be no one left alive in a position to contradict him. Even if there were, his goal would have been achieved. He cared nothing for Guo's Hundred Year Marathon. It only mattered that the renegade Chinese General had made Ryu's dream of revenge a reality. And in his heart, he would know that he had not betrayed his nation: he had saved it.

He prayed that future generations of Koreans would have cause to thank him for cutting the insane tyrant from the thread of history, even if they were never to know the name of Ryu Sang-Chul.

He unplugged his netbook, packed it into his attaché case and left the shack, taking care to lock the door behind him. He ran to the *Kozlik*, started its rattling engine, and did a U-turn, descending the hill via the road on which he'd come.

There was a place to hide nearby, accessible to his noisy but rugged little vehicle. The boxy ravine featured a creek fed by a small waterfall, a grove of tightly spaced trees, and a flat, well-drained clearing beneath them where he could pitch his tent. The bed of the *Kozlik* held warm clothes, enough food to sustain him for weeks, radiation protection and outdoor survival gear, including a water filter.

With luck, the high walls of the ravine would shelter him from the worst of what was soon to come. Ryu had no illusions about which side would win. He'd seen the videos from the wars in the Middle East. He knew what the American technology could do. The inescapable ravine would not be along the path of retreat of his fellow soldiers. He hoped to be able to surrender to the invading forces without being shot when the fighting died down.

If fate had something else in store for him, he would die content, knowing that the Kim dynasty had met its end.

CHAPTER FORTY-NINE

Struve Technologies Coyote Hill Campus, Palo Alto, California

John Shea slammed the door behind him.

His vision had narrowed to a red-tinged tunnel. The thunder of blood pumping through his head was so loud he wouldn't have been surprised to find it spraying out of his ears.

He managed to find the kitchen at the end of the hallway. Bob Christie and João Amaral were still there, drinking sodas and talking in low voices. Like most of the security contractors, they worked for John's former employer, Verity Services. Good men, even if they were just Army pukes. They went silent when they saw Shea, turning slightly pale when they caught a good look at his expression.

He growled, "Blaise is under arrest. He doesn't leave that room unless it's with me, Agent Wynn or one of the PAPD detectives."

"Right," said Bob, the shorter and more senior of the two security contractors. They tossed their drinks in the recycling bin and went back down the hall.

He called after them, "And I want someone in there with him to make sure he doesn't hang himself."

They stopped, turned and stared at him. "Right," repeated Bob. He thumped João on the shoulder and they trotted down the hall to Blaise's room.

John stood there after they left, quivering with rage. Unable to contain it any longer, he aimed a punch at a nearby wall, turning it into a blow from the heel of his palm at the last instant. The boom of the strike echoed down the hallway.

Laurel came running. "Are you all right?" she blurted, looking at the huge dent in the drywall with wide eyes.

John rubbed his palm. If he'd struck with his knuckles, he'd have laid them open to the bone. "Aidan fucking O'Keefe. He killed Peter, and he killed Emily and Jason, and Eric Dalton, and all those people at the hospital—I swear to God, Laurel, if I ever see him again, I am going to cut him open and hang him with his own guts!"

"I wouldn't blame you," she said. "I have to get this report back to Moffett Field. The command center has got to know."

He lowered his voice. "Is there a nuke out in the Bay? Is that what this is all about?"

Her silence was all the answer he needed.

"Goddamned need-to-know security rules," he breathed. "I thought I left that shit behind when I left the Corps. What the hell are we going to do if it goes off?"

She drew close and whispered, "Will you keep this between us?"

He nodded.

"You heard about the accident with the ship in Redwood City?"

"Of course."

"We got lucky. The ship ran into a robot sub carrying a short range missile. The NTSB investigator called in the NEST team. They disarmed the warhead. It was big enough to take out the whole Valley."

John felt dizzy. He pulled a chair away from a dining table and collapsed into it. "Thank God they found it," he whispered.

"We're not out of the woods, John. The attack in Moss Landing probably involved a different sub. The ROV from Monterey Bay Aquarium found big metal boxes on the sea floor, under the spot where the Coast Guard vessel was attacked. Probably part of whatever it was transferring to Aidan's crew. There might be another missile sub out there. Maybe more than one."

The moment of relief evaporated like a snowball in a blast furnace. "God damn it, Laurel."

"That's not the worst of it. All the evidence from the sub wreckage had Korean writing on it, but if Blaise is right, his contact is *Chinese*. What if this is a Chinese sneak attack, and they're trying to pin the blame on the Norks?"

"And what if Blaise is wrong? What if he can't tell a Chinese guy from a Korean?"

She shook her head. "It doesn't matter. General Dorsey needs to know. If we go to DEFCON 1, it'll mean war. Do you want us to nuke an innocent country, even if it is those crazy shitheads in North Korea?"

"No," he said after an instant's thought. "You're right. Call 'em."

"This isn't the kind of thing you can talk about on the phone. If news of this gets out, it'll start a stampede. I've got to get back to Moffett.

Anyway, if things here go sideways, I'm not going to be much help." She glanced down at the standard-issue 9mm Beretta on her hip. "I can shoot, but I'm no soldier." Then she checked her watch. "Jesus, the HyperQUBE test is about to start. Is there any way you can talk Jack into aborting? We've got to get the people and the QUBEs to Livermore."

"I already tried, twice. Anyway, it's too late. The test is underway. The HyperQUBE is already in the deep freeze."

She turned on her heel and left the kitchen at a run.

He followed, shaking his throbbing hand. "Laurel!"

She didn't slow down.

He chased her across the grass to the rear entrance of the Pauling Building. The guards stopped her. She looked at John impatiently. He gestured for them to let her in. She took the fire stairs at a run instead of waiting for the ponderous freight elevator. He followed, cursing under his breath. He badged her in to Mission Control. She flung the heavy door open.

The control room was strangely empty. More than half of the consoles were unoccupied. The rest were manned by the members of Jack's team. Amber D'Agostino, Stathis Sotiropoulos, and a pretty Hispanic engineer named Cat Moreno stood watching the big screens at the front of the room. Every eye turned to them as they entered.

"Laurel?" Jack's voice came from the back of the room, where he was leaning over Ed Black's shoulder, looking at the Flight Director's screen. He trotted down the stairs. He wore the same faded black AC/DC sweatshirt he'd worn on his first day at StruvePharma. His face was drawn with fatigue, but he looked happy. "Glad you could make it! I suspended the dress code for the occasion." His smile died when he saw their faces. "What's going on?"

"Call this off," she said without preamble. "The situation is getting really bad. We need to get the convoy on the move, right now."

"We can't."

"Jack!" she shouted.

"Laurel. We *can't*. The HyperQUBE's at operating temperature. Even if we stopped now, it will still take more than an hour to bring it back up. We can't use the rapid shutdown sequence until we know the case can survive it. If there's any defect in the structure, it could shatter."

Laurel's face grew panicked. "Can you at least cut the tests short? Do the least necessary to make sure it works?"

"We already trimmed the schedule to the bare minimum. There's no slack in the timeline. The test is going to start in seven minutes."

John gripped Jack by the shoulder and pulled him into a corner. Laurel followed.

Jack gaped at him. "What. The. Fuck."

John released him and said in a low tone, "Blaise Thierry was the other mole. He had a breakdown. He confessed. He was the reason the bad guys paying Eric Dalton knew about the QUBE. He said Aidan O'Keefe was behind the attack that killed Emily. He was trying to discredit Peter Struve and take control of the company, and it went wrong. He also said that Aidan made him use QUBE Delta to create a synthetic virus. He infected Peter with it in the bathroom the night of the party. It was targeted for Peter's genes. That's what killed him."

Jack paled. "Good Christ. I was in that bathroom!"

John grasped both of the scientist's shoulders, this time to keep him from falling down. "Hold onto yourself. He said Aidan has a big crew getting ready to assault this place, and that they probably have heavy arms. He didn't know the specifics, but he says Aidan has fifty or sixty mercenaries. Professionals. Ex-military. And there might be a fucking nuclear missile out in the Bay. They might be planning to nuke the lab after the attack to keep the technology out of the government's hands. We have got to *go*." He saw Laurel grimace at his broken promise. He snapped, "We don't have time to fuck around." He released his grip on Jack's shoulders.

Jack whispered, "Oh, my God." He shook his head as if to clear it. He croaked, "I wasn't kidding about the schedule. There isn't any slack. The tests are about to start. They run for twenty-one minutes, and then we can bring the HyperQUBE back up to room temperature. It'll take about an hour and a half if everything goes perfectly."

"Jack!" hissed Laurel. "We're talking about your life!"

He looked at John. "Didn't you tell her?"

John shook his head. "There wasn't time."

"Tell me what?" said Laurel.

Jack moved closer to her. He took her right hand in his. "I did it, Laurel. I solved it. I have the Grand Unified Theory. We spent most of the night reprogramming three of the HyperQUBE tests. They should prove whether I'm right or not, beyond a shadow of a doubt." His eyes turned pleading. "We can't stop it now. Running the test just takes twenty-one minutes."

"Your life is more important than any goddamned test—"

Jack spread his hands to encompass the lab, the engineers and scientists standing across the room, his former students at the test consoles gaping down at them. "This *is* my life, Laurel. This was Emily's life. We have the answer now. We have to test it. If the theory is right, it changes everything. *Everything.*"

"Goddammit! You stubborn son of a bitch!" she cried.

He smiled, but his face was full of pain. "That's part of my charm."

Laurel took out her cell phone and tried to make a call. It made a loud, fast beeping sound. "Shit!" She put the phone back in her pocket, embraced Jack, then kissed him fiercely. "Don't get yourself killed, you fucking idiot." She ran to the door.

"Wait! Where are you going?" Jack shouted.

"To get more help."

John followed her out of the building at a flat-out run. She was faster than he was, and many years younger.

He caught up with her as she closed the door of her Humvee. "I'll try to hold down the fort until you get here. Bring reinforcements."

"I'll bring everybody," she snarled. "Keep safe. Take care of Jack. Call Robbie on a land line and tell him to get troops down to Morgan Hill. Maybe Aidan hasn't left yet."

"Fat chance, but I'll try."

"Thanks, John." She turned to her driver. "Go! Go go go!"

The Humvee surged forward and left by the south gate, heavy tires squealing as it rounded the corner.

John grabbed the mic from his shoulder and pushed the button as he ran back to the office. "This is John Shea! Section heads to the main security office, on the double!"

CHAPTER FIFTY

Palo Alto, California

Tom's burner rang. He muted the TV and answered it.

Bobby Boykin's voice was garbled but still comprehensible. "Boss? This is the fourth time... to... you. Phones... getting unreliable...."

The phone made a squawking sound and the line went dead.

"Goddammit," Tom grated, hanging up. Everyone in the Bay Area must be calling everybody else just now. They'd have to switch to their radios if it got any worse.

Boykin and one of the contractors were in the oak trees atop the hill overlooking Page Mill Road. The sniper and his spotter were the first of his men in position, watching events at ST from a safe distance. They weren't supposed to break communications silence unless they had a damned good reason.

Tom waited impatiently for his phone to ring again. He glanced at the TV. It showed a jumpy, narrow cell phone video of a Coast Guard cutter racing along the shore of the Bay in hot pursuit of a speed boat.

The phone rang. "Make it quick!" he snapped.

The connection was better this time. Boykin said, "A Humvee just peeled out of here at top speed. Same one that came in a little while ago. Two people on board, just like before. Pretty sure one of them was that FBI bitch. All the troops around the perimeter took cover. They even pulled the Humvees inside the fence. Something's up."

"Shit. Did the MRAPs get there yet?" Blaise had told them that the trucks that would ferry the QUBEs to Lawrence Livermore would arrive around noon.

"No sign of them."

Tom felt relief wash over him. Disabling the huge up-armored transports without killing the occupants would have been hard. "I don't think we can wait. You guys be ready in five minutes."

"Are you serious? We're two hours ahead of schedule!"

"Just do it!"

"All right, all right!"

Tom hung up. He went out to the truck and pounded on the passenger side window. Gonzo jumped and looked at him accusingly as he reached over and rolled down the window.

"Schedule's moving up. Five minutes," Tom said quietly.

"Jesus," said Gonzo. He nodded and jumped out of the truck, taking a yellow and black plastic toolbox with him.

Tom went next door to Dead Geek Manor. Nick and Chucky were also glued to the TV. "Get ready, five minutes!" he barked. They scrambled for their gear. Then he dialed Aidan's burner.

"What's up, Tom?"

"Something put all the troops at ST on alert. The convoys aren't here yet, but we need to get this show on the road. Move up the schedule. We go in five minutes."

"We haven't heard from Blaise yet."

Tom glanced at his watch. "I think they figured Blaise out. There was a lot of movement right after he arrived, and just now everybody got behind cover. They're expecting us. We have to make sure those convoys don't get here, and it's going to take longer to take down the guards now that they're ready for us. And then we have to get into the building. It's time to go."

There was a long pause. "All right," said Aidan. "Five minutes, then. We'll alert the other crews and set the remote timers. Good hunting."

"Thanks."

Tom hung up the phone, took a deep breath and released it slowly. His heart slowed as the familiar cool detachment he always felt before battle came over him. This was what he was born for. The stakes had never been higher. *Win or die,* he thought. *Win or die.*

His phone buzzed with an incoming text message. He ignored it. He already knew what it said. Aidan was sending the same message to everyone on the team. In a dozen houses within a mile radius of the ST campus, crews would be scrambling to reach their positions in time for the big show.

Gonzo's nail gun went off with a muffled bang.

He went outside, a faint smile on his lips. He pulled a small, folded aluminized Mylar bag from his back pocket, unzipped it and dropped his cell phone and belt radio inside before zipping it closed again. He removed a pair of rubber earplugs from the bag and held onto them. He'd put them in at the proper moment.

As an afterthought, he went back into the house and opened the living room drapes. He'd be able to see the big flat panel display from outside.

The next few minutes would be very interesting.

CHAPTER FIFTY-ONE

San Francisco, California

Devilfish Two's sensor buoy was permanently deployed now, its tiny ballast tanks half-filled with seawater to keep it low in the water. Only its sat-phone antenna and the low-resolution panoramic camera were exposed.

The satellite phone receiver got a call. The encrypted message was decoded and authenticated.

A few minutes earlier, Colonel Ryu's message had cleared the path for the Devilfish to complete its mission. The newest message advanced the deadline yet again. The Devilfish's tiny brain was incapable of surprise. It merely obeyed.

Its computer began the five-minute countdown.

The cargo bay doors opened with excruciating slowness to produce as little sound as possible. Inside was a huge, featureless metal cylinder. In the turbid green depths of its hiding place next to Alcatraz Island, there was no chance of visual detection, but the magnetic field cloak was now compromised.

The panoramic camera on the surface revealed no aircraft in the vicinity, but the passive sonar array heard one in the distance. It was growing closer. If there was any indication of detection, the splash of sonobuoys into the water, or active sonar pings, the payload would deploy instantly.

At the front end of the cylinder nestled inside the payload bay, panels fell away to expose deflated rubberized bags. The Devilfish quietly fed its remaining store of argon and oxygen from its no-longer-necessary fuel supply into the bags. If necessary, it could inflate them explosively in less than five seconds.

The buoyancy of the slowly inflating bags levered the cylinder upright. Its base was anchored to the cargo pod by a dozen heavy, noiseless polymer cables. The cylinder now pointed straight at the surface, more than a hundred feet above the muddy floor of the Bay.

Four minutes of the countdown remained.

* * *

The Sausalito marina was busy in spite of the curfew. Everyone was preparing to leave, wrestling boxes and coolers and luggage onto boats and then staring out at the water with fear in their eyes. Amplified voices from police launches cautioned people to stay put. So far, no one had dared to challenge the order. So far.

An Army helicopter screamed past at low altitude. The soldier sitting in the open waist door clutched the handles of a heavy machine gun swivel-mounted to the chopper's frame.

Dawid Swart watched from the folding chair on the rear deck of the *Cool Runnings,* a two-decked, twin-engine sport fishing boat whose owner now rested in peace inside the small cabin.

His boat was moored tail-first in a slip that opened directly onto the expanse of placid water inside the small harbor's breakwater. He'd volunteered for the lookout spot in Sausalito, knowing how close it was to the Golden Gate Bridge, and to freedom. His boat was bigger and faster than the police launches stationed near the gap in the breakwater. With a little luck, he figured he could get past them. He had plenty of fuel, enough to reach Bodega Bay to the north, or Monterey to the south.

The helicopter roared off toward the Golden Gate Bridge.

Adam had selected Dawid and four other mercs from the crew for this special duty. He hadn't said why he was paying them so much more to do this job, but Dawid was no fool.

Cell phone reception had degraded so much he couldn't watch the Fox News online feed anymore. He kept up with the events with Google News. Once the action started, he had to get away, and *fast*. The other four were in their own boats in various spots along the shore.

Dawid was beholden only to himself. He could flee right now. The money had already been transferred to his account—he'd checked. Simple pride kept him here. He was going to earn his pay.

His cheap flip phone buzzed in his pocket.

He stood up, dug the phone out and read the screen.

GO. BLACK C-130 NO 1 PRIORITY.

Without a wasted motion, Dawid unhooked the mooring ropes from the cleats at the tail and along the rails, dropping the phone into the water at the same time.

He knelt and opened the two big, black plastic boxes on the deck. They were hidden from the police by the boat's superstructure.

He looked around and craned his head to listen.

In the distance, over the diminishing *whump-whump-whump* of the chopper, he heard the faint but unmistakable sound of turboprop aircraft engines. The sound grew louder, and louder still.

He looked up.

The weird black cargo plane with the bulbous nose was about to pass directly overhead. It was three or four hundred meters above the water.

"*Uitstekende,*" said Dawid ferociously. It was well within range, and too slow to get away in case he needed a second shot.

He grunted as he lifted one of the launchers to his shoulder. It was heavy, but the South African mercenary was built like a linebacker, and this wasn't his first time using a man-portable air defense system. He'd turned both MANPADs on fifteen minutes ago when the GET READY message arrived.

He sighted, heard the warble of the target lock, and fired.

The Stinger missile shot out of the launcher tube, propelled by a small initiator rocket. Once it was a safe distance away, the big motor caught. The missile arced upward.

The plane began a sharp turn to the left. Brilliant white flares sprayed out from a dispenser on the tail, but the Stinger was quick, modern, and very, very smart.

In less time than it took for him to draw breath, the missile reached its target. It lanced into the inboard engine on the plane's port wing and exploded.

The wing tumbled away from the fuselage in a huge cloud of orange flame. The blazing wreckage spun down to the Bay. The fuselage crashed into the rocks at the base of the north end of the Golden Gate Bridge. The sound reached his ears seconds later.

Dawid dropped the launcher and climbed the ladder to the controls. *The other guys can take care of the big white planes,* he thought. He'd dealt with the primary target. Pride was satisfied.

He started the twin engines, pushed all the way forward on the throttle levers—

—and found himself looking up at the sky.

The boat's engines screamed. The boat bounced and surged against something hard and unyielding. His body flopped on the deck. He couldn't feel his arms or legs, much less control them. The only sensation he had was confusion.

The boat crashed hard against something. *The breakwater,* he realized. The boat was slamming against the rocks of the breakwater without him to turn the wheel.

He had another moment of clarity when he understood that someone must have shot him. A cop, maybe, or some busybody civilian. The bullet must have entered his spine very high for him not to feel anything at all.

Splinters erupted from the deck all around him. His ears were pounded by a thumping, rattling roar.

The helicopter passed above him, the waist gunner's mouth wide with fury as he fired the machine gun down at him.

So. Not a civilian, then.

The boat bucked and heaved like a mad bull. He flopped forward onto his face. His view of the sky was replaced with one of the shattered wooden deck, now awash with his blood.

The world grew dark and guttered out.

The Devilfish performed its final readiness check.

The engine noise from low-flying aircraft had died, one after the other cutting off in quick succession, ending with thumping explosions and the *staccato* patter of debris raining into the water.

The large ship with its side-scanning sonar array was motionless, its sonar emitters offline.

The passive sonar detected no surface or submarine threats in the vicinity.

All systems were fully operational.

At precisely the designated time, the missile's tail-mounted chemical gas generator explosively pressurized the launch tube.

The overpressure blew the top off the tube, which separated into four petal-like sections.

The blunt spherical nose of the missile pushed past them effortlessly. The porous nose and sides of the missile emitted streams of millions of tiny bubbles that ensheathed its surface with air. The cavitation bubbles acted like a lubricant, allowing the missile to lance toward the surface at an astonishing two hundred miles an hour.

The weapon broached the surface.

The gas generator fell away.

The seven-meter long, graphite-black missile leapt out of the sea, slowing as the velocity of its launch was arrested by the force of gravity. When it reached the zenith of its skyward arc, more than fifty feet above the water, its powerful solid fuel booster ignited.

One point four seconds after it left the water, the rocket's stolen guidance system tried to acquire the United States' GPS satellites. It failed. The Americans had scrambled the signals from its Global Positioning System as part of their defense response to an imminent missile attack.

The European Galileo satellites were also scrambling their signals as they passed within range of the North American continent.

If the missile failed its last available option, it would merely ascend to a certain altitude and explode.

Since the emergence of the new cold war, the Russians had been uninterested in coordinating GPS signal shutdowns with the United States. Their GLONASS satellites were working normally.

Their signals told the missile all it needed to know about its position, speed, and trajectory.

It angled toward its designated target.

The closest Patriot battery had been positioned on the broken runway of the former Alameda Naval Air Station. By the time the launch was detected and the battery had a radar lock, the "North Korean" missile was already halfway to its destination.

The Patriot operators had enabled the automatic launch mode after Gort and the Navy's old Orion anti-submarine planes were shot down.

All four of the hypervelocity PAC-3 missiles blasted away from the truck-mounted launcher at the same instant.

More seconds elapsed as the interceptors speared toward the black missile.

They were just three hundred yards from it when it reached its target, 1.65 miles above San Francisco's Alamo Square Playground.

CHAPTER FIFTY-TWO

San Francisco, California

H-Hour

The human mind evolved on the grassy plains of Africa. Homo sapiens sapiens *was endowed with sharp vision, decent hearing, a passable sense of smell, rudimentary teeth and merely decorative claws, compared to those of the other predators of the savannah. Yet humans emerged from Africa to conquer the world because of their astonishing brains—the largest of any species in the history of the planet relative to body size, and inarguably the most inventive.*

It was the human mind that allowed it to defeat all competitors in the natural world, to extend its habitat from pole to pole, from the depths of the ocean to the cold vacuum of outer space. In the last century, the accumulation of knowledge accelerated radically. The human understanding of the world transformed so constantly that each astounding new revelation was taken in stride, without reflection or appreciation, as something merely to be expected, as inevitable as the rising of the sun.

Yet human understanding had its limits.

Only one who had seen the wrath of a thermonuclear explosion could truly understand its appalling power. America's last above-ground nuclear test had been in the early 1960s. Many people had seen films or video of nuclear explosions, either in documentaries or in popular entertainment, but these were not even shadows of the real thing.

No populated city had suffered an attack by an atomic weapon since 1945. Few who had witnessed the attack remained alive anywhere in the world when the Devilfish warhead exploded above San Francisco. Even they, had they been unfortunate enough to witness it, would not have been prepared for the havoc it would bring.

In every possible way, the weapon's effects exceeded the human capacity to comprehend them.

Within a millionth of a second of initiation, the temperature at the heart of the fusion explosion exceeded three hundred million degrees Celsius—thirty times hotter than the core of the sun.

A fraction of the mass of the weapon was converted directly to energy. A spherical wave front of gamma rays, X-radiation, visible light, heat, and radio waves exploded away from the center of the blast at the speed of light. The casing of the bomb became star-hot plasma as the energy wave swept over it, its vaporized metals emitting even more X-rays as the electrons around their atoms were stripped away.

The force of the staggering detonation was the equivalent of three point one million tons of TNT—greater than the combined explosive power of every bullet, grenade, rocket, conventional and atomic bomb expended in the entire six-year span of World War II.

The four inbound Patriot interceptor missiles simply evaporated.

The flash was visible to observers standing on the ground more than a hundred and fourteen miles away, and further still to those at higher altitudes. The light was so intense that anyone in the Bay Area who happened to be looking in the direction of San Francisco was blinded—some temporarily, most permanently.

The light from the blast dimmed for an instant as the explosive force of the shockwave heated and compressed the air so much that it became opaque. As the hypersonic shockwave advanced, the air cooled enough to become transparent again, allowing the hellish flash to pass without impediment. The transcendent heat from the explosion scoured the land beneath it, igniting everything combustible within a radius of seven miles.

In moments, the searing fireball swelled to a mile in diameter, a globe of total annihilation in the shocked air above the city.

The heat was strong enough to create third-degree burns on unprotected skin more than twelve miles from the explosion. Even twenty miles away it was still hot enough to redden the skin.

Closer to the fireball, the heat was utterly beyond description. People walking on the streets below the explosion were vaporized. Their nerves didn't even have enough time to relay the light of the flash from their eyes to their brains before they simply ceased to exist. All that remained of them were the shadows of their bodies on the smoking asphalt, until the shock wave reduced the streets to boiling gravel.

They were the lucky ones.

The altitude of the detonation had been calculated to maximize its airburst effects. The blast wave pulverized every building from Buena Vista Park to Cathedral Hill, from the University of San Francisco to City Hall.

The FA-18 fighter aircraft on patrol over the city were smashed by the shockwave. Their blinded pilots screamed as their planes tumbled out of control. "Grease" McNally and his weapons system officer managed to bail out, but their ejection seats plummeted into the fireball and were consumed. Not even ash remained.

The dozens of helicopters flying low over the Bay were swatted from the air like a swarm of annoying insects.

Only a handful of pedestrians perished when the searing shock-wave struck the city's two great bridges, currently vacant because of the curfew and road closures. Cables snapped and spans fell into the steaming waters of the Bay.

The explosion was a mile and a half above ground level, yet even from that distance its incandescent fury blasted a dish-shaped crater two thousand feet across and as deep as the height of a forty-story building into the heart of the city, hurling molten debris into the sky.

The spherical shock wave expanded away from the crater faster than the speed of sound. As the high-pressure wave passed, rings of clouds condensed in the rarefied sea air, circling the flaming cloud as it rose.

Further away, the buildings fared little better. The newer towers of the Financial District were built to withstand the massive earthquakes of California. Many remained upright, though no one within them survived the colossal blast, the hellish heat, or the lethal storm of neutrons. The superheated air fleeing the hypocenter turned windows, office furniture, and the more fragile parts of the buildings themselves into a sleet of shrapnel, scouring the towers clean of life before setting them ablaze.

Older structures were simply ripped apart.

Everything within a circle two and a half miles from the blast's center was seared and smashed as if by a flaming, God-sized ham-mer.

Then the wreckage was struck again as the vacuum created by the rising fireball induced a second hurricane, this time in the opposite direction. Smoke, soil, and pulverized concrete were sucked into the air, but fell again as the force of the vortex was spent. Many fires were snuffed out by the tornadic force of the recoil, but the flames would soon return.

Infants, children, adults, and elderly alike had no time to flee and nowhere to hide.

Countless thousands who did not die instantly from heat or radiation perished as the titanic blast of pressure slammed through their bodies, tearing lungs and intestines apart. Those few left alive in the heart of the city would die later, from lethal burns, fractures, cuts and punctures, from the acute effects of radiation, or even from injuries that would under normal circumstances be treatable.

For within the city limits, not a single hospital was untouched, nor fire house, nor ambulance company, nor police station. Even if by some miracle they had remained intact, there was no way for rescuers to reach the tens of thousands of wounded buried in the crumbled devastation of the once-vibrant city. The entire northern end of the San Francisco Peninsula had been ground into unrecognizable debris.

The sole mercy shown to the inhabitants of the Bay Area was that the airburst was too high to produce appreciable amounts of radioactive fallout.

Electrical currents induced by the bomb's electromagnetic pulse traveled away from the city along transmission lines at the speed of light. Every length of wire longer than the wavelength of the pulse conducted electromagnetic fury away from the center of the explosion. Transformers burst into flame as arcing, spitting bolts of man-made lightning forked down into the earth.

Automatic circuit breakers and the destruction of the power lines themselves limited the spread of the electrical storm, but the damage was bad enough. The cascade of power surges tripped circuits as far away as Los Angeles, Las Vegas, and Portland.

The shockwave lost force as its distance from the hypocenter grew. It was still more than sufficient to level smoldering wooden Victorians and ticky-tacky box houses more than six miles away in the suburb of Daly City.

The ring of devastation even reached towns across the waters of the Bay. Buildings were flattened in Sausalito and Tiburon, in Emeryville and along the dockyards of Oakland Harbor.

The crewmen of the BCL Barinthus unlucky enough to be on deck were blinded, seared and then deafened. Captain Anneke Van den Broeke fell down a ladder, shrieking a scream she could not hear. She landed on her chin two levels down, snapping her neck.

The colossal blast blew out windows up to fourteen miles away, from towns north of the ruins of the Golden Gate Bridge, along the entire shore of the East Bay across from the city, and well beyond San Francisco Airport to the south.

The shockwave dissipated into thundering echoes that seemed to go on forever.

The superheated mushroom cloud boiled into the livid blue sky. Concentric, delicate-looking rings condensed around its stem. It would not stop climbing until it reached the stratosphere, eighty thousand feet above.

All of San Francisco lay in smoking ruins beneath it.

The flames began to spread.

CHAPTER FIFTY-THREE

Palo Alto, California

H-Hour

Tom Reed watched the action on CNN through the living room window.

A correspondent on Fisherman's Wharf reported the trail of smoke leaping up from the marina in Sausalito. The cameraman whirled in time to record the big black plane going down in flames. The old-looking white Navy turboprops went down seconds later. Coast Guard boats surged into action around the Bay, heading for the sources of the antiaircraft missiles.

Tom couldn't suppress a slow smile.

The reporter shook with reaction, trying to describe the events while people ran past him, away from the end of the pier, screaming with terror over the rising wail of sirens and alarms. The studio commentators went berserk.

The image from the camera dissolved into static an instant before the TV went dead.

Tom turned away from the window and looked up curiously. The blue morning sky had grown pale. The trees around the house were too high and dense for him to see the blast itself. The mild effect was oddly disappointing. "Bummer," he said.

The pale sky quickly deepened to its former blue.

Tom dug his phone out of the Mylar bag and turned it on. It was still functional, but there was no signal. Aidan had told him that most of what people knew about EMP from movies was total horseshit. He'd even sent Tom an Internet link to a technical article he hadn't bothered to read. This close to the ground, the EMP would only affect electronics and power lines very close to the explosion, though the surges would probably knock out the power grid. The simple aluminized bag would be enough to shield his phone and radio from damage. *Aidan's right again*, he thought without surprise. He usually was.

Gonzo came around the truck and said, "Hey, where the hell are the—"

A series of distant booms echoed through the neighborhood.

"Ah, there they are," the wannabe Colombian said with satisfaction.

Tom smirked.

Adam's South African contractors had spent days locating and planting high explosives next to as many of the internet service companies, telephone central offices and data centers they could find. They weren't easy to track down. Internet service providers put them in deliberately anonymous buildings in drab, unremarkable business parks. But find them they had, and used detonators with cell-phone programmable timers to take out their generators. They'd set the explosions to happen an instant before the Big One. It just took a while for the sound of the smaller, nearer blasts to reach them.

The power grid was out. The cell network would also be down or disrupted, and so now would phones and internet services—any that survived the effects of the EMP, that is.

They couldn't do anything about HAM radio operators, but with luck the interference from the nuke would make it harder on them. Aidan had told him not to count on that, but Tom remained hopeful. In any case the airwaves would be jammed with people trying to reach rescuers or survivors. If the power came back online, the computer networks would be swamped just as quickly. Communications should be disrupted long enough for them to take the QUBEs and the scientists and make their way to the coast.

Nick and Chucky emerged from Dead Geek Manor, dressed in their camo gear and body armor, rifles held at the low-ready, barrels pointed down.

An elderly neighbor came out to see what was going on, but hobbled back into his house with a warbling wail when he saw the armed men.

Tom checked his EMP-proof mechanical watch. About ten seconds had elapsed since the power went out. "Okay, the blast will get here in about two minutes. Let's move. Gonzo, start it up."

Gonzo unhooked the grounding wire he'd driven into the asphalt next to the truck. They'd put a lot of effort into installing copper Faraday cages and tightly wrapped aluminum foil around the delicate electronics of the engines of their trucks. Aidan had insisted on the precautions in spite of his assurances that the EMP shouldn't be a problem. Tom had agreed. He didn't believe in taking pointless chances.

The truck's engine turned over easily.

"Good deal," said Tom. He threw open the back of the truck and jumped in.

The cargo box was full of knee-high metal crates, packed close together and tied down with heavy nylon straps. The area closest to the door remained empty. Tom's and Gonzo's body armor and gray-green camo gear were draped across the crates closest to the door. Their Kevlar helmets were there too, but they wouldn't put those on until the action was about to get heavy.

Gonzo joined him a few seconds later.

Nick and Chucky took up positions on either side of the truck, eyes wary, guns ready.

As Tom and Gonzo put on their battle dress, the truck trembled, as if someone had jumped on the tail gate. The motion subsided a few seconds later.

"Earthquake?" asked Gonzo.

"Shock wave," said Tom. "From the bomb. Sound travels a lot faster through the ground."

"Fuck me," Gonzo marveled. "Thirty miles away and we can still feel it. We gonna need the radiation suits?"

"Not yet. Maybe not at all. Depends on the wind. Airbursts don't make much fallout anyway, and it's supposed to rain later. Should settle any ash in the air. Just keep an eye on your dosimeter badge."

They were fully dressed and equipped for battle before the crashing boom of the explosion hammered through the neighborhood.

"FUCK ME!" chortled Gonzo, his eyes alight with homicidal glee.

Crazy asshole, Tom thought. *Maybe a million people just died.* Then he wondered at his own reaction: disgust at Gonzo's bloodthirsty laugh, and nothing else. Words from a book he read a long time ago popped into his mind: *A single death is a tragedy. A million deaths is a statistic.*

Screams from neighboring houses were audible over the grinding echoes of the blast.

"That's torn it," Tom said as he finished attaching his ammo harness. He checked his watch. He lifted the top of one of the metal crates and handed out Etymōtic GunSport Pro earplugs, radios and headsets.

Then he pulled out his new weapon and the heavy ammo harness that accompanied it.

Gonzo put his earplugs in, turned his headset on and raised his eyebrows when he saw the monstrous, ugly gun.

"I like to keep this handy... for close encounters," Tom quoted with a straight face.

Gonzo laughed. Last night they'd watched *Aliens* on the rental home's huge TV after disposing of the geeks and enjoying their bratwursts. "It's not Belgian, *patrón*. But it'll do." He jumped out, still chuckling, and ran to the cabin.

Chucky joined Tom in the open back of the truck while Nick went forward to ride shotgun with Gonzo. They donned their earplugs and radio headsets, and clipped the transmitters to their belts. The truck lurched into motion. They both took a knee and held onto the rubberized bumpers running the length of the truck's cargo box.

"Radio check," said Tom into his voice-activated microphone.

They responded by the numbers.

"This is a nice neighborhood," said Chucky as Gonzo threaded the big truck through the narrow streets. They both braced themselves as Gonzo turned onto Peter Coutts Road. "You think the fire will reach all the way down here?"

Behind them, people were starting to emerge from their houses, watching them drive past with wide eyes. They ran for cover when they saw the guns.

"Maybe," said Tom. "Aidan said it could be a firestorm. Like in Dresden."

"Where?"

Tom rolled his eyes. "Germany. World War II, numb nuts." He'd seen a documentary about it on the History Channel once. The Allies bombed the shit out of Dresden with incendiaries. The fire burned so hot all the oxygen was sucked out of the air. People fainted in the streets and then got burned to ashes. The temperatures in the center of the fire were hotter than in a blast furnace.

Conditions in San Francisco would be a thousand times worse after a nuke. God only knew how far the fire would spread, or how long it would last. The whole Bay Area could burn if the forecasted rain didn't materialize. If the fire was hot enough, it might all burn down anyway.

He shook his head. Best not to think about it. The mission was everything now. They would be fine as long as they could stay ahead of the fire. It would take a long time for it to reach Palo Alto.

The truck halted abruptly. *"Road's blocked, boss,"* said Gonzo over the radio.

Tom and Chucky jumped down and crouch-walked forward, eyes on the thick brush next to the road. Nick was already out of the cabin, covering the other side of the truck.

Peter Coutts Road was blocked by a twenty-foot concrete rail just before the intersection with Page Mill. It was much too heavy to lift, but they could still pull it out of the way. They were prepared to clear obstacles a lot bigger than this one.

Tom crept forward and looked over the rail onto the road, his massive gun held low.

Page Mill was vacant in both directions, but it wasn't going to stay that way. The National Guard checkpoint at Page Mill and Foothill Expressway was just over the rise to his right, out of sight.

"Okay, rig it," he said. He turned around and froze. Over the tops of the trees, he saw the monstrous gray mushroom cloud billowing slowly into the sky to the north.

The gruesome reality of what they were doing finally came home to him. It was like taking a ball peen hammer blow right between the eyes. A million more deaths to add to his personal tally of innocents. He could try to blame Aidan, but he was just as guilty.

He swallowed the nausea rising in his throat. *Ignore it!* he told himself savagely. He had a job to do.

He stood guard while the others busied themselves with the barrier.

Nick and Chucky anchored a block and tackle to the base of a nearby tree while Gonzo turned the truck around. They hitched a braided nylon line to one of the metal loops at the end of the rail, threaded it through the pulley and tied it to the hitch on the back of the truck. In short order they towed the rail far enough out of the intersection to get the truck past it.

Tom turned his eyes back to Page Mill.

A CHP cruiser was driving slowly up the hill toward them.

"Shit fire," he breathed. He unlimbered his gun and ducked behind a tree trunk.

Suddenly the cruiser surged forward, lights flashing. It screeched to a tire-smoking halt about fifty yards away.

"Good eyes, trooper," growled Tom. Aidan was right again. In the movies, every car in a thousand miles would have been knocked out by the EMP. He shouted, "Cover! Nobody shoot!"

His men dropped their ropes and took shelter behind the trees and the truck.

The two highway patrolmen jumped out and took cover behind their car doors, guns drawn.

Tom raised his heavy gun to his shoulder.

It was a prototype, but it had been tested extensively in Afghanistan and Iraq. The troops loved it. Its official designation was the XM25 Counter Defilade Target Engagement system, in full-on Army "take the fun out of everything" naming mode. The troops promptly dubbed it "The Punisher." It wasn't a rifle. It was a 25mm smart-grenade launcher, with a sophisticated laser sight and an onboard computer.

Since pulling the ugly thing out of the Cosmoline-packed box of arms and ammo provided by their Chinese allies, Tom had been dying to try it. They only had six of them, and just three hundred of the insanely expensive handmade grenades. The gun wasn't in full-scale production yet. That the Chinese had managed to get their hands on these was something of a minor miracle.

Tom didn't think twice about trying it now. He had to know how well it worked in battle. Their plan might depend on it.

He pulled the charging handle to chamber an airburst round. He flicked the targeting system on with a thumb and sighted on the driver's side mirror of the police cruiser. He pressed the thumb button to get the range. He saw the driver lift a microphone to his lips.

"This is the police!" the cop's amplified voice said, as if there were any doubt. "Put down your weapons and come out with your hands up!"

Gonzo's sinister chuckle sounded in Tom's headphones.

He checked the rangefinder display. It showed a distance of 45.2 meters. The Punisher was supposed to be good for five hundred. He pressed a thumb switch, adding half a meter to the range, and sighted on the center of the cruiser's windshield. He let out a breath, instinctively waited for a pause between heartbeats, and fired.

The grenade burst from the Punisher's huge rifled barrel. Its big round shell was programmed with the distance he'd selected, just beyond the hard glass of the windshield. It counted rotations as it spun along its long axis to track how far it had gone down range.

It punched through the windshield and exploded inside the car. The windows blew out, sending fragments of glass in all directions. The light bar on the roof shattered into a spray of plastic shards.

The CHP officers shrieked and fell. The passenger collapsed behind his door like a puppet whose strings had been cut. The driver tried to crawl away, but stopped after a few fruitless seconds, blood pooling beneath his body.

Smoke began to rise from beneath the police car's hood. In moments the cruiser was fully engulfed in flames.

"Wow," said Gonzo.

"Fuckin' A," said Tom, deeply impressed. The Punisher's recoil wasn't as bad as he expected. It was heavy as hell, but dead easy to operate. As long as they didn't have any misfires or rounds going off inside the gun—a problem that had delayed its transition to full scale production—the plan should work. Taking cover behind sandbags or HESCO bastions just wouldn't cut it against this baby. The grenades sprayed a dumbbell-shaped pattern of high-velocity ball shrapnel, taking out anything immediately in front or or behind the blast. Just add a meter or two to the range and aim over the top of the barrier, and that's all she wrote. Anyone crouching behind it was toast.

Tom shouted, "They probably heard that at the campus. They know we're coming. No point in waiting." He reached for the radio at his belt.

"Hey, it's too early!" protested Chucky. "You said we had to wait until people started getting out on the roads!"

Tom glared at Chucky. "If Blaise spilled his guts, ST probably knows what we're going to do. It'll take twice as long to get into the building now, and we don't want to wait for the roads to get jammed. And I don't have time to waste in a fucking argument with you. *Capisce?*"

"Okay, boss," muttered Chucky, his goblin face flushing red.

"We're just going to have to chance it. Now let's get to position one. Move it!"

"Roger," said his men in ragged unison. They ran back to the truck and secured the block and tackle and ropes. They might need them again.

Tom twisted the channel knob on his belt radio. He clicked the transmit key three times in quick succession.

Two hissing, staticky clicks sounded in his earphones. A few seconds later he heard the heavy reports of sniper rifles in the distance.

The attack on Struve Technologies was finally underway.

He switched frequency again, clicking the transmitter four times, putting the anti-aircraft missile teams on alert. Three clicks came back to acknowledge the command.

Tom frowned, considering. Then he clicked the key again and said, "Rogue One, this is Red Leader. How do you read?"

"Five by five," said Stu Cooper. The scout's voice was crystal-clear.

"Good. Red Leader out." He shook his head again. Fucking Gonzo had insisted on code names from *Star Wars*.

So the long-range radios are fully operational. They'd used the click codes because even Aidan hadn't known how clear the voices would be following the EMP. Evidently it wasn't an issue. Another Hollywood myth down the crapper.

He loped toward the truck, cradling the massive Punisher in his hands. It was a whole lot more fun than his Belgian F2000. It was even a bullpup design, with the trigger in front of the magazine. He said to it, "I think this is the beginning of a beautiful friendship."

CHAPTER FIFTY-FOUR

Mountain View, California

H-Hour

Laurel was looking down at her cell phone, trying to send a message to Robbie Holmes, when searing white light blasted silently into the cabin through the rear window of the Humvee.

"Jesus *Christ!*" shrieked Laurel's driver.

"Stop the car! Stop! Cover your eyes!" she screamed. She dropped her iPhone and did as she'd told him.

Corporal Berry slammed on the brakes. The tires squealed. She surged forward against the shoulder harness as the Humvee came to a skidding halt.

Heat prickled on the back of her neck. The glare reflecting from the gray interior of the vehicle drove through her hands and eyelids, jamming spears of red light into her panicked brain.

"Oh, Christ!" moaned Berry.

The heat on her neck faded, as did the redness filtering through her eyelids.

A series of sharp blasts rippled through the shocked morning air, making Laurel jump in her seat. They sounded close, but none were big enough to be from *that*.

She lowered her hands and wiped tears from her streaming eyes. *Oh Christ, no. No, please God, no.*

She tried to get a sense of where they were.

The Humvee had stopped diagonally across two lanes in the center of the empty freeway. Morning sunlight slanted into the cabin through the front window. They were on Highway 101, just short of the Shoreline Boulevard exit, perhaps a quarter mile from the Highway 85 interchange. Its arching overpass was empty of traffic.

She turned to Berry. "Are you okay?"

"No, Jesus Christ, no!" The driver clutched his face with both hands. "I'm blind! I saw it in the rear view mirrors! Fuck, they *nuked* us!"

"Calm down," she said, far more coolly than she would have believed possible. "Don't stop the engine! God knows if we could start it again. Put it in park and get into my seat. I'll get us back to Moffett." She opened the door and jumped out, then stopped, transfixed by the ghastly ball of fire crawling silently into the sky above the distant city San Francisco.

She could still feel its heat on the back of her neck, like a sunburn. *Or a radiation burn,* she thought anxiously. Even now, as the infernal, glowing cloud faded from orange to red, she felt it on her face like the warmth from a just-opened oven.

"Oh, dear Lord, no," she sobbed. She put her hands over her mouth to keep herself from screaming. *No,* she told herself. *Not now. Keep your head. Cry later. Act now!*

She heard distant shouts and horrified screams from the tree-lined neighborhoods on either side of the walled freeway.

Her blood froze in her veins as she realized that those freeways would shortly be choked with every living human being on the San Francisco Peninsula.

The realization hit her like a hammer-blow.

This was why they'd been nuked.

"Oh, Jack," she whispered.

Get off the freeway, she told herself. Get back to Moffett while you can. Get help.

She banished the tears with a savage swipe of her sleeve and shook herself back into action.

Corporal Berry had clambered over the high center console between the seats. He sat in the passenger seat, hands on his eyes, moaning.

She buckled him in, slammed the door, and ran around the idling Humvee, silently thanking God that the military spent so much effort hardening its vehicles and infrastructure against EMP.

She jumped into the driver's seat, checked to make sure Berry was okay, threw the transmission into DRIVE and floored it.

She had just reached the Ellis Street off-ramp when a crashing BOOM slammed them like the blast of every gun in the world going off at the same time.

"Holy shit!" she yelped. She jerked the wheel, almost sending them off the road.

Berry screamed a curse.

She regained control and said, "It's all right, it's all right." With the ringing in her ears and the growling echoes of the explosion, her voice was barely audible, even to herself. "Oh, my God," she gasped. Her stomach began to threaten rebellion. *Stay in control, stay in control!*

She rode out the nausea and turned toward the base.

The four guards aimed their M4s at her as she approached the gate. Fortunately, one of them recognized her, and ordered the others to let her through.

The base was a madhouse. Big trucks and Humvees roared along the perimeter road. A squadron of heavy attack helicopters were spinning up on the apron in front of the skeletal Hangar One. Fighter jets were already lining up on the taxiway, waiting their turns to roar into the sky.

She managed to get them to the apron next to Hangar Two. She stopped outside the dark green Mobile Command Post, next to the big tent where she'd attended her first briefing. She shouted "Medic!" over the rumble of a dozen backup generators.

A corpsman ran over. She handed the weeping corporal over to him and ran to the CP.

The huge tent was filled with tables, laptops, and furious soldiers. Andrew Seigart stood to one side, looking old and lost.

"Sir," she said. Her voice echoed weirdly inside her skull. Her hearing hadn't recovered from the blast of the nuke. "Sir! Where's General Dorsey?"

He looked at her, but his eyes didn't quite focus. "I... I don't know."

She could barely hear him over the din of the soldiers and the screams of aircraft engines. She looked around, seized an unoccupied folding chair, and put it next to Seigart. "You'd better sit down, sir," she said, and gently coaxed him into doing it.

He's in shock, she realized. *And he's in his late sixties.* She knelt next to him. "I'm going to find the General, sir. You stay here."

"He's busy," said Seigart distantly. He looked down at his trembling hands.

She left him there. She searched the huge, chaotic tent for endless, crucial minutes. She found Robbie. His face was a mask of pain. His apartment had been in Corona Heights. He was unmarried and childless, but everyone he knew in San Francisco was probably dead. She gave him a quick hug and whispered, "Did your parents get away?"

He nodded. "They caught a plane out of San Jose right before they shut the airport down."

"Thank God. I have to find General Dorsey. Can you take care of Seigart? He's... out of it."

Robbie nodded solemnly and went to Seigart's side.

She hunted fruitlessly for the General. At last she concluded that he wasn't in the command tent. She went to the exit and nearly ran into him as he pushed past the flap.

"General!" she said. "I have to talk to you!"

"Not now, Agent Wynn," he growled, and tried to step around her.

She blocked him. "This can't wait! I know why all this happened!"

He grimaced. Behind him were the other generals she recognized from the briefing. He looked at them and jerked his chin toward the interior of the tent. They glanced sternly at her as they filed past.

Dorsey turned on his heel and went outside, crooking a finger at her to follow. He led her about ten feet from the entrance. Behind him, the fatal cloud over San Francisco clawed its way toward the stratosphere.

"One minute," he snapped. "Go."

"This is all part of Aidan O'Keefe's plan."

His mouth tightened into a razor-thin line.

She added quickly, "There was another mole, a scientist high up in the organization. He confessed. I tried to get you a message."

"It's been a little busy here, Agent Wynn!"

"Yes, sir. Blaise Thierry was working with Aidan O'Keefe and an Asian agent named Adam, maybe Chinese, maybe not. He wasn't sure. O'Keefe was behind the original attempt to steal the QUBE, and the attack on Moss Landing. They're working out of a farm equipment company compound down in Morgan Hill. They took a shipment of heavy weapons from the sub, maybe even missiles, things too big to smuggle into the country. Blaise didn't know what they were, but O'Keefe and this Adam were pretty smug about it."

A flicker of interest kindled in his eyes. "Gort and the Orions were shot down by surface-to-air missiles just before the bomb went off."

Oh, Jesus, thought Laurel.

He gave her a considering look, then glanced at his watch. "You just bought yourself another minute. Step it up. Then get the address of that compound to Captain Morton."

"Yes sir. Blaise was supposed to message O'Keefe when he got to the campus this morning, and again after the HyperQUBE test was completed. I think they got nervous when he didn't contact them, so they moved the schedule up. The bomb in San Francisco was a diversion."

"A diversion?"

"Blaise knew they had something planned, something they were *absolutely* certain would keep attention off them while they attack ST. They're going to take the QUBE and kidnap the scientists. Blaise was supposed to disable the internal security systems and the vehicle barriers at the gates."

"Jesus Christ, Wynn, do you know how crazy this sounds?" Dorsey roared.

"Yes, sir!" she exploded. "But it's the only theory that fits all the facts! The nuke off Redwood City was probably intended to destroy the lab and cover their tracks. They can't use it now, so they're going to have to use the panic as cover to get away. They'll be moving delicate equipment, the QUBEs and a ton of hard drives, and as many prisoners as they can take alive. I think they're headed for an airport, or maybe trying to make their way to the shore and get on a boat. And that sub off Moss Landing was never found. They could be planning to use it to get the equipment away. Then they can blend into the refugees. We have to get help to ST, sir," she said. *We have to help Jack.*

Dorsey said, "Every person still alive south of San Francisco is going to be trying to get away. They're already pouring out onto the roads, and I've told my people to help them get out. That's my number one priority now."

"Sir, we can't let them take the ST scientists. God only knows what the enemy could do with that technology. You have no idea, sir. Blaise confessed to helping Aidan O'Keefe kill Peter Struve. They built a synthetic virus that targeted Struve's DNA, and killed him without leaving a trace. Blaise got it past the Secret Service at the dinner party with the President. It was supposed to be a demo to prove to whoever's sponsoring them that they can do what they claim, and it worked. Jesus Christ, did it work."

Dorsey's eyes grew wide. "Holy God," he whispered.

"The Chinese have to be behind this, sir," she said. "The North Koreans couldn't do this on their own."

Dorsey shook his head. "You haven't seen the latest intel. Come with me."

He led her back into the tent. Andrew Seigart still sat to one side, looking down at his hands. She felt Robbie Holmes' eyes on her as they strode past.

Dorsey stopped in front of a high, portable table. The other Generals crowded around it, leafing through a pile of printouts and schematics. Dorsey said, "This just came in. A North Korean Colonel of intelligence named Ryu sent it to every goddamned newspaper and magazine in the Western Hemisphere." He riffled through the printouts, plucked one out and handed it to her. "Here, read this. Excuse me for a minute." He pulled his advisors away for a whispered conversation.

Laurel's heart began to pound as she skimmed the North Korean spy's detailed confession.

"This can't be right," she said. She picked up other papers and scanned them quickly. The detail was overwhelming, the evidence damning. She didn't believe any of it.

"Sir, this just can't be right," she repeated loudly. "The North Koreans don't have the resources."

Dorsey rounded on her. "We've already got confirmation of some of this stuff from the NSA. Shit, lady, you told us yourself just yesterday that the Norks were probably involved in this!"

"I reconsidered, sir. Building those subs would have bankrupted them. I've been researching their industrial intel for years. They just couldn't do it. Not alone. And Blaise said the agent working with O'Keefe was probably Chinese."

Dorsey shook his head. "No, ma'am! *Probably* doesn't cut it. The Chinese already called us. They promised to help us track down whoever did this. There were a lot of Chinese expats in San Francisco. Emphasis on *were*. I can't tell my bosses to do what needs to be done on the basis of *probably*."

"But, sir—"

"We're at DEFCON 1, Agent Wynn, and your two minutes are up." He took a deep breath and expelled it slowly. "All right. I'm not going to leave you high and dry." He turned to the Marine Major General and said, "Dutch, I want you to help her get those people at ST out. Do what you can. And if you can't rescue them, then I want you to take them out."

"What?" she cried, aghast. "Sir, Jack Dura just completed a theory that—"

"Agent Wynn," he snapped. "I accept that these people are valuable. But if what you say is true, we absolutely cannot allow them to fall into enemy hands. Under any circumstances. We are at war, Agent Wynn! The one thing you *do not do* in war is allow the enemy to take his objective! You have your orders. Dutch, get her out of here."

The Marine's big hands closed around her forearm. He gingerly led her out of the CP.

"All right, Agent Wynn," shouted Dutch Holland as a Navy fighter jet took off nearby. The short, brawny Marine looked up at her with a fearsome stare. "You wanted help. You got it."

She fought down a scream of frustration. "Sir, the scientists in that lab are the most important people on Planet Earth right now. We have to save them."

We have to save him.

CHAPTER FIFTY-FIVE

Struve Technologies Coyote Hill Campus, Palo Alto, California

H-Hour

John Shea stood just inside the door to Mission Control, arms crossed over his chest, watching the scientists prepare for the test. This was the first time he'd worn his Santa's Workshop body armor since the night he took down the eco-sniper. The twice-daily workouts had paid off. With the ACU on top, the armor was still unpleasantly hot to wear for long periods, but there was now ample room around his waist. And that was the only comforting thought in his head this morning.

The room was much emptier than usual. Aside from the security staff and the near-catatonic Blaise Thierry in the Crick Building, the only ST employees on campus were in this room. John had insisted, and even Jack had balked at arguing for more.

Ed Black and Jack Dura supervised from the top row of workstations at the back of the room. Jack's former students and the two engineers from ZMPC had been trained to operate the other consoles. Three of Santa's Elves were there to help with the transfer of the HyperQUBE to the convoy: Amber D'Agostino, the Greek, and the senior cryo systems specialist, Cat Moreno.

"Power?" boomed Ed Black's voice over the loudspeakers.

John looked up as the lights flickered.

"Transfer to local power complete," said Hank Drummond from behind one of the consoles. "We're off the grid and stable."

"Network ops?" said Black.

Xu Chao-Xing replied, "All systems are green."

Ed said something else, but Ana Katsumata's crackling voice in John's earpiece drowned it out. *"Sir! We have a situation! We need you in Security, right now!"*

Shea grabbed the trigger on his shoulder mic and said, "Be right there." He waved to Jack and pointed at his earpiece, receiving a wave of acknowledgment. He turned, opened the door, and slipped outside.

Alex Southall was supposed to be just outside in the short hallway, next to the door. He wasn't.

John said, "Alex! Where the hell are you?"

He barreled out into Main Street.

The brawny former SEAL stood next to the armor glass window at Broadway and Main Street. From there he'd be able to see most of the ST campus, but he wasn't looking down.

Bright orange light slanted past him. His body cast a long, moving shadow on the spotless concrete floor.

John thought, *That's wrong. Those windows face west.* It was ten in the morning.

Only then did it hit him that the sun never moved that fast.

The shaft of light slowly faded to a sullen red.

"Alex!" Shea shouted.

The young former SEAL turned. His face was ashen, and his mouth hung open. He tried to speak, but succeeded only in making a guttural, coughing sound. He pointed out the window.

John rushed forward. When he reached Alex's side, he froze, staring out the window at a vast, fiery cloud ballooning into the blue sky to the northwest. The city itself was mercifully invisible beyond the limb of the hill across from the campus.

He croaked, "Mother of God."

The younger man's eyes were huge, his mouth working soundlessly.

He slapped Alex across the face, hard.

Awareness snapped back into Alex's watering eyes. "The flash lit up the hallway," he muttered. "If I'd been in front of the window—"

"But you weren't! Can you see?"

"Spots. Afterimages. Like looking into a searchlight. I'll be okay." Horror distorted his face. "Holy Christ, Gunny. Somebody nuked San Francisco."

"Stay here. I'm sending someone else up to help. Get back to your post. Nobody but me goes into Mission Control. Understood?"

Alex nodded sharply.

John spun on his heel and ran down the hall to the fire stairs, spewing a mantra of curses. He threw open the door to the security office, past the dozen or so men and women gathered there, and bolted into the surveillance room. Cord Walker ducked in an instant later, his dark skin beaded with sweat.

Ana Katsumata and the new security operator sat in the room, stunned expressions on their faces. They stared at an image of the mushroom cloud on one of the monitors.

John snapped, "Ana! Sitrep!"

Ana looked at him. "The rest of the campus lost power when the—when the bomb went off. Our building was isolated and on generators for the test. No reports of casualties. A few people are seeing spots. Nothing worse than that." Her voice was shaky.

John glanced at Cord. "Get someone to stand guard at Mission Control with Alex. He's got the spots, too. He says he's okay but I want to make sure. Nobody gets into that room without my authority."

"Got it." Cord slipped out of the room.

"Do we have radio contact with the perimeter?"

"No, sir," said Ana. "The roof antenna's dead. EMP from the explosion, probably. If we hadn't been off the grid already because of the test, we'd probably be dead in the water too."

John mentally blessed the architects they'd enlisted to design the Pauling Building. Even the water pipes were joined to external sources with polymer couplers, and were shut off and drained during QUBE runs. This building was as isolated from the ceaseless electromagnetic yammer of the twenty-first-century world as it was possible to be.

The floor trembled sharply. The walls creaked.

John had been through any number of small quakes as a resident of the Bay Area. This one felt different. It was as if someone had dropped a heavy weight on the ceiling from the room above.

"Oh, my God," Ana said.

He grabbed her shoulder and squeezed it. "Get a hold of yourself, soldier. We've got a job to do. You'll get through it. Just focus on the work."

She nodded up at him. "Yes sir." Her voice was choked with emotion.

"Is the PA system still working?"

"It should be," she said. She grabbed the PA mic and handed it to him.

"Testing, testing," he said as he pressed the button. He heard his voice from the ceiling speakers in the next room. The amplifiers on the roof of the Pauling Building would carry his voice across the entire campus.

Ana nodded to him.

"Attention. This is John Shea. I have some bad... some awful news to report. There was a large explosion over San Francisco a minute ago. It looks like someone attacked the city with a nuclear weapon."

He could hear the people in the main security room shout with horror and astonishment. The door opened and the people beyond began to shout questions at him.

Cord Walker pushed past them and shouted, "SHUT THE FUCK UP!"

The room fell silent. They'd never heard Cord shout before. His drill-instructor's voice was like a cannon.

John keyed the mic again and said, "Listen to me, everyone! I know this is a shock. You've got to get control of yourselves. I have something I have to tell you." He raced through a bare-bones summary of Blaise Thierry's confession, the broken submarine and its nuclear payload off the port of Redwood City, and Laurel Wynn's all-too-accurate guess about their being another missile sub.

Everyone within eyeshot stared at him, their shocked faces reflecting the horror he felt at having to speak those words aloud.

He said, "Laurel thinks the attack is a diversion to allow them to steal the QUBEs. There's a good chance that we're going to be hit with heavy weapons at any moment. She is sending help." *Assuming she made it back to Moffett Field.* He kept that depressing thought to himself. "We'll put a replacement antenna on the roof and hand out new radios to anyone who needs them." He looked meaningfully at Cord, who nodded back, pushed the onlookers back into the main room and relayed John's orders. Men raced out of the room to carry them out.

WHAM

The titanic sound was brutally loud even deep inside the building. Brave men and women shouted, cursed and screamed.

John felt a wave of cold terror race through him. Even after seeing the mushroom cloud and feeling the tremor of the ground wave, it had all seemed unreal, like a half-forgotten late night movie—until he heard that sound.

Get hold of yourself, Marine. This is reality. Fucking deal with it.

The thunder echoed through the building for many seconds. John shouted for people to calm down. It took way too long to restore a semblance of order. He keyed the mic again.

"Listen, people. You know how bad things could get if an enemy got hold of Emily and Jack's work. We can't let that happen. Keep your heads. Stay behind cover. Don't take any stupid chances, but we can't let them take us down. We've got to hold out until help arrives. We've *got* to. Whoever's backing Aidan O'Keefe just killed God knows how many people to get this technology. We can't let them have it. We owe it to everyone who just died—and to everyone who probably will."

"Oorah!" bellowed Cord Walker. The rest of the crew in the security room shouted it as well. Soon the halls were echoing with the battle cry of the Marines. Even the non-Marines were shouting.

"OORAH! OORAH! OORAH!"

John released the mic.

Cord drew a hand across his neck in a cutting gesture. "Now get to your posts! Move!"

The outer room emptied.

Ana and Leo Patrusky stared up at him. Their expressions no longer looked stricken. They were furiously determined.

"Get Blaise and the PAPD cops over here," he said to Cord. "We're going to seal the underground passageways and prepare to button this building up if the enemy get into the perimeter. Tell everyone to retreat to the loading dock if we get overrun, and prepare to raise the emergency barrier once everyone's in."

"Roger that," Cord said. He said in a low voice, "The outer fence is twelve inches thick, Gunny. The gates are lined with HESCOs and Guardsmen with itchy trigger fingers. The vehicle barriers could stop an M1 Abrams. Do you really think they can get in?"

"Depends on how much heavy shit they got off that boat at Moss Landing. They could have missiles, C4, who knows what. We'll burn that bridge when we come to it. Turn to, Cord! We don't have a second to waste."

Cord gave him the practiced alpha-male nod and disappeared.

"Ana, get Mikey, Norbert and Oscar ready to go. When the shit hits the fan I want them in the air. In the meantime, mirror the windows. I don't want those bastards to see what we're doing in here."

"Roger that," she said crisply, unlimbering the drone controls almost before he finished his sentence.

John yelped, "Patrusky! Are you fully checked out on these?" He jerked a thumb at the consoles and view screens recently installed by Laurel's friends at the NSA.

"Yes sir."

"Good. Keep your eyes peeled and sing out on the radio as soon as you see movement. I'm headed outside to check with the Guard commander."

When John Shea's PA address ended, Jack sat down heavily in the chair behind his console. Everyone else stood, staring up at him, their faces contorted with fear.

"Is it true, boss?" Hank asked, his voice trembling.

"It must be," he grated. He hadn't wanted to believe it. The terrible thunder of the bomb still seemed to echo in his ears. It had been stunningly loud even through the thick walls and the armor glass of the Pauling Building. He couldn't imagine what it had been like to hear it outside. "I knew that motherfucker O'Keefe was crazy, but I didn't know how crazy."

"My parents," said Terry Blau bleakly. "My sister." Then he burst into tears. Jack remembered suddenly that Terry was from San Francisco. "Sweet Jesus, why?"

"They want this," said Jack, sweeping an arm to indicate the whole of Struve Technologies. "They want *us*. And if O'Keefe finds out that we cracked the Grand Unified Theory—oh, holy Christ. I could barely sleep last night, thinking about the implications. I think we could manage direct conversion of matter to energy. It would make H-bombs seem like firecrackers. O'Keefe and his allies could rule the world, or reduce it to a burned out cinder."

"Oh, my God," said Amber D'Agostino. She collapsed into a chair at one of the workstations. "What are we going to do?"

Jack looked carefully at the faces of everyone in the room. Everyone stared at him in return, eyes wide and glassy with shock and terror.

"I'm sorry I got you into this," he said quietly. "I really am. I need a minute to think."

Lizbeth cried, "Let's just go! Let's get out of here!"

"We can't," he said, trying to sound calm. "Shea's people have the place buttoned up tight as a drum. We can't get out until the convoys get here—if they ever do. They weren't supposed to be here until sometime after noon. Oh. Shit. Every road is going to be jammed with people trying to get away from the city."

Chao-Xing moaned a phrase in her native tongue. She put her head in her hands and cried softly.

Everyone else waited, staring blankly at the screens, sniffling, weeping or just gaping in silent amazement. He stood and paced back and forth behind the row of consoles at the rear of the room.

Fury rose in his chest, forming a knot in his throat so hard it felt like he would choke on it. Aidan fucking O'Keefe. He killed Emily and her technician. He'd had all those people at Stanford killed just to silence his trigger man. He and Blaise murdered Peter in cold blood.

Jack's anger ramped up a notch. Fucking Blaise Thierry! How had Aidan turned him? Was it the promise of fame, fabulous riches, or both? Had he blackmailed him somehow?

Did it matter? The damage was done.

Jack had never liked the arrogant little Belgian, but he had to admit, Blaise had talent. The molecular designer was supremely capable in the lab, and a genuine wizard with the E-ware systems. He had an excellent grasp of quantum mechanics. Thinking back on it, Aidan had probably put him up to pumping Jack for details in his five-hour marathon talk to the staff about the HyperQUBE. And he'd designed a demonic weapon and tested it with no apparent compunction on the very man who'd made it all possible.

Jack remembered Blaise's studied blandness at the party at the Four Seasons, how calm and even bored he'd seemed just minutes before administering the lethal virus. He'd heard Blaise singing the Allyvil jingle with Peter from his stall in the bathroom. *Jesus, that was cold.* And if Blaise hadn't been such a good molecular designer, the virus could very well have killed Jack as well. The prospect of killing millions with a nuclear weapon had apparently broken him. If he hadn't cracked under the pressure and confessed—

Jack slapped his forehead with his open palm. "Think, goddammit!" He paced back and forth for another furious half-minute before his brain started moving forward again. He stopped and said, "There's a hundred-plus soldiers, former SEALs and Marines guarding us. Even if the bad guys get past them, this building is like a fortress. Santa's special plate glass windows, remember? But if they *can* get in, we're going to need leverage. We've got to finish the test."

"Are you out of your mind?" shouted Ben Holcombe. "What good is the HyperQUBE if they break in here and kill us all? We have to get out! We've got to get to our families!"

"We can't," said Stathis Sotiropoulos. "Jack's right. I know all about the emergency procedures. You can check with John Shea if you want to. We're locked in for the duration."

There was a long, tense silence.

Jack broke it. "Is the board still green?" he asked Ed Black.

The glazed look in the rotund Flight Director's eyes faded. He looked down at the three consoles arrayed before him. He looked up and nodded mutely.

"No damage from the... from the vibration?" Jack didn't want to say *from the bomb blast.*

Black shook his head. "The San Andreas fault is just over the hill from here. We get a dozen tiny quakes a day. The QUBE pillar is on active vibration isolation. The whole cryo facility is mounted on springs. Like NORAD headquarters, inside Cheyenne Mountain." His voice was harsh with tightly leashed emotion.

Jack looked at the rest of the team. "If it works, the HyperQUBE will be the most valuable thing in the world. They're coming for it. They won't do anything to endanger it. Or us, for that matter. We know how it works. We're the only people who can build more of them. Let's finish the test. That's our leverage, folks—if it works. Come on. Let's go." He said it gently, but firmly.

They looked at him, their faces bleak, but they shuffled back to their stations.

"Ed, do the honors," he said. Then he bounded down the stairs, grabbed Amber D'Agostino and the Greek by the forearms and pulled them out into the hallway behind him.

He led the two scientists out of earshot of the two guards. He whispered, "What other goodies do you have in Santa's Workshop we can use if those fuckers get inside? Anything we can use to slow them down or stop them. Anything at all."

The Greek exchanged a glance with Amber. He said, "Oh, yeah. We have some things."

"Get them ready and tell John Shea."

The Greek nodded.

Amber said, "*Can* they get in?"

Jack shrugged. "Aidan helped build this place. He designed the security systems, remember? If anyone knows a weakness, it's him."

The Greek nodded. His mouth twisted in a feral smile completely unsuited to his boyish face. "Come on, Amber. I have some ideas. Some *really* nasty ideas."

CHAPTER FIFTY-SIX

Near the Struve Technologies Campus, Palo Alto, California

H-Hour

Bobby Boykin watched the mushroom cloud climb toward heaven.

He and his spotter, a stumpy, sunburned Afrikaner he knew only as Hans, were hidden in a clump of oak trees on a hill to the northwest of the ST campus.

The defenders had infrared cameras and drones. Bobby and his spotter kept out of sight on the north-facing slope of the hillside, below the peak of the ridge. Only the tops of the Afrikaner's periscope binoculars were exposed. They were supposed to move into firing position only after the sound of the bomb reached them. It was as good a signal as any. Aidan O'Keefe had promised it would be impossible to miss.

They'd sneaked into position in the early morning hours, and had been hiding from hikers trudging up the hill on the paved walking paths since dawn.

They'd both worn ultra-dark glacier glasses and had their faces turned away from the blast. The flash lit up the hillside like a searchlight. Heat washed over the unprotected skin of his hands and neck. *Jesus. Thirty miles away and I still felt it.* When the fiery light died away, he'd turned to watch the aftermath with horrified fascination. He could even see the shockwave moving through the air, raising a white line of foam on the distant waters of the South Bay.

When the sound smashed against his stoppered ears, he'd been unable to stifle a shocked curse. It didn't matter. Who would hear him over *that?*

The hikers on the nearby trails had fled down the hill, some of them guiding weeping people who'd been unlucky enough to be looking toward San Francisco when the flash went off. The hillside was now deserted.

The mushroom cloud filled a great swath of the northern sky now. Its roiling white top continued to climb. It had to be in the stratosphere by now.

San Francisco was engulfed by a thick and swiftly spreading pall of black smoke. The firestorm was well underway. The smoke seemed to be drifting toward the hills of the East Bay. As long as it didn't come here. Fighting in gas masks and radiation clothes would be a serious bitch.

Hans slapped him on the shoulder. "Let's get to work!" He had to say it twice.

Bobby cursed, pulled the earplugs out, and tossed them away.

Hans opened a silvery plastic bag and handed Bobby his noise-canceling earphones and radio headset. Hans had already donned his.

Bobby inserted the earphones and put the headset on over them, turning on the radio as he did so, making sure it was tuned to the common frequency. He clipped the radio to his belt and the cable to his mottled yellow and gold camo shirt.

"It's time," said the South African. "Let's move."

They scrambled out of their hideout and hustled down the hillside, leaving the heavy periscope binoculars behind. Bobby carried the case for the Barrett M-98B sniper rifle. Hans held the handle of the big metal ammo box in his left hand, and a black .45 in his right. His spotter's scope was in his bulging backpack.

They crouch-walked toward their preselected location beneath another grove of oak trees on a lower ridge, directly overlooking the north side of the Struve Technologies campus. Bobby had scouted it himself two days ago. It gave a nice clear view of Page Mill as well as the whole length of Coyote Hill Road, and provided good concealment well below the top of the ridge. The other three sniper crews had picked similar sites nearby, bracketing the ST campus—and the only two gates in the high concrete fence.

The National Guard had set up roadblocks on Page Mill and machine gun nests on either side of the north gate. The campus was hidden behind the perimeter fence and a continuous row of narrow, sixty-foot cypress trees. From ground level, there was no way to see targets inside the fence. Only rooftops and the top two floors of the giant Pauling Building were visible from his vantage point. Its windows were now as reflective as mirrors. "Huh," he grunted. He hadn't known they could do that.

It didn't matter. Bobby's mission was to keep the guards' heads down, to let the guys with the Punishers get close enough to start blasting them behind their sandbags and HESCO bastions. And if anyone was stupid enough to peek over those sandbags—well, Bobby had been raised in Wyoming, where hunting was almost compulsory, and he'd trained with Tom Reed for years. He could take out any target he could see up to a thousand yards away. He was no Chris Kyle, but he practiced every chance he got. If Tom Reed said you were good enough, you were.

They reached their sniper's nest without incident. Hans began to set up his spotting scope, a big, weird-looking German thing with a laser rangefinder.

Bobby rolled his eyes. The Barrett Optical Ranging System sight on his rifle was all he needed, but the laser rangefinder would give more accurate results. Anyway, it was helpful to have a spotter to look for other targets, and to watch for anyone who might try to creep up and take them out. And of course Hans had another task to carry out once the perimeter was secured.

Bobby pulled a rolled-up sheet of canvas from his own pack. He unfurled it lengthwise on top of the weeds. He opened the heavy carrying case and quickly assembled his customized Barrett. It was a big but surprisingly light, even with the ten round magazine loaded with his own wildcat .338 Lapua loads. The heavy copper-jacketed rounds slipped through crosswinds with ease. They could penetrate all but the toughest body armor like it was made of cardboard.

Hans opened the ammo box and pulled out five loaded magazines. He put them on the canvas to Bobby's right, within easy reach. He closed the box and left it next to the canvas. "There are ten more in there if you need them, and two hundred more rounds in my pack if we need to reload."

Bobby nodded his thanks. He attached the full-length lens hood to the BORS sight and deployed the gun's bipod arms and the small monopod under the end of the stock. He lay prone on the canvas and got comfortable, putting his long-brimmed cap on backwards. The morning sun was high enough that it wouldn't interfere with his vision.

He ran through the calibration and setup procedure for the BORS sight in seconds. The tiny LCD display would tell him all he needed to know about how to adjust for elevation. It was even smart enough to consider air density and temperature. He didn't have the luxury of zeroing the scope with a practice shot or two, of course, but he figured he could adjust it when the shit started to fly.

He aimed at the Pauling Building and looked through the sight. He swept the scope along the length of the roof. Most of the air conditioning equipment was clustered in the middle, toward the edge of the building closest to the big hump of Coyote Hill. There was no place for an ST or National Guard rifleman to hide.

The only movement he saw on the roof was hot, smoky air rising from the tops of six short smoke stacks, presumably connected to the building's underground generators. Even through the scope, the windows were completely reflective. He frowned. Someone on the other side could be staring at him right now, and he'd never know it.

He tried to push that unsettling thought from his mind.

Hans pushed a metal rod into the ground nearby and screwed a swivel-mounted wind velocity meter onto it. Its tiny vanes remained motionless. Good. No wind up here on the unprotected ridge probably meant no wind down there.

Bobby shifted his position so he could cover Coyote Hill Road. Finally, he began to look for targets.

From this short distance he didn't need the scope to see that the barricades outside the campus were unmanned. The sandbagged nests next to the gate were empty. The Humvees with their big roof-mounted .50 cal machine guns were missing, too.

"Shit," he whispered. "Do you see anyone out there?"

"Not yet," said Hans, scanning the road with his spotter's scope.

The "go" signal wasn't long in coming. Three clicks sounded on his headset.

Bobby might not have seen anything, but apparently someone did. Two heavy booms echoed across the valley. He heard shouting and a scream of pain. The other snipers were all contractors, and if they'd left their targets alive enough to scream, they'd screwed the pooch. *Goddamned amateurs,* he thought.

"Target," Hans said. "Peeking out of the gate, looking toward us. Range... 331.4 meters."

Bobby quickly found the target: a helmeted head protruding just past the near edge of the gate. The soldier's dark-skinned forehead and eyes were exposed.

He quickly dialed in the sight, glanced at the LCD screen mounted over the scope to make sure it was correct, and re-sighted on his target, pushing forward a tiny bit to put some tension on the bipod. The soldier had leaned a little bit further out, and was now looking up Coyote Hill Road in the other direction.

"So long, stupid," Bobby whispered. He took a normal breath, held it, waited for the space between heartbeats, and smoothly pulled back on the trigger. As always, when he knew he had a good clean shot, the rifle charged into his shoulder at precisely the time he anticipated. The trick was not flinching against the recoil. The image through the sight barely twitched.

The round took the Guardsman at the base of his skull, just below the edge of his Kevlar helmet. A spray of red misted the air on the far side of the soldier's head. He dropped instantly, all of his strings cut.

Bobby let his breath out slowly and kept his finger curled around the trigger for a long second. *Not a bad way to go,* he reflected silently. *Not even enough time to feel the pain.* He didn't like punching National-al Guardsmen's tickets this way, but if he had to do it, he wanted to do it clean.

He worked the bolt and chambered another round.

"Goeie skiet!" whispered Hans. "I mean, good shooting, sorry."

Bobby glanced at the South African. His enthusiasm was a little disgusting. "Whatever, man. Just look for more targets."

They searched in vain. The other snipers' guns remained silent. Apparently the Guard had gotten the message.

"Yellow Squad," Tom's voice crackled in his earphones. "Report, by the numbers."

"Guess the EMP isn't a problem," muttered Hans.

Bobby clicked the VOX button on his radio, turning the voice-activated microphone on. "Yellow Leader, all secure."

The other snipers reported the same message.

"Take out the perimeter cameras," said Tom over the radio.

Hans dug into the backpack and removed a device that looked like a long silver flashlight mounted to a rifle stock. It also had a telescopic sight. He sat down, his left leg curled beneath him, and rested the weird gun-like contraption on his right knee. He took careful aim and squeezed the "gun's" trigger.

The blue laser was bright enough for Bobby to see it light up motes of dust in the air near the barrel, but it was so thin it became invisible just a few feet away from the end of the "flashlight."

Bobby chanced a quick look through his gun sight at one of the omnidirectional cameras mounted on poles in the middle of the row of cypress trees. Harsh bluish light sparkled from its spherical glass cover. Smoky haze filled the globe a few seconds later. The blue sparkles winked out as Hans moved on to the next camera tower.

Bobby snorted. They'd built the lasers with diodes harvested from Blu-ray players, following instructions they found on YouTube. Aidan O'Keefe had said a bullet wouldn't do much against the kind of glass they used on the perimeter cameras, but the blue laser light would go right through it. The light was intense enough to burn out the camera's sensors almost instantly. Bobby had told the spotters to keep the lasers on target until they saw smoke, just to be safe.

Hans said into his radio, "Yellow Two, here. All assigned cameras are down."

Bobby returned his attention to the north gate. Still no soldiers. No one would dare show themselves after the devastating demonstration of sniper fire.

The other three spotters reported in a few seconds later. All of the pole-mounted cameras were now out of commission. The defenders inside the ST campus were blind.

Tom's voice said, "Blue Squad, take your positions. They just launched two drones. Yellow Squad spotters, take them out if you can."

Bobby kept his eye on the north gate. No movement. The sixteen members of the Blue squads would now be creeping across the grassy fields toward the gates: two groups of four men on either side of the campus. Three men of each squad would have light machine guns to lay down suppressing fire for the one with the devastating XM-25 Punisher grenade launcher.

It didn't take long for the ratcheting sound of machine guns to fill the air. Bobby fired blindly into the trees near the gate, hoping to hit some of the Guardsmen, or at least make them pull back a bit. He heard the heavy booms of the other snipers doing the same thing from their hidden positions on the hills.

From the corner of his eye, he saw Hans holding his laser at the ready, scanning back and forth at the air above the campus, trying to locate the ST drones. Aidan had said they'd be a bitch to see or hear. Even the simple commercial drones they'd practiced against at the Morgan Hill compound had been nearly impossible to bring down.

Well, that works both ways, thought Bobby. He heard the buzzing whine of their own drones, operated by a pair of two-man crews hidden in a grove atop a nearby hillside. They'd give Tom and the other squad leaders a bird's eye view of the troops inside the campus.

He heard a heavy bang that could only be a Punisher grenade, followed by screams from inside the campus walls instant later.

Inside the gates, the big vehicle barriers made a curved steel wall about four feet high. There was about a foot of clearance on either side: enough room for defenders to fire out, but also room for attackers to fire in.

The Punisher grenadiers had the advantage of being able to duck below the cover provided by the vehicle barrier. They could fire their grenades above the sandbags and HESCO bastions lining the roads. The airburst rounds could take out the defenders, as long as the Punisher crews could get decent intel on their locations. The tree-filled campus was big. Cover was plentiful. And there were only so many grenades. Their drones would provide the critical information. Then it would be a turkey shoot.

The unmistakable thumping boom of .50 cal machine guns echoed across the shallow valley. The Blue squad members dropped to the grass, crawling as fast as they could away from the front of the gate.

Bobby tried to guess where the Humvees with the roof mounted guns had to be. He fired through the trees, but to no apparent effect. He stopped after five shots. His supply of ammo was limited, too.

"Shit," said Hans. "I can't see their fucking drones!"

A big box truck came into view on Page Mill Road just below them. He recognized the fake Allied Van Lines logo.

The truck lumbered through the National Guard's wooden barricade at the corner of Page Mill and Coyote Hill Road. It slowed well short of the gate and rolled up onto the embankment next to the fence.

Four men jumped out. They crept toward the gate, keeping as close to the fence as possible, firing occasionally. Bobby knew that Tom Reed was among them. He felt a swell of pride in his boss. Tom Reed sure as shit didn't lead from behind.

Bobby watched the Blue squads move forward again, the machine gunners spraying rounds toward the gate. He couldn't tell how much return fire they were getting, but the noise was immense, even from this distance.

The .50 cals inside the campus opened up again. One of the Blue gunners strayed a little too close to the opening. He was suddenly minus his head. His body pitched backward, blood fountaining from the severed veins in his neck, painting the brown grass a gaudy crimson clearly visible even from this distance.

The Punisher operators lagged well behind, staying low. One of them scrambled forward and fired a grenade into the gate. There was a loud bang and the .50 cal fell silent. The Punisher operator fired four more rounds in quick succession. More screams and shouts came from inside the campus. The Punisher guy dropped to the grass and crawled away as a withering barrage of light machine gun fire started up. He managed to get away, apparently unharmed.

There was a small explosion in the grass not far from the lead Blue gunner. Another one followed. The Blue gunner scrambled to find cover. Bobby searched the tree line along the gate, trying to find whoever was throwing the grenades. He saw nothing, but the sniper across from him apparently did. The report of a Barrett rifle rang out, and the explosions in the grass did not happen again.

Bobby said, "Ha. That'll show you." He decided to put in a fresh magazine while he wasn't busy. You never knew when you'd need all ten rounds in a hurry.

Another vehicle appeared at the top of the rise of Coyote Hill Road on the far side of the campus. Bobby looked at it through the BORS sight. It was one of theirs: a light gray Hummer, the commercial version of the Army's Humvee. Aidan and that Chinese guy would be inside.

The Hummer stopped before cresting the summit. Behind it was a big lumbering truck with a huge white tank. It stopped behind the Hummer. A front-end loader with its bucket raised moved forward and stopped just to the right of the Hummer. A quartet of armed men took positions in front of the vehicles, their guns pointed down Coyote Hill Road toward the gate.

Bobby heard the roar of car engines pushed to their limits. Apparently the roadblocks were starting to go down. A few cars arrowed down Page Mill Road, heading toward the nearby I-280 freeway. In seconds the few became many.

The tidal wave of refugees was finally underway.

Bobby muttered a curse. He'd hoped the EMP would disable more of the cars. It always did in movies. Aidan O'Keefe had told them not to count on it. *Score another one for the evil genius.*

A torrent of cars and trucks skidded past the splintered remains of the barricade at Page Mill and Coyote Hill Road, heedless of the battle going on a few yards away.

Traffic ground to a halt as the expressway filled. Cars jumped the weedy median, driving toward the freeway on the wrong side of the road. Others veered onto the shoulder, trying to get around the vehicles stopped in front of them. In less than a minute they'd jammed the expressway from edge to edge. Horns blared and drivers screamed. It made no difference. The road was impassable.

One super-genius in a red Charger made the mistake of smashing through the roadblock and turning onto Coyote Hill Road, probably trying to loop around the campus. There was a back way onto the southbound I-280 ramp via a small road that went under the freeway.

The Charger slewed to a tire-scorching halt before it reached the gate. Dozens of machine gun rounds raked it from inside and outside the campus. Shards of bloody glass scattered across the roadway. The car lurched forward and crashed through the short barbed wire fence across from the north gate, smoke boiling from under the hood.

That didn't stop a whole platoon of fellow geniuses from trying to follow it.

"Fuck," Bobby said. He had orders for this situation.

He went to one knee and raised the rifle. Fortunately, it was light enough to be usable even hand-held. There wasn't time to dial in the distance, so he'd just have to wing it.

He aimed just in front of the lead car's hood and fired, anticipating where the car would be when the round intersected its path. He worked the bolt, aimed at the next car and fired, again and again with robotic precision.

"Reload!" he shouted as he released the spent magazine. Hans slapped a full mag into his hand. He put it in and worked another round in the chamber before he realized he didn't need to fire again.

Bobby had put six of the ten heavy copper-jacketed rounds through engine blocks. Six motionless cars now slanted across the intersection of Page Mill and Coyote Hill Road, effectively blocking it. The M-98B was almost as good at stopping cars and small trucks as people.

One car had escaped his barrage. The .50 cal inside the campus joined in the massive crossfire as it tried to get past the gate. Sparks showered from the car as it was shredded. It veered crazily and smashed into the concrete fence next to the gate. Flames erupted from it and spread in a burning pool. Bobby cursed as the smoke obscured the gate from view.

Three of the cars he'd disabled were now burning. The drivers fled on foot toward the freeway. More people whose cars were stuck in the jam jumped out and followed, carrying suitcases or backpacks or children, screaming and crying.

"Good work, Yellow Leader," said Tom over the radio.

Bobby grinned as Hans chucked him on the shoulder.

"Red Leader, this is Blue Three. I just saw one of our drones go down."

"Copy that. White Leader, do you confirm?"

"Red Leader, roger, we lost one." The lead drone operator said something inaudible. Then: "What the...? Another one?"

"White Leader! What's going on?" Tom's voice was coldly furious.

"Red Leader, something's taking out our drones. That's another one! Three down now!"

"Get them the fuck out of here!" Tom yelled.

There as a long pause. "Sorry, Red Leader. All four are down. There was static from their cameras, then nothing. I think the ST guys fried them somehow."

"Fuck," snarled Tom. "Did we get any pictures? Disposition of their troops? Defensive positions?"

"Some," said the drone operator. "Not enough. There's hundreds of trees on that campus. We needed more time to get the full picture."

"And their drones are still up there?"

"Yes, sir."

Even with the Punishers, a frontal assault without knowing where the defenders were would be suicide, especially with those .50 cals still working. The line of closely spaced cypress trees made it impossible for them to toss grenades over the fence. They'd probably wind up killing more of themselves than the defenders.

Based on their surveillance of the campus over the last three days, there were more than a hundred armed men in there. They could spread out in the trees and cut down the invaders from a distance. They'd have the advantage of cover and eyes in the sky.

Bobby could almost feel Tom's frustration boiling across the radio. "Then we're going to the fallback plan. Everyone take cover. Orange Leader, strike pattern one, fire for effect. All forward squads, danger close in one minute!"

"Shit," said Bobby. A shot of adrenaline burst into his bloodstream. He dug his helmet out of his pack and put it on. Hans did likewise. They both lay down as flat as they could. He prayed that the GPS satellites were still online.

"Are we far enough away?" whispered the South African mercenary.

"Sure." I hope so, anyway.

CHAPTER FIFTY-SEVEN

Struve Technologies Coyote Hill Campus, Palo Alto, California

John Shea stood behind the surveillance operators, watching the battle unfold on the wall of flat panel screens.

He wrung his hands together in frustration. He was in charge of the building defense. He couldn't get out there and lend a hand, though it went against every instinct he had as a former Marine. The National Guard commander had made it clear that he was in charge outside. John was relegated to his original job as head of ST security, and nothing more.

He'd slung his M4 over his shoulder, and had his Kimber .45 on his belt, but unless things went seriously tits-up, he wouldn't be using them. All he could do now was watch.

He thanked God that Janine and the kids were in Santa Barbara visiting his mother. If he had to worry about them too, he'd go out of his fucking mind.

The only positive thing he'd seen so far was the enemy drones disappearing from the millimeter-wave radar scanner one by one. The Zap Gun on the roof had made short work of them. Alex and his defense contractor buddy would be proud.

The attackers had somehow blinded the pole-mounted cameras all the way around the campus. Fortunately, the pinhole cameras embedded at infrequent intervals in the walls themselves were too small to be seen from a distance, and John hadn't bothered to mention them to anyone in the senior staff. Aidan O'Keefe wouldn't know squat about them. The images they produced were distorted and low resolution, but they were better than nothing.

Fortunately, the cameras inside the tree line around the campus were still working. The rooftop cameras could see over the trees and across the road, but they didn't have an angle on anything close to the fence.

And they still had the Greek's drones.

The stealthy drones were painted a dull gray that was nearly invisible against the sky. Mikey and Norbert were high above, well out of credible gunshot range. Oscar was still on the Pauling Building rooftop, ready to join them if necessary. The big hexacopters could stay in the air for twenty minutes on their lithium-ion batteries. The attackers might be able to take them out when they landed for automated battery swaps, but it was a risk they'd have to take. Ana had them orbiting the campus outside the perimeter.

Mikey and Norbert showed a number of vehicles nearby: a dirty gray Hummer, a big white tanker truck and a bulldozer at the head of Coyote Hill Road; a convoy of smaller commercial trucks and Jeeps around the corner from the south gate atop Deer Creek Road. The drones had also proven that none of the attackers were trying to climb the fence. The Guards could concentrate their defenses on the gates.

The thirty-foot lines of blocky, water-soaked HESCO bastions on both sides of the road near the gates provided good cover. The Guards had to shoot from a standing position over the vehicle barriers to hit the attackers creeping in from the fields across the streets. They fired from behind tall but hastily erected lines of sandbags at the ends of the HESCO-lined "corridors." They'd done well until one of the attackers fired some kind of grenade down the corridor. It had exploded above and behind the defenders crouching behind the sandbags.

Several died instantly in spite of their body armor and Kevlar helmets. The Guards dragged the dead and wounded away from the sandbags and stayed behind the tall HESCOs from then on, firing outward and then ducking back when receiving fire. At that point they rolled Humvees with roof-mounted .50 cal machine guns up to the line of sandbags and began to fire out through the gate. The murderous fire kept the attackers at bay, but they had to be conservative with the ammo. A grenade killed the .50 cal gunner at the north gate, but another Guard took his place.

Three young men had died from sniper's bullets. Ten men and two women had perished from the terrifying rifle-launched grenades, or whatever they were. At least a dozen more Guards had taken wounds ranging from light to life-threatening. They'd brought them back to the Pauling Building. The two National Guard medics were trying to keep them alive in the auditorium.

A 1:1 wounded-to-killed ratio. That fucking sucks. John shook his head. In modern combat, it was usually more like seven or eight to one. Those grenades were too damned effective.

Luckily, ST had plenty of emergency supplies on hand, including frozen O-negative blood and plasma donated by members of the staff. It had been meant for use by the Rapid Response Team. They'd also recently gotten XStat applicators—tiny sterile sponges that could be injected with a big hypodermic-shaped device directly into a gunshot wound, stopping even arterial bleeding in seconds.

When Peter had recruited John and described the nature of the technology they were developing, the paranoid defensive measures they'd planned had included contingencies for protracted stays inside the safety of the fortress-like Pauling Building.

They hadn't expected to face the kind of effort the attackers were showing today, though.

John took a deep breath and let it out slowly. This situation was fucking *insane*. Thank God for the FQG armor glass. If there was a way to get through that, he sure as hell didn't know what it was. He prayed that Aidan O'Keefe didn't know it, either. He added a silent prayer for Laurel Wynn to have gotten back to Moffett Field, and that she would send help soon. The Guards were doing a great job, but they hadn't brought enough ammo to fend off a prolonged siege.

"Sir," said Leo Patrusky, the rookie surveillance operator. He pointed at a console showing a view from one of the pinhole cameras. It showed a group of men creeping along the outside fence. The one in the lead was talking into a radio headset. He was a slender man with angular features and cruel-looking blue eyes. His face was contorted with anger. A strand of blond hair protruded from beneath his camouflage-pattern helmet. He carried a short, blocky rifle—or was it a rifle?

John's heart skipped a beat when he recognized the weapon. "Shit," he said. "Those are Punishers. Smart grenade launchers. I saw a TV show about them a few years ago. They're still in the prototype stage. How the fuck did they get hold of them? Ana, tell everyone to stay the hell clear of anyone carrying one of those things."

"Yes, sir," she replied, and relayed the instructions over the radio.

The blond man moved a little closer to the pinhole camera. His lips were clearly visible. He said something into the radio and then dropped out of sight.

Patrusky said, "Did he just take cover?"

"*Outside* the fence?" said John, nonplussed.

Fear jolted through him.

He barked, "Run that video back ten seconds! And slow it down!"

John had spent many years operating behind enemy lines in Marine Force Recon. He'd forgotten how many nights he'd spent watching the enemy through telescopic gun sights, and he was a quick study with languages. He could speak and lip-read in English, Spanish, Arabic, Farsi and Pashto. In his business, it was a survival skill.

Patrusky played the video. The blond man's lips moved slowly on the screen.

"Shit," said John as the blond man dropped slowly out of sight again. It had been a long time since he'd done this. "I didn't get it. Play it again!"

This time John's brain matched the lip movements with words.

Something pattern one, fire for effect, all something squads, danger close in one minute.

The video feeds from Mikey and Norbert showed the helmeted attackers in the fields dropping prone in the knee-high grass, covering their necks with gloved hands.

"Oh, fuck!" said John.

DANGER CLOSE IN ONE MINUTE.

More than thirty seconds of that minute had already run out while he replayed the video.

He grabbed the PA mic from the desk in front of Ana and mashed down the button. "Everyone back to the Pauling Building, now! Incoming! *We've got incoming in less than thirty seconds! Get to the loading dock! MOVE YOUR ASSES!*"

He dropped the PA mic and raced down the main hall to the front of the building. He grabbed his shoulder mic and said, "Cord! Unlock the turnstile! Bring the emergency barriers up the second the last guy's in! We're going to total lockdown!"

"*Roger, Gunny!*" replied his second-in-command.

"God *damn* you!" he raged at himself as he ran. "Thirty seconds wasted! You are too fucking old for this, Marine!"

He skidded to a halt in the lobby. It had been sealed months ago, when the emergency barrier was raised from its compartment just inside the armor glass front of the building. It provided an extra fifteen inches of alternating layers of ultra-strong FQG and shock-dissipating gel. Nothing was getting in this way.

The garage and tunnel entrances were sealed. The only way in was through the loading dock in the rear. It had better cover than the front, being close to the high fence next to Coyote Hill.

John watched the Guards, the Verity Services contractors and his own men and women run flat out down Watson Road toward him.

"Come on! Come on, you sons of bitches! *Move it!*" He pounded on the armor glass with the side of his fist. It didn't even vibrate, much less make a sound. It was like hitting a slab of rain-slick marble.

There was a barely perceptible whistling whine, descending in pitch with terrifying speed.

The fastest runners from the north gate were still a dozen yards from the building when something exploded in the air just above them.

Instinctively, John threw himself to the floor.

The sound of the blast was muffled to a dull *crump* by the armor glass.

Fighting the animal instinct to hide, John made himself look.

Debris, flame, shrapnel and body parts pelted the armor glass and dropped away, leaving it untouched.

Another explosion followed the first, then another, and another. And another.

John pushed himself up from the floor and forced himself to watch, flinching violently at every muffled blast.

The world outside the windows became a churning maelstrom of smoke and fire. Explosion followed explosion, again and again and again. The blasts sounded like distant thunder.

He turned and ran as fast as his tottering legs would take him to the loading dock at the rear of the building.

The armor glass doors that spanned the loading dock were closed, but the external emergency barrier had not yet been raised. The sound of explosions was louder here, but not much.

John stared at Cord Walker.

The former drill instructor winced. "I had to shut 'em, Gunny," he said. "If one of those rounds lands back here—"

"I know," said John. "You did the right thing."

The four men standing watch with Cord looked through the windows, their faces gray.

"Did anyone else get in?" asked John.

Cord shook his head. The others stared at John in mute horror.

He looked down at the floor. He couldn't meet their eyes.

If only I'd been faster.

Cord rasped, "How the fuck did they get artillery into the Bay Area?"

"Mortars, probably," said John. "They offloaded a lot of heavy stuff from the boat. Or so I'm told." He gave a bitter snort. "If those bastards can get a hydrogen bomb, I guess GPS-guided mortars wouldn't be much of a challenge."

The conversation died. They waited for the barrage to end, or for a survivor to rush to the closed outer door.

The explosions finally stopped a minute later.

No one came.

John looked at the men who'd been standing watch with Cord. They were all from the original Rapid Response Team: Guy Harris, Armando Diego, Sy Hamilton and Martín Garza.

All of the Guardsmen and the contractors from Verity Services had been on the perimeter duty rotation. As had about half of the permanent ST security staff.

And all of them were probably dead.

John said, "See if you can spot any survivors through the windows. Don't set foot outside unless you clear it with me."

They nodded and dispersed into the building.

He walked unsteadily back to the surveillance room.

Ana Katsumata and Leo Patrusky didn't look at him when he entered. They stared at the screens showing the smoke-filled views from Mikey and Norbert.

"Oh, my God," said John.

The mortar barrage had been incredibly precise. Not a single round had fallen outside the high concrete fence. Inside, the campus grounds had been blown to hell.

Some of the cypress trees on the edge of the campus were still standing. Every other tree inside the perimeter had been blasted into tinder.

The nine-foot tall HESCO bastions lining Watson Road were still there. Some of them were torn, the damp earth inside spilling onto the ground, but no one had found shelter behind them.

All of the pole-mounted cameras were down. The Humvees near the gates and the Guard transport trucks parked in front of the Jenner Building had been shredded.

The Pauling Building hadn't even been scratched. Every other structure on campus was a fiery ruin.

There were dozens of uniformed bodies, all of them blood-soaked and motionless. If there were any survivors, they weren't visible from the drones.

John reached up slowly for his shoulder mic. "Attention," he croaked. "If anyone sees anyone alive, say so now."

He waited thirty seconds for an answer. The drone video showed machine-gun-bearing attackers running around the still-raised vehicle barriers, past the HESCO bastions and the flaming remains of the Humvees, onto the shattered, smoking grounds of the campus.

Your fault, a voice inside him shrilled silently.

It was the same voice he'd heard when his last mission in Iraq blew up in his face. It nearly cost him his career.

Four fellow Marines and the Air Force pilot they'd been trying to rescue had perished. He'd held himself responsible, even if the board of inquiry hadn't. He hadn't been fast enough to see how the situation was turning bad. At least once or twice a month in the many years since, he awakened with a cold sweat and the anguished voices of his men echoing in his ears.

You weren't fast enough. You weren't smart enough. Your fault, your fault, YOUR FAULT.

He told that voice to go to hell.

He couldn't afford to crack up or wallow in self-recrimination. He still had a job to do. He might lie awake at night for the rest of his life, but right now, he still had people to protect. If he could.

"Ana, land the drones and swap out the batteries. We might need them later. The rooftop cameras will do for now."

"Yes, sir," she replied, her voice cracking with grief.

He clicked his shoulder mic again. "Cord. Bring up the rest of the emergency barriers. Now."

"Wilco, Gunny."

He took one of the wheeled chairs from the newly installed console and sat down heavily.

He looked up at the shiny new monitors. Advanced millimeter wave radar, ultra-sensitive infrared cameras, seismic ground sensors and who knows what other fancy toys Laurel had wheedled out of the NSA, all now as useless as tits on a boar. They didn't need to find the enemy. They were everywhere.

A quote from the famous Chesty Puller swam into his consciousness. *Great. Now we can shoot at those bastards from every direction.*

"Jesus," he whispered. "What the fuck do I do now?"

CHAPTER FIFTY-EIGHT

Struve Technologies Coyote Hill Campus, Palo Alto, California

Tom Reed looked stood in front of the Pauling Building, hands on hips, considering the next move.

Men muttered on the radio. "Keep the channel clear," Tom growled. "Switch your radios off VOX if you need to talk." He took his own advice and turned off his voice-activated microphone.

Al Sanderson trotted up to him, head on a swivel, looking for threats, holding his M4 carbine at the low-ready position. "You sure you want to be this close?"

Tom shrugged. "Why not? They can't exactly shoot at me through a window." He looked up at the huge armor glass structure. The GPS-guided mortar strike pattern had been designed to spare it, of course, but it was amazing to see it standing untouched in the gritty, stinking smoke. Its mirrored windows gleamed in the late morning sunlight, looking as if they had just been washed.

The attack had been risky. The government had undoubtedly disabled GPS signals from its own satellite network as part of the standard DEFCON 1 procedures. Fortunately, their Chinese benefactors had retrofitted the 81mm mortar guidance systems with multi-function chips that could pull signals from European Galileo satellites as well as Russian GLONASS and even the BeiDou-2 systems, though the coverage area of the Chinese GPS network was still confined to the western Pacific. Evidently, at least one of the other systems had still been functional. All of the mortars had struck inside the walls of the ST campus.

Tom took off his helmet and wiped sweat away with his forearm. The heat from the burning buildings was becoming oppressive, but the smoke was going almost straight up. That wouldn't last, but at least for now, radioactive fallout wasn't falling on their heads. They could leave their masks in their bags for a little while longer.

He examined the sky. Lacy threads of cirrus clouds were building high in the west. Tufts of cumulus had started to form above the Santa

Cruz Mountains, drifting down into the valleys like fog from a dry ice machine. He grimaced. The predicted overcast was pretty goddamned late in coming, but at least it was on the way.

With clouds would come wind, almost certainly blowing down the length of the peninsula from the direction of San Francisco. The prevailing winds here were pretty consistent, when they blew at all. Smoke from the firestorm would come. It would give them invaluable cover from aerial surveillance, but they'd have to put on their masks and radiation gear. It would also send the refugees into an all-consuming panic as they tried to get away. The convoy of MRAPs would never get through them.

Unlike the military, Tom and his men wouldn't hesitate to clear a path through the evacuees with their bulldozers. The route across the hills to the sea was long, but with the cover of smoke and rain, they should be able to make it to the beach, where men with inflatable Zodiacs waited to ferry them to the boat. A quick dash down the coast, a transfer to ground vehicles, and all that remained would be to melt into the millions of refugees fleeing the Bay Area, until they could smuggle their captives and their precious equipment into Tijuana. From there they could bribe their way to their destination.

The radio crackled. "North gate vehicle barrier is down. Repeat, the north gate is clear."

Tom pressed the mic switch on his headset. "Clear the road and bring in the trucks. Get the south gate open and set the guard. Yellow Squad, keep both roads clear of refugees. Orange Squad, take down any airborne threats. I don't want any surprises."

The acknowledgements sounded in his ears.

He turned to Al Sanderson. "Get some crews on gate duty and take charge of the perimeter. I don't want anyone sneaking up on us."

"Will do." Al loped away.

Tom smiled grimly. The attack had gone almost perfectly, in spite of their having to use the mortars to clear the campus grounds. Sixty-three of his men were still in perfect health, including the other five Punisher operators. The same couldn't be said for the Guardsmen. Their bodies had been shredded by the mortar airbursts.

His ears were still ringing from the barrage. He'd much rather have taken the Guards out with the Punishers. The unmistakable sound of the mortars would have told everyone for miles that a military-scale attack was underway.

The mortars and their launchers had comprised most of the payload they'd gotten from the sub. The remainder had been the Punishers and about a third of the anti-aircraft missiles they'd been expecting. A good number of those had gone north with the contractors tasked with downing the anti-submarine planes.

One thing he *was* sure of: if anyone was coming to ST's rescue, they would not come by ground. Not through the million-strong horde of refugees headed south. He hoped there were enough Stingers left to give their airborne guests a very warm welcome.

The front end loader rumbled in through the north gate. Its steel bucket clanged against the asphalt and made a hideous scraping noise as it scooped debris off the road. It took only two minutes to clear a path to the front of the Pauling Building, but every passing second felt like an eternity.

Aidan's Hummer rolled in next. It came to a stop on the grassy shoulder of the main road.

Aidan ambled over to Tom, looking ridiculous in his oversized camouflage uniform, body armor and heavy boots. Two of the South African contractors trailed him, peering around suspiciously, submachine guns at the ready. Adam followed, looking far more credible in his soldier's kit.

"Well done," said Aidan. His eyes swiveled toward the Pauling Building. "Now all we have to do is get through this." He walked forward and rubbed a gloved hand against the flawless surface of the armor glass. "Adam? Look at it. It's almost frictionless. It came through the attack without a scratch."

Adam moved to the window and touched it lightly. "Amazing." He even sounded sincere for a change.

The mirror sheen of the window in front of him disappeared.

Tom jumped back and grabbed his pistol.

Beyond the thick glass stood a tall man in a baggy gray-green Army Combat Uniform. He had close-cropped, graying blond hair, a lantern jaw, and was built like a linebacker. The bulges in his uniform betrayed the presence of body armor underneath. He stared down at them, his mouth contorted into a savage scowl.

The man was alone in what was apparently the building's main lobby. Around him were comfortable-looking modern chairs and couches. The overhead lights were off. Behind the man, details of the interior were lost in darkness.

Aidan walked up to the window and waggled his fingers in sardonic greeting.

The tall man's unblinking eyes shifted to Aidan, but he made no move to respond.

Aidan turned and gestured toward the man behind the glass. "Tom, Adam, let me introduce John Shea, head of security. He will try to kill me today. Kindly make sure he doesn't."

A young man with dark, curly hair appeared out of the darkness behind Shea. The tall man turned to look at him. The newcomer wore jeans, sneakers and a blue T-shirt with the phrase "BACK OFF MAN, I'M A SCIENTIST" in bold white letters across the front. He held a small round can in one hand. He showed it to John Shea and said something, looking fearfully at Tom, Aidan and Adam as he did so. His voice didn't penetrate the thick glass.

"Stathis Sotiropoulos," murmured Aidan, his voice no longer quite so jolly.

Shea turned from the young man and looked out at Aidan. His scowl had been replaced by an evil smile.

Aidan crossed his arms. "Hmm."

Shea touched the microphone clipped to his shoulder loop and said something. The window became a mirror again.

"Who was that?" asked Adam before Tom could.

"A very inventive young man," said Aidan. He turned a grim eye on Tom. "He could make a great deal of trouble for us."

Adam growled, "Be sure to kill him when we get inside."

"No!" barked Aidan. "Adam, you really have no idea what they can do with this technology, do you? Even after the virus, and seeing this?" He gestured to the spotless armor glass. "That young man invented this. We need these people alive. If we can bend those minds to our purposes, everything they do will be to your master's benefit."

Adam frowned but said nothing.

Tom muttered, "They don't look like they want to go quietly."

Aidan shifted away from a drifting cloud of smoke. He coughed and said, "Then you'll really earn your pay today, my friend. I want everyone but the guards alive. No exceptions." He took a long drink from a canteen at his belt.

They all moved upwind as the smoke thickened around them. It was then that Tom realized that a cooling wind was beginning to pick up.

Cotton ball clouds drifted by, a few hundred feet up. More were coming in from the northwest.

Thank God, he thought. The cloud cover was finally taking shape. He touched his headset mic and said, "Yellow Leader, keep an eye out for smoke and fallout from the City. Give us a five-minute warning when it starts to get close."

"Roger that," replied Bobby Boykin.

The big tanker truck rumbled to a stop in front of the building. Big blue letters on the white tank read "FROSTY'S CRYO-GAS SERVICES." There was also a comical drawing of a shivering snowman. Men jumped down from the cab and began to unroll long white hoses toward the front of the building.

A pick-up truck with a tailgate lift rolled up behind the tanker. A pair of men jumped out, climbed into the back and dollied a pair of heavy gas tanks onto the lift, which lowered them gently to the ground. They rolled the tanks up to the left side of the building, then raced back to the truck to offload a portable generator.

Tom led the others to the street to let the breaching teams get started.

"Who do you think will get in first?" Aidan asked cheerfully. "My money's on the torch."

"I'd guess the liquid nitrogen," Tom said. "They can freeze a big area and then smash out each layer with the sledges. Rinse and repeat. Say, a thousand bucks?"

"Let's make it interesting. How about ten?"

Tom smiled. If they survived, ten grand wouldn't even qualify as pocket change. "You're on."

Adam snorted. "You are making bets at a time like this?"

"Adam, dear Adam," said Aidan, shaking his head in pity. "You need to learn about this thing we call *fun.*"

A voice said on the radio, "Red Leader, this is Green Leader. South gate's open."

He smiled and touched the mic switch. "Green Leader, roger. Assault teams, assemble in front of the building. Let's try to get someone on the roof. We need to disable those drones. Yellow Squad, if anyone's up there, take them out or at least keep their heads down."

The acknowledgements came in quick order.

Aidan crossed his arms. "Now all we have to do is wait."

Tom added, "And hope the military doesn't crash the party."

Aidan frowned. "Don't be a spoilsport. Listen." He swept his hands wide. Around the campus were the sounds of abject panic on a monumental scale: shouts and screams, car horns, racing engines, and gunshots near and far. "Tom. Seriously. Do you think they're really going to be able to get here through *that?*"

Tom shrugged. "Through it? No. *Over* it? That's a different story."

He kept a wary eye on the thickening clouds as the breaching teams began their work.

CHAPTER FIFTY-NINE

Moffett Field, Mountain View, California

Laurel Wynn stood outside the main command tent and let the two female Marines strap the body armor over her new dark brown and gray Marine Corps camo fatigues.

She shivered slightly. The high clouds had thickened enough to dim the late morning sun, and the breeze was strengthening. A low, brooding cloud deck was starting to pour over the tops of the Santa Cruz Mountains.

Major General Holland—or "Dutch," as his commander called him—had told her it would take half an hour to assemble the detail and refuel the Ospreys. It had taken closer to forty minutes. The fuel trucks were servicing the combat air patrols first. Now, finally, they were almost ready to go.

She watched a Super Hornet take off as the Marines finished their work. She didn't want to see that awful cloud towering over San Francisco anymore. Friends she'd known for many years in the San Francisco Field Office had undoubtedly perished today. "Cowboy" Bob Sheridan, for one. He'd been her mentor for her first posting after graduating from the Defense Analysis program down in Monterey. She couldn't even imagine what Robbie Holmes was going through.

The Marines helped her don her heavy Kevlar vest. It had pockets for an improbable number of gray ceramic plates. They should protect her torso from small-arms fire, even from modest armor-piercing rounds. It wasn't the kind of full-body coverage used by John Shea's men at ST, but it was very reassuring.

When the armorers finished, she'd put on about thirty pounds. She'd carried heavier packs when backpacking in the wilderness, but the weight distribution was different. Hopefully she'd live long enough to get used to it.

The armorer, whose name tag read MONTOYA, stuffed Laurel's vest pockets with loaded magazines for her 9mm Beretta. The other Marine handed her a sloshing canteen with a green nylon shoulder strap and a camouflaged bag large enough to carry a 35mm camera.

"What the hell is this for?" Laurel said, holding the bag uncertainly.

"Gas mask. Fallout," replied Montoya. "You don't want to breathe that shit in, ma'am." Then she pointed toward the apron next to Hangar Two.

The six gray MV-22 Ospreys were there, loading ramps extended, lines of Marines behind them waiting their turn to embark. One of the planes was already spinning up its pair of giant three-bladed prop-rotors. The giant up-tilted engine nacelles on the ends of the stubby wings looked about half the size of the Osprey's big troop compartment.

"Two minutes!" yelled the armorer.

Laurel shouted back, "I'll be there!"

Montoya handed Laurel a Kevlar helmet, jerked her chin at the other Marine and said, *"¡Ándale!"* The armorers pelted toward Hangar Two.

Laurel put on the helmet, strapped the gas mask bag to her belt, looped the canteen over her neck and ran—or *tried* to run, managing only a trudging quick-step—to the Mobile Command Post tent.

As before, it was a madhouse. Everyone was still shouting, but now there was a rough order to it that had been missing on her first arrival.

The folding chairs where Robbie Holmes and Andrew Seigart had been sitting were empty. She looked around and quickly found them. Seigart stood to one side of the tent, talking animatedly with the intelligence officer, Captain Deborah Morton. Holmes stood next to him, watching.

Laurel caught Robbie's eye.

He walked over to her. His naturally doleful expression was bleaker than ever.

"How is he doing?" she asked. She didn't need to ask how Robbie was. She put a hand on his arm and squeezed once.

"Better," he said, straining to be heard over the din. "Seems to be back in full control. Guess it was just the shock. What the hell are you doing in that getup?"

"Going to rescue Jack. Hopefully."

He shook his head. "No way, Laurel! You need to see this." He grabbed her wrist and pulled her to a spot where she could see the big projection screens in front of the soldiers pounding on laptops.

The screens were filled with video from hovering aircraft, showing the conditions of the freeways. The nearest showed a section of Highway 101, probably close to San Francisco Airport, judging by the big hangar-shaped buildings on the right side. Both sides of the freeway were jammed with vehicles. There wasn't even room to get by on the shoulders.

Cars and trucks spilled off the edge of the roadway, some moving, most abandoned. A few had crashed into the chain-link fence. Refugees climbed over the wrecks onto the airport grounds, perhaps hoping to get out by airplane. Most of them stuck to the freeway, picking their way through the tight maze of cars and trucks, climbing onto hoods if there wasn't enough room to get between them. She couldn't count how many collisions she saw.

As she watched, a gasoline tanker truck bloomed into a massive ball of flame so bright it washed out the image. The camera pulled back, the image darkening as its sensor compensated for the brightness. The flames engulfed both sides of the freeway. Burning figures stumbled away from the explosion. They didn't get far.

"Oh, my God," she said. She looked away.

Robbie shouted, "Every goddamned road on the Peninsula is like that, Laurel! You can't get there!"

She shook her head. "We're flying. General Holland has six Ospreys outside ready to go. I just came in to tell you and the Director where I'm going."

"Laurel."

She turned. It was Seigart. His craggy face was grim, but the light of intelligence shone from his eyes again.

"Thank God you're all right, sir."

He frowned. "There've been reports of heavy gunfire and explosions coming from the area of the ST campus. One of the reports described it as an artillery attack. They stopped about half an hour ago."

Her stomach clenched. "It's Aidan O'Keefe. He's trying to steal the HyperQUBE and take the scientists."

"Dorsey told me your theory after I... after I snapped out of it. I agree with you. He also told me they're going to bomb that area flat if Holland doesn't get them back." His eyes softened. "Don't go. We need you here. I need you here."

"I have to, sir. They need a guide. I know that facility inside and out. I'm the only one here who does."

He took a deep breath and expelled it slowly. "Goddammit it."

"Did anyone get any pictures of the campus?"

Seigart shook his heads. "The Global Hawks are still looking for missile subs in the Bay. I asked Dorsey, and he turned me down flat. There's no time to retask them before you get there, anyway. Clouds are moving in. All military air traffic's being routed around the area. You'll be going in with the first responders, Laurel."

"Can we get air support?" she asked. "We're going to need it."

Seigart raised his hands helplessly. "We know the bad guys have anti-aircraft missiles. They shot down the laser plane and the Orions. God knows what else they got off that damned sub. Most of the Army choppers got knocked out of the air by the bomb. Dorsey ordered an A-10 squadron in from Nellis but they're still about an hour out. The Marines from Pendleton won't be here until mid-afternoon. Airlift scheduling snafu."

"Holy Christ." It just keeps getting better and better.

"All of the fighters here were armed for air-to-air or anti-sub combat. Dorsey's not willing to commit them to ground support without forward air controllers on the scene. They're sending a couple along with you." Seigart shook his head. "No one expected a full-on ground war complete with artillery and missiles. An attempted break-in, yes. Maybe an assault on one of the convoys. They figured the Guard could handle whatever was thrown at them."

"I hope to God they did," said Laurel. Nothing would make her happier than to find that she'd called in the Marines for a false alarm.

Seigart's frown told her what he thought of that. "No one's been able to reach anyone at ST since the bomb went off."

Hope died before it could bloom.

He said, "Dorsey's been ordered to focus on finding any other subs and on search and rescue. He's commandeered every civilian helicopter in the Bay Area. There aren't any gunships to spare."

"Did we get anyone down to the compound in Morgan Hill?"

"State Police managed to get a SWAT team in. It was deserted, but there were ammo crates all over the place."

Laurel shook her head. "It was a long shot, anyway."

A male voice roared from the front of the tent, "AGENT WYNN! WE ARE LEAVING!"

Seigart drew her into a quick hug. "Keep your head down. Be careful."

She squeezed him back, fighting tears. She nodded to Robbie, and then jogged heavily to the exit.

Two of the Ospreys had already taken off. A third was revving up, blasting twin tornadoes of broiling, kerosene-rich air behind it as its huge prop-rotors hauled it toward the runway. The heat was astonishing even from a hundred yards away.

A Marine corporal with a dark green flight helmet ran in front of her, urging her to move faster with an exaggerated scooping wave. He led her to the closest Osprey. She was just beginning to get the hang of running in the heavy vest when she reached it.

"Get on, get on!" the Marine shouted, pushing her past a heavy machine gun swivel-mounted on one side of the ramp.

Weirdly, her eyes fastened on the ribbed plastic tube protruding from the bottom of the gun. It projected out past the end of the ramp—clearly designed to catch the brass ejected by the gun and funnel it outside.

The darkened troop compartment was anything but pretty. Hoses, ducts, and bundles of cables ran from one end of the low ceiling to the other. Morning light struggled in through a pair of side windows halfway down the length of the compartment, and through a smaller window in the closed side door next to the cockpit.

There were maybe twenty or so hulking Marines already jammed into the narrow seats along the walls. They wore flight helmets instead of camouflaged Kevlar brain buckets. Their M4 carbines were between their legs, stocks resting on the black composite floor. Their faces betrayed their opinion of the cramped space. It looked a lot bigger from the outside.

The corporal pushed her through the packed compartment to one of two empty seats closest to the cockpit. To her left was a huge switch panel; across from her was the closed side door.

The corporal handed her a small oxygen bottle and a big green flight helmet. He grabbed her gas mask bag and shoved it into her lap. He strapped her into the jump seat, fastening the shoulder straps to an almost painful tightness. He showed her the quick release and shouted instructions to her: what to do in case there was a hard landing or if they ditched in the water. Most of what he said was lost in the whining roar of the revved-up engines. *Water landing? What water?* she wondered dazedly.

She managed to put her combat helmet under her seat and squeezed her head into the flight helmet. The corporal cinched her chin strap tight and pressed something on the side of her helmet. The engine sounds from outside dropped to a tolerable level. *Noise-canceling headphones,* she guessed.

The corporal retreated to the rear of the Osprey, attached a safety line dangling from the back of his harness to a metal loop in the floor, and took a seat on the still-lowered ramp. He swiveled the machine gun into position in front of him and pulled the charging handle.

The other Marines looked at her, conspicuously taking note of her lack of rank insignia.

"I'm your guide!" she shouted, not knowing if her voice would carry more than a few feet in this din.

"You don't have to yell," drawled another Marine as he shoved past the seated men. His conversational voice was clear in her headphones. It was Major General Holland.

The squat, rugged man dropped into the last empty seat across from her. He already had his flight helmet on. He pulled the waist belt tight. His broad shoulders pushed against the Marine seated next to him. He turned toward the others and said, "You men! Listen up. This is Senior Special Agent Wynn. FBI. She knows the ground and she knows the players. You keep her alive at all costs. Got me?"

"Aye aye, sir!" chorused the Marines.

Her heart skipped a few beats. The reality of impending combat finally came home, and hard. She clutched her hands together to keep them from shaking.

The thumping of the prop-rotors beat against her helmet, trying hard to get in. The Osprey lurched, rolled, turned, and surged forward. The engines thundered. A few seconds later the concrete of the runway dropped away. They banked sharply almost as soon as they were airborne. Hangar Two passed behind them as they turned, its giant Red Cross flag rippling in the late morning breeze.

Laurel's stomach did a slow barrel roll.

She felt a sharp tap on her knee.

She looked at General Holland.

"Keep your eyes inside!" he said. "It's easier that way. Now, tell us what to expect."

"Yes, sir!" she replied, swallowing her nausea. "I don't have any new intel. Director Seigart said there hasn't been any contact with ST or the

National Guards since the bomb went off." Her eyes strayed to the window to the left of the General's head. She instantly wished they hadn't.

They were a couple of hundred feet above Highway 101. The freeway was a crush of intact and broken vehicles and running people: a mob scene of animal panic that stretched the length of the peninsula, as far as the eye could see.

Far beyond was the maelstrom that had once been San Francisco.

The bomb's mushroom cloud had drifted far to the east, but now a massive column of oil-black smoke boiled up from the place where San Francisco had been. It looked like photos of the Mount Saint Helens volcanic explosion. She'd seen them in one of her dad's old *National Geographic* magazines.

The cloud had fanned out in every direction, but it looked like it was starting to come their way.

Laurel swallowed hard and looked back at the General. "Seigart told me the enemy has anti-aircraft missiles." Her tongue felt thick in her mouth.

"Yep," said Holland, apparently unperturbed.

"Where are we landing?"

"Depends. The lead Thunder Chicken is gonna do a low pass across the campus, take some photos. Then we'll see what we'll see. Excuse me." His Oklahoma drawl rendered *photos* as two distinct words: *pho toes.* He looked away from her and pressed something on the side of his helmet. His mouth moved, but she could no longer hear him.

They call these planes Thunder Chickens? An involuntary smile ghosted across her lips. She looked at the other Marines. They were either just as relaxed as Dutch Holland, or they were doing a good imitation of it. She couldn't imagine how. She was scared to death.

The cityscape of Silicon Valley slid behind them as they neared the hills. The sunlight dimmed as they flew through a low cloud, then brightened as they emerged. She glanced out the small window across from her. They flew into clouds again, and the landscape was replaced by a field of uniform gray. Water droplets raced in diagonal tracks across the outside of the window. They flew in cloudy dimness for an endless minute, maneuvering from time to time. Her nausea began to abate.

Bright light flooded in through the side window. She narrowed her eyelids against the sudden brightness. The white top of a low cloud streamed by.

Then the Osprey made a violent dive. A stream of flares trailing behind them filled the troop compartment with a fierce white light.

Laurel's stomach jumped into her throat. The oxygen bottle the corporal had given her slipped out of her grasp. It banged against the ceiling before it sailed out through the open ramp door.

She clutched her shoulder straps with both hands and clamped her jaws on the scream that tried to tear loose from her chest.

The Osprey jerked from side to side, then banked hard.

A cracking BOOM stabbed through the roar of wind and engines.

Light beamed in through countless new holes in the rear half of the compartment.

At the same instant, something banged hard against the side of her helmet. White-hot pain speared through her left shoulder.

Her scream joined a chorus.

The plane creaked and shuddered.

A voice in her earphones blared over the cries of pain. *"Hard landing! Prepare for hard landing!"*

The Osprey tilted and spun. The engines shrieked.

The corporal at the machine gun flew upward, tethered by his restraining strap, silhouetted against a cyclone of blue and white.

The Osprey leveled out.

The corporal smashed head-first against the ramp.

Laurel saw trees behind him.

Then there was noise and chaos.

Her helmet whipped back against the unyielding wall of the compartment.

All went black.

CHAPTER SIXTY

Struve Technologies Coyote Hill Campus, Palo Alto, California

Ed Black said something, but Jack didn't register it.

Barely a word had been spoken since the explosions had stopped outside. After an all-too brief silence, a distant *CRACK* echoed through the second-floor halls. The relentless sound repeated about twice a minute.

Jack stared at his hands. This was supposed to be a day of triumph, the peak of his professional career—and if his new tests passed, certain proof of his Grand Unified Theory. Now he wondered if he or anyone else in this building would make it to nightfall alive.

He'd been trying to figure out a way out of this mess, but his thoughts flowed with all the speed of molasses down a glacier. He kept coming up with the same useless ideas again and again. *Get outside. Run. Run now. Outside. Run and never stop.* But running was useless. There were dozens of armed men out there. They'd be caught. They'd be taken. They'd never see home again.

Aidan would have them.

The psychopath wouldn't stop until they gave him everything he wanted, and more.

Ed spoke again.

Jack looked up. "What?"

"It passed."

"Passed what?"

"The tests, Jack," Ed said softly. "All of them. Including the new ones. The HyperQUBE works. It proves your theory."

Jack straightened from his slumped position behind the three low screens and glanced around.

Everyone in Mission Control was looking at him. Their faces were tight with barely controlled panic.

"Yay," he croaked, utterly without enthusiasm.

"What now, boss?" asked Hank Drummond, his voice cracking.

Jack drew his hands down his face, rubbed his eyes, and stifled a monstrously inappropriate yawn. His brain began a slow struggle back to functionality. He looked at Deepthi. "Did the strain gauges show any irregularities during cool down? Any variations in contraction velocity? Anything indicating a crack or an assembly error?"

The ZMPC engineer looked at her screens for a moment. "Nothing," she said shortly. "No significant variations." She beckoned Cat Moreno over to the console.

The slender cryo specialist reviewed the data on the screen and looked up, nodding. "Better than QUBE Delta at this point. It looks totally solid."

"Then start the rapid shutdown sequence. Bring it out of deep freeze, now."

"Jack!" barked Ben Holcombe.

"We can't leave it in the cryo facility. We're out of time."

Chao-Xing said, "Can the—" She fumbled for a term. "Can *they* really get in?" The Taiwanese post-doc looked much younger than her twenty-six years.

"Assume they can. Get started, Deepthi. Do it. I'll check with John. See how much time we have."

Jack bounded down the stairs, galvanized into action.

The cracking sound was louder outside Mission Control. Alex Southall trailed behind him as he leaped down the stairs to the first floor lobby.

John Shea was there. He stood with his arms crossed, peering out through the darkened armor glass.

The bad guys were trying to get in.

The massive emergency barrier still held, but a ragged, oblong crater about six feet tall and eight wide had been dug into the front lobby armor glass about twenty feet to the right of the doorway. A man wearing an aluminized hood, jacket, pants and gloves held a heavy white hose that spilled boiling liquid across the still-intact surface of the window.

Jack traced the hose back to a big white tanker truck bearing the label FROSTY'S CRYO-GAS SERVICES. In small black letters under the company name was written NITROGEN, REFRIGERATED LIQUID.

"Uh oh," said Jack.

Then the devastation beyond the window finally registered in his depression-fogged consciousness.

Every building was on fire, sending plumes of black smoke into the partly cloudy sky. Every tree that wasn't simply missing had been stripped of leaves and limbs. Twisted metal, splintered wood, shredded foliage and shattered, unidentifiable debris littered the ground. Some of it was dark, red, and glistening.

"Holy *fuck!*" he said, aghast.

John turned and looked at him. "Everyone who was outside is dead or missing." His monotone roughened. "At least a hundred and twenty-three people."

"Jesus wept," Jack said. Numbness closed in around him again. He couldn't think of anything else to say.

He watched the man with the hose stop the flow of liquid nitrogen and step back.

Another man dressed in similar gear strode forward. He carried a heavy-looking tool consisting of a red, wedge-shaped metal head at the end of a long black handle.

Splitting maul, Jack's mind dredged up out of some catalog he'd seen once.

The man swung the maul at the armor glass.

CRACK.

A layer of glass inside the ragged crater turned white. Then it splintered and spalled away, falling to the ground in glittering fragments, like flakes of mica. The glass inside the crater was clear again.

"Fuck me," breathed Jack. "It gets brittle at low temperatures."

John sighed. "We never thought anyone would be able to drive a liquid nitrogen tanker right up to the side of the building."

Two more men with push brooms moved forward to sweep the pulverized armor glass away. Some of it drifted into the air, glittering like snowflakes in a winter breeze.

John smiled grimly. "They'll probably get lung cancer, breathing that stuff in. I sure as hell ain't gonna tell 'em."

The man with the hose moved forward and began to shower the glass wall with frothing liquid again.

"They tried a torch first," said John, pointing at a section of window twenty feet down the wide hallway that ran inside the front wall of the building.

There was a small scarred patch in the otherwise flawless glass, about four feet from the ground, surrounded by an odd, rainbow-hued discoloration. Two pairs of booted feet protruded from a scavenged fire blanket on the ground nearby.

John said, "The first layer of impact gel caught fire and sprayed out the hole. Fried those motherfuckers but good. The blond guy over there shot them. Cold as ice, that one. Didn't even bat an eyelash."

CRACK.

Jack fought a surge of nausea for a long moment. Eventually he found his voice. "How long will it take them to get through the glass?"

"Half an hour. Maybe more, maybe less. Assuming they don't run out of liquid nitrogen. They're getting faster, but the emergency barrier is twice as thick as the outer layer."

"God damn it," snarled Jack. "Can't we do something about it? Drop some grenades on them or something!"

"There's not enough cover near the front edge of the roof. They have at least two snipers out there, maybe more. One of 'em's on top of Coyote Hill. We can't get close enough. Alex tried. Nearly didn't make it back."

"Shit. We can't use the drones?"

"Too risky. Stathis would have to build a new release mechanism to pull the pin. There's not enough time. And we need the drones to keep tabs on those bastards."

CRACK.

Jack flinched away from the sound. Recovering, he caught sight of Aidan O'Keefe, standing behind the men working on the glass.

Next to O'Keefe were two other men: the slender blond man John Shea had mentioned, and a fit-looking Asian. All of them wore combat uniforms. The blond man was expressionless. The Asian man looked annoyed.

Aidan smiled. He laughed.

Jack ran up to the window. He slapped his hands uselessly against it. "You goddamned maniac! I'll fucking kill you!"

"He can't see you," John said mildly. "The glass is mirrored. For now, anyway. Don't know how long *that* will last."

Jack stepped back, his palms stinging. "Jesus Christ."

John said, "Good thing they don't have RPGs. Or maybe they do, but they're not too keen on setting this building on fire with us in it. Or you scientists, rather." He smiled at Jack crookedly. "I can guess what they have in mind for the rest of us."

CRACK.

Outside, a man with a big rifle-shaped grappling hook launcher strode forward. A helper brought a long coil of bright orange rope and threaded its end into the hook. The first man stood back, aimed high, and fired.

The rope uncoiled rapidly. The man with the launcher smiled. His helper pulled hard on the rope, then stumbled backward. The rope slithered back down. The helper picked up the end and showed it to the guy with the launcher. The end of the rope looked like it had been cut by a scalpel.

Jack looked at John.

The former Marine shrugged. "Guess Aidan didn't know about the rope cutters on the eaves. We installed those two months ago. Q3-graphane blades. They're not getting up that way."

CRACK.

They watched as the grappling hook crew tried again, with the same result.

"What are we going to do?" asked Alex Southall in a leaden voice.

Jack looked at his watch. Barely an hour and a half had elapsed since San Francisco died. He shot a look at John. "How many of your team are left?"

"Six. Seven if you include me. Two surveillance operators, checked out on pistols but without body armor. There's a dozen or so wounded Guardsmen in the auditorium. Two corpsmen. Blaise and the two Palo Alto cops. And you scientists." He counted silently, his lips moving. "Thirty-five people, all told, and only seven serious combat vets."

Jack gaped at him. "That's it?"

"Yep."

"Holy shit." Jack sat down heavily in one of the lobby's soft chairs. "Any chance that the convoy will get here?"

John snorted. "Page Mill is a war zone. The view from the roof cameras is on the screens in the surveillance room. Go look if you want. Probably every road in the Bay Area is like that. Nobody's getting through on the ground. Not in time. They're probably using the MRAPs for evacuation now, anyway."

CRACK.

"Any way to get to anyone on the radio?"

John shook his head. "We tried. Every goddamned frequency is jammed. Every HAM in the country is talking. You can't even pick up local radio stations. Power went out when the bomb went off. Probably EMP fried the transmission lines. Even the satellite phone is on the fritz. They might be using jammers on us. We are on our own."

Alex said, "We can barricade inside the Black Box."

"They can cut through the wall with the torch."

Jack said, "Are there any safe rooms, like in the dorm?"

John's face was bleak. "We thought the whole building *was* a safe room."

"Can we hide someplace?"

"It's a big building, but we couldn't stay hidden forever, and Aidan knows every inch of it."

"We just need to hold out until Laurel gets here."

John didn't reply.

Jack knew what the security chief was thinking. Laurel might be dead or injured. She might not be able to convince anyone else to come. Even if she did, God only knew how long it would take them to get here, and what kind of evil reception Aidan O'Keefe had waiting them. After a long moment he grated, "Did the Greek talk with you yet?"

"Yeah. He has a few things that will keep them busy for a while. Slow 'em down getting to the upper floors, anyway."

CRACK.

Jack snarled, "I don't want them busy. I want them dead." He stared at Aidan O'Keefe, still laughing with his friends. "Especially him."

Alex growled, "Works for me."

John said, "Then let's go talk with the Elves."

Jack took a long, lingering look at Aidan O'Keefe. He'd killed Emily and countless others just to take what she had built. Nothing would please Jack more than to choke the life out of him, but he'd settle for watching him die from a distance.

He heaved himself to his feet, about to follow John.

At that instant, a spark of an idea began to glow in a dark crevice of his subconsciousness.

He froze, staring out the ever-weakening window at Aidan O'Keefe, thinking hard.

A plan began to coalesce in his mind.

CRACK.

"Boss?" prompted Alex Southall.

"Go on up," said Jack distractedly. "I need to think."

"Roger that," said Alex. He followed John up the fire stairs.

Jack's mind churned. So many things could go wrong. He had to chart a course between the infinite number of paths that led to failure to find the one that could lead to success. And he had to face the possibility that Laurel wasn't coming.

Aidan O'Keefe couldn't be allowed to get his hands on the QUBEs.

And success didn't necessarily mean survival.

Jack watched the man hit the window with the splitting maul four more times. He was at least half an inch into the fifteen-inch emergency barrier already.

Fourteen and a half to go.

CRACK.

Jack turned and ran up the stairs, growling with fury.

Santa had to find a few lumps of coal for some very bad kids.

CHAPTER SIXTY-ONE

Los Altos Hills, California

When Laurel came to, she was being dragged by the arms, and it *hurt*.

Her left shoulder was on fire. A tiny man with a big hammer smacked the back of her head with every heartbeat. Her neck was bent back by the weight of her helmet. Her eyes were open, but she would never remember what she saw in those first terrible moments of consciousness.

She was vaguely aware of a shrill keening in her ears.

"Put her down, put her down!" said a young male. His voice had an unmistakable African-American inflection.

She felt herself being lowered onto grass. The pressure came off her shoulder. The keening faded. She realized belatedly that she'd been its source. She nearly wept with relief.

Another sound still filled the air, a weird, high-pitched warbling, glissandoing up and down the scale. She couldn't make sense of it.

She focused on a black face with wide, anxious eyes. Behind his head was a crazed background of white, blue, black and gray. "You okay, ma'am? Where you hurt?"

"Arm," she croaked. "Left shoulder."

She screamed again as the injury was probed by iron-hard fingers. "Flesh wound, through and through," her rescuer said. "Bone's intact. Didn't go through the joint. Hang on, ma'am! I'll be back!"

Then he disappeared.

She lay on the grass for a long moment, staring into what she finally realized was a cloudy sky. She lifted her head, then lowered it with a groan when her shoulder responded with a stab of white-hot agony.

She'd recovered enough of her faculties to understand where she was. She lay in a squarish field surrounded by trees. The dry, patchy grass around her was littered with chunks of metal, mangled tree branches, and bodies.

The weird, unidentifiable rising and falling sound resolved itself into screams. The screams of men.

She scissored her legs, pushing herself onto her right side, ignoring the fire in her left shoulder, the uncomfortable lump of her pistol under her hip, and the hammer still pounding the back of her head.

She had to see.

Her Osprey had smashed through the trees on the other side of the small field, the huge prop-rotors turning branches into confetti. The plane's nose and fuselage had dug a trench into the field. A herringbone pattern of progressively deeper gouges ran alongside it, presumably scooped out by the tips of the rotors. The trench passed beyond her feet and out of sight.

She lowered herself onto her back. She couldn't roll onto her left side because of her shoulder, not to mention the bulky gas mask bag at her waist. Instead she rolled her helmeted head to the left. She instantly wished that she hadn't.

The left—*port*, her father's voice whispered in her head—the *port* wing of the Osprey had been sheared off close to the root. The engine nacelle and the remains of the wing had cartwheeled through a row of stumpy, dry-looking trees, down a low embankment, and into a small, yellow, metal-roofed building a few hundred feet beyond.

There were faded white stripes painted on the asphalt between the trees and the distant, burning building. The pattern jogged an old memory. It was a hopscotch square.

There were chalk lines on the grassy field beneath her. Her mind made the connection then. This was a playing field. They'd crashed next to a school. The engine had set fire to a temporary classroom.

"Oh, Christ," she whispered. She craned her head, listening. She heard distant shouting, adult wails of grief, the mechanical howls of car horns and revving engines. Even a few gunshots. Most of the sounds were a long way off, and none of them sounded like kids. She prayed they'd all been evacuated to... to somewhere else.

Is anywhere safe? she wondered dizzily. The vast black cloud filling the northern sky didn't bode well for it. The Bay Area was overgrown with parched vegetation after a wet winter. The firestorm might march all the way down the Peninsula and beyond.

She tried to put the burning school building out of her mind. She couldn't do anything about it anyway. She looked around and tried to understand her situation.

The ruined Osprey now faced the way it had come. Black smoke poured from the starboard engine nacelle. Its giant prop-rotor blades had been snapped off. Two of them were nowhere to be seen. The third lay on the ground next to the burning engine. There was less fire than she'd have expected, but God only knew how long that would last.

The plane's bulbous nose had been mashed in. The broad, curved cockpit windows were missing, apparently popped out by the force of the impact. The rear half of the troop compartment was peppered with countless holes. Some were big enough to put her fist through.

The ground between her and the wreck was littered with blood-stained, uniformed bodies. Most were motionless. Some writhed and screamed.

A few Marines were still moving. They shouted as they dove back into the burning plane through the still-extended loading ramp.

Two of them dragged the limp body of Major General Everett "Dutch" Holland out. They hustled him toward Laurel and set him down on the grass. She recognized the African-American NCO who'd checked her shoulder wound. He said, "He's out cold, but I think he'll be okay." The soldiers ran back to the wreckage.

There was a loud popping sound, followed by a liquid hiss and a frenzy of shouting. She looked up. The small engine fire had become a conflagration. The rescuers pelted back out of the fuselage with seconds to spare.

She put her head down and shielded her face from the furnace-like heat as the two soldiers dragged the few survivors further away from the wreckage. Eventually they came for her.

The black Marine wasn't a Marine. A silver caduceus—a winged staff twined by a pair of serpents—was pinned above the U.S. NAVY patch on his left breast. It marked him as a corpsman. His camo uniform was bluer than the dark mottled colors of the Marine's urban MARPAT cloth. His insignia had three stripes on it, but she'd never really understood Navy enlisted ranks. All she knew is that they didn't call them sergeants. His name tag read COLLINS.

"Help me stand up," she said.

The corpsman shook his head. "No way, ma'am! You might have a concussion." He and a red-faced corporal named Thursby picked her up as gently as they could and carried her further from the wreck. She clenched her jaw to contain a howl of pain.

Another Osprey thundered by overhead, just feet above the trees.

The two men flinched away from the sound, almost dropping her.

Her shoulder blazed as Thursby jostled it. The scream finally got out, but she managed to throttle it down to a screeching moan.

"I'm sorry, ma'am," Thursby panted. His accent was soft and Southern.

They put her down next to the trees at the far end of the field. The *whomp-whomp-whomp* of the Osprey's prop-rotors was getting louder. It was coming back.

Collins shouted, "Don't you move, ma'am! We'll be back ASAP!" He and Thursby disappeared.

The Osprey passed overhead, props tilted skyward, moving low and slow. The hot, fuel-rich downwash battered her with hurricane force. She threw her hand across her face.

Mercifully, the tilt-rotor plane moved away. It set down on the far side of the field, upwind of the smoke from the crash. Marines stormed out, M4s at the ready. The grass under the engines caught fire before the prop-rotors began to spin down, but it wasn't quite dry enough to spread.

The additional manpower made short work of moving the remaining survivors away from the spreading flames. She lay back, tried not to move, and listened helplessly to the moans and shrieks until they were drowned out by the sound of another Osprey landing somewhere nearby. Collins and another corpsman dealt with the injuries as best they could.

"Anti-aircraft missile," someone said. His voice had an Oklahoma twang.

She twisted her head gingerly to her right.

General Dutch Holland was sitting up, prodding a knot on his forehead the size of a robin's egg. "Could've been worse," he growled, looking around. "Missile must've had a proximity fuze. Flares drew it off but it still exploded." He shook his head took a deep breath. "How's the shoulder?"

"Not great," she said through gritted teeth.

Holland called one of the new arrivals over, a senior sergeant, judging by the six stripes on his insignia badge. Soon he and the sergeant were deep in a hushed conversation.

Laurel lay back again and waited for Collins to return, praying that the General wouldn't call off the mission and just bomb the campus into oblivion.

The corpsman finally arrived, carrying a big backpack full of medical supplies. He checked her neck carefully before helping her remove her flight helmet. Then he cut away her bloody left sleeve with an angled pair of scissors. She sucked in her breath when he prodded the injury again, and felt blood trickling as the wound was reopened. Three needle-pricks high on her shoulder gave rise to blessed numbness. She let out a huge sigh of relief. "Oh, my God. Thanks."

"You hurt anywhere else, ma'am?" asked Collins.

"Got bonked in the head. Other than that, no." Even the hammering in the back of her head was beginning to subside. "I could use some aspirin."

"Can you sit? I gotta stitch this up."

She pushed herself upright with her right hand, struggling against the dead weight of her body armor vest, and let him do his work. All she could feel was an occasional tug as he looped the sutures through the skin. He peppered her with questions about her head, whether she felt dizzy or sick to her stomach, and what she remembered after coming to.

"Don't think you have a concussion," he said as he taped a dressing over the wound. "You lucked out, ma'am. This is gonna hurt like a sumbitch when the local wears off, but you should be able to walk. I can give you some codeine to take the edge off. You allergic?"

"No."

He handed her a pair of big yellow tablets in a plastic wrapper. "These are the extra strength kind. I'll get you a sling. Back in a minute." He picked up his bag and left at the run.

General Holland growled, "Lucky you." He lay flat on the ground again, shielding his eyes from the cloud-filtered sunlight. The sergeant he'd been talking to had disappeared. He said, "Double vision. Concussion for sure. I'm gonna have to wait for medevac." Then he turned on his side and retched—facing away from Laurel, fortunately.

Her own stomach heaved, but she managed to control it. The sound of vomiting had always made her want to hurl, too.

Holland gasped, wiped his mouth and lay flat again. "Top?" he called weakly.

The senior sergeant came at a run. He was a tall, rangy man in his late thirties. His name tag read AMES. The many stripes on his collar insignia surrounded a small silver diamond. His brown hair was salted with gray, and his weathered skin was tanned so dark it looked like the bark of an oak tree. His ropy neck was white with scars, including a spectacular one that ran from the base of his left ear halfway to his Adam's apple.

He knelt next to the general. "Here, sir." His voice was a bone-saw rasp.

"Agent Wynn, this is First Sergeant Ames. Call him Top."

Laurel exchanged nods with the gnarled veteran.

"Give her the situation," growled Holland. He put his forearm across his eyes as he listened to Ames' depressing news.

Four of the six Ospreys had been shot down. There was no chance of survivors from the other three. Both pilots of Laurel's Osprey were dead, as were twelve of the twenty-four passengers. Two of the twelve survivors were in critical condition. Five were still mission-capable.

Ames' Osprey had flown point, reconnoitering the ST campus at low altitude. The whole work site was devastated, probably by mortars. Bodies and parts of bodies were everywhere. Every building was shattered or ablaze but one: a big four-story structure that looked untouched.

The Pauling Building, Laurel thought. Relief gusted through her like a cool spring breeze. She expelled the breath she hadn't known she was holding. Jack and his team had been in the Pauling Building when she left the campus. If they had stayed inside, they were probably safe. Probably.

Ames continued his report. The few people they'd glimpsed on the broken campus grounds had been wearing the outdated gray, brown and green camo fatigues known as Battle Dress Uniforms, commonly available on the open market, and not well suited to urban combat. There was no sign of the ACU-clad National Guard troops.

Holland's mouth tightened at this news, but he just nodded to Ames to finish.

Ames' Osprey had taken small arms fire from the ground and had returned it from the tail-mounted machine gun. A missile had been launched but this time the flares drew it off. No one aboard had been injured. They'd contacted the other surviving plane, doubled back and spotted the crashed Osprey on the playing field. "Thank God you made it," Ames said. "Your pilots sure had the right stuff, sir."

"Jesus Harold Christ on a pogo stick," growled Holland. "Cluster-fucked before we even get started."

Laurel felt like she was about to faint. More than a hundred National Guardsmen at the campus were dead or out of commission, and four of the six Ospreys were down, too. Her muzzy brain struggled with the mental math. *Fifty-three Marines are left. It should be enough—but only if our luck changes.* She cleared her throat. "General—"

He held up his hand to cut her off. "Top, how far are we from the campus?"

The sergeant squinted thoughtfully. "Maybe three klicks. Lots of streets between here and there, though. About a zillion panicky civilians all over those roads. Gonna be a bitch."

Holland looked at Laurel. "Are you okay to go with them?"

"Yes, sir." The pounding in her head had settled down to a regular headache. As long as the local anesthetic held out, she'd be okay. She unwrapped one of the yellow horse pills Collins had given her and dry-swallowed it, remembering too late the canteen at her waist.

Holland said, "Top. Did you see where those missiles came from?"

"Some of 'em, sir. Hilltop west-northwest of here. Saw some smoke trails. There might be three or four missile squads out there. Probably the same crews who mortared the campus."

"There was a JTAC in your stick, right?"

"Yes, sir. We got two Raven crews, too."

"Good man. I'm in no shape to go. You're in command, Top. Take Agent Wynn and every able-bodied Marine and get the job done. Leave as soon as that corpsman gets the wounded stabilized. Take him with you. You'll probably need him more than we will. And find out when those A-10s are gonna get here, goddammit!" Holland lifted himself up long enough to take a swig from his canteen. He spat the water out and groaned as he lay down again. "Lord, why didn't I listen to my mama? She told me to be a dentist."

The wiry sergeant deadpanned, "Cuz you'd rather stick your finger in the enemy's eye than put it in somebody's stinking wet mouth all day?"

Holland managed a pained smile. "That must be it. Okay, you have your orders. Turn to."

"Aye aye, sir," Ames said. He stood, saluted and held out a hand to Laurel. He pulled her upright effortlessly. His hands felt like leather over steel cables. He looked at her with narrowed eyes. "You up for this?"

"I have to be." The wound in her left shoulder was a distant throbbing ache. Her head ached abominably, but she'd lived through migraines that were worse. When and if the codeine took effect, she should be okay. She hoped.

"All right." He whistled and gathered his troops.

She looked around for her combat helmet. Then she remembered that she'd stowed it under her jump seat in the Osprey. It was probably a puddle of melted plastic by now. Her bulky flight helmet wouldn't be much protection against bullets, and it might restrict her vision or movements. Regretfully, she decided to leave it on the grass. *Well, at least I'll be cooler.*

Two of the Marines were lightly armed and wore big square backpacks. Everyone aside from them and the two radio operators had smaller field packs.

A dozen of the bigger men cradled big machine guns with bipod arms folded forward along the long muzzle. Three others had long, sinister black rifles slung from their shoulders.

The rest carried the usual M4 carbines, many equipped with blunt grenade launcher tubes under the barrels. They also had ammo belts, grenades, gas mask bags, canteens and expressions running the gamut from angry to murderous.

Ames briefed them, speaking in choppy sentences as spare and lean as he was. Then he said something in an undertone to one of the radio operators, who nodded and busied himself with his pack-mounted transmitter.

Laurel fought with impatience. Every passing second brought the bad guys closer to Jack. She jumped as Navy medic Collins cleared his throat. He helped her put on a sling jury-rigged from camouflage-patterned cloth.

"Thanks," she said.

He nodded to her as he shouldered his pack. "You let me know if you get dizzy or have problems walking, okay?"

"Sure." She rested her right hand on her holstered 9mm. She wouldn't be doing any Krav Maga for a while, but at least she hadn't lost the use of her gun arm.

The radio operator shouted, "Top! I got General Dorsey!"

Ames pulled the radio man aside and took the proffered radio handset.

She was too far away to hear either side of the brief conversation.

Ames gave the radio operator the handset. "Listen up!" he bellowed. "The big boss cleared the revised mission. Air cover's inbound, about forty-five minutes out. Good to go?"

"Oorah!" his men bellowed.

Ames' eyes flicked to Laurel.

She nodded.

"Outstanding!" he shouted. "Let's move!"

They moved.

CHAPTER SIXTY-TWO

Struve Technologies Coyote Hill Campus, Palo Alto, California

John Shea stared at the three disassembled drones on the black workbench.

The Greek had commandeered an empty fourth floor lab. He'd wanted to get the drones from the roof himself but John had vetoed that idea. He wasn't about to risk Stathis Sotiropoulos going outside. Instead, he sent Alex Southall and Sy Hamilton.

The two former SEALS had retrieved the three gray hexacopter drones from their rooftop enclosures. Now they and Martín Garza were busily taking apart the cases of three new-looking PC laptops. The screwdrivers looked absurdly tiny in their thick-fingered hands.

A wad of reddened gauze was taped high on Sy Hamilton's left cheek. He'd narrowly missed getting hit by a sniper's bullet. Chips of concrete from the impact on the low wall would have taken out an eye if he hadn't been wearing protective gear.

All of the combatants were ready to rock: Santa's Special helmets and combat visors on, concussion and fragmentation grenades scavenged from the injured Guardsmen on their belts, pouches filled with extra magazines strapped across their chests, gas masks and canteens in easy reach.

"How long?" asked John.

"Twenty, thirty minutes, maybe," grunted the Greek. He wiped sweat from his forehead before he gingerly removed the motherboard from a drone's case. "I gotta take the transmitters out of these—" He gestured at the laptops the SEALs were disassembling. "—and wire 'em into the drones and hook up the booster antennas. Then I gotta install the drivers and config the software."

"You can't go any faster?"

"Not if you want it to work."

"How much extra range will we get?"

"Maybe a mile. Maybe two. But they won't stay in the air as long. These laptop wifi cards take more juice."

"Christ," John said under his breath.

The Greek looked up, eyes flashing. "You know, if I hadn't built these drones in the first place we'd be talking hours. Hard stuff takes time! This isn't some goddamned episode of *24*, you know. I can't just tell Chloe to open a fucking socket!"

John raised a placating hand. "Sorry, Stathis. I'll try to buy you as much time as I can. Alex, you and Sy get to the second floor and finish up there as soon as he's done with you. We got maybe five minutes before those bastards get through the armor glass. Martín, you stay here and lend a hand if Stathis needs it." He put a hand on the Greek's shoulder. "What you and Amber did for us downstairs will slow them down. A lot. Hopefully enough."

The Greek looked up at him, his face growing pale. "Jesus," he said. His protuberant Adam's apple betrayed his gulp. "I'll go faster."

John gave him an approving nod and left.

The personnel elevators were locked at sub-basement level 3, where most of the scientists, the wounded Guardsmen and their corpsmen, the two Palo Alto cops and that goddamned traitor Blaise Thierry were hiding. Armando Diego and Guy Harris were down there with them, both to keep them calm and act as their last line of defense, if it should come to that.

They should all be safe, if Jack's plan went by the numbers. Even if the bad guys pried open the elevator doors and rappelled down the shaft, they'd still have to get through the top of the elevator, which had been treated with the last of the FQG—what Jack called "Santa's Magic Window Spray." They'd need a diamond drill to get through now. There were a few other surprises awaiting them as well, courtesy of Amber D'Agostino and the Greek.

John checked the main freight elevator on Main Street, and then the backup elevator way over on Sunset Strip. The fireman's override had been engaged. His men had blocked the doors open with stout curtain rods they'd taken from one of the lounges. No one would get to the fourth floor this way.

A distant cracking sound echoed faintly through the halls.

"Boss!" said Ana Katsumata's voice on his earpiece. "Cord says they're almost through the inner barrier!"

"Everyone to positions!" he shouted.

He put on his combat gloves and unslung his M4. He carried it in both hands as he jogged down Wall Street to Stairwell 2, in the northeast corner of the floor. Someone had taped a white sheet of paper onto the floor in front of the first step. The word "NO" was written in big black letters on the sheet. "Good," he grunted.

He loped down the outermost corridors, checking the other stairwells. Only Stairwell 4, in the southeast corner, was without a "NO" sign.

He started down the armor glass steps to the third floor.

Another *crack* echoed up from below.

He took the rest of the stairs two at a time.

Ana and her fellow surveillance op, Leo Patrusky, nearly ran into him as he reached the landing. They both carried big binoculars and tiny laptops. They ducked out of his way.

Ana said, "We're ready, Gunny!"

"Good!" he replied as he bounded past.

He found Jack standing next to the window at the third-floor intersection of Broadway and Main Street, looking down at the devastated ST campus. He'd changed into ACUs, combat boots and a bullet-proof vest they'd liberated from one of the wounded Guardsmen. A radio earpiece protruded from his left ear.

John joined him and followed his gaze.

Three stories below them, the enemy troops were massing for the attack. Aidan O'Keefe, easily identified by the un-soldier-like bulge around his belly, was putting on his helmet.

Aidan's icy blond friend was looking up at them.

John felt a surge of unease, even though he knew the outside surface of the window was still mirrored. He was suddenly sure that the blond man was the one who'd shot everyone in the Stanford ICU.

Kill that bastard last, he told himself. Slowly.

He turned and looked down Main Street. Halfway down the wide hallway was a rolling desk chair next to two plastic boxes filled with soft black foam rubber. Jack's borrowed helmet was on the chair.

The glittering silver tops of QUBE Delta and the HyperQUBE were just visible over the lips of the boxes.

Next to the chair was a small flat-panel screen and keyboard mounted on a spindly-looking three-wheeled stand. He'd seen Luke's guys using them in the server rooms. Cables snaked from the stand down the hall and into the open door of the main heating and electrical closet.

He turned his gaze back to Jack. The scientist looked down at the enemy troops, his face impassive, his stare unwavering.

John asked, "Are you sure you want to go through with this? There's still time for you to hole up with the others."

"If those bastards don't get something out of this, they'll burn the building to the ground and kill everyone in it. We've gotta give them something to give the others a chance." Jack's mouth twitched. "And that something is me."

"You have the GPS tracker in your boot."

"They'll find it."

"We'll track you with the drones until Laurel gets here. The Greek's improvements should give us plenty of extra range."

"If she does get here..." Jack sighed. "Tell her I'm looking forward to not working with her again. Soon. *Real* soon."

"Huh?"

"She'll know what I mean."

John took a deep breath. "Are you ready for this?"

Jack turned to face him. "Is my team safe?"

"As safe as I can make them."

"Then I'm ready."

John offered his hand. "Good luck. I hope you know what you're doing, you crazy fucker."

Jack shook it. "Me, too. You'd better get down there."

"Grenade!" shouted Cord Walker in John's earpiece.

John pulled the charging handle of his M4. A round slid into the chamber. "Get your helmet on!" he barked.

An ear-punishing thunderclap came from two floors below.

"They're through!" shouted Cord.

John ran for Stairwell 1.

Toward the sound.

Toward battle.

CHAPTER SIXTY-THREE

Struve Technologies Coyote Hill Campus, Palo Alto, California

Aidan crouched behind the rampart of sandbags Tom's men had stacked in front of the Pauling Building. Next to him, Adam held a pistol at the ready. On both sides of them knelt men with assault rifles, ducking below the top row of sandbags.

"Fire in the hole!" shouted someone with a South African accent.

There was a loud BANG.

The riflemen surged up to cover the breach with their guns. Aidan stayed low.

Adam peeked over the top of the sandbags a moment later.

It took about a minute for Tom to shout, "Clear!"

Adam stood. Aidan followed suit.

The riflemen advanced on the new entrance, still aiming their guns into the building's dark interior. About a foot of armor glass on either side of the hole was transparent now, but the rest of the building was still mirror-shiny. ST guards could be anywhere behind them.

The grenade blast had sent flakes of pulverized armor glass everywhere. They were still drifting to the ground outside, sparkling like snowflakes in the sun. This time no one bothered to clean them up. Aidan pulled a handkerchief from a back pocket and held it over his nose and mouth. He wasn't keen to inhale the tiny shards.

Tom pulled Aidan away from the front of the hole. He growled, "We breached off to the side for a reason, dammit! If we'd gone straight in the front, they could have picked us off from the other end of Main Street. Do me a favor? Don't get shot. You're as important to the plan as Jack Dura."

Aidan nodded. It wasn't hubris to acknowledge that simple fact. He knew more about the QUBE support systems and E-ware than anyone else alive.

Tom glanced up at the sky. His perpetual calm had evaporated when the low-flying helicopter-plane hybrid buzzed the campus some fifteen minutes ago. Now he was as jumpy as a long-tailed cat in a room full of rocking chairs, as Aidan's Virginian grandfather would've put it.

"Time's running out," whispered Tom. "We've got to move fast. You should stay out here, Aidan."

"No. You're going to need me if they have any surprises for us."

"Goddammit, if you die, this whole mission is fucked."

"And if you die because you missed something I would've spotted, we're equally fucked. Let's get on with it."

Tom frowned at him. "Then stay low and clear of any action. I mean it."

"Whatever you say. You're in command."

"Apparently not," Tom fumed. He turned on his heel and strode up to the breach.

Aidan followed Tom's men, staying well to the right of the ragged hole.

A squat, bulldog-faced man in his mid-thirties waited for them there. Aidan blinked. The mercenary was completely hairless, without a hint of beard or even eyebrows. He aimed his ugly-looking rifle into the lobby.

"Nothing," he said. "Not even furniture. Fire doors are closed on Broadway. Main Street's clear at least as far as the atrium."

Aidan frowned. When he'd last seen John Shea glaring at him from the other side of the armor glass, the lobby behind him had been full of colorful chairs and sofas.

He tried to peer over the shoulders of the men queued up in front of the breach. They were tall and he wasn't. He couldn't see anything except for one of the lobby's two massive support columns. He looked through the transparent strip of armor glass to the right of the breach. The lobby was as the bald man described it.

Tom said, "Aidan? Can we do anything about these cameras?" He jerked a chin at the small mirrored domes at ten-foot intervals across the expansive ceiling.

"Not really," he replied. "The domes are FQG. You could try the Blu-Ray lasers but most of the light will just reflect off."

Tom frowned. "All right, Igmar," he said, turning back to the mercenary. "You're first man in."

The hairless man stepped into the building. He gave a startled grunt. His body dropped out of sight.

There was a commotion at the front of the queue of mercenaries, accompanied by stifled curses.

Then Aidan saw the bald South African through the transparent section of armor glass. He was sliding across the polished concrete floor of the lobby as if it were made of ice. He windmilled his arms, trying fruitlessly to stop himself, an expression of pure confusion on his ugly face. He slid out of view behind a still-mirrored pane of glass.

Two shots echoed from deep inside the building.

"Fuck!" shouted Tom.

Aidan said, "Get out of the way!" He shoved through the men to Tom's side.

The lobby had indeed been cleared. The concrete floor was spotless. *Too* spotless. There wasn't a trace of debris from the armor glass pane shattered by the grenade.

The mercenary Tom had called Igmar was dead, but his body was still moving. Face up and spread-eagled, it spun slowly back toward the breach, rivers of blood snaking across the floor behind it. The blood pooled and oscillated like blobs of crimson mercury. Igmar's head rotated into view. The undamaged half of his face was contorted into an expression of utter bafflement.

Tom grabbed the dead mercenary and hauled his body outside. He looked at Aidan. "What the *fuck?*"

Aidan knelt just outside the breach. Crumbled armor glass crunched beneath his knee pads. He ran a hand across the concrete floor inside. "They coated it with FQG. It's the same material as the armor glass. Almost frictionless."

One of the mercenaries snarled something in Afrikaans.

"What do we do now?" whispered Tom, his face pale.

Aidan thought about it. "They were getting close to the end of the last production run when I left. I doubt they would've made any more. We can freeze it and shatter it, if there's any liquid nitrogen left. Is there?"

He and Tom stared hard at the leader of the breaching team.

The man smiled. "Plenty."

Aidan looked inside. Igmar's blood supply had pooled in the far corner of the lobby, near the entrance to the Pauling Auditorium's atrium. Evidently the floor wasn't quite level.

Tom said, "The slippery part's not glossy. I can't tell where it ends, if it ever does."

His words touched off a rapid fire sequence of thoughts. Aidan glanced back at him. "Get me some rocks."

"What the hell is he doing?" whispered Cord Walker.

John and Cord crouched behind their own waist-high line of sand-bags at the end of Main Street, just outside the entrance to the loading dock. They stared at John's small iPad. It showed a ceiling camera's wide-angle view of the main lobby at the far end of the hall.

On the screen, Aidan O'Keefe was sliding small objects across the ice-slick lobby floor. *Stones*, John realized. They ricocheted from wall to support column to wall again. Most of them wound up in the sticky pool of mercenary blood in one corner of the lobby. Some bounced into the atrium and were still sliding around, making a dull *clunk* and slowing a bit each time they struck the baseboard.

John murmured, "He's trying to figure out how much of the floor we managed to coat."

Just then a lucky throw sent a stone through the atrium and into the hallway beyond. It bounced as it slid off the friction-free FQG coating onto polished but comparatively rough concrete. They had run out about thirty feet down Main Street, just past the atrium.

On the screen, Aidan's head twitched.

"Hell," said Cord. "He heard that."

Another stone followed the last one, retracing its path almost exactly. It, too, found the edge of the nearly frictionless coating. It, too, clattered to a stop.

Aidan stood and retreated from the breach. A man dressed from head to toe in aluminized fabric hauled a big white hose inside and turned a valve at its tip. Bubbling fluid frothed out. He sluiced it back and forth across the lobby floor.

"Well," John breathed. "Now they know how much FQG coating we had left. We knew it wouldn't keep them out forever." *But goddammit, I sure wish it had taken them longer to figure that out. Fucking Aidan O'Keefe!*

Cord growled, "We can still pick 'em off when they try to come down Main Street."

"No, we can't. I saw at least two of them with Punishers out there, and one was that blond psycho who looks like he's in charge. If that's Tom Reed, our only chance is to stay away from him."

"Well shit, Gunny, you sure know how to take all the fun out of a fight."

John's lips twitched at Cord's weak attempt at humor. "I think they'll try to get around us through the fire door first."

Cord smiled grimly. "I sure hope you're right."

Aidan watched through the strip of transparent armor glass to the left of the breach as the man with the splitting maul smashed it down on the frozen lobby floor.

CRACK!

A roughly circular region of floor about three feet in diameter turned gray. Tiny glittering flakes drifted up from it.

"Try stepping on it," ordered Tom.

Two men in the breaching team grabbed the man carrying the maul to keep him from falling as he prodded the gray area floor with an outstretched toe. When he didn't slip, he put more of his weight on it. "It's good," he said, nodding. "Not slippery at all anymore."

"Then what the fuck are you waiting for? Clear the way to the fire door!" Tom growled.

The brawny mercenary did as he was told, holding the maul vertically and pounding the end on the floor again and again. It cracked easily for a few moments, then began to resist him. Another treatment with the liquid nitrogen followed by more maul-work did the trick.

The massive fire door was now in reach. It was as wide as the corridor, hinged at the interior wall. It was locked in place by a steel post installed against the armor glass.

One of the other mercenaries stepped forward, holding a small metal cylinder that looked like a roadside emergency flare. He pressed the cylinder against the fire door's lock. A blazing yellow-white jet speared out, sending a cloud of acrid smoke in all directions. It made short work of the lock. When the door began to swing open, he darted back into the lobby, clearing the path for a squad of armored mercenaries with machine guns.

Aidan lost sight of the crew as soon as they went through the door. *"Hall's clear,"* he heard on his radio headset. *"Floor's good. We're headed to the next door."* A few seconds later, the screams began.

"I love it when a plan comes together," said John, watching the surviving mercenaries retreat from Broadway in a blind panic. His lips were taut with a vicious smile. "I only wish we had audio from that camera."

Only one of the four mercenaries had escaped injury. He helped the two bleeding survivors back to the lobby.

The leader was very, very dead. He'd run straight into the invisible Q3 monofilaments crisscrossing the hall.

He'd led with his left foot, sliding forward in case there was more of the slick coating on the concrete. A strand of fluorine-coated super-diamond fiber had found the gap between his boot and the composite shin guard. It was only a few hundred atomic diameters thick—far thinner than a wavelength of visible light—sharper than any razor and as strong as a piano wire. It had sliced his lower leg off as cleanly as a surgeon's scalpel.

Unbalanced, the screaming merc had pitched forward into a web of monofilaments, bound to the glass wall, the ceiling and the floor at crazy angles with Amber D'Agostino's insanely expensive patent-pending molecular adhesive.

The deadly strands couldn't penetrate the body armor head-on, but as his body fell, they carved long gouges in the carbon composites until they found fabric or flesh.

The force of his momentum and body weight sliced him into pieces.

The others had been following close. They'd suffered minor injuries, at least by comparison, but they were no longer in the fight.

"Jesus Christ," said Cord, swallowing. He looked away from the ghastly image on the iPad. "If that doesn't slow them down, nothing will."

John nodded. "Five minutes, five tangos down. I'll take it."

Tom's face turned an alarming shade of red. "What the *fuck*, Aidan!"

"How was I to know?" His reply sounded peevish even in his own ears. He should have thought of the Q3 monofilaments. It was obvious in retrospect. His respect for Stathis Sotiropoulos went up another notch. Maybe it would be better to eliminate him, after all. He was proving a little *too* inventive.

"What else is in there? Robots? Dinosaurs? Goddamn Jedi Knights?"

"Calm down," said Aidan. His own temper began to rise. "I'm trying to think."

"Fuck this!" said Tom. "We don't have time to wade through all these goddamned traps! They don't even have to shoot at us, and we're still losing men! You!" he shouted, pointing at the squad of gunmen inside the lobby, covering the atrium entryway. "Clear out of there!"

The men left the building at a trot.

Tom turned to Al Sanderson. "Get me an RPG, and every round you can find for it. And those wall-breaching charges."

Aidan grabbed Sanderson by the arm before he could obey. "No! You can't shoot rockets into the building!"

Tom grabbed Aidan's wrist and pried it free without apparent effort. "Do it!" he said to Sanderson, who turned and ran to the closest truck.

His fingers still clamped tight, Tom pulled Aidan off to the side. "We do not have time to dick around! John Shea's playing for time. The Marines could come over the hill any second. You want to go up against *Marines*, Aidan? I sure as shit don't! We have got to get though these defenses, and I mean *now*." He let Aidan go.

"If you destroy the QUBEs, this is all for nothing," snarled Aidan, rubbing his wrist.

Tom glared at him. "If we're not alive to use them, who gives a flying fuck?"

"You can't use explosives above the ground floor! There are toxic chemicals everywhere!"

"Then you'll just have to tell us where we *can* use them! You know this building's layout. Make yourself useful, goddammit!"

"Gentlemen," said Adam.

Aidan's head whipped around. He hadn't heard the Chinese agent approach.

"May I suggest that you get on with it?" said Adam in a low, deadly tone. "We do not have much time."

Sanderson returned, toting the ugly Soviet-style rocket propelled grenade launcher. Four men followed him, carrying crates presumably full of ammunition for the hideous device.

"Don't piss yourself," Tom snapped as he shouldered the launcher and checked its rudimentary controls. "Your precious QUBEs will be as far from this action as they can get them. And so will Jack Dura."

Aidan clamped his jaw shut on the retort. His head swam with fury. When this was all over, he and Tom would have words about this.

Tom strode to the breach. "What's on the other side of this wall?"

Aidan said, "The security offices."

Tom aimed the launcher. "Not for long. Clear!"

Men jumped away from the space behind him.

He fired.

CHAPTER SIXTY-FOUR

Los Alto Hills, California

The local anesthetic wore off all too soon. Knives lanced into Laurel's shoulder wound with every jouncing step she took toward the ST campus. The sling didn't do much for her while she ran. *Thank God and Corpsman Collins for the super-codeine.* Without it, she wasn't sure she'd be able to fight down the whimpers queuing up in her chest, waiting for an unfortunate moment to emerge.

"Top" Ames took them north along La Cresta Drive, a narrow, tree-lined road that ran along the summit of a ridge of the Los Altos Hills. The neighborhood was almost deserted. Most of the civilians had already headed downhill, toward Highway 101, on foot, carrying whatever they valued most. Children. Pets. Computers. One older man with a toupee dangling from the side of his sweat-beaded head carried nothing but an antique table lamp.

The crowds grew even thinner as they went uphill, but the roads were jammed with abandoned cars, which slowed them down terribly.

They tried to avoid contact with the few remaining groups of refugees. They weren't always successful.

Laurel tried to ignore the cries and shouts of the people they encountered, begging for their help. "Go south! Get away from the smoke!" Top told them. "Fallout coming! We can't stop for you!"

A couple of brawny young men yelled furiously at one of the Marines to stop and help them. Their two female companions stood well back from the roadside, next to a huge pile of luggage.

The two men tried to grab the Marine as he jogged past.

He reversed his M4 and thumped the first one in the forehead with the butt, then smashed it across the second man's chin in a single fluid motion.

The two men fell. The women screamed curses.

The Marine didn't even break stride.

Laurel's breath hitched in her chest, but she kept going as well.

They moved faster when they finally reached La Cresta Drive. The narrow road was mostly clear, aside from a few abandoned wrecks.

The last one before they reached their objective was the worst. A SmartCar and a big, dirty pickup truck had smashed into each other on a blind corner. The SmartCar was in surprisingly good shape, but the older man who'd been driving it was face-down on the asphalt, his legs still inside the open door, his head a bloody ruin. He'd been beaten to death with a tire iron.

They couldn't stop for that, either.

When Top finally called a halt, they were all sweat-soaked and panting. Hauling full field packs on a forced march through an urban environment was not for wimps. Laurel carried only her sidearm, gas mask and canteen, but the shoulder wound had sapped her endurance. She hunched over, propping herself up with her right hand on her knee, and waited for the black dots in her vision to fade away. When they did, she straightened and tried to figure out where they were.

They had stopped in front of a large, upscale house. Based on the topo map Top Ames had shown her, it should command a good view of the surrounding hilltops, including the summit of Coyote Hill.

The Marines checked for occupants inside and found none.

They stayed outside, crouching in the trees behind the line of low shrubs that bordered the crescent-shaped back yard. The trees on the far side of the yard were far enough downslope that they didn't obstruct the view. She didn't envy the gardener who had to mow that lawn.

Top said, "We're here for a few minutes. Rest up while you can."

Laurel sat down with her back to a tree and took a long swig from her canteen. Corpsman Collins adjusted her sling and offered her another shot of lidocaine to take the edge off the pain from her wound. She refused it. He crooked a dubious eyebrow at her but shrugged and walked away.

Idiot, she chided herself. Who cares if they think you're a wimp?

Clouds scudded low overhead, providing welcome relief from the sun, but the air was growing moist and cold, making her sweat all the more uncomfortable.

Top called for the scouts.

Three lean young men converged on him. He murmured instructions.

They dropped their packs but took their guns, fading silently into the trees with astonishing speed.

A distant, muffled explosion echoed through the hills. It was followed by two more. They'd been hearing them for about half an hour now.

"Let's get some eyes on the prize," said Top.

The two big men hauling the biggest backpacks unslung them and assembled their contents into a pair of small gray Ravens.

The little drones weren't big enough to carry weapons. They were much more conventional than the Greek's homemade hexacopters. These looked more like her mostly-forgotten old boyfriend's little Cessna. They were little more than high-mounted wings, a nose-mounted camera pod, and a small pusher propeller attached to the back. They didn't even have landing gear.

The two Raven operators made themselves useful while the two big Marines who'd carried them put them together. They set up a pair of tripod-mounted antennas. One of them tied a length of yellow and black striped tape to one of them. Laurel guessed it was an improvised wind sock. It flapped fitfully toward the south.

The operators sat cross-legged in the shade and unpacked their ruggedized laptops. They talked coordinates and bearings for a couple of minutes. Then they traded their laptops for big Gameboy-like controllers. When they gave the signal, the Marines who'd hauled and assembled the Ravens moved out of the trees and drew their arms back, ready to throw them into the air like kiddie model airplanes. Their propellers spun up with a startlingly loud whine.

The Marines faced the breeze, chorused "Launch launch launch!" and hurled the Ravens skyward. One of them buzzed up and away. The other one spiraled into the grass at the far end of the yard. It came apart like it had been fastened together with paper clips.

"Goddamn these fucking things," grumbled the Marine who'd launched it, jogging down to collect the pieces. A minute later he'd reassembled it and they tried to launch it again. This time it stayed up. "Thank God," he said.

The little planes climbed steeply into the sky. They were invisible once they went in front of the low cloud deck, but the whine of their tiny engines took a long time to fade away.

The other Marines checked their weapons and silently got their game faces on.

One of the radio operators handed an old-fashioned looking telephone handset to Top Ames. Laurel was too far away to hear his side of the conversation clearly, but his eyes narrowed and his lips curved upward as he listened.

He said something and handed the handset back to the radio operator. He saw Laurel watching and came over to her. "Air support's twenty minutes out. Now all we have to do is find those missile crews. And take 'em out. And assault the campus. And win."

"Yeah," she said, her voice as neutral as she could make it. "That's all." She tried to keep the smile from getting to her lips. There was a real chance, now.

A chance.

CHAPTER SIXTY-FIVE

Struve Technologies Coyote Hill Campus, Palo Alto, California

Cord stood on the middle step of the southeast corner stairwell, aiming his M4 carbine down the short stretch of hallway between him and the bolted loading dock door.

"Hurry!" he shouted.

John darted down the stairs in front of Cord and took a knee.

He held a small plastic tube in one hand and Amber's 3D-printed monofilament applicator in the other. The improvised device looked like a grocer's price tag gun, except for the tiny black light the Greek had mounted at the business end.

He dabbed a tiny blob of hyper-glue onto the armor glass interior wall of the stairwell, more or less at knee height. He pushed the tip of the filament applicator into the blob of glue. Then he squeezed the trigger four times to unreel what he hoped was about a foot of invisible super-diamond fiber. He pointed the black light at the glue and pressed the thumb switch.

The ultraviolet radiation catalyzed a chemical reaction in the glue. It spread out to form an invisible film, hopefully bonding the super-diamond filament permanently onto the surface. He tugged on the applicator. It resisted his pull. *Thank God,* he thought fervently. The fiber had been captured by the glue.

He couldn't afford any mistakes now. He'd laid down dozens of super-diamond booby traps throughout the building, but he wasn't as fast as Alex Southall or his buddy Sy Hamilton. The smug former SEALs took every opportunity to remind him of it. *Rat-bastard squids.*

The molecular glue was as tough as the FQG armor glass. It wasn't coming loose without a fight. If he accidentally glued his finger to the wall, he'd have to leave skin behind to get away.

"Come on, Gunny," urged Cord. "Let's go, let's go!"

John moved the applicator to the other side of the stairwell and did the same trick again, taking up as much slack in the fiber as he could before fixing the glue with the UV light. He popped the tube of glue into a vest pocket and pulled the filament cutter from another. It was a little black box with two thick copper electrodes sticking out of one end. It looked like an old-fashioned self-defense stun gun.

He pulled on the applicator to put some tension on the line, then placed the electrodes on either side of where he guessed the fiber had to be. He pressed the square button on the cutter's top surface.

Blue-white electricity buzzed between the electrodes. He moved them across the space between the applicator and the spot where the fiber was attached to the wall. The tension on the applicator vanished as the electric current cut through the super-diamond.

He backed away from the lethal, invisible strand now stretched across the stairway. It was as dangerous to him as to the enemy, but unlike them, he knew it was there.

An explosion rattled the loading dock door in its frame, but it held firm.

Cord shouted, "Come on, John! Get the next one ready as soon as I'm up there!"

"Roger that!" John darted up the stairs. As he turned the corner, he saw a white jet of flame and sparks spewing from the door's lock into the hallway. He kept going until he reached the top stair.

The door banged open.

Cord managed to bring two tangos down with armor-piercing rounds before anyone managed to return fire. He ducked back around the corner. Bullets smashed into the stairwell glass behind him. He stumbled but recovered.

"You okay?" shouted John.

"Took one in the shin." He hobbled up the stairs.

John waited for Cord to limp past him. Then he bent to add another super diamond fiber across the opening of the stairway.

"Watch it!" shouted Cord. He grabbed John's arm and pulled him around the corner just as someone on the first floor cut loose with a Punisher.

Five explosions went off inside the stairwell. The ear-splitting concussions were slightly muffled by the thick armor glass walls. Ball shrapnel pinged on the stairs and into the second floor hall like a blizzard of steel hailstones. If the stairwell walls had been normal glass or drywall, they'd both be dead now, in spite of their Elf-made body armor.

John shouted, "Thanks, man!" as he pulled the pin on a bulb-shaped fragmentation grenade. He waited a second, then tossed it around the corner and down the stairs.

It bounced into the hallway below.

Someone down there yelled, "Grenade!"

Then it went off. The shouts ramped from alarm to agony.

John slapped Cord on the side of the helmet. "Go!"

Cord retreated a few feet down South Avenue toward Broadway.

John quickly fixed the super-diamond fiber in place, crossing the top of the stairwell around knee-height.

There was a sheet of paper with the word "NO" scrawled across it taped on the floor in front of the stairs leading up to the third floor. He grabbed it and took it with him. They didn't want the enemy knowing that Stairwell Four had already been booby-trapped. *Let those fuckers find out the hard way.*

They went about halfway down South Avenue.

Alex Southall and Sy Hamilton waited with more of Amber's improvised monofilament guns. John ran past them and turned around, aiming his carbine toward the stairwell they'd just come up.

Cord did likewise, grumbling about the sting of taking a machine gun round in the shin. If it hadn't been for his souped-up body armor, his leg probably would have been blown off.

Alex and Sy fixed the loose ends of their strands in place, cut them, then fell back, alternating with each other to add more fibers at unpredictable angles and intervals as they retreated down South Avenue to Broadway. They closed and locked the heavy fire doors behind them. Anything to slow the enemy down and make it harder for his guys to be shot at. They had already placed dozens of filaments across hallways and doors elsewhere on the floor. Now they were trapping the only remaining open path to the upper two stories.

Their enemies had changed tactics after losing four men to the first super-diamond filaments. Instead of using the hallways, they were blasting through walls with RPGs and shaped charges of plastic explosive. Ana Katsumata and Leo Patrusky kept tabs on their progress from the Greek's lab on the fourth floor. They were patched into the *Argus* surveillance feeds with their laptops.

Fortunately, the enemy troops hadn't destroyed anything important yet. Aidan O'Keefe appeared to be keeping the blond man from going completely berserk. They'd limited their demolition work to rooms containing non-critical infrastructure: offices, custodial closets, even bathrooms. Anything to avoid walking directly down the halls.

Luckily, none of the fires they'd started with their explosives had spread. The sprinkler system was disabled because of the QUBE test, when the valves connecting the building to the municipal water supply were closed and drained. No one had thought to reconnect them, and it was too late to do it now. The air conditioners howled as they tried to clear the pall of smoke from the building.

The *Argus* system was also too well protected for them to disable. Its power source was the network cabling itself, and there were literally thousands of miles of it in the vast Pauling Building. The only way the bad guys could disable it would be to track down and destroy every router on the floor. The only problem with that idea was the existence of multiple, independent wiring paths from many of the cameras to well-hidden routers on adjacent floors.

The attackers couldn't cut power to the whole building. The conduits were buried in tough, reinforced concrete walls, hidden from inspection. Each floor had independent wiring all the way to the sub-basement generators, which were safely inaccessible—for now, at any rate.

Even if they got into the electrical closets and shut down the power for each floor one at a time, a good number of cameras would keep running. They could cover the camera domes with opaque material, but there were hundreds of them on every floor. The tangos hadn't bothered. They seemed rather pressed for time.

The bad news was that the enemy had figured out that they could burn through the super-diamond monofilament with the torch they'd first tried on the armor glass.

Ana and Leo had seen them use the torch via the *Argus* feeds. They still had to find the deadly, invisible strands, though: a hazardous task until some genius stumbled onto a trick that worked all too well. The enemy troops now slowly probed the hallway air with long metal poles. They slowed down even more after one of their men sliced two gloved fingers off by advancing a little too quickly down the hall.

The first pole was from a *torchiere* lamp taken from the ground floor security office. They'd actually managed to cut the thin metal tube in half with a too-vigorous swing. They replaced it with a crowbar they found in the custodian's closet. Even the super-diamond couldn't do more than scuff the drop-forged carbon steel crowbar. They could even

break the filaments with a powerful enough swing, but it was dangerous, and it took more effort than they seemed willing to expend.

They finally settled on fishing the monofilaments from the air with
the hooked end of the crowbar, then bringing up the torch and quickly
burning the fiber in two.

Hauling the torch's fuel tank around exposed the attackers to a non-
zero probability of being blown up, if only John or one of his team
could get a shot at them. Sadly, their enemies were all too aware of this
danger. Two Punishers covered the fiber-cutting crew at all times.

Their progress had become depressingly rapid.

John and Cord couldn't even hide around a corner and duck out to
take an occasional shot. The men with the Punishers routinely fired a
few deadly airburst grenades to clear the corners. They were appalling-
ly good shots. Fortunately, John and his men had the home field
advantage, not to mention two excellent surveillance operators watching the bad guys via *Argus*. They had managed to keep two turns ahead
of the enemy so far, but the margin was getting uncomfortably close.

"Ana, let us know when they come up the stairs," John said.

"Roger, Gunny," came her response. "You knocked about eight of
them out of the fight with that grenade. They're hauling the dead and
wounded out now. It'll take 'em a few minutes to regroup."

"Did we get the torch?"

"No, it was too far back."

"Shit," they chorused.

"You did get one of the Punisher guys that time, though. They're
looking at the gun. Looks like it's out of commission."

"Good. Fuck that guy," snarled Cord.

They backed onto Broadway, gluing down a dozen more of the lethal
fibers at random intervals until they reached the intersection with Main
Street. One by one, they ran out of the irreplaceable monofilament.
Thank God the other half of Broadway had already been prepped.

Alex was the last one to run out of line. He handed the empty applicator gun to John, who had collected the others.

"Cord, make sure our last little surprise is ready to go."

"Roger that, Gunny."

Cord ducked into the first lab on Main Street while John went to the
bathroom at the far end of the hall and tossed them into the trash. It
wouldn't do to leave the spent applicators sitting out where the bad

guys could see them, but they'd figure out pretty quickly that there were no fibers on Main Street.

It didn't matter. They always knew they would run out at some point. They were lucky to have gotten as far as they did.

He walked slowly back down Main Street to his men.

Cord reappeared, closing the lab door behind him. "Ready to rock."

"Outstanding," said John.

"Damn," gasped Alex. He grabbed his canteen and downed a healthy swallow. "My aching back."

John took a drink from his own canteen. "Well, that's it, then. Now it's all up to Jack."

"Jesus," said Cord. "Is he crazy, or what?"

"Crazy as a loon, but he's also chock full of *or what*," John said, smiling tightly. "And who knows? The cavalry might still ride to the rescue."

"Fat fucking chance," growled Sy Hamilton. He swiped at the trickle of blood running from beneath the soaked patch of gauze taped to his left cheek.

John said, "Stow the negativity, Sy."

Cord gave him a crooked smile. "That ain't negativity. Just good old entitled United Stated armed forces NCO grousing."

"They're getting ready to come up Stairwell One, Boss," said Ana.

John barked, "Okay, let's give the other bastards something to grouse about."

Alex pulled the keyboard-video-monitor cart out of the doorway where they'd stowed it. He put it in the middle of the hall while Sy plugged an extension cord into an outlet in the hallway.

There was a tiny Mac computer strapped to the back of the monitor. John flicked it on. The friendly Apple logo appeared on screen for a few seconds. Then a window opened and a video image of Jack Dura's face appeared on the center of the screen.

"Hey, guys," said Jack, his tinny voice emerging from the small computer's speaker. *"Can you move the camera up a bit?"*

John adjusted the small webcam Velcroed to the top of the monitor.

"Perfect. Ana says the bad guys are gonna get there in about ten minutes, and they're going to be pissed."

John looked at his crew. "Okay, guys. It's show time. Get to positions."

CHAPTER SIXTY-SIX

Struve Technologies Coyote Hill Campus, Palo Alto, California

The reports from the scouts started coming in only minutes after they disappeared into the trees. The radio operators, whom Top Ames confusingly called "Sparks One" and "Sparks Two," relayed the intelligence to the field commander as soon as it came in.

The enemy anti-aircraft missile crew was the first target to be located. Top knelt next to their Joint Tactical Air Controller, a Filipino senior sergeant whose job was to track and direct aircraft fire onto battlefield targets.

The JTAC's name was Bathala Dimasalang, known to everyone as "Bat." Laurel hadn't known that foreign nationals were allowed to join the US military. His accent was so thick it was nearly indecipherable to her, but everyone else seemed to understand him without any effort. Evidently there were plenty of Filipinos in the Marines.

When he and Top finished talking, Bat nodded, gave a squinty smile, grabbed his pack and clambered up onto the gabled roof of the multi-story house. Fortunately, it was covered with asphalt shingles instead of cedar shake or Spanish tile, making the climb easier, safer, and quieter. She lost sight of him as he crawled sideways across the roof, keeping his head well below the ridge.

"He's gonna light up the missile crew with an IR laser when the Hogs get here."

Laurel jumped. She hadn't heard Top walk over to her. "Good to know," she said, blinking up at him.

"We found two of their snipers, too. One on the back of Coyote Hill, another one on the big hill across the road. There's probably a few others out there, but we'll find 'em, don't you worry."

"I'm not worried," she said, and found that she meant it. All of her anxiety was taken up by the thought of Jack Dura not making it out of that building alive.

"Fifteen minutes," Top murmured. "Then the fun begins. All right, Devil Dogs! Let's get down there."

The explosions from downstairs had stopped. There hadn't been any gunfire for what seemed a long time, but was probably only minutes.

Stathis looked up from his bench where he continued to work on the drone. "Martín, could you get me a drink? I'm about to die here."

"Sure thing," said the SEAL. "Back in a sec."

Stathis felt a stab of guilt as his friend left the room. "It's all in a good cause," he murmured to himself. Jack had given him specific instructions. It was all up to him now. He couldn't let Jack down.

He was alone. Ana and Leo had moved to outer hallways of the fourth floor where they could spot the enemy positions.

He'd chosen the empty lab in room 482 for its distance from the two lounges. Stathis figured he probably had about thirty seconds to do his work.

He glanced at his laptop. Ana had patched it into the *Argus* feed before she left. The bad guys on the second floor were about halfway up South Avenue now, clearing the monofilament traps just in front of the last closed fire door before they reached Broadway. One more right turn, one more nasty little surprise he and Amber had cooked up, and half the length of Broadway to go before they reached Main Street. Then Jack would take over.

There wasn't much time now. Minutes, maybe.

Stathis pulled the batteries out of their compartments on each of the three drones. He took the three tiny fingernail-sized USB flash drives from his pocket. There was a roll of double-sided sticky tape on the table. He applied a strip to each flash drive and used a long handled pair of forceps to position them in the small space between the terminals in the battery compartments. He felt adrenaline squirt into his blood when he couldn't shove the first battery in all the way. He pressed harder and felt the reassuring click of the latches as the battery slid home.

Two seconds after Stathis shoved the last battery pack in, Martín returned, carrying not one Coke but three. He'd also brought some plastic-wrapped snacks. "Just in case," he said.

Stathis plastered an answering smile on his face and nodded. He popped the top on an ice-cold can, took a swig, and returned to his work.

"Stathis!" came Ana's voice on the radio. *"There's a raven out here!"*

He picked up the walkie on the desk and pressed the TRANSMIT button. "So what?"

"Not a raven, a Raven! A military recon drone! Hurry up! I'll try to keep it in sight. Come on!"

"Okay, okay!" Renewed hope sent adrenaline through him. The cavalry might be just over the next hill.

It took him two more minutes to complete the wifi extension mods on the last of the hexacopters. Ana called him twice to urge him to work faster. He screwed the cases together with the speed only someone who had built them in the first place could manage. He'd lied to John about having to install and test new driver software. He'd needed the extra time to fill up the USB thumb drives. He felt a stab of guilt. *All in a good cause,* he reminded himself.

He used the hand controller to test each drone in turn, making them spin up, hover for a moment, move a few feet in each direction and then settle gently back to the bench when he was satisfied. He turned to his laptop and started the scripts that would send the drones away at high speed and different directions when he released them on the roof.

"All right, Ana, I'm going to launch them," he said into the walkie. "Gimme a hand with these?" he asked the former SEAL. "We got one minute 'til they fly."

Bobby Boykin was bored to tears. He could see a lot more of the campus now, thanks to the tree-shredding mortars, but there wasn't much to look at. Burning buildings. Fragments of corpses.

A group of maybe ten of his "coworkers" dealt with the twenty or so wounded mercs lying on the grass in front of the Pauling Building, well away from the smoke and fire.

Better them than me. He'd rather be bored up here than dead down there. The ST guys inside the building were apparently putting up a pretty good fight.

He looked around. The tide of refugees had finally learned to steer clear of Page Mill Road. They were hoofing it south on Foothill Expressway now.

Big helicopters beat their way up and down the Peninsula. Since the Stinger guys brought down the Ospreys, the military clearly knew to keep well clear of ST—at least until they could bring some more serious firepower to bear.

"Hurry up, guys," he murmured. "We need to get the hell out of Dodge."

He happened to be looking through the scope at the rooftop of the Pauling Building when he caught movement out of the corner of his eye.

A small gray object flew up into the cloudy sky at a ridiculous speed.

Hans cursed. "Did you see it?"

"Yeah, I saw it." It was one of those goddamned ST drones, back in the air.

He tried to figure out where it had come from. Then he saw another one pop up, racing off in a different direction. It had come from a place near the base of the generator smoke stacks.

He saw a dark object moving on the rooftop, behind an air conditioner unit.

Hans said, "Target!"

Bobby didn't bother to reply. He aimed and fired.

Martín dropped the drone and collapsed.

An instant later, Stathis heard the report of a rifle echo across the grounds.

He rose from his crouch next to the rooftop door and dragged Martín's limp body by the legs.

Something whipped past his head and smashed into the wall behind him, blasting him with stinging debris. The sound of another shot rang out from across the valley.

He ducked lower and managed to get Martín back to the door. There was no blood, but there was a long gouge in the thick graphane material of his helmet.

Stathis checked the former SEAL's pulse. It was there, rapid but regular. "Thank You, Jesus," he moaned.

He crawled low to retrieve the drone. It was Norbert. It had taken a bad fall. The little OLED screen he'd fastened to it had broken off. The fact that its rotors weren't spinning spoke of more serious damage inside. They could use it as a wifi relay if he could get it back into the air, but it couldn't carry messages to would-be rescuers anymore, and he didn't have time to fix it. With Ana on lookout duty, he was the only one left to fly the drones.

He thought about taping a walkie to it, but the heavy radio would weigh the drone down so much its range would be radically reduced. That was the reason they'd gone with the lightweight screen modification in the first place. They might need every last millimeter of that range. "Damn it!" he whispered.

"Hey, watch your mouth," slurred Martín. "My virgin ears."

Stathis scrambled to his friend's side. "Are you okay?"

"Got my bell rung pretty bad," Martín whispered. "Help me sit up."

Stathis struggled to prop the soldier up against the low wall just inside the door. "Shit. I can't get you downstairs by myself."

"Don't try, man. You gotta fly the drones. Come on, those batteries won't last forever."

Stathis hesitated.

"Get a move on!" ordered Martín faintly. "I'll be okay. I'm just gonna look at the sky for a little while. Should be safe here. You gotta track down one of those Ravens."

"I'll be back." He took the broken drone with him.

"Stathis!" Ana cried into her headset mic. She stared through the binoculars at the gray plane-like drone, praying it wouldn't disappear before he answered. "Damn it! Where could he be? Stathis! Come on!"

"Here!" replied the Greek breathlessly. *"Martín's hurt but he'll be okay. Probably. Mikey and Oscar are in the air. Norbert's screen is—"*

"Stathis! Shut up! You're gonna have to burn a battery to catch up. That drone is really moving. Now, listen to me very carefully..."

The Marines were close to the campus now, walking in a widely spaced file along a long, narrow private driveway, staying under the cover provided by the trees. Ahead was the intersection of Arastradero and Deer Creek Roads. Just above them, behind a bunch of office buildings, was the shoulder of Coyote Hill.

They stopped to catch their breaths and assess the situation. Laurel's shoulder pulsed with agony. She felt a trickle of blood running down from the soaked dressing. She was just about ready to ask Corpsman Collins for another shot of the local.

The Raven operator in front of her said in a quiet voice, "Top! You gotta see this!"

Top Ames scrambled back to the Raven operator and peered at the video screen in the hand controller. "Holy fuck," he murmured. He stared at the expanse of open road in front of them, chewing his thin lips. Then he checked his watch. "Okay. I guess we'll start the party a little early. Sparks! Tell Chazz to cross off the two on Coyote Hill. We're can't let them see where it comes down."

"Where what comes down?" whispered Laurel.

Top didn't reply.

Less than a minute later, the radio operator said, "Chazz reports his sniper and spotter are down, Top."

Laurel whistled noiselessly. They were only a few hundred yards from the summit of Coyote Hill. She'd heard no gunshots.

"Outstanding," growled the grizzled sergeant. He turned to the Raven operator. "Okay, Placer, bring 'em in."

She heard the whine of the returning Raven long before she saw it. It seemed to materialize out of the gray sky. It plowed into the driveway and came apart. Apparently that was just the way you landed it. It didn't come with landing gear, after all. No one made a move to retrieve the pieces.

Behind it was a small hexacopter drone. It glided gracefully down, rotated and traversed the ground toward her. It landed gently not more than three feet from her boots. Its six rotors stopped turning.

There was a small white length of hand-lettered tape on the gray body of the drone. It read TAKE ME TO LAUREL WYNN.

Her eyes filled with tears.

"Look," the Raven operator said. He picked up the drone and rotated it to show her.

She wiped her eyes and looked. It was a small black display screen, obviously hand-wired. Next to it was a professional looking label that read "OSCAR."

The drone's camera swiveled toward her.

Tiny words flowed across the screen.

> HELLO GORGEOUS! AM I GLAD TO SEE YOU! THIS IS STATHIS. JACK IS OKAY BUT THE BAD GUYS ARE CLOSE. WE KNOW WHERE MOST OF THEM ARE. GET SOMETHING TO WRITE THIS DOWN. ANA HAS COORDINATES FOR SNIPERS AND AA MISSILE CREW. WE CAN SEE THEM FROM UP HERE. YOU'RE GOING TO HAVE TO TAKE THEM OUT BEFORE YOU TRY TO GET INTO THE CAMPUS. THERE'S A MIC ON THE DRONE. JUST TALK! I CAN HEAR EVERYTHING YOU SAY, BUT HURRY! OSCAR IS RUNNING LOW ON POWER.

"Thank God," she said with feeling, unable to keep the quaver from her voice. "I've got fifty Marines with me, Stathis. We're close, too. Tell Jack. Tell everyone!"

"Holy shit, that guy types fast," breathed the Raven operator.

She laughed. "You have no idea."

> I HAVE A PRIVATE MESSAGE FOR YOU FROM JACK FIRST. IT'LL ONLY TAKE A MINUTE BUT IT'S ABSOLUTELY CONFIDENTIAL.

She looked at the Marines gathered around her. "Do you mind?"

They shook their heads, though Top Ames hesitated for a long second before doing so.

She took the drone from the Raven operator and turned its screen so that only she could see it. "Go ahead, Stathis."

Words flew across the screen. Her heart sank into her boots as the import of what she read struck home. *Oh, Jack, what are you getting me into now?* It got worse with every word that scrolled across the tiny display.

The final sentence was a question.

Laurel closed her eyes. If I do this, it could mean my career. My freedom. My life.

If anyone but Jack Dura had asked, she'd say "no."

Back at Lake San Antonio, she'd told him she was with him. Now was the time to prove it.

She opened her eyes and said, "Yes."

I'LL LET HIM KNOW. THANKS! NOW GIVE ME BACK
TO THE MARINES. I HAVE TO RELAY ANA'S INTEL
AND THE BATTERY REALLY IS GETTING LOW.

She nodded to the camera.

The screen went blank.

She handed the drone back to the Raven operator, ignoring Top's flinty gaze. Then she turned away, murmured a quick, heartfelt prayer, and looked for the medic.

CHAPTER SIXTY-SEVEN

Struve Technologies Coyote Hill Campus, Palo Alto, California

Aidan, Tom and Adam trailed the men clearing the second floor hallways by a good fifty feet. Tom had insisted.

Aidan wasn't about to argue, especially after the grenade near the stairwell. He walked slowly behind the others, craning his neck to see.

Six men were in Broadway ahead of them. One held a crowbar. One held the torch. Another wheeled the gas tank behind the torch man. Two Punisher operators were there as well. They stood well to either side, covering the opening to Main Street, just in front of them.

The crowbar swept slowly up and down, probing for filaments. The group inched forward, step by careful step.

Adam growled, "This is taking too long."

"Yeah?" snapped Tom. "Feel free to give them a hand, then."

The Chinese agent frowned sidelong at Tom but stayed where he was.

"That's odd," said Aidan. "The light's different there."

"What?" said Tom.

"The light through the window, just where they are in the corridor. It's darker and kind of bluish." A horrible thought snaked into the back of his mind. "Tell them to come back."

"Aidan, what the fuck—?"

"COME BACK! NOW! RUN!"

The men were just beginning to turn to look at him when it happened.

A dozen forks of blue-white electricity arced across the width of the hallway, accompanied by a series of hollow, popping bangs. The bolts transfixed the men where they stood. They didn't even have time to scream. They just collapsed.

Adam took a step forward.

Aidan opened his mouth to shout again, but Tom grabbed his arm and squeezed painfully.

Aidan closed his mouth.

Tom moved up next to Adam. "Holy shit, did you see that?" he said, pointing at the closest of the fallen men.

"What?" said Adam, taking another step.

"That!" Tom got behind Adam and shoved with all his might.

Adam stumbled forward, wind-milling his arms and crying out in wordless alarm.

Another bolt of lightning reached out for him.

The Chinese agent pitched forward onto the floor. He didn't move again.

Aidan sighed. "Alas, poor Adam." He added in a fake English accent, "I knew him, Horatio," and chuckled darkly. The smell of roasting meat and the ozone tang of summer thunderstorms began to fill the hallway.

"Waste not, want not," Tom grated. He raised his Punisher to his shoulder and covered the hallway. "Aidan, get back to the lounge." He spoke into his mic. "This is Reed! We need every available man up here, now!"

Aidan did as Tom directed. He couldn't contain an admiring laugh. "Stathis, you sneaky bastard," he murmured. He went to the counter, poured himself a glass of sparkling water, and took a long drink. Watching a battle was thirsty work, and the water in his canteen had turned stale far too quickly.

So, seven more dead. More than half of the crew that had started the assault was either dead or disabled now. Yet it wasn't a total loss. Adam had been subtracted from the equation very neatly. That would make things easier. If he and Tom had been forced to put the Chinese agent down in view of the other men, there would have been questions too delicate to answer. The other men didn't know who sponsored their operation, and they had never been told their destination.

Now they'd never know that Adam's plan had never been Aidan's plan.

The halls echoed with running footsteps. Eight men ran past the lounge without sparing a glance for him. He recognized most of them as Ableman Security employees. Tom's hand-picked men.

He heard Tom murmur, "This is it?"

"Yes sir," said Al Sanderson. "We're it. The snipers and missile guys are still out in the hills, and we needed the rest to cover the gates and deal with the injured." A pause, then: "Jesus. What a sight. Aw, fuck, is that Freddy? And Eric too. Goddamn. Good thing the gas tank didn't blow up."

"No shit. Cover this hall." Tom called, "Aidan, it's safe now."

Aidan took a long drink from his glass as he walked back to Tom.

His old friend glared at him. "Take your goddamned time, why don't you."

"I'm still thinking about this. Give me a minute."

Aidan halted next to Tom and peered at the bluish section of armor glass down the hall. He put the glass on the floor, took a pair of small binoculars from a pouch on his vest, and carefully scanned both sides of the corridor.

He said, "Unless I miss my guess, that is Amber's ultra-capacitor film. Carbon nanotubes packed in parallel to boost the surface area. Stores enough electrical charge to... well, to electrocute a bunch of men. I've seen it in the lab. I had no idea they'd made so much of it."

Tom shouted, "What the hell do we do about it!"

"It's connected to the wall power. Look at the baseboard. There are two wires running along the floor, attached to either end of the film. Probably connected to a wall socket somewhere." Aidan aimed the binoculars down the hall. A length of gray duct tape was strung across the far end of Broadway next to the stairwell, running along a seam in the concrete floor, disguising the pair of gray wires running along the armor glass wall. *Well done*, he thought. The tape was almost the color of the concrete. He'd never have seen it without the binoculars. He lowered them. "Just shoot the wires."

Tom barked, "Al! Do it."

Al Sanderson thumbed a selector on his machine gun, took careful aim and squeezed off a shot.

The wires at the base of the armor glass jumped. Another bolt of lightning sizzled across the hallway. The next shot severed the wires at the bottom of the wallboard. There was no electrical arc this time.

"That should do it," Aidan said. "Just keep an eye out for more wires."

"Al, get up there," ordered Tom. "See if any of those guys are still alive."

They weren't.

Some of the men kept watch, guns pointed down the hall and into Main Street, while the rest dragged the bodies to one side of the broad corridor.

"Okay," said Tom. "Back at it."

They found and cut the last of the fibers in short order.

Al crouched next to the corner that led to Main Street. The others took up covering fire positions. Al pulled a telescoping rod from a vest pocket. It had a small round mirror on one end. He angled it to give him a view down the corridor.

"That's weird," he said. "Nothing there but one of those computer video monitors on a rolling stand. There's a video of some geek on it. No guards, nothing else in the hallway. The fire doors are open all the way to Wall Street."

Aidan exchanged a glance with Tom.

Tom said, "Okay, advance. Punishers, put some rounds around those corners."

An amplified voice said, "*DON'T.*"

Aidan smiled. "Jack? Nice to hear your voice. How've you been?"

"JUST PEACHY. I'M READY TO TALK. YOU CAN COME DOWN THE HALLWAY. THERE AREN'T ANY MORE SUPER-DIAMOND FIBERS. WE RAN OUT. JUST STICK TO MAIN STREET AND YOU'LL BE FINE. I WOULDN'T GO ANY FURTHER DOWN BROADWAY, THOUGH."

Aidan looked at Tom, who shook his head. He addressed the empty air again. "You won't mind if we don't take your word for that?"

"SUIT YOURSELF."

"You're very loud, by the way. Could you turn it down a notch?"

"Fine. I've got something to show you on the monitor when you quit fucking around. There's no one else on this floor. Shoot all you want, but not the video cart, or I'll do something you will not like."

Tom said, "Chucky, you and Nick stay here and keep an eye on that end of Broadway. The rest of you, get moving."

The men advanced down the corridor at the same deliberate pace as before, checking for fibers with the crowbar. They gave the video cart a wide berth. Al looked it over quickly and called, "Looks okay to me. I don't see anything weird, any explosives or anything."

"Keep going, but pick up the pace," Tom replied. He looked at his watch.

Even Aidan was starting to feel nervous about the time. The Marine Corps plane hadn't been back. There was no telling what mischief they could be getting up to out there, beyond the campus walls.

Al and his five men reached the end of Broadway without incident. "He wasn't lying about the fibers. It's clear."

"Just stay there for now," Jack's amplified voice rang out. "Aidan, get up to that video screen. I need you to see something."

Aidan laughed. "I don't think so, Jack. I'll just watch from here, if you don't mind." He pulled his binoculars from his vest pocket again and raised them to his eyes. "You need a shave, my friend."

"Fuck you, psycho."

"Eloquent, as always." From the corner of his eye, he saw Tom raise his own pair of binoculars.

"Just watch."

The monitor switched to a view from a ceiling camera in a large room with bare concrete walls.

In the center was the huge hydraulic shear shredder. Aidan had used it to dispose of his old MacBook after throwing it at the door of his office, when he'd failed to decipher Jack's formulas on the whiteboard. He remembered the way the notched, spinning shafts had consumed his laptop without as much as slowing down.

The Dura Party was crowded in front of the big wedge-shaped collection bin, holding small rectangular objects. Hundreds of them were piled in front of the shredder in neat, knee-high stacks.

"What is this, Jack?" he asked, his heart starting to pound.

"Keep watching. And keep in mind that you will never get to the basement in time to do squat about it. Okay, Ben, do it."

The thirtyish man with receding hair held up an oblong object. *"Here we go,"* his tinny voice said over the PA speakers.

He dropped the object into the bin. There was an unpleasant crunching sound.

The rest of Jack's former students pitched in.

The grinding noise became louder.

Jack said, *"You know all those hard drives we were getting ready to haul out of here? You know, the ones containing the modeling data you've accumulated over all these years? The ones you were probably counting on us keeping in a nice safe vault so you couldn't get to them, and then you'd make us take you to them at gunpoint?"*

On the screen, the Dura Party continued to shove drives into the shredder's collection bin. The grinding sound grew into a roar.

"You are bluffing," squeaked Aidan. "You're a scientist! Your whole life is about the search for knowledge! Emily's life work is on those drives!"

"Listen to me very carefully, you sick motherfucker. I. Don't. Bluff."

Aidan's stomach clenched. He'd said the same thing to Alberto di Mottura the night Emily died.

"Blaise told us what you did to Peter. The synthetic virus you made. The recipe was on the first drive Ben dropped into the grinder. The oil synthesizer. The diamond fiber. The structure of FQG. Everything. You think we'd give that to you? You just killed hundreds of thousands of people. Wave bye-bye, Aidan. Wave bye-bye."

"I will blow your fucking head off," shouted Tom Reed.

"I don't think so," Jack said. *"In about ten minutes, this head's going to be the only place in the world to find the formula."*

Aidan screamed, "What formula?"

The video mercifully switched away from the scene of intellectual carnage going on in the basement. Jack's unshaven face replaced it. *"Didn't Blaise tell you, Aidan? I cracked it. Quantinuum theory. The Grand Unified Theory. It's all in here."* He tapped his helmeted temple. *"We've been busy. We destroyed every file, every printout, every video. The Hadoop cluster in the server farm. Erased. The hard copies of the QUBE schematics. The oil synthesizer demo unit. Everything from Santa's Workshop. In the shredder. Every bit of knowledge gathered over the course of seven long years. Gone. Except for this."*

Jack backed away from the camera. He was wearing a bullet-proof vest as well as the helmet. He held a familiar glittering silver sphere in his right hand.

"QUBE Delta. And this."

He held up his left hand.

"The HyperQUBE. Which works perfectly, by the way."

Jack stared at the video camera, his dark, red-rimmed eyes gleaming, Satan's own smile on his lips.

Aidan's mind went blank. His hand drooped. The binoculars fell to the floor. His heart felt like it would burst. He went to a wall to steady himself.

As if from a great distance, he heard Tom say, "You said you were ready to talk. So talk."

"Here's the deal. Aidan comes up here, alone and unarmed. I ask a few questions. He answers. Then I go with you. You leave everyone else alive. Or else I will do this to the HyperQUBE."

Aidan closed his eyes, knowing what was coming next. The crunching sound was like a dagger through his mind.

"So much for QUBE Delta. So what do you say? Aidan?" His tone turned sickly-sweet. *"Buddy?"*

Aidan straightened. "All right." He stooped, picked up the binoculars, wrapped the cord around them and put them carefully into his breast pocket. "I'll do it."

Tom grabbed his arm. He whispered, "Are you out of your mind?"

He shrugged the hand off. "He's scorched the earth. There aren't any options left."

"You're just going to take him at his word that he destroyed the hard drives?"

Aidan hissed, "Do we have time to do an inventory of the whole building? We've got to get this done, now, or we're finished! If we don't take him out of here of his own will, we've lost everything."

"Dura," said Tom.

"Yeah?"

"He's coming up. But understand this. His mic will be on VOX. I will hear everything you two will say. If you hurt him or kill him, I will dig your eyes out of your skull with a spoon. And then I'll burn this fucking building down and bury your precious students alive. You got that? Did you see my guys planting thermite all over the first floor? Sprinklers will just make it worse. It'll keep burning until it hits bedrock. I don't bluff, either. You've got five minutes, and then we're coming up."

"Fair enough. I'm sending someone down. Tell your men to back away from the end of the hall. We have cameras everywhere. I'll know if they don't."

Tom's mouth tightened. "Tell your messenger to come unarmed."

"Sure."

"Al. Take two guys and get those incendiaries wired up. Move it!" He turned to Aidan. "Don't do anything dumb."

For once, Aidan couldn't think of a reply. He unholstered his never-used pistol, handed it to Tom, and trudged to the other end of Broadway, passing the other men as they jogged back to their leader's side.

He stood there, numb, until John Shea walked into view at the other end of Main Street.

Shea was unarmed, as far as he could tell, but he knew the big former Marine could kill him with his bare hands without breaking a sweat.

He walked down to meet Shea. It didn't even occur to him until he reached the end that they could easily have lured him into a deadly web of diamond filaments. He wouldn't have cared. He felt hollow, like someone had scooped his entrails out with a sharpened shovel.

Grief? Sorrow? He knew the words, but not the feelings to which they were supposed to be attached. The only emotion he really understood was anger. He embraced it now. He let it course through him until he was giddy with it.

Jack Dura had done this to him.

He'd bow to the profane bastard until they reached the getaway. And then he would take great pleasure in ripping every one of Jack Dura's secrets from his screaming mouth.

"I'm ready," he said to Shea.

The big man scowled. "Come with me." He turned to the left.

Aidan followed.

CHAPTER SIXTY-EIGHT

Lieutenant General Bradford Albert Dorsey stood behind Captain Zoe Franks, the lead communications officer of the San Francisco Theater of what had been christened "Operation Eternal Resolve."

The sound of aircraft taking off and landing outside the Mobile Command Post muted the roar inside the tent to a dull buzz. Dorsey scarcely noticed the noise anymore.

He stared at the tactical map displayed on the big projection screen.

The cluster of dots to the north of the Bay Area represented twenty B-1B bombers of the 28th Bomb Wing, flying from Ellsworth Air Force Base near Rapid City, South Dakota. They were moving across the simulated terrain with appreciable speed.

From the south approached thirty-five B-1Bs from the 9th and 28th Bomb Squadrons of the 7th Bomb Wing. They had come from Dyess Air Force Base outside Abilene, Texas.

The sleek, supersonic bombers had broken windows across half of the continental United States to get here as fast as possible, emptying a whole fleet of airborne tankers along the way. Their payloads were a mixture of heavy GPS-guided 2000-pound JDAM bombs and many more 250-pound Small Diameter Bombs.

There were only so many places in San Francisco Bay where another of the North Korean drone subs could hide. It was unlikely to have been close enough to San Francisco to have been damaged by the first bomb, which left the shipping channels of the North and South Bay.

The destroyers *Decatur* and *Kidd* couldn't do the job by themselves, and the others on their way up from San Diego wouldn't arrive until well after nightfall. In any case, the southern half of the Golden Gate Bridge was heavily damaged. Big sections of the roadway had already dropped into the channel, and several more were dangling. It was too dangerous to bring any of the warships into the Bay. Their only real alternative was air power.

It would have to be done carefully. The JDAMs could use their tail fins to steer themselves, and the SDBs with their small extensible wings could "fly" to their targets for even greater distances. It was possible to deliver them so they would all strike at almost the same instant. The concept was named "time on target," frequently used in artillery, but seldom applied to aerial bombing.

No one had ever tried anything on this scale before. If their attack was successful, most if not all of the bombs would hit the channel within seconds of each other, hopefully too quickly for a drone sub to panic-launch its warhead before being destroyed.

Air Force Major General Ken Cook had brought Dorsey the plan five minutes after the nuke erased San Francisco. He'd given Cook the green light without hesitation. There wasn't any time to waste.

The only comforting fact was that the Russians had finally disabled their GLONASS satellites after the Air Force received clearance to cook three of them with secret ground based lasers. The President had taken the gloves off.

As Dorsey watched, he saw one blip detach from the northbound group of bombers. It veered west, toward the Peninsula. The tiny altitude marker under its unit label began to increment. It had a special role to play in this battle. Dorsey prayed it would never be used. It had been selected because it had more fuel than any of the other bombers. The crew estimated they could loiter overhead for no more than twenty minutes, if they pulled every trick in the book to conserve fuel. The rest would be running on fumes when they got here, if they managed to get here at all. One bomber had already run dry. Its crew had punched out over the hills west of the Central Valley town of Los Banos.

There was another blip on the tactical map, moving quickly toward Mountain View, at the southern end of the Bay. It passed directly above the label marked "Moffett Field" even as he watched.

The whistling of wings and the whine of jet engines pierced the roar in the tent, dropping in pitch as the A-10 squadron flew north. The sounds quickly faded into the background noise.

Cook waved a hand, getting Dorsey's attention. "They're here. We go in five minutes," said the Air Force general, one hand on his earphones.

Dorsey nodded. He tapped Captain Franks on the shoulder.

She looked up at him, her dark eyes alert in a face the color of teak.

"Send the word," Dorsey told her. "Get every chopper away from those shipping channels, right now. Tell them they have three minutes to get clear."

"Yes sir," she said, relaying his commands.

"Franks?" he said.

She looked up at him. "Sir?"

"Tell Sergeant Ames the Hogs are almost here. If I don't hear that he has control of the Pauling Building in fifteen minutes, we're going to flatten it."

"You should stay here," Top said to Laurel.

"No way! I am coming with you!" She clutched her forehead with her right hand.

"Your arm, goddammit! Your whole sleeve is covered with blood! And you're as pale as a sheet!"

"The corpsman gave me another local. I can still hold a gun!" she said, groaning slightly. She didn't want to overdo it.

"You're benched. We got Ana on the radio. She told us how to get through the building. We're good. Grab some dirt. Doc, see if she needs to be patched up real quick. We gotta beat feet, and I mean now."

She sank to the ground next to the driveway with exaggerated clumsiness. *I'm not winning any Academy Awards for this performance,* she thought, heat rising to her cheeks. She couldn't believe Ames was falling for it. Maybe he was the kind of guy who believed women still had fainting couches at home. *Or maybe he's not used to someone on his side lying to him,* she thought with a pang of guilt.

Corpsman Collins raced over to her, peeled back the edges of her uniform's sleeve where he'd cut it to apply the dressing, and shrugged. "You all right?" he asked her. "This doesn't look too bad, just a little seepage."

Ames growled, "Looks bad enough to me. Ms. Wynn. We'll be back for you. Stay under the tree, away from the edge of the road. Here. You don't want those Warthog pilots to mistake you for a bad guy." He handed her an elastic band with a black knob of plastic fixed to it. "This is an IFF beacon. *Identification, friend or foe,* that is. Anyone watching you in infrared will see it blink, and know you're one of us." He narrowed his eyes at her. "Where's your helmet?"

"Melted."

"Well, turn it on and hang it around your neck or something."

It was then that she noticed all of the Marines had similar beacons strapped to their helmets.

"Thanks," she said woefully, leaning back against a reddish-brown madrone tree trunk.

Top tapped "Sparks Two" on the shoulder. "Tell Bat to light up that missile crew. Let's hope Ana's coordinates for the other positions are still good." He called in a low voice, "Devil Dogs, weapons free. Let's get into this war!"

"Oorah," they chorused softly, unslinging their long guns.

They ran low, fast, and only a few at a time across Arastradero Road. They disappeared into the woods.

Laurel listened to the sound of their footfalls fade as they hiked the gentle slope toward Coyote Hill.

She was alone.

She didn't hesitate. She scrambled to her feet and found the bush where the Raven operator had hidden the drone named Oscar.

She pulled the spent lithium-ion battery out of its compartment. The USB memory stick was there, just as Stathis had said it would be.

She had to find a stick to pry it loose. It popped out, bouncing off her leg and into the leaf-strewn grass. She found it quickly, blew debris out of the connector, and put it in her breast pocket, making sure to Velcro it shut.

Right now it was the most valuable thumb drive on Earth, containing one of only three copies of Jack's research notes and the rough draft of the paper he'd been writing on his quantinuum theory.

The other two were inside the battery compartments of Mikey and Norbert. She hoped Stathis would be able to retrieve Mikey. He'd landed it on top of Coyote Hill after the Marines told him the sniper there had been taken care of. It should still have enough juice to let them communicate with him inside the building. He'd probably already gotten rid of the thumb drive he'd put inside Norbert.

She hoped she'd survive to carry out the task Jack had asked of her.

She knelt to put the drone back in the bush in more or less the same position it had been in when she'd found it. It would probably be out here until some kid found it and carried it away. She doubted anyone would ever think to look for it.

"Bye, Oscar. You were a good drone."

She stood, brushed her pants off, drew her 9mm, and headed after the Marines. Stathis had described how to avoid the remaining super-diamond fiber booby traps inside the building. She knew the building better than any of them. His directions burned bright in her mind.

Sorry, Jack. Your mission is going to have to wait. No way am I going to sit this fight out.

Aidan O'Keefe followed John Shea down Wall Street. He trailed the big Marine by ten feet, quietly narrating a description of their path into his headset microphone. Tom might need to know.

Shea turned left onto Park Avenue, right at Maple, through a warren of scientists' offices, then left again onto North Avenue.

They went past the second-floor lounge and up Stairwell 1, at the northwest corner of the building. Shea walked straight down the third floor's Broadway and turned left when he reached Main.

Aidan followed.

Jack Dura sat in the middle of the hall in a Herman Miller desk chair, helmeted and wearing an ill-fitting bulletproof vest over baggy ACUs. He cradled the HyperQUBE in his lap. To his right was another of the rolling keyboard-video-mouse stands. To his left was a large, empty plastic box.

On the floor in front of him were the shattered ruins of QUBE Delta. Golden metallic flakes had drifted across the wide hallway, like autumn leaves.

Shea walked past Jack, nodding once. He kept going. He turned right when he reached the far end of Main Street and disappeared.

Aidan stopped about twenty feet from the grubby scientist. He looked at the wreckage of QUBE Delta and shook his head. "I'm surprised at you, Jack. I'd never have thought you ruthless enough to destroy your wife's life work."

"The most important parts still exist. In here," Jack said, tapping his forehead. "That kind of puts me in the driver's seat, doesn't it? Anyway, Emily stopped being my wife a long time ago. Thanks to you."

Aidan absorbed Jack's stony glare. "You said you had some questions. We have five minutes until Tom comes up."

"Will you answer honestly?"

Aidan sighed. "Why not?"

"When did you decide to take Emily away from me?"

"Just after she joined the faculty. Long before you were married. She was special. Smarter than me. Smarter than you. Smarter than anyone. A unique resource, and, in her own way, rather intoxicating. It took me a long time to earn her trust, but you helped with that, Jack. She said you had quite a temper."

Jack's lips thinned into a line. "We both did."

"True. You were like fire and oil together, in more ways than one. It's a good thing you never hit her, Jack. I'd have killed you for that. I came to feel... very protective of her."

"I would never have hit her!" Jack stood, grasping the HyperQUBE in both hands. The chair shot backwards down the hall.

Aidan's heart skipped a beat, but he continued as if nothing had happened. "No. You were not abusive. Not in that way. But there's too much anger in you. It makes you unpredictable. Frightening. It wasn't hard to convince her it could become more than that."

Jack's mouth worked furiously for a long moment. When he spoke again, it was in a throaty whisper. "Why did you have Emily killed?"

"That was never part of the plan. Folstad was supposed to steal QUBE Charlie and hold it for ransom, not kidnap Emily. That was arranged by my backers, without my knowledge. I've dealt with them accordingly. Emily's death was an accident."

"No. It was murder. And you're responsible."

"Folstad was. I had him and everyone else involved put down for it. If it had gone my way, no one would have been injured, much less killed. Except, of course, for Folstad."

"You're pretty goddamned kind to yourself, aren't you? What about Peter? Did he *accidentally* inhale a virus that could only kill him?"

Aidan crossed his arms. "I wanted to show the Board that Peter didn't have what it took to run the company. That he wasn't competent to secure its most valuable assets. I was the only logical choice as his successor. When that didn't work out, I had to take other measures. I didn't expect Laurel Wynn to dig into my affairs quite so quickly. I underestimated her tenacity. Blaise and I started work on the virus before I was forced to run. He deployed it at the dinner party to prove to our new benefactors that we could do it. It's unfortunate. I liked Peter, as much as I'm capable of liking anyone. He was just in the way."

"You really are a psychopath, aren't you?" Jack's said in a wondering tone.

"There's some controversy over that word. I've done a lot of reading on the subject. I don't really think there's a term for—for what I am." He smiled. "I am what I am, and that's all that I am."

Jack shook his head. "It doesn't even faze you, does it? Emily and Peter dead. Hundreds more outside. God knows how many more in San Francisco."

"We projected about eight hundred thousand fatalities, more or less." Aidan looked at his watch. "Three minutes."

Jack's mouth fell open. He shook his head. "Holy Christ," he croaked at last. "And all for this." He stared down at the HyperQUBE.

"Jack, you must understand. I didn't do this for myself. I did it for humanity."

The scientist looked up at him, eyes narrowing.

"Look at our world," said Aidan, entreating. "Everywhere civilization is in decay. Terrorism is rampant. Intellectual discourse is dying. The Internet was supposed to bring people closer together. All it does is drive them further apart. People these days don't believe in anything. They're so skeptical they think merely questioning an idea is the same as disproving it. Do you know how dangerous that is? A people that believes in nothing can be made to believe in anything."

He took a step closer to Jack. "Do you think a generation like this one will be able to stand up to the forces of darkness rising all around us? How much longer will it be before the terrorist leaders of the world get their hands on nuclear bombs, or biological weapons? Millions of people hunger for Armageddon, Jack, and our leaders seem to want to give it to them. I don't want to destroy the world. I want to save it. At least, the part of it that's worth saving."

Jack hissed, "You son of a bitch. You just nuked a city!"

"I didn't give the final orders. I didn't build the submarines or the warheads. There are thousands of missiles poised to annihilate civilization right now. Did I create them? My acts in this little drama don't even register on that scale of madness."

Jack stormed, "Then what's your solution, you sick fuck?"

"To leave."

Jack's brow furrowed.

That got his attention. "It's very simple, Jack. The human race has too many eggs in one small, flammable basket. We have to go. We need to leave this charnel house of a world behind and let the savages eat each other. The materials and technologies the QUBE can unlock will make that feasible. We can spread out into the solar system, create sustainable habitats on the Moon or on orbit. Perhaps even terraform Venus or Mars. There's an endless supply of metal and carbon and water in the outer solar system. All we have to do is go get it. I plan to make that happen."

"You get to choose who goes and stays."

"Someone has to."

"And you get to call the shots. You decide who benefits from the technology."

Aidan couldn't help smiling. "And who doesn't."

"Why didn't you just leave us in peace? The whole world should share in this!"

"And hasten the fall? How naïve you are. You actually *believed* the government wouldn't seize this technology as soon as it became portable. Why do you think they provided so many guards, and offered to relocate you to their lab at no cost? Out of charity? Governments have no charity. Just legions of petty technocratic vampires who live to suck the life-blood out of their constituents. Peter didn't have what it took to keep them from taking it away. I do. Contrary to what you think, I took no joy from sacrificing all of those people, but it's nothing compared to what will happen if the true villains out there get hold of it."

Jack gave a bitter laugh. "And you think your new Communist buddies won't take it away from you? You really are nuts."

Aidan shook his head, "That was never going to happen. Tom and I have a place in—" He glanced up at the cameras in the ceiling. "—ah, let's just say it's very far away, and very safe. If your ultra-capacitor hadn't cooked him first, Adam was going to have a little accident before we left the building. I must leave a note to thank Amber and Stathis for that. Adam's masters supplied us with tools, but they will never enjoy the fruits of our labors."

"You're not afraid they're going to come after you."

"I suspect they're going to have their hands full dealing with matters closer to home. Millions of starving refugees are about to cross their border."

"How the hell are you planning to get away, anyway?"

Aidan snorted. "Sorry. You won't be leaving a trail of breadcrumbs on video." He looked at his watch again. "Speaking of which, time's up."

"Just one more question."

"Quickly, then."

Jack opened his mouth to speak. His eyes flicked to something behind Aidan. They widened.

How feeble. Aidan scoffed, "Really, Jack, do you think I'll fall for—" Then all hell broke loose.

First Sergeant Avery Hammond "Top" Ames lay prone under an oak tree at the summit of Coyote Hill, watching the A-10s begin their run.

The anti-aircraft missile crew was the first to go. They were concealed in a similar grove of gnarled oaks on a hilltop about a kilometer to the west-northwest. Unknown to them, Bat Dimasalang's infrared laser designator was lighting them up for the incoming aircraft.

The Hellfire missile streaked across the valley from right to left. It flew into the oak grove with pinpoint precision. The fiery blast annihilated the trees and their inhabitants. A flat boom echoed across the valley. Ames saw a body fly into the air. It tumbled about thirty yards before it crashed bonelessly into the downslope.

Secondary explosions from the surface-to-air missiles followed, sending flaming debris corkscrewing into the sky in every direction.

The cross-shaped gray aircraft wheeled away to the west, its quiet, high-bypass turbofan engines whining softly. It left a fan of glaring white flares in its wake before soaring into the clouds.

An instant later, something moving incredibly fast shrieked directly over their heads. It arced over the roof of the Pauling Building and arrowed downward. A searing orange cloud exploded into the air on the far side of the huge laboratory. The flames transformed into a pall of blackness that mingled with the smoke already boiling from the other blazing structures. Debris pattered to earth for long seconds afterward.

A Warthog swooped overhead. It cleared the few remaining cypresses along Page Mill Road by no more than fifty feet.

A shocking, ratcheting roar stunned Ames' ears as the tank-buster's 30mm Gatling gun cut loose. The two-second burst seemed to last forever.

Plumes of sand and earth spewed from the low ridge on the hill across Page Mill Road. The A-10 kept right on going, grazing the trees on the top of the hill before it turned right and arced into the darkening sky. Its flares bounced across the hillside, setting fire to the tinder-dry grass.

"Scratch one sniper!" shouted one of the Marines behind him.

Another barrage of depleted uranium shells tore into another hillside to their left. The roar of the Gatling gun thrummed through him a second later. A third A-10 barreled through the air above the campus. It cleared the ridge by less than a wingspan before soaring into the low deck of clouds.

It was easy to see why the Al Qaeda and ISIS *mujahideen* called the A-10 "the Devil's Cross."

"Damage assessment!" Ames shouted.

His men scoured the scenery with their binoculars.

Sparks Two yelled, "Top! Ana reports the Hellfire scratched every one of the bad guys in front of the building. There are still some near the gates."

"Missile crew is gone, First Sergeant!" came Bat's unmistakable babble over the radio.

"Bat, tell 'em to lob some more Hellfires in there! I want those gates clear!"

"Wilco, Top!"

Sergeant Drake said, "Two sniper crews down, Top!"

"Top!" called the Navy corpsman, Collins. "Laurel Wynn is up here!"

Ames turned and looked back. Sure enough, Laurel Wynn was scrambling up the grassy hillside behind him. He growled, "Goddammit!"

Something moved in the corner of his eye. That one something became many.

He ducked instinctively, trying to figure out what it was. Then his eyes swiveled toward the Bay.

"Holy fuck!" he gasped.

The placid surface of San Francisco Bay had exploded.

Massive black and white clouds erupted everywhere, running the whole length of the Bay, or as much of it as he could see from this hilltop. Hundreds of spherical shockwaves lensed the air, expanding away from the center of each explosion at the speed of sound.

"They're hitting the shipping channel!" Laurel Wynn shouted in his ear. "To take out any other subs!"

"No shit!" he barked. She'd crawled up the slope next to him, propping herself up with her right arm. She seemed a lot livelier than when he'd seen her last. "What the hell are you doing, sneaking up on us like that? You could've been shot!"

"Your men recognized me," she said. "You might want to cover your ears!" She jammed her hands over hers just as the first sound reached them.

BOOM-boom-boom-BOOMBOOMBBBBBOOOOOOOOOOMMMMM

His noise-canceling earplugs helped, but not much.

The rolling thunder was joined by the shrieking roar of near-supersonic aircraft. He saw some of them now: giant, arrowhead-shaped B-1B Lancers, more than he'd ever seen in one place before. There had to be dozens of them, spaced a mile or two apart, swing-wings all the way back, afterburners blazing. They rocketed south just under the high cloud deck, one after the other, moving much faster than anything that big had a right to move. He could even see cone-shaped shockwaves form and dissipate behind their swept-back wings.

As he watched, the fiery, blue-hot spears of exhaust from the engines of one of the bombers winked out. The plane instantly pulled up, its swing-wings spreading wide as it arced up and to the west. It slowed as it rose, seeming almost to come to a standstill before pitching forward suddenly. Four jets of flame burst away from its cockpit, sending small dark objects tumbling into the sky. The plane fell, disappearing briefly behind the clouds for a moment before spinning into the hills perhaps a mile to the northwest.

Parachutes deployed from the objects that had ejected from the plane. They dropped slowly behind the line of hills to the north of the campus.

The din continued to grow, and grow, and grow, as hundreds of massive explosions mixed with the demonic howl of bombers flying at just under the speed of sound. The crash of the bomber was barely noticeable in that unholy din.

The blasts seemed like they would last forever. Every refugee heading south would shit their pants at that sound, and with good reason. The raw might of the blasts was starkly terrifying, even to him.

He barely heard the second salvo of Hellfires over that awful noise, but he sure saw them. Two more orange death-blossoms rose skyward from either side of the campus grounds.

The two A-10s that had delivered them were going head-to-head. They turned on their sides and crossed within feet of each other, directly over the center of the campus, their wingtips carving through the smoke, leaving horizontal tornadoes and dozens of glaring white flares bouncing across the campus behind them.

Ames turned to the radio operator. "Get on the horn to our rides and tell them to get in the air. They can land on Deer Creek Road. It's pretty clear. We might need medevac."

"Yes, First Sergeant!"

"We still got one more sniper, Top!" shouted Sergeant Drake, pointing.

Ames saw something dark and fast drop down from the clouds. He grinned at his subordinate. "Not for long."

When Bobby Boykin saw the last of the guards at the gates blown to burning gobbets, he finally shook himself out of his astonished paralysis. He hissed, "Jesus Christ!"

Another A-10 swooped down from the lowering sky.

It turned in his direction.

He shouted, "Fuck this!" He dropped his rifle and ran.

Hans struggled to keep up. But Bobby already knew it was too late.

There was an awful sound behind him, like a thousand men pounding the hillside with baseball bats.

He had just enough time to think that being fired at by an A-10 wasn't like being shot at by a machine gun.

It was more like being on the business end of a meteor storm.

Ames watched the ridge top across Page Mill Road dissolve beneath a rain of depleted uranium shells.

He checked his watch. They had less than ten minutes to secure that building before Dorsey's bomber started its run. It was time to go.

He raised his voice and said, "Come on, you sons of bitches, you want to live forever? Assault teams, move in!"

He got to his feet, unslung his M4, flicked off the safety and joined the rush toward the long concrete fence at the bottom of Coyote Hill.

He scowled when he saw Laurel Wynn sprinting down the hillside to join them, but her safety was her problem. She'd made it clear enough that she wasn't going to obey his orders.

586

When the fireball erupted outside, Tom Reed leaped back from the window. He threw himself to the floor and covered his head with his arms in sheer, blind instinct. His Punisher fell out of his hands and bounced into Broadway. Into the part they hadn't cleared.

A keening *CLANG* rang through the building as the thick glass absorbed the blast. Miraculously, it held firm.

Static roared in his earpiece, then was just as suddenly cut off. An instant later it was filled with a gurgling, agonized scream.

He screamed uselessly into his own headset, "Take your radios off VOX! Turn off the mic, you stupid fuck!"

Distant booming crashes echoed through the halls, mixing with the banshee roar of God knew how many jet engines.

The Air Force had arrived.

The scream in his earphones suddenly cut off, only to be replaced by someone else's.

He heard the muffled, unmistakable sound of Gatling gun fire outside. Then two more explosions shook the building.

Tom raised his head in time to see an A-10 ground attack jet flying toward him, ridiculously close to the ground. It rolled onto its side as it came, flying right through the rising cloud of flame and smoke above the north gate, where a missile had struck. The tip of its wing clipped branches from the top of one of the few trees still standing along the fence. It flashed by, directly in the front of the building, not fifty feet away. For an instant he could see directly into the cockpit.

Another A-10 blasted past it, flying in the opposite direction, spraying arc-lamp bright flares in its wake. A pair of smoky cyclones trailed behind the plane as it raced into the sky.

Speechless with rage, Tom stood and grabbed the screaming radio at his belt. He ripped his headset cable free and threw the transceiver at the wall, shattering it.

He stared dumbly out the window. It was no longer pristine. Dozens of inch-long diamond-shaped metal shards stuck out of it. The tips had penetrated to a depth of about half an inch.

The smoke from the latest blasts began to clear. He looked down and saw what he feared to see, strewn in bloody chunks across the shredded lawn.

All of the wounded and the men who'd been treating them were dead.

He saw movement in the corner of his eye. Armed Marines had gotten past the shattered gates. They were converging on the Pauling Building. Not many, but enough to overwhelm his tiny band of survivors.

A smaller figure carrying only a pistol trailed just behind the soldiers coming in from the left.

As he watched, it sprinted past them.

Tom looked at his men as they picked themselves up off the floor. He recognized Nick, Chucky and Gonzo. The other two were contractors whose names he couldn't remember. They stared at him mutely, their eyes filled with terror.

Then he looked at his Punisher, resting on the floor down the hall. A long streak of shiny steel had been gouged out of its barrel—proof that were diamond fibers in the hallway. He didn't dare to retrieve it.

He stared at the gun, mouth open.

When he heard shouts and many footsteps echoing up from the ground floor, he looked at his men. "Surrender," he said bleakly. "Put down your guns, lie down on the floor and put your hands behind your heads. Try to run. Or let them mow you down. Whatever makes you happy. We're finished."

He pulled his 9mm from its holster and thumbed the safety off.

"But I have something to take care of first."

He ran to the other end of Main Street, praying that he'd remember all of Aidan's radioed directions.

Jack ducked instinctively as a fiery cloud boiled into the air outside the window at the far end of Main Street. He managed to keep his grip on the HyperQUBE, but just barely.

Aidan jumped back as the blast rang through the building.

Adrenaline flooded through him. *This is it!*

"Air assault on the enemy is underway!" shouted Ana Katsumata in Jack's earpiece.

A sound like God's fly being unzipped came from outside.

"It's over," Jack said, straightening.

Aidan turned to stare at him, his eyes huge in a face utterly drained of color.

Distant explosions thumped through the halls, accompanied by the high keening whine of jet engines.

Aidan's mouth moved, but he said nothing.

There were two more huge blasts of orange fire outside. An instant later, two cross-shaped airplanes nearly flew into each other right in front of the window.

John Shea charged around the corner, his M4 at his shoulder. "Get out of the way, Jack!" he yelled.

He looked over his shoulder at John. "No."

"Let me put that son of a bitch down!" John sidled over, trying to get an angle. Sy Hamilton and Alex Southall ran up to join him, crouching behind the corners at the end of the hall.

Jack moved to block their shots. "I still have one question to ask." He walked up to Aidan, staring into his eyes, unblinking.

Aidan backed away.

"Marines are entering the building!" cried Ana on the radio.

"Jack, goddammit! Move!" John roared.

Ana's voice came over the PA system now. "One tango, on the second floor, on the move. Armed with a pistol."

"You were with Emily that day," hissed Jack. "The day Eddie died. So I know you didn't set the fire."

There was a distant sound of shouting.

"Five tangos surrendered!" Ana shouted. "Only one left! Second floor, North Avenue now, heading to Stairwell One!"

Aidan kept backing up. He was about ten feet from the end of Main Street.

Jack kept pace with him.

The hallways echoed with rapid, distant footsteps, quickly growing louder.

"Who did it, Aidan?" Jack whispered. "Who did you send to kill my son?"

Aidan's head whipped to his left.

The cruel-looking blond gunman ran into view at the far end of Broadway. His pistol was already raised. He halted just short of the intersection with Main Street.

John and his men wouldn't be able to hit him from there.

Jack moved to put Aidan between himself and the gunman. In the corner of his eye, he saw that John Shea and his men were running toward him. *Too late,* he thought bleakly.

"Aidan," said the gunman. "Get behind me."

Aidan didn't move. His mouth gaped wide.

The gunman shouted, "Aidan!"

Aidan seemed to snap out of it. "Tom, what are you doing?"

The gunman's face was red with fury. "We lost! If we can't have it, no one can!" He took aim, sighting through Aidan's head directly at Jack. "AIDAN!" he screamed. "DROP NOW!"

Aidan dropped.

Jack hurled the HyperQUBE at the gunman and dove to his right.

The silver object flying at his face distracted the blond man, but not enough. He let it fly past his head and fired twice as he ducked.

The first round hit Jack in the chest. He reeled back against the wall just inside Main Street. The second bullet must have gone wide.

The HyperQUBE smashed into the armor glass behind the gunman, exploding into silver and golden shards.

A woman's voice echoed down the hall. "TOM REED!"

Startled, the gunman glanced back.

A single gunshot rang out, followed by a fusillade of machine gun fire from Shea and his men.

The gunman was already falling when the machine gun rounds hammered him. The gun flew from his hand. He dropped to the floor, limp as a rag. His helmet bounced away. Blood poured from the hole in the back of his head, just above the neck.

Jack gasped. The gunman's bullet had smacked into the ceramic plate in the center of his chest. It felt like a mule had kicked him in the breast bone.

Something hot flowed down his leg.

He looked down. When he saw the dark redness spreading across his camouflage pants, he finally felt it. Agony knifed through his gut. He grabbed for the wound.

The second bullet hadn't gone wide.

It had missed the bottom of his vest by less than an inch and entered his abdomen just to the right of his navel. He pressed his hand over the wound, but blood was also pouring down his back.

He gasped, "Son of a fucking bitch!"

Aidan's answer was a scream of despair.

Jack looked up.

Aidan cradled the dead gunman's head in his hands. "Oh, Tom! Oh, no! No!"

Then Jack knew.

"It was him, wasn't it?" he gasped.

Aidan looked up, eyes unseeing. "What?"

"He killed my son. On your orders."

Aidan's only answer was an anguished wail.

"Jack!" a woman called to him from somewhere close by. It was a familiar voice. But he had eyes only for Aidan O'Keefe.

"He killed my son. And you killed Emily."

Rage snuffed out his pain.

Jack launched himself at Aidan O'Keefe.

He felt something crunch before they managed to pry his bloody hands from the weeping monster's throat.

They got him onto his back and stripped the vest away. Someone shouted, "Get the XStat applicator! Go, go, go!"

The world dissolved into chaos. The rage drained away. The void was filled with agony, worse than anything he'd felt since the fire. Yet he was strangely content.

Faces stared down at him. He recognized John Shea, his face contorted with fury. There was Alex Southall, the friendly young bull who'd escorted him into the building his first day at what was then called StruvePharma. There was a young black man, too, someone he didn't know, wearing a bluish camouflage uniform with an embroidered caduceus logo on a patch. He seemed very busy.

There was a sharp prick in his arm. Cool relief surged through him. The agony faded away.

Then he saw Laurel, panting for breath, her eyes shining with unshed tears.

"Hello, beautiful," he whispered. He spotted the torn uniform and the bloody bandage on her left shoulder. "Oh, no, you got hurt."

"Shh, Jack," she said between gasps. "Just relax. I'm fine."

"Was it you? You got him? The blond guy?"

"Yes. I got him."

He felt a surge of panic. "Oh, no. You shouldn't... shouldn't be here. Did you get it?"

"Yes," she said, glancing up at the others. "I got your message. I love you, too."

He smiled. *Clever. I almost gave it all away.* "Can't wait to... to take you to that hotel in Tahiti. Remember? Told you about it... first time we met. Said I'd take you there on our honeymoon. There's this really great bar. Walk on the beach. See you in a bathing suit. Wow." He swallowed with difficulty. "It's a magical place."

"It sounds great, Jack," she said. Tears fell onto his face. They felt like rain.

The young black man said, "We gotta get him to the hospital. Now."

A leather-faced sergeant came into view, looking down at him. "Osprey just touched down. We got a cart or a gurney or something?"

"We're just gonna have to carry him. I gotta sedate him and put in a tube first."

"Oh, crap," he mumbled. "Laurel..."

"Yes, Jack?"

"Take care of the kids for me. I love—"

There was another sharp pain in his arm, and the world went away.

Laurel went with them as they carried him to the Osprey and carefully put him inside.

To her astonishment, four Marines carried the limp body of Aidan O'Keefe into the troop compartment as well. There was blood on his throat, and a small plastic tube sticking out of the emergency tracheotomy. She heard breath whistling through the tube as the Marines shoved past her. They placed him on the floor next to Jack.

Collins knelt on Jack's other side, holding an IV bag up with one hand. He gave her a thumbs-up, but when he turned away and leaned over Jack's motionless form, his mouth was set in a grimace.

She watched from the wrecked campus gate as the Osprey clawed its way into the air. She turned and walked back to the Pauling Building. Jack had asked her to take care of the kids. They were still sealed in the basement.

It took nearly an hour to restore the backup freight elevator to full working order. They were in communication with them the whole time. They were never in any danger. They were afraid, but not for themselves. For Jack.

There was a brief, somber reunion as they came out of the elevator and found her there to greet them. The Marines helped move the wounded Guardsmen and their caretakers back up to the auditorium. They also rescued Martín Garza from the roof. He was still woozy, but the corpsmen said he'd be fine.

Laurel waited with her friends in the fourth-floor lounge while John Shea and his men cleared the remaining super-diamond monofilaments from the hallways.

Stathis tracked her down. "Got Mikey back," he said briefly. "Battery low but still good enough for a couple of minutes flying. How was Oscar when you saw him?" He looked at her meaningfully.

"Fine," she said. "He's in a bush a few blocks away. You should send someone to get him."

"Sounds good. Everything's taken care of here." He sat down and joined the vigil.

She kept her self-control until John Shea walked in. His face was bleak. He walked up to her and looked down with brimming eyes.

She stood unsteadily. "When?" she asked, her voice breaking.

"About half an hour ago," he grated. "They couldn't stop the bleeding."

When she came back to herself, she was standing in the lobby, looking out through the ragged breach in the armor glass wall.

Smoke curled into the threatening sky from the shattered remains of the campus grounds. The air was filled with the harsh chemical reek of burning plastic and the ghastly stench of a slaughterhouse.

It isn't true, she thought. It's just a cover story. He's fine.

As she watched, flakes of charcoal-colored ash began to fall.

"I'm sorry," said John.

She started. She hadn't realized he'd come with her. "I'm sorry, too." She sighed. "What about Aidan?"

"No idea." His voice trembled with unspent fury.

She wiped her eyes and took stock of herself. She still had her canteen and her gas mask in its big camouflage pouch. Her 9mm pistol was back in its holster. She realized then that she was still wearing her vest and body armor. She'd managed to get used to the weight, after all.

It isn't true. He's alive. He's fine. Focus. Finish the job.

She put the magazines for her pistol into a pocket, then unstrapped the vest and let it fall to the floor.

"I need to go for a walk," she said.

"In that?" he said, pointing at the thickening rain of ash.

"In that. I need to clear my head, John." She unbuckled the pouch and took out the gas mask.

She met his eyes.

Eventually, he nodded. "They're sending some Blackhawks to evac everybody. Should be here in an hour or so."

"I'll see you then." She put the mask on, pulled the straps taut, and walked out.

After calling off the fruitless hunt for survivors, the Marines had pulled back into the Pauling Building to escape the fallout. No one was outside to stop her.

She went out the south gate and turned left onto Deer Creek Road.

She powered off her cell phone and dropped it into a storm drain before she was a mile from the campus.

She checked a dozen abandoned houses in Los Altos Hills before she found all of the supplies she needed.

When she emerged from her final stop, she was fully equipped with good hiking gear, a backpack full of freeze-dried camping food, three big bottles of water, a tiny gas stove, two cans of fuel, a first aid kit with plenty of gauze bandages and tape, a small tent, a book of local area day hikes, and a summer-weight sleeping bag. The gear was heavy but not as bad as the body armor. The camping enthusiasts even had the foresight to buy a decent water filtration unit. Laurel guessed that they'd been out of town when the nuke hit.

The camping-nut wife or girlfriend had been a pretty good match for Laurel's size. The only parts of her uniform that she kept were her sturdy, well-fitted boots, her canteen, her gas mask, her pistol, and the spare magazines. She threw a lightweight Gore-Tex poncho over her shoulders and pack to shelter them from falling ash before she left. She disposed of her blood-stained ACUs in a trash can at the end of the block.

She hiked west, into the hills. Cold rain began to pelt her long before she reached the treeless summit and found a place with good drainage. There was just enough light for her to pitch her tent before true darkness fell.

The wind was blowing strongly from the west now, and there was no more evidence of ash. She stripped to the skin and washed herself in the rain to make sure she didn't track fallout in with her before she went inside. She cursed herself for forgetting to steal a towel.

It isn't true. He's fine. He's perfectly fine.

She let herself air-dry in front of the meager cooking stove until she could stand the cold no more. She taped a fresh dressing onto her shoulder, turned off the stove and jammed herself into her sleeping bag to shiver herself to sleep.

She was too exhausted to dream, but the wind beating on the tent woke her up frequently.

It's not true, she chanted to herself, again and again as she tried to get back to sleep.

But there had been so much blood.

The rain lasted all night, culminating with a heavy downpour just before dawn.

When she emerged from her tent the following morning, aching and exhausted, the sun was high and the wind still blew briskly to the east. She could not see San Francisco directly from her camp site, but volcano-like clouds of smoke still violated the otherwise pristine blue sky to the north. Fortunately, the clouds were headed away from the Peninsula. She hoped the soaking rainfall would keep the fires from spreading too much further south.

She used the hiking book to find her way to the coast. She took her time, careful of her stiff, throbbing shoulder, avoiding the few other refugees she heard stumbling through the woods.

He's alive, he's alive, he's alive, she chanted silently, keeping time with the rhythm of her footfalls.

She came across a cabin near the end of the first full day of her hike. The doors were open. The inside was trashed. The looters had taken all the food and electronics, but they'd left the bath towels.

Laurel finally arrived at the intersection of Highway 1 and State Road 84 just after noon on November 4, three days after walking away from the carnage at ST.

Other than the ever-present pile-ups, the only vehicles she saw were Army trucks in the middle distance. She hurriedly crossed the highway and found herself at San Gregorio State Beach.

There were thousands of others camped on the hills overlooking the long, sandy beach. It was orderly enough, but much too crowded for her tastes. Tanker trucks were dispensing drinking water, so she dumped and refilled her canteen.

National Guards handed out plastic-wrapped Meals Ready to Eat from the back of a big canvas-covered truck. She stood in the hundreds-long line and collected one, wolfing its contents eagerly. Hiking burned a lot of calories, and she'd grown thoroughly sick of the rehy-drated camping food after the second day. She eyed the Guardsmen and tried not to think of the mangled, ACU-clad bodies she'd run past on her way to the Pauling Building.

Around her, everyone was talking about the war with North Korea. She had trouble concentrating on anything but the food. The only information she took away from the confused babble of rumors was that the Kim dynasty would no longer be a bother to anyone.

When she finished, she decided to go north to Half Moon Bay. There was a harbor just north of the town, sheltered behind the arms of two boulder-strewn breakwaters. The others were talking about refugees getting out on ships leaving from there. It wasn't too far, if her memory served.

Her memory didn't. Pillar Point Harbor was much further away than she remembered. She arrived just after sunset, having cadged a ride on a northbound bus half-filled with dejected refugees.

The last time she'd been here, the slips in Pillar Point Harbor had been full of pleasure craft, sailboats, and working fisherman's vessels. Now they were empty, but at least the lights were back on.

Vacant slips notwithstanding, the marina was busy. Dozens of big ships were anchored well beyond the breakwater. A warship cruised south, the marine fog layer hovering like a gray curtain wall just behind it. Navy and Coast Guard launches ferried people away from the long pier that jutted out into the harbor.

She waited behind hundreds of others for her turn to board one of the boats. Volunteers from a local restaurant handed out rolls of sourdough bread, bottled water and small cups of clam chowder. She blinked tears of gratitude away as she consumed them.

Two days later she found herself at a refugee processing center on Coronado Island in San Diego. She claimed to have lost her ID. She gave a fake name to the nattily dressed lieutenant who interviewed her. The camp was too crowded for them to bother with niceties like fingerprints.

Shortly thereafter she was bussed to a refugee camp somewhere in the hot, dry Imperial Valley, well inland of the beautiful coastal city. From the smell of rotting fish, it had to be somewhere downwind of the landlocked Salton Sea.

She got on the waiting list for the public computers. Everyone else in the camp without a working cell phone was waiting their turn to get in touch with loved ones via the Internet. The list was amazingly long, and each person was granted only ten minutes at a time.

The corpsmen in the hospital tent clucked when the saw the condition of her wound, but she'd kept it clean and it wasn't infected. It would leave an ugly scar. They dismissed her after giving her a clean dressing, a shot of antibiotics, a paltry handful of pain killers, and a schoolmarm scolding.

When her turn for the computer finally came, she plugged in the USB thumb drive she'd taken from Oscar's battery compartment, signed up to a file sharing service using a fake name she'd used in the past for work, uploaded the drive's contents and made them publicly accessible.

Then she sent emails with the link to that file share to every newspaper and magazine she could think of. With her background in electronic espionage, she had amassed quite a list.

Someone would look. Perhaps many. Her email had been crisp and concise. If working in the FBI had taught her anything, it was how to write an attention-getting memo.

She unplugged the thumb drive, signed off, and went back to her cot in the huge, poorly air-conditioned barracks tent. She lay down and stared up at the flapping canvas roof.

That's it, Jack. Mission accomplished. I'll find you. I'll find you soon. If you're... if you're still...

She would not allow herself to think it.

Unconsciousness swept over her like the incoming tide.

She opened her eyes when she felt someone shaking her shoulder gently.

It was the middle of the night. There were three men standing over her. She recognized one of them.

She said, "Special Agent Robert Stephen Holmes. You just can't let me get a good night's sleep, can you?"

The few refugees awake nearby stared at them fearfully.

Robbie didn't smile. He knelt next to her cot and took her hand. "I'm so sorry," he said, his voice cracking.

The two policemen behind him looked at the floor.

Desolation swept through her.

She burst into tears.

EPILOGUE

When he woke up, he was in a room with plain white walls and a faint odor of antiseptic.

An old man in a somber black suit sat in a chair at the foot of his bed, reading a book. He was as bald as an egg and had a hawk's merciless stare.

Behind the old man was an open window. Sunlight streamed through the sheer drapes.

The air rippling through the fabric smelled clean and fresh. It carried a naggingly familiar scent. He'd been here for days, now, and he still couldn't identify it, but it smelled good.

He looked at the old man and said in a high, querulous voice, "Gandalf?" Then he coughed half a dozen times. "Shit. Ruined it."

"That's all right. I didn't get it, anyway." The old man stood, went to his bedside table and handed him a plastic glass of water with a bendy straw in it.

He raised his head and took a long, cool sip. "Thanks. Seriously, you never saw *The Lord of the Rings?* You're missing out. Great movie. Seemed like every time Frodo woke up, Gandalf was sitting at the end of the bed."

"Young man, the last movie I saw in the theater was *The Star Wars.* It's what made me stop going to the theater."

"The *Star Wars?* Egad. So who the hell are you?"

"My name is Andrew Seigart, Dr. Dura. I'm the Secretary of Homeland Security."

"Please. All my girlfriends' bosses call me Jack. Congratulations on the promotion. Where the hell is she?"

"Thank you, Jack. Actually, Laurel's part of the reason I'm here. She's in a lot of trouble, thanks to you."

Jack hit the button that raised the bed into a semi-reclining position. He winced as his stitches complained. "You found her? Is she all right?" He'd asked everyone about Laurel since he first woke up in this anonymous hospital. The doctors, nurses, and scrupulously nondescript orderlies had claimed to know nothing.

"She's fine. She's in custody."

"What the *fuck?* It's *my* theory. I asked her to send it out. It's a free country, or at least, it was. I didn't violate any trade secrets agreements with ST. And what if I did? I forgive myself. I'm the CEO."

"Not anymore." He opened the big book he'd been reading and pulled out a newspaper clipping.

"They have this thing called the Internet, Gramps," Jack said, glad of the chance to use Hank's line. He felt a sudden pang as he realized how much he missed the lanky young man, not to mention Lizbeth, Terry and Chao-Xing. The two newcomers from ZMPC. Even John Shea.

"Yes, I've heard of the Internet," Seigart said dryly. "I'd show you on my iPad if they allowed them in here." He handed Jack the clipping. It unfolded several times to a length of at least two feet.

It was an article about him.

When he looked up from it, his heart was pounding. "So I died while they were trying to rescue me, eh?"

Seigart plucked the clipping from his unresisting fingers. "That's the way it is. That's the way it's going to stay. Before you ask, it's the only way to keep you safe." He moved his chair closer to Jack's bedside and sat down wearily.

Jack shook his head. "I have seen this shit in so many movies, you wouldn't believe it. It never works."

"Let me clue you in about what's happened since you got your little tummy ache. We fought a very one-sided nuclear war with North Korea. They lost. Every North Korean who can walk is headed into China. South Korea was badly hurt, too, when Kooky Kim Junior decided to fire every artillery piece and medium-range missile he had before we turned Pyongyang into a glowing crater."

Seigart talked and talked. By the time he finished, Jack thought he was going to throw up.

Over a million and a half people were thought to have died in the blackened ruins of the Bay Area. Everyone else had fled, creating a refugee crisis the likes of which America had never seen.

Tens of millions had died in North and South Korea. God only knew how many more would starve to death before they reached help.

After the attack, the search for the reason for the horrors began. The inside story of Struve Technologies went public.

It didn't matter that all the QUBEs were destroyed. The capabilities of the technology they'd developed shocked the world at a time when everyone hoped the shocks were already past.

Within hours, the oil futures market collapsed. The economies of nations dependent on oil plummeted as well. The populations of those nations rose up to bring down their leaders. Then they turned on each other. Long-dormant sectarian and tribal feuds flared back to life across the globe.

When they saw that the great powers were utterly consumed with their own problems, the *jihadis* trying to restore a global Islamic Caliphate attacked Israel. Astonishingly, Egypt joined Israel in fighting them off. Hezbollah responded with chlorine and sarin gas attacks. When Gaza, Beirut, Damascus and Tehran were reduced to smoking holes in the desert, the *jihadis* suddenly decided they had better things to do at home. When they ran out of bullets, they switched to swords.

The global stock market crashed to the ground and as yet showed no signs of reviving. Trillions of dollars had been lost, perhaps forever.

China was on the brink of another revolution. The Great Firewall had sprung a hundred leaks. The shell game that was the Chinese command economy had been exposed. In a world where few had money, no one was buying what they were trying to sell. Their domestic consumption, never strong, had nearly collapsed. There were rumors about members of the Standing Committee disappearing in suspicious circumstances. The Chinese were painting radar on everything that moved on sea, land or air near their borders. They'd even fired warning shots at a Japanese Coast Guard ship near some islands the two nations had been arguing over for years.

China wasn't the only country on the verge of ruin. The EU was tee-tering on the brink. The poorer members were calling for the richer members to prop them up, only there weren't any rich members anymore, only less impoverished ones. Nationalism suddenly reassert-ed itself across the continent. Some of the larger members of the EU had announced plans to leave it. The bureaucrats in Brussels were aghast at the prospect of a full-fledged monetary dissolution. And the Russians were on the move. They'd already taken back the rest of Ukraine, and were now massing on the borders of their former satel-lites.

In spite of the attack on San Francisco, the U.S. economy was the least-worst off. Even here, assuming a full-scale nuclear war didn't settle things for good, conditions were expected to be worse than the Great Depression of the Thirties.

Seigart rubbed his scalp. "I could go on, but I think you get the gist."

"I don't believe it," Jack croaked.

"I'm not surprised. It's a lot to take in all at once." Seigart stood up, went to the door, and opened it. "Could you bring those in here, please?"

A dark-skinned orderly brought in an armful of newspapers.

"Just put them on the bed, there," Seigart said.

The orderly complied and left without a word.

Seigart said, "You might want to look through those, while they're still printing them. They'll be switching to online-only soon. Paper's getting scarce."

Jack saw a copy of the Santa Fe *New Mexican* on top of the pile. The headline screamed RUSSIANS PAUSE AT HUNGARIAN BORDER in two-inch letters.

"The *New Mexican?*" He looked up. "That orderly was Hopi," he said wonderingly.

"If you say so," said Seigart, sitting back down with a grunt.

Now he knew what he'd smelled through the open window. Piñon and juniper. Sagebrush and mesquite. The heady scent of ponderosa pines, drifting down from the slopes of the Jemez Mountains.

"So, I'm home."

"Got it in one," said Seigart. "Welcome to Los Alamos National Laboratory, home of the atomic bomb. If we can't keep you a secret here, we can't keep it anywhere. Now, let's talk about Laurel Wynn. When she walked out of Palo Alto, the information on that thumb drive wasn't classified. By the time she posted it, it was. As classified as it gets. Right up there with nuclear weapons data. There's a whole new law, approved by Congress and everything."

"She couldn't have known that!"

"Really? She must have thought it was possible. Otherwise, why walk away from the campus and hike out with the refugees? Don't try to play me, Jack. I've been doing this kind of work for a long, long time. Laurel's smart. She must have known the curtain was going to come down."

"Goddammit, you can't classify an entire science! Someone would have figured it out eventually."

"Possibly, but you two have made that question kind of academic, now, haven't you?"

Jack fumed but didn't respond.

"What the hell were you thinking?" Seigart asked mildly.

"Quantinuum theory is too big for one owner. It's too much power to give to one company, or one country. It's science, man. You can't keep science a secret. Either everyone shares in the knowledge, or no one does. You don't get to decide. I don't get to decide. *They* get to decide."

Seigart shook his head. "God save us from idealists."

Jack snorted. "We recorded everything in the Pauling Building. Did you see the video of Aidan O'Keefe trying to talk me into going with him?"

"Several times."

"Then you know what I'm talking about. He wasn't interested in saving the world. He said those things to try to get me to come with him willingly. He just wanted power." He looked pointedly at the old man. "This world is full of people just like him. The only way to prevent them from monopolizing power is to give it to everyone."

Seigart studied him for a long moment, obviously unconvinced. "Well, it doesn't matter now. Thanks to you, the secret's out. Congratulations, Prometheus. You and your girlfriend set fire to the world. Now I'm going to give you a chance to help put it out."

Seigart talked for a long time.

When he finished, he stared at Jack. "Well?"

Jack leaned back against the pillow and closed his eyes. "Let me think about it. Come back tomorrow."

Seigart's knees popped as he stood. "Fair enough. I'll be back after lunch. I hear you like the local food. I'll have them bring you a burrito or something."

Jack studied the papers for hours after Seigart left. When he could stand no more, he shoved the pile onto the floor, lay back and closed his eyes.

Sleep was a long time coming.

Seigart was as good as his word. The next day, the same Hopi orderly who'd brought the papers carted in a take-out box filled to bursting with a giant burrito drenched with hot green chile sauce. Jack's gray mood dissipated instantly. "Oh, my God, that smells unbelievable. Chili Works?"

The orderly nodded, looking at Jack with curiosity as he rolled the table into position.

"I grew up here. What's your name?"

"Dan Tewanima."

"Dan, I accept you as my personal savior. Thank you." He offered his hand. Tewanima shook it, smiling shyly.

Jack inhaled the burrito, slashing at it with the plastic knife and shoveling it into his maw with the plastic spork. *"Carne asada,"* he mumbled happily. "Oh, God, green chile." From what Seigart was saying, there was no guarantee that little stores like the one that made this burrito would even be functioning a few months from now. He prayed the old man was wrong. Life without New Mexican food just wasn't worth living.

Seigart walked in just after Dan Tewanima took away the empty box, now torn apart and thoroughly licked clean.

"Feeling better?" asked the old man. He was dressed just as he had been the previous day. Jack wondered if Seigart did the Einstein thing and filled his wardrobe with the same black suit for every occasion.

"Didn't sleep well, but the burrito took the edge off."

"Glad to hear it," he said in a voice as dry as the Sahara. He dragged his chair from its spot near the window and brought it to Jack's bedside. He lowered himself gingerly into it, folded his hands across his stomach, and looked at Jack expectantly.

Jack returned Seigart's gaze without blinking. "I have two conditions."

November 12

When she woke up, a key was rattling in the lock of her cell.

She stood quickly, wincing at the sharp protest from the healing wound in her shoulder, and brushed at her orange prison overalls to flatten the wrinkles.

Robbie Holmes walked in. His dolorous face wasn't as grim as usual.

"Did you hear from your parents?" she asked anxiously.

He nodded, actually smiling a little. "They're fine. And I have some good news. They're letting you go. All charges dropped. All you have to do is sign a confidentiality agreement."

Relief flooded through her, then a wave of suspicion. "Why?"

"Hell if I know, Laurel, but if I were you, I'd take it. Beats turning big rocks into little rocks at Leavenworth for the rest of your life."

"I'll take it."

Two hours of mind-numbing processing later, she emerged blinking into warm, autumnal California sunlight. They'd cleaned her stolen hiking clothes. She silently swore an oath never to wear anything orange again.

Robbie walked out with her to the parking lot.

She looked at the sign in front of the maximum security prison. "Seriously? George Bailey Detention Center? Frank Capra's rolling in his grave."

"I don't even know what that means."

"George Bailey? *It's a Wonderful Life?* Didn't you ever watch TV around Christmas? Jimmy Stewart? 'Merry Christmas, movie house?'"

He just looked at her blankly.

"Never mind. I told you I've been hanging around Jack Dura too long."

Oh, I shouldn't have said that.

He held her awkwardly until the tears stopped. He handed her a clean, folded handkerchief. "Keep it," he said after she blew her nose into it. "I've got others."

"What now?" she said, voice hitching. She looked at the desolate, treeless hills around the prison.

A rental car pulled into the parking lot in front of them. The passenger side window rolled down.

The driver was John Shea.

Laurel hugged Robbie one last time and got in.

John pulled the car away from the curb. "I understand you lost your job."

"Yeah," she sighed. "For some reason, the FBI seems to think I'm a security risk."

"Want a new one?"

"Yes, please. Doing what?"

"You'll see."

The flight to Tennessee took about six hours, with a layover in Denver. There weren't many people on the plane. The airports were nearly empty. People weren't traveling unless they had to.

They were picked up at the Knoxville Airport by a pair of unsmiling, bullet-headed young men in nondescript dark gray suits. They were even less amusing than the two men who'd picked her up for her fighter-jet ride to Moffett Field, a hundred years ago.

They drove through the gate of the Oak Ridge National Laboratory well after sundown. There wasn't much to see except lights on poles and generically pleasant office buildings with red trim and lots of windows.

Their two escorts walked them into the lobby of one of the buildings.

It was a Dura Party reunion. Everyone was there: Hank and Lizbeth, Ben and Deepthi, Chao-Xing and Terry, everyone dressed in casual clothing and wearing smiles. Many hugs were exchanged.

Amber D'Agostino and Stathis Sotiropoulos arrived a few minutes after Laurel. She shook Amber's listless hand, but when Stathis extended his, she pulled him into an embrace, kissed him on the cheek, and looked into his eyes. "Thank *God* for the Greek," she whispered. "If it hadn't been for you, Stathis—" She couldn't say any more.

His blush was its own reward. "No. Thank God for you, Laurel. You saved us all."

Not everyone. She willed the incipient tears away and tried to laugh. "Let's just agree that we all saved each other, and leave it at that."

She had just enough time to learn that most of them had reunited with their loved ones in the Bay Area—Amber D'Agostino being the notable and heartbroken exception—when the lobby doors opened again.

Philip Mayhew walked in. Behind him was Andrew Seigart.

She nodded to them both. Mayhew's frown was back with a vengeance. He'd either lost or given up on the hairpiece. He actually looked pretty good without it, though his down-turned mouth was beginning to make him look like Beaker from *The Muppet Show.*

Seigart returned her nod with a hint of a smile. Now that is something you don't see every day. Or ever.

"Thanks for coming on such short notice," Seigart said. He looked at one of the bullet-headed guards. "Dr. Eiseley said you'd show us to room 31."

"Yes, sir, it's all been arranged. Please follow me."

At length they found themselves in a conference room, seated around an oblong table. There was a water cooler with paper cups in the corner, a big flat panel display on the far wall, and a whiteboard with about a hundred dry-erase markers heaped on the bottom rail.

"So here's the deal," said Seigart. "Luckily for you, according to the bylaws of the agreement he signed with the Board of Directors, God rest their souls, Philip Mayhew is now the Chairman of Struve Technologies, version 2.0. And he has a billion and a half dollars in cash, for what that's worth. He's agreed to restart the company, and wants to offer you all continued employment. And to hire Laurel Wynn as a security consultant, working for Mr. Shea. Arrest record expunged. Security clearance restored." He looked around the table at every face in turn. "Well?"

"Excuse me, sir," said Terry Blau. "But the lab's still in Palo Alto."

"Not for long. It's coming here. Just as soon as they can grow a replacement HyperQUBE."

"What?" gasped Ben Holcombe. "You have people working at the campus right now? Downwind of San Francisco?"

"They're well protected," said Seigart in a mild tone. "We tracked down about two thirds of Santa's Elves, as you call them, and they were able to scavenge enough of the raw materials from the last two QUBEs to build a new one. By the way, the President asked me to thank you for not destroying the data or the schematics."

"We're not insane," snapped Amber D'Agostino. "We weren't going to flush seven years of work down the drain. You can't tell one hard drive from another on those cameras, and we had hundreds of spares for the Hadoop cluster. We used to lose fifty drives a week."

"I saw the video. It certainly scared me. You were all very convincing. I wouldn't play poker with any of you."

"Why here?" blurted Laurel.

Seigart turned his hawkish eyes on her. "We can defend you here. We're hundreds of miles from any coastline. The security is so tight a mosquito won't be able to get through, much less a human being or a missile. On that, you have my guarantee. And besides, it's a nice place. Green. Beautiful hills. Pretty good whisky. Would you rather be in Los Alamos?" He shuddered visibly. "I was just there. I never did like deserts."

Chao-Xing said, "I don't want to live in an armed camp."

"We'll make it better than it was in Palo Alto," said Seigart. "The countryside for miles is inside the perimeter, and we're adding a lot more. We plan to build a whole new town for ST scientists and engineers. Shopping malls, schools, a library. The works."

"We," said Laurel, mental antennae twitching.

"Yes, Ms. Wynn, 'we.' ST will be an independent company, but you'll have one and only one customer, at least for now. We will have an active hand in making you a success. Eventually this whole laboratory is going to be working on your discoveries. We have a lot of work to do to keep the world from falling apart. We need your help."

"Fuck that," said Hank Drummond. Lizbeth grasped his arm and tried to shush him, but he looked at her, frowning, and she let go. "Jack would never just knuckle under to this heavy-handed government bullshit."

Seigart's smile emerged fully now. "Now, there's where you're wrong." He picked up a remote control and aimed it at the flat panel across the room.

The screen came to life.

Jack Dura's face beamed at her from a hospital bed.

"Hi, gorgeous. Miss me?"

Joyous bedlam swept through the room.

Laurel's hands leaped to her mouth. She squeaked, "Jack! You... you...!"

This time, she didn't even try to hold the tears back.

Time and Date Unknown

When he woke up, he was completely disoriented. It took him many long minutes to come back to himself.

He felt weightless, as if he were floating in water. All around him was darkness and quiet. He heard nothing. He saw nothing. He couldn't move. The only thing he was conscious of was a burning pain in his throat.

A voice floated out of the depths: a male voice, old, quavering, but full of confidence and vitality.

"Welcome back, Dr. O'Keefe. No, don't try to move or talk. You can't, anyway. Jack Dura crushed your larynx, and you didn't receive any attention from the corpsman for several minutes. I'm afraid there might have been some permanent brain damage."

Lights began to glimmer in the darkness.

"Good, good." The speaker muttered, "Generalized activity across the visual cortex. Excellent." His voice resumed its former level. "We're going to try some test patterns, Dr. O'Keefe. Just watch." He added in a murmur, "Like he has a choice."

A quiet female chuckle sounded in his ears.

Simple geometric patterns appeared in front of him: lines, circles, squares, in various colors, some moving, some almost stationary.

The voice once said, "Good, there's that little spike over in Brodmann's 17. Let's calibrate the ventral stream, shall we?"

The shapes became more complex. Household objects. Plants. Pets. Houses of various types. He recognized some of the styles. Craftsman. Prairie. Victorian.

"He likes architecture. Let's focus on that."

The pictures of buildings became more and more complex and varied. He couldn't close his eyes. They never seemed to get dry, though, which he found puzzling. He also couldn't move them. His focus was fixed on a single point, and the images moved past them. Sometimes, when they stopped, they melted into a shimmering gray haze.

The eyes have to move to see, he remembered. Always moving, to keep the retinal rods and cones stimulated. They can only sense changes in light intensity and color. Stop the eye completely, and the image goes away.

His eyes were paralyzed. *He* was paralyzed. He couldn't move. Maybe he *couldn't* move.

"Heart rate is jumping," a woman's voice said in his left ear. "Right on schedule."

"Dr. O'Keefe," said the old man with the shaky but powerful voice. "Dr. O'Keefe! You must calm down. Yes, we've temporarily paralyzed you. It's required for the protocol." He sighed and whispered with obvious exasperation, "Every single time."

"Well, what do you expect?" said the woman.

"Dr. O'Keefe! That's right. Just calm down. I'll explain what's happening."

The woman hissed, "Oh goody. This again. I'm going out for a cigarette."

The old man said warmly, "Everything's fine. That's right. Now I'll tell you what's going on. I'm Doctor Nagy. You did suffer some brain damage from asphyxia, but more importantly, you can't speak anymore because of your neck injury. If you'd cooperate with us, we wouldn't have to use this special procedure. Are you ready to do that?"

He tried to make sense of what he was hearing.

The old man's voice continued, "We can get you out of the scanner and have you back in your cell in about an hour. You can write or type the answers instead of making us go prospecting through your brain. I can only ask this once a day, when you're still lucid. The drugs interfere with your long-term memory consolidation. You won't remember a word of this tomorrow. So. Do you want to cooperate? Your friend Blaise is helping us. He gets three square meals a day and all the books he can read. It's not much of a life, but it's a life."

Aidan raged silently inside his skull.

This time, the old man's sigh was resigned. "Well, it was worth a try. So, let me tell you what we're going to do. You're wearing goggles that keep your eyelids apart and your eyes moist. They project images right onto your retinas. You have headphones on your ears. We show you a series of pictures and sounds. This lets us map the activity inside your brain with the PET scanner, just like in the hospital. Except here, we calibrate your neural responses to various stimuli for the big computer server farm to analyze."

Nagy paused. "It's all very expensive, you know. You should feel honored." He paused again. "You don't? Ah well. Once the calibration is complete, we start with the questions. The answers are very simple: true or false. We ask, and you'll answer, whether you want to or not. All we have to do is flash it in front of your eye to see whether you agree with it or not. Your brain just can't help forming a response. It's a reflex, like recognizing a picture of a kitty cat. The signal takes longer to form if your response is a lie. This delay is physiological. It's the way human brains work. You can't think your way around it. Don't waste energy trying."

Aidan would have screamed if he'd been capable of making any sound at all.

"This protocol works, Dr. O'Keefe. Trust me. I've been using this same procedure on other prisoners here in Guantanamo for about a year now. We uncovered a lot of very interesting things about our enemies, and some of our so-called friends. By the way, if you're hoping for a lawyer to ride to the rescue, don't hold your breath. You've been stripped of your citizenship by an act of Congress. You're what they call an SEC. A stateless enemy combatant. The rules have changed since The Day."

Aidan didn't have to ask what day.

"Ah, that got your attention, didn't it? Do you want to cooperate, or do we use the scanner? No? Okay, the scanner it is." His voice descended to a whisper. "I really wish this hurt, Dr. O'Keefe. My niece lived in

San Francisco. I shall have to be content with knowing that you will never leave this building while you are alive. But cheer up! Quite a lot of radioactive tracer goes into your bloodstream every morning. You'll probably die of cancer in a few years. But until then, we will keep excavating your secrets, one by one. Anyone who helped you is going to pay. Never fear."

The woman returned shortly after the calibration procedure was complete. She said, "Yesterday we found out the name of the agent you were working with. Adam. Today we want to find out where he came from."

"Time for the cocktail," Dr. Nagy said.

He felt a sudden warmth. His attention began to wander.

A question flowed in front of his eyes.

ADAM'S COUNTRY STARTS WITH A LETTER BETWEEN "A" AND "M"

"True," said Dr. Nagy.

ADAM'S COUNTRY STARTS WITH A LETTER BETWEEN "A" AND "F"

The woman said, "Ah, he tried to lie. That's a very bad boy, Aidan." Nagy said, "So, also true."

ADAM'S COUNTRY STARTS WITH A LETTER BETWEEN "A" AND "C"

The goggles on Aidan's eyes kept him from weeping.

The world stepped up to the brink, stared thoughtfully into the abyss, and finally decided to step back.

The Greater Depression lasted for six anguished years. The intermingling of the world's economies ensured that no nation was spared, but some fared much worse than others. Pestilence, war, famine and death reigned over the Middle East, South Asia and Oceania. The world's population plummeted from seven to just over four billion by the end of those awful years.

The tide began to turn when Struve Technologies astounded the world with the announcement of its return. Working in secret, they had perfected a new kind of power, even more efficient than the promising but never perfected fusion reactors, based on newly discovered scientific principles.

They demonstrated the so-called Dura reactor in grand style. They replaced the aging Tennessee Valley Authority's Allen Fossil Plant with a single, massive, orange box the size of a locomotive. It appeared to consume nothing. It produced no waste products. All it needed was cold water flowing through the jacket around the giant electrical bus bars, to keep them from melting. Even the water could be air-cooled and recycled in a closed loop, wasting nothing.

The orange box generated just over a gigawatt of electricity.

Struve Technologies issued no press releases describing the technology behind the Dura reactor. They merely showed that it worked, described the awful things that would happen if anyone managed to break through the nearly indestructible walls of the reactor vessel, and began accepting orders—but only from peaceful democratic nations.

Within three years, Dura reactors replaced all other forms of power generation in North America, Europe and India.

Then one was sold to a company that was a carefully concealed front for a government unfriendly to the United States.

The new owners of the Dura reactor ignored the terrifying warnings imprinted on the case. With great difficulty, they eventually cracked it open.

Rumors circulated for decades afterward that the U.S. had deliberately allowed the reactor to fall into the wrong hands. The only government spokesmen who would dignify any questions on that topic with a response was Andrew Seigart. Just before he retired, he quipped, "Think of it as evolution in action."

The crater in the mountains of northeast Pakistan was visible from the Moon. Immediate fatalities were estimated at over three hundred thousand, even in that thinly populated region. No one wanted to venture into the devastation to count the dead.

The sound of the explosion was still detectable on ultra-sensitive barographs eleven days later as it echoed and re-echoed around the word. It blasted enough vaporized rock and soil into the upper atmosphere to create a year without a summer, much like the one after the steam explosion that pulverized the island volcano of Krakatoa in 1883.

Global temperature dropped an average of 1.5 degrees Celsius for four years. The final death toll from secondary effects of the explosion were eventually estimated at just over seventy million.

Fortunately, the bread baskets of the world quickly returned to productivity. With hastily erected greenhouses the size of large cities sheltering their crops, widespread starvation did not stage a comeback.

ST played a major part in solving that problem, too. They set up manufacturing lines to create incredibly thin but durable sheets of a slippery, transparent material they called FQG. The roofs of the greenhouses were made from it. They required no cleaning. Water and snow did not cling to them. They soon found uses in architecture and ship building, electric car and airplane manufacture.

ST eventually released a new type of FQG that collected water from the air and funneled it into pipes to irrigate those enclosed farms. It could even generate solar electricity to run the water pumps, making the entire system self-sustaining. Greenhouses made with panes of FQG began to appear all over the world, providing food and water in even the driest climates.

The deserts bloomed.

If Americans had cared to conquer the world in those years, they could have. They were still licking their own wounds, but they were quick to preempt anyone who looked like they planned to inflict more of them. A few small wars ended almost before they really began. With a few noisy exceptions, Americans no longer believed that a world without a policeman was a good idea. Whether other nations believed it was no longer of much concern. The world couldn't tolerate another day like The Day.

A few pounds of flesh were exacted from those who had conspired to attack the United States. Colonel Ryu Sang-Chul had been found, half-dead from starvation, in a ravine not far from the former border with South Korea. He cracked under the Nagy Protocol much faster than Aidan O'Keefe, who held on for seven grim months before giving up and agreeing to cooperate. Unknown to everyone at ST, O'Keefe and Thierry were moved from Guantanamo to a top-secret lab in Washington state, where a new HyperQUBE awaited them.

A few months later, eleven senior Chinese military officers mysteriously died of heart attacks within an hour of each other. Among them was General Guo Qiang.

Shortly thereafter, the US ambassador had a four-hour meeting with the Chinese President, behind closed doors and alone. A few carrots were brandished, along with a great many sticks. When the meeting ended, the unsmiling ambassador was escorted away. The shaken President did not sleep that night, but the next day, he had word that Dura reactors would be arriving in mainland China within the week.

The new *Pax Americana* was enforced rigorously and without hesitation. The warlike nations of the world gradually turned their attention to other pursuits. Those that persisted in their attempts to destabilize the new order soon found their leaders dying of heart attacks, in large numbers, often within minutes or hours of each other.

The terrorist problem was solved by application of a simple and merciless formula: no terrorist, no problem. The war-weary peoples of the lands where they held sway were easily convinced to collect dishes or glassware used by the terrorists and ship them in sterilized containers to collection points. Their DNA went into a very secret database in an equally secret lab, which shipped minute quantities of customized viruses back.

The DNA samples were cross-checked against intelligence gathered from human and robotic sources before a hunter-killer virus was generated. Undoubtedly a few innocents perished as well, but the terrorists expired in much larger numbers.

The statesmen who had made such free use of terrorism in the twentieth and early twenty-first centuries soon decided they'd had enough. The despotic regimes that did not collapse of their own accord were finally pulled down by their own citizens—with a judicious application of help.

The economies of the world eventually began to recover. Ten years after the Day, the Dow Jones index had clawed its way back to 10,000 points. Abundant and nearly free electrical power had revived the West. Ten years later, it had done the same for the pacified East, and the Dow hovered just below yet another so-called "magic number" of 60,000.

Once the Hard Years were acknowledged by all to be over, ST returned to its roots as a biomedical company. They announced a cure for senile dementia twenty-three years after the Day. The cure for all of the many forms of cancer followed two years later.

The next year they announced a viral treatment that would destroy aged, senescent cells and encourage the body to replace them with healthy ones, repairing damaged DNA and extending lifespans far past their original limits. The media promptly dubbed it "the Fountain of Youth." A few hardline Greens objected to the use of genetic engineering and retroviral treatments, but given ST's track record, few paid any attention to them.

Jack had focused all of his attention on the rejuvenation treatment in order to help those who'd suffered from the fallout created on The Day. When they finally received all the FDA approvals and shipped the first batch, he breathed a giant sigh of relief, celebrated with his friends and family for a grand total of ten minutes, and got back to work.

ST went public a year later, on the twenty-seventh anniversary of Jack Dura's joining the company. At the conclusion of the first day of trading, its stock was valued at $11,000 a share.

The next year, researchers in France announced the invention of a new kind of computer technology. They'd reasoned from Jack's research and from first principles how to develop a quantinuum processor about twice the speed of the old QUBE Delta. It was an admirable achievement, though it was still a long way from being a competitor to the eleventh-generation HyperQUBE, much less the other exotic technologies ST had developed over the intervening decades.

The French team was awarded the Nobel Prize.

The Dura Party held a consolation party for Jack, complete with a fake Nobel medal that turned out to be gold foil around a disc of white chocolate. Laurel had made it herself. He'd never told her that he detested white chocolate. When he was fourteen years old, he'd eaten too much of it and barfed it up all over the back seat of his parents' truck on a camping trip to Lake Navajo.

Jack ate his wife's chocolate and somehow managed to keep it down. He might be CTO of Struve Technologies again, but Laurel had climbed the corporate ladder to succeed Philip Mayhew as CEO, and she absolutely did not take any shit. He swallowed a series of snarky comments along with the chocolate, but by way of compensation, he got gloriously drunk on twenty-four-year-old cask-strength A'bunadh Scotch whisky.

His thirty-year agreement with the late Andrew Seigart would soon expire. In the meantime, he was chained to Oak Ridge, doing his penance.

He had little to complain about. The high-walled fortress of a town that had grown up next to the National Laboratory was a lovely place to live. He'd never been in danger of starvation or even hunger, though he'd consciously decided to limit his caloric intake as he reached his late sixties.

He and Laurel shared a beautiful big house on a hilltop overlooking a long, narrow green valley. He learned how to cook New Mexican food, since the spiciest ingredient used in the local cuisine was black pepper. His friends lived next door to him, and their families shared all the typical joys and pains of family life.

Jack wasn't reflective by nature, but every once in a long while the guilt got to him. The weeks after the conversion reactor explosion in Pakistan had been really bad. He consoled himself with the fact that far more people had benefited from his work than had suffered from it, but he hid his eyes from every blood-red sunset for years afterward.

His brain still shied away from thoughts of his old life in the Bay Area. Even after millions of man-years of work, and the efforts of all of the ST staff to build new technologies for the clean-up, it was only now becoming livable again.

Laurel was his only real comfort when he couldn't stand the guilt any longer. She held him into the long, merciless nights when he woke up screaming. She told him that he was a good man. He even managed to believe her, at least until the next time the night terrors came for a visit.

He still had his work, of course, and the company of an ever-larger community of friends and fellow researchers, delving into every nook and cranny the natural world had to offer. He regained his freedom when the term of his agreement with Andrew Seigart elapsed, but he could never resume his public identity of Jack Dura. When he traveled, which wasn't often, he went by an alias and a valid, if fictitious, passport.

He and Laurel had been too consumed with work to feel comfortable raising children of their own. They enjoyed the frequent visits from Hank and Lizbeth's kids, some of whom were now in college. They doted on Eileen Dupree Sotiropoulos' new baby. She and Stathis had waited until they'd both recovered from rejuvenation therapy to start their own family.

Stathis grinned like a Halloween pumpkin for a month after little John was born. He asked Jack to be his son's godfather, and Eileen recruited Laurel as godmother.

"John would've been proud to have you name your son after him," Jack said to Stathis before the ceremony.

Stathis looked down at the wooden floor of the church. He'd taken John's stroke and sudden death hard.

Jack beamed at the once-again youthful scientist. "And I'm proud to pinch-hit for him. Just this once. I'm just glad you didn't name the kid Giacomo. Don't wish that on anyone. Always choose a name that won't get your kid beat up in the schoolyard."

Stathis smiled. "Have you seen the names people are choosing these days? I never heard of half of them. 'John' sounds like something from the seventeen-hundreds now. Hey, when are you going to take the rejuvenation pill, Jack? You're getting pretty wrinkly."

"Soon enough, you young whippersnapper, soon enough. I'm too busy right now. Mind your own beeswax, and get offa my lawn."

"Busy with what?"

His eyes twinkled. "Something wonderful."

Some years later, ST made the biggest announcement of all.

Forty Years After The Day

Jack knelt on the grass in front of Emily's grave.

El Carmelo Cemetery was just as beautiful as he remembered, even if the surrounding town of Pacific Grove was a lot busier.

"I came to say goodbye," Jack said. He shifted, wincing. His knees were pretty creaky now, which was no surprise for a man of eighty-one years. Geriatric drugs had kept his mind sharp and his major organs functioning, but short of full rejuvenation, there still wasn't much they could do about advanced arthritis.

He looked at Eddie's grave marker. The memory of his son's arms beating against his back from his perch in the baby carrier as he laughed at the lighthouse filled his mind.

Tears trickled down his face, but he smiled.

"I don't know when I'll be back," he said to his son, his voice thick with emotion. "I might not be. I just wanted you to know... I guess... I just needed to tell you that you'll always be in my heart." He looked at Emily's marker. "Both of you."

He brushed his fingertips to his lips, and touched each of the markers in turn.

"Goodbye," he said.

Laurel helped him stand. She had completed the rejuvenation therapy more than a year ago. She looked just as she'd looked in her twenties. He'd seen the pictures.

He spared a single glance at the empty plot next to Eddie's grave. Well, I probably won't be needing that. But I'll keep it. Just in case.

He took a final look around. The lighthouse across Asilomar Road was still trim and well-kept. Deer still walked among the tombstones, nuzzling the short, manicured lawn. The tang of iodine and sea salt was strong in his nostrils. Low clouds drifted overhead. Sunbeams rippled across the hazy sky, like the pleats of celestial curtains ruffling in the gentle sea breeze.

"This *is* a beautiful place," he said at last. He looked at Laurel. "It's nice to be anywhere besides Oak Ridge for a change. Even if it is a cemetery."

"It is," she agreed. "You could have come here years ago, you know."

"Busy. Offa my lawn. You know the drill."

"You can't fool me. You just couldn't drag yourself away from the lab."

"Have I mentioned how smokin' hot you look today?" he said. He glanced at her legs, displayed to great advantage below the hem of her short skirt. "Yowza."

"Come on, geezer. Let's get going. You're going to conk out once the rejuve pill kicks in. Why did you take it right now? You're going to sleep through all the best parts."

"I didn't want to waste any more time."

"You could have taken it years ago!"

"Yeah, well. I wanted to make sure it didn't have any long-term ill effects."

"You moron. You helped invent it. Did I have any ill effects? Just look at me." She twirled, doing amazing things to her skirt.

"Don't mind if I do."

"You'll be back to your old self in no time, dirty old man. And I can't wait. I have all the hormones of a twenty-year old again." She gave him a lingering kiss.

When it ended, he said, "I said it once, and I'll say it again. Yowza."

They walked arm-in-arm to the parking lot.

"Oh, crap. We never did make it to Tahiti," he said mournfully.

"Don't worry. I'm sure we'll find a beach where we're going."

"I hope so. Can't wait to see you in a bikini."

Their red rental skycar dusted off, rising quickly to a thousand feet under computer control before angling toward the Monterey International Airport.

"Wow," Jack said. He swept an arm toward the city. "This place has gotten *big*."

"A lot of refugees from the Bay Area resettled here."

"Of course, of course. Carmel looks the same." He squinted. "Damn. Too far away to see if the Lone Cypress is still there." He suddenly grinned at her. "Holy crap, Laurel. We're in an air car. How cool is that?"

She laughed. "I've been using them for years."

"Ha. Andrew Seigart had me chained to a rock for forty years."

"Pretty cushy rock, Prometheus. And it was only thirty years. You did the last ten for free."

"Have I said 'get offa my lawn' yet today?"

"Six or seven times. And we don't have a lawn anymore. Or a house."

"No," Jack said, smiling with deep satisfaction. "We have something a lot better." He looked out the spacious window and whistled the theme music from *The Jetsons*.

The skycar grounded next to Del Monte Aviation's private terminal. Stathis, Eileen, young John and their youngest, Laurie, were there to greet them.

"Where's everyone else?" groused Jack.

"They left an hour ago," said Eileen with mock severity. "Where *were* you?"

Jack said, "Had some things to do. One last lunch at Pepper's. Visited Emily and Eddie. Don't sass your elders."

"You're only five years older than I am," she pointed out.

"Yeah, but *I* don't look like I'm twenty-one."

"Not yet, anyway."

Stathis and Eileen led them to the shuttle. It was about the size of a small private jet, horizontal stabilizers at the nose, twin turbine engines mounted near the tail above swept-back wings whose tips curved to form gracefully upturned winglets.

MIKEY was stenciled on the nose, next to a painting of a grinning kid eating cereal.

Laurel said, "Beautiful. Looks like an old Beechcraft Starship. You did a nice job, Stathis."

"Thanks."

Eileen said, "Hard to believe you could cram a conversion drive into something this small."

"Yep."

Jack didn't mention that the military had been cramming far smaller matter-energy conversion units into variable-yield smart bombs for two decades. *Thank God they never had to use them.* He took a final look around. "Okay. Let's get this show on the road."

Laurel took the pilot's seat. Jack sat next to her. The window was immense, wrapping around the entire front end of the vehicle, giving them a stunning panoramic view. Made of FQG, no doubt, as was most of the airplane's fuselage.

"How did you learn how to fly this thing?" Jack asked, putting his hands to his mouth in mock terror.

"They have this thing called the Internet, Gramps," she shot back as she put on a spindly augmented reality headset. She blinked as the tiny laser emitters in the hair-thin imager loop in front of her eyes calibrated themselves. "I've had a pilot's license for twenty years now. I still think it's weird not to have to do a preflight. There's just not much that can go wrong in these things anymore."

She studied the virtual instrument panel projected on her retinas for a moment before saying, "Monterey Ground, experimental niner one seven three kilo with information zulu, manual mode, taxi for unlimited takeoff, VFR, then oscar india tango as filed."

A computer-generated voice replied, "Niner one seven three kilo, roger, taxi and hold short runway two eight left. Oscar india tango approved at pilot's discretion. Contact Monterey Tower on ATAC golf papa whisky."

Jack looked back at Stathis and Eileen as the shuttle began to roll down the taxiway. They returned his gaze with happy smiles. Their kids were behind them, staring eagerly out the windows.

He tilted his head to indicate Laurel. "Isn't she awesome?" he said, waggling his eyebrows. "*My* wife."

In moments they were pressed back into their seats. The ground dropped away. The takeoff was astoundingly quiet. The air-breathing turbines were electric, powered by the miniature conversion reactor.

Green hills and blue sea slid beneath them.

Laurel's left wrist twitched on the stick, and the shuttle veered north. "Just wanted to give you one last look," she said.

In minutes they were high above the coast of the San Francisco Peninsula. The old city was gone, but a new one had risen in its place. Gold and silver spires gleamed in the afternoon sunlight. Coit Tower had been rebuilt, as had the Opera House and City Hall. Jack's heart beat faster when he saw the restored Golden Gate Bridge, and the many new, graceful spans that arched across the placid waters.

"Thank you," he said, meeting Laurel's perfect blue eyes. Then he yawned.

"See? I told you. You're going to miss everything."

She angled the ship toward the vertical. The wind noise faded as the atmosphere grew thinner. Then the Dura drive kicked in.

Jack felt a moment of roller-coaster weightlessness as the artificial gravity field slowly engaged. Soon it was as if the ship was back on solid ground again. There was no sense of motion whatever. If it weren't for the swiftly darkening sky ahead and the Earth dropping away behind, they'd never have known they were moving.

The sky turned black. It was filled with stars.

A synthetic voice emerged from a speaker on the control panel. "Niner one seven three kilo experimental, this is Grissom Station. You're cleared for outbound insertion track as filed. Contact Challenger Approach Control on ORBCOMM channel 41. Good day."

Laurel acknowledged the communications. "Now watch this." She grasped a lever on the console and pushed it forward. "I'm going to dim the cabin lights."

"Wow," the kids chorused, looking behind them through the wraparound window.

Jack turned his head to see, yawning again.

Behind them, a circular, blue-white wall filled half the sky.

As they watched, it began to shrink.

Ahead of them, the fingernail sliver of the moon began to grow.

The journey lasted thirty minutes. The first time men had ventured to lunar orbit, it had taken three or four days.

Jack was nodding long before the long silver spike of the *Challenger* appeared in the starry void, one of many being built from the materials mined from the vast black asteroid behind them. Nearby was her nearly-completed sister ship, the *Columbia*.

By the time they docked in the giant shuttle bay of the first true starship, Jack was fast asleep.

Laurel carried him to the sickbay herself, bearing his weight easily with her augmented muscles. She saw him safely tucked into bed, IVs inserted to keep him fed and hydrated during the four-day coma of the initial phase of his rejuvenation.

She stayed to look at him for a while. He'd be up and about in a week, sore for a month, and complaining of headaches and nausea for months after that, but he would be young again, and far faster and stronger than he'd ever been. Even the burn scars on his arms and back would fade and disappear, just like the bullet scar formerly on her left shoulder.

There were millions of planets in this galaxy alone. Four generations of space telescopes had proved it. There were thousands of small, rocky worlds with liquid water and oxygen atmospheres. Many might prove suitable for human life.

Once they found a new home, after giving much of their lives to public service, restored to health and youthful vitality, she and Jack could finally start working on a family of their own.

Laurel felt a pang as she thought of the world they were leaving behind. It had taken many years for scientists throughout the world to catch up to Struve Technologies. They weren't there yet, but they were close.

The Earth was growing troubled again. The *Pax Americana* wouldn't last much longer. At some point, the knowledge gap would close entirely. God only knew what would happen then. There was no getting rid of humanity's predilection for causing itself problems, it seemed. Hopefully in a world with unlimited material prosperity there would be fewer things to fight about. Hopefully. She wasn't planning to hold her breath.

Aidan O'Keefe had been right about one thing: Earth was much too fragile for it to be humanity's only home. They had to leave. And thanks to Jack Dura, they could.

They and their friends had sunk much of their collective fortune into moving the asteroid into lunar orbit, creating the technologies to build the ships, developing the nanotech robots to construct them in the span of three years, and testing Jack's drive. There was a universe out there to discover. Infinite universes, in fact, though only one was within reach.

Laurel smiled as she looked at her sleeping husband. *One little universe should be enough.*

She walked to the bridge and sat in the big chair. Around her were many of her old friends from ST, sitting in front of the controls: Stathis and Eileen, Hank and Lizbeth, Terry and Xu Chao-Xing. Ben and Deepthi were down in Engineering.

The large view screen at the front of the bridge had been designed to look like the one from *Star Trek*. Jack had insisted. But he'd been outvoted when it came to naming their ship. They decided to pay tribute to real heroes, not make-believe ones.

So it was that Jack Dura, the man who perfected the QUBE, who discovered the quantinuum and the Grand Unified Theory of physics, the genius who invented the matter-energy conversion reactor and eventually the star drive, was fast asleep when his wife, Laurel Wynn, Captain of the United States Starship *Challenger*, gave the order to go.

624

IF YOU ENJOYED THIS BOOK

I'd be grateful if you would post a brief review on Amazon.com. Self-published books live and die by reviews. I'd prefer mine not to die. Smiley-face.

If you've come across an error or have other feedback you'd like to send me, please let me know via the book's official home page. I'll make every effort to respond promptly.

Thanks, and I hope to see you online!

http://theprometheusoption.com

AFTERWORD

A book this big takes a long time to write.

I first conceived of the story that would turn into *The Prometheus Option* in 2005, eleven years before I wrote the final page. I even completed a full outline. However, I quickly lost interest in writing it. It turns out that plotting the whole story from stem to stern took a lot of the fun out of it. Filling it in just seemed like drudgery.

Between 2008 and 2009, I wrote a big, wordy fantasy novel called *The Storm Winds Rise*. I gave myself the freedom to explore the threads of the story wherever they led. Writing it was a joy. Unfortunately, there were *way* too many threads. I also made the mistake of writing the book as the first of a trilogy. The chances of selling a trilogy with only one book in hand didn't seem great to me. I didn't even bother trying to find an agent.

My beta readers enjoyed the book, but it never quite satisfied me. I didn't feel like it was the best work I could deliver. Truth to tell, I was a little embarrassed by it. I decided to put it in the drawer and come back to it someday in the future when I had an established body of work, and might actually stand a chance of selling a multi-volume series.

A few years ago, the urge to write returned with a vengeance.

I dug out the old, half-completed manuscript and plot outline of *The Prometheus Option*, read enough of it to renew my excitement about the story, and decided to try again. Only this time, I wouldn't work from the old plot outline at all. I would write it linearly, one chapter at a time, with only a rather vague knowledge of where I wanted the story to go. I would pose myself only one key question and let the chips fall where they may.

The question was simply this: "What would happen if a Silicon Valley company created not just the Next Big Thing, but the Biggest Thing of All—not just some hokey new computer or phone widget, but the most disruptive technology in the history of technology?"

That made all the difference. I'd been working in the Valley for many years. I know the place and I know a lot of players. I followed that sage old advice: "Write what you know." And I followed my own self-imposed discipline of writing the book as a single, continuous string of scenes. Not one chapter has budged a single iota from the order in which I wrote it, though many of the sentences have.

Writing *The Prometheus Option* was a ball. It wasn't *all* "skittles and beer," as they say, especially the constant fights with Microsoft Word on the iPad, and it took a lot longer than I expected, but I got there in the end.

"On the iPad?" you might say. Yes, on the iPad. Although I usually write on a MacBook or my iMac, when I'm on the train to and from work, I use the iPad. It's great to be able to use Dropbox and have the Word doc automatically synched up between the desktop, laptop and mobile device. For whatever reason, I find it much easier to edit when using the iPad. Maybe it's because it's more like a book. It's possible, although painful, to write on the iPad using the on-screen keyboard. I entered a couple of chapters like that when I was flat on my back with a compressed nerve injury last year. But Microsoft really needs to do some work on the editing UI. I don't know how many times I accidentally introduced extra spaces or periods because of the blatantly stupid way it handles cut-and-paste. Smarten up, app!

Don't get me started about what a horrible thing auto-correct is, either. Oh! There. See? You got me started.

Auto-correct is the Devil. If you ever feel compelled to write on the iPad, just turn auto-correct the hell off. It will correct your spelling, sure enough, but you'll wind up with any number of perfectly spelled and nearly impossible-to-find wrong words in place of typos, which any spell checker worth its salt will immediately flag for your attention. My beta readers were purely mystified at some of the doozies that crept into my revision draft.

Get thee behind me, auto-correct!

Enough grousing.

A brief note on the subject of the pervasive use of strong language in the book: sorry, but this really is the way it is in the Valley. I've been in meetings with nerdy engineers using language harsh enough to cause a whole platoon of Marines to faint dead away. If anything, I think I played it down a bit.

Finally, I'd like to discuss the origin of some of the scientific, technological, and political topics I described in the book. A number of my readers have asked me which are fictional and which aren't. While the following is by no means exhaustive, I will try to cover some of the more interesting and potentially controversial elements of the story.

Please bear in mind that although I trained as a scientist, even going so far as completing two years in a Ph.D. program in molecular cell biology, I am not a professional. I bring only an interested layman's knowledge to these subjects.

Quantum computing is real. Or at least, if it isn't today, it soon will be, and computer scientists are excited. I confess, I find it just as baffling as you probably do, but I expect it will in fact become a reality soon, and it will probably be just as revolutionary as the original binary computers were when they were first built in the 1940s. Parallel-universe quantum entanglement is fictitious, but wouldn't that be cool? *I* think it would be cool.

Genetic algorithms are real. My first introduction to the concept was in a wonderful book about evolution by Richard Dawkins, *The Blind Watchmaker*. Dawkins created a (Mac) program that he included with the book that illustrated how complex organism "designs" could arise from simple variations of simple patterns coupled with a selection process, in this case, the user's sense of esthetics. That book has always stuck with me.

The Protein Folding Problem is very real, and as far as I know, it's still a very real problem. There have been some massively parallel computation efforts to simulate protein folding, notably the "Folding at Home" screen saver, which tries to harness the power of zillions of home computers for this noble purpose. I do hope that quantum computing can make a difference here.

I have been and continue to be an extremely amateur aficionado of aviation, space, firearms, and military history. Every piece of military hardware described in the book is real, including the XM25 CDTE "Punisher" grenade launcher. The sole exceptions are the XC-130J "Gort" laser aircraft and the Devilfish, though fiber lasers, IMOD display technology and (at least in principle) anti-magnetic metamate-rials are also real. I would not be terribly surprised to find that many governments are pursuing stealthy drone submarines programs.

A bit more on Gort. I really hope we build it. High-power, solid-state fiber laser weapons systems are just becoming practical. There are plenty of videos online showing experimental laser interceptions of missiles, drone aircraft and boats. It's a hard problem to lick, but it's absolutely worth pursuing. The giant Boeing 747-mounted, chemical-powered Airborne Laser system was cancelled, but I sincerely hope that we will build more modest systems for use as counter-terrorism weapons, and as quickly as practical. If fictional Gort hadn't been shot down, it might have prevented the destruction of fictional San Francisco. If Gort were *really* built, it might be able to prevent the same thing from happening to a real city. *Klaatu barada nikto.* There. I said the words.

(And if that mystifies you, it's time to watch *Army of Darkness* and *The Day the Earth Stood Still.* The good version.)

Michael Pillsbury's fascinating book, *The Hundred Year Marathon: China's Secret Strategy to Replace America as the Global Superpower,* informed the corresponding plot thread of my novel. China's attempts to expand its influence and exert sole dominion over the South China Sea and surrounding islands are also matters of record. General Guo, Colonel Ryu and their co-conspirators are purely fictitious, but Chinese espionage in both military and industrial contexts is all too real. If you doubt this, look up the new Chinese J-31 fighter and compare it to the U.S. F-35. Coincidence? You be the judge.

Cyber-attacks against infrastructure targets such as power plants, hospitals, and the electrical grid are entirely plausible and have already happened. The first weaponized computer virus was the so-called STUXNET virus, targeting a component used in uranium gas centrifuges in the secret Iranian nuclear program. It is widely thought that this virus was designed by computer scientists working for the U.S. government. While I applaud this particular use of a computer virus, it is entirely likely that someone unfriendly to the U.S. will eventually hit us with something at least as damaging. If we aren't conducting a crash program to identify and fix these vulnerabilities, *a la* the fictitious HERMES BROADHEAD program mentioned in my story, we certainly should be. The danger is real.

My description of the thermonuclear weapon and its effects on San Francisco was informed by Alex Wellerstein's NukeMAP web site, which purports to calculate the effects of a nuclear weapon on a target of your choice. The site is reputed to be highly accurate, which is both amazing and horrifying.

My earnest prayer is that we will never again see any city in any nation visited by these terrible weapons, or by anything even more ghastly that might succeed them. At the same time, I would encourage you to visit the NukeMAP site and try it out. The more informed we are of the appalling power of these weapons, the less likely we are to wish to use them. Would that everyone currently or soon to be in possession of nuclear weapons felt the same way.

You can find NukeMAP at http://nuclearsecrecy.com/nukemap

The technologies of StruvePharma (later Struve Technologies), including the oil synthesizer, the QUBE and HyperQUBE, FQG, super-diamond filaments and the rest, are of course fictitious. The only "invention" of theirs that's likely to be close to reality is the carbon-nanotube ultra-capacitor. This technology is in fact under development and is extremely promising. I would be very surprised if any of the other inventions were to come to fruition during my lifetime, but I wouldn't mind seeing that rejuvenation pill, and sooner rather than later. And I surely would relish getting a chance to visit another solar system or two.

Go, science, go!

Lastly, I hope my portrayal of law enforcement officers and soldiers in the branches of the U.S. military represented in this book doesn't cause any real cops or soldiers to gripe, growl, or groan. I have nothing but respect for the men and women in uniform, past and present. I tried hard to depict them honestly and honorably. They have desperately difficult jobs and they aren't appreciated enough by half. To them I say: thank you sincerely for your service.

ACKNOWLEDGEMENTS

Writing *The Prometheus Option* took me nearly three years.

I enjoyed the constant encouragement of my wonderful, loving wife, Valerie Aidan. She was my first reader and had enormous influence on the decisions I made about characters and storyline. She is not a big fan of the techno thriller or science fiction genres, but I figured if I could capture her attention, I might really have something. I did, and I think I do. The story benefited hugely from her feedback, and from the fact that she did not murder me for writing during many holiday vacations. I love you, baby.

I'd like to acknowledge the *John Batchelor Show*, which I listen to in podcast form. John Batchelor's thoughtful interviews with primary sources in the military and political arenas provided much fertile ground for the backstory of this book. Keep on truckin', John, for many years to come. You're one of the good guys.

I would also like to pay tribute to my friends and beta readers who furnished me with invaluable advice and criticism: Tony di Croce, Paul von Heyking, Don Louv, Jeff Jensen, my sister Kim Birnbaum and brother-in-law Marc. Special thanks are due to Allie Williams, Mike Kobb, and especially my two buddies, both former Marines, Archie Campbell and Max Pruden *(semper fi, Devil Dogs!)* for detailed, trenchant feedback, criticism, and support.

I would be remiss if I didn't give Max Pruden the Supreme "Holy Cow" Award for a truly monumental quantity of feedback, suggestions, corrections and ideas. Holy cow, Max! You blew my socks off. Way beyond the call. I can't thank you enough. I owe you a Coke.

Any errors remaining in this novel, be they factual, grammatical, historical, attitudinal or intellectual, are solely my responsibility.

Finally—and it really is finally—I dedicate this book to my mother, Doris Eugenia Baker Johnson, who passed away in 1996. She instilled in me a love for learning and reading, for music and language, and always with her patented desert-dry sense of humor.

This one's for you, mom. I'll love you forever.

May 14, 2016

San Francisco Bay Area, California
Santa Monica, California
Las Vegas, Nevada
Santa Fe, New Mexico
Paris, France
Munich, Germany
London, United Kingdom
Newport, Oregon

ABOUT THE AUTHOR

Jeff Kirk is a long-time veteran of Silicon Valley. He studied biology and chemistry at the New Mexico Institute of Mining and Technology, the University of New Mexico, and the University of California at Berkeley. Then he found out he liked being a computer geek, and against all odds, he still does. He's worked for start-ups as well as some of the most successful companies in the technology business, including Microsoft and Google.

Jeff lives and works in the San Francisco Bay Area with his wife Valerie and their two cats, O'Maley and Gus.

Visit his home page at http://jeffkirk.online